THE LOST WORLD
& Other Stories

THE LOST WORLD
& Other Stories

Sir Arthur Conan Doyle

WORDSWORTH CLASSICS

This edition published 1995 by
Wordsworth Editions Limited
Cumberland House, Crib Street, Ware,
Hertfordshire SG12 9ET

ISBN 1 85326 245 5

*Printed and bound in Great Britain
by Mackays of Chatham plc, Chatham, Kent
Typeset in the UK by R & B Creative Services Ltd*

INTRODUCTION

THERE CAN BE NO DOUBT that Sir Arthur Conan Doyle was a master storyteller. The various collected editions of his works have attracted introductory accolades and reverential bows from such literary stars as Graham Greene, Angus Wilson, C P Snow, Mary Renault, John Fowles, Len Deighton, Elizabeth Longford and Anthony Burgess. And of course his most famous characters, Sherlock Holmes and Dr Watson, are known and loved throughout the world.

Besides the intricate and detailed unravellings of Holmes and Watson, Doyle was the creator of great historical novels which Winston Churchill liked 'even more than the detective stories'. The third major strand in Doyle's *oeuvre* was science fiction in which he stands alongside Jules Verne and H G Wells as one of the founders of the tradition. His most memorable creation was the maddening, fascinating and irascible character who thunders through adventure after adventure, the memorable Professor George Edward Challenger.

Professor Challenger, 'a cave-man in a lounge suit', is mad scientist, explorer and hunter all in one. When not hurling abuse and attacking people without warning, or throwing young journalists bodily out of his house, he is (with the help of his friends Edward Malone, Professor Summerlee and Lord John Roxton) bringing back evidence of Pterodactyls in a lost world in South America, or foretelling cosmic catastrophe indicated by 'the blurring and shifting of Frauenhofer lines', a world bacterial plague, and a nerve poison that sweeps the earth killing everyone in its path – or does it? Then there are the other stories, *The Land of Mist* and *The Disintegration Machine*.

But perhaps the most powerful and thought-provoking story in this complete collection of Professor Challenger adventures is the climactic and awesome *When the World Screamed*. It may have seemed a fanciful and fantastic notion in the early years of the twentieth century, that Professor Challenger, the man whose handwriting 'looked like . . . barbed wire', should feel 'the world upon which we live is itself an organism . . . with a circulation, a respiration, and a nervous system of its own'. He sets out to bore an eight-mile shaft through the earth's crust to reach the living matter of our mother planet. The result is a terrifying revelation which readers will judge for themselves.

In this age of growing ecological awareness, of poisoned seas, of destruction of rain forests, we may perhaps see some of the adventures and wild ideas of Sir Arthur Conan Doyle's 'cave-man in a lounge suit' in a sympathetic light.

Arthur Conan Doyle was born in Edinburgh in 1859. He was educated at Stonyhurst and Edinburgh University where he qualified as a doctor. He practised at Southsea from 1882 until 1890, after which date he devoted himself entirely to writing. Though the Sherlock Holmes stories are the best-known of his works, Doyle himself thought more highly of his historical romances of which Rodney Stone, Sir Nigel *and* The White Company *are fine examples. He was knighted in 1902 and died in 1930.*

Further reading:

L D Carr: *Life of Arthur Conan Doyle* 1949 & 1987
A C Doyle: *Autobiography* 1924
O Dudley-Edwards: *Life of Arthur Conan Doyle* 1983

CONTENTS

The Lost World

I.	There are Heroisms All Round Us	1
II.	Try Your Luck with Professor Challenger	5
III.	He is a Perfectly Impossible Person	11
IV.	It's Just the Very Biggest Thing in the World	17
V.	Question!	30
VI.	I Was the Flail of the Lord	40
VII.	To-morrow We Disappear Into the Unknown	47
VIII.	The Outlying Pickets of the New World	55
IX.	Who Could Have Foreseen It?	66
X.	The Most Wonderful Things Have Happened	84
XI.	For Once I Was the Hero	95
XII.	It Was Dreadful in the Forest	108
XIII.	A Sight I Shall Never Forget	119
XIV.	Those Were the Real Conquests	131
XV.	Our Eyes Have Seen Great Wonders	142
XVI.	A Procession! A Procession!	155

The Poison Belt

I.	The Blurring of the Lines	173
II.	The Tide of Death	186
III.	Submerged	198
IV.	A Diary of the Dying	211
V.	The Dead World	220
VI.	The Great Awakening	231

The Land of Mist

I. In Which Our Special Commissioners Make A Start   241

II. Which Describes an Evening in Strange Company   247

III. In Which Professor Challenger Gives His Opinion   259

IV. Which Describes Some Strange Doings in Hammersmith   263

V. Where our Commissioners Have a Remarkable Experience   283

VI. In Which the Reader is Shown the Habits of a Notorious Criminal   297

VII. In Which the Notorious Criminal Gets What the British Law Considers to be His Deserts   308

VIII. In Which Three Investigators Come Upon a Dark Soul   318

IX. Which Introduces Some Very Physical Phenomena   334

X. De Profundis   341

XI. Here Silas Linden Comes Into His Own   352

XII. There are Heights and there are Depths   361

XIII. In Which Professor Challenger Goes Forth to Battle   370

XIV. In Which Challenger Meets a Strange Colleague   381

XV. In Which Traps are Laid for a Great Quarry   390

XVI. In Which Challenger Has the Experience of His Lifetime   399

XVII. Where the Mists Clear Away   410

Appendices   415

The Disintegration Machine   423

When the World Screamed   437

THE LOST WORLD

CHAPTER I

There are Heroisms All Round Us

MR. HUNGERTON, her father, really was the most tactless person upon earth – a fluffy, feathery, untidy cockatoo of a man, perfectly good-natured, but absolutely centred upon his own silly self. If anything could have driven me from Gladys, it would have been the thought of such a father-in-law. I am convinced that he really believed in his heart that I came round to the Chestnuts three days a week for the pleasure of his company, and very especially to hear his views upon bimetallism – a subject upon which he was by way of being an authority.

For an hour or more that evening I listened to his monotonous chirrup about bad money driving out good, the token value of silver, the depreciation of the rupee, and the true standards of exchange.

'Suppose,' he cried, with feeble violence, 'that all the debts in the world were called up simultaneously and immediate payment insisted upon. What, under our present conditions, would happen then?'

I gave the self-evident answer that I should be a ruined man, upon which he jumped from his chair, reproved me my habitual levity, which made it impossible for him to discuss any reasonable subject in my presence, and bounced off out of the room to dress for a Masonic meeting.

At last I was alone with Gladys, and the moment of fate had come! All that evening I had felt like the soldier who awaits the signal which will send him on a forlorn hope, hope of victory and fear of repulse alternating in his mind.

She sat with that proud, delicate profile of hers outlined against the red curtain. How beautiful she was! And yet how aloof! We had been friends, quite good friends; but never could I get beyond the same comradeship which I might have established with one of my fellow-reporters upon the *Gazette* – perfectly frank, perfectly kindly, and perfectly unsexual. My instincts are all against a woman being too frank and at her ease with me. It is no compliment to a man.

Where the real sex feeling begins, timidity and distrust are its companions, heritage from old wicked days when love and violence went often hand in hand. The bent head, the averted eye, the faltering voice, the wincing figure – these, and not the unshrinking gaze and frank reply, are the true signals of passion. Even in my short life I had learned as much as that – or had inherited it in that race-memory which we call instinct.

Gladys was full of every womanly quality. Some judged her to be cold and hard, but such a thought was treason. That delicately-bronzed skin, almost Oriental in its colouring, that raven hair, the large liquid eyes, the full but exquisite lips – all the stigmata of passion were there. But I was sadly conscious that up to now I had never found the secret of drawing it forth. However, come what might, I should have done with suspense and bring matters to a head to-night. She could but refuse me, and better be a repulsed lover than an accepted brother.

So far my thoughts had carried me, and I was about to break the long and uneasy silence when two critical dark eyes looked round at me, and the proud head was shaken in smiling reproof.

'I have a presentiment that you are going to propose, Ned. I do wish you wouldn't, for things are so much nicer as they are.'

I drew my chair a little nearer.

'Now, how did you know that I was going to propose?' I asked, in genuine wonder.

'Don't women always know? Do you suppose any woman in the world was ever taken unawares? But, oh, Ned, our friendship has been so good and so pleasant! What a pity to spoil it! Don't you feel how splendid it is that a young man and a young woman should be able to talk face to face as we have talked?'

'I don't know, Gladys. You see, I can talk face to face with – with the station-master.' I can't imagine how that official came into the matter, but in he trotted and set us both laughing. 'That does not satisfy me in the least. I want my arms round you and your head on my breast, and, oh, Gladys, I want –'

She had sprung from her chair as she saw signs that I proposed to demonstrate some of my wants.

'You've spoiled everything, Ned,' she said. 'It's all so beautiful and natural until this kind of thing comes in. It is such a pity. Why can't you control yourself?'

'I didn't invent it,' I pleaded. 'It's nature. It's love!'

'Well, perhaps if both love it may be different. I have never felt it.'

'But, you must – you, with your beauty, with your soul! Oh, Gladys, you were made for love! You must love!'

'One must wait till it comes.'

'But why can't you love me, Gladys? Is it my appearance, or what?'

She did unbend a little. She put forward a hand – such a gracious, stooping attitude it was – and she pressed back my head. Then she looked into my upturned face with a very wistful smile.

'No, it isn't that,' she said at last. 'You're not a conceited boy by nature, and so I can safely tell you that it is not that. It's deeper.'

'My character?'

She nodded severely.

'What can I do to mend it? Do sit down and talk it over. No, really I won't, if you'll only sit down!'

She looked at me with a wondering distrust which was much more to my mind than her whole-hearted confidence How primitive and bestial it looks when you put it down in black and white! And perhaps after all it is only a feeling peculiar to myself. Anyhow, she sat down.

'Now tell me what's amiss with me.'

'I'm in love with somebody else,' said she.

It was my turn to jump out of my chair.

'It's nobody in particular,' she explained, laughing at the expression of my face, 'only an ideal. I've never met the kind of man I mean.'

'Tell me about him. What does he look like?'

'Oh, he might look very much like you.'

'How dear of you to say that! Well, what is it that he does that I don't do? Just say the word – teetotal, vegetarian, aeronaut, Theosophist, Superman – I'll have a try at it, Gladys, if you will only give me an idea what would please you.'

She laughed at the elasticity of my character. 'Well, in the first place, I don't think my ideal would speak like that,' she said. 'He would be a harder, sterner man, not so ready to adapt himself to a silly girl's whim. But above all he must be a man who could do, who could act, who would look death in the face and have no fear of him – a man of great deeds and strange experiences. It is never a man that I should love, but always the glories he had won, for they would be reflected upon me. Think of Richard Burton! When I read his wife's life of him I could so understand her love. And Lady Stanley! Did you ever read the wonderful last chapter of that book about her husband? These are the sort of men that a woman could worship with all her soul and yet be the greater, not the less, on account of her love, honoured by all the world as the inspirer of noble deeds.'

She looked so beautiful in her enthusiasm that I nearly brought down the whole level of the interview. I gripped myself hard, and went on with the argument.

'We can't all be Stanleys and Burtons,' said I. 'Besides, we don't get the chance – at least, I never had the chance. If I did I should try to take it.'

'But chances are all around you. It is the mark of the kind of man I mean that he makes his own chances. You can't hold him back. I've never met him, and yet I seem to know him so well. There are heroisms all round us waiting to be done. It's for men to do them, and for women to reserve their love as a reward for such men. Look at that young Frenchman who went up last week in a balloon. It was blowing a gale of wind, but because he was announced to go he insisted on starting. The wind blew him one thousand five hundred miles in twenty-four hours, and he fell in the middle of Russia. That was the kind of man I mean. Think of the woman he loved, and how other women must have envied her! That's what I should like – to be envied for my man.'

'I'd have done it to please you.'

'But you shouldn't do it merely to please me. You should do it because you can't help it, because it's natural to you – because the man in you is crying out for heroic expression. Now, when you described the Wigan coal explosion last month, could you not have gone down and helped those people, in spite of the choke-damp?'

'I did.'

'You never said so.'

'There was nothing worth bucking about.'

'I didn't know.' She looked at me with rather more interest. 'That was brave of you.'

'I had to. If you want to write good copy you must be where the things are.'

'What a prosaic motive! It seems to take all the romance out of it. But still, whatever your motive, I am glad that you went down that mine.' She gave me her hand, but with such sweetness and dignity that I could only stoop and kiss it. 'I dare say I am merely a foolish woman with a young girl's fancies. And yet it is so real with me, so entirely part of my very self, that I cannot help acting upon it. If I marry, I do want to marry a famous man.'

'Why should you not?' I cried. 'It is women like you who brace men up. Give me a chance and see if I will take it! Besides, as you say, men ought to *make* their own chances, and not wait until they are given. Look at Clive – just a clerk, and he conquered India. By George! I'll do something in the world yet!'

She laughed at my sudden Irish effervescence.

'Why not?' she said. 'You have everything a man could have – youth, health, strength, education, energy. I was sorry you spoke. And now I am glad – so glad – if it wakens these thoughts in you.'

'And if I do – ?'

Her hand rested like warm velvet upon my lips.

'Not another word, sir. You should have been at the office for evening duty half an hour ago, only I hadn't the heart to remind you. Some day, perhaps, when you have won your place in the world, we shall talk it over again.'

And so it was that I found myself that foggy November evening pursuing the Camberwell tram with my heart glowing within me, and with the eager determination that not another day should elapse before I should find some deed which was worthy of my lady. But who in all this wide world could ever have imagined the incredible shape which that deed was to take, or the strange steps by which I was led to the doing of it?

And, after all, this opening chapter will seem to the reader to have nothing to do with my narrative; and yet there would have been no narrative without it, for it is only when a man goes out into the world with the thought that there are heroisms all round him, and with the desire all alive in his heart to follow any which may come within sight of him, that he breaks away as I did from the life he knows, and ventures forth into the wonderful mystic twilight land where lie the great adventures and the great rewards. Behold me, then, at the office of the *Daily Gazette*, on the staff of which I was a most insignificant unit, with the settled determination that very night, if possible, to find the quest which should be worthy of my Gladys! Was it hardness, was it selfishness, that she should ask me to risk my life for her own glorification? Such thoughts may come to middle age, but never to ardent three-and-twenty in the fever of his first love.

CHAPTER II

Try Your Luck with Professor Challenger

I ALWAYS LIKED MCARDLE, the crabbed old, round backed, red-headed news editor, and I rather hoped that he liked me. Of course,

Beaumont was the real boss, but he lived in the rarified atmosphere of some Olympian height from which he could distinguish nothing smaller than an international crisis or a split in the Cabinet. Sometimes we saw him passing in lonely majesty to his inner sanctum with his eyes staring vaguely and his mind hovering over the Balkans or the Persian Gulf. He was above and beyond us. But McArdle was his first lieutenant, and it was he that we knew. The old man nodded as I entered the room, and he pushed his spectacles far up on his bald forehead.

'Well, Mr. Malone, from all I hear, you seem to be doing very well,' said he, in his kindly Scotch accent.

I thanked him.

'The colliery explosion was excellent. So was the Southwark fire. You have the true descreeptive touch. What did you want to see me about?'

'To ask a favour.'

He looked alarmed and his eyes shunned mine.

'Tut! tut! What is it?'

'Do you think, sir, that you could possibly send me on some mission for the paper? I would do my best to put it through and get you some good copy.'

'What sort of a meesion had you in your mind, Mr. Malone?'

'Well, sir, anything that had adventure and danger in it. I would really do my very best. The more difficult it was the better it would suit me.'

'You seem very anxious to lose your life.'

'To justify my life, sir.'

'Dear me, Mr. Malone, this is very – very exalted. I'm afraid the day for this sort of thing is rather past. The expense of the "special meesion" business hardly justifies the result, and, of course, in any case it would only be an experienced man with a name that would command public confidence who would get such an order. The big blank spaces in the map are all being filled in, and there's no room for romance anywhere. Wait a bit, though!' he added, with a sudden smile upon his face. 'Talking of the blank spaces of the map gives me an idea. What about exposing a fraud – a modern Munchausen – and making him rideeculous? You could show him up as the liar that he is! Eh, man, it would be fine. How does it appeal to you?'

'Anything – anywhere – I care nothing.'

McArdle was plunged in thought for some minutes.

'I wonder whether you could get on friendly – or at least on talking terms with the fellow,' he said, at last. 'You seem to have a sort of genius for establishing relations with people – seempathy, I suppose, or animal magnetism, or youthful vitality, or something. I am conscious of it myself.'

'You are very good, sir.'

'So why should you not try your luck with Professor Challenger, of Enmore Park?'

I dare say I looked a little startled.

'Challenger!' I cried. 'Professor Challenger, the famous zoologist! Wasn't he the man who broke the skull of Blundell, of the *Telegraph*?'

The news editor smiled grimly.

'Do you mind? Didn't you say it was adventures you were after?'

'It is all in the way of business, sir,' I answered.

'Exactly. I don't suppose he can always be so violent as that. I'm thinking that Blundell got him at the wrong moment, maybe, or in the wrong fashion. You may have better luck, or more tact in handling him. There's something in your line there, I am sure, and the *Gazette* should work it.'

'I really know nothing about him,' said I. 'I only remember his name in connection with the police-court proceedings, for striking Blundell.'

'I have a few notes for your guidance, Mr. Malone. I've had my eye on the Professor for some little time.' He took a paper from a drawer. 'Here is a summary of his record. I give it you briefly: –

' "Challenger, George Edward. *Born:* Largs, N.B., 1863. *Educ.:* Largs Academy; Edinburgh University. British Museum Assistant, 1892. Assistant-Keeper of Comparative Anthropology Department, 1893. Resigned after acrimonious Correspondence same year. Winner of Crayston Medal for Zoological Research. Foreign Member of" – well, quite a lot of things, about two inches of small type – "Société Belge, American Academy of Sciences, La Plata, etc., etc. Ex-President Palæontological Society. Section H, British Association" so on, so on! – "Publications: 'Some Observations Upon a Series of Kalmuck Skulls'; 'Outlines of Vertebrate Evolution'; and numerous papers, including 'The Underlying Fallacy of Weissmannism,' which caused heated discussion at the Zoological Congress of Vienna. *Recreations:* Walking, Alpine climbing. *Address:* Enmore Park, Kensington, W."

'There, take it with you. I've nothing more for you tonight.'

I pocketed the slip of paper.

'One moment, sir,' I said, as I realized that it was a pink bald head, and not a red face, which was fronting me. 'I am not very clear yet why I am to interview this gentleman. What has he done?'

The face flashed back again.

'Went to South America on a solitary expedeetion two years ago. Came back last year. Had undoubtedly been to South America, but refused to say exactly where. Began to tell his adventures in a vague way, but somebody started to pick holes, and he just shut up like an oyster. Something wonderful happened – or the man's a champion liar, which is the more probable supposeetion. Had some damaged photographs, said to be fakes. Got so touchy that he assaults anyone who asks questions, and heaves reporters doun the stairs. In my opinion he's just a homicidal megalomaniac with a turn for science. That's your man, Mr. Malone. Now, off you run, and see what you can make of him. You're big enough to look after yourself. Anyway, you are all safe. Employers' Liability Act, you know.'

A grinning red face turned once more into a pink oval, fringed with gingery fluff: the interview was at an end.

I walked across to the Savage Club, but instead of turning into it I leaned upon the railings of Adelphi Terrace and gazed thoughtfully for a long time at the brown, oily river. I can always think most sanely and clearly in the open air. I took out the list of Professor Challenger's exploits, and I read it over under the electric lamp. Then I had what I can only regard as an inspiration. As a Pressman, I felt sure from what I had been told that I could never hope to get into touch with this cantankerous Professor. But these recriminations, twice mentioned in his skeleton biography, could only mean that he was a fanatic in science. Was there not an exposed margin there upon which he might be accessible? I would try.

I entered the club. It was just after eleven, and the big room was fairly full, though the rush had not yet set in. I noticed a tall, thin, angular man seated in an arm-chair by the fire. He turned as I drew my chair up to him. It was the man of all others whom I should have chosen – Tarp Henry of the staff of *Nature*, a thin, dry, leathery creature, who was full, to those who knew him, of kindly humanity. I plunged instantly into my subject.

'What do you know of Professor Challenger?'

'Challenger?' He gathered his brows in scientific disapproval. 'Challenger was the man who came with some cock-and-bull story from South America.'

'What story?'

'Oh, it was rank nonsense about some queer animals he had discovered. I believe he has retracted since. Anyhow, he has suppressed it all. He gave an interview to Reuter's, and there was such a howl that he saw it wouldn't do. It was a discreditable business. There were one or two folk who were inclined to take him seriously, but he soon choked them off.'

'How?'

'Well, by his insufferable rudeness and impossible behaviour. There was poor old Wadley, of the Zoological Institute. Wadley sent a message: "The President of the Zoological Institute presents his compliments to Professor Challenger, and would take it as a personal favour if he would do them the honour to come to their next meeting." The answer was unprintable.'

'You don't say?'

'Well, a bowdlerized version of it would run: "Professor Challenger presents his compliments to the President of the Zoological Institute, and would take it as a personal favour if he would go to the devil." '

'Good Lord!'

'Yes, I expect that's what old Wadley said. I remember his wail at the meeting, which began: "In fifty years' experience of scientific intercourse –" It quite broke the old man up.'

'Anything more about Challenger?'

'Well, I'm a bacteriologist, you know. I live in a nine-hundred-diameter microscope. I can hardly claim to take serious notice of anything that I can see with my naked eye. I'm a frontiersman from the extreme edge of the Knowable, and I feel quite out of place when I leave my study and come into touch with all you great, rough, hulking creatures. I'm too detached to talk scandal, and yet at scientific conversaziones I *have* heard something of Challenger, for he is one of those men whom nobody can ignore. He's as clever as they make 'em – a full-charged battery of force and vitality, but a quarrelsome, ill-conditioned faddist, and unscrupulous at that. He had gone the length of faking some photographs over the South American business.'

'You say he is a faddist. What is his particular fad?'

'He has a thousand, but the latest is something about Weissmann and Evolution. He had a fearful row about it in Vienna, I believe.'

'Can't you tell me the point?'

'Not at the moment, but a translation of the proceedings exists. We have it filed at the office. Would you care to come?'

'It's just what I want. I have to interview the fellow, and I need some lead up to him. It's really awfully good of you to give me a lift. I'll go with you now, if it is not too late.'

Half an hour later I was seated in the newspaper office with a huge tome in front of me, which had been opened at the article 'Weissmann *versus* Darwin,' with the subheading, 'Spirited Protest at Vienna. Lively Proceedings.' My scientific education having been somewhat neglected I was unable to follow the whole argument, but it was evident that the English Professor had handled his subject in a very aggressive fashion, and had thoroughly annoyed his Continental colleagues. 'Protests,' 'Uproar,' and 'General appeal to the Chairman' were three of the first brackets which caught my eye. Most of the matter might have been written in Chinese for any definite meaning that it conveyed to my brain.

'I wish you could translate it into English for me,' I said, pathetically, to my helpmate.

'Well, it is a translation.'

'Then I'd better try my luck with the original.'

'It is certainly rather deep for a layman.'

'If I could only get a single good, meaty sentence which seemed to convey some sort of definite human idea, it would serve my turn. Ah, yes, this one will do. I seem in a vague way almost to understand it. I'll copy it out. This shall be my link with the terrible Professor.'

'Nothing else I can do?'

'Well, yes; I propose to write to him. If I could frame the letter here, and use your address, it would give atmosphere.'

'We'll have the fellow round here making a row and breaking the furniture.'

'No, no; you'll see the letter – nothing contentious, I assure you.'

'Well, that's my chair and desk. You'll find paper there. I'd like to censor it before it goes.'

It took some doing, but I flatter myself that it wasn't such a bad job when it was finished. I read it aloud to the critical bacteriologist with some pride in my handiwork.

'DEAR PROFESSOR CHALLENGER,' it said. 'As a humble student of Nature, I have always taken the most profound interest in your speculations as to the differences between Darwin and Weissmann. I have recently had occasion to refresh my memory by re-reading –'

'You infernal liar!' murmured Tarp Henry.

–'by re-reading your masterly address at Vienna. That lucid and admirable statement seems to be the last word in the matter. There is one sentence in it, however – namely: "I protest strongly against the insufferable and entirely dogmatic assertion that each separate *id* is a microcosm possessed of an historical architecture elaborated slowly through the series of generations." Have you no desire, in view of later research, to modify this statement? Do you not think that it is over-accentuated? With your permission, I would ask the favour of an interview, as I feel strongly upon the subject, and have certain suggestions which I could only elaborate in a personal conversation. With your consent, I trust to have the honour of calling at eleven o'clock the day after to-morrow (Wednesday) morning.

'I remain, Sir, with assurances of profound respect, yours very truly,

EDWARD D. MALONE.'

'How's that?' I asked, triumphantly.

'Well, if your conscience can stand it –'

'It has never failed me yet.'

'But what do you mean to do?'

'To get there. Once I am in his room I may see some opening. I may even go the length of open confession. If he is a sportsman he will be tickled.'

'Tickled, indeed! He's much more likely to do the tickling. Chain mail, or an American football suit – that's what you'll want. Well, good-bye. I'll have the answer for you here on Wednesday morning – if he ever deigns to answer you. He is a violent, dangerous, cantankerous character, hated by everyone who comes across him, and the butt of the students, so far as they dare take a liberty with him. Perhaps it would be best for you if you never heard from the fellow at all.'

CHAPTER III

He is a Perfectly Impossible Person

MY FRIEND'S FEAR or hope was not destined to be realized. When I called on Wednesday there was a letter with the West Kensington postmark upon it, and my name scrawled across the envelope in a handwriting which looked like a barbed-wire railing. The contents were as follows: –

'Enmore Park, W.

'Sir, – I have duly received your note, in which you claim to endorse my views, although I am not aware that they are dependent upon endorsement either from you or anyone else. You have ventured to use the word "speculation" with regard to my statement upon the subject of Darwinism, and I would call your attention to the fact that such a word in such a connection is offensive to a degree. The context convinces me, however, that you have sinned rather through ignorance and tactlessness than through malice, so I am content to pass the matter by. You quote an isolated sentence from my lecture, and appear to have some difficulty in understanding it. I should have thought that only a sub-human intelligence could have failed to grasp the point, but if it really needs amplification I shall consent to see you at the hour named, though visits and visitors of every sort are exceedingly distasteful to me. As to your suggestion that I may modify my opinion, I would have you know that it is not my habit to do so after a deliberate expression of my mature views. You will kindly show the envelope of this letter to my man, Austin, when you call, as he has to take every precaution to shield me from the intrusive rascals who call themselves "journalists."

'Yours faithfully,
GEORGE EDWARD CHALLENGER.'

This was the letter that I read aloud to Tarp Henry, who had come down early to hear the result of my venture. His only remark was, 'There's some new stuff, cuticura or something, which is better than arnica.' Some people have such extraordinary notions of humour.

It was nearly half-past ten before I had received my message, but a taxicab took me round in good time for my appointment. It was an imposing porticoed house at which we stopped, and the heavily-curtained windows gave every indication of wealth upon the part of this formidable Professor. The door was opened by an odd, swarthy, dried-up person of uncertain age, with a dark pilot jacket and brown leather gaiters. I found afterwards that he was the chauffeur, who filled the gaps left by a succession of fugitive butlers. He looked me up and down with a searching light blue eye.

'Expected?' he asked.

'An appointment.'

'Got your letter?'

I produced the envelope.

'Right!' He seemed to be a person of few words. Following him down the passage I was suddenly interrupted by a small woman, who stepped out from what proved to be the dining-room door. She was a bright, vivacious, dark-eyed lady, more French than English in her type.

'One moment,' she said. 'You can wait, Austin. Step in here, sir. May I ask if you have met my husband before?'

'No, madam, I have not had the honour.'

'Then I apologize to you in advance. I must tell you that he is a perfectly impossible person – absolutely impossible. If you are forewarned you will be the more ready to make allowances.'

'It is most considerate of you, madam.'

'Get quickly out of the room if he seems inclined to be violent. Don't wait to argue with him. Several people have been injured through doing that. Afterwards there is a public scandal, and it reflects upon me and all of us. I suppose it wasn't about South America you wanted to see him?'

I could not lie to a lady.

'Dear me! That is his most dangerous subject. You won't believe a word he says – I'm sure I don't wonder. But don't tell him so, for it makes him very violent. Pretend to believe him, and you may get through all right. Remember he believes it himself. Of that you may be assured. A more honest man never lived. Don't wait any longer or he may suspect. If you find him dangerous – really dangerous – ring the bell and hold him off until I come. Even at his worst I can usually control him.'

With these encouraging words the lady handed me over to the taciturn Austin, who had waited like a bronze statue of discretion during our short interview, and I was conducted to the end of the passage. There was a tap at a door, a bull's bellow from within, and I was face to face with the Professor.

He sat in a rotating chair behind a broad table, which was covered with books, maps, and diagrams. As I entered, his seat spun round to face me. His appearance made me gasp. I was prepared for something strange, but not for so overpowering a personality as this. It was his size which took one's breath away – his size and his imposing presence. His head was enormous, the largest I have ever seen upon a human being. I am sure that his top-hat, had I ventured to don it, would have slipped over me entirely and rested on my shoulders. He had the face and beard which I associate with an Assyrian bull; the former florid, the latter so black as almost to have a suspicion of blue, spade-shaped and rippling down over his chest. The hair was peculiar, plastered down in front in a long, curving wisp over his massive forehead. The eyes were blue-grey under great black tufts, very clear, very critical, and very masterful. A huge spread of shoulders and a chest like a barrel were the other parts of him which appeared above the table, save for two enormous hands covered with long black hair. This and a bellowing, roaring, rumbling voice made up my first impression of the notorious Professor Challenger.

'Well?' said he, with a most insolent stare. 'What now?'

I must keep up my deception for at least a little time longer, otherwise here was evidently an end of the interview.

'You were good enough to give me an appointment, sir,' said I, humbly, producing his envelope.

He took my letter from his desk and laid it out before him.

'Oh, you are the young person who cannot understand plain English, are you? My general conclusions you are good enough to approve, as I understand?'

'Entirely, sir – entirely!' I was very emphatic.

'Dear me! That strengthens my position very much, does it not? Your age and appearance make your support doubly valuable. Well, at least you are better than that herd of swine in Vienna, whose gregarious grunt is, however, not more offensive than the isolated effort of the British hog.' He glared at me as the present representative of the beast.

'They seem to have behaved abominably,' said I.

'I assure you that I can fight my own battles, and that I have no possible need of your sympathy. Put me alone, sir, and with my back to the wall. G. E. C. is happiest then. Well, sir, let us do what we can to curtail this visit, which can hardly be agreeable to you, and is inexpressibly irksome to me. You had, as I have been led to believe, some comments to make upon the proposition which I advanced in my thesis.'

There was a brutal directness about his methods which made evasion difficult. I must still make play and wait for a better opening. It had seemed simple enough at a distance. Oh, my Irish wits, could they not help me now, when I needed help so sorely? He transfixed me with two sharp, steely eyes. 'Come, come!' he rumbled.

'I am, of course, a mere student,' said I, with a fatuous smile, 'hardly more, I might say, than an earnest inquirer. At the same time, it seemed to me that you were a little severe upon Weissmann in this matter. Has not the general evidence since that date tended to – well, to strengthen his position?'

'What evidence?' He spoke with a menacing calm.

'Well, of course, I am aware that there is not any what you might call *definite* evidence. I alluded merely to the trend of modern thought and the general scientific point of view, if I might so express it.'

He leaned forward with great earnestness.

'I suppose you are aware,' said he, checking off points upon his fingers, 'that the cranial index is a constant factor?'

'Naturally,' said I.

'And that telegony is still *sub judice*?'

'Undoubtedly.'

'And that the germ plasm is different from the parthenogenetic egg?'

'Why, surely!' I cried, and gloried in my own audacity.

'But what does that prove?' he asked, in a gentle, persuasive voice.

'Ah, what indeed?' I murmured. 'What does it prove?'

'Shall I tell you?' he cooed.

'Pray do.'

'It proves,' he roared, with a sudden blast of fury, 'that you are the rankest impostor in London – a vile, crawling journalist, who has no more science than he has decency in his composition!'

He had sprung to his feet with a mad rage in his eyes. Even at that moment of tension I found time for amazement at the discovery that he was quite a short man, his head not higher than my shoulder – a stunted Hercules whose tremendous vitality had all run to depth, breadth, and brain.

'Gibberish!' he cried, leaning forward, with his fingers on the table and his face projecting. 'That's what I have been talking to you, sir – scientific gibberish! Did you think you could match cunning with me – you with your walnut of a brain? You think you are omnipotent, you infernal scribblers, don't you? That your praise can make a man and your blame can break him? We must all bow to you, and try to get a favourable word, must we? This man shall have a leg up, and this man shall have a dressing down! Creeping vermin, I know you! You've got out of your station. Time was when your ears were clipped. You've lost your sense of proportion. Swollen gas-bags! I'll keep you in your proper place. Yes, sir, you haven't got over G. E. C. There's one man who is still your master. He warned you off, but if you *will* come, by the Lord you do it at your own risk. Forfeit, my good Mr. Malone, I claim forfeit! You have played a rather dangerous game, and it strikes me that you have lost it.'

'Look here, sir.' said I, backing to the door and opening it; 'you can be as abusive as you like. But there is a limit. You shall not assault me.'

'Shall I not?' He was slowly advancing in a peculiarly menacing way, but he stopped now and put his big hands into the side pockets of a rather boyish short jacket which he wore. 'I have thrown several of you out of the house. You will be the fourth or fifth. Three pound fifteen each – that is how it averaged. Expensive, but very necessary. Now, sir, why should you not follow your brethren? I rather think you must.' He resumed his unpleasant and stealthy advance, pointing his toes as he walked, like a dancing master.

I could have bolted for the hall door, but it would have been too ignominious. Besides, a little glow of righteous anger was springing up within me. I had been hopelessly in the wrong before, but this man's menaces were putting me in the right.

'I'll trouble you to keep your hands off, sir. I'll not stand it.'

'Dear me!' His black moustache lifted and a white fang twinkled in a sneer. 'You won't stand it, eh?'

'Don't be such a fool, Professor!' I cried. 'What can you hope for? I'm fifteen stone, as hard as nails, and play centre three-quarter every Saturday for the London Irish. I'm not the man –'

It was at that moment that he rushed me. It was lucky that I had opened the door, or we should have gone through it. We did a Catherine-wheel together down the passage. Somehow we gathered up a chair upon our way, and bounded on with it towards the street. My mouth was full of his beard, our arms were locked, our bodies intertwined, and that infernal chair radiated its legs all round us. The watchful Austin had thrown open the hall door. We went with a back somersault down the front steps. I have seen the two Macs attempt something of the kind at the halls, but it appears to take some practice to do it without hurting oneself. The chair went to matchwood at the bottom, and we rolled apart into the gutter. He sprang to his feet, waving his fists and wheezing like an asthmatic.

'Had enough?' he panted.

'You infernal bully!' I cried, as I gathered myself together.

Then and there we should have tried the thing out, for he was effervescing with fight, but fortunately I was rescued from an odious situation. A policeman was beside us, his notebook in his hand.

'What's all this? You ought to be ashamed,' said the policeman. It was the most rational remark which I had heard in Enmore Park. 'Well,' he insisted, turning to me, 'what is it, then?'

'This man attacked me,' said I.

'Did you attack him?' asked the policeman.

The Professor breathed hard and said nothing.

'It's not the first time, either,' said the policeman, severely, shaking his head. 'You were in trouble last month for the same thing.

You've blackened this young man's eye. Do you give him in charge, sir?'

I relented.

'No,' said I, 'I do not.'

'What's that?' said the policeman.

'I was to blame myself. I intruded upon him. He gave me fair warning.'

The policeman snapped up his notebook.

'Don't let us have any more such goings-on,' said he. 'Now, then! Move on, there, move on!' This to a butcher's boy, a maid, and one or two loafers who had collected. He clumped heavily down the street, driving this little flock before him. The Professor looked at me, and there was something humorous at the back of his eyes.

'Come in!' said he. 'I've not done with you yet.'

The speech had a sinister sound, but I followed him none the less into the house. The man-servant, Austin, like a wooden image, closed the door behind us.

CHAPTER IV

It's Just the Very Biggest Thing in the World

HARDLY WAS IT SHUT THAN Mrs. Challenger darted out from the dining-room. The small woman was in a furious temper. She barred her husband's way like an enraged chicken in front of a bulldog. It was evident that she had seen my exit, but had not observed my return.

'You brute, George!' she screamed. 'You've hurt that nice young man.'

He jerked backwards with his thumb.

'Here he is, safe and sound behind me.'

She was confused, but not unduly so.

'I am sorry, I didn't see you.'

'I assure you, madam, that it is all right.'

'He has marked your poor face! Oh, George, what a brute you are! Nothing but scandals from one end of the week to the other. Everyone hating and making fun of you. You've finished my patience. This ends it.'

'Dirty linen,' he rumbled.

'It's not a secret,' she cried. 'Do you suppose that the whole street – the whole of London, for that matter – Get away, Austin, we

don't want you here. Do you suppose they don't all talk about you?
Where is your dignity? You, a man who should have been Regius
Professor at a great University with a thousand students all revering
you. Where is your dignity, George?'

'How about yours, my dear?'

'You try me too much. A ruffian – a common brawling ruffian –
that's what you have become.'

'Be good, Jessie.'

'A roaring, raging bully!'

'That's done it! Stool of penance!' said he.

To my amazement he stooped, picked her up, and placed her sitting upon a high pedestal of black marble in the angle of the hall. It
was at least seven feet high, and so thin that she could hardly balance upon it. A more absurd object than she presented cocked up
there with her face convulsed with anger, her feet dangling, and her
body rigid for fear of an upset, I could not imagine.

'Let me down!' she wailed.

'Say "please."'

'You brute, George! Let me down this instant!'

'Come into the study, Mr. Malone.'

'Really, sir –!' said I, looking at the lady.

'Here's Mr. Malone pleading for you, Jessie. Say "please," and
down you come.'

'Oh, you brute! Please! please!'

He took her down as if she had been a canary.

'You must behave yourself, dear. Mr. Malone is a Pressman. He
will have it all in his rag to-morrow, and sell an extra dozen among
our neighbours. "Strange story of high life" – you felt fairly high on
that pedestal, did you not? Then a subtitle, "Glimpse of a singular
ménage." He's a foul feeder, is Mr. Malone, a carrion eater, like all
of his kind – *porcus ex grege diaboli* – a swine from the devil's herd.
That's it, Malone – what?'

'You are really intolerable!' said I, hotly.

He bellowed with laughter.

'We shall have a coalition presently,' he boomed, looking from
his wife to me and puffing out his enormous chest. Then, suddenly
altering his tone, 'Excuse this frivolous family badinage, Mr.
Malone. I called you back for some more serious purpose than to
mix you up with our little domestic pleasantries. Run away, little
woman, and don't fret.' He placed a huge hand upon each of her
shoulders. 'All that you say is perfectly true. I should be a better
man if I did what you advise, but I shouldn't be quite George

Edward Challenger. There are plenty of better men, my dear, but only one G. E. C. So make the best of him.' He suddenly gave her a resounding kiss, which embarrassed me even more than his violence had done. 'Now, Mr. Malone,' he continued, with a great accession of dignity, 'this way if *you* please.'

We re-entered the room which we had left so tumultuously ten minutes before. The Professor closed the door carefully behind us, motioned me into an arm-chair, and pushed a cigar-box under my nose.

'Real San Juan Colorado,' he said. 'Excitable people like you are the better for narcotics. Heavens! don't bite it! Cut – and cut with reverence! Now lean back, and listen attentively to whatever I may care to say to you. If any remark should occur to you, you can reserve it for some more opportune time.

'First of all, as to your return to my house after your most justifiable expulsion' – he protruded his beard, and stared at me as one who challenges and invites contradiction – 'after, as I say, your well-merited expulsion. The reason lay in your answer to that most officious policeman, in which I seemed to discern some glimmering of good feeling upon your part – more, at any rate, than I am accustomed to associate with your profession. In admitting that the fault of the incident lay with you, you gave some evidence of a certain mental detachment and breadth of view which attracted my favourable notice. The sub-species of the human race to which you unfortunately belong has always been below my mental horizon. Your words brought you suddenly above it. You swam up into my serious notice. For this reason I asked you to return with me, as I was minded to make your further acquaintance. You will kindly deposit your ash in the small Japanese tray on the bamboo table which stands at your left elbow.'

All this he boomed forth like a professor addressing his class. He had swung round his revolving-chair so as to face me, and he sat all puffed out like an enormous bull-frog, his head laid back, and his eyes half-covered by supercilious lids. Now he suddenly turned himself sideways, and all I could see of him was tangled hair with a red, protruding ear. He was scratching about among the litter of papers upon his desk. He faced me presently with what looked like a very tattered sketch-book in his hand.

'I am going to talk to you about South America,' said he. 'No comments if you please. First of all, I wish you to understand that nothing I tell you now is to be repeated in any public way unless you have my express permission. That permission will, in all human probability, never be given. Is that clear?'

'It is very hard,' said I. 'Surely a judicious account –'

He replaced the notebook upon the table.

'That ends it,' said he. 'I wish you a very good morning.'

'No, no!' I cried. 'I submit to any conditions. So far as I can see, I have no choice.'

'None in the world,' said he.

'Well, then, I promise.'

'Word of honour?'

'Word of honour.'

He looked at me with doubt in his insolent eyes.

'After all, what do I know about your honour?' said he.

'Upon my word, sir,' I cried, angrily, 'you take very great liberties! I have never been so insulted in my life.'

He seemed more interested than annoyed at my outbreak.

'Round-headed,' he muttered. 'Brachycephalic, grey-eyed, black-haired, with suggestion of the negroid. Celtic, I presume?'

'I am an Irishman, sir.'

'Irish Irish?'

'Yes, sir.'

'That, of course, explains it. Let me see; you have given me your promise that my confidence will be respected? That confidence, I may say, will be far from complete. But I am prepared to give you a few indications which will be of interest. In the first place, you are probably aware that two years ago I made a journey to South America – one which will be classical in the scientific history of the world? The object of my journey was to verify some conclusions of Wallace and of Bates, which could only be done by observing their reported facts under the same conditions in which they had themselves noted them. If my expedition had no other results it would still have been noteworthy, but a curious incident occurred to me while there which opened up an entirely fresh line of inquiry.

'You are aware – or probably, in this half-educated age, you are not aware – that the country round some parts of the Amazon is still only partially explored, and that a great number of tributaries, some of them entirely uncharted, run into the main river. It was my business to visit this little-known back-country and to examine its fauna, which furnished me with the materials for several chapters for that great and monumental work upon zoology which will be my life's justification. I was returning, my work accomplished, when I had occasion to spend a night at a small Indian village at a point where a certain tributary – the name and position of which I withhold – opens into the main river. The natives were Cucama Indians, an amiable but degraded race, with mental powers hardly superior to the average Londoner. I had effected some cures among them upon my way up the river, and had impressed them considerably with my personality, so that I was not surprised to find myself eagerly awaited upon my return. I gathered from their signs that someone had urgent need of my medical services, and I followed the chief to one of his huts. When I entered I found that the sufferer to whose aid I had been summoned had that instant expired. He was, to my surprise, no Indian, but a white man; indeed, I may say a very white man, for he was flaxen-haired and had some characteristics of an albino. He was clad in rags, was very emaciated, and bore every trace of prolonged hardship. So far as I could understand the account of the natives, he was a complete stranger to them, and had come upon their village through the woods alone and in the last stage of exhaustion.

'The man's knapsack lay beside the couch, and I examined the contents. His name was written upon a tab within it – Maple White, Lake Avenue, Detroit, Michigan. It is a name to which I am prepared always to lift my hat. It is not too much to say that it will rank level with my own when the final credit of this business comes to be apportioned.

'From the contents of the knapsack it was evident that this man had been an artist and poet in search of effects. There were scraps of verse. I do not profess to be a judge of such things, but they appeared to me to be singularly wanting in merit. There were also some rather commonplace pictures of river scenery, a paint-box, a box of coloured chalks, some brushes, that curved bone which lies upon my inkstand, a volume of Baxter's "Moths and Butterflies," a cheap revolver, and a few cartridges. Of personal equipment he either had none or he had lost it in his journey. Such were the total effects of this strange American Bohemian.

'I was turning away from him when I observed that something projected from the front of his ragged jacket. It was this sketchbook, which was as dilapidated then as you see it now. Indeed, I can assure you that a first folio of Shakespeare could not be treated with greater reverence than this relic has been since it came into my possession. I hand it to you now, and I ask you to take it page by page and to examine the contents.'

He helped himself to a cigar and leaned back with a fiercely critical pair of eyes, taking note of the effect which this document would produce.

I had opened the volume with some expectation of a revelation, though of what nature I could not imagine. The first page was disappointing, however, as it contained nothing but the picture of a very fat man in a pea-jacket, with the legend, 'Jimmy Colver on the Mail-boat,' written beneath it. There followed several pages which were filled with small sketches of Indians and their ways. Then came a picture of a cheerful and corpulent ecclesiastic in a shovel hat, sitting opposite a very thin European, and the inscription: 'Lunch with Fra Cristofero at Rosario.' Studies of women and babies accounted for several more pages, and then there was an unbroken series of animal drawings with such explanations as 'Manatee upon Sandbank,' 'Turtles and their Eggs,' 'Black Ajouti under a Miriti Palm' – the latter disclosing some sort of pig-like animal; and finally came a double page of studies of long-snouted and very unpleasant saurians. I could make nothing of it, and said so to the Professor.

'Surely these are only crocodiles?'

'Alligators! Alligators! There is hardly such a thing as a true crocodile in South America. The distinction between them –'

'I meant that I could see nothing unusual – nothing to justify what you have said.'

He smiled serenely.

'Try the next page,' said he.

I was still unable to sympathize. It was a full-page sketch of a landscape roughly tinted in colour – the kind of painting which an open-air artist takes as a guide to a future more elaborate effort. There was a pale-green foreground of feathery vegetation, which sloped upwards and ended in a line of cliffs dark red in colour, and curiously ribbed like some basaltic formations which I have seen. They extended in an unbroken wall right across the background. At one point was an isolated pyramidal rock, crowned by a great tree, which appeared to be separated by a cleft from the main crag. Behind it all, a blue tropical sky. A thin green line of vegetation fringed the summit of the ruddy cliff. On the next page was another water-colour wash of the same place, but much nearer, so that one could clearly see the details.

'Well?' he asked.

'It is no doubt a curious formation,' said I, 'but I am not geologist enough to say that it is wonderful.'

'Wonderful!' he repeated. 'It is unique. It is incredible. No one on earth has ever dreamed of such a possibility. Now the next.'

I turned it over, and gave an exclamation of surprise. There was a full-page picture of the most extraordinary creature that I had ever seen. It was the wild dream of an opium smoker, a vision of delirium. The head was like that of a fowl, the body that of a bloated lizard, the trailing tail was furnished with upward-turned spikes, and the curved back was edged with a high serrated fringe, which looked like a dozen cocks' wattles placed behind each other. In front of this creature was an absurd mannikin, or dwarf in the human form, who stood staring at it.

'Well, what do you think of that?' cried the Professor, rubbing his hands with an air of triumph.

'It is monstrous – grotesque.'

'But what made him draw such an animal?'

'Trade gin, I should think.'

'Oh, that's the best explanation you can give, is it?'

'Well, sir, what is yours?'

'The obvious one that the creature exists. That it is actually sketched from the life.'

I should have laughed only that I had a vision of our doing another Catherine-wheel down the passage.

'No doubt,' said I, 'no doubt,' as one humours an imbecile. 'I confess, however,' I added, 'that this tiny human figure puzzles me. If it were an Indian we could set it down as evidence of some pigmy race in America, but it appears to be a European in a sun-hat.'

The Professor snorted like an angry buffalo. 'You really touch the limit,' said he. 'You enlarge my view of the possible. Cerebral paresis! Mental inertia! Wonderful!'

He was too absurd to make me angry. Indeed, it was a waste of energy, for if you were going to be angry with this man you would be angry all the time. I contented myself with smiling wearily. 'It struck me that the man was small,' said I.

'Look here!' he cried, leaning forward and dabbing a great hairy sausage of a finger on to the picture. 'You see that plant behind the animal; I suppose you thought it was a dandelion or a brussels sprout – what? Well, it is a vegetable ivory palm, and they run to about fifty or sixty feet. Don't you see that the man is put in for a purpose? He couldn't really have stood in front of that brute and lived to draw it. He sketched himself in to give a scale of heights. He was, we will say, over five feet high. The tree is ten times bigger, which is what one would expect.'

'Good heavens!' I cried. 'Then you think the beast was – Why, Charing Cross Station would hardly make a kennel for such a brute!'

'Apart from exaggeration, he is certainly a well-grown specimen,' said the Professor, complacently.

'But,' I cried, 'surely the whole experience of the human race is not to be set aside on account of a single sketch' – I had turned over the leaves and ascertained that there was nothing more in the book – 'a single sketch by a wandering American artist who may have done it under hashish, or in the delirium of fever, or simply in order to gratify a freakish imagination. You can't, as a man of science, defend such a position as that.'

For answer the Professor took a book down from a shelf.

'This is an excellent monograph by my gifted friend, Ray Lankester!' said he. 'There is an illustration here which would interest you. Ah, yes, here it is! The inscription beneath it runs: "Probable appearance in life of the Jurassic Dinosaur Stegosaurus. The hind leg alone is twice as tall as a full-grown man." Well, what do you make of that?'

He handed me the open book. I started as I looked at the picture. In this reconstructed animal of a dead world there was certainly a very great resemblance to the sketch of the unknown artist.

'That is certainly remarkable,' said I.

'But you won't admit that it is final?'

'Surely it might be a coincidence, or this American may have seen a picture of the kind and carried it in his memory. It would be likely to recur to a man in a delirium.'

'Very good,' said the Professor, indulgently; 'we leave it at that. I will now ask you to look at this bone.' He handed over the bone which he had already described as part of the dead man's possessions. It was about six inches long, and thicker than my thumb, with some indications of dried cartilage at one end of it.

'To what known creature does that bone belong?' asked the Professor.

I examined it with care, and tried to recall some half-forgotten knowledge.

'It might be a very thick human collar-bone,' I said.

My companion waved his hand in contemptuous deprecation.

'The human collar-bone is curved. This is straight. There is a groove upon its surface showing that a great tendon played across it, which could not be the case with a clavicle.'

'Then I must confess that I don't know what it is.'

'You need not be ashamed to expose your ignorance, for I don't suppose the whole South Kensington staff could give a name to it.' He took a little bone the size of a bean out of a pill-box. 'So far as I am a judge this human bone is the analogue of the one which you hold in your hand. That will give you some idea of the size of the creature. You will observe from the cartilage that this is no fossil specimen, but recent. What do you say to that?'

'Surely in an elephant –'

He winced as if in pain.

'Don't! Don't talk of elephants in South America. Even in these days of Board Schools –'

'Well,' I interrupted, 'any large South American animal – a tapir, for example.'

'You may take it, young man, that I am versed in the elements of my business. This is not a conceivable bone either of a tapir or of any other creature known to zoology. It belongs to a very large, a very strong, and, by all analogy, a very fierce animal which exists upon the face of the earth, but has not yet come under the notice of science. You are unconvinced?'

'I am at least deeply interested.'

'Then your case is not hopeless. I feel that there is reason lurking in you somewhere, so we will patiently grope round for it. We will now leave the dead American and proceed with my narrative. You can imagine that I could hardly come away from the Amazon without probing deeper into the matter. There were indications as to the direction from which the dead traveller had come. Indian legends would alone have been my guide, for I found that rumours of a strange land were common among all the riverine tribes. You have heard, no doubt, of Curupuri?'

'Never.'

'Curupuri is the spirit of the woods, something terrible, something malevolent, something to be avoided. None can describe its shape or nature, but it is a word of terror along the Amazon. Now all tribes agree as to the direction in which Curupuri lives. It was the same direction from which the American had come. Something terrible lay that way. It was my business to find out what it was.'

'What did you do?' My flippancy was all gone. This massive man compelled one's attention and respect.

'I overcame the extreme reluctance of the natives – a reluctance which extends even to talk upon the subject – and by judicious persuasion and gifts, aided, I will admit, by some threats of coercion, I got two of them to act as guides. After many adventures which I need not describe, and after travelling a distance which I will not mention, in a direction which I withhold, we came at last to a tract of country which has never been described, nor, indeed, visited save by my unfortunate predecessor. Would you kindly look at this?'

He handed me a photograph – half-plate size.

'The unsatisfactory appearance of it is due to the fact,' said he, 'that on descending the river the boat was upset and the case which contained the undeveloped films was broken, with disastrous results. Nearly all of them were totally ruined – an irreparable loss. This is one of the few which partially escaped. This explanation of deficiencies or abnormalities you will kindly accept. There was talk of faking. I am not in a mood to argue such a point.'

The photograph was certainly very off-coloured. An unkind critic might easily have misinterpreted that dim surface. It was a dull grey landscape, and as I gradually deciphered the details of it I realized that it represented a long and enormously high line of cliffs exactly like an immense cataract seen in the distance, with a sloping, tree-clad plain in the foreground.

'I believe it is the same place as the painted picture,' said I.

'It *is* the same place,' the Professor answered. 'I found traces of the fellow's camp. Now look at this.'

It was a nearer view of the same scene, though the photograph was extremely defective. I could distinctly see the isolated, tree-crowned pinnacle of rock which was detached from the crag.

'I have no doubt of it at all,' said I.

'Well, that is something gained,' said he. 'We progress, do we not? Now, will you please look at the top of that rocky pinnacle? Do you observe something there?'

'An enormous tree.'

'But on the tree?'

'A large bird,' said I.

He handed me a lens.

'Yes,' I said, peering through it, 'a large bird stands on the tree. It appears to have a considerable beak. I should say it was a pelican.'

'I cannot congratulate you upon your eyesight,' said the Professor. 'It is not a pelican, nor, indeed, is it a bird. It may interest you to know that I succeeded in shooting that particular specimen. It was the only absolute proof of my experiences which I was able to bring away with me.'

'You have it, then?' Here at last was tangible corroboration.

'I had it. It was unfortunately lost with so much else in the same boat accident which ruined my photographs. I clutched at it as it disappeared in the swirl of the rapids, and part of its wing was left in my hand. I was insensible when washed ashore, but the miserable remnant of my superb specimen was still intact; I now lay it before you.'

From a drawer he produced what seemed to me to be the upper portion of the wing of a large bat. It was at least two feet in length, a curved bone, with a membranous veil beneath it.

'A monstrous bat!' I suggested.

'Nothing of the sort,' said the Professor, severely. 'Living, as I do, in an educated and scientific atmosphere, I could not have conceived that the first principles of zoology were so little known. Is it possible that you do not know the elementary fact in comparative anatomy, that the wing of a bird is really the forearm, while the wing of a bat consists of three elongated fingers with membranes between? Now, in this case, the bone is certainly not the forearm, and you can see for yourself that this is a single membrane hanging upon a single bone, and therefore that it cannot belong to a bat. But if it is neither bird nor bat, what is it?'

My small stock of knowledge was exhausted.

'I really do not know,' said I.

He opened the standard work to which he had already referred me.

'Here,' said he, pointing to the picture of an extraordinary flying monster, 'is an excellent reproduction of the dimorphodon, or pterodactyl, a flying reptile of the Jurassic period. On the next page is a diagram of the mechanism of its wing. Kindly compare it with the specimen in your hand.'

A wave of amazement passed over me as I looked. I was convinced. There could be no getting away from it. The cumulative proof was overwhelming. The sketch, the photographs, the narrative, and now the actual specimen – the evidence was complete. I said so – I said so warmly, for I felt that the Professor was an ill-used man. He leaned back in his chair with drooping eyelids and a tolerant smile, basking in this sudden gleam of sunshine.

'It's just the very biggest thing that I ever heard of!' said I, though it was my journalistic rather than my scientific enthusiasm that was roused. 'It is colossal. You are a Columbus of science who has discovered a lost world. I'm really awfully sorry if I seemed to doubt you. It was all so unthinkable. But I understand evidence when I see it, and this should be good enough for anyone.'

The Professor purred with satisfaction.

'And then, sir, what did you do next?'

'It was the wet season, Mr. Malone, and my stores were exhausted. I explored some portion of this huge cliff, but I was unable to find any way to scale it. The pyramidal rock upon which I saw and shot the pterodactyl was more accessible. Being something of a cragsman, I did manage to get half way to the top of that. From that height I had a better idea of the plateau upon the top of the crags. It appeared to be very large; neither to east nor to west could I see any end to the vista of green-capped cliffs. Below, it is a swampy, jungly region, full of snakes, insects, and fever. It is a natural protection to this singular country.'

'Did you see any other trace of life?'

'No, sir, I did not; but during the week that we lay encamped at the base of the cliff we heard some very strange noises from above.'

'But the creature that the American drew? How do you account for that?'

'We can only suppose that he must have made his way to the summit and seen it there. We know, therefore, that there *is* a way up. We know equally that it must be a very difficult one, otherwise the creatures would have come down and overrun the surrounding country. Surely that is clear?'

'But how do they come to be there?'

'I do not think that the problem is a very obscure one,' said the Professor; 'there can only be one explanation. South America is, as you may have heard, a granite continent. At this single point in the interior there has been, in some far distant age, a great, sudden volcanic upheaval. These cliffs, I may remark, are basaltic, and therefore plutonic. An area, as large perhaps as Sussex, has been lifted up *en bloc* with all its living contents, and cut off by perpendicular precipices of a hardness which defies erosion from all the rest of the continent. What is the result? Why, the ordinary laws of nature are suspended. The various checks which influence the struggle for existence in the world at large are all neutralized or altered. Creatures survive which would otherwise disappear. You will observe that both the pterodactyl and and the stegosaurus are Jurassic, and therefore of a great age in the order of life. They have been artificially conserved by those strange accidental conditions.'

'But surely your evidence is conclusive. You have only to lay it before the proper authorities.'

'So, in my simplicity, I had imagined,' said the Professor, bitterly. 'I can only tell you that it was not so, that I was met at every turn by incredulity, born partly of stupidity and partly of jealousy. It is not my nature, sir, to cringe to any man, or to seek to prove a fact if my word has been doubted. After the first I have not condescended to show such corroborative proofs as I possess. The subject became hateful to me – I would not speak of it. When men like yourself, who represent the foolish curiosity of the public, came to disturb my privacy I was unable to meet them with dignified reserve. By nature I am, I admit, somewhat fiery, and under provocation I am inclined to be violent. I fear you may have remarked it.'

I nursed my eye and was silent.

'My wife has frequently remonstrated with me upon the subject, and yet I fancy that any man of honour would feel the same. To-night, however, I propose to give an extreme example of the control of the will over the emotions. I invite you to be present at the exhi-bition.' He handed me a card from his desk. 'You will perceive that Mr. Percival Waldron, a naturalist of some popular repute, is announced to lecture at eight-thirty at the Zoological Institute's Hall upon "The Record of the Ages." I have been specially invited to be present upon the platform, and to move a vote of thanks to the lecturer. While doing so, I shall make it my business, with infi-nite tact and delicacy, to throw out a few remarks which may arouse the interest of the audience and cause some of them to desire to go more deeply into the matter. Nothing contentious, you understand, but only an indication that there are greater deeps beyond. I shall hold myself strongly in leash, and see whether by this self-restraint I attain a more favourable result.'

'And I may come?' I asked eagerly.

'Why, surely,' he answered, cordially. He had an enormously massive genial manner, which was almost as over-powering as his violence. His smile of benevolence was a wonderful thing, when his cheeks would suddenly bunch into two red apples, between his half-closed eyes and his great black beard. 'By all means, come. It will be a comfort to me to know that I have one ally in the hall, however inefficient and ignorant of the subject he may be. I fancy there will be a large audience, for Waldron, though an absolute charlatan, has a considerable popular following. Now, Mr. Malone, I have given you rather more of my time than I had intended. The individual must not monopolize what is meant for the world. I shall be pleased to see you at the lecture to-night. In the meantime, you will under-stand that no public use is to be made of any of the material that I have given you.'

'But Mr. McArdle – my news editor, you know – will want to know what I have done.'

'Tell him what you like. You can say, among other things, that if he sends anyone else to intrude upon me I shall call upon him with a riding whip. But I leave it to you that nothing of all this appears in print. Very good. Then the Zoological Institute's Hall at eight-thirty tonight.' I had a last impression of red cheeks, blue rippling beard, and intolerant eyes, as he waved me out of the room.

CHAPTER V

Question!

WHAT WITH THE PHYSICAL SHOCKS incidental to my first interview with Professor Challenger and the mental ones which accompanied the second, I was a somewhat demoralized journalist by the time I found myself in Enmore Park once more. In my aching head the one thought was throbbing that there really *was* truth in this man's story, that it was of tremendous consequence, and that it would work up into inconceivable copy for the *Gazette* when I could obtain permission to use it. A taxicab was waiting at the end of the road, so I sprang into it and drove down to the office. McArdle was at his post as usual.

'Well,' he cried, expectantly, 'what may it run to? I'm thinking, young man, you have been in the wars. Don't tell me that he assaulted you.'

'We had a little difference at first.'

'What a man it is! What did you do?'

'Well, he became more reasonable and we had a chat. But I got nothing out of him – nothing for publication.'

'I'm not so sure about that. You got a black eye out of him, and that's for publication. We can't have this reign of terror, Mr. Malone. We must bring the man to his bearings. I'll have a lead-erette on him to-morrow that will raise a blister. Just give me the material and I will engage to brand the fellow for ever. Professor Munchausen – how's that for an inset headline? Sir John Mande-ville redivivus – Cagliostro – all the impostors and bullies in history. I'll show him up for the fraud he is.'

'I wouldn't do that, sir.'

'Why not?'

'Because he is not a fraud at all.'

'What!' roared McArdle. 'You don't mean to say you really believe this stuff of his about mammoths and mastodons and great sea sairpents?'

'Well, I don't know about that. I don't think he makes any claims of that kind. But I do believe that he has got something new.'

'Then for Heaven's sake, man, write it up!'

'I'm longing to, but all I know he gave me in confidence and on condition that I didn't.' I condensed into a few sentences the Professor's narrative. 'That's how it stands.'

McArdle looked deeply incredulous.

'Well, Mr. Malone,' he said at last, 'about this scientific meeting to-night; there can be no privacy about that, anyhow. I don't suppose any paper will want to report it, for Waldron has been reported already a dozen times, and no one is aware that Challenger will speak. We may get a scoop, if we are lucky. You'll be there in any case, so you'll just give us a pretty full report. I'll keep space up to midnight.'

My day was a busy one, and I had an early dinner at the Savage Club with Tarp Henry, to whom I gave some account of my adventures. He listened with a sceptical smile on his gaunt face, and roared with laughter on hearing that the Professor had convinced me.

'My dear chap, things don't happen like that in real life. People don't stumble upon enormous discoveries and then lose their evidence. Leave that to the novelists. The fellow is as full of tricks as the monkey-house at the Zoo. It's all absolute bosh.'

'But the American poet?'

'He never existed.'

'I saw his sketch-book.'

'Challenger's sketch-book.'

'You think he drew that animal?'

'Of course he did. Who else?'

'Well, then, the photographs?'

'There was nothing in the photographs. By your own admission you only saw a bird.'

'A pterodactyl.'

'That's what he says. He put the pterodactyl into your head.'

'Well, then, the bones?'

'First one out of an Irish stew. Second one vamped up for the occasion. If you are clever and you know your business you can fake a bone as easily as you can a photograph.'

I began to feel uneasy. Perhaps, after all, I had been premature in my acquiescence. Then I had a sudden happy thought.

'Will you come to the meeting?' I asked.

Tarp Henry looked thoughtful.

'He is not a popular person, the genial Challenger,' said he. 'A lot of people have accounts to settle with him. I should say he is about the best-hated man in London. If the medical students turn out there will be no end of a rag. I don't want to get into a bear-garden.'

'You might at least do him the justice to hear him state his own case.'

'Well, perhaps it's only fair. All right. I'm your man for the evening.'

When we arrived at the hall we found a much greater concourse than I had expected. A line of electric broughams discharged their little cargoes of white-bearded professors, while the dark stream of humbler pedestrians, who crowded through the arched doorway, showed that the audience would be popular as well as scientific. Indeed, it became evident to us as soon as we had taken our seats that a youthful and even boyish spirit was abroad in the gallery and the back portions of the hall. Looking behind me, I could see rows of faces of the familiar medical student type. Apparently the great hospitals had each sent down their contingent. The behaviour of the audience at present was good-humoured, but mischievous. Scraps of popular songs were chorused with an enthusiasm which was a strange prelude to a scientific lecture, and there was already a tendency to personal chaff which promised a jovial evening to others, however embarrassing it might be to the recipients of these dubious honours.

Thus, when old Doctor Meldrum, with his well-known curly-brimmed opera-hat, appeared upon the platform, there was such a universal query of 'Where *did* you get that tile?' that he hurriedly removed it, and concealed it furtively under his chair. When gouty Professor Wadley limped down to his seat there were general affectionate inquiries from all parts of the hall as to the exact state of his poor toe, which caused him obvious embarrassment. The greatest demonstration of all, however, was at the entrance of my new acquaintance, Professor Challenger, when he passed down to take his place at the extreme end of the front row of the platform. Such a yell of welcome broke forth when his black beard first protruded round the corner that I began to suspect Tarp Henry was right in his surmise, and that this assemblage was there not merely for the sake of the lecture, but because it had got rumoured abroad that the famous Professor would take part in the proceedings.

There was some sympathetic laughter on his entrance among the front benches of well-dressed spectators, as though the demonstration of the students in this instance was not unwelcome to them. That greeting was, indeed, a frightful outburst of sound, the uproar of the carnivora cage when the step of the bucket-bearing keeper is heard in the distance. There was an offensive tone in it, perhaps, and yet in the main it struck me as mere riotous outcry, the noisy reception of one who amused and interested them, rather than of one they disliked or despised. Challenger smiled with weary and tolerant contempt, as a kindly man would meet the yapping of a litter of puppies. He sat slowly down, blew out his chest, passed his hand caressingly down his beard, and looked with drooping eyelids and supercilious eyes at the crowded hall before him. The uproar of his advent had not yet died away when Professor Ronald Murray, the Chairman, and Mr. Waldron, the lecturer, threaded their way to the front, and the proceedings began.

Professor Murray will, I am sure, excuse me if I say that he has the common fault of most Englishmen of being inaudible. Why on earth people who have something to say which is worth hearing should not take the slight trouble to learn how to make it heard is one of the strange mysteries of modern life. Their methods are as reasonable as to try to pour some precious stuff from the spring to the reservoir through a non-conducting pipe, which could by the least effort be opened. Professor Murray made several profound remarks to his white tie and to the water-carafe upon the table, with a humorous, twinkling aside to the silver candlestick upon his right. Then he sat down, and Mr. Waldron, the famous lecturer, rose amid a general murmur of applause. He was a stern, gaunt man, with a harsh voice and an aggressive manner, but he had the merit of knowing how to assimilate the ideas of other men, and to pass them on in a way which was intelligible and even interesting to the lay public, with a happy knack of being funny about the most unlikely objects, so that the precession of the Equinox or the formation of a vertebrate became a highly humorous process as treated by him.

It was a bird's-eye view of creation, as interpreted by science, which, in language always clear and sometimes picturesque, he unfolded before us. He told us of the globe, a huge mass of flaming gas, flaring through the heavens. Then he pictured the solidification, the cooling, the wrinkling which formed the mountains, the steam which turned to water, the slow preparation of the stage upon which was to be played the inexplicable drama of life. On the origin of life itself he was discreetly vague. That the germs of it could hardly have survived the original roasting was, he declared, fairly certain. Therefore it had come later. Had it built itself out of the cooling, inorganic elements of the globe? Very likely. Had the germs of it arrived from outside upon a meteor? It was hardly conceivable. On the whole, the wisest man was the least dogmatic upon the point. We could not – or at least we had not succeeded up to date in making organic life in our laboratories out of inorganic materials. The gulf between the dead and the living was something which our chemistry could not as yet bridge. But there was a higher and subtler chemistry of Nature, which, working with great forces over long epochs, might well produce results which were impossible for us. There the matter must be left.

This brought the lecturer to the great ladder of animal life, beginning low down in molluscs and feeble sea creatures, then up rung by rung through reptiles and fishes, till at last we came to a kangaroo-rat, a creature which brought forth its young alive, the direct ancestor of all mammals, and presumably, therefore, of everyone in the audience. ('No, no,' from a sceptical student in the back row.) If the young gentleman in the red tie who cried 'No, no,' and who presumably claimed to have been hatched out of an egg, would wait upon him after the lecture, he would be glad to see such a curiosity. (Laughter.) It was strange to think that the climax of all the age-long processes of Nature had been the creation of that gentleman in the red tie. But had the process stopped? Was this gentleman to be taken as the final type – the be-all and end-all of development? He hoped that he would not hurt the feelings of the gentleman in the red tie if he maintained that, whatever virtues that gentleman might possess in private life, still the vast processes of the universe were not fully justified if they were to end entirely in his production. Evolution was not a spent force, but one still working, and even greater achievements were in store.

Having thus, amid a general titter, played very prettily with his interrupter, the lecturer went back to his picture of the past, the drying of the seas, the emergence of the sand-bank, the sluggish, viscous life which lay upon their margins, the overcrowded lagoons, the tendency of the sea creatures to take refuge upon the mud-flats, the abundance of food awaiting them, their consequent enormous growth. 'Hence, ladies and gentlemen,' he added, 'that frightful brood of saurians which still afright our eyes when seen in the Wealden or in the Solenhofen slates, but which were fortunately extinct long before the first appearance of mankind upon this planet.'

'Question!' boomed a voice from the platform.

Mr. Waldron was a strict disciplinarian with a gift of acid humour, as exemplified upon the gentleman with the red tie, which made it perilous to interrupt him. But this interjection appeared to him so absurd that he was at a loss how to deal with it. So looks the Shakespearean who is confronted by a rancid Baconian, or the astronomer who is assailed by a flat-earth fanatic. He paused for a moment, and then, raising his voice, repeated slowly the words: 'Which were extinct before the coming of man.'

'Question!' boomed the voice once more.

Waldron looked with amazement along the line of professors upon the platform until his eyes fell upon the figure of Challenger, who leaned back in his chair with closed eyes and an amused expression, as if he were smiling in his sleep.

'I see!' said Waldron, with a shrug. 'It is my friend Professor Challenger,' and amid laughter he renewed his lecture as if this was a final explanation and no more need be said.

But the incident was far from being closed. Whatever path the lecturer took amid the wilds of the past seemed invariably to lead him to some assertion as to extinct or prehistoric life which instantly brought the same bull's bellow from the Professor. The audience began to anticipate it and to roar with delight when it came. The packed benches of students joined in, and every time Challenger's beard opened, before any sound could come forth, there was a yell of 'Question!' from a hundred voices, and an answering counter cry of 'Order!' and 'Shame!' from as many more. Waldron, though a hardened lecturer and a strong man, became rattled. He hesitated, stammered, repeated himself, got snarled in a long sentence, and finally turned furiously upon the cause of his troubles.

'This is really intolerable!' he cried, glaring across the platform. 'I must ask you, Professor Challenger, to cease these ignorant and unmannerly interruptions.'

There was a hush over the hall, the students rigid with delight at seeing the high gods on Olympus quarrelling among themselves. Challenger levered his bulky figure slowly out of his chair.

'I must in turn ask you, Mr. Waldron,' he said, 'to cease to make assertions which are not in strict accordance with scientific fact.'

The words unloosed a tempest. 'Shame! Shame!' 'Give him a hearing!' 'Put him out!' 'Shove him off the platform!' 'Fair play!' emerged from a general roar of amusement or execration. The chairman was on his feet flapping both his hands and bleating excitedly. 'Professor Challenger – personal – views – later,' were the solid peaks above his clouds of inaudible mutter. The interrupter bowed, smiled, stroked his beard, and relapsed into his chair. Waldron, very flushed and warlike, continued his observations. Now and then, as he made an assertion, he shot a venomous glance at his opponent, who seemed to be slumbering deeply, with the same broad, happy smile upon his face.

At last the lecture came to an end – I am inclined to think that it was a premature one, as the peroration was hurried and disconnected. The thread of the argument had been rudely broken, and the audience was restless and expectant. Waldron sat down, and, after a chirrup from the chairman, Professor Challenger rose and advanced to the edge of the platform. In the interests of my paper I took down his speech verbatim.

'Ladies and Gentlemen,' he began, amid a sustained interruption from the back. 'I beg pardon – Ladies, Gentlemen, and Children – I must apologize, I had inadvertently omitted a considerable section of this audience' (tumult, during which the Professor stood with one hand raised and his enormous head nodding sympathetically, as if he were bestowing a pontifical blessing upon the crowd), 'I have been selected to move a vote of thanks to Mr. Waldron for the very picturesque and imaginative address to which we have just listened. There are points in it with which I disagree, and it has been my duty to indicate them as they arose, but, none the less, Mr. Waldron has accomplished his object well, that object being to give a simple and interesting account of what he conceives to have been the history of our planet. Popular lectures are the easiest to listen to, but Mr. Waldron' (here he beamed and blinked at the lecturer) 'will excuse me when I say that they are necessarily both superficial and misleading, since they have to be graded to the comprehension of an ignorant audience.' (Ironical cheering.) 'Popular lecturers are in their nature parasitic.' (Angry gesture of protest from Mr. Waldron.) 'They exploit for fame or cash the work which has been done by the indigent and unknown brethren. One smallest new fact obtained in the laboratory, one brick built into the temple of science, far outweighs any second-hand exposition which passes an idle hour, but can leave no useful result behind it. I put forward this obvious reflection, not out of any desire to disparage Mr. Waldron in particular, but that you may not lose your sense of proportion and mistake the acolyte for the high priest.' (At this point Mr. Waldron whispered to the chairman, who half rose and said something severely to his water-carafe.) 'But enough of this!' (Loud and prolonged cheers.) 'Let me pass to some subject of wider interest. What is the particular point upon which I, as an original investigator, have challenged our lecturer's accuracy? It is upon the permanence of certain types of animal life upon the earth. I do not speak

upon this subject as an amateur, nor, I may add, as a popular lecturer, but I speak as one whose scientific conscience compels him to
adhere closely to facts, when I say that Mr. Waldron is very wrong
in supposing that because he has never himself seen a so-called prehistoric animal, therefore these creatures no longer exist. They are
indeed, as he has said, our ancestors, but they are, if I may use the
expression, our contemporary ancestors, who can still be found with
all their hideous and formidable characteristics if one has but the
energy and hardihood to seek their haunts. Creatures which were
supposed to be Jurassic, monsters who would hunt down and
devour our largest and fiercest mammals, still exist.' (Cries of
'Bosh!' 'Prove it!' 'How do *you* know?' 'Question!') 'How do I
know? you ask me. I know because I have visited their secret haunts.
I know because I have seen some of them.' (Applause, uproar, and a
voice, 'Liar!') 'Am I a liar?' (General hearty and noisy assent.) 'Did I
hear someone say that I was a liar? Will the person who called me a
liar kindly stand up that I may know him?' (A voice, 'Here he is, sir!'
and an inoffensive little person in spectacles, struggling violently,
was held up among a group of students.) 'Did you venture to call
me a liar?' ('No, sir, no!' shouted the accused, and disappeared like a
Jack-in-the-box.) 'If any person in this hall dares to doubt my veracity, I shall be glad to have a few words with him after the lecture.'
('Liar!') 'Who said that?' (Again the inoffensive one, plunging desperately, was elevated high in the air.) 'If I come down among you –'
(General chorus of 'Come, love, come!' which interrupted the proceedings for some moments, while the chairman, standing up and
waving both his arms, seemed to be conducting the music. The
Professor, with his face flushed, his nostrils dilated, and his beard
bristling, was now in a proper Berserk mood.) 'Every great discov-
erer has been met with the same incredulity – the sure brand of a
generation of fools. When great facts are laid before you, you have
not the intuition, the imagination which would help you to understand them. You can only throw mud at the men who have risked
their lives to open new fields to science. You persecute the
prophets! Galileo, Darwin, and I –' (Prolonged cheering and complete interruption.)

All this is from my hurried notes taken at the time, which give
little notion of the absolute chaos to which the assembly had by this
time been reduced. So terrific was the uproar that several ladies had
already beaten a hurried retreat. Grave and reverend seniors seemed
to have caught the prevailing spirit as badly as the students, and I
saw white-bearded men rising and shaking their fists at the obdurate

Professor. The whole great audience seethed and simmered like a boiling pot. The Professor took a step forward and raised both his hands. There was something so big and arresting and virile in the man that the clatter and shouting died gradually away before his commanding gesture and his masterful eyes. He seemed to have a definite message. They hushed to hear it.

'I will not detain you,' he said. 'It is not worth it. Truth is truth, and the noise of a number of foolish young men – and, I fear I must add, of their equally foolish seniors – cannot affect the matter. I claim that I have opened a new field of science. You dispute it.' (Cheers.) 'Then I put you to the test. Will you accredit one or more of your own number to go out as your representatives and test my statement in your name?'

Mr. Summerlee, the veteran Professor of Comparative Anatomy, rose among the audience, a tall, thin, bitter man, with the withered aspect of a theologian. He wished, he said, to ask Professor Challenger whether the results to which he had alluded in his remarks had been obtained during a journey to the headwaters of the Amazon made by him two years before.

Professor Challenger answered that they had.

Mr. Summerlee desired to know how it was that Professor Challenger claimed to have made discoveries in those regions which had been overlooked by Wallace, Bates, and other previous explorers of established scientific repute.

Professor Challenger answered that Mr. Summerlee appeared to be confusing the Amazon with the Thames; that it was in reality a somewhat larger river; that Mr. Summerlee might be interested to know that with the Orinoco, which communicated with it, some fifty thousand miles of country were opened up, and that in so vast a space it was not impossible for one person to find what another had missed.

Mr. Summerlee declared, with an acid smile, that he fully appreciated the difference between the Thames and the Amazon, which lay in the fact that any assertion about the former could be tested, while about the latter it could not. He would be obliged if Professor Challenger would give the latitude and the longitude of the country in which prehistoric animals were to be found.

Professor Challenger replied that he reserved such information for good reasons of his own, but would be prepared to give it with proper precautions to a committee chosen from the audience. Would Mr. Summerlee serve on such a committee and test his story in person?

Mr. Summerlee: 'Yes, I will.' (Great cheering.)

Professor Challenger: 'Then I guarantee that I will place in your hands such material as will enable you to find your way. It is only right, however, since Mr. Summerlee goes to check my statement that I should have one or more with him who may check his. I will not disguise from you that there are difficulties and dangers. Mr. Summerlee will need a younger colleague. May I ask for volunteers?'

It is thus that the great crisis of a man's life springs out at him. Could I have imagined when I entered that hall that I was about to pledge myself to a wilder adventure than had ever come to me in my dreams? But Gladys – was it not the very opportunity of which she spoke? Gladys would have told me to go. I had sprung to my feet. I was speaking, and yet I had prepared no words. Tarp Henry, my companion, was plucking at my skirts and I heard him whispering, 'Sit down, Malone! Don't make a public ass of yourself.' At the same time I was aware that a tall, thin man, with dark gingery hair, a few seats in front of me, was also upon his feet. He glared back at me with hard angry eyes, but I refused to give way.

'I will go, Mr. Chairman,' I kept repeating over and over again.

'Name! Name!' cried the audience.

'My name is Edward Dunn Malone. I am the reporter of the *Daily Gazette*. I claim to be an absolutely unprejudiced witness.'

'What is *your* name, sir?' the chairman asked of my tall rival.

'I am Lord John Roxton. I have already been up the Amazon, I know all the ground, and have special qualifications for this investigation.'

'Lord John Roxton's reputation as a sportsman and a traveller is, of course, world-famous,' said the chairman; 'at the same time it would certainly be as well to have a member of the Press upon such an expedition.'

'Then I move,' said Professor Challenger, 'that both these gentlemen be elected, as representatives of this meeting, to accompany Professor Summerlee upon his journey to investigate and to report upon the truth of my statements.'

And so, amid shouting and cheering, our fate was decided, and I found myself borne away in the human current which swirled towards the door, with my mind half stunned by the vast new project which had risen so suddenly before it. As I emerged from the hall I was conscious for a moment of a rush of laughing students down the pavement, and of an arm wielding a heavy umbrella, which rose and fell in the midst of them. Then, amid a mixture of groans and cheers, Professor Challenger's electric brougham slid from the kerb, and I found myself walking under the silvery lights of Regent Street, full of thoughts of Gladys and of wonder as to my future.

Suddenly there was a touch at my elbow. I turned, and found myself looking into the humorous, masterful eyes of the tall, thin man who had volunteered to be my companion on this strange quest.

'Mr. Malone, I understand,' said he. 'We are to be companions – what? My rooms are just over the road, in the Albany. Perhaps you would have the kindness to spare me half an hour, for there are one or two things that I badly want to say to you.'

CHAPTER VI

I Was the Flail of the Lord

LORD JOHN ROXTON and I turned down Vigo Street together and through the dingy portals of the famous aristocratic rookery. At the end of a long drab passage my new acquaintance pushed open a door and turned on an electric switch. A number of lamps shining through tinted shades bathed the whole great room before us in a ruddy radiance. Standing in the doorway and glancing round me, I had a general impression of extraordinary comfort and elegance combined with an atmosphere of masculine virility. Everywhere there were mingled the luxury of the wealthy man of taste and the careless untidiness of the bachelor. Rich furs and strange iridescent mats from some Oriental bazaar were scattered upon the floor. Pictures and prints which even my unpractised eyes could recognize as being of great price and rarity hung thick upon the walls. Sketches of boxers, of ballet-girls, and of racehorses alternated with a sensuous Fragonard, a martial Girardet, and a dreamy Turner. But amid these varied ornaments there were scattered the trophies which brought back strongly to my recollection the fact that Lord John Roxton was one of the great all-round sportsmen and athletes of his day. A dark-blue oar crossed with a cherry-pink one above his mantel-piece spoke of the old Oxonian and Leander man, while the foils and boxing-gloves above and below them were the tools of a man who had won supremacy with each. Like a dado round the room was the jutting line of splendid heavy game-heads, the best of their sort from every quarter of the world, with the rare white rhinoceros of the Lado Enclave drooping its supercilious lip above them all.

In the centre of the rich red carpet was a black and gold Louis Quinze table, a lovely antique, now sacrilegiously desecrated with marks of glasses and the scars of cigar-stumps. On it stood a silver tray of smokables and a burnished spirit-stand, from which and an adjacent siphon my silent host proceeded to charge two high glasses. Having indicated an arm-chair to me and placed my refreshment near it, he handed me a long, smooth Havana. Then, seating himself opposite to me, he looked at me long and fixedly with his strange, twinkling, reckless eyes – eyes of a cold light blue, the colour of a glacier lake.

Through the thin haze of my cigar smoke I noted the details of a face which was already familiar to me from many photographs – the strongly-curved nose. the hollow, worn cheeks, the dark, ruddy hair, thin at the top, the crisp, virile moustaches, the small, aggressive tuft upon his projecting chin. Something there was of Napoleon III, something of Don Quixote, and yet again something which was the essence of the English country gentleman, the keen, alert, open-air lover of dogs and of horses. His skin was of a rich flower-pot red from sun and wind. His eyebrows were tufted and overhanging, which gave those naturally cold eyes an almost ferocious aspect, an impression which was increased by his strong and furrowed brow. In figure he was spare, but very strongly built – indeed, he had often proved that there were few men in England capable of such sustained exertions. His height was a little over six feet, but he seemed shorter on account of a peculiar rounding of the shoulders. Such was the famous Lord John Roxton as he sat opposite to me, biting hard upon his cigar and watching me steadily in a long and embarrassing silence.

'Well,' said he, at last, 'we've gone and done it, young fellah-my-lad.' (This curious phrase he pronounced as if it were all one word – 'young fellah-my-lad.') 'Yes, we've taken a jump, you an' me. I suppose, now, when you went into that room there was no such notion in your head – what?'

'No thought of it.'

'The same here. No thought of it. And here we are, up to our necks in the tureen. Why, I've only been back three weeks from Uganda, and taken a place in Scotland, and signed the lease and all. Pretty goin's on – what? How does it hit you?'

'Well, it is all in the main line of my business. I am a journalist on the *Gazette.*'

'Of course – you said so when you took it on. By the way I've got a small job for you, if you'll help me.'

'With pleasure.'

'Don't mind takin' a risk, do you?'

'What is the risk?'

'Well, it's Ballinger – he's the risk. You've heard of him?'

'No.'

'Why, young fellah, where *have* you lived? Sir John Ballinger is the best gentleman jock in the north country. I could hold him on the flat at my best, but over jumps he's my master. Well, it's an open secret that when he's out of trainin' he drinks hard – strikin' an average, he calls it. He got delirium on Toosday, and has been ragin' like a devil ever since. His room is above this. The doctors say that it is all up with the old dear unless some food is got into him, but as he lies in bed with a revolver on his coverlet, and swears he will put six of the best through anyone that comes near him, there's been a bit of a strike among the serving-men. He's a hard nail, is Jack, and a dead shot, too, but you can't leave a Grand National winner to die like that – what?'

'What do you mean to do, then?' I asked.

'Well, my idea was that you and I could rush him. He may be dozin', and at the worst he can only wing one of us, and the other should have him. If we can get his bolster-cover round his arms and then 'phone up a stomach-pump, we'll give the old dear the supper of his life.'

It was rather a desperate business to come suddenly into one's day's work. I don't think that I am a particularly brave man. I have an Irish imagination which makes the unknown and the untried more terrible than they are. On the other hand, I was brought up with a horror of cowardice and with a terror of such a stigma. I dare say that I could throw myself over a precipice, like the Hun in the history books, if my courage to do it were questioned, and yet it would surely be pride and fear, rather than courage, which would be my inspiration. Therefore, although every nerve in my body shrank from the whisky-maddened figure which I pictured in the room above, I still answered, in as careless a voice as I could command, that I was ready to go. Some further remark of Lord Roxton's about the danger only made me irritable.

'Talking won't make it any better,' said I. 'Come on.'

I rose from my chair and he from his. Then, with a little confidential chuckle of laughter, he patted me two or three times on the chest, finally pushing me back into my chair.

'All right, sonny my lad – you'll do,' said he.

I looked up in surprise.

'I saw after Jack Ballinger myself this mornin'. He blew a hole in the skirt of my kimono, bless his shaky old hand, but we got a jacket on him, and he's to be all right in a week. I say, young fellah, I hope you don't mind – what? You see, between you an' me close-tiled, I look on this South American business as a mighty serious thing, and if I have a pal with me I want a man I can bank on. So I sized you down, and I'm bound to say that you came well out of it. You see, it's all up to you and me, for this old Summerlee man will want dry-nursin' from the first. By the way, are you by any chance the Malone who is expected to get his Rugby cap for Ireland?'

'A reserve, perhaps.'

'I thought I remembered your face. Why, I was there when you got that try against Richmond – as fine a swervin' run as I saw the whole season. I never miss a Rugby match if I can help it, for it is the manliest game we have left. Well, I didn't ask you in here just to talk sport. We've got to fix our business. Here are the sailin's, on the first page of *The Times*. There's a Booth boat for Para next Wednesday week and if the Professor and you can work it, I think we should take it – what? Very good, I'll fix it with him. What about your outfit?'

'My paper will see to that.'

'Can you shoot?'

'About average Territorial standard.'

'Good Lord! as bad as that? It's the last thing you young fellahs think of learnin'. You're all bees without stings, so far as lookin' after the hive goes. You'll look silly, some o' these days, when someone comes along an' sneaks the honey. But you'll need to hold your gun straight in South America, for, unless our friend the Professor is a madman or a liar, we may see some queer things before we get back. What gun have you?'

He crossed to an oaken cupboard, and as he threw it open I caught a glimpse of glistening rows of parallel barrels, like the pipes of an organ.

'I'll see what I can spare you out of my own battery,' said he.

One by one he took out a succession of beautiful rifles, opening and shutting them with a snap and a clang, and then patting them as he put them back into the rack as tenderly as a mother would fondle her children.

'This is a Bland's .577 axite express,' said he. 'I got that big fellow with it.' He glanced up at the white rhinoceros. 'Ten more yards, and he'd have added me to *his* collection.

> "On that conical bullet his one chance hangs,
> 'Tis the weak one's advantage fair."

Hope you know your Gordon, for he's the poet of the horse and the gun and the man that handles both. Now, here's a useful tool – .470, telescopic sight, double ejector, point-blank up to three-fifty. That's the rifle I used against the Peruvian slave-drivers three years ago. I was the flail of the Lord up in those parts, I may tell you, though you won't find it in any Blue-book. There are times, young fellah, when every one of us must make a stand for human right and justice, or you never feel clean again. That's why I made a little war on my own. Declared it myself, waged it myself, ended it myself. Each of those nicks is for a slave murderer – a good row of them – what? That big one is for Pedro Lopez, the king of them all, that I killed in a backwater of the Putomayo River. Now, here's something that would do for you.' He took out a beautiful brown-and-silver rifle. 'Well rubbered at the stock, sharply sighted, five cartridges to the clip. You can trust your life to that.' He handed it to me and closed the door of his oak cabinet. 'By the way,' he continued, coming back to his chair, 'what do you know of this Professor Challenger?'

'I never saw him till to-day.'

'Well, neither did I. It's funny we should both sail under sealed orders from a man we don't know. He seemed an uppish old bird. His brothers of science don't seem too fond of him, either. How came you to take an interest in the affair?'

I told him shortly my experiences of the morning, and he listened intently. Then he drew out a map of South America and laid it on the table.

'I believe every single word he said to you was the truth,' said he, earnestly, 'and, mind you, I have something to go on when I speak like that. South America is a place I love, and I think, if you take it right through from Darien to Fuego, it's the grandest, richest, most wonderful bit of earth upon this planet. People don't know it yet, and don't realize what it may become. I've been up an' down it from end to end, and had two dry seasons in those very parts, as I told you when I spoke of the war I made on the slave-dealers. Well, when I was up there I heard some yarns of the same kind – traditions of Indians and the like, but with somethin' behind them, no doubt. The more you knew of that country, young fellah, the more you would understand that anythin' was possible – *anythin'*. There are just some narrow water-lanes along which folk travel, and outside that it is all darkness. Now, down here in the Matto Grosso' – he swept his cigar over a part of the map – 'or up in this corner where three countries meet, nothin' would surprise me. As that chap said to-night, there are fifty thousand miles of water-way runnin' through a forest that is very near the size of Europe. You and I could be as far away from each other as Scotland is from Constantinople, and yet each of us be in the same great Brazilian forest. Man has just made a track here and a scrape there in the maze. Why, the river rises and falls the best part of forty feet, and half the country is a morass that you can't pass over. Why shouldn't somethin' new and wonderful lie in such a country? And why shouldn't we be the men to find it out? Besides,' he added, his queer, gaunt face shining with delight, 'there's a sportin' risk in every mile of it. I'm like an old golfball – I've had all the white paint knocked off me long ago. Life can whack me about now and it can't leave a mark. But a sportin' risk, young fellah, that's the salt of existence. Then it's worth livin' again. We're all gettin' a deal too soft and dull and comfy. Give me the great waste lands and the wide spaces, with a gun in my fist and somethin' to look for that's worth findin'. I've tried war and steeplechasin' and aeroplanes, but this huntin' of beasts that look like a lobster-supper dream is a brand-new sensation.' He chuckled with glee at the prospect.

Perhaps I have dwelt too long upon this new acquaintance, but he is to be my comrade for many a day, and so I have tried to set him down as I first saw him, with his quaint personality and his queer little tricks of speech and of thought. It was only the need of getting in the account of my meeting which drew me at last from his company. I left him seated amid his pink radiance, oiling the lock of his favourite rifle, while he still chuckled to himself at the thought of the adventures which awaited us. It was very clear to me that if dangers lay before us I could not in all England have found a cooler head or a braver spirit with which to share them.

That night, wearied as I was after the wonderful happenings of the day, I sat with McArdle, the news editor, explaining to him the whole situation, which he thought important enough to bring next morning before the notice of Sir George Beaumont, the chief. It was agreed that I should write home full accounts of my adventures in the shape of successive letters to McArdle, and that these should either be edited for the *Gazette* as they arrived, or held back to be published later, according to the wishes of Professor Challenger, since we could not yet know what conditions he might attach to those directions which should guide us to the unknown land. In response to a telephone inquiry, we received nothing more definite than a fulmination against the Press, ending up with the remark that if we would notify our boat he would hand us any directions which he might think it proper to give us at the moment of starting. A second question from us failed to elicit any answer at all, save a plaintive bleat from his wife to the effect that her husband was in a very violent temper already, and that she hoped we would do nothing to make it worse. A third attempt, later in the day, provoked a terrific crash, and a subsequent message from the Central Exchange that Professor Challenger's receiver had been shattered. After that we abandoned all attempt at communication.

And now, my patient readers, I can address you directly no longer. From now onwards (if, indeed, any continuation of this narrative should ever reach you) it can only be through the paper which I represent. In the hands of the editor I leave this account of the events which have led up to one of the most remarkable expeditions of all time, so that if I never return to England there shall be some record as to how the affair came about. I am writing these last lines in the saloon of the Booth liner *Francisca*, and they will go back by the pilot to the keeping of Mr. McArdle. Let me draw one last picture before I close the notebook – a picture which is the last memory of the old country which I bear away with me. It is a wet, foggy morning in the late spring; a thin, cold rain is falling. Three shining mackintoshed figures are walking down the quay, making for the gang-plank of the great liner from which the blue-peter is flying. In front of them a porter pushes a trolley piled high with trunks, wraps, and gun-cases. Professor Summerlee, a long, melancholy figure, walks with dragging steps and drooping head, as one who is already profoundly sorry for himself. Lord John Roxton steps briskly, and his thin, eager face beams forth between his hunting-cap and his muffler. As for myself, I am glad to have got the bustling days of preparation and the pangs of leave-taking behind me, and I have no doubt that I show it in my bearing. Suddenly, just as we reach the vessel, there is a shout behind us. It is Professor Challenger, who had promised to see us off. He runs after us, a puffing, red-faced, irascible figure.

'No, thank you,' says he; 'I should much prefer not to go aboard. I have only a few words to say to you, and they can very well be said where we are. I beg you not to imagine that I am in any way indebted to you for making this journey. I would have you to understand that it is a matter of perfect indifference to me, and I refuse to entertain the most remote sense of personal obligation. Truth is truth, and nothing which you can report can affect it in any way, though it may excite the emotions and allay the curiosity of a number of very ineffectual people. My directions for your instruction and guidance are in this sealed envelope. You will open it when you reach a town upon the Amazon which is called Manaos, but not until the date and hour which is marked upon the outside. Have I made myself clear? I leave the strict observance of my conditions entirely to your honour. No, Mr. Malone, I will place no restriction upon your correspondence, since the ventilation of the facts is the object of your journey; but I demand that you shall give no particulars as to your exact destination, and that nothing be actually published until your return. Good-bye sir. You have done something to mitigate my feelings for the loathsome profession to which you unhappily belong. Good-bye, Lord John. Science is, as I understand, a sealed book to you; but you may congratulate yourself upon the hunting-field which awaits you. You will, no doubt, have the opportunity of describing in the *Field* how you brought down the rocketing dimorphodon. And good-bye to you also, Professor Summerlee. If you are still capable of self-improvement, of which I am frankly unconvinced, you will surely return to London a wiser man.'

So he turned upon his heel, and a minute later from the deck I could see his short, squat figure bobbing about in the distance as he made his way back to his train. Well, we are well down Channel now. There's the last bell for letters, and it's good-bye to the pilot. We'll be 'down, hull-down, on the old trail' from now on. God bless all we leave behind us, and send us safely back.

CHAPTER VII

To-morrow We Disappear Into the Unknown

I WILL NOT BORE THOSE whom this narrative may reach by an account of our luxurious voyage upon the Booth liner, nor will I tell of our week's stay at Para (save that I should wish to acknowledge the great kindness of the Pereira da Pinta Company in helping us to get together our equipment). I will also allude very briefly to our river journey, up a wide, slow-moving, clay-tinted stream, in a steamer which was little smaller than that which had carried us across the Atlantic. Eventually we found ourselves through the narrows of Obidos and reached the town of Manaos. Here we were rescued from the limited attractions of the local inn by Mr. Shortman, the representative of the British and Brazilian Trading Company. In his hospitable fazenda we spent our time until the day when we were empowered to open the letter of instructions given to us by Professor Challenger. Before I reach the surprising events of that date I would desire to give a clearer sketch of my comrades in this enterprise, and of the associates whom we had already gathered together in South America. I speak freely, and I leave the use of my material to your own discretion, Mr. McArdle, since it is through your hands that this report must pass before it reaches the world.

The scientific attainments of Professor Summerlee are too well known for me to trouble to recapitulate them. He is better equipped for a rough expedition of this sort than one would imagine at first sight. His tall, gaunt, stringy figure is insensible to fatigue, and his dry, half-sarcastic, and often wholly unsympathetic manner is uninfluenced by any change in his surroundings. Though in his sixty-sixth year, I have never heard him express any dissatisfaction at the occasional hardships which we have had to encounter. I had regarded his presence as an encumbrance to the expedition, but, as a matter of fact, I am now well convinced that his power of endurance is as great as my own. In temper he is naturally acid and sceptical. From the beginning he has never concealed his belief that Professor Challenger is an absolute fraud, that we are all embarked upon an absurd wild-goose chase and that we are likely to reap nothing but disappointment and danger in South America, and corresponding ridicule in England. Such are the views which, with much passionate distortion of his thin features and wagging of his thin, goat-like beard, he poured into our ears all the way from Southampton to Manaos. Since landing from the boat he has obtained some consolation from the beauty and variety of the insect and bird life around him, for he is absolutely whole-hearted in his devotion to science. He spends his days flitting through the woods with his shot-gun and his butterfly-net, and his evenings in mounting the many specimens he has acquired. Among his minor peculiarities are that he is careless as to his attire, unclean in his person, exceedingly absent-minded in his habits, and addicted to smoking a short briar pipe, which is seldom out of his mouth. He has been upon several scientific expeditions in his youth (he was with Robertson in Papua), and the life of the camp and the canoe is nothing fresh to him.

Lord John Roxton has some points in common with Professor Summerlee and others in which they are the very antithesis to each other. He is twenty years younger, but has something of the same spare, scraggy physique. As to his appearance, I have, as I recollect, described it in that portion of my narrative which I have left behind me in London. He is exceedingly neat and prim in his ways, dresses always with great care in white drill suits and high brown mosquito-boots, and shaves at least once a day. Like most men of action, he is laconic in speech, and sinks readily into his own thoughts, but he is always quick to answer a question or join in a conversation, talking in a queer, half-humorous fashion. His knowledge of the world and very especially of South America, is surprising, and he has a whole-hearted belief in the possibilities of our journey which is not to be dashed by the sneers of Professor Summerlee. He has a gentle voice and a quiet manner, but behind his twinkling blue eyes there lurks a capacity for furious wrath and implacable resolution, the more dangerous because they are held in leash. He spoke little of his own exploits in Brazil and Peru, but it was a revelation to me to find the excitement which was caused by his presence among the riverine natives, who looked upon him as their champion and protector. The exploits of the Red Chief, as they called him, had become legends among them, but the real facts, as far as I could learn them, were amazing enough.

These were that Lord John had found himself some years before in that no-man's-land which is formed by the half-defined frontiers between Peru, Brazil, and Colombia. In this great district the wild rubber tree flourishes, and has become, as in the Congo, a curse to the natives which can only be compared to their forced labour under the Spaniards upon the old silver mines of Darien. A handful of villainous half-breeds dominated the country, armed such Indians as would support them, and turned the rest into slaves, terrorizing them with the most inhuman tortures in order to force them to gather the india-rubber, which was then floated down the river to Para. Lord John Roxton expostulated on behalf of the wretched victims, and received nothing but threats and insults for his pains. He then formally declared war against Pedro Lopez, the leader of the slave-drivers, enrolled a band of runaway slaves in his service, armed them, and conducted a campaign, which ended by his killing with his own hands the notorious half-breed and breaking down the system which he represented.

No wonder that the ginger-headed man with the silky voice and the free and easy manners was now looked upon with deep interest upon the banks of the great South American river, though the feelings he inspired were naturally mixed, since the gratitude of the natives was equalled by the resentment of those who desired to exploit them. One useful result of his former experiences was that he could talk fluently in the Lingoa Geral, which is the peculiar talk, one-third Portuguese and two-thirds Indian, which is current all over Brazil.

I have said before that Lord John Roxton was a South Americomaniac. He could not speak of that great country without ardour, and this ardour was infectious, for, ignorant as I was, he fixed my attention and stimulated my curiosity. How I wish I could reproduce the glamour of his discourses; the peculiar mixture of accurate knowledge and of racy imagination which gave them their fascination, until even the Professor's cynical and sceptical smile would gradually vanish from his thin face as he listened. He would tell the history of the mighty river so rapidly explored (for some of the first conquerors of Peru actually crossed the entire continent upon its waters), and yet so unknown in regard to all that lay behind its ever-changing banks.

'What is there?' he would cry, pointing to the north. 'Wood and marsh and unpenetrated jungle. Who knows what it may shelter? And there to the south? A wilderness of swampy forests, where no white man has ever been. The unknown is up against us on every side. Outside the narrow lines of the rivers what does anyone know? Who will say what is possible in such a country? Why should old man Challenger not be right?' At which direct defiance the stubborn sneer would reappear upon Professor Summerlee's face, and he would sit, shaking his sardonic head in unsympathetic silence, behind the cloud of his briar-root pipe.

So much, for the moment, for my two white companions, whose characters and limitations will be further exposed as surely as my own, as this narrative proceeds. But already we have enrolled certain retainers who may play no small part in what is to come. The first is a gigantic negro named Zambo, who is a black Hercules, as willing as any horse, and about as intelligent. Him we enlisted at Para, on the recommendation of the steamship company, on whose vessels he had learned to speak a halting English.

It was at Para also that we engaged Gomez and Manuel, two half-breeds from up the river, just come down with a cargo of red-wood. They were swarthy fellows, bearded and fierce, as active and wiry as panthers. Both of them had spent their lives in those upper waters of the Amazon which we were about to explore, and it was this recommendation which had caused Lord John to engage them. One of them, Gomez, had the further advantage that he could speak excellent English. These men were willing to act as our personal servants, to cook, to row, or to make themselves useful in any way at a payment of fifteen dollars a month. Besides these, we had engaged three Mojo Indians from Bolivia, who are the most skilful at fishing and boat work of all the river tribes. The chief of these we called Mojo, after his tribe, and the others are known as José and Fernando. Three white men, then, two half-breeds, one negro, and three Indians made up the personnel of the little expedition which lay waiting for its instructions at Manaos, before starting upon its singular quest.

At last after a weary week, the day had come and the hour. I ask you to picture the shaded sitting-room of the Fazenda Santa Ignacio, two miles inland from the town of Manaos. Outside lay the yellow, brassy glare of the sunshine, with the shadows of the palm trees as black and definite as the trees themselves. The air was calm, full of the eternal hum of insects, a tropical chorus of many octaves, from the deep drone of the bee to the high, keen pipe of the mosquito. Beyond the veranda was a small cleared garden, bounded with cactus hedges and adorned with clumps of flowering shrubs, round which the great blue butterflies and the tiny humming-birds fluttered and darted in crescents of sparkling light. Within we were seated round the cane table, on which lay a sealed envelope. Inscribed upon it, in the jagged handwriting of Professor Challenger, were the words:

'Instructions to Lord John Roxton and party. To be opened at Manaos upon July 15th, at 12 o'clock precisely.'

Lord John had placed his watch upon the table beside him.

'We have seven more minutes,' said he. 'The old dear's very precise.'

Professor Summerlee gave an acid smile as he picked up the envelope in his gaunt hand.

'What can it possibly matter whether we open it now or in seven minutes?' said he. 'It is all part and parcel of the same system of quackery and nonsense for which I regret to say that the writer is notorious.'

'Oh, come, we must play the game accordin' to rules,' said Lord John. 'It's old man Challenger's show and we are here by his good will, so it would be rotten bad form if we didn't follow his instructions to the letter.'

'A pretty business it is!' cried the Professor, bitterly. 'It struck me as preposterous in London, but I'm bound to say that it seems even more so upon closer acquaintance. I don't know what is inside this envelope, but, unless it is something pretty definite, I shall be much tempted to take the next down-river boat and catch the *Bolivia* at Para. After all, I have some more responsible work in the world than to run about disproving the assertions of a lunatic. Now, Roxton, surely it is time.'

'Time it is,' said Lord John. 'You can blow the whistle.' He took up the envelope and cut it with his penknife. From it he drew a folded sheet of paper. This he carefully opened out and flattened on the table. It was a blank sheet. He turned it over. Again it was blank. We looked at each other in a bewildered silence, which was broken by a discordant burst of derisive laughter from Professor Summerlee.

'It is an open admission,' he cried. 'What more do you want? The fellow is a self-confessed humbug. We have only to return home and report him as the brazen impostor that he is.'

'Invisible ink!' I suggested.

'I don't think!' said Lord Roxton, holding the paper to the light. 'No, young fellah-my-lad, there is no use deceiving yourself. I'll go bail for it that nothing has ever been written upon this paper.'

'May I come in?' boomed a voice from the veranda.

The shadow of a squat figure had stolen across the patch of sunlight. That voice! That monstrous breadth of shoulder! We sprang to our feet with a gasp of astonishment as Challenger, in a round, boyish straw-hat with a coloured ribbon – Challenger, with his hands in his jacket-pockets and his canvas shoes daintily pointing as he walked – appeared in the open space before us. He threw back his head, and there he stood in the golden glow with all his old Assyrian luxuriance of beard, all his native insolence of drooping eyelids and intolerant eyes.

'I fear,' said he, taking out his watch, 'that I am a few minutes too late. When I gave you this envelope I must confess that I had never intended that you should open it, for it had been my fixed intention to be with you before the hour. The unfortunate delay can be apportioned between a blundering pilot and an intrusive sandbank. I fear that it has given my colleague, Professor Summerlee, occasion to blaspheme.'

'I am bound to say, sir,' said Lord John, with some sternness of voice, 'that your turning up is a considerable relief to us, for our mission seemed to have come to a premature end. Even now I can't for the life of me understand why you should have worked it in so extraordinary a manner.'

Instead of answering, Professor Challenger entered, shook hands with myself and Lord John, bowed with ponderous insolence to Professor Summerlee, and sank back into a basket-chair, which creaked and swayed beneath his weight.

'Is all ready for your journey?' he asked.

'We can start to-morrow.'

'Then so you shall. You need no chart of directions now, since you will have the inestimable advantage of my own guidance. From the first I had determined that I would myself preside over your investigation. The most elaborate charts would, as you will readily admit, be a poor substitute for my own intelligence and advice. As to the small ruse which I played upon you in the matter of the envelope, it is clear that, had I told you all my intentions, I should have been forced to resist unwelcome pressure to travel out with you.'

'Not from me, sir!' exclaimed Professor Summerlee, heartily. 'So long as there was another ship upon the Atlantic.'

Challenger waved him away with his great hairy hand.

'Your common sense will, I am sure, sustain my objection and realize that it was better that I should direct my own movements and appear only at the exact moment when my presence was needed. That moment has now arrived. You are in safe hands. You will not now fail to reach your destination. From henceforth I take command of this expedition, and I must ask you to complete your preparations to-night, so that we may be able to make an early start in the morning. My time is of value, and the same thing may be said, no doubt, in a lesser degree of your own. I propose, therefore, that we push on as rapidly as possible, until I have demonstrated what you have come to see.'

Lord John Roxton had chartered a large steam-launch, the *Esmeralda*, which was to carry us up the river. So far as climate goes, it was immaterial what time we chose for our expedition, as the temperature ranges from seventy-five to ninety degrees both summer and winter, with no appreciable difference in heat. In moisture, however, it is otherwise; from December to May is the period of the rains, and during this time the river slowly rises until it attains a height of nearly forty feet above its low-water mark. It floods the banks, extends in great lagoons over a monstrous waste of country, and forms a huge district, called locally the Gapo, which is for the most part too marshy for foot-travel and too shallow for boating. About June the waters begin to fall, and are at their lowest at October or November. Thus our expedition was at the time of the dry season, when the great river and its tributaries were more or less in a normal condition.

The current of the river is a slight one, the drop being not greater than eight inches in a mile. No stream could be more convenient for navigation, since the prevailing wind is south-east, and sailing boats may make a continuous progress to the Peruvian frontier, dropping down again with the current. In our own case the excellent engines of the *Esmeralda* could disregard the sluggish flow of the stream, and we made as rapid progress as if we were navigating a stagnant lake. For three days we steamed north-westwards up a stream which even here, a thousand miles from its mouth, was still so enormous that from its centre the two banks were mere shadows upon the distant skyline. On the fourth day after leaving Manaos we turned into a tributary which at its mouth was little smaller than the main stream. It narrowed rapidly, however, and after two more days' steaming we reached an Indian village, where the Professor insisted that we should land, and that the *Esmeralda* should be sent back to Manaos. We should soon come upon rapids, he explained, which would make its further use impossible. He added privately that we were now approaching the door of the unknown country, and that the fewer whom we took into our confidence the better it would be. To this end also he made each of us give our word of honour that we would publish or say nothing which would give any exact clue as to the whereabouts of our travels, while the servants were all solemnly sworn to the same effect. It is for this reason that I am compelled to be vague in my narrative, and I would warn my readers that in any map or diagram which I may give the relation of places to each other may be correct, but the points of the compass are carefully confused, so that in no way can it be taken as an actual guide to the country. Professor Challenger's reasons for secrecy may be valid or not, but we had no choice but to adopt them, for he was prepared to abandon the whole expedition rather than modify the conditions upon which he would guide us.

It was August 2nd when we snapped our last link with the outer world by bidding farewell to the *Esmeralda*. Since then four days have passed, during which we have engaged two large canoes from the Indians, made of so light a material (skins over a bamboo framework) that we should be able to carry them round any obstacle. These we have loaded with all our effects, and have engaged two additional Indians to help us in the navigation. I understand that they are the very two – Ataca and Ipetu by name – who accompanied Professor Challenger upon his previous journey. They appeared to be terrified at the prospect of repeating it, but the chief has patriarchal powers in these countries, and if the bargain is good in his eyes the clansman has little choice in the matter.

So to-morrow we disappear into the unknown. This account I am transmitting down the river by canoe, and it may be our last word to those who are interested in our fate. I have, according to our arrangement, addressed it to you, my dear Mr. McArdle, and I leave it to your discretion to delete, alter, or do what you like with it. From the assurance of Professor Challenger's manner – and in spite of the continued scepticism of Professor Summerlee – I have no doubt that our leader will make good his statement and that we are really on the eve of some most remarkable experiences.

CHAPTER VIII

The Outlying Pickets of the New World

OUR FRIENDS AT HOME may well rejoice with us, for we are at our goal, and up to a point, at least, we have shown that the statement of Professor Challenger can be verified. We have not, it is true, ascended the plateau, but it lies before us, and even Professor Summerlee is in a more chastened mood. Not that he will for an instant admit that his rival could be right, but he is less persistent in his incessant objections, and has sunk for the most part into an observant silence. I must hark back, however, and continue my narrative from where I dropped it. We are sending home one of our local Indians who is injured, and I am committing this letter to his charge, with considerable doubts in my mind as to whether it will ever come to hand.

When I wrote last we were about to leave the Indian village where we had been deposited by the *Esmeralda*. I have to begin my report by bad news, for the first serious personal trouble (I pass over the incessant bickerings between the Professors) occurred this evening, and might have had a tragic ending. I have spoken of our English-speaking half-breed, Gomez – a fine worker and a willing fellow, but afflicted, I fancy, with the vice of curiosity, which is common enough among such men. On the last evening he seems to have hid himself near the hut in which we were discussing our plans, and, being observed by our huge negro Zambo, who is as faithful as a dog and has the hatred which all his race bear to the half-breeds, he was dragged out and carried into our presence. Gomez whipped out his knife, however, and but for the huge strength of his captor, which enabled him to disarm him with one hand, he would certainly have stabbed him. The matter has ended in reprimands, the opponents have been compelled to shake hands, and there is every hope that all will be well. As to the feuds of the two learned men, they are continuous and bitter. It must be admitted that Challenger is provocative in the last degree, but Summerlee has an acid tongue, which makes matters worse. Last night Challenger said that he never cared to walk on the Thames Embankment and look up the river, as it was always sad to see one's own eventual goal. He is convinced, of course, that he is destined for Westminster Abbey. Summerlee retorted, however, with a sour smile, by saying that he understood that Millbank Prison had been pulled down. Challenger's conceit is too colossal to allow him to be really annoyed. He only smiled in his beard and repeated 'Really! really!' in the pitying tone one would use to a child. Indeed, they are children both – the one wizened and cantankerous, the other formidable and overbearing, yet each with a brain which has put him in the front rank of his scientific age. Brain, character, soul – only as one sees more of life does one understand how distinct is each.

The very next day we did actually make our start upon this remarkable expedition. We found that all our possessions fitted very easily into the two canoes, and we divided our personnel, six in each, taking the obvious precaution in the interests of peace of putting one Professor into each canoe. Personally, I was with Challenger, who was in a beatific humour, moving about as one in a silent ecstasy and beaming benevolence from every feature. I have had some experience of him in other moods, however, and shall be the less surprised when the thunderstorms suddenly come up amidst the sunshine. If it is impossible to be at your ease, it is equally impossible to be dull in his company, for one is always in a state of half-tremulous doubt as to what sudden turn his formidable temper may take.

For two days we made our way up a good-sized river, some hundreds of yards broad, and dark in colour, but transparent, so that one could usually see the bottom. The affluents of the Amazon are, half of them, of this nature, while the other half are whitish and opaque, the difference depending upon the class of country through which they have flowed. The dark indicate vegetable decay, while the others point to clayey soil. Twice we came across rapids, and in each case made a portage of half a mile or so to avoid them. The woods on either side were primeval, which are more easily penetrated than woods of the second growth, and we had no great difficulty in carrying our canoes through them. How shall I ever forget the solemn mystery of it? The height of the trees and the thickness of the boles exceeding anything which I in my town-bred life could have imagined, shooting upwards in magnificent columns until, at an enormous distance above our heads, we could dimly discern the spot where they threw out their side-branches into Gothic upward curves which coalesced to form one great matted roof of verdure, through which only an occasional golden ray of sunshine shot downwards to trace a thin dazzling line of light amidst the majestic obscurity. As we walked noiselessly amid the thick, soft carpet of decaying vegetation the hush fell upon our souls which comes upon us in the twilight of the Abbey, and even Professor Challenger's full-chested notes sank into a whisper. Alone, I should have been ignorant of the names of these giant growths, but our men of science pointed out the cedars, the great silk cotton trees, and the redwood trees, with all that profusion of various plants which has made this continent the chief supplier to the human race of those gifts of nature which depend upon the vegetable world, while it is the most backward in those products which come from animal life. Vivid orchids and wonderful coloured lichens smouldered upon the swarthy tree-trunks, and where a wandering shaft of light fell full upon the golden allamanda, the scarlet star-clusters of the tacsonia, or the rich deep blue of ipomæa the effect was as a dream of fairyland. In these great wastes of forest, life, which abhors darkness, struggles ever upwards to the light. Every plant, even the smaller ones, curls and writhes to the green surface, twining itself round its stronger and taller brethren in the effort. Climbing plants are monstrous and luxuriant, but others which have never been known to climb elsewhere learn the art as an escape from that sombre shadow, so that the common nettle, the jasmine, and even the jacitara palm tree can be seen circling the stems of the cedars and striving to reach their crowns. Of animal life there was no movement amid the majestic vaulted aisles which stretched from us as we walked, but a constant movement far above our heads told of that multitudinous world of snake and monkey, bird and sloth, which lived in the sunshine, and looked down in wonder at our tiny, dark, stumbling figures in the obscure depths immeasurably below them. At dawn and at sunset the howler monkeys screamed together and the parakeets broke into shrill chatter, but during the hot hours of the day, only the full drone of insects like the beat of a distant surf, filled the ear, while nothing moved amid the solemn vistas of stupendous trunks, fading away into the darkness which held us in. Once some bandy-legged, lurching creature, an ant-eater or a bear, scuttled clumsily amid the shadows. It was the only sign of earth life which I saw in this great Amazonian forest.

And yet there were indications that even human life itself was not far from us in those mysterious recesses. On the third day out we were aware of a singular deep throbbing in the air, rhythmic and solemn, coming and going fitfully throughout the morning. The two boats were paddling within a few yards of each other when we first heard it, and our Indians remained motionless, as if they had been turned to bronze, listening intently with expressions of terror upon their faces.

'What is it, then?' I asked.

'Drums,' said Lord John, carelessly; 'war drums. I have heard them before.'

'Yes, sir, war drums,' said Gomez, the half-breed. 'Wild Indians, bravos, not mansos; they watch us every mile of the way; kill us if they can.'

'How can they watch us?' I asked, gazing into the dark, motionless void.

The half-breed shrugged his broad shoulders.

'The Indians know. They have their own way. They watch us. They talk the drum talk to each other. Kill us if they can.'

By the afternoon of that day – my pocket diary shows me that it was Tuesday, August 18th – at least six or seven drums were throbbing from various points. Sometimes they beat quickly, sometimes slowly, sometimes in obvious question and answer, one far to the east breaking out in a high staccato rattle, and being followed after a pause by a deep roll from the north. There was something indescribably nerve-shaking and menacing in that constant mutter, which seemed to shape itself into the very syllables of the half-breed, endlessly repeated, 'We will kill you if we can. We will kill you if we can.' No one ever moved in the silent woods. All the peace and soothing of quiet Nature lay in that dark curtain of vegetation, but away from behind there came ever the one message from our fellow-man. 'We will kill you if we can,' said the men in the east. 'We will kill you if we can,' said the men in the north.

All day the drums rumbled and whispered, while their menace reflected itself in the faces of our coloured companions. Even the hardy, swaggering half-breed seemed cowed. I learned, however, that day once for all that both Summerlee and Challenger possessed that highest type of bravery, the bravery of the scientific mind. Theirs was the spirit which upheld Darwin among the gauchos of the Argentine or Wallace among the head-hunters of Malaya. It is decreed by a merciful Nature that the human brain cannot think of two things simultaneously, so that if it be steeped in curiosity as to science it has no room for merely personal considerations. All day amid that incessant and mysterious menace our two Professors watched every bird upon the wing, and every shrub upon the bank, with many a sharp wordy contention, when the snarl of Summerlee came quick upon the deep growl of Challenger, but with no more sense of danger and no more reference to drum-beating Indians than if they were seated together in the smoking-room of the Royal Society's Club in St. James's Street. Once only did they condescend to discuss them.

'Miranha or Amajuaca cannibals,' said Challenger, jerking his thumb towards the reverberating wood.

'No doubt, sir,' Summerlee answered. 'Like all such tribes, I shall expect to find them of polysynthetic speech and of Mongolian type.'

'Polysynthetic certainly,' said Challenger, indulgently. 'I am not aware that any other type of language exists in this continent, and I have notes of more than a hundred. The Mongolian theory I regard with deep suspicion.'

'I should have thought that even a limited knowledge of comparative anatomy would have helped to verify it,' said Summerlee, bitterly.

Challenger thrust out his aggressive chin until he was all beard and hat-rim. 'No doubt, sir, a limited knowledge would have that effect. When one's knowledge is exhaustive, one comes to other conclusions.' They glared at each other in mutual defiance, while all round rose the distant whisper, 'We will kill you – we will kill you if we can.'

That night we moored our canoes with heavy stones for anchors in the centre of the stream, and made every preparation for a possible attack. Nothing came, however, and with the dawn we pushed upon our way, the drum-beating dying out behind us. About three o'clock in the afternoon we came to a very steep rapid, more than a mile long – the very one in which Professor Challenger had suffered disaster upon his first journey. I confess that the sight of it consoled me, for it was really the first direct corroboration, slight as it was, of the truth of his story. The Indians carried first our canoes and then our stores through the brushwood, which is very thick at this point, while we four whites, our rifles on our shoulders, walked between them and any danger coming from the woods. Before evening we had successfully passed the rapids, and made our way some ten miles above them, where we anchored for the night. At this point I reckoned that we had come not less than a hundred miles up the tributary from the main stream.

It was in the early forenoon of the next day that we made the great departure. Since dawn Professor Challenger had been acutely uneasy, continually scanning each bank of the river. Suddenly he gave an exclamation of satisfaction and pointed to a single tree, which projected at a peculiar angle over the side of the stream.

'What do you make of that?' he asked.

'It is surely an Assai palm,' said Summerlee.

'Exactly. It was an Assai palm which I took for my landmark. The secret opening is half a mile onwards upon the other side of the river. There is no break in the trees. That is the wonder and the mystery of it. There where you see light-green rushes instead of dark-green undergrowth, there between the great cotton woods, that is my private gate into the unknown. Push through, and you will understand.'

It was indeed a wonderful place. Having reached the spot marked by a line of light-green rushes, we poled our two canoes through them for some hundreds of yards, and eventually emerged into a placid and shallow stream, running clear and transparent over a sandy bottom. It may have been twenty yards across, and was banked in on each side by most luxuriant vegetation. No one who had not observed that for a short distance reeds had taken the place of shrubs could possibly have guessed the existence of such a stream or dreamed of the fairyland beyond.

For a fairyland it was – the most wonderful that the imagination of man could conceive. The thick vegetation met overhead, interlacing into a natural pergola, and through this tunnel of verdure in a golden twilight flowed the green, pellucid river, beautiful in itself, but marvellous from the strange tints thrown by the vivid light from above filtered and tempered in its fall. Clear as crystal, motionless as a sheet of glass, green as the edge of an iceberg, it stretched in front of us under its leafy archway, every stroke of our paddles sending a thousand ripples across its shining surface. It was a fitting avenue to a land of wonders. All sign of the Indians had passed away, but animal life was more frequent, and the tameness of the creatures showed that they knew nothing of the hunter. Fuzzy little black-velvet monkeys, with snow-white teeth and gleaming mocking eyes, chattered at us as we passed. With a dull, heavy splash an occasional cayman plunged in from the bank. Once a dark, clumsy tapir stared at us from a gap in the bushes, and then lumbered away through the forest; once, too, the yellow, sinuous form of a great puma whisked amid the brushwood, and its green, baleful eyes glared hatred at us over its tawny shoulder. Bird life was abundant, especially the wading birds, stork, heron, and ibis gathering in little groups, blue, scarlet, and white, upon every log which jutted from the bank, while beneath us the crystal water was alive with fish of every shape and colour.

For three days we made our way up this tunnel of hazy green sunshine. On the longer stretches one could hardly tell as one looked ahead where the distant green water ended and the distant green archway began. The deep peace of this strange waterway was unbroken by any sign of man.

'No Indian here. Too much afraid. Curupuri,' said Gomez.

'Curupuri is the spirit of the woods,' Lord John explained. 'It's the name for any kind of devil. The poor beggars think that there is something fearsome in this direction, and therefore they avoid it.'

On the third day it became evident that our journey in the canoes could not last much longer, for the stream was rapidly growing more shallow. Twice in as many hours we stuck upon the bottom. Finally we pulled the boats up among the brushwood and spent the night on the bank of the river. In the morning Lord John and I made our way for a couple of miles through the forest, keeping parallel with the stream; but as it grew ever shallower we returned and reported, what Professor Challenger had already suspected, that we had reached the highest point to which the canoes could be brought. We drew them up, therefore, and concealed them among the bushes, blazing a tree with our axes, so that we should find them again. Then we distributed the various burdens among us – guns, ammunition, food, a tent, blankets, and the rest – and, shouldering our packages, we set forth upon the more laborious stage of our journey.

An unfortunate quarrel between our pepperpots marked the outset of our new stage. Challenger had from the moment of joining us issued directions to the whole party, much to the evident discontent of Summerlee. Now, upon his assigning some duty to his fellow-Professor (it was only the carrying of an aneroid barometer), the matter suddenly came to a head.

'May I ask, sir,' said Summerlee, with vicious calm, 'in what capacity you take it upon yourself to issue these orders?'

Challenger glared and bristled.

'I do it, Professor Summerlee, as leader of this expedition.'

'I am compelled to tell you, sir, that I do not recognize you in that capacity.'

'Indeed!' Challenger bowed with unwieldy sarcasm. 'Perhaps you would define my exact position.'

'Yes, sir. You are a man whose veracity is upon trial, and this committee is here to try it. You walk sir, with your judges.'

'Dear me!' said Challenger, seating himself on the side of one of the canoes. 'In that case you will, of course, go on your way, and I will follow at my leisure. If I am not the leader you cannot expect me to lead.'

Thank heaven that there were two sane men – Lord John Roxton and myself – to prevent the petulance and folly of our learned Professors from sending us back empty-handed to London. Such arguing and pleading and explaining before we could get them mollified! Then at last Summerlee, with his sneer and his pipe, would move forwards, and Challenger would come rolling and grumbling after. By some good fortune we discovered about this time that both our savants had the very poorest opinion of Dr. Illingworth of Edinburgh. Thenceforward that was our one safety, and every strained situation was relieved by our introducing the name of the Scotch zoologist, when both our Professors would form a temporary alliance and friendship in their detestation and abuse of this common rival.

Advancing in single file along the bank of the stream, we soon found that it narrowed down to a mere brook, and finally that it lost itself in a great green morass of sponge-like mosses, into which we sank up to our knees. The place was horribly haunted by clouds of mosquitoes and every form of flying pest, so we were glad to find solid ground again and to make a circuit among the trees, which enabled us to outflank this pestilent morass, which droned like an organ in the distance, so loud was it with insect life.

On the second day after leaving our canoes we found that the whole character of the country changed. Our road was persistently upwards, and as we ascended the woods became thinner and lost their tropical luxuriance. The huge trees of the alluvial Amazonian plain gave place to the Phœnix and coco palms, growing in scattered clumps, with thick brushwood between. In the damper hollows the Mauritia palms threw out their graceful drooping fronds. We travelled entirely by compass, and once or twice there were differences of opinion between Challenger and the two Indians, when, to quote the Professor's indignant words, the whole party agreed to 'trust the fallacious instincts of undeveloped savages rather than the highest product of modern European culture.' That we were justified in doing so was shown upon the third day, when Challenger admitted that he recognized several landmarks of his former journey, and in one spot we actually came upon four fire-blackened stones, which must have marked a camping-place.

The road still ascended, and we crossed a rock-studded slope which took two days to traverse. The vegetation had again changed, and only the vegetable ivory tree remained, with a great profusion of wonderful orchids, among which I learned to recognize the rare *Nuttonia Vexillaria* and the glorious pink and scarlet blossoms of Cattleya and odontoglossum. Occasional brooks with pebbly bottoms and fern-draped banks gurgled down the shallow gorges in the hill, and offered good camping-grounds every evening on the banks of some rock-studded pool, where swarms of little blue-backed fish, about the size and shape of English trout, gave us a delicious supper.

On the ninth day after leaving the canoes, having done, as I reckon, about a hundred and twenty miles, we began to emerge from the trees, which had grown smaller until they were mere shrubs. Their place was taken by an immense wilderness of bamboo, which grew so thickly that we could only penetrate it by cutting a pathway with the machetes and bill-hooks of the Indians. It took us a long day, travelling from seven in the morning till eight at night, with only two breaks of one hour each, to get through this obstacle. Anything more monotonous and wearying could not be imagined, for, even at the most open places, I could not see more than ten or twelve yards, while usually my vision was limited to the back of Lord John's cotton jacket in front of me, and to the yellow wall within a foot of me on either side. From above came one thin knife-edge of sunshine, and fifteen feet over our heads one saw the tops of the reeds swaying against the deep blue sky. I do not know what kind of creatures inhabit such a thicket, but several times we heard the plunging of large, heavy animals quite close to us. From their sounds Lord John judged them to be some form of wild cattle. Just as night fell we cleared the belt of bamboos, and at once formed our camp, exhausted by the interminable day.

Early next morning we were again afoot, and found that the character of the country had changed once again. Behind us was the wall of bamboo, as definite as if it marked the course of a river. In front was an open plain, sloping slightly upwards and dotted with clumps of tree-ferns, the whole curving before us until it ended in a long, whale-backed ridge. This we reached about midday, only to find a shallow valley beyond, rising once again into a gentle incline which led to a low, rounded sky-line. It was here, while we crossed the first of these hills, that an incident occurred which may or may not have been important.

Professor Challenger, who, with the two local Indians, was in the van of the party, stopped suddenly and pointed excitedly to the right. As he did so we saw, at the distance of a mile or so, something which appeared to be a huge grey bird flap slowly up from the ground and skim smoothly off, flying very low and straight, until it was lost among the tree-ferns.

'Did you see it?' cried Challenger, in exultation. 'Summerlee, did you see it?'

His colleague was staring at the spot where the creature had disappeared.

'What do you claim that it was?' he asked.

'To the best of my belief, a pterodactyl.'

Summerlee burst into derisive laughter. 'A ptero-fiddlestick!' said he. 'It was a stork, if ever I saw one.'

Challenger was too furious to speak. He simply swung his pack upon his back and continued upon his march. Lord John came abreast of me, however, and his face was more grave than was his wont. He had his Zeiss glasses in his hand.

'I focused it before it got over the trees,' said he. 'I won't undertake to say what it was, but I'll risk my reputation as a sportsman that it wasn't any bird that ever I clapped eyes on in my life.'

So there the matter stands. Are we really just at the edge of the unknown, encountering the outlying pickets of this lost world of which our leader speaks? I give you the incident as it occurred and you will know as much as I do. It stands alone, for we saw nothing more which could be called remarkable.

And now, my readers, if ever I have any, I have brought you up the broad river, and through the screen of rushes, and down the green tunnel, and up the long slope of palm trees, and through the bamboo brake, and across the plain of tree-ferns. At last our destination lay in full sight of us. When we had crossed the second ridge we saw before us an irregular, palm-studded plain, and then the line of high red cliffs which I have seen in the picture. There it lies, even as I write, and there can be no question that it is the same. At the nearest point it is about seven miles from our present camp, and it curves away, stretching as far as I can see. Challenger struts about like a prize peacock, and Summerlee is silent, but still sceptical.

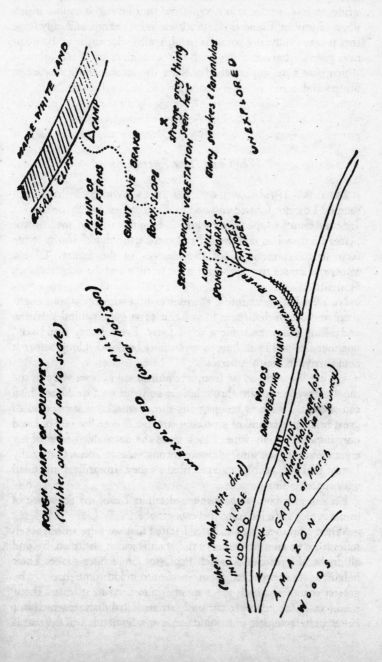

MAPLE-WHITE LAND

BASALT CLIFF

△ CAMP

PLAIN OF TREE FERNS

GIANT CANE BRAKE

ROCKY SLOPE

✕ strange grey thing seen here

SEMI-TROPICAL VEGETATION

LOW HILLS

SPONGY MORASS

many smokes & tarantulas

UNEXPLORED

CANOES HIDDEN

RIVER CONCEALED

HILLS

UNEXPLORED (in far horizon)

ROUGH CHART OF JOURNEY
(Neither oriented nor to scale)

EXPLORED (in far horizon)

WOODS

DRUM BEATING INDIANS

RAPIDS
(where Challenger lost specimens in first journey)

INDIAN VILLAGE
ODOOO
(where Maple White died)

GAPO or MARSH

AMAZON

WOODS

WOODS

Another day should bring some of our doubts to an end. Meanwhile, as José, whose arm was pierced by a broken bamboo, insists upon returning, I send this letter back in his charge, and only hope that it may eventually come to hand. I will write again as the occasion serves. I have enclosed with this a rough chart of our journey, which may have the effect of making the account rather easier to understand.

CHAPTER IX

Who Could Have Foreseen It?

A DREADFUL THING HAS HAPPENED TO US. Who could have foreseen it? I cannot foresee any end to our troubles. It may be that we are condemned to spend our whole lives in this strange, inaccessible place. I am still so confused that I can hardly think clearly of the facts of the present or of the chances of the future. To my astounded senses the one seems most terrible and the other as black as night.

No men have ever found themselves in a worse position; nor is there any use in disclosing to you our exact geographical situation and asking our friends for a relief party. Even if they could send one, our fate will in all human probability be decided long before it could arrive in South America.

We are, in truth, as far from any human aid as if we were in the moon. If we are to win through, it is only our own qualities which can save us. I have as companions three remarkable men, men of great brain-power and of unshaken courage. There lies our one and only hope. It is only when I look upon the untroubled faces of my comrades that I see some glimmer through the darkness. Outwardly I trust that I appear as unconcerned as they. Inwardly I am filled with apprehension.

Let me give you, with as much detail as I can, the sequence of events which have led us to this catastrophe.

When I finished my last letter I stated that we were within seven miles from an enormous line of ruddy cliffs which encircled, beyond all doubt, the plateau of which Professor Challenger spoke. Their height, as we approached them, seemed to me in some places to be greater than he had stated – running up in parts to at least a thousand feet – and they were curiously striated, in a manner which is, I believe, characteristic of basaltic upheavals. Something of the sort is to be seen in Salisbury Crags at Edinburgh. The summit showed every sign of a luxuriant vegetation, with bushes near the edge, and farther back many high trees. There was no indication of any life that we could see.

That night we pitched our camp immediately under the cliff – a most wild and desolate spot. The crags above us were not merely perpendicular, but curved outwards at the top, so that ascent was out of the question. Close to us was the high, thin pinnacle of rock which I believe I mentioned earlier in this narrative. It is like a broad red church spire, the top of it being level with the plateau, but a great chasm gaping between. On the summit of it there grew one high tree. Both pinnacle and cliff were comparatively low – some five or six hundred feet, I should think.

'It was on that,' said Professor Challenger, pointing to this tree, 'that the pterodactyl was perched. I climbed half-way up the rock before I shot him. I am inclined to think that a good mountaineer like myself could ascend the rock to the top, though he would, of course, be no nearer to the plateau when he had done so.'

As Challenger spoke of his pterodactyl I glanced at Professor Summerlee, and for the first time I seemed to see some signs of a dawning credulity and repentance. There was no sneer upon his thin lips, but, on the contrary, a grey, drawn look of excitement and amazement. Challenger saw it, too, and revelled in the first taste of victory.

'Of course,' said he, with his clumsy and ponderous sarcasm, 'Professor Summerlee will understand that when I speak of a pterodactyl I mean a stork – only it is the kind of stork which has no feathers, a leathery skin, membranous wings, and teeth in its jaws.' He grinned and blinked and bowed until his colleague turned and walked away.

In the morning, after a frugal breakfast of coffee and manioc – we had to be economical of our stores – we held a council of war as to the best method of ascending to the plateau above us.

Challenger presided with a solemnity as if he were the Lord Chief Justice on the Bench. Picture him seated upon a rock, his absurd boyish straw hat tilted on the back of his head, his supercilious eyes dominating us from under his drooping lids, his great black beard wagging as he slowly defined our present situation and our future movements.

Beneath him you might have seen the three of us – myself, sunburnt, young, and vigorous after our open-air tramp; Summerlee, solemn, but still critical, behind his eternal pipe; Lord John, as keen as a razor-edge, with his supple, alert figure leaning upon his rifle, and his eagle eyes fixed eagerly upon the speaker. Behind us were grouped the two swarthy half-breeds and the little knot of Indians, while in front and above us towered those huge, ruddy ribs of rocks which kept us from our goal.

'I need not say,' said our leader, 'that on the occasion of my last visit I exhausted every means of climbing the cliff, and where I failed I do not think that anyone else is likely to succeed, for I am something of a mountaineer. I had none of the appliances of a rock-climber with me, but I have taken the precaution to bring them now. With their aid I am positive I could climb that detached pin-nacle to the summit; but so long as the main cliff overhangs, it is vain to attempt ascending that. I was hurried upon my last visit by the approach of the rainy season and by the exhaustion of my sup-plies. These considerations limited my time, and I can only claim that I have surveyed about six miles of the cliff to the east of us, finding no possible way up. What, then, shall we now do?'

'There seems to be only one reasonable course,' said Professor Summerlee. 'If you have explored the east, we should travel along the base of the cliff to the west, and seek for a practicable point for our ascent.'

'That's it,' said Lord John. 'The odds are that this plateau is of no great size, and we shall travel round it until we either find an easy way up it, or come back to the point from which we started.'

'I have already explained to our young friend here,' said Chal-lenger (he has a way of alluding to me as if I were a school child ten years old), 'that it is quite impossible that there should be an easy way up anywhere, for the simple reason that if there were the summit would not be isolated, and those conditions would not obtain which have effected so singular an interference with the gen-eral laws of survival. Yet I admit that there may very well be places where an expert human climber may reach the summit, and yet a cumbrous and heavy animal be unable to descend. It is certain that there *is* a point where an ascent is possible.'

'How do you know that, sir?' asked Summerlee, sharply.

'Because my predecessor, the American Maple White, actually made such an ascent. How otherwise could he have seen the mon-ster which he sketched in his notebook?'

'There you reason somewhat ahead of the proved facts,' said the stubborn Summerlee. 'I admit your plateau, because I have seen it; but I have not as yet satisfied myself that it contains any form of life whatever.'

'What you admit, sir, or what you do not admit, is really of inconceivably small importance. I am glad to perceive that the plateau itself has actually obtruded itself upon your intelligence.' He glanced up at it, and then, to our amazement, he sprang from his rock, and, seizing Summerlee by the neck, he tilted his face into the air. 'Now, sir!' he shouted, hoarse with excitement. 'Do I help you to realize that the plateau contains some animal life?'

I have said that a thick fringe of green overhung the edge of the cliff. Out of this there had emerged a black, glistening object. As it came slowly forth and overhung the chasm, we saw that it was a very large snake with a peculiar flat spade-like head. It wavered and quivered above us for a minute, the morning sun gleaming upon its sleek, sinuous coils. Then it slowly drew inwards and disappeared.

Summerlee had been so interested that he had stood unresisting while Challenger tilted his head into the air. Now he shook his colleague off and came back to his dignity.

'I should be glad, Professor Challenger,' said he, 'if you could see your way to make any remarks which may occur to you without seizing me by the chin. Even the appearance of a very ordinary rock python does not appear to justify such a liberty.'

'But there is life upon the plateau all the same,' his colleague replied in triumph. 'And now, having demonstrated this important conclusion so that it is clear to anyone, however prejudiced or obtuse, I am of opinion that we cannot do better than break up our camp and travel westward until we find some means of ascent.'

The ground at the foot of the cliff was rocky and broken, so that the going was slow and difficult. Suddenly we came, however, upon something which cheered our hearts. It was the site of an old encampment, with several empty Chicago meat tins, a bottle labelled 'Brandy,' a broken tin-opener, and a quantity of other travellers' debris. A crumpled, disintegrated newspaper revealed itself as the *Chicago Democrat*, though the date had been obliterated.

'Not mine,' said Challenger. 'It must be Maple White's.'

Lord John had been gazing curiously at a great tree-fern which overshadowed the encampment. 'I say, look at this,' said he. 'I believe it is meant for a sign-post.'

A slip of hard wood had been nailed to the tree in such a way as to point to the westward.

'Most certainly a sign-post,' said Challenger. 'What else? Finding himself upon a dangerous errand, our pioneer has left this sign so that any party which follows him may know the way he has taken. Perhaps we shall come upon some other indications as we proceed.'

We did indeed, but they were of a terrible and most unexpected nature. Immediately beneath the cliff there grew a considerable patch of high bamboo, like that which we had traversed in our journey. Many of these stems were twenty feet high, with sharp, strong tops, so that even as they stood they made formidable spears. We were passing along the edge of this cover when my eye was caught by the gleam of something white within it. Thrusting in my head between the stems, I found myself gazing at a fleshless skull. The whole skeleton was there, but the skull had detached itself and lay some feet nearer to the open.

With a few blows from the machetes of our Indians we cleared the spot and were able to study the details of this old tragedy. Only a few shreds of clothes could still be distinguished, but there were the remains of boots upon the bony feet, and it was very clear that the dead man was a European. A gold watch by Hudson, of New York, and a chain which held a stylographic pen, lay among the bones. There was also a silver cigarette-case, with 'J. C., from A. E. S.,' upon the lid. The state of the metal seemed to show that the catastrophe had occurred no great time before.

'Who can he be?' asked Lord John. 'Poor devil! every bone in his body seems to be broken.'

'And the bamboo grows through his smashed ribs,' said Summerlee. 'It is a fast-growing plant, but it is surely inconceivable that this body could have been here while the canes grew to be twenty feet in length.'

'As to the man's identity,' said Professor Challenger, 'I have no doubt whatever upon that point. As I made my way up the river before I reached you at the fazenda I instituted very particular inquiries about Maple White. At Para they knew nothing. Fortunately, I had a definite clue, for there was a particular picture in his sketch-book which showed him taking lunch with a certain ecclesiastic at Rosario. This priest I was able to find, and though he proved a very argumentative fellow, who took it absurdly amiss that I should point out to him the corrosive effect which modern science must have upon his beliefs, he none the less gave me some positive information. Maple White passed Rosario four years ago, or two years before I saw his dead body. He was not alone at the time, but there was a friend, an American named James Colver, who remained in the boat and did not meet this ecclesiastic. I think, therefore, that there can be no doubt that we are now looking upon the remains of this James Colver.'

'Nor,' said Lord John, 'is there much doubt as to how he met his death. He has fallen or been chucked from the top, and so been impaled. How else could he come by his broken bones, and how could he have been stuck through by these canes with their points so high above our heads?'

A hush came over us as we stood round these shattered remains and realized the truth of Lord John Roxton's words. The beetling head of the cliff projected over the cane-brake. Undoubtedly he had fallen from above. But *had* he fallen? Had it been an accident? Or – Already ominous and terrible possibilities began to form round that unknown land.

We moved off in silence, and continued to coast round the line of cliffs, which were as even and unbroken as some of those monstrous Antarctic ice-fields which I have seen depicted as stretching from horizon to horizon and towering high above the mast-heads of the exploring vessel. In five miles we saw no rift or break. And then suddenly we perceived something which filled us with new hope. In a hollow of the rock, protected from rain, there was drawn a rough arrow in chalk, pointing still to the westward.

'Maple White again,' said Professor Challenger. 'He had some presentiment that worthy footsteps would follow close behind him.'

'He had chalk, then?'

'A box of coloured chalks was among the effects I found in his knapsack. I remember that the white one was worn to a stump.'

'That is certainly good evidence,' said Summerlee. 'We can only accept his guidance and follow on to the westward.'

We had proceeded some five more miles when again we saw a white arrow upon the rocks. It was at a point where the face of the cliff was for the first time split into a narrow cleft. Inside the cleft was a second guidance mark, which pointed right up it with the tip somewhat elevated, as if the spot indicated were above the level of the ground.

It was a solemn place, for the walls were so gigantic and the slit of blue sky so narrow and so obscured by a double fringe of verdure that only a dim and shadowy light penetrated to the bottom. We had had no food for many hours, and we were very weary with the stony and irregular journey, but our nerves were too strung to allow us to halt. We ordered the camp to be pitched, however, and, leaving the Indians to arrange it, we four, with the two half-breeds, proceeded up the narrow gorge.

It was not more than forty feet across at the mouth, but it rapidly closed until it ended in an acute angle, too straight and smooth for an ascent. Certainly it was not this which our pioneer had attempted to indicate. We made our way back – the whole gorge was not more than a quarter of a mile deep – and then suddenly the quick eyes of Lord John fell upon what we were seeking. High up above our heads, amid the dark shadows, there was one circle of deeper gloom. Surely it could only be the opening of a cave.

The base of the cliff was heaped with loose stones at the spot, and it was not difficult to clamber up. When we reached it, all doubt was removed. Not only was it an opening into the rock, but on the side of it was marked once again the sign of the arrow. Here was the point, and this the means by which Maple White and his ill-fated comrade had made their ascent.

We were too excited to return to the camp, but must make our first exploration at once. Lord John had an electric torch in his knapsack, and this had to serve us as light. He advanced, throwing his little clear circlet of yellow radiance before him, while in single file we followed at his heels.

The cave had evidently been water-worn, the sides being smooth and the floor covered with rounded stones. It was of such a size that a single man could just fit through by stooping. For fifty yards it ran almost straight into the rock, and then it ascended at an angle of forty-five. Presently this incline became even steeper, and we found ourselves climbing upon hands and knees among loose rubble which slid from beneath us. Suddenly an exclamation broke from Lord Roxton.

'It's blocked!' said he.

Clustering behind him we saw in the yellow field of light a wall of broken basalt which extended to the ceiling.

'The roof has fallen in!'

In vain we dragged out some of the pieces. The only effect was that the larger ones became detached and threatened to roll down the gradient and crush us. It was evident that the obstacle was far beyond any efforts which we could make to remove it. The road by which Maple White had ascended was no longer available.

Too much cast down to speak, we stumbled down the dark tunnel and made our way back to the camp.

One incident occurred, however, before we left the gorge, which is of importance in view of what came afterwards.

We had gathered in a little group at the bottom of the chasm, some forty feet beneath the mouth of the cave, when a huge rock rolled suddenly downwards and shot past us with tremendous force. It was the narrowest escape for one or all of us. We could not ourselves see whence the rock had come, but our half-breed servants, who were still at the opening of the cave, said that it had flown past them, and must therefore have fallen from the summit. Looking upwards, we could see no sign of movement above us amidst the green jungle which topped the cliff. There could be little doubt, however, that the stone was aimed at us, so the incident surely pointed to humanity – and malevolent humanity – upon the plateau!

We withdrew hurriedly from the chasm, our minds full of this new development and its bearing upon our plans. The situation was difficult enough before, but if the obstructions of Nature were increased by the deliberate opposition of man, then our case was indeed a hopeless one. And yet, as we looked up at that beautiful fringe of verdure only a few hundreds of feet above our heads, there was not one of us who could conceive the idea of returning to London until we had explored it to its depths.

On discussing the situation, we determined that our best course was to continue to coast round the plateau in the hope of finding some other means of reaching the top. The line of cliffs, which had decreased considerably in height, had already begun to trend from west to north, and if we could take this as representing the arc of a circle, the whole circumference could not be very great. At the worst, then, we should be back in a few days at our starting-point.

We made a march that day which totalled some two-and-twenty miles, without any change in our prospects. I may mention that our aneroid shows us that in the continual incline which we have ascended since we abandoned our canoes we have risen to no less than three thousand feet above sea-level. Hence there is a considerable change both in the temperature and in the vegetation. We have shaken off some of that horrible insect life which is the bane of tropical travel. A few palms still survive, and many tree-ferns, but the Amazonian trees have been all left behind. It was pleasant to see the convolvulus, the passion-flower, and the begonia, all reminding me of home, here among these inhospitable rocks. There was a red begonia just the same colour as one that is kept in a pot in the window of a certain villa in Streatham – but I am drifting into private reminiscence.

That night – I am still speaking of the first day of our circumnavigation of the plateau – a great experience awaited us, and one which for ever set at rest any doubt which we could have had as to the wonders so near us.

You will realize as you read it, my dear Mr. McArdle, and possibly for the first time, that the paper has not sent me on a wild-goose chase, and that there is inconceivably fine copy waiting for the world whenever we have the Professor's leave to make use of it. I shall not dare to publish these articles unless I can bring back my proofs to England, or I shall be hailed as the journalistic Munchausen of all time. I have no doubt that you feel the same way yourself, and that you would not care to stake the whole credit of the *Gazette* upon this adventure until we can meet the chorus of criticism and scepticism which such articles must of necessity elicit. So this wonderful incident, which would make such a headline for the old paper, must still wait its turn in the editorial drawer.

And yet it was all over in a flash, and there was no sequel to it, save in our own convictions.

What occurred was this. Lord John had shot an ajouti – which is a small, pig-like animal – and, half of it having been given to the Indians, we were cooking the other half upon our fire. There is a chill in the air after dark, and we had all drawn close to the blaze. The night was moonless, but there were some stars, and one could see for a little distance across the plain. Well, suddenly out of the darkness, out of the night, there swooped something with a swish like an aeroplane. The whole group of us were covered for an instant by a canopy of leathery wings, and I had a momentary vision of a long, snake-like neck, a fierce, red, greedy eye, and a great snapping beak, filled, to my amazement, with little, gleaming teeth. The next instant it was gone – and so was our dinner. A huge black shadow, twenty feet across, skimmed up into the air; for an instant the monster wings blotted out the stars, and then it vanished over the brow of the cliff above us. We all sat in amazed silence round the fire, like the heroes of Virgil when the Harpies came down upon them. It was Summerlee who was the first to speak.

'Professor Challenger,' said he, in a solemn voice, which quavered with emotion, 'I owe you an apology. Sir, I am very much in the wrong, and I beg that you will forget what is past.'

It was handsomely said, and the two men for the first time shook hands. So much we have gained by this clear vision of our first pterodactyl. It was worth a stolen supper to bring two such men together.

But if prehistoric life existed upon the plateau, it was not superabundant, for we had no further glimpse of it during the next three days. During this time we traversed a barren and forbidding country, which alternated between stony desert and desolate marshes full of many wild-fowl, upon the north and east of the cliffs. From that direction the place is really inaccessible, and, were it not for a hardish ledge which runs at the very base of the precipice, we should have had to turn back. Many times we were up to our waists in the slime and blubber of an old, semi-tropical swamp. To make matters worse, the place seemed to be a favourite breeding-place of the Jaracaca snake, the most venomous and aggressive in South America. Again and again these horrible creatures came writhing and springing towards us across the surface of this putrid bog, and it was only by keeping our shot guns for ever ready that we could feel safe from them. One funnel-shaped depression in the morass, of a livid green in colour from some lichen which festered in it, will always remain as a nightmare memory in my mind. It seems to have been a special nest of these vermin, and the slopes were alive with them, all writhing in our direction, for it is a peculiarity of the Jaracaca that it will always attack man at first sight. There were too many for us to shoot, so we fairly took to our heels and ran until we were exhausted. I shall always remember as we looked back how far behind we could see the heads and necks of our horrible pursuers rising and falling amid the reeds. Jaracaca Swamp we named it in the map which we are constructing.

The cliffs upon the farther side had lost their ruddy tint, being chocolate-brown in colour; the vegetation was more scattered along the top of them, and they had sunk to three or four hundred feet in height, but in no place did we find any point where they could be ascended. If anything, they were more impossible than at the first point where we had met them. Their absolute steepness is indicated in the photograph which I took over the stony desert.

'Surely,' said I, as we discussed the situation, 'the rain must find its way down somehow. There are bound to be water-channels in the rocks.'

'Our young friend has glimpses of lucidity,' said Professor Challenger, patting me upon the shoulder.

'The rain must go somewhere,' I repeated.

'He keeps a firm grip upon actuality. The only drawback is that we have conclusively proved by ocular demonstration that there are *no* water channels down the rocks.'

'Where, then, does it go?' I persisted.

'I think it may be fairly assumed that if it does not come outwards it must run inwards.'

'Then there is a lake in the centre.'

'So I should suppose.'

'It is more than likely that the lake may be an old crater,' said Summerlee. 'The whole formation is, of course, highly volcanic. But however that may be, I should expect to find the surface of the plateau slope inwards with a considerable sheet of water in the centre, which may drain off, by some subterranean channel, into the marshes of the Jaracaca Swamp.'

'Or evaporation might preserve an equilibrium,' remarked Challenger, and the two learned men wandered off into one of their usual scientific arguments, which were as comprehensible as Chinese to the layman.

On the sixth day we completed our circuit of the cliffs, and found ourselves back at the first camp, beside the isolated pinnacle of rock. We were a disconsolate party, for nothing could have been more minute than our investigation, and it was absolutely certain that there was no single point where the most active human being could possibly hope to scale the cliff. The place which Maple White's chalk-marks had indicated as his own means of access was now entirely impassable.

What were we to do now? Our stores of provisions, supplemented by our guns, were holding out well, but the day must come when they would need replenishment. In a couple of months the rains might be expected, and we should be washed out of our camp. The rock was harder than marble, and any attempt at cutting a path for so great a height was more than our time or resources would admit. No wonder that we looked gloomily at each other that night, and sought our blankets without hardly a word exchanged. I remember that as I dropped off to sleep my last recollection was that Challenger was squatting, like a monstrous bull-frog, by the fire, his huge head in his hands, sunk apparently in the deepest thought, and entirely oblivious to the good-night which I wished him.

But it was a very different Challenger who greeted us in the morning – a Challenger with contentment and self-congratulation shining from his whole person. He faced us as we assembled for breakfast with a deprecating false modesty in his eyes, as who should say, 'I know that I deserve all that you can say, but I pray you to spare my blushes by not saying it.' His beard bristled exultantly, his chest was thrown out, and his hand was thrust into the front of his jacket. So, in his fancy, may he see himself sometimes, gracing the vacant pedestal in Trafalgar Square, and adding one more to the horrors of the London streets.

'Eureka!' he cried, his teeth shining through his beard. 'Gentlemen, you may congratulate me and we may congratulate each other. The problem is solved.'

'You have found a way up?'

'I venture to think so.'

'And where?'

For answer he pointed to the spire-like pinnacle upon our right.

Our faces – or mine, at least – fell as we surveyed it. That it could be climbed we had our companion's assurance. But a horrible abyss lay between it and the plateau.

'We can never get across,' I gasped.

'We can at least all reach the summit,' said he. 'When we are up I may be able to show you that the resources of an inventive mind are not yet exhausted.'

After breakfast we unpacked the bundle in which our leader had brought his climbing accessories. From it he took a coil of the strongest and lightest rope, a hundred and fifty feet in length, and climbing irons, clamps, and other devices. Lord John was an experienced mountaineer, and Summerlee had done some rough climbing at various times, so that I was really the novice at rock-work of the party; but my strength and activity may have made up for my want of experience.

It was not in reality a very stiff task, though there were moments which made my hair bristle upon my head. The first half was perfectly easy, but from there upwards it became continually steeper, until, for the last fifty feet, we were literally clinging with our fingers and toes to tiny ledges and crevices in the rock. I could not have accomplished it, nor could Summerlee, if Challenger had not gained the summit (it was extraordinary to see such activity in so unwieldy a creature) and there fixed the rope round the trunk of the considerable tree which grew there. With this as our support, we were soon able to scramble up the jagged wall until we found ourselves upon the small grassy platform, some twenty-five feet each way, which formed the summit.

The first impression which I received when I had recovered my breath was the extraordinary view over the country which we traversed. The whole Brazilian plain seemed to lie beneath us, extending away and away until it ended in dim blue mists upon the farthest sky-line. In the foreground was the long slope, strewn with rocks and dotted with tree-ferns; farther off in the middle distance, looking over the saddle-back hill, I could just see the yellow and green mass of bamboos through which we had passed; and then, gradually, the vegetation increased until it formed the huge forest which extended as far as the eyes could reach, and for a good two thousand miles beyond.

I was still drinking in this wonderful panorama when the heavy hand of the Professor fell upon my shoulder.

'This way, my young friend,' said he; *'vestigia nulla restrorsum.* Never look rearwards, but always to our glorious goal.'

The level of the plateau, when I turned, was exactly that on which we stood, and the green bank of bushes, with occasional trees, was so near that it was difficult to realize how inaccessible it remained. At a rough guess the gulf was forty feet across, but, so far as I could see, it might as well have been forty miles. I placed one arm round the trunk of the tree and leaned over the abyss. Far down were the small dark figures of our servants, looking up at us. The wall was absolutely precipitous, as was that which faced me.

'This is indeed curious,' said the creaking voice of Professor Summerlee.

I turned, and found that he was examining with great interest the tree to which I clung. That smooth bark and those small, ribbed leaves seemed familiar to my eyes. 'Why,' I cried, 'it's a beech!'

'Exactly,' said Summerlee. 'A fellow-countryman in a far land.'

'Not only a fellow-countryman, my good sir,' said Challenger, 'but also, if I may be allowed to enlarge your simile, an ally of the first value. This beech tree will be our saviour.'

'By George!' cried Lord John, 'a bridge!'

'Exactly, my friends, a bridge! It is not for nothing that I expended an hour last night in focusing my mind upon the situation. I have some recollection of once remarking to our young friend here that G. E. C. is at his best when his back is to the wall. Last night you will admit that all our backs were to the wall. But where will-power and intellect go together, there is always a way out. A drawbridge had to be found which could be dropped across the abyss. Behold it!'

It was certainly a brilliant idea. The tree was a good sixty feet in height, and if it only fell the right way it would easily cross the chasm. Challenger had slung the camp axe over his shoulder when he ascended. Now he handed it to me.

'Our young friend has the thews and sinews,' said he. 'I think he will be the most useful at this task. I must beg, however, that you will kindly refrain from thinking for yourself, and that you will do exactly what you are told.'

Under his direction I cut such gashes in the sides of the tree as would ensure that it should fall as we desired. It had already a strong, natural tilt in the direction of the plateau, so that the matter was not difficult. Finally I set to work in earnest upon the trunk, taking turn and turn with Lord John. In a little over an hour there was a loud crack, the tree swayed forward, and then crashed over, burying its branches among the bushes on the farther side. The severed trunk rolled to the very edge of our platform, and for one terrible second we all thought that it was over. It balanced itself, however, a few inches from the edge, and there was our bridge to the unknown.

All of us, without a word, shook hands with Professor Challenger, who raised his straw hat and bowed deeply to each in turn.

'I claim the honour,' said he, 'to be the first to cross to the unknown land – a fitting subject, no doubt, for some future historical painting.'

He had approached the bridge when Lord John laid his hand upon his coat.

'My dear chap,' said he, 'I really cannot allow it.'

'Cannot allow it, sir!' The head went back and the beard forward.

'When it is a matter of science, don't you know, I follow your lead because you are by way of bein' a man of science. But it's up to you to follow me when you come into my department.'

'Your department, sir?'

'We all have our professions, and soldierin' is mine. We are, accordin' to my ideas, invadin' a new country, which may or may not be chock-full of enemies of sorts. To barge blindly into it for want of a little common sense and patience isn't my notion of management.'

The remonstrance was too reasonable to be disregarded. Challenger tossed his head and shrugged his heavy shoulders.

'Well, sir, what do you propose?'

'For all I know there may be a tribe of cannibals waitin' for lunch-time among those very bushes,' said Lord John, looking across the bridge. 'It's better to learn wisdom before you get into a cookin'-pot; so we will content ourselves with hopin' that there is no trouble waitin' for us, and at the same time we will act as if there were. Malone and I will go down again, therefore, and we will fetch up the four rifles, together with Gomez and the other. One man can then go across and the rest will cover him with guns, until he sees that it is safe for the whole crowd to come along.'

Challenger sat down upon the cut stump and groaned his impatience; but Summerlee and I were of one mind that Lord John was our leader when such practical details were in question. The climb was a more simple thing now that the rope dangled down the face of the worst part of the ascent. Within an hour we had brought up the rifles and a shot-gun. The half-breeds had ascended also, and under Lord John's orders they had carried up a bale of provisions in case our first exploration should be a long one. We had each bandoliers of cartridges.

'Now, Challenger, if you really insist upon being the first man in,' said Lord John, when every preparation was complete.

'I am much indebted to you for your gracious permission,' said the angry Professor; for never was a man so intolerant of every form of authority. 'Since you are good enough to allow it, I shall most certainly take it upon myself to act as pioneer upon this occasion.'

Seating himself with a leg overhanging the abyss on each side, and his hatchet slung upon his back, Challenger hopped his way across the trunk and was soon at the other side. He clambered up and waved his arms in the air.

'At last!' he cried; 'at last!'

I gazed anxiously at him, with a vague expectation that some terrible fate would dart at him from the curtain of green behind him. But all was quiet, save that a strange, many-coloured bird flew up from under his feet and vanished among the trees.

Summerlee was the second. His wiry energy is wonderful in so frail a frame. He insisted upon having two rifles slung upon his back, so that both Professors were armed when he had made his transit. I came next, and tried not to look down into the horrible gulf over which I was passing. Summerlee held out the butt-end of his rifle, and an instant later I was able to grasp his hand. As to Lord John, he walked across – actually walked, without support! He must have nerves of iron.

And there we were, the four of us, upon the dreamland, the lost world, of Maple White. To all of us it seemed the moment of our supreme triumph. Who could have guessed that it was the prelude to our supreme disaster? Let me say in a few words how the crushing blow fell upon us.

We had turned away from the edge, and had penetrated about fifty yards of close brushwood, when there came a frightful rending crash from behind us. With one impulse we rushed back the way we had come. The bridge was gone!

Far down at the base of the cliff I saw, as I looked over, a tangled mass of branches and splintered trunk. It was our beech tree. Had the edge of the platform crumbled and let it through? For a moment this explanation was in all our minds. The next, from the farther side of the rocky pinnacle before us a swarthy face, the face of Gomez the half-breed, was slowly protruded. Yes, it was Gomez, but no longer the Gomez of the demure smile and the mask-like expression. Here was a face with flashing eyes and distorted features, a face convulsed with hatred and with the mad joy of gratified revenge.

'Lord Roxton!' he shouted. 'Lord John Roxton!'

'Well,' said our companion, 'here I am.'

A shriek of laughter came across the abyss.

'Yes, there you are, you English dog, and there you will remain! I have waited and waited, and now has come my chance. You found it hard to get up; you will find it harder to get down. You cursed fools, you are trapped, every one of you!'

We were too astounded to speak. We could only stand there staring in amazement. A great broken bough upon the grass showed whence he had gained his leverage to tilt over our bridge. The face had vanished, but presently it was up again, more frantic than before.

'We nearly killed you with a stone at the cave,' he cried, 'but this is better. It is slower and more terrible. Your bones will whiten up there, and none will know where you lie or come to cover them. As you lie dying, think of Lopez, whom you shot five years ago on the Putomayo River. I am his brother, and, come what will I die happy now, for his memory has been avenged.' A furious hand was shaken at us and then all was quiet.

Had the half-breed simply wrought his vengeance and then escaped, all might have been well with him. It was that foolish, irresistible Latin impulse to be dramatic which brought his own downfall. Roxton, the man who had earned himself the name of the Flail of the Lord through three countries, was not one who could be safely taunted. The half-breed was descending on the farther side of the pinnacle; but before he could reach the ground Lord John had run along the edge of the plateau and gained a point from which he could see his man. There was a single crack of his rifle, and, though we saw nothing, we heard the scream and then the distant thud of the falling body. Roxton came back to us with a face of granite.

'I have been a blind simpleton,' said he, bitterly. 'It's my folly that has brought you all into this trouble. I should have remembered that these people have long memories for blood-feuds, and have been more upon my guard.'

'What about the other one? It took two of them to lever that tree over the edge.'

'I could have shot him, but I let him go. He may have had no part in it. Perhaps it would have been better if I had killed him, for he must, as you say, have lent a hand.'

Now that we had the clue to his action, each of us could cast back and remember some sinister act upon the part of the half-breed – his constant desire to know our plans, his arrest outside our tent when he was over-hearing them, the furtive looks of hatred which from time to time one or other of us had surprised. We were still discussing it, endeavouring to adjust our minds to these new conditions, when a singular scene in the plain below arrested our attention.

A man in white clothes, who could only be the surviving half-breed, was running as one does run when Death is the pacemaker. Behind him, only a few yards in his rear, bounded the huge ebony figure of Zambo, our devoted negro. Even as we looked, he sprang upon the back of the fugitive and flung his arms round his neck. They rolled on the ground together. An instant afterwards Zambo rose, looked at the prostrate man, and then, waving his hand joyously to us, came running in our direction. The white figure lay motionless in the middle of the great plain.

Our two traitors had been destroyed, but the mischief that they had done lived after them. By no possible means could we get back to the pinnacle. We had been natives of the world; now we were natives of the plateau. The two things were separate and apart. There was the plain which led to the canoes. Yonder, beyond the violet, hazy horizon, was the stream which led back to civilization. But the link between was missing. No human ingenuity could suggest a means of bridging the chasm which yawned between ourselves and our past lives. One instant had altered the whole conditions of our existence.

It was at such a moment that I learned the stuff of which my three comrades were composed. They were grave, it is true, and thoughtful, but of an invincible serenity. For the moment we could only sit among the bushes in patience and wait the coming of Zambo. Presently his honest black face topped the rocks and his Herculean figure emerged upon the top of the pinnacle.

'What I do now?' he cried. 'You tell me and I do it.'

It was a question which it was easier to ask than to answer. One thing only was clear. He was our one trusty link with the outside world. On no account must he leave us.

'No, no!' he cried. 'I not leave you. Whatever come, you always find me here. But no able to keep Indians. Already they say too much, Curupuri live on this place, and they go home. Now you leave them me no able to keep them.'

'Make them wait till to-morrow, Zambo,' I shouted; 'then I can send letter back by them.'

'Very good, sarr! I promise they wait till to-morrow,' said the negro. 'But what I do for you now?'

There was plenty for him to do, and admirably the faithful fellow did it. First of all, under our directions, he undid the rope from the tree-stump and threw one end of it across to us. It was not thicker than a clothes-line, but it was of great strength, and though we could not make a bridge of it, we might well find it invaluable if we had any climbing to do. He then fastened his end of the rope to the package of supplies which had been carried up, and we were able to drag it across. This gave us the means of life for at least a week, even if we found nothing else. Finally he descended and carried up two other packets of mixed goods – a box of ammunition and a number of other things, all of which we got across by throwing our rope to him and hauling it back. It was evening when he at last climbed down, with a final assurance that he would keep the Indians till next morning.

And so it is that I have spent nearly the whole of this our first night upon the plateau writing up our experiences by the light of a single candle-lantern.

We supped and camped at the very edge of the cliff, quenching our thirst with two bottles of Apollinaris which were in one of the cases. It is vital to us to find water, but I think even Lord John himself had had adventures enough for one day, and none of us felt inclined to make the first push into the unknown. We forbore to light a fire or to make any unnecessary sound.

To-morrow (or to-day, rather, for it is already dawn as I write) we shall make our first venture into this strange land. When I shall be able to write again – or if I ever shall write again – I know not. Meanwhile, I can see that the Indians are still in their place, and I am sure that the faithful Zambo will be here presently to get my letter. I only trust that it will come to hand.

P.S. – The more I think the more desperate does our position seem. I see no possible hope of our return. If there were a high tree near the edge of the plateau we might drop a return bridge across, but there is none within fifty yards. Our united strength could not carry a trunk which would serve our purpose. The rope, of course, is far too short that we could descend by it. No, our position is hopeless – hopeless!

CHAPTER X

The Most Wonderful Things Have Happened

THE MOST WONDERFUL THINGS HAVE HAPPENED and are continually happening to us. All the paper that I possess consists of five old note-books and a lot of scraps, and I have only the one stylographic pencil; but so long as I can move my hand I will continue to set down our experiences and impressions, for, since we are the only men of the whole human race to see such things, it is of enormous importance that I should record them whilst they are fresh in my memory and before that fate which seems to be constantly impending does actually overtake us. Whether Zambo can at last take these letters to the river, or whether I shall myself in some miraculous way carry them back with me, or, finally, whether some daring explorer, coming upon our tracks, with the advantage, perhaps, of a perfected monoplane, should find this bundle of manuscript, in any case I can see that what I am writing is destined to immortality as a classic of true adventure.

On the morning after our being trapped upon the plateau by the villainous Gomez we began a new stage in our experiences. The first incident in it was not such as to give me a very favourable opin-ion of the place to which we had wandered. As I roused myself from a short nap after day had dawned, my eyes fell upon a most singular appearance upon my own leg. My trouser had slipped up, exposing a few inches of my skin above my sock. On this there rested a large, purplish grape. Astonished at the sight, I leaned forward to pick it off, when, to my horror, it burst between my finger and thumb, squirting blood in every direction. My cry of disgust had brought the two Professors to my side.

'Most interesting,' said Summerlee, bending over my shin. 'An enormous blood-tick, as yet I believe, unclassified.'

'The first-fruits of our labours,' said Challenger in his booming, pedantic fashion. 'We cannot do less than call it *Ixodes Maloni*. The very small inconvenience of being bitten, my young friend, cannot, I am sure, weigh with you as against the glorious privilege of having your name inscribed in the deathless roll of zoology. Unhappily you have crushed this fine specimen at the moment of satiation.'

'Filthy vermin!' I cried.

Professor Challenger raised his great eyebrows in protest, and placed a soothing paw upon my shoulder.

'You should cultivate the scientific eye and the detached scientific mind,' said he. 'To a man of philosophic temperament like myself the blood-tick, with its lancet-like proboscis and its distending stomach, is as beautiful a work of Nature as the peacock, or, for that matter, the aurora borealis. It pains me to hear you speak of it in so unappreciative a fashion. No doubt, with due diligence, we can secure some other specimen.'

'There can be no doubt of that,' said Summerlee, grimly, 'for one has just disappeared behind your shirt-collar.'

Challenger sprang into the air bellowing like a bull, and tore frantically at his coat and shirt to get them off. Summerlee and I laughed so that we could hardly help him. At last we exposed that monstrous torso (fifty-four inches, by the tailor's tape). His body was all matted with black hair, out of which jungle we picked the wandering tick before it had bitten him. But the bushes round were full of the horrible pests, and it was clear that we must shift our camp.

But first of all it was necessary to make our arrangements with the faithful negro, who appeared presently on the pinnacle with a number of tins of cocoa and biscuits, which he tossed over to us. Of the stores which remained below he was ordered to retain as much as would keep him for two months. The Indians were to have the remainder as a reward for their services and as payment for taking our letters back to the Amazon. Some hours later we saw them in single file far out upon the plain, each with a bundle on his head, making their way back along the path we had come. Zambo occupied our little tent at the base of the pinnacle, and there he remained, our one link with the world below.

And now we had to decide upon our immediate movements. We shifted our position from among the tick-laden bushes until we came to a small clearing thickly surrounded by trees upon all sides. There were some flat slabs of rock in the centre, with an excellent well close by, and there we sat in cleanly comfort while we made our first plans for the invasion of this new country. Birds were calling among the foliage – especially one with a peculiar whooping cry which was new to us – but beyond these sounds there were no signs of life.

Our first care was to make some sort of list of our own stores, so that we might know what we had to rely upon. What with the things we had ourselves brought up and those which Zambo had sent across on the rope, we were fairly well supplied. Most important of all, in view of the dangers which might surround us, we had our four rifles and one thousand three hundred rounds, also a shot-gun, but not more than a hundred and fifty medium pellet car-tridges. In the matter of provisions we had enough to last for several weeks, with a sufficiency of tobacco and a few scientific implements, including a large telescope and a good field-glass. All these things we collected together in the clearing, and as a first precaution, we cut down with our hatchet and knives a number of thorny bushes, which we piled round in a circle some fifteen yards in diameter. This was to be our headquarters for the time – our place of refuge against sudden danger and the guard-house for our stores. Fort Challenger, we called it.

It was midday before we had made ourselves secure, but the heat was not oppressive, and the general character of the plateau, both in its temperature and in its vegetation, was almost temperate. The beech, the oak, and even the birch were to be found among the tangle of trees which girt us in. One huge gingko tree, topping all the others, shot its great limbs and maidenhair foliage over the fort which we had constructed. In its shade we continued our discussion, while Lord John, who had quickly taken command in the hour of action, gave us his views.

'So long as neither man nor beast has seen or heard us, we are safe,' said he. 'From the time they know we are here our troubles begin. There are no signs that they have found us out as yet. So our game surely is to lie low for time and spy out the land. We want to have a good look at our neighbours before we get on visitin' terms.'

'But we must advance,' I ventured to remark.

'By all means, sonny my boy! We will advance. But with common sense. We must never go so far that we can't get back to our base. Above all, we must never, unless it is life or death, fire off our guns.'

'But *you* fired yesterday,' said Summerlee.

'Well, it couldn't be helped. However, the wind was strong and blew outwards. It is not likely that the sound could have travelled far into the plateau. By the way, what shall we call this place? I sup-pose it is up to us to give it a name?'

There were several suggestions, more or less happy, but Chal-lenger's was final.

'It can only have one name,' said he. 'It is called after the pioneer who discovered it. It is Maple White Land.'

Maple White Land it became, and so it is named in that chart which has become my special task. So it will, I trust, appear in the atlas of the future.

The peaceful penetration of Maple White Land was the pressing subject before us. We had the evidence of our own eyes that the place was inhabited by some unknown creatures, and there was that of Maple White's sketch-book to show that more dreadful and more dangerous monsters might still appear. That there might also prove to be human occupants and that they were of a malevolent character was suggested by the skeleton impaled upon the bamboos, which could not have got there had it not been dropped from above. Our situation, stranded without possibility of escape in such a land, was clearly full of danger, and our reason endorsed every measure of caution which Lord John's experience could suggest. Yet it was surely impossible that we should halt on the edge of this world of mystery when our very souls were tingling with impatience to push forward and to pluck the heart from it.

We therefore blocked the entrance to our zareba by filling it up with several thorny bushes, and left our camp with the stores entirely surrounded by this protecting hedge. We then slowly and cautiously set forth into the unknown, following the course of the little stream which flowed from our spring, as it should always serve us as a guide on our return.

Hardly had we started when we came across signs that there were indeed wonders awaiting us. After a few hundred yards of thick forest, containing many trees which were quite unknown to me, but which Summerlee, who was the botanist of the party, recognized as forms of conifera and of cycadaceous plants which have long passed away in the world below, we entered a region where the stream widened out and formed a considerable bog. High reeds of a peculiar type grew thickly before us, which were pronounced to be equisetacea, or mare's-tails, with tree-ferns scattered amongst them, all of them swaying in a brisk wind. Suddenly Lord John, who was walking first, halted with uplifted hand.

'Look at this!' said he. 'By George, this must be the trail of the father of all birds!'

An enormous three-toed track was imprinted in the soft mud before us. The creature, whatever it was, had crossed the swamp and had passed on into the forest. We all stopped to examine that monstrous spoor. If it were indeed a bird – and what animal could leave such a mark? – its foot was so much larger than an ostrich's that its height upon the same scale must be enormous. Lord John looked eagerly round him and slipped two cartridges into his elephant-gun.

'I'll stake my good name as a shikaree,' said he, 'that the track is a fresh one. The creature has not passed ten minutes. Look how the water is still oozing into that deeper print! By Jove! See, here is the mark of a little one!'

Sure enough, smaller tracks of the same general form were running parallel to the large ones.

'But what do you make of this?' cried Professor Summerlee, triumphantly, pointing to what looked like the huge print of a five-fingered human hand appearing among the three-toed marks.

'Wealden!' cried Challenger, in an ecstasy. 'I've seen them in the Wealden clay. It is a creature walking erect upon three-toed feet, and occasionally putting one of its five-fingered fore-paws upon the ground. Not a bird, my dear Roxton – not a bird.'

'A beast?'

'No; a reptile – a dinosaur. Nothing else could have left such a track. They puzzled a worthy Sussex doctor some ninety years ago; but who in the world could have hoped – hoped – to have seen a sight like that?'

His words died away into a whisper, and we all stood in motionless amazement. Following the tracks, we had left the morass and passed through a screen of brushwood and trees. Beyond was an open glade, and in this were five of the most extraordinary creatures that I have ever seen. Crouching down among the bushes, we observed them at our leisure.

There were, as I say, five of them, two being adults and three young ones. In size they were enormous. Even the babies were as big as elephants, while the two large ones were far beyond all creatures I have ever seen. They had slate-coloured skin, which was scaled like a lizard's and shimmered where the sun shone upon it. All five were sitting up, balancing themselves upon their broad, powerful tails and their huge three-toed hind-feet, while with their small five-fingered front-feet they pulled down the branches upon which they browsed. I do not know that I can bring their appearance home to you better than by saying that they looked like monstrous kangaroos, twenty feet in length, and with skins like black crocodiles.

I do not know how long we stayed motionless gazing at this marvellous spectacle. A strong wind blew towards us and we were well concealed, so there was no chance of discovery. From time to time the little ones played round their parents in unwieldy gambols, the great beasts bounding into the air and falling with dull thuds upon the earth. The strength of the parents seemed to be limitless, for one of them, having some difficulty in reaching a bunch of foliage which grew upon a considerable-sized tree, put his fore-legs round the trunk and tore it down as if it had been a sapling. The action seemed, as I thought, to show not only the great development of its muscles, but also the small one of its brain, for the whole weight came crashing down upon the top of it, and it uttered a series of shrill yelps to show that, big as it was, there was a limit to what it could endure. The incident made it think, apparently, that the neighbourhood was dangerous, for it slowly lurched off through the wood, followed by its mate and its three enormous infants. We saw the shimmering slatey gleam of their skins between the tree-trunks, and their heads undulating high above the brushwood. Then they vanished from our sight.

I looked at my comrades. Lord John was standing at gaze with his finger on the trigger of his elephant-gun, his eager hunter's soul shining from his fierce eyes. What would he not give for one such head to place between the two crossed oars above the mantelpiece in his snuggery at the Albany! And yet his reason held him in, for all our exploration of the wonders of this unknown land depended upon our presence being concealed from its inhabitants. The two professors were in silent ecstasy. In their excitement they had unconsciously seized each other by the hand, and stood like two little children in the presence of a marvel, Challenger's cheeks bunched up into a seraphic smile, and Summerlee's sardonic face softening for the moment into wonder and reverence.

'*Nunc dimittis!*' he cried at last. 'What will they say in England of this?'

'My dear Summerlee, I will tell you with great confidence exactly what they will say in England,' said Challenger. 'They will say that you are an infernal liar and a scientific charlatan, exactly as you and others said of me.'

'In the face of photographs?'

'Faked, Summerlee! Clumsily faked!'

'In the face of specimens?'

'Ah, there we may have them! Malone and his filthy Fleet Street crew may be all yelping our praises yet. August the twenty-eighth – the day we saw five live iguanodons in a glade of Maple White Land. Put it down in your diary, my young friend, and send it to your rag.'

'And be ready to get the toe-end of the editorial boot in return,' said Lord John. 'Things look a bit different from the latitude of London, young fellah-my-lad. There's many a man who never tells his adventures, for he can't hope to be believed. Who's to blame them? For this will seem a bit of a dream to ourselves in a month or two. What did you say they were?'

'Iguanodons,' said Summerlee. 'You'll find their foot-marks all over the Hastings sands, in Kent, and in Sussex. The South of England was alive with them when there was plenty of good lush green-stuff to keep them going. Conditions have changed, and the beasts died. Here it seems that the conditions have not changed, and the beasts have lived.'

'If ever we get out of this alive, I must have a head with me,' said Lord John. 'Lord, how some of that Somaliland-Uganda crowd would turn a beautiful pea-green if they saw it! I don't know what you chaps think, but it strikes me that we are on mighty thin ice all this time.'

I had the same feeling of mystery and danger around us. In the gloom of the trees there seemed a constant menace, and as we looked up into their shadowy foliage vague terrors crept into one's heart. It is true that these monstrous creatures which we had seen were lumbering, inoffensive brutes which were unlikely to hurt anyone, but in this world of wonders what other survivals might there not be – what fierce, active horrors ready to pounce upon us from their lair among the rocks or brushwood? I knew little of pre-historic life, but I had a clear remembrance of one book which I had read in which it spoke of creatures who would live upon our lions and tigers as a cat lives upon mice. What if these also were to be found in the woods of Maple White Land!

It was destined that on this very morning – our first in the new country – we were to find out what strange hazards lay around us. It was a loathsome adventure, and one of which I hate to think. If, as Lord John said, the glade of the iguanodons will remain with us as a dream, then surely the swamp of the pterodactyls will for ever be our nightmare. Let me set down exactly what occurred.

We passed very slowly through the woods, partly because Lord John acted as scout before he would let us advance, and partly because at every second step one or other of our professors would fall, with a cry of wonder, before some flower or insect which presented him with a new type. We may have travelled two or three miles in all, keeping to the right of the line of the stream, when we came upon a considerable opening in the trees. A belt of brushwood led up to a tangle of rocks – the whole plateau was strewn with boulders. We were walking slowly towards these rocks, among bushes which reached over our waists, when we became aware of a strange low gabbling and whistling sound, which filled the air with a constant clamour and appeared to come from some spot immediately before us. Lord John held up his hand as a signal for us to stop, and he made his way swiftly, stooping and running, to the line of rocks. We saw him peep over them and give a gesture of amazement. Then he stood staring as if forgetting us, so utterly entranced was he by what he saw. Finally he waved us to come on, holding up his hand as a signal for caution. His whole bearing made me feel that something wonderful but dangerous lay before us.

Creeping to his side, we looked over the rocks. The place into which we gazed was a pit, and may, in the early days, have been one of the smaller volcanic blow-holes of the plateau. It was bowl-shaped, and at the bottom, some hundreds of yards from where we lay, were pools of green-scummed, stagnant water, fringed with bulrushes. It was a weird place in itself, but its occupants made it seem like a scene from the Seven Circles of Dante. The place was a rookery of pterodactyls. There were hundreds of them congregated within view. All the bottom area round the water-edge was alive with their young ones, and with hideous mothers brooding upon their leathery, yellowish eggs. From this crawling flapping mass of obscene reptilian life came the shocking clamour which filled the air and the mephitic horrible, musty odour which turned us sick. But above perched each upon its own stone, tall, grey, and withered, more like dead and dried specimens than actual living creatures, sat the horrible males, absolutely motionless save for the rolling of their red eyes or an occasional snap of their rat-trap beaks as a dragon-fly went past them. Their huge, membranous wings were closed by folding their forearms, so that they sat like gigantic old women, wrapped in hideous web-coloured shawls, and with their ferocious heads protruding above them. Large and small, not less than a thousand of these filthy creatures lay in the hollow before us.

Our professors would gladly have stayed there all day, so entranced were they by this opportunity of studying the life of a prehistoric age. They pointed out the fish and dead birds lying about among the rocks as proving the nature of the food of these creatures, and I heard them congratulating each other on having cleared up the point why the bones of this flying dragon are found in such great numbers in certain well-defined areas, as in the Cambridge Green-sand, since it was now seen that, like penguins, they lived in gregarious fashion.

Finally, however, Challenger, bent upon proving some point which Summerlee had contested, thrust his head over the rock and nearly brought destruction upon us all. In an instant the nearest male gave a shrill, whistling cry, and flapped its twenty-foot span of leathery wings as it soared up into the air. The females and young ones huddled together beside the water, while the whole circle of sentinels rose one after the other and sailed off into the sky. It was a wonderful sight to see at least a hundred creatures of such enormous size and hideous appearance all swooping like swallows with swift, shearing wing-strokes above us; but soon we realized that it was not one on which we could afford to linger. At first the great brutes flew round in a huge ring, as if to make sure what the exact extent of the danger might be. Then, the flight grew lower and the circle narrower, until they were whizzing round and round us, the dry, rustling flap of their huge slate-coloured wings filling the air with a volume of sound that made me think of Hendon aerodrome upon a race day.

'Make for the wood and keep together,' cried Lord John, clubbing his rifle. 'The brutes mean mischief.'

The moment we attempted to retreat the circle closed in upon us, until the tips of the wings of those nearest to us nearly touched our faces. We beat at them with the stocks of our guns, but there was nothing solid or vulnerable to strike. Then suddenly out of the whizzing, slate-coloured circle a long neck shot out, and a fierce beak made a thrust at us. Another and another followed. Summerlee gave a cry and put his hand to his face, from which the blood was streaming. I felt a prod at the back of my neck, and turned dizzy with the shock. Challenger fell, and as I stooped to pick him up I was again struck from behind and dropped on the top of him. At the same instant I heard the crash of Lord John's elephant-gun, and, looking up, saw one of the creatures with a broken wing struggling upon the ground, spitting and gurgling at us with a wide-opened beak and blood-shot, goggled eyes, like some devil in a mediæval picture. Its comrades had flown higher at the sudden sound, and were circling above our heads.

'Now,' cried Lord John, 'now for our lives!'

We staggered through the brushwood, and even as we reached the trees the harpies were on us again. Summerlee was knocked down, but we tore him up and rushed among the trunks. Once there we were safe, for those huge wings had no space for their sweep beneath the branches. As we limped homewards, sadly mauled and discomfited, we saw them for a long time flying at a great height against the deep blue sky above our heads, soaring round and round, no bigger than wood-pigeons, with their eyes no doubt still following our progress. At last, however, as we reached the thicker woods they gave up the chase, and we saw them no more.

'A most interesting and convincing experience,' said Challenger, as we halted beside the brook and he bathed a swollen knee. 'We are exceptionally well informed, Summerlee, as to the habits of the enraged pterodactyl.'

Summerlee was wiping the blood from a cut in his forehead, while I was tying up a nasty stab in the muscle of the neck. Lord John had the shoulder of his coat torn away, but the creature's teeth had only grazed the flesh.

'It is worth noting,' Challenger continued, 'that our young friend has received an undoubted stab, while Lord John's coat could only have been torn by a bite. In my own case, I was beaten about the head by their wings, so we have had a remarkable exhibition of their various methods of offence.'

'It has been touch and go for our lives,' said Lord John, gravely, 'and I could not think of a more rotten sort of death than to be outed by such filthy vermin. I was sorry to fire my rifle, but, by Jove! there was no great choice.'

'We should not be here if you hadn't,' said I, with conviction.

'It may do no harm,' said he. 'Among these woods there must be many loud cracks from splitting or falling trees which would be just like the sound of a gun. But now, if you are of my opinion, we have had thrills enough for one day, and had best get back to the surgical box at the camp for some carbolic. Who knows what venom these beasts may have in their hideous jaws?'

But surely no men ever had just such a day since the world began. Some fresh surprise was ever in store for us. When, following the course of our brook, we at last reached our glade and saw the thorny barricade of our camp, we thought that our adventures were at an end. But we had something more to think of before we could rest. The gate of Fort Challenger had been untouched, the walls were unbroken, and yet it had been visited by some strange and powerful creature in our absence. No foot-mark showed a trace of its nature, and only the overhanging branch of the enormous gingko tree suggested how it might have come and gone; but of its malevolent strength there was ample evidence in the condition of our stores. They were strewn at random all over the ground, and one tin of meat had been crushed into pieces so as to extract the contents. A case of cartridges had been shattered into matchwood, and one of the brass shells lay shredded into pieces beside it. Again the feeling of vague horror came upon our souls, and we gazed round with frightened eyes at the dark shadows which lay around us, in all of which some fearsome shape might be lurking. How good it was when we were hailed by the voice of Zambo, and, going to the edge of the plateau, saw him sitting grinning at us upon the top of the opposite pinnacle.

'All well, Massa Challenger, all well!' he cried. 'Me stay here. No fear. You always find me when you want.'

His honest black face, and the immense view before us, which carried us half-way back to the affluent of the Amazon, helped us to remember that we really were upon this earth in the twentieth century, and had not by some magic been conveyed to some raw planet in its earliest and wildest state. How difficult it was to realise that the violet line upon the far horizon was well advanced to that great river upon which huge steamers ran, and folk talked of the small affairs of life, while we, marooned among the creatures of a bygone age, could but gaze towards it and yearn for all that it meant!

One other memory remains with me of this wonderful day, and with it I will close this letter. The two professors, their tempers aggravated no doubt by their injuries, had fallen out as to whether our assailants were of the genus pterodactylus or dimorphodon, and high words had ensued. To avoid their wrangling I moved some little way apart, and was seated smoking upon the trunk of a fallen tree, when Lord John strolled over in my direction.

'I say, Malone,' said he, 'do you remember that place where those beasts were?'

'Very clearly.'

'A sort of volcanic pit, was it not?'

'Exactly,' said I.

'Did you notice the soil?'

'Rocks.'

'But round the water – where the reeds were?'

'It was a bluish soil. It looked like clay.'

'Exactly. A volcanic tube full of blue clay.'

'What of that?' I asked.

'Oh, nothing, nothing,' said he, and strolled back to where the voices of the contending men of science rose in a prolonged duet, the high, strident note of Summerlee rising and falling to the sonorous bass of Challenger. I should have thought no more of Lord John's remark were it not that once again that night I heard him mutter to himself: 'Blue clay – clay in a volcanic tube!' They were the last words I heard before I dropped into an exhausted sleep.

CHAPTER XI

For Once I Was the Hero

LORD JOHN ROXTON was right when he thought that some specially toxic quality might lie in the bite of the horrible creatures
which had attacked us. On the morning after our first adventure
upon the plateau, both Summerlee and I were in great pain and
fever, while Challenger's knee was so bruised that he could hardly
limp. We kept to our camp all day, therefore, Lord John busying
himself, with such help as we could give him, in raising the height
and thickness of the thorny walls which were our only defence. I
remember that during the whole long day I was haunted by the
feeling that we were closely observed, though by whom or whence
I could give no guess.

So strong was the impression that I told Professor Challenger of
it, who put it down to the cerebral excitement caused by my fever.
Again and again I glanced round swiftly, with the conviction that I
was about to see something, but only to meet the dark tangle of our
hedge or the solemn and cavernous gloom of the great trees which
arched above our heads. And yet the feeling grew ever stronger in
my own mind that something observant and something malevolent
was at our very elbow. I thought of the Indian superstition of the
Curupuri – the dreadful, lurking spirit of the woods – and I could
have imagined that his terrible presence haunted those who have
invaded his most remote and sacred retreat.

That night (our third in Maple White Land) we had an experience which left a fearful impression upon our minds, and made us
thankful that Lord John had worked so hard in making our retreat
impregnable. We were all sleeping round our dying fire when we
were aroused – or, rather, I should say, shot out of our slumbers –
by a succession of the most frightful cries and screams to which I
have ever listened. I know no sound to which I could compare this
amazing tumult, which seemed to come from some spot within a
few hundred yards of our camp. It was as ear-splitting as any whistle
of a railway-engine; but whereas the whistle is a clear, mechanical,
sharp-edged sound, this was far deeper in volume and vibrant with
the uttermost strain of agony and horror. We clapped our hands to
our ears to shut out that nerve-shaking appeal. A cold sweat broke
out over my body, and my heart turned sick at the misery of it. All

the woes of tortured life, all its stupendous indictment of high heaven, its innumerable sorrows, seemed to be centred and condensed into that one dreadful, agonized cry. And then, under this high-pitched, ringing sound there was another, more intermittent, a low, deep-chested laugh, a growling, throaty gurgle of merriment which formed a grotesque accompaniment to the shriek with which it was blended. For three or four minutes on end the fearsome duet continued, while all the foliage rustled with the rising of startled birds. Then it shut off as suddenly as it began. For a long time we sat in horrified silence. Then Lord John threw a bundle of twigs upon the fire, and their red glare lit up the intent faces of my companions and flickered over the great boughs above our heads.

'What was it?' I whispered.

'We shall know in the morning,' said Lord John. 'It was close to us – not farther than the glade.'

'We have been privileged to overhear a prehistoric tragedy, the sort of drama which occurred among the reeds upon the border of some Jurassic lagoon, when the greater dragon pinned the lesser among the slime,' said Challenger, with more solemnity than I had ever heard in his voice. 'It was surely well for man that he came late in the order of creation. There were powers abroad in earlier days which no courage and no mechanism of his could have met. What could his sling, his throwing-stick, or his arrow avail him against such forces as have been loose to-night? Even with a modern rifle it would be all odds on the monster.'

'I think I should back my little friend,' said Lord John, caressing his Express. 'But the beast would certainly have a good sporting chance.'

Summerlee raised his hand.

'Hush!' he cried. 'Surely I hear something?'

From the utter silence there emerged a deep, regular pat-pat. It was the tread of some animal – the rhythm of soft but heavy pads placed cautiously upon the ground. It stole slowly round the camp, and then halted near our gateway. There was a low, sibilant rise and fall – the breathing of the creature. Only our feeble hedge separated us from this horror of the night. Each of us had seized his rifle, and Lord John had pulled out a small bush to make an embrasure in the hedge.

'By George!' he whispered. 'I think I can see it!'

I stooped and peered over his shoulder through the gap. Yes, I could see it, too. In the deep shadow of the tree there was a deeper shadow yet, black, inchoate, vague – a crouching form full of savage vigour and menace. It was no higher than a horse, but the dim outline suggested vast bulk and strength. That hissing pant, as regular and full-volumed as the exhaust of an engine, spoke of a monstrous organism. Once, as it moved, I thought I saw the glint of two terrible, greenish eyes. There was an uneasy rustling, as if it were crawling slowly forward.

'I believe it is going to spring!' said I, cocking my rifle.

'Don't fire! Don't fire!' whispered Lord John. 'The crash of a gun in this silent night would be heard for miles. Keep it as a last card.'

'If it gets over the hedge we're done,' said Summerlee, and his voice crackled into a nervous laugh as he spoke.

'No, it must not get over,' cried Lord John; 'but hold your fire to the last. Perhaps I can make something of the fellow. I'll chance it, anyhow.'

It was as brave an act as ever I saw a man do. He stooped to the fire, picked up a blazing branch, and slipped in an instant through a sallyport which he had made in our gateway. The thing moved forward with a dreadful snarl. Lord John never hesitated, but, running towards it with a quick, light step, he dashed the flaming wood into the brute's face. For one moment I had a vision of a horrible mask like a giant toad's, of a warty, leprous skin, and of a loose mouth all beslobbered with fresh blood. The next, there was a crash in the underwood and our dreadful visitor was gone.

'I thought he wouldn't face the fire,' said Lord John, laughing, as he came back and threw his branch among the faggots.

'You should not have taken such a risk!' we all cried.

'There was nothing else to be done. If he had got among us we should have shot each other in tryin' to down him. On the other hand, if we had fired through the hedge and wounded him he would soon have been on the top of us – to say nothin' of giving ourselves away. On the whole, I think that we are jolly well out of it. What was he, then?'

Our learned men looked at each other with some hesitation.

'Personally, I am unable to classify the creature with any certainty,' said Summerlee, lighting his pipe from the fire.

'In refusing to commit yourself you are but showing a proper scientific reserve,' said Challenger, with massive condescension. 'I am not myself prepared to go farther than to say in general terms that we have almost certainly been in contact to-night with some form of carnivorous dinosaur. I have already expressed my anticipation that something of the sort might exist upon this plateau.'

'We have to bear in mind,' remarked Summerlee, 'that there are many prehistoric forms which have never come down to us. It would be rash to suppose that we can give a name to all that we are likely to meet.'

'Exactly. A rough classification may be the best that we can attempt. To-morrow some further evidence may help us to an identification. Meantime we can only renew our interrupted slumbers.'

'But not without a sentinel,' said Lord John, with decision. 'We can't afford to take chances in a country like this. Two-hour spells in the future, for each of us.'

'Then I'll just finish my pipe in starting the first one,' said Professor Summerlee; and from that time onwards we never trusted ourselves again without a watchman.

In the morning it was not long before we discovered the source of the hideous uproar which had aroused us in the night. The iguanodon glade was the scene of a horrible butchery. From the pools of blood and the enormous lumps of flesh scattered in every direction over the green sward we imagined at first that a number of animals had been killed, but on examining the remains more closely we discovered that all this carnage came from one of these unwieldy monsters, which had been literally torn to pieces by some creature not larger, perhaps, but far more ferocious, than itself.

Our two professors sat in absorbed argument, examining piece after piece, which showed the marks of savage teeth and of enormous claws.

'Our judgment must still be in abeyance,' said Professor Challenger, with a huge slab of whitish-coloured flesh across his knee. 'The indications would be consistent with the presence of a sabre-toothed tiger, such as are still found among the breccia of our caverns; but the creature actually seen was undoubtedly of a larger and more reptilian character. Personally, I should pronounce for allosaurus.'

'Or megalosaurus,' said Summerlee.

'Exactly. Any one of the larger carnivorous dinosaurs would meet the case. Among them are to be found all the most terrible types of animal-life that have ever cursed the earth or blessed a museum.' He laughed sonorously at his own conceit, for, though he had little sense of humour, the crudest pleasantry from his own lips moved him always to roars of appreciation.

'The less noise the better,' said Lord John, curtly. 'We don't know who or what may be near us. If this fellah comes back for his breakfast and catches us here we won't have so much to laugh at. By the way, what is this mark upon the iguanodon's hide?'

On the dull, scaly, slate-coloured skin, somewhere above the shoulder, there was a singular black circle of some substance which looked like asphalt. None of us could suggest what it meant, though Summerlee was of opinion that he had seen something similar upon one of the young ones two days before. Challenger said nothing, but looked pompous and puffy, as if he could if he would, so that finally Lord John asked his opinion direct.

'If your lordship will graciously permit me to open my mouth, I shall be happy to express my sentiments,' said he, with elaborate sarcasm. 'I am not in the habit of being taken to task in the fashion which seems to be customary with your lordship. I was not aware that it was necessary to ask your permission before smiling at a harmless pleasantry.'

It was not until he had received his apology that our touchy friend would suffer himself to be appeased. When at last his ruffled feelings were at ease, he addressed us at some length from his seat upon a fallen tree, speaking, as his habit was, as if he were imparting most precious information to a class of a thousand.

'With regard to the marking,' said he, 'I am inclined to agree with my friend and colleague, Professor Summerlee, that the stains are from asphalt. As this plateau is, in its very nature, highly volcanic, and as asphalt is a substance which one associates with Plutonic forces, I cannot doubt that it exists in the free liquid state, and that the creatures may have come in contact with it. A much more important problem is the question as to the existence of the carnivorous monster which has left its traces in this glade. We know roughly that this plateau is not larger than an average English county. Within this confined space a certain number of creatures, mostly types which have passed away in the world below, have lived together for innumerable years. Now, it is very clear to me that in so long a period one would have expected that the carnivorous creatures, multiplying unchecked, would have exhausted their food supply and have been compelled to either modify their flesh-eating habits or die of hunger. This we see has not been so. We can only imagine therefore, that the balance of Nature is preserved by some check which limits the numbers of these ferocious creatures. One of the many interesting problems, therefore, which await our solution is to discover what that check may be and how it operates. I venture to trust that we may have some future opportunity for the closer study of the carnivorous dinosaurs.'

'And I venture to trust that we may not,' I observed.

The Professor only raised his great eyebrows, as the schoolmaster meets the irrelevant observation of the naughty boy.

'Perhaps Professor Summerlee may have an observation to make,' he said, and the two *savants* ascended together into some rarified scientific atmosphere, where the possibilities of a modification of the birth-rate were weighed against the decline of the food supply as a check in the struggle for existence.

That morning we mapped out a small portion of the plateau, avoiding the swamp of the pterodactyls, and keeping to the east of our brook instead of to the west. In that direction the country was still thickly wooded, with so much undergrowth that our progress was very slow.

I have dwelt up to now upon the terrors of Maple White Land; but there was another side to the subject, for all that morning we wandered among lovely flowers – mostly, as I observed, white or yellow in colour, these being, as our professors explained, the primitive flower-shades. In many places the ground was absolutely covered with them, and as we walked ankle-deep on that wonderful yielding carpet, the scent was almost intoxicating in its sweetness and intensity. The homely English bee buzzed everywhere around us. Many of the trees under which we passed had their branches bowed down with fruit, some of which were of familiar sorts, while other varieties were new. By observing which of them were pecked by the birds we avoided all danger of poison and added a delicious variety to our food reserve. In the jungle which we traversed were numerous hard-trodden paths made by the wild-beasts, and in the more marshy places we saw a profusion of strange foot-marks, including many of the iguanodon. Once in a grove we observed several of these great creatures grazing, and Lord John, with his glass, was able to report that they also were spotted with asphalt, though in a different place to the one which we had examined in the morning. What this phenomenon meant we could not imagine.

We saw many small animals, such as porcupines, a scaly anteater, and a wild pig, piebald in colour and with long curved tusks. Once, through a break in the trees, we saw a clear shoulder of green hill some distance away, and across this a large dun-coloured animal was travelling at a considerable pace. It passed so swiftly that we were unable to say what it was; but if it were a deer, as was claimed by Lord John, it must have been as large as those monstrous Irish elk which are still dug up from time to time in the bogs of my native land.

Ever since the mysterious visit which had been paid to our camp we always returned to it with some misgivings. However, on this occasion we found everything in order. That evening we had a grand discussion upon our present situation and future plans, which I must describe at some length, as it led to a new departure by which we were enabled to gain a more complete knowledge of Maple White Land than might have come in many weeks of exploring. It was Summerlee who opened the debate. All day he had been querulous in manner, and now some remark of Lord John's as to what we should do on the morrow brought all his bitterness to a head.

'What we ought to be doing to-day, to-morrow, and all the time,' said he, 'is finding some way out of the trap into which we have fallen. You are all turning your brains towards getting into this country. I say that we should be scheming how to get out of it.'

'I am surprised, sir,' boomed Challenger, stroking his majestic beard, 'that any man of science should commit himself to so ignoble a sentiment. You are in a land which offers such an inducement to the ambitious naturalist as none ever has since the world began, and you suggest leaving it before we have acquired more than the most superficial knowledge of it or of its contents. I expected better things of you, Professor Summerlee.'

'You must remember,' said Summerlee, sourly, 'that I have a large class in London who are at present at the mercy of an extremely inefficient *locum tenens*. This makes my situation different from yours, Professor Challenger, since, so far as I know, you have never been entrusted with any responsible educational work.'

'Quite so,' said Challenger. 'I have felt it to be a sacrilege to divert a brain which is capable of the highest original research to any lesser object. That is why I have sternly set my face against any proffered scholastic appointment.'

'For example?' asked Summerlee, with a sneer; but Lord John hastened to change the conversation.

'I must say,' said he, 'that I think it would be a mighty poor thing to go back to London before I know a great deal more of this place than I do at present.'

'I could never dare to walk into the back office of my paper and face old McArdle,' said I. (You will excuse the frankness of this report, will you not, sir?) 'He'd never forgive me for leaving such unexhausted copy behind me. Besides, so far as I can see, it is not worth discussing, since we can't get down, even if we wanted.'

'Our young friend makes up for many obvious mental lacunæ by some measure of primitive common sense,' remarked Challenger. 'The interests of his deplorable profession are immaterial to us; but, as he observes, we cannot get down in any case, so it is a waste of energy to discuss it.'

'It is a waste of energy to do anything else,' growled Summerlee from behind his pipe. 'Let me remind you that we came here upon a perfectly definite mission, entrusted to us at the meeting of the Zoological Institute in London. That mission was to test the truth of Professor Challenger's statements. Those statements, as I am bound to admit, we are now in a position to endorse. Our ostensible work is therefore done. As to the detail which remains to be worked out upon this plateau, it is so enormous that only a large expedition, with a very special equipment, could hope to cope with it. Should we attempt to do so ourselves, the only possible result must be that we shall never return with the important contribution to science which we have already gained. Professor Challenger has devised means for getting us on to this plateau when it appeared to be inaccessible; I think that we should now call upon him to use the same ingenuity in getting us back to the world from which we came.'

I confess that as Summerlee stated his view it struck me as altogether reasonable. Even Challenger was affected by the consideration that his enemies would never stand confuted if the confirmation of his statements should never reach those who had doubted them.

'The problem of the descent is at first sight a formidable one,' said he, 'and yet I cannot doubt that the intellect can solve it. I am prepared to agree with our colleague that a protracted stay in Maple White Land is at present inadvisable, and that the question of our return will soon have to be faced. I absolutely refuse to leave, however, until we have made at least a superficial examination of this country, and are able to take back with us something in the nature of a chart.'

Professor Summerlee gave a snort of impatience.

'We have spent two long days in exploration,' said he, 'and we are no wiser as to the actual geography of the place than when we started. It is clear that it is all thickly wooded, and it would take months to penetrate it and to learn the relations of one part to another. If there were some central peak it would be different, but it all slopes downwards, so far as we can see. The farther we go the less likely it is that we will get any general view.'

It was at that moment that I had my inspiration. My eyes chanced to light upon the enormous gnarled trunk of the gingko tree which cast its huge branches over us. Surely, if its bole exceeded that of all the others, its height must do the same. If the rim of the plateau was indeed the highest point, then why should this mighty tree not prove to be a watch-tower which commanded the whole country?

Now, ever since I ran wild as a lad in Ireland I have been a bold and skilled tree-climber. My comrades might be my masters on the rocks, but I knew that I would be supreme among those branches. Could I only get my legs on to the lowest of the giant off-shoots, then it would be strange indeed if I could not make my way to the top. My comrades were delighted at my idea.

'Our young friend,' said Challenger, bunching up the red apples of his cheeks, 'is capable of acrobatic exertions which would be impossible to a man of a more solid, though possibly of a more commanding, appearance. I applaud his resolution.'

'By George, young fellah, you've put your hand on it!' said Lord John, clapping me on the back. 'How we never came to think of it before I can't imagine! There's not more than an hour of daylight left, but if you take your notebook you may be able to get some rough sketch of the place. If we put these three ammunition cases under the branch, I will soon hoist you on to it.'

He stood on the boxes while I faced the trunk, and was gently raising me when Challenger sprang forward and gave me such a thrust with his huge hand that he fairly shot me into the tree. With both arms clasping the branch, I scrambled hard with my feet until I had worked, first my body, and then my knees, on to it. There were three excellent off-shoots, like huge rungs of a ladder, above my head, and a tangle of convenient branches beyond, so that I clambered onwards with such speed that I soon lost sight of the ground and had nothing but foliage beneath me. Now and then I encountered a check, and once I had to shin up a creeper for eight or ten feet, but I made excellent progress, and the booming of Challenger's voice seemed to be a great distance beneath me. The tree was, however, enormous, and, looking upwards, I could see no thinning of the leaves above my head. There was some thick, bush-like clump which seemed to be a parasite upon a branch up which I was swarming. I leaned my head round it in order to see what was beyond, and I nearly fell out of the tree in my surprise and horror at what I saw.

A face was gazing into mine – at the distance of only a foot or two. The creature that owned it had been crouching behind the parasite, and had looked round it at the same instant that I did. It was a human face – or at least it was far more human than any monkey's that I have ever seen. It was long, whitish, and blotched with pimples, the nose flattened, and the lower jaw projecting, with a bristle of coarse whiskers round the chin. The eyes, which were under thick and heavy brows, were bestial and ferocious, and as it opened its mouth to snarl what sounded like a curse at me I observed that it had curved, sharp canine teeth. For an instant I read hatred and menace in the evil eyes. Then, as quick as a flash, came an expression of overpowering fear. There was a crash of broken boughs as it dived wildly down into the tangle of green. I caught a glimpse of a hairy body like that of a reddish pig, and then it was gone amid a swirl of leaves and branches.

'What's the matter?' shouted Roxton from below. 'Anything wrong with you?'

'Did you see it?' I cried with my arms round the branch and all my nerves tingling.

'We heard a row, as if your foot had slipped. What was it?'

I was so shocked at the sudden and strange appearance of this ape-man that I hesitated whether I should not climb down again and tell my experience to my companions. But I was already so far up the great tree that it seemed a humiliation to return without having carried out my mission.

After a long pause therefore, to recover my breath and my courage, I continued my ascent. Once I put my weight upon a rotten branch and swung for a few seconds by my hands, but in the main it was all easy climbing. Gradually the leaves thinned around me, and I was aware, from the wind upon my face, that I had topped all the trees of the forest. I was determined, however, not to look about me before I had reached the very highest point, so I scrambled on until I had got so far that the topmost branch was bending beneath my weight. There I settled into a convenient fork, and, balancing myself securely, I found myself looking down at a most wonderful panorama of this strange country in which we found ourselves.

The sun was just above the western sky-line, and the evening was a particularly bright and clear one, so that the whole extent of the plateau was visible beneath me. It was, as seen from this height, of an oval contour, with a breadth of about thirty miles and a width of twenty. Its general shape was that of a shallow funnel, all the sides sloping down to a considerable lake in the centre. This lake may have been ten miles in circumference, and lay very green and beautiful in the evening light, with a thick fringe of reeds at its edges, and with its surface broken by several yellow sandbanks, which gleamed golden in the mellow sunshine. A number of long dark objects, which were too large for alligators and too long for canoes, lay upon the edges of these patches of sand. With my glass I could clearly see that they were alive, but what their nature might be I could not imagine.

From the side of the plateau on which we were, slopes of wood-land, with occasional glades, stretched down for five or six miles to the central lake. I could see at my very feet the glade of the iguan-odons, and farther off was a round opening in the trees which marked the swamp of the pterodactyls. On the side facing me, how-ever, the plateau presented a very different aspect. There the basalt cliffs of the outside were reproduced upon the inside, forming an escarpment about two hundred feet high, with a woody slope beneath it. Along the base of these red cliffs, some distance above the ground, I could see a number of dark holes through the glass, which I conjectured to be the mouths of caves. At the opening of one of these something white was shimmering, but I was unable to make out what it was. I sat charting the country until the sun had set and it was so dark that I could no longer distinguish details. Then I climbed down to my companions waiting for me so eagerly at the bottom of the great tree. For once I was the hero of the expe-dition. Alone I had thought of it, and alone I had done it; and here was the chart which would save us a month's blind groping among unknown dangers. Each of them shook me solemnly by the hand. But before they discussed the details of my map I had to tell them of my encounter with the ape-man among the branches.

'He has been there all the time,' said I.

'How do you know that?' asked Lord John.

'Because I have never been without that feeling something malev-olent was watching us. I mentioned it to you, Professor Challenger.'

'Our young friend certainly said something of the kind. He is also the one among us who is endowed with that Celtic temperament which would make him sensitive to such impressions.'

'The whole theory of telepathy –' began Summerlee filling his pipe.

'Is too vast to be now discussed,' said Challenger, with decision. 'Tell me, now,' he added, with the air of a bishop addressing a Sunday-school, 'did you happen to observe whether the creature could cross its thumb over its palm?'

'No, indeed.'

'Had it a tail?'

'No.'

'Was the foot prehensile?'

'I do not think it could have made off so fast among the branches if it could not get a grip with its feet.'

'In South America there are, if my memory serves me – you will check the observation, Professor Summerlee – some thirty-six

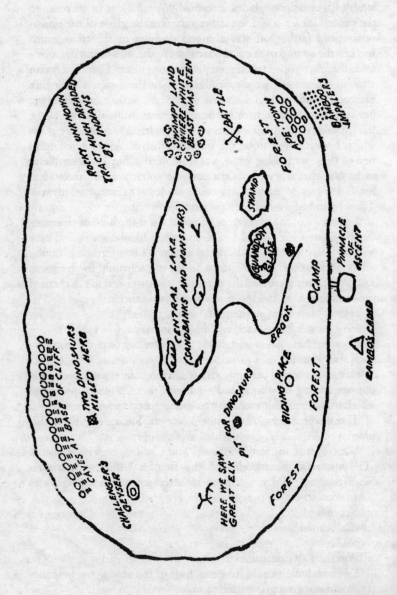

species of monkeys, but the anthropoid ape is unknown. It is clear, however, that he exists in this country, and that he is not the hairy, gorilla-like variety, which is never seen out of Africa or the East.' (I was inclined to interpolate, as I looked at him, that I had seen his first cousin in Kensington.) 'This is a whiskered and colourless type, the latter characteristic pointing to the fact that he spends his days in arboreal seclusion. The question which we have to face is whether he approaches more closely to the ape or the man. In the latter case, he may well approximate to what the vulgar have called the "missing link." The solution of this problem is our immediate duty.'

'It is nothing of the sort,' said Summerlee, abruptly. 'Now that, through the intelligence and activity of Mr. Malone' (I cannot help quoting the words), 'we have got our chart, our one and only immediate duty is to get ourselves safe and sound out of this awful place.'

'The flesh-pots of civilization,' groaned Challenger.

'The ink-pots of civilization, sir. It is our task to put on record what we have seen, and to leave the further exploration to others. You all agreed as much before Mr. Malone got us the chart.'

'Well,' said Challenger, 'I admit that my mind will be more at ease when I am assured that the result of our expedition has been conveyed to our friends. How we are to get down from this place I have not as yet an idea. I have never yet encountered any problem, however, which my inventive brain was unable to solve, and I promise you that to-morrow I will turn my attention to the question of our descent.'

And so the matter was allowed to rest. But that evening, by the light of the fire and of a single candle, the first map of the lost world was elaborated. Every detail which I had roughly noted from my watch-tower was drawn out in its relative place. Challenger's pencil hovered over the great blank which marked the lake.

'What shall we call it?' he asked.

'Why should you not take the chance of perpetuating your own name?' said Summerlee, with his usual touch of acidity.

'I trust, sir, that my name will have other and more personal claims upon posterity,' said Challenger, severely. 'Any ignoramus can hand down his worthless memory by imposing a mountain or a river. I need no such monument.'

Summerlee, with a twisted smile, was about to make some fresh assault when Lord John hastened to intervene.

'It's up to you, young fellah, to name the lake,' said he. 'You saw it first, and, by George, if you choose to put "Lake Malone" on it, no one has a better right.'

'By all means. Let our young friend give it a name,' said Challenger.

'Then,' said I, blushing, I dare say, as I said it, 'let it be named Lake Gladys.'

'Don't you think the Central Lake would be more descriptive?' remarked Summerlee.

'I should prefer Lake Gladys.'

Challenger looked at me sympathetically, and shook his great head in mock disapproval. 'Boys will be boys,' said he. 'Lake Gladys let it be.'

CHAPTER XII

It Was Dreadful in the Forest

I HAVE SAID – or perhaps I have not said, for my memory plays me sad tricks these days – that I glowed with pride when three such men as my comrades thanked me for having saved, or at least greatly helped, the situation. As the youngster of the party, not merely in years, but in experience, character, knowledge, and all that goes to make a man, I had been overshadowed from the first. And now I was coming into my own. I warmed at the thought. Alas! for the pride which goes before a fall! That little glow of self-satisfaction, that added measure of self-confidence, were to lead me on that very night to the most dreadful experience of my life, ending with a shock which turns my heart sick when I think of it.

It came about in this way. I had been unduly excited by the adventure of the tree, and sleep seemed to be impossible. Summerlee was on guard, sitting hunched over our small fire, a quaint, angular figure, his rifle across his knees and his pointed, goat-like beard wagging with each weary nod of his head. Lord John lay silent, wrapped in the South American poncho which he wore, while Challenger snored with a roll and rattle which reverberated through the woods. The full moon was shining brightly, and the air was crisply cold. What a night for a walk! And then suddenly came the thought, 'Why not?' Suppose I stole softly away, suppose I made my way down to the central lake, suppose I was back at breakfast with some record of the place – would I not in that case be thought an even more worthy associate? Then, if Summerlee carried the day and some means of escape were found, we should return to London with first-hand knowledge of the central mystery of the plateau, to which I alone, of all men, would have penetrated. I thought of Gladys, with her 'There are heroisms all round us.' I seemed to hear her voice as she said it. I thought also of McArdle. What a three-column article for the paper! What a foundation for a career! A correspondentship in the next great war might be within my reach. I clutched at a gun – my pockets were full of cartridges – and, parting the thorn bushes at the gate of our zareba, I quickly slipped out. My last glance showed me the unconscious Summerlee, most futile of sentinels, still nodding away like a queer mechanical toy in front of the smouldering fire.

I had not gone a hundred yards before I deeply repented my rashness. I may have said somewhere in this chronicle that I am too imaginative to be a really courageous man, but that I have an overpowering fear of seeming afraid. This was the power which now carried me onwards. I simply could not slink back with nothing done. Even if my comrades should not have missed me, and should never know of my weakness, there would still remain some intolerable self-shame in my own soul. And yet I shuddered at the position in which I found myself, and would have given all I possessed at that moment to have been honourably free of the whole business.

It was dreadful in the forest. The trees grew so thickly and their foliage spread so widely that I could see nothing of the moonlight save that here and there the high branches made a tangled filigree against the starry sky. As the eyes became more used to the obscurity one learned that there were different degrees of darkness among the trees – that some were dimly visible, while between and among them there were coal-black shadowed patches, like the mouths of caves, from which I shrank in horror as I passed. I thought of the despairing yell of the tortured iguanodon – that dreadful cry which had echoed through the woods. I thought, too, of the glimpse I had in the light of Lord John's torch of that bloated, warty, blood-slavering muzzle. Even now I was on its hunting-ground. At any instant it might spring upon me from the shadows – this nameless and horrible monster. I stopped, and, picking a cartridge from my pocket, I opened the breech of my gun. As I touched the lever my heart leaped within me. It was the shot-gun, not the rifle, which I had taken!

Again the impulse to return swept over me. Here, surely, was a most excellent reason for my failure – one for which no one would think the less of me. And again the foolish pride fought against that very word. I could not – must not – fail. After all, my rifle would probably have been as useless as a shot-gun against such dangers as

I might meet. If I were to go back to camp to change my weapon I could hardly expect to enter and to leave again without being seen. In that case there would be explanations, and my attempt would no longer be all my own. After a little hesitation, then, I screwed up my courage and continued upon my way, my useless gun under my arm.

The darkness of the forest had been alarming, but even worse was the white, still flood of moonlight in the open glade of iguanodons. Hid among the bushes, I looked out at it. None of the great brutes were in sight. Perhaps the tragedy which had befallen one of them had driven them from their feeding ground. In the misty, silvery night I could see no sign of any living thing. Taking courage, therefore, I slipped rapidly across it, and among the jungle on the farther side I picked up once again the brook which was my guide. It was a cheery companion, gurgling and chuckling as it ran, like the dear old trout stream in the West Country where I have fished at night in my boyhood. So long as I followed it down I must come to the lake, and so long as I followed it back I must come to the camp. Often I had to lose sight of it on account of the tangled brushwood but I was always within earshot of its tinkle and splash.

As one descended the slope the woods became thinner, and bushes, with occasional high trees, took the place of the forest. I could make good progress, therefore, and I could see without being seen. I passed close to the pterodactyl swamp, and as I did so, with a dry, crisp, leathery rattle of wings, one of these great creatures – it was twenty feet at least from tip to tip – rose up from somewhere near me and soared into the air. As it passed across the face of the moon the light shone clearly through the membranous wings, and it looked like a flying skeleton against the white, tropical radiance. I crouched low among the bushes, for I knew from past experience that with a single cry the creature could bring a hundred of its loathsome mates about my ears. It was not until it had settled again that I dared to steal onwards upon my journey.

The night had been exceedingly still, but as I advanced I became conscious of a low, rumbling sound, a continuous murmur somewhere in front of me. This grew louder as I proceeded, until at last it was clearly quite close to me. When I stood still the sound was constant, so that it seemed to come from some stationary cause. It was like a boiling kettle or the bubbling of some great pot. Soon I came upon the source of it, for in the centre of a small clearing I found a lake – or a pool, rather, for it was not larger than the basin of the Trafalgar Square fountain – of some black, pitch-like stuff, the surface of which rose and fell in great blisters of bursting gas. The air above it was shimmering with heat, and the ground round was so hot that I could hardly bear to lay my hand on it. It was clear that the great volcanic outburst which had raised this strange plateau so many years ago had not yet entirely spent its forces. Blackened rocks and mounds of lava I had already seen everywhere peeping out from amid the luxuriant vegetation which draped them, but this asphalt pool in the jungle was the first sign that we had of actual existing activity on the slopes of the ancient crater. I had no time to examine it further, for I had need to hurry if I was to be back in camp in the morning.

It was a fearsome walk, and one which will be with me so long as memory holds. In the great moonlit clearings I slunk along among the shadows on the margin. In the jungle I crept forward, stopping with a beating heart whenever I heard, as I often did, the crash of breaking branches as some wild beast went past. Now and then great shadows loomed up for an instant and were gone – great, silent shadows which seemed to prowl upon padded feet. How often I stopped with the intention of returning, and yet every time my pride conquered my fear, and sent me on again until my object should be attained.

At last (my watch showed that it was one in the morning) I saw the gleam of water amid the openings of the jungle, and ten minutes later I was among the reeds upon the borders of the central lake. I was exceedingly dry, so I lay down and took a long draught of its waters, which were fresh and cold. There was a broad pathway with many tracks upon it at the spot which I had found, so that it was clearly one of the drinking-places of the animals. Close to the water's edge there was a huge isolated block of lava. Up this I climbed, and, lying on the top, I had an excellent view in every direction.

The first thing which I saw filled me with amazement. When I described the view from the summit of the great tree, I said that on the farther cliff I could see a number of dark spots, which appeared to be the mouths of caves. Now as I looked up at the same cliffs, I saw discs of light in every direction, ruddy, clearly-defined patches, like the port-holes of a liner in the darkness. For a moment I thought it was the lava-glow from some volcanic action; but this could not be so. Any volcanic action would surely be down in the hollow, and not high among the rocks. What, then, was the alternative? It was wonderful, and yet it must surely be. These ruddy spots must be the reflection of fires within the caves – fires which could only be lit by the hand of man. There were human beings, then, upon the plateau. How gloriously my expedition was justified! Here was news indeed for us to bear back with us to London!

For a long time I lay and watched these red, quivering blotches of light. I suppose they were ten miles off from me, yet even at that distance one could observe how, from time to time, they twinkled or were obscured as someone passed before them. What would I not have given to be able to crawl up to them, to peep in, and to take back some word to my comrades as to the appearance and character of the race who lived in so strange a place! It was out of the question for the moment, and yet surely we could not leave the plateau until we had some definite knowledge upon the point.

Lake Gladys – my own lake – lay like a sheet of quicksilver before me, with a reflected moon shining brightly in the centre of it. It was shallow, for in many places I saw low sandbanks protruding above the water. Everywhere upon the still surface I could see signs of life, sometimes mere rings and ripples in the water, sometimes the gleam of a great silver-sided fish in the air, sometimes the arched, slate-coloured back of some passing monster. Once upon a yellow sandbank I saw a creature like a huge swan, with a clumsy body and a high, flexible neck, shuffling about upon the margin. Presently it plunged in, and for some time I could see the arched neck and darting head undulating over the water. Then it dived, and I saw it no more.

My attention was soon drawn away from these distant sights and brought back to what was going on at my very feet. Two creatures like large armadillos had come down to the drinking place, and were squatting at the edge of the water, their long, flexible tongues like red ribbons shooting in and out as they lapped. A huge deer, with branching horns, a magnificent creature which carried itself like a king, came down with its doe and two fawns and drank beside the armadillos. No such deer exists anywhere else upon earth, for the moose or elks which I have seen would hardly have reached its shoulders. Presently it gave a warning snort and was off with its family among the reeds, while the armadillos also scuttled for shelter. A new-comer, a most monstrous animal, was coming down the path.

For a moment I wondered where I could have seen that ungainly shape, that arched back with triangular fringes along it, that strange bird-like head held close to the ground. Then it came back to me. It was the stegosaurus – the very creature which Maple White had preserved in his sketch-book, and which had been the first object which arrested the attention of Challenger! There he was – perhaps the very specimen which the American artist had encountered. The ground shook beneath his tremendous weight, and his gulpings of water resounded through the still night. For five minutes he was so close to my rock that by stretching out my hand I could have touched the hideous waving hackles upon his back. Then he lumbered away and was lost among the boulders.

Looking at my watch, I saw that it was half-past two o'clock, and high time, therefore, that I started upon my homeward journey. There was no difficulty about the direction in which I should return, for all along I had kept the little brook upon my left, and it opened into the central lake within a stone's-throw of the boulder upon which I had been lying. I set off, therefore, in high spirits, for I felt that I had done good work and was bringing back a fine budget of news for my companions. Foremost of all, of course, were the sight of the fiery caves and the certainty that some troglodytic race inhabited them. But besides that I could speak from experience of the central lake. I could testify that it was full of strange creatures, and I had seen several land forms of primæval life which we had not before encountered. I reflected as I walked that few men in the world could have spent a stranger night or added more to human knowledge in the course of it.

I was plodding up the slope, turning these thoughts over in my mind, and had reached a point which may have been half-way to home, when my mind was brought back to my own position by a strange noise behind me. It was something between a snore and a growl, low, deep, and exceedingly menacing. Some strange creature was evidently near me, but nothing could be seen, so I hastened more rapidly upon my way. I had traversed half a mile or so when suddenly the sound was repeated, still behind me, but louder and more menacing than before. My heart stood still within me as it flashed across me that the beast, whatever it was, must surely be after *me*. My skin grew cold and my hair rose at the thought. That these monsters should tear each other to pieces was a part of the strange struggle for existence, but that they should turn upon modern man, that they should deliberately track and hunt down the predominant human, was a staggering and fearsome thought. I remembered again the blood-slobbered face which we had seen in the glare of Lord John's torch, like some horrible vision from the deepest circle of Dante's hell. With my knees shaking beneath me, I stood and glared with starting eyes down the moonlit path which lay behind me. All was quiet as in a dream landscape. Silver clearings and the black patches of the bushes – nothing else could I see.

Then from out of the silence, imminent and threatening, there came once more that low, throaty croaking, far louder and closer than before. There could no longer be a doubt. Something was on my trail, and was closing in upon me every minute.

I stood like a man paralyzed, still staring at the ground which I had traversed. Then suddenly I saw it. There was movement among the bushes at the far end of the clearing which I had just traversed. A great dark shadow disengaged itself and hopped out into the clear moonlight. I say 'hopped' advisedly, for the beast moved like a kangaroo, springing along in an erect position upon its powerful hind-legs, while its front ones were held bent in front of it. It was of enormous size and power, like an erect elephant, but its movements, in spite of its bulk, were exceedingly alert. For a moment, as I saw its shape, I hoped that it was an iguanodon, which I knew to be harmless, but, ignorant as I was, I soon saw that this was a very different creature. Instead of the gentle, deer-shaped head of the great three-toed leaf-eater, this beast had a broad, squat, toad-like face like that which had alarmed us in our camp. His ferocious cry and the horrible energy of his pursuit both assured me that this was surely one of the great flesh-eating dinosaurs, the most terrible beasts which have ever walked this earth As the huge brute loped along it dropped forward upon its fore-paws and brought its nose to the ground every twenty yards or so. It was smelling out my trail. Sometimes, for an instant, it was at fault. Then it would catch it up again and come bounding swiftly along the path I had taken.

Even now when I think of that nightmare the sweat breaks out upon my brow. What could I do? My useless fowling-piece was in my hand. What help could I get from that? I looked desperately round for some rock or tree, but I was in a bushy jungle with nothing higher than a sapling within sight, while I knew that the creature behind me could tear down an ordinary tree as though it were a reed. My only possible chance lay in flight. I could not move swiftly over the rough, broken ground, but as I looked round me in despair I saw a well-marked, hard-beaten path which ran across in front of me. We had seen several of the sort, the runs of various wild beasts, during our expeditions. Along this I could perhaps hold my own, for I was a fast runner, and in excellent condition. Flinging away my useless gun, I set myself to do such a half mile as I have never done before or since. My limbs ached, my chest heaved, I felt that my throat would burst for want of air, and yet with that horror behind me I ran and I ran and I ran. At last I paused, hardly able to move. For a moment I thought that I had thrown him off. The path lay still behind me. And then suddenly, with a crashing and a rending, a thudding of giant feet and a panting of monster lungs, the beast was upon me once more. He was at my very heels. I was lost.

Madman that I was to linger so long before I fled! Up to then he had hunted by scent, and his movement was slow. But he had actually seen me as I started to run. From then onwards he had hunted by sight, for the path showed him where I had gone. Now, as he came round the curve, he was springing in great bounds. The moonlight shone upon his huge projecting eyes, the row of enormous teeth in his open mouth, and the gleaming fringe of claws upon his short, powerful forearms. With a scream of terror I turned and rushed wildly down the path. Behind me the thick, gasping breathing of the creature sounded louder and louder. His heavy footfall was beside me. Every instant I expected to feel his grip upon my back. And then suddenly there came a crash – I was falling through space, and everything beyond was darkness and rest.

As I emerged from my unconsciousness – which could not, I think, have lasted more than a few minutes – I was aware of a most dreadful and penetrating smell. Putting out my hand in the darkness I came upon something which felt like a huge lump of meat, while my other hand closed upon a large bone. Up above me there was a circle of starlit sky, which showed me that I was lying at the bottom of a deep pit. Slowly I staggered to my feet and felt myself all over. I was stiff and sore from head to foot, but there was no limb which would not move, no joint which would not bend. As the circumstances of my fall came back into my confused brain, I looked up in terror, expecting to see that dreadful head silhouetted against the paling sky. There was no sign of the monster, however, nor could I hear any sound from above. I began to walk slowly round, therefore, feeling in every direction to find out what this strange place could be into which I had been so opportunely precipitated.

It was, as I have said, a pit, with sharply-sloping walls and a level bottom about twenty feet across. This bottom was littered with great gobbets of flesh, most of which was in the last state of putridity. The atmosphere was poisonous and horrible. After tripping and stumbling over these lumps of decay, I came suddenly against something hard, and I found that an upright post was firmly fixed in the centre of the hollow. It was so high that I could not reach the top of it with my hand, and it appeared to be covered with grease.

Suddenly I remembered that I had a tin box of wax-vestas in my pocket. Striking one of them, I was able at last to form some opinion of this place into which I had fallen. There could be no question as to its nature. It was a trap – made by the hand of man. The post in the centre, some nine feet long, was sharpened at the upper end, and was black with the stale blood of the creatures who had been impaled upon it. The remains scattered about were fragments of the victims, which had been cut away in order to clear the stake for the next who might blunder in. I remembered that Challenger had declared that man could not exist upon the plateau, since with his feeble weapons he could not hold his own against the monsters who roamed over it. But now it was clear enough how it could be done. In their narrow-mouthed caves the natives, whoever they might be, had refuges into which the huge saurians could not penetrate, while with their developed brains they were capable of setting such traps, covered with branches, across the paths which marked the run of the animals as would destroy them in spite of all their strength and activity. Man was always the master.

The sloping wall of the pit was not difficult for an active man to climb, but I hesitated long before I trusted myself within reach of the dreadful creature which had so nearly destroyed me. How did I know that he was not lurking in the nearest clump of bushes, waiting for my reappearance? I took heart, however, as I recalled a conversation between Challenger and Summerlee upon the habits of the great saurians. Both were agreed that the monsters were practically brainless, that there was no room for reason in their tiny cranial cavities, and that if they have disappeared from the rest of the world it was assuredly on account of their own stupidity, which made it impossible for them to adapt themselves to changing conditions.

To lie in wait for me now would mean that the creature had appreciated what had happened to me, and this in turn would argue some power connecting cause and effect. Surely it was more likely that a brainless creature, acting solely by vague predatory instinct, would give up the chase when I disappeared, and, after a pause of astonishment, would wander away in search of some other prey? I clambered to the edge of the pit and looked over. The stars were fading, the sky was whitening, and the cold wind of morning blew pleasantly upon my face. I could see or hear nothing of my enemy. Slowly I climbed out and sat for a while upon the ground, ready to spring back into my refuge if any danger should appear. Then, reassured by the absolute stillness and by the growing light, I took my courage in both hands and stole back along the path which I had come. Some distance down it I picked up my gun, and shortly afterwards struck the brook which was my guide. So, with many a frightened backward glance, I made for home.

And suddenly there came something to remind me of my absent companions. In the clear, still morning air there sounded far away the sharp, hard note of a rifle-shot. I paused and listened, but there was nothing more. For a moment I was shocked at the thought that some sudden danger might have befallen them. But then a simpler and more natural explanation came to my mind. It was now broad daylight. They had imagined that I was lost in the woods, and had fired this shot to guide me home. It is true that we had made a strict resolution against firing, but if it seemed to them that I might be in danger they would not hesitate. It was for me now to hurry on as fast as possible, and so to reassure them.

I was weary and spent, so my progress was not as fast as I wished; but at last I came into regions which I knew. There was the swamp of the pterodactyls upon my left; there in front of me was the glade of the iguanodons. Now I was in the last belt of trees which separated me from Fort Challenger. I raised my voice in a cheery shout to allay their fears. My heart sank at that ominous stillness. I quickened my pace into a run. The zareba rose before me, even as I had left it, but the gate was open. I rushed in. In the cold morning light it was a fearful sight which met my eyes. Our effects were scattered in wild confusion over the ground; my comrades had disappeared, and close to the smouldering ashes of our fire the grass was stained crimson with a hideous pool of blood.

I was so stunned by this sudden shock that for a time I must have nearly lost my reason. I have a vague recollection, as one remembers a bad dream, of rushing about through the woods all round the empty camp, calling wildly for my companions. No answer came back from the silent shadows. The horrible thought that I might never see them again, that I might find myself abandoned all alone in that dreadful place, with no possible way of descending into the world below, that I might live and die in that nightmare country, drove me to desperation. I could have torn my hair and beaten my head in my despair. Only now did I realize how I had learned to lean upon my companions, upon the serene self-confidence of Challenger, and upon the masterful, humorous coolness of Lord Roxton. Without them I was like a child in the dark, helpless and powerless. I did not know which way to turn or what I should do first.

After a period, during which I sat in bewilderment, I set myself to try and discover what sudden misfortune could have befallen my companions. The whole disordered appearance of the camp showed that there had been some sort of attack, and the rifle shot no doubt marked the time when it had occurred. That there should have been only one shot showed that it had been all over in an instant. The rifles still lay upon the ground, and one of them – Lord John's – had the empty cartridge in the breech. The blankets of Challenger and of Summerlee beside the fire suggested that they had been asleep at the time. The cases of ammunition and of food were scattered about in a wild litter, together with our unfortunate cameras and plate-carriers, but none of them were missing. On the other hand, all the exposed provisions – and I remembered that there were a consider-able quantity of them – were gone. They were animals, then, and not natives, who had made the inroad, for surely the latter would have left nothing behind.

But if animals, or some single terrible animal, then what had become of my comrades? A ferocious beast would surely have destroyed them and left their remains. It is true that there was that one hideous pool of blood, which told of violence. Such a monster as had pursued me during the night could have carried away a victim as easily as a cat could a mouse. In that case the others would have followed in pursuit. But then they would assuredly have taken their rifles with them. The more I tried to think it out with my con-fused and weary brain the less could I find any plausible explana-tion. I searched round in the forest, but could see no tracks which could help me to a conclusion. Once I lost myself, and it was only by good luck, and after an hour of wandering, that I found the camp once more.

Suddenly a thought came to me and brought some little comfort to my heart. I was not absolutely alone in the world. Down at the bottom of the cliff, and within call of me, was waiting the faithful Zambo. I went to the edge of the plateau and looked over. Sure enough, he was squatting among his blankets beside his fire in his little camp. But, to my amazement, a second man was seated in front of him. For an instant my heart leaped for joy, as I thought that one of my comrades had made his way safely down. But a second glance dispelled the hope. The rising sun shone red upon the man's skin. He was an Indian. I shouted loudly and waved my handkerchief. Presently Zambo looked up, waved his hand, and turned to ascend the pinnacle. In a short time he was standing close to me and listening with deep distress to the story which I told him.

'Devil got them sure, Massa Malone,' said he. 'You got into the devil's country, sah, and he take you all to himself. You take advice, Massa Malone, and come down quick, else he get you as well.'

'How can I come down, Zambo?'

'You get creepers from trees, Massa Malone. Throw them over here. I make fast to this stump, and so you have bridge.'

'We have thought of that. There are no creepers here which could bear us.'

'Send for ropes, Massa Malone.'

'Who can I send, and where?'

'Send to Indian village, sah. Plenty hide-rope in Indian village. Indian down below; send him.'

'Who is he?'

'One of our Indians. Other ones beat him and take away his pay. He come back to us. Ready now to take letter, bring rope – anything.'

To take a letter! Why not? Perhaps he might bring help; but in any case he would ensure that our lives were not spent for nothing, and that news of all that we had won for Science should reach our friends at home. I had two completed letters already waiting. I would spend the day in writing a third, which would bring my experiences absolutely up to date. The Indian could bear this back to the world. I ordered Zambo, therefore, to come again in the evening, and I spent my miserable and lonely day in recording my own adventures of the night before. I also drew up a note, to be given to any white merchant or captain of a steam-boat whom the Indian could find, imploring them to see that ropes were sent to us, since our lives must depend upon it. These documents I threw to Zambo in the evening, and also my purse, which contained three English sovereigns. These were to be given to the Indian, and he was promised twice as much if he returned with the ropes.

So now you will understand, my dear Mr. McArdle, how this communication reaches you, and you will also know the truth, in case you never hear again from your unfortunate correspondent. To-night I am too weary and too depressed to make my plans. To-morrow I must think out some way by which I shall keep in touch with this camp, and yet search round for any traces of my unhappy friends.

CHAPTER XIII

A Sight I Shall Never Forget

JUST AS THE SUN WAS SETTING UPON that melancholy night I saw the lonely figure of the Indian upon the vast plain beneath me, and I watched him, our one faint hope of salvation, until he disappeared in the rising mists of evening which lay, rose-tinted from the setting sun, between the far-off river and me.

It was quite dark when I at last turned back to our stricken camp, and my last vision as I went was the red gleam of Zambo's fire, the one point of light in the wide world below, as was his faithful presence in my own shadowed soul. And yet I felt happier than I had done since this crushing blow had fallen upon me, for it was good to think that the world should know what we had done, so that at the worst our names should not perish with our bodies, but should go down to posterity associated with the result of our labours.

It was an awesome thing to sleep in that ill-fated camp; and yet it was even more unnerving to do so in the jungle. One or the other it must be. Prudence, on the one hand, warned me that I should remain on guard, but exhausted Nature, on the other, declared that I should do nothing of the kind. I climbed up on to a limb of the great gingko tree, but there was no secure perch on its rounded surface, and I should certainly have fallen off and broken my neck the moment I began to doze. I got down, therefore, and pondered over what I should do. Finally, I closed the door of the zareba, lit three separate fires in a triangle, and having eaten a hearty supper dropped off into a profound sleep, from which I had a strange and most welcome awakening. In the early morning, just as day was breaking, a hand was laid upon my arm, and starting up, with all my nerves in a tingle and my hand feeling for a rifle, I gave a cry of joy as in the cold grey light I saw Lord John kneeling beside me.

It was he – and yet it was not he. I had left him calm in his bearing, correct in his person, prim in his dress. Now he was pale and wild-eyed, gasping as he breathed like one who has run far and fast. His gaunt face was scratched and bloody, his clothes were hanging in rags, and his hat was gone. I stared in amazement, but he gave me no chance for questions. He was grabbing at our stores all the time he spoke.

'Quick, young fellah! Quick!' he cried. 'Every moment counts. Get the rifles, both of them. I have the other two. Now, all the cartridges you can gather. Fill up your pockets. Now, some food. Half a dozen tins will do. That's all right! Don't wait to talk or think. Get a move on, or we are done!'

Still half-awake, and unable to imagine what it all might mean, I found myself hurrying madly after him through the wood, a rifle under each arm and a pile of various stores in my hands. He dodged in and out through the thickest of the scrub until he came to a dense clump of brushwood. Into this he rushed, regardless of thorns, and threw himself into the heart of it, pulling me down by his side.

'There!' he panted. 'I think we are safe here. They'll make for the camp as sure as fate. It will be their first idea. But this should puzzle 'em.'

'What is it all?' I asked, when I had got my breath. 'Where are the professors? And who is it that is after us?'

'The ape-men,' he cried. 'My God, what brutes! Don't raise your voice, for they have long ears – sharp eyes, too, but no power of scent, so far as I could judge, so I don't think they can sniff us out. Where have you been, young fellah? You were well out of it.'

In a few sentences I whispered what I had done.

'Pretty bad,' said he, when he had heard of the dinosaur and the pit. 'It isn't quite the place for a rest cure. What? But I had no idea what its possibilities were until those devils got hold of us. The man-eatin' Papuans had me once, but they are Chesterfields compared to this crowd.'

'How did it happen?' I asked.

'It was in the early mornin'. Our learned friends were just stirrin'. Hadn't even begun to argue yet. Suddenly it rained apes. They came down thick as apples out of a tree. They had been assemblin' in the dark, I suppose, until that great tree over our heads was heavy with them. I shot one of them through the belly, but before we knew where we were they had us spread-eagled on our backs. I call them apes, but they carried sticks and stones in their hands and jabbered talk to each other, and ended up by tyin' our hands with creepers, so they are ahead of any beast that I have seen in my wanderin's. Ape-men – that's what they are – Missin' Links, and I wished they had stayed missin'. They carried off their wounded comrade – he was bleedin' like a pig – and then they sat around us, and if ever I saw frozen murder it was in their faces. They were big fellows, as big as a man and a deal stronger. Curious glassy grey eyes they have, under red tufts, and they just sat and gloated and gloated. Challenger is no chicken, but even he was cowed. He managed to struggle on to his feet, and yelled out at them to have done with it and get it over. I think he had gone a bit off his head at the suddenness of it, for he raged and cursed at them like a lunatic. If they had been a row of his favourite Pressmen he could not have slanged them worse.'

'Well, what did they do?' I was enthralled by the strange story which my companion was whispering into my ear, while all the time his keen eyes were shooting in every direction and his hand grasping his cocked rifle.

'I thought it was the end of us, but instead of that it started them on a new line. They all jabbered and chattered together. Then one of them stood out beside Challenger. You'll smile, young fellah, but 'pon my word they might have been kinsmen. I couldn't have believed it if I hadn't seen it with my own eyes. This old ape-man – he was their chief – was a sort of red Challenger, with every one of our friend's beauty points, only just a trifle more so. He had the short body, the big shoulders, the round chest, no neck, a great ruddy frill of a beard, the tufted eyebrows, the "What do *you* want, damn you!" look about the eyes, and the whole catalogue. When the ape-man stood by Challenger and put his paw on his shoulder, the thing was complete. Summerlee was a bit hysterical, and he laughed till he cried. The ape-men laughed too – or at least they put up the devil of a cacklin' – and then they set to work to drag us off through the forest. They wouldn't touch the guns and things – thought them dangerous, I expect – but they carried away all our loose food. Summerlee and I got some rough handlin' on the way – there's my skin and my clothes to prove it – for they took us a bee-line through the brambles, and their own hides are like leather. But Challenger was all right. Four of them carried him shoulder high, and he went like a Roman emperor. What's that?'

It was a strange clicking noise in the distance, not unlike castanets.

'There they go!' said my companion, slipping cartridges into the second double-barrelled 'Express.' 'Load them all up, young fellah-my-lad, for we're not going to be taken alive, and don't you think it! That's the row they make when they are excited. By George! they'll have something to excite them if they put us up. The "Last Stand of the Greys" won't be in it. "With their rifles grasped in their stiffened hands, 'mid a ring of the dead and dyin'," as some fathead sings. Can you hear them now?'

'Very far away.'

'That little lot will do no good, but I expect their search parties are all over the wood. Well, I was tellin' you my tale of woe. They got us soon to this town of theirs – about a thousand huts of branches and leaves in a great grove of trees near the edge of the cliff. It's three or four miles from here. The filthy beasts fingered me all over, and I feel as if I should never be clean again. They tied us up – the fellow who handled me could tie like a bo'sun – and there we lay with our toes up, beneath a tree, while a great brute stood guard over us with a club in his hand. When I say "we" I mean Summerlee and myself. Old Challenger was up a tree, eatin' pines and havin' the time of his life. I'm bound to say that he managed to get some fruit to us, and with his own hands he loosened our bonds. If you'd seen him sittin' up in that tree hob-nobbin' with his twin brother – and singin' in that rollin' bass of his, "Ring out wild bells," 'cause music of any kind seemed to put 'em in a good humour, you'd have smiled; but we weren't in much mood for laughin', as you can guess. They were inclined, within limits, to let him do what he liked, but they drew the line pretty sharply at us. It was a mighty consolation to us all to know that you were runnin' loose and had the archives in your keepin'.

'Well now, young fellah, I'll tell you what will surprise you. You say you saw signs of men, and fires, traps, and the like. Well, we have seen the natives themselves. Poor devils they were, down-faced little chaps, and had enough to make them so. It seems that the humans hold one side of this plateau – over yonder, where you saw the caves – and the ape-men hold this side, and there is bloody war between them all the time. That's the situation, so far as I could follow it. Well, yesterday the ape-men got hold of a dozen of the humans and brought them in as prisoners. You never heard such a jabberin' and shriekin' in your life. The men were little red fellows, and had been bitten and clawed so that they could hardly walk. The ape-men put two of them to death there and then – fairly pulled the arm off one of them – it was perfectly beastly. Plucky little chaps they are, and hardly gave a squeak. But it turned us absolutely sick. Summerlee fainted, and even Challenger had as much as he could stand. I think they have cleared, don't you?'

We listened intently, but nothing save the calling of the birds broke the deep peace of the forest. Lord John went on with his story.

'I think you have had the escape of your life, young fellah-my-lad. It was catchin' those Indians that put *you* clean out of their heads, else they would have been back to the camp for you as sure as fate and gathered you in. Of course, as you said, they have been watchin' us from the beginnin' out of that tree, and they knew perfectly well that we were one short. However, they could think only of this new haul; so it was I, and not a bunch of apes, that dropped in on you in the morning. Well, we had a horrid business afterwards. My God! what a nightmare the whole thing is! You remember the great bristle of sharp canes down below where we found the skeleton of the American? Well, that is just under ape-town, and that's the jumpin'-off place of their prisoners. I expect there's heaps of skeletons there, if we looked for 'em. They have a sort of clear parade ground on the top, and they make a proper ceremony about it. One by one the poor devils have to jump, and the game is to see whether they are merely dashed to pieces or whether they get skewered on the canes. They took us out to see it, and the whole tribe lined up on the edge. Four of the Indians jumped, and the canes went through 'em like knitting needles through a pat of butter. No wonder we found that poor Yankee's skeleton with the canes growin' between his ribs. It was horrible but it was doocedly interestin' too. We were all fascinated to see them take the dive, even when we thought it would be our turn next on the spring-board.

'Well, it wasn't. They kept six of the Indians up for to-day – that's how I understood it – but I fancy we were to be the star performers in the show. Challenger might get off, but Summerlee and I were in the bill. Their language is more than half signs, and it was not hard to follow them. So I thought it was time we made a break for it. I had been plottin' it out a bit, and had one or two things clear in my mind. It was all on me, for Summerlee was useless and Challenger not much better. The only time they got together they got slangin', because they couldn't agree upon the scientific classification of these red-headed devils that had got hold of us. One said it was the dryopithecus of Java, the other said it was pithecanthropus. Madness, I call it – loonies – both. But, as I say, I had thought out one or two points that were helpful. One was that these brutes could not run as fast as a man in the open. They have short, bandy legs, you see, and heavy bodies. Even Challenger could give a few yards in a hundred to the best of them, and you or I would be a perfect Shrubb. Another point was that they knew nothin' about guns. I don't believe they ever understood how the fellow I shot came by his hurt. If we could get at our guns there was no sayin' what we could do.

'So I broke away early this mornin', gave my guard a kick in the tummy that laid him out, and sprinted for the camp. There I got you and the guns, and here we are.'

'But the professors!' I cried, in consternation.

'Well, we must just go back and fetch 'em. I couldn't bring 'em with me. Challenger was up the tree, and Summerlee was not fit for the effort. The only chance was to get the guns and try a rescue. Of course they may scupper them at once in revenge. I don't think they would touch Challenger, but I wouldn't answer for Summerlee. But they would have had him in any case. Of that I am certain. So I haven't made matters any worse by boltin'. But we are honour bound to go back and have them out or see it through with them. So you can make up your soul, young fellah-my-lad, for it will be one way or the other before evenin'.'

I have tried to imitate here Lord Roxton's jerky talk, his short, strong sentences, the half-humorous, half-reckless tone that ran through it all. But he was a born leader. As danger thickened his jaunty manner would increase, his speech become more racy, his cold eyes glitter into ardent life, and his Don Quixote moustache bristle with joyous excitement. His love of danger, his intense appreciation of the drama of an adventure – all the more intense for being held tightly in – his consistent view that every peril in life is a form of sport, a fierce game betwixt you and Fate, with Death as a forfeit, made him a wonderful companion at such hours. If it were not for our fears as to the fate of our companions, it would have been a positive joy to throw myself with such a man into such an affair. We were rising from our brushwood hiding-place when suddenly I felt his grip upon my arm.

'By George!' he whispered, 'here they come!'

From where we lay we could look down a brown aisle, arched with green, formed by the trunks and branches. Along this a party of the ape-men were passing. They went in single file, with bent legs and rounded backs, their hands occasionally touching the ground, their heads turning to left and right as they trotted along. Their crouching gait took away from their height, but I should put them at five feet or so, with long arms and enormous chests. Many of them carried sticks, and at the distance they looked like a line of very hairy and deformed human beings. For a moment I caught this clear glimpse of them. Then they were lost among the bushes.

'Not this time,' said Lord John, who had caught up his rifle. 'Our best chance is to lie quiet until they have given up the search. Then we shall see whether we can't get back to their town and hit 'em where it hurts most. Give 'em an hour and we'll march.'

We filled in the time by opening one of our food tins and making sure of our breakfast. Lord Roxton had had nothing but some fruit since the morning before and ate like a starving man. Then, at last, our pockets bulging with cartridges and a rifle in each hand, we started off upon our mission of rescue. Before leaving it we carefully marked our little hiding-place among the brushwood and its bearing to Fort Challenger, that we might find it again if we needed it. We slunk through the bushes in silence until we came to the very edge of the cliff, close to the old camp. Then we halted, and Lord John gave me some idea of his plans.

'So long as we are among the thick trees these swine are our masters,' said he. 'They can see us and we cannot see them. But in the open it is different. There we can move faster than they. So we must stick to the open all we can. The edge of the plateau has fewer large trees than further inland. So that's our line of advance. Go slowly, keep your eyes open and your rifle ready. Above all, never let them get you prisoner while there is a cartridge left – that's my last word to you, young fellah.'

When we reached the edge of the cliff I looked over and saw our good old black Zambo sitting smoking on a rock below us. I would have given a great deal to have hailed him and told him how we were placed, but it was too dangerous, lest we should be heard. The woods seemed to be full of the ape-men, again and again we heard their curious clicking chatter. At such times we plunged into the nearest clump of bushes and lay still until the sound had passed away. Our advance, therefore, was very slow, and two hours at least must have passed before I saw by Lord John's cautious movements that we must be close to our destination. He motioned to me to lie still, and he crawled forward himself. In a minute he was back again, his face quivering with eagerness.

'Come!' said he. 'Come quick! I hope to the Lord we are not too late already!'

I found myself shaking with nervous excitement as I scrambled forward and lay down beside him, looking out through the bushes at a clearing which stretched before us.

It was a sight which I shall never forget until my dying day – so weird, so impossible, that I do not know how I am to make you realize it, or how in a few years I shall bring myself to believe in it if I live to sit once more on a lounge in the Savage Club and look out on the drab solidity of the Embankment. I know that it will seem then to be some wild nightmare, some delirium of fever. Yet I will set it down now, while it is still fresh in my memory, and one at least, the man who lay in the damp grasses by my side, will know if I have lied.

A wide, open space lay before us – some hundreds of yards across – all green turf and low bracken growing to the very edge of the cliff. Round this clearing there was a semicircle of trees with curious huts built of foliage piled one above the other among the branches. A rookery, with every nest a little house, would best convey the idea. The openings of these huts and the branches of the trees were thronged with a dense mob of ape-people, whom from their size I took to be the females and infants of the tribe. They formed the background of the picture, and were all looking out with eager interest at the same scene which fascinated and bewildered us.

In the open, and near the edge of the cliff, there had assembled a crowd of some hundred of these shaggy red-haired creatures, many of them of immense size, and all of them horrible to look upon. There was a certain discipline among them, for none of them attempted to break the line which had been formed. In front there stood a small group of Indians – little, clean-limbed, red fellows, whose skins glowed like polished bronze in the strong sunlight. A tall, thin white man was standing beside them, his head bowed, his arms folded, his whole attitude expressive of his horror and dejection. There was no mistaking the angular form of Professor Summerlee.

In front of and around this dejected group of prisoners were several ape-men who watched them closely and made all escape impossible. Then, right out from all the others and close to the edge of the cliff, were two figures, so strange, and under other circumstances so ludicrous, that they absorbed my attention. The one was our comrade, Professor Challenger. The remains of his coat still hung from his shoulders, but his shirt had been all torn out, and his great beard merged itself in the black tangle which covered his mighty chest. He had lost his hat, and his hair, which had grown long in our wanderings, was flying in wild disorder. A single day seemed to have changed him from the highest product of modern civilization to the most desperate savage in South America. Beside him stood his master the king of the ape-men. In all things he was, as Lord John had said, the very image of our Professor, save that his colouring was red instead of black. The same short, broad figure, the same heavy shoulders, the same forward hang of the arms, the same bristling beard merging itself in the hairy chest. Only above the eyebrows, where the sloping forehead and low, curved skull of the ape-man were in sharp contrast to the broad brow and magnificent cranium of the European, could one see any marked difference. At every other point the king was an absurd parody of the Professor.

All this, which takes me so long to describe, impressed itself upon me in a few seconds. Then we had very different things to think of, for an active drama was in progress. Two of the ape-men had seized one of the Indians out of the group and dragged him forward to the edge of the cliff. The king raised his hand as a signal. They caught the man up by his leg and arm, and swung him three times back-wards and forwards with tremendous violence. Then, with a fright-ful heave they shot the poor wretch over the precipice. With such force did they throw him that he curved high in the air before beginning to drop. As he vanished from sight, the whole assembly, except the guards, rushed forward to the edge of the precipice, and there was a long pause of absolute silence, broken by a mad yell of delight. They sprang about, tossing their long, hairy arms in the air and howling with exultation. Then they fell back from the edge, formed themselves again into line, and waited for the next victim.

This time it was Summerlee. Two of his guards caught him by the wrists and pulled him brutally to the front. His thin figure and long limbs struggled and fluttered like a chicken being dragged from a coop. Challenger had turned to the king and waved his hands frantically before him. He was begging, pleading, imploring for his comrade's life. The ape-man pushed him roughly aside and shook his head. It was the last conscious movement he was to make upon earth. Lord John's rifle cracked, and the king sank down, a tangled red sprawling thing, upon the ground.

'Shoot into the thick of them! Shoot! sonny, shoot!' cried my companion.

There are strange red depths in the soul of the most common-place man. I am tender-hearted by nature, and have found my eyes moist many a time over the scream of a wounded hare. Yet the blood lust was on me now. I found myself on my feet emptying one magazine, then the other, clicking open the breech to re-load, snap-ping it to again, while cheering and yelling with pure ferocity and joy of slaughter as I did so. With our four guns the two of us made a horrible havoc. Both the guards who held Summerlee were down, and he was staggering about like a drunken man in his amazement, unable to realize that he was a free man. The dense mob of ape-men ran about in bewilderment, marvelling whence this storm of death was coming or what it might mean. They waved, gesticulated, screamed, and tripped up over those who had fallen. Then, with a sudden impulse, they all rushed in a howling crowd to the trees for shelter, leaving the ground behind them spotted with their stricken comrades. The prisoners were left for the moment standing alone in the middle of the clearing.

Challenger's quick brain had grasped the situation. He seized the bewildered Summerlee by the arm, and they both ran towards us. Two of their guards bounded after them and fell to two bullets from Lord John. We ran forward into the open to meet our friends, and pressed a loaded rifle into the hands of each. But Summerlee was at the end of his strength. He could hardly totter. Already the ape-men were recovering from their panic. They were coming through the brushwood and threatening to cut us off. Challenger and I ran Summerlee along, one at each of his elbows, while Lord John covered our retreat, firing again and again as savage heads snarled at us out of the bushes. For a mile or more the chattering brutes were at our very heels. Then the pursuit slackened, for they learned our power and would no longer face that unerring rifle. When we had at last reached the camp, we looked back and found ourselves alone.

So it seemed to us; and yet we were mistaken. We had hardly closed the thorn-bush door of our zareba, clasped each other's hands, and thrown ourselves panting upon the ground beside our spring, when we heard a patter of feet and then a gentle, plaintive crying from outside our entrance. Lord Roxton rushed forward, rifle in hand, and threw it open. There, prostrate upon their faces, lay the little red figures of the four surviving Indians, trembling with fear of us and yet imploring our protection. With an expressive sweep of his hands one of them pointed to the woods around them, and indicated that they were full of danger. Then, darting forward, he threw his arms round Lord John's legs and rested his face upon them.

'By George!' cried Lord John, pulling at his moustache in great perplexity, 'I say – what the dooce are we to do with these people? Get up, little chappie, and take your face off my boots.'

Summerlee was sitting up and stuffing some tobacco into his old briar.

'We've got to see them safe,' said he. 'You've pulled us all out of the jaws of death. My word! it was a good bit of work!'

'Admirable!' cried Challenger. 'Admirable! Not only we as individuals, but European science collectively, owe you a deep debt of gratitude for what you have done. I do not hesitate to say that the disappearance of Professor Summerlee and myself would have left an appreciable gap in modern zoological history. Our young friend here and you have done most excellently well.'

He beamed at us with the old paternal smile, but European science would have been somewhat amazed could they have seen their chosen child, the hope of the future, with his tangled, unkempt head, his bare chest, and his tattered clothes. He had one of the meat tins between his knees, and sat with a large piece of cold Australian mutton between his fingers. The Indian looked up at him, and then, with a little yelp, cringed to the ground and clung to Lord John's leg.

'Don't you be scared, my bonnie boy,' said Lord John, patting the matted head in front of him. 'He can't stick your appearance, Challenger; and, by George! I don't wonder. All right, little chap, he's only a human, just the same as the rest of us.'

'Really, sir!' cried the Professor.

'Well, it's lucky for you, Challenger, that you *are* a little out of the ordinary. If you hadn't been so like the king –'

'Upon my word, Lord John Roxton, you allow yourself great latitude.'

'Well, it's a fact.'

'I beg, sir, that you will change the subject. Your remarks are irrelevant and unintelligible. The question before us is what are we to do with these Indians? The obvious thing is to escort them home, if we knew where their home was.'

'There is no difficulty about that,' said I. 'They live in the caves on the other side of the central lake.'

'Our young friend here knows where they live. I gather that it is some distance.'

'A good twenty miles,' said I.

Summerlee gave a groan.

'I, for one, could never get there. Surely I hear those brutes still howling upon our track.'

As he spoke, from the dark recesses of the woods we heard far away the jibbering cry of the ape-men. The Indians once more set up a feeble wail of fear.

'We must move, and move quick!' said Lord John. 'You help Summerlee, young fellah. These Indians will carry stores. Now, then, come along before they can see us.'

In less than half an hour we had reached our brushwood retreat and concealed ourselves. All day we heard the excited calling of the ape-men in the direction of our old camp, but none of them came our way, and the tired fugitives, red and white, had a long, deep sleep. I was dozing myself in the evening when someone plucked my sleeve, and I found Challenger kneeling beside me.

'You keep a diary of these events, and you expect eventually to publish it, Mr. Malone,' said he, with solemnity.

'I am only here as a Press reporter,' I answered.

'Exactly. You may have heard some rather fatuous remarks of Lord John Roxton's which seemed to imply that there was some – some resemblance –'

'Yes, I heard them.'

'I need not say that any publicity given to such an idea – any levity in your narrative of what occurred – would be exceedingly offensive to me.'

'I will keep well within the truth.'

'Lord John's observations are frequently exceedingly fanciful, and he is capable of attributing the most absurd reasons to the respect which is always shown by the most undeveloped races to dignity and character. You follow my meaning?'

'Entirely.'

'I leave the matter to your discretion.' Then, after a long pause, he added: 'The king of the ape-men was really a creature of great distinction – a most remarkably handsome and intelligent personality. Did it not strike you?'

'A most remarkable creature,' said I.

And the Professor, much eased in his mind, settled down to his slumber once more.

CHAPTER XIV

Those Were the Real Conquests

WE HAD IMAGINED THAT OUR PURSUERS, the ape-men, knew nothing of our brushwood hiding-place, but we were soon to find out our mistake. There was no sound in the woods – not a leaf moved upon the trees and all was peace around us – but we should have been warned by our first experience how cunningly and how patiently these creatures can watch and wait until their chance comes. Whatever fate may be mine through life, I am very sure that I shall never be nearer death than I was that morning. But I will tell you the thing in its due order.

We all awoke exhausted after the terrific emotions and scanty food of yesterday. Summerlee was still so weak that it was an effort for him to stand; but the old man was full of a sort of surly courage which would never admit defeat. A council was held, and it was agreed that we should wait quietly for an hour or two where we were, have our much-needed breakfast, and then make our way across the plateau and round the central lake to the caves where my observations had shown that the Indians lived. We relied upon the fact that we could count upon the good word of those whom we had rescued to ensure a warm welcome from their fellows. Then, with our mission accomplished and possessing a fuller knowledge of the secrets of Maple White Land, we should turn our whole thoughts to the vital problem of our escape and return. Even Challenger was ready to admit that we should then have done all for which we had come, and that our first duty from that time onwards was to carry back to civilization the amazing discoveries we had made.

We were able now to take a more leisurely view of the Indians whom we had rescued. They were small men, wiry, active, and well-built, with lank black hair tied up in a bunch behind their heads with a leathern thong, and leathern also were their loin-clothes. Their faces were hairless, well formed, and good-humoured. The lobes of their ears, hanging ragged and bloody, showed that they had been pierced for some ornaments which their captors had torn out. Their speech, though unintelligible to us, was fluent among themselves, and as they pointed to each other and uttered the word 'Accala' many times over, we gathered that this was the name of their nation. Occasionally, with faces which were convulsed with fear and hatred, they shook their clenched hands at the woods round and cried: 'Doda! Doda!' which was surely their term for their enemies.

'What do you make of them, Challenger?' asked Lord John. 'One thing is very clear to me, and that is that the little chap with the front of his head shaved is a chief among them.'

It was indeed evident that this man stood apart from the others, and that they never ventured to address him without every sign of deep respect. He seemed to be the youngest of them all, and yet, so proud and high was his spirit, that upon Challenger laying his great hand upon his head he started like a spurred horse and, with a quick flash of his dark eyes, moved further away from the Professor. Then, placing his hand upon his breast and holding himself with great dignity, he uttered the word 'Maretas' several times. The Professor, unabashed, seized the nearest Indian by the shoulder and proceeded to lecture upon him as if he were a potted specimen in a class-room.

'The type of these people,' said he in his sonorous fashion, 'whether judged by cranial capacity, facial angle, or any other test, cannot be regarded as a low one; on the contrary, we must place it as considerably higher in the scale than many South American tribes which I can mention. On no possible supposition can we explain the evolution of such a race in this place. For that matter, so great a gap separates these ape-men from the primitive animals which have survived upon this plateau, that it is inadmissible to think that they could have developed where we find them.'

'Then where the dooce did they drop from?' asked Lord John.

'A question which will, no doubt, be eagerly discussed in every scientific society in Europe, and America,' the Professor answered. 'My own reading of the situation for what it is worth' – he inflated his chest enormously and looked insolently around him at the words – 'is that evolution has advanced under the peculiar conditions of this country up to the vertebrate stage, the old types surviving and living on in company with the newer ones. Thus we find such modern creatures as the tapir – an animal with quite a respectable length of pedigree – the great deer, and the anteater in the companionship of reptilian forms of Jurassic type. So much is clear. And now come the ape-men and the Indian. What is the scientific mind to think of their presence? I can only account for it by an invasion from outside. It is probable that there existed an anthropoid ape in South America, who in past ages found his way to this place, and that he developed into the creatures we have seen, some of which' – here he looked hard at me – 'were of an appearance and shape which if it had been accompanied by corresponding intelligence, would, I do not hesitate to say, have reflected credit upon any living race. As to the Indians I cannot doubt that they are more recent immigrants from below. Under the stress of famine or of conquest they have made their way up here. Faced by ferocious creatures which they had never before seen, they took refuge in the caves which our young friend has described, but they have no doubt had a bitter fight to hold their own against wild beasts, and especially against the ape-men who would regard them as intruders, and wage a merciless war upon them with a cunning which the larger beasts would lack. Hence the fact that their numbers appear to be limited. Well, gentlemen, have I read you the riddle aright, or is there any point which you would query?'

Professor Summerlee for once was too depressed to argue, though he shook his head violently as a token of general disagreement. Lord John merely scratched his scanty locks with the remark that he couldn't put up a fight as he wasn't in the same weight or class. For my own part I performed my usual *rôle* of bringing things down to a strictly prosaic and practical level by the remark that one of the Indians was missing.

'He has gone to fetch some water,' said Lord Roxton. 'We fitted him up with an empty beef tin and he is off.'

'To the old camp?' I asked.

'No, to the brook. It's among the trees there. It can't be more than a couple of hundred yards. But the beggar is certainly taking his time.'

'I'll go and look after him,' said I. I picked up my rifle and strolled in the direction of the brook, leaving my friends to lay out the scanty breakfast. It may seem to you rash that even for so short a distance I should quit the shelter of our friendly thicket, but you will remember that we were many miles from Ape-town, that so far as we knew the creatures had not discovered our retreat, and that in any case with a rifle in my hands I had no fear of them. I had not yet learned their cunning or their strength.

I could hear the murmur of our brook somewhere ahead of me, but there was a tangle of trees and brushwood between me and it. I was making my way through this at a point which was just out of sight of my companions, when, under one of the trees, I noticed something red huddled among the bushes. As I approached it, I was shocked to see that it was the dead body of the missing Indian. He lay upon his side, his limbs drawn up, and his head screwed round at a most unnatural angle, so that he seemed to be looking straight over his own shoulder. I gave a cry to warn my friends that something was amiss, and running forwards I stooped over the body. Surely my guardian angel was very near to me then, for some instinct of fear, or it may have been some faint rustle of leaves, made me glance upwards. Out of the thick green foliage which hung low over my head, two long muscular arms covered with reddish hair were slowly descending. Another instant and the great stealthy hands would have been round my throat. I sprang backwards, but quick as I was, those hands were quicker still. Through my sudden spring they missed a fatal grip, but one of them caught the back of my neck and the other my face. I threw my hands up to protect my throat, and the next moment the huge paw had slid down my face and closed over them. I was lifted lightly from the ground, and I felt an intolerable pressure forcing my head back and back until the strain upon the cervical spine was more than I could bear. My senses swam, but I still tore at the hand and forced it out from my chin. Looking up I saw a frightful face with cold inexorable light blue eyes looking down into mine. There was something hypnotic in those terrible eyes. I could struggle no longer. As the creature felt me grow limp in his grasp, two white canines gleamed for a moment at each side of the vile mouth, and the grip tightened still more upon my chin, forcing it always upwards and back. A thin, opal-tinted mist formed before my eyes and little silvery bells tinkled in my ears. Dully and far off I heard the crack of a rifle and was feebly aware of the shock as I was dropped to the earth, where I lay without sense or motion.

I awoke to find myself on my back upon the grass in our lair within the thicket. Someone had brought the water from the brook, and Lord John was sprinkling my head with it, while Challenger and Summerlee were propping me up, with concern in their faces. For a moment I had a glimpse of the human spirits behind their scientific masks. It was really shock, rather than any injury, which had prostrated me, and in half an hour, in spite of aching head and stiff neck, I was sitting up and ready for anything.

'But you've had the escape of your life, young fellah-my-lad,' said Lord John. 'When I heard your cry and ran forward, and saw your head twisted half-off and your stohwassers kickin' in the air, I thought we were one short. I missed the beast in my flurry, but he dropped you all right and was off like a streak. By George! I wish I had fifty men with rifles. I'd clear out the whole infernal gang of them and leave this country a bit cleaner than we found it.'

It was clear now that the ape-men had in some way marked us down, and that we were watched on every side. We had not so much to fear from them during the day, but they would be very likely to rush us by night; so the sooner we got away from their neighbourhood the better. On three sides of us was absolute forest, and there we might find ourselves in an ambush. But on the fourth side – that which sloped down in the direction of the lake – there was only low scrub, with scattered trees and occasional open glades. It was, in fact, the route which I had myself taken in my solitary journey, and it led us straight for the Indian caves. This then must for every reason be our road.

One great regret we had, and that was to leave our old camp behind us, not only for the sake of the stores which remained there, but even more because we were losing touch with Zambo, our link with the outside world. However, we had a fair supply of cartridges and all our guns, so, for a time at least, we could look after ourselves, and we hoped soon to have a chance of returning and restoring our communications with our negro. He had faithfully promised to stay where he was, and we had not a doubt that he would be as good as his word.

It was in the early afternoon that we started upon our journey. The young chief walked at our head as our guide, but refused indignantly to carry any burden. Behind him came the two surviving Indians with our scanty possessions upon their backs. We four white men walked in the rear with rifles loaded and ready. As we started there broke from the thick silent woods behind us a sudden great ululation of the ape-men, which may have been a cheer of triumph at our departure or a jeer of contempt at our flight. Looking back we saw only the dense screen of trees, but that long-drawn yell told us how many of our enemies lurked among them. We saw no sign of pursuit, however, and soon we had got into more open country and beyond their power.

As I tramped along, the rearmost of the four, I could not help smiling at the appearance of my three companions in front. Was this the luxurious Lord John Roxton who had sat that evening in the Albany amidst his Persian rugs and his pictures in the pink radiance of the tinted lights? And was this the imposing Professor who had swelled behind the great desk in his massive study at Enmore Park? and finally, could this be the austere and prim figure which had risen before the meeting at the Zoological Institute? No three tramps that one could have met in a Surrey lane could have looked more hopeless and bedraggled. We had, it is true, been only a week or so upon the top of the plateau, but all our spare clothing was in our camp below, and the one week had been a severe one upon us all, though least to me who had not to endure the handling of the ape-men. My three friends had all lost their hats, and had now bound handkerchiefs round their heads, their clothes hung in ribbons about them, and their unshaven grimy faces were hardly to be recognized. Both Summerlee and Challenger were limping heavily, while I still dragged my feet from weakness after the shock of the morning, and my neck was as stiff as a board from the murderous grip that held it. We were indeed a sorry crew, and I did not wonder to see our Indian companions glance back at us occasionally with horror and amazement on their faces.

In the late afternoon we reached the margin of the lake, and as we emerged from the bush and saw the sheet of water stretching before us our native friends set up a shrill cry of joy and pointed eagerly in front of them. It was indeed a wonderful sight which lay before us. Sweeping over the glassy surface was a great flotilla of canoes coming straight for the shore upon which we stood. They were some miles out when first we saw them, but they shot forward with great swiftness, and were soon so near that the rowers could distinguish our persons. Instantly a thunderous shout of delight burst from them, and we saw them rise from their seats, waving their paddles and spears madly in the air. Then, bending to their work once more, they flew across the intervening water, beached their boats upon the sloping sand, and rushed up to us, prostrating themselves with loud cries of greeting before the young chief. Finally one of them, an elderly man, with a necklace and bracelet of great lustrous glass beads and the skin of some beautiful mottled amber-coloured animal slung over his shoulders, ran forward and embraced most tenderly the youth whom we had saved. He then looked at us and asked some questions, after which he stepped up with much dignity and embraced us also each in turn. Then, at his order, the whole tribe lay down upon the ground before us in homage. Personally I felt shy and uncomfortable at this obsequious adoration, and I read the same feeling in the faces of Lord John and Summerlee, but Challenger expanded like a flower in the sun.

'They may be undeveloped types,' said he, stroking his beard and looking round at them, 'but their deportment in the presence of their superiors might be a lesson to some of our more advanced Europeans. Strange how correct are the instincts of the natural man!'

It was clear that the natives had come out upon the warpath, for every man carried his spear – a long bamboo tipped with bone – his bow and arrows, and some sort of club or stone battle-axe slung at his side. Their dark, angry glances at the woods from which we had come, and the frequent repetition of the word 'Doda,' made it clear enough that this was a rescue party who had set forth to save or revenge the old chief's son, for such we gathered that the youth must be. A council was now held by the whole tribe squatting in a circle, whilst we sat near on a slab of basalt and watched their proceedings. Two or three warriors spoke, and finally our young friend made a spirited harangue with such eloquent features and gestures that we could understand it all as clearly as if we had known the language.

'What is the use of returning?' he said. 'Sooner or later the thing must be done. Your comrades have been murdered. What if I have returned safe? These others have been done to death. There is no safety for any of us. We are assembled now and ready.' Then he pointed to us. 'These strange men are our friends. They are great fighters, and they hate the ape-men even as we do. They command,' here he pointed up to heaven, 'the thunder and the lightning. When shall we have such a chance again? Let us go forward, and either die now or live for the future in safety. How else shall we go back unashamed to our women?'

The little red warriors hung upon the words of the speaker, and when he had finished they burst into a roar of applause, waving their rude weapons in the air. The old chief stepped forward to us, and asked us some question, pointing at the same time to the woods. Lord John made a sign to him that he should wait for an answer and then he turned to us.

'Well, it's up to you to say what you will do,' said he; 'for my part I have a score to settle with these monkey-folk, and if it ends by wiping them off the face of the earth I don't see that the earth need fret about it. I'm goin' with our little red pals and I mean to see them through the scrap. What do you say, young fellah?'

'Of course I will come.'

'And you, Challenger?'

'I will assuredly co-operate.'

'And you, Summerlee?'

'We seem to be drifting very far from the object of this expedition, Lord John. I assure you that I little thought when I left my professorial chair in London that it was for the purpose of heading a raid of savages upon a colony of anthropoid apes.'

'To such base uses do we come,' said Lord John, smiling. 'But we are up against it, so what's the decision?'

'It seems a most questionable step,' said Summerlee, argumentative to the last, 'but if you are all going, I hardly see how I can remain behind.'

'Then it is settled,' said Lord John, and turning to the chief he nodded and slapped his rifle. The old fellow clasped our hands, each in turn, while his men cheered louder than ever. It was too late to advance that night, so the Indians settled down into a rude bivouac. On all sides their fires began to glimmer and smoke. Some of them who had disappeared into the jungle came back presently driving a young iguanodon before them. Like the others, it had a daub of asphalt upon its shoulder, and it was only when we saw one of the natives step forward with the air of an owner and give his consent to the beast's slaughter that we understood at last that these great creatures were as much private property as a herd of cattle, and that these symbols which had so perplexed us were nothing more than the marks of the owner. Helpless, torpid, and vegetarian, with great limbs and a minute brain, they could be rounded up and driven by a child. In a few minutes the huge beast had been cut up and slabs of him were hanging over a dozen camp fires, together with great scaly ganoid fish which had been speared in the lake.

Summerlee had lain down and slept upon the sand, but we others roamed round the edge of the water, seeking to learn something more of this strange country. Twice we found pits of blue clay, such as we had already seen in the swamp of the pterodactyls. These were old volcanic vents, and for some reason excited the greatest interest in Lord John. What attracted Challenger, on the other hand, was a bubbling, gurgling mud geyser, where some strange gas formed great bursting bubbles upon the surface. He thrust a hollow reed into it and cried out with delight like a schoolboy when he was able, on touching it with a lighted match to cause a sharp explosion and a blue flame at the far end of the tube. Still more pleased was he when, inverting a leathern pouch over the end of the reed, and so filling it with the gas, he was able to send it soaring up into the air.

'An inflammable gas, and one markedly lighter than the atmosphere. I should say beyond doubt that it contains a considerable proportion of free hydrogen. The resources of G. E. C. are not yet exhausted, my young friend. I may yet show you how a great mind moulds all Nature to its use.' He swelled with some secret purpose, but would say no more.

There was nothing which we could see upon the shore which seemed to me so wonderful as the great sheet of water before us. Our numbers and our noise had frightened all living creatures away, and save for a few pterodactyls, which soared round high above our heads while they waited for the carrion, all was still around the camp. But it was different out upon the rose-tinted waters of the Central Lake. It boiled and heaved with strange life. Great slate-coloured backs and high serrated dorsal fins shot up with a fringe of silver, and then rolled down into the depths again. The sandbanks far out were spotted with uncouth crawling forms, huge turtles, strange saurians, and one great flat creature like a writhing palpitating mat of black greasy leather, which flopped its way slowly to the lake. Here and there high serpent heads projected out of the water, cutting swiftly through it with a little collar of foam in front, and a long swirling wake behind, rising and falling in graceful, swan-like undulations as they went. It was not until one of these creatures wriggled on to a sand-bank within a few hundred yards of us, and exposed a barrel-shaped body and huge flippers behind the long serpent neck, that Challenger and Summerlee, who had joined us, broke out into their duet of wonder and admiration.

'Plesiosaurus! A fresh-water Plesiosaurus!' cried Summerlee. 'That I should have lived to see such a sight! We are blessed, my dear Challenger, above all zoologists since the world began!'

It was not until the night had fallen, and the fires of our savage allies glowed red in the shadows, that our two men of science could be dragged away from the fascinations of that primæval lake. Even in the darkness as we lay upon the strand, we heard from time to time the snort and plunge of the huge creatures who lived therein.

At earliest dawn our camp was astir and an hour later we had started upon our memorable expedition. Often in my dreams have I thought that I might live to be a war correspondent. In what wildest one could I have conceived the nature of the campaign which it should be my lot to report? Here then is my first despatch from a field of battle:

Our numbers had been reinforced during the night by a fresh batch of natives from the caves, and we may have been four or five hundred strong when we made our advance. A fringe of scouts was thrown out in front, and behind them the whole force in a solid column made their way up the long slope of the bush country until we were near the edge of the forest. Here they spread out into a long straggling line of spearmen and bowmen. Roxton and Summerlee took their position upon the right flank, while Challenger and I were on the left. It was a host of the stone age that we were accompanying to battle – we with the last word of the gunsmith's art from St. James's Street and the Strand.

We had not long to wait for our enemy. A wild shrill clamour rose from the edge of the wood and suddenly a body of ape-men rushed out with clubs and stones, and made for the centre of the Indian line. It was a valiant move but a foolish one, for the great bandy-legged creatures were slow of foot, while their opponents were as active as cats. It was horrible to see the fierce brutes with foaming mouths and glaring eyes, rushing and grasping, but for ever missing their elusive enemies, while arrow after arrow buried itself in their hides. One great fellow ran past me roaring with pain, with a dozen darts sticking from his chest and ribs. In mercy I put a bullet through his skull, and he fell sprawling among the aloes. But this was the only shot fired, for the attack had been on the centre of the line, and the Indians there had needed no help of ours in repulsing it. Of all the ape-men who had rushed out into the open, I do not think that one got back to cover.

But the matter was more deadly when we came among the trees. For an hour or more after we entered the wood, there was a desperate struggle in which for a time we hardly held our own. Springing out from among the scrub the ape-men with huge clubs broke in upon the Indians and often felled three or four of them before they could be speared. Their frightful blows shattered everything upon which they fell. One of them knocked Summerlee's rifle to matchwood and the next would have crushed his skull had an Indian not stabbed the beast to the heart. Other ape-men in the trees above us hurled down stones and logs of wood, occasionally dropping bodily on to our ranks and fighting furiously until they were felled. Once our allies broke under the pressure, and had it not been for the execution done by our rifles they would certainly have taken to their heels. But they were gallantly rallied by their old chief and came on with such a rush that the ape-men began in turn to give way. Summerlee was weaponless, but I was emptying my magazine as quick as I could fire, and on the further flank we heard the continuous cracking of our companions' rifles. Then in a moment came the panic and the collapse. Screaming and howling, the great creatures rushed away in all directions through the brushwood, while our allies yelled in their savage delight, following swiftly after their flying enemies. All the feuds of countless generations, all the hatreds and cruelties of their narrow history, all the memories of ill-usage and persecution were to be purged that day. At last man was to be supreme and the man-beast to find for ever his allotted place. Fly as they would the fugitives were too slow to escape from the active savages, and from every side in the tangled woods we heard the exultant yells, the twanging of bows, and the crash and thud as ape-men were brought down from their hiding-places in the trees.

I was following the others, when I found that Lord John and Summerlee had come across to join us.

'It's over,' said Lord John. 'I think we can leave the tidying up to them. Perhaps the less we see of it the better we shall sleep.'

Challenger's eyes were shining with the lust of slaughter.

'We have been privileged,' he cried, strutting about like a game-cock, 'to be present at one of the typical decisive battles of history – the battles which have determined the fate of the world. What, my friends, is the conquest of one nation by another? It is meaningless. Each produces the same result. But those fierce fights, when in the dawn of the ages the cave-dwellers held their own against the tiger folk, or the elephants first found that they had a master, those were the real conquests – the victories that count. By this strange turn of fate we have seen and helped to decide even such a contest. Now upon this plateau the future must ever be for man.'

It needed a robust faith in the end to justify such tragic means. As we advanced together through the woods we found the ape-men lying thick, transfixed with spears or arrows. Here and there a little group of shattered Indians marked where one of the anthropoids had turned to bay, and sold his life dearly. Always in front of us we heard the yelling and roaring which showed the direction of the pursuit. The ape-men had been driven back to their city, they had made a last stand there, once again they had been broken, and now we were in time to see the final fearful scene of all. Some eighty or a hundred males, the last survivors, had been driven across that same little clearing which led to the edge of the cliff, the scene of our own exploit two days before. As we arrived the Indians, a semicircle of spearmen, had closed in on them, and in a minute it was over. Thirty or forty died where they stood. The others, screaming and clawing, were thrust over the precipice, and went hurtling down, as their prisoners had of old, on to the sharp bamboos six hundred feet below. It was as Challenger had said, and the reign of man was assured for ever in Maple White Land. The males were exterminated, Ape Town was destroyed, the females and young were driven away to live in bondage, and the long rivalry of untold centuries had reached its bloody end.

For us the victory brought much advantage. Once again we were able to visit our camp and get at our stores. Once more also we were able to communicate with Zambo, who had been terrified by the spectacle from afar of an avalanche of apes falling from the edge of the cliff.

'Come away, Massas, come away!' he cried, his eyes starting from his head. 'The debbil get you sure if you stay up there.'

'It is the voice of sanity!' said Summerlee with conviction. 'We have had adventures enough and they are neither suitable to our character or our position. I hold you to your word, Challenger. From now onwards you devote your energies to getting us out of this horrible country and back once more to civilization.'

CHAPTER XV

Our Eyes Have Seen Great Wonders

I WRITE THIS FROM DAY TO DAY, but I trust that before I come to the end of it, I may be able to say that the light shines, at last, through our clouds. We are held here with no clear means of making our escape, and bitterly we chafe against it. Yet, I can well imagine that the day may come when we may be glad that we were kept, against our will, to see something more of the wonders of this singular place, and of the creatures who inhabit it.

The victory of the Indians and the annihilation of the ape-men marked the turning point of our fortunes. From then onwards, we were in truth masters of the plateau, for the natives looked upon us with a mixture of fear and gratitude, since by our strange powers we had aided them to destroy their hereditary foe. For their own sakes they would, perhaps, be glad to see the departure of such formidable and incalculable people, but they have not themselves suggested any way by which we may reach the plains below. There had been, so far as we could follow their signs, a tunnel by which the place could be approached, the lower exit of which we had seen from below. By this, no doubt, both ape-men and Indians had at different epochs reached the top, and Maple White with his companion had taken the same way. Only the year before, however, there had been a terrific earthquake, and the upper end of the tunnel had fallen in and completely disappeared. The Indians now could only shake their heads and shrug their shoulders when we expressed by signs our desire to descend. It may be that they cannot, but it may also be that they will not help us to get away.

At the end of the victorious campaign the surviving ape-folk were driven across the plateau (their wailings were horrible) and established in the neighbourhood of the Indian caves, where they would, from now onwards, be a servile race under the eyes of their masters. It was a rude, raw, primæval version of the Jews in Babylon or the Israelites in Egypt. At night we could hear from amid the trees the long-drawn cry, as some primitive Ezekiel mourned for fallen greatness and recalled the departed glories of Ape Town. Hewers of wood and drawers of water, such were they from now onwards.

We had returned across the plateau with our allies two days after the battle, and made our camp at the foot of their cliffs. They would have had us share their caves with them, but Lord John would by no means consent to it, considering that to do so would put us in their power if they were treacherously disposed. We kept our independence therefore, and had our weapons ready for any emergency, while preserving the most friendly relations. We also continually visited their caves, which were most remarkable places, though whether made by man or by Nature we have never been able to determine. They were all on the one stratum, hollowed out of some soft rock which lay between the volcanic basalt forming the ruddy cliffs above them, and the hard granite which formed their base.

The openings were about eighty feet above the ground, and were led up to by long stone stairs, so narrow and steep that no large animal could mount them. Inside they were warm and dry, running in straight passages of varying length into the side of the hill, with smooth grey walls decorated with many excellent pictures done with charred sticks and representing the various animals of the plateau. If every living thing were swept from the country the future explorer would find upon the walls of these caves ample evidence of the strange fauna – the dinosaurs, iguanodons and fish lizards which had lived so recently upon earth.

Since we had learned that the huge iguanodons were kept as tame herds by their owners, and were simply walking meat-stores, we had conceived that man, even with his primitive weapons, had established his ascendancy upon the plateau. We were soon to discover that it was not so, and that he was still there upon tolerance. It was on the third day after our forming our camp near the Indian caves that the tragedy occurred. Challenger and Summerlee had gone off together that day to the lake, where some of the natives, under their direction, were engaged in harpooning specimens of the great lizards. Lord John and I had remained in our camp, while a number of the Indians were scattered about upon the grassy slope in front of the caves engaged in different ways. Suddenly there was a shrill cry of alarm, with the word 'Stoa' resounding from a hundred tongues. From every side men, women and children were rushing wildly for shelter, swarming up the staircases and into the caves in a mad stampede.

Looking up, we could see them waving their arms from the rocks above and beckoning to us to join them in their refuge. We had both seized our magazine rifles and ran out to see what the danger could be. Suddenly from the near belt of trees there broke forth a group of twelve or fifteen Indians, running for their lives, and at their very heels two of those frightful monsters which had disturbed our camp and pursued me upon my solitary journey. In shape they were like horrible toads, and moved in a succession of springs, but in size they were of an incredible bulk, larger than the largest elephant. We had never before seen them save at night, and indeed they are nocturnal animals save when disturbed in their lairs, as these had been. We now stood amazed at the sight, for their blotched and warty skins were of a curious fish-like iridescence, and the sunlight struck them with an ever-varying rainbow bloom as they moved.

We had little time to watch them, however, for in an instant they had overtaken the fugitives and were making a dire slaughter among them. Their method was to fall forward with their full weight upon each in turn, and, leaving him crushed and mangled, to bound on after the others. The wretched Indians screamed with terror, but were helpless, run as they would, before the relentless purpose and horrible activity of these monstrous creatures. One after another they went down, and there were not half a dozen surviving by the time my companion and I could come to their help. But our aid was of little avail and only involved us in the same peril. At the range of a couple of hundred yards we emptied our magazines, firing bullet after bullet into the beasts, but with no more effect than if we were pelting them with pellets of paper. Their slow reptilian natures cared nothing for wounds, and the springs of their lives, with no special brain centre but scattered throughout their spinal cords, could not be tapped by any modern weapons. The most that we could do was to check their progress by distracting their attention with the flash and roar of our guns, and so to give both the natives and ourselves time to reach the steps which led to safety. But where the conical explosive bullets of the twentieth century were of no avail the poisoned arrows of the natives, dipped in the juice of stro-phanthus and steeped afterwards in decayed carrion, could succeed. Such arrows were of little avail to the hunter who attacked the beast, because their action in that torpid circulation was slow, and before its powers failed it could certainly overtake and slay its assailant. But now, as the two monsters hounded us to the very foot of the stairs, a drift of darts came whistling from every chink in the cliff above them. In a minute they were feathered with them, and yet with no sign of pain they clawed and slobbered with impotent rage at the steps which would lead them to their victims, mounting clumsily up for a few yards and then sliding down again to the ground. But at last the poison worked. One of them gave a deep rumbling groan and dropped his huge squat head on to the earth. The other bounded round in an eccentric circle with shrill, wailing cries, and then lying down writhed in agony for some minutes before it also stiffened and lay still. With yells of triumph the Indi-ans came flocking down from their caves and danced a frenzied dance of victory round the dead bodies, in mad joy that two more of the most dangerous of all their enemies had been slain. That night they cut up and removed the bodies, not to eat – for the poison was still active – but lest they should breed a pestilence. The great rep-tilian hearts, however, each as large as a cushion, still lay there, beating slowly and steadily, with a gentle rise and fall, in horrible independent life. It was upon the third day that the ganglia ran down and the dreadful things were still.

Some day, when I have a better desk than a meat-tin and more helpful tools than a worn stub of pencil and a last, tattered note-book, I will write some fuller account of the Accala Indians – of our life amongst them, and of the glimpses which we had of the strange conditions of wondrous Maple White Land. Memory, at least, will never fail me, for so long as the breath of life is in me every hour and every action of that period will stand out as hard and clear as do the first strange happenings of our childhood. No new impressions could efface those which are so deeply cut. When the time comes I will describe that wondrous moonlit night upon the great lake when a young ichthyosaurus – a strange creature, half seal, half fish, to look at, with bone-covered eyes on each side of his snout, and a third eye fixed upon the top of his head – was entangled in an Indian net, and nearly upset our canoe before we towed it ashore; the same night that a green water-snake shot out from the rushes and carried off in its coils the steersman of Challenger's canoe. I will tell, too, of the great nocturnal white thing – to this day we do not know whether it was beast or reptile – which lived in a vile swamp to the east of the lake, and flitted about with a faint phosphorescent glimmer in the darkness. The Indians were so terrified of it that they would not go near the place, and, though we twice made expeditions and saw it each time, we could not make our way through the deep marsh in which it lived. I can only say that it seemed to be larger than a cow and had the strangest musky odour. I will tell also of the huge bird which chased Challenger to the shelter of the rocks one day – a great running bird, far taller than an ostrich, with a vulture-like neck and cruel head which made it a walking death. As Challenger climbed to safety one dart of that savage curving beak shore off the heel of his boot as if it had been cut with a chisel. This time at least modern weapons prevailed and the great creature, twelve feet from head to foot – phororachus its name, according to our panting but exultant Professor – went down before Lord Roxton's rifle in a flurry of waving feathers and kicking limbs, with two remorseless yellow eyes glaring up from the midst of it. May I live to see that flattened vicious skull in its own niche amid the trophies of the Albany. Finally, I will surely give some account of the toxodon, the giant ten-foot guinea pig, with projecting chisel teeth, which we killed as it drank in the grey of the morning by the side of the lake.

All this I shall some day write at fuller length, and amidst these more stirring days I would tenderly sketch in those lovely summer evenings, when with the deep blue sky above us we lay in good comradeship among the long grasses by the wood and marvelled at the strange fowl that swept over us and the quaint new creatures which crept from their burrows to watch us, while above us the boughs of the bushes were heavy with luscious fruit, and below us strange and lovely flowers peeped at us from among the herbage; or those long moonlit nights when we lay out upon the shimmering surface of the great lake and watched with wonder and awe the huge circles rippling out from the sudden splash of some fantastic monster; or the greenish gleam, far down in the deep water, of some strange creature upon the confines of darkness. These are the scenes which my mind and my pen will dwell upon in every detail at some future day.

But, you will ask, why these experiences and why this delay, when you and your comrades should have been occupied day and night in the devising of some means by which you could return to the outer world? My answer is, that there was not one of us who was not working for this end, but that our work had been in vain. One fact we had very speedily discovered: The Indians would do nothing to help us. In every other way they were our friends – one might almost say our devoted slaves – but when it was suggested that they should help us to make and carry a plank which would bridge the chasm, or when we wished to get from them thongs of leather or liana to weave ropes which might help us, we were met by a good-humoured, but an invincible, refusal. They would smile, twinkle their eyes, shake their heads, and there was the end of it. Even the old chief met us with the same obstinate denial, and it was only Maretas, the youngster whom we had saved, who looked wistfully at us and told us by his gestures that he was grieved for our thwarted wishes. Ever since their crowning triumph with the ape-men they looked upon us as supermen, who bore victory in the tubes of strange weapons, and they believed that so long as we remained with them good fortune would be theirs. A little red-skinned wife and a cave of our own were freely offered to each of us if we would but forget our own people and dwell for ever upon the plateau. So far all had been kindly, however far apart our desires might be; but we felt well assured that our actual plans of a descent must be kept secret, for we had reason to fear that at the last they might try to hold us by force.

In spite of the danger from dinosaurs (which is not great save at night, for as I may have said before they are nocturnal in their habits) I have twice in the last three weeks been over to our old camp in order to see our negro who still kept watch and ward below the cliff. My eyes strained eagerly across the great plain in the hope of seeing afar off the help for which we had prayed. But the long cactus-strewn levels still stretched away, empty and bare, to the distant line of the cane-brake.

'They will come soon now, Massa Malone. Before another week pass Indian come back and bring rope and fetch you down.' Such was the cheery cry of our excellent Zambo.

I had one strange experience as I came from this second visit which had involved my being away for a night from my companions. I was returning along the well-remembered route, and had reached a spot within a mile or so of the marsh of the pterodactyls, when I saw an extraordinary object approaching me. It was a man who walked inside a framework made of bent canes so that he was enclosed on all sides in a bell-shaped cage. As I drew nearer I was more amazed still to see that it was Lord John Roxton. When he saw me he slipped from under his curious protection and came towards me laughing, and yet, as I thought, with some confusion in his manner.

'Well, young fellah,' said he, 'who would have thought of meetin' you up here?'

'What in the world are you doing?' I asked.

'Visitin' my friends, the pterodactyls,' said he.

'But why?'

'Interestin' beasts, don't you think? But unsociable! Nasty rude ways with strangers, as you may remember. So I rigged this framework which keeps them from bein' too pressin' in their attentions.'

'But what do you want in the swamp?'

He looked at me with a very questioning eye, and I read hesitation in his face.

'Don't you think other people besides Professors can want to know things?' he said at last. 'I'm studyin' the pretty dears. That's enough for you.'

'No offence,' said I.

His good-humour returned and he laughed.

'No offence, young fellah. I'm goin' to get a young devil chick for Challenger. That's one of my jobs. No, I don't want your company. I'm safe in this cage, and you are not. So long, and I'll be back in camp by nightfall.'

He turned away and I left him wandering on through the wood with his extraordinary cage around him.

If Lord John's behaviour at this time was strange, that of Challenger was more so. I may say that he seemed to possess an extraordinary fascination for the Indian women, and that he always carried a large spreading palm branch with which he beat them off as if they were flies, when their attentions became too pressing. To see him walking, like a comic opera Sultan, with this badge of authority in his hand, his black beard bristling in front of him, his toes pointing at each step, and a train of wide-eyed Indian girls behind him, clad in their slender drapery of bark cloth, is one of the most grotesque of all the pictures which I will carry back with me. As to Summerlee, he was absorbed in the insect and bird life of the plateau, and spent his whole time (save that considerable portion which was devoted to abusing Challenger for not getting us out of our difficulties) in cleaning and mounting his specimens.

Challenger had been in the habit of walking off by himself every morning and returning from time to time with looks of portentous solemnity, as one who bears the full weight of a great enterprise upon his shoulders. One day, palm branch in hand, and his crowd of adoring devotees behind him, he led us down to his hidden workshop and took us into the secret of his plans.

The place was a small clearing in the centre of a palm grove. In this was one of those boiling mud geysers which I have already described. Around its edge were scattered a number of leathern thongs cut from iguanodon hide, and a large collapsed membrane which proved to be the dried and scraped stomach of one of the great fish lizards from the lake. This huge sack had been sewn up at one end and only a small orifice left at the other. Into this opening several bamboo canes had been inserted and the other ends of these canes were in contact with conical clay funnels which collected the gas bubbling up through the mud of the geyser. Soon the flaccid organ began to slowly expand and show such a tendency to upward movements that Challenger fastened the cords which held it to the trunks of the surrounding trees. In half an hour a good-sized gas-bag had been formed, and the jerking and straining upon the thongs showed that it was capable of considerable lift. Challenger, like a glad father in the presence of his first-born, stood smiling and stroking his beard in silent, self-satisfied content as he gazed at the creation of his brain. It was Summerlee who first broke the silence.

'You don't mean us to go up in that thing, Challenger?' said he, in an acid voice.

'I mean, my dear Summerlee, to give you such a demonstration of its powers that after seeing it you will, I am sure, have no hesitation in trusting yourself to it.'

'You can put it right out of your head now, at once,' said Summerlee with decision; 'nothing on earth would induce me to commit such a folly. Lord John, I trust that you will not countenance such madness?'

'Dooced ingenious, I call it,' said our peer. 'I'd like to see how it works.'

'So you shall,' said Challenger. 'For some days I have exerted my whole brain force upon the problem of how we shall descend these cliffs. We have satisfied ourselves that we cannot climb down and that there is no tunnel. We are also unable to construct any kind of bridge which may take us back to the pinnacle from which we came. How then shall I find a means to convey us? Some little time ago I had remarked to our young friend here that free hydrogen was evolved from the geyser. The idea of a balloon naturally followed. I was, I will admit, somewhat baffled by the difficulty of discovering an envelope to contain the gas, but the contemplation of the immense entrails of these reptiles supplied me with a solution to the problem. Behold the result!'

He put one hand in the front of his ragged jacket and pointed proudly with the other.

By this time the gas-bag had swollen to a goodly rotundity and was jerking strongly upon its lashings.

'Midsummer madness!' snorted Summerlee.

Lord John was delighted with the whole idea. 'Clever old dear, ain't he?' he whispered to me, and then louder to Challenger. 'What about a car?'

'The car will be my next care. I have already planned how it is to be made and attached. Meanwhile I will simply show you how capable my apparatus is of supporting the weight of each of us.'

'All of us, surely?'

'No it is part of my plan that each in turn shall descend as in a parachute, and the balloon be drawn back by means which I shall have no difficulty in perfecting. If it will support the weight of one and let him gently down, it will have done all that is required of it. I will now show you its capacity in that direction.'

He brought out a lump of basalt of a considerable size, constructed in the middle so that a cord could be easily attached to it. This cord was the one which we had brought with us on the plateau after we had used it for climbing the pinnacle. It was over a hundred feet long, and though it was thin it was very strong. He had prepared a sort of collar of leather with many straps depending from it. This collar was placed over the dome of the balloon, and the hanging thongs were gathered together below, so that the pressure of any weight would be diffused over a considerable surface. Then the lump of basalt was fastened to the thongs and the rope was allowed to hang from the end of it, being passed three times round the Professor's arm.

'I will now,' said Challenger, with a smile of pleased anticipation, 'demonstrate the carrying power of my balloon.' As he said so he cut with a knife the various lashings that held it.

Never was our expedition in more imminent danger of complete annihilation. The inflated membrane shot up with frightful velocity into the air. In an instant Challenger was pulled off his feet and dragged after it. I had just time to throw my arms round his ascending waist when I was myself whipped up into the air. Lord John had me with a rat-trap grip round the legs, but I felt that he also was coming off the ground. For a moment I had a vision of four adventurers floating like a string of sausages over the land that they had explored. But, happily, there were limits to the strain which the rope would stand, though none apparently to the lifting powers of this infernal machine. There was a sharp crack, and we were in a heap upon the ground with coils of rope all over us. When we were able to stagger to our feet we saw far off in the deep blue sky one dark spot where the lump of basalt was speeding upon its way.

'Splendid!' cried the undaunted Challenger, rubbing his injured arm. 'A most thorough and satisfactory demonstration! I could not have anticipated such a success. Within a week, gentlemen, I promise that a second balloon will be prepared, and that you can count upon taking in safety and comfort the first stage of our homeward journey.'

So far I have written each of the foregoing events as it occurred. Now I am rounding off my narrative from the old camp, where Zambo has waited so long, with all our difficulties and dangers left like a dream behind us upon the summit of those vast ruddy crags which tower above our heads. We have descended in safety, though in a most unexpected fashion, and all is well with us. In six weeks or two months we shall be in London, and it is possible that this letter may not reach you much earlier than we do ourselves. Already our hearts yearn and our spirits fly towards the great mother city which holds so much that is dear to us.

It was on the very evening of our perilous adventure with Challenger's home-made balloon that the change came in our fortunes. I have said that the one person from whom we had had some sign of sympathy in our attempts to get away was the young chief whom we had rescued. He alone had no desire to hold us against our will in a strange land. He had told us as much by his expressive language of signs. That evening, after dusk, he came down to our little camp, handed me (for some reason he had always shown his attentions to me, perhaps because I was the one who was nearest his age) a small roll of the bark of a tree, and then pointing solemnly up at the row of caves above him, he had put his finger to his lips as a sign of secrecy and had stolen back again to his people.

I took the slip of bark to the firelight and we examined it together. It was about a foot square, and on the inner side there was a singular arrangement of lines, which I here reproduce:

They were neatly done in charcoal upon the white surface, and looked to me at first sight like some sort of rough musical score.

'Whatever it is, I can swear that it is of importance to us,' said I. 'I could read that on his face as he gave it.'

'Unless we have come upon a primitive practical joker,' Summerlee suggested, 'which I should think would be one of the most elementary developments of man.'

'It is clearly some sort of script,' said Challenger.

'Looks like a guinea puzzle competition,' remarked Lord John, craning his neck to have a look at it. When suddenly he stretched out his hand and seized the puzzle.

'By George!' he cried, 'I believe I've got it. The boy guessed right the very first time. See here! How many marks are on that paper? Eighteen. Well, if you come to think of it there are eighteen cave openings on the hill-side above us.'

'He pointed up to the caves when he gave it to me,' said I.

'Well, that settles it. This is a chart of the caves. What! Eighteen of them all in a row, some short, some deep, some branching, same as we saw them. It's a map, and here's a cross on it. What's the cross for? It is placed to mark one that is much deeper than the others.'

'One that goes through,' I cried.

'I believe our young friend has read the riddle,' said Challenger. 'If the cave does not go through I do not understand why this person, who has every reason to mean us well, should have drawn our attention to it. But if it *does* go through and comes out at the corresponding point on the other side, we should not have more than a hundred feet to descend.'

'A hundred feet!' grumbled Summerlee.

'Well, our rope is still more than a hundred feet long,' I cried. 'Surely we could get down.'

'How about the Indians in the cave?' Summerlee objected.

'There are no Indians in any of the caves above our heads,' said I. 'They are all used as barns and storehouses. Why should we not go up now at once and spy out the land?'

There is a dry bituminous wood upon the plateau – a species of araucaria, according to our botanist – which is always used by the Indians for torches. Each of us picked up a faggot of this, and we made our way up weed-covered steps to the particular cave which was marked in the drawing. It was, as I had said, empty, save for a great number of enormous bats, which flapped round our heads as we advanced into it. As we had no desire to draw the attention of the Indians to our proceedings, we stumbled along in the dark until we had gone round several curves and penetrated a considerable distance into the cavern. Then, at last, we lit our torches. It was a beautiful dry tunnel, with smooth grey walls covered with native symbols, a curved roof which arched over our heads, and white glistening sand beneath our feet. We hurried eagerly along it until, with a deep groan of bitter disappointment, we were brought to a halt. A sheer wall of rock had appeared before us, with no chink through which a mouse could have slipped. There was no escape for us there.

We stood with bitter hearts staring at this unexpected obstacle. It was not the result of any convulsion, as in the case of the ascending tunnel. It was, and had always been, a *cul-de-sac*.

'Never mind, my friends,' said the indomitable Challenger. 'You have still my firm promise of a balloon.'

Summerlee groaned.

'Can we be in the wrong cave?' I suggested.

'No use, young fellah,' said Lord John, with his finger on our chart. 'Seventeen from the right and second from the left. This is the cave sure enough.'

I looked at the mark to which his finger pointed, and gave a sudden cry of joy.

'I believe I have it! Follow me! Follow me!'

I hurried back along the way we had come, my torch in my hand. 'Here,' said I, pointing to some matches upon the ground, 'is where we lit up.'

'Exactly.'

'Well, it is marked as a forked cave, and in the darkness we passed the fork before the torches were lit. On the right side as we go out we should find the longer arm.'

It was as I had said. We had not gone thirty yards before a great black opening loomed in the wall. We turned into it to find that we were in a much larger passage than before. Along it we hurried in breathless impatience for many hundreds of yards. Then, suddenly, in the black darkness of the arch in front of us we saw a gleam of dark red light. We stared in amazement. A sheet of steady flame seemed to cross the passage and to bar our way. We hastened towards it. No sound, no heat, no movement came from it, but still the great luminous curtain glowed before us, silvering all the cave and turning the sand to powdered jewels, until as we drew closer it discovered a circular edge.

'The moon, by George!' cried Lord John. 'We are through boys! We are through!'

It was indeed the full moon which shone straight down the aperture which opened upon the cliffs. It was a small rift, not larger than a window, but it was enough for all our purposes. As we craned our necks through it we could see that the descent was not a very difficult one, and that the level ground was no very great way below us. It was no wonder that from below we had not observed the place, as the cliffs curved overhead and an ascent at the spot would have seemed so impossible as to discourage close inspection. We satisfied ourselves that with the help of our rope we could find our way down, and then returned, rejoicing, to our camp to make our preparations for the next evening.

What we did we had to do quickly and secretly, since even at this last hour the Indians might hold us back. Our stores we would leave behind us, save only our guns and cartridges. But Challenger had some unwieldy stuff which he ardently desired to take with him, and one particular package, of which I may not speak, which gave us more labour than any. Slowly the day passed, but when the darkness fell we were ready for our departure. With much labour we got our things up the steps, and then, looking back, took one last long survey of that strange land, soon I fear to be vulgarised, the prey of hunter and prospector, but to each of us a dreamland of glamour and romance, a land where we had dared much, suffered much, and learned much – *our* land, as we shall ever fondly call it. Along upon our left the neighbouring caves each threw out its ruddy cheery firelight into the gloom. From the slope below us rose the voices of the Indians as they laughed and sang. Beyond was the long sweep of the woods, and in the centre, shimmering vaguely through the gloom, was the great lake, the mother of strange monsters. Even as we looked a high whickering cry, the call of some weird animal, rang clear out of the darkness. It was the very voice of Maple White

Land bidding us good-bye. We turned and plunged into the cave which led to home.

Two hours later, we, our packages, and all we owned, were at the foot of the cliff. Save for Challenger's luggage we had never a difficulty. Leaving it all where we descended, we started at once for Zambo's camp. In the early morning we approached it, but only to find, to our amazement, not one fire but a dozen upon the plain. The rescue party had arrived. There were twenty Indians from the river, with stakes, ropes, and all that could be useful for bridging the chasm. At least we shall have no difficulty now in carrying our packages, when to-morrow we begin to make our way back to the Amazon.

And so, in humble and thankful mood, I close this account. Our eyes have seen great wonders and our souls are chastened by what we have endured. Each is in his own way a better and deeper man. It may be that when we reach Para we shall stop to refit. If we do, this letter will be a mail ahead. If not, it will reach London on the very day that I do. In either case, my dear Mr. McArdle, I hope very soon to shake you by the hand.

CHAPTER XVI

A Procession! A Procession!

I SHOULD WISH TO PLACE upon record here our gratitude to all our friends upon the Amazon for the very great kindness and hospitality which was shown to us upon our return journey. Very particularly would I thank Signor Penalosa and other officials of the Brazilian Government for the special arrangements by which we were helped upon our way, and Signor Pereira of Para, to whose forethought we owe the complete outfit for a decent appearance in the civilized world which we found ready for us at that town. It seemed a poor return for all the courtesy which we encountered that we should deceive our hosts and benefactors, but under the circumstances we had really no alternative, and I hereby tell them that they will only waste their time and their money if they attempt to follow upon our traces. Even the names have been altered in our accounts, and I am very sure that no one, from the most careful study of them, could come within a thousand miles of our unknown land.

The excitement which had been caused through those parts of South America which we had to traverse was imagined by us to be purely local, and I can assure our friends in England that we had no notion of the uproar which the mere rumour of our experiences had caused through Europe. It was not until *Ivernia* was within five hundred miles of Southampton that the wireless messages from paper after paper and agency after agency, offering huge prices for a short return message as to our actual results, showed us how strained was the attention not only of the scientific world but of the general public. It was agreed among us, however, that no definite statement should be given to the Press until we had met the members of the Zoological Institute, since as delegates it was our clear duty to give our first report to the body from which we had received our commission of investigation. Thus, although we found Southampton full of Pressmen, we absolutely refused to give any information, which had the natural effect of focusing public attention upon the meeting which was advertised for the evening of November 7th. For this gathering, the Zoological Hall, which had been the scene of the inception of our task, was found to be far too small, and it was only in the Queen's Hall in Regent Street that accommodation could be found. It is now common knowledge that the promoters might have ventured upon the Albert Hall and still found their space too scanty.

It was for the second evening after our arrival that the great meeting had been fixed. For the first, we had each, no doubt, our own pressing personal affairs to absorb us. Of mine I cannot yet speak. It may be that as it stands further from me I may think of it, and even speak of it, with less emotion. I have shown the reader in the beginning of this narrative where lay the springs of my action. It is but right, perhaps, that I should carry on the tale and show also the results. And yet the day may come when I would not have it otherwise. At least I have been driven forth to take part in a wondrous adventure, and I cannot but be thankful to the force that drove me.

And now I turn to the last supreme eventful moment of our adventure. As I was racking my brain as to how I should best describe it, my eyes fell upon the issue of my own journal for the morning of the 8th of November with the full and excellent account of my friend and fellow-reporter Macdona. What can I do better than transcribe his narrative – head-lines and all? I admit that the paper was exuberant in the matter, out of compliment to its own enterprise in sending a correspondent, but the other great dailies were hardly less full in their account. Thus, then, friend Mac in his report:

THE NEW WORLD
GREAT MEETING AT THE QUEEN'S HALL
SCENES OF UPROAR
EXTRAORDINARY INCIDENT
WHAT WAS IT?
NOCTURNAL RIOT IN REGENT STREET

(Special)

'The much-discussed meeting of the Zoological Institute, convened to hear the report of the Committee of Investigation sent out last year to South America to test the assertions made by Professor Challenger as to the continued existence of prehistoric life upon that continent, was held last night in the greater Queen's Hall, and it is safe to say that it is likely to be a red-letter date in the history of Science, for the proceedings were of so remarkable and sensational a character that no one present is ever likely to forget them.' (Oh, brother scribe Macdona, what a monstrous opening sentence!) 'The tickets were theoretically confined to members and their friends, but the latter is an elastic term, and long before eight o'clock, the hour fixed for the commencement of the proceedings, all parts of the Great Hall were tightly packed. The general public, however, which most unreasonably entertained a grievance at having been excluded, stormed the doors at a quarter to eight, after a prolonged *mêlée* in which several people were injured, including Inspector Scoble of H Division, whose leg was unfortunately broken. After this unwarrantable invasion, which not only filled every passage, but even intruded upon the space set apart for the Press, it is estimated that nearly five thousand people awaited the arrival of the travellers. When they eventually appeared, they took their places in the front of a platform which already contained all the leading scientific men, not only of this country, but of France and of Germany. Sweden was also represented, in the person of Professor Sergius, the famous Zoologist of the University of Upsala. The entrance of the four heroes of the occasion was the signal for a remarkable demonstration of welcome, the whole audience rising and cheering for some minutes. An acute observer might, however, have detected some signs of dissent amid the applause, and gathered that the proceedings were likely to become more lively than harmonious. It may safely be prophesied, however, that no one could have foreseen the extraordinary turn which they were actually to take.

'Of the appearance of the four wanderers little need be said, since their photographs have for some time been appearing in all the papers. They bear few traces of the hardships which they are said to have undergone. Professor Challenger's beard may be more shaggy, Professor Summerlee's features more ascetic, Lord John Roxton's figure gaunt, and all three may be burned to a darker tint than when they left our shores, but each appeared to be in most excellent health. As to our own representative, the well-known athlete and international Rugby football player, E. D. Malone, he looks trained to a hair, and as he surveyed the crowd a smile of good-humoured contentment pervaded his honest but homely face.' (All right, Mac, wait till I get you alone!)

'When quiet had been restored and the audience resumed their seats after the ovation which they had given to the travellers, the chairman, the Duke of Durham, addressed the meeting. "He would not," he said, "stand for more than a moment between that vast assembly and the treat which lay before them. It was not for him to anticipate what Professor Summerlee, who was the spokesman of the committee, had to say to them, but it was common rumour that their expedition had been crowned by extraordinary success." (Applause.) "Apparently the age of romance was not dead, and there was common ground upon which the wildest imaginings of the novelist could meet the actual scientific investigations of the searcher for truth. He would only add, before he sat down, that he rejoiced – and all of them would rejoice – that these gentlemen had returned safe and sound from their difficult and dangerous task, for it cannot be denied that any disaster to such an expedition would have inflicted a well-nigh irreparable loss to the cause of zoological science." ' (Great applause, in which Professor Challenger was observed to join.)

'Professor Summerlee's rising was the signal for another extraordinary outbreak of enthusiasm, which broke out again at intervals throughout his address. That address will not be given *in extenso* in these columns, for the reason that a full account of the whole adventures of the expedition is being published as a supplement from the pen of our own special correspondent. Some general indications will therefore suffice. Having described the genesis of their journey, and paid a handsome tribute to his friend Professor Challenger, coupled with an apology for the incredulity with which his assertions, now fully vindicated, had been received, he gave the actual course of their journey, carefully withholding such information as would aid the public in any attempt to locate this remarkable plateau. Having described, in general terms, their course from the main river up to the time that they actually reached the base of the cliffs, he enthralled his hearers by his account of the difficulties encountered by the expedition in their repeated attempts to mount them, and finally described how they succeeded in their desperate endeavours, which cost the lives of their two devoted half-breed servants.' (This amazing reading of the affair was the result of Summerlee's endeavours to avoid raising any questionable matter at the meeting.)

'Having conducted his audience in fancy to the summit, and marooned them there by reason of the fall of their bridge, the Professor proceeded to describe both the horrors and the attractions of that remarkable land. Of personal adventures he said little, but laid stress upon the rich harvest reaped by Science in the observations of the wonderful beast, bird, insect and plant life of the plateau. Peculiarly rich in the coleoptera and in the lepidoptera, forty-six new species of the one and ninety-four of the other had been secured in the course of a few weeks. It was, however, in the larger animals, and especially in the larger animals supposed to have been long extinct, that the interest of the public was naturally centred. Of these he was able to give a goodly list, but had little doubt that it would be largely extended when the place had been more thoroughly investigated. He and his companions had seen at least a dozen creatures, most of them at a distance, which corresponded with nothing at present known to Science. These would in time be duly classified and examined. He instanced a snake, the cast skin of which, deep purple in colour, was fifty-one feet in length, and mentioned a white creature, supposed to be mammalian, which gave forth well-marked phosphorescence in the darkness; also a large black moth, the bite of which was supposed by the Indians to be highly poisonous. Setting aside these entirely new forms of life, the plateau was very rich in known prehistoric forms, dating back in some cases to Early Jurassic times. Among these he mentioned the gigantic and grotesque stegosaurus, seen once by Mr. Malone at a drinking-place by the lake, and drawn in the sketchbook of that adventurous American who had first penetrated this unknown world. He described also the iguanodon and the pterodactyl – two of the first of the wonders which they had encountered. He then thrilled the assembly by some account of the terrible carnivorous dinosaurs, which had on more than one occasion pursued members of the party, and which were the most formidable of all the creatures which they had encountered. Thence he passed to the huge and ferocious bird, the phororachus, and to the great elk which still roams upon this upland. It was not, however, until he sketched the mysteries of the central lake that the full interest and enthusiasm of the audience were aroused. One had to pinch oneself to be sure that one was awake as one heard this sane and practical Professor in cold, measured tones describing the monstrous three-eyed fish-lizards and the huge water-snakes which inhabit this enchanted sheet of water. Next he touched upon the Indians, and upon the extraordinary colony of anthropoid apes, which might be looked upon as an advance upon the pithecanthropus of Java, and as coming therefore nearer than any known form to that hypothetical creation, the missing link. Finally he described, amongst some merriment, the ingenious but highly dangerous aeronautic invention of Professor Challenger, and wound up a most memorable address by an account of the methods by which the committee did at last find their way back to civilization.

'It had been hoped that the proceedings would end there, and that a vote of thanks and congratulation, moved by Professor Sergius, of Upsala University, would be duly seconded and carried; but it was soon evident that the course of events was not destined to flow so smoothly. Symptons of opposition had been evident from time to time during the evening, and now Dr. James Illingworth, of Edinburgh, rose in the centre of the hall. Dr. Illingworth asked whether an amendment should not be taken before a resolution.

'The Chairman: "Yes, sir, if there must be an amendment."

'Dr. Illingworth: "Your Grace, there must be an amendment."

'The Chairman: "Then let us take it at once."

'Professor Summerlee (springing to his feet): "Might I explain, your Grace, that this man is my personal enemy ever since our controversy in the 'Quarterly Journal of Science' as to the true nature of Bathybius?"

'The Chairman: "I fear I cannot go into personal matters. Proceed."

'Dr. Illingworth was imperfectly heard in part of his remarks on account of the strenuous opposition of the friends of the explorers. Some attempts were also made to pull him down. Being a man of enormous physique, however, and possessed of a very powerful voice, he dominated the tumult and succeeded in finishing his speech. It was clear, from the moment of his rising, that he had a number of friends and sympathisers in the hall, though they formed a minority in the audience. The attitude of the greater part of the public might be described as one of attentive neutrality.

'Dr. Illingworth began his remarks by expressing his high appreciation of the scientific work both of Professor Challenger and of Professor Summerlee. He much regretted that any personal bias should have been read into his remarks, which were entirely dictated by his desire for scientific truth. His position, in fact, was substantially the same as that taken up by Professor Summerlee at the last meeting. At that last meeting Professor Challenger had made certain assertions which had been queried by his colleague. Now this colleague came forward himself with the same assertions and expected them to remain unquestioned. Was this reasonable? ("Yes," "No," and prolonged interruption, during which Professor Challenger was heard from the Press box to ask leave from the Chairman to put Dr. Illingworth into the street.) A year ago one man said certain things. Now four men said other and more startling ones. Was this to constitute a final proof where the matters in question were of the most revolutionary and incredible character? There had been recent examples of travellers arriving from the unknown with certain tales which had been too readily accepted. Was the London Zoological Institute to place itself in this position? He admitted that the members of the committee were men of character. But human nature was very complex. Even Professors might be misled by the desire for notoriety. Like moths, we all love best to flutter in the light. Heavy-game shots liked to be in a position to cap the tales of their rivals, and journalists were not averse from sensational *coups*, even when imagination had to aid fact in the process. Each member of the committee had his own motive for making the most of his results. ("Shame! shame!") He had no desire to be offensive. ("You are!" and interruption.) The corroboration of these wondrous tales was really of the most slender description. What did it amount to? Some photographs. Was it possible that in this age of ingenious manipulation photographs could be accepted as evidence? What more? We have a story of a flight and a descent by ropes which precluded the production of larger specimens. It was ingenious, but not convincing. It was understood that Lord John Roxton claimed to have the skull of a phororachus. He could only say that he would like to see that skull.

'Lord John Roxton: "Is this fellow calling me a liar?" (Uproar.)

'The Chairman: "Order! order! Dr. Illingworth, I must direct you to bring your remarks to a conclusion and to move your amendment."

'Dr. Illingworth: "Your Grace, I have more to say, but I bow to your ruling. I move, then, that, while Professor Summerlee be thanked for his interesting address, the whole matter shall be regarded as '*non-proven*,' and shall be referred back to a larger, and possibly more reliable Committee of Investigation."

'It is difficult to describe the confusion caused by this amendment. A large section of the audience expressed their indignation at such a slur upon the travellers by noisy shouts of dissent and cries of "Don't put it!" "Withdraw!" "Turn him out!" On the other hand, the malcontents — and it cannot be denied that they were fairly numerous — cheered for the amendment, with cries of "Order!" "Chair!" and "Fair play!" A scuffle broke out in the back benches, and blows were freely exchanged among the medical students who crowded that part of the hall. It was only the moderating influence of the presence of large numbers of ladies which prevented an absolute riot. Suddenly, however, there was a pause, a hush, and then complete silence. Professor Challenger was on his feet. His appearance and manner are peculiarly arresting, and as he raised his hand for order the whole audience settled down expectantly to give him a hearing.

' "It will be within the recollection of many present," said Professor Challenger, "that similar foolish and unmannerly scenes marked the last meeting at which I have been able to address them. On that occasion Professor Summerlee was the chief offender, and though he is now chastened and contrite, the matter could not be entirely forgotten. I have heard to-night similar, but even more offensive, sentiments from the person who has just sat down, and though it is a conscious effort of self-effacement to come down to that person's mental level, I will endeavour to do so, in order to allay any reasonable doubt which could possibly exist in the minds of anyone." (Laughter and interruption.) "I need not remind this audience that, though Professor Summerlee, as the head of the Committee of Investigation, has been put up to speak to-night, still it is I who am the real prime mover in this business, and that it is mainly to me that any successful result must be ascribed. I have safely conducted these three gentlemen to the spot mentioned, and I have, as you have heard, convinced them of the accuracy of my previous account. We had hoped that we should find upon our return that no one was so dense as to dispute our joint conclusion. Warned, however, by my previous experience, I have not come without such proofs as may convince a reasonable man. As explained by Professor Summerlee, our cameras have been tampered with by the ape-men when they ransacked our camp, and most of our negatives ruined." (Jeers, laughter, and "Tell us another!" from the back.) "I have mentioned the ape-men, and I cannot forbear from saying that some of the sounds which now meet my ears bring back most vividly to my recollection my experiences with those interesting creatures." (Laughter.) "In spite of the destruction of so many invaluable negatives, there still remains in our collection a certain number of corroborative photographs showing the conditions of life upon the plateau. Did they accuse them of having forged these photographs?" (A voice, "Yes," and considerable interruption which ended in several men being put out of the hall.) "The negatives were open to the inspection of experts. But what other evidence had they? Under the conditions of their escape it was naturally impossible to bring a large amount of baggage, but they had rescued Professor Summerlee's collections of butterflies and beetles, containing many new species. Was this not evidence?" (Several voices, "No.") "Who said no?"

'Dr. Illingworth (rising): "Our point is that such collection might have been made in other places than a prehistoric plateau." (Applause.)

'Professor Challenger: "No doubt, sir, we have to bow to your scientific authority, although I must admit that the name is unfamiliar. Passing, then, both the photographs and the entomological collection, I come to the varied and accurate information which we bring with us upon points which have never before been elucidated. For example, upon the domestic habits of the pterodactyl – (A voice: "Bosh," and uproar) – I say, that upon the domestic habits of the pterodactyl we can throw a flood of light. I can exhibit to you from my portfolio a picture of that creature taken from life which would convince you –"

'Dr. Illingworth: "No picture could convince us of anything."

'Professor Challenger: "You would require to see the thing itself?"

'Dr. Illingworth: "Undoubtedly."

'Professor Challenger: "And you would accept that?"

'Dr. Illingworth (laughing): "Beyond a doubt."

'It was at this point that the sensation of the evening arose – a sensation so dramatic that it can never have been paralleled in the history of scientific gatherings. Professor Challenger raised his hand in the air as a signal, and at once our colleague, Mr. E. D. Malone, was observed to rise and to make his way to the back of the platform. An instant later he re-appeared in company of a gigantic negro, the two of them bearing between them a large square packing-case. It was evidently of great weight, and was slowly carried forward and placed in front of the Professor's chair. All sound had hushed in the audience and everyone was absorbed in the spectacle before them. Professor Challenger drew off the top of the case, which formed a sliding lid. Peering down into the box he snapped his fingers several times and was heard from the Press seat to say, "Come, then, pretty, pretty!" in a coaxing voice. An instant later, with a scratching, rattling sound, a most horrible and loathsome creature appeared from below and perched itself upon the side of the case. Even the unexpected fall of the Duke of Durham into the orchestra, which occurred at this moment, could not distract the petrified attention of the vast audience. The face of the creature was like the wildest gargoyle that the imagination of a mad mediæval builder could have conceived. It was malicious, horrible, with two small red eyes as bright as points of burning coal. Its long, savage mouth, which was held half-open, was full of a double row of shark-like teeth. Its shoulders were humped, and round them were draped what appeared to be a faded grey shawl. It was the devil of our childhood in person. There was a turmoil in the audience – someone screamed, two ladies in the front row fell senseless from their chairs, and there was a general movement upon the platform to follow their chairman into the orchestra. For a moment there was danger of a general panic. Professor Challenger threw up his hands to still the commotion, but the movement alarmed the creature beside him. Its strange shawl suddenly unfurled, spread, and fluttered as a pair of leathery wings. Its owner grabbed at its legs, but too late to hold it. It had sprung from the perch and was circling slowly round the Queen's Hall with a dry, leathery flapping of its ten-foot wings, while a putrid and insidious odour pervaded the room. The cries of the people in the galleries, who were alarmed at the near approach of those glowing eyes and that murderous beak, excited the creature to a frenzy. Faster and faster it flew, beating against the walls and chandeliers in a blind frenzy of alarm. "The window! For heaven's sake shut that window!" roared the Professor from the platform, dancing, and wringing his hands in an agony of apprehension. Alas, his warning was too late! In a moment the creature, beating and bumping along the wall like a huge moth within a gas shade, came upon the opening, squeezed its hideous bulk through it, and was gone. Professor Challenger fell back into his chair with his face buried in his hands, while the audience gave one long, deep sigh of relief as they realized that the incident was over.

'Then – oh! how shall one describe what took place then – when the full exuberance of the majority and the full reaction of the minority united to make one great wave of enthusiasm, which rolled from the back of the hall, gathering volume as it came, swept over the orchestra, submerged the platform, and carried the four heroes away upon its crest?' (Good for you, Mac.) 'If the audience had done less than justice, surely it made ample amends. Everyone was on his feet. Everyone was moving, shouting, gesticulating. A dense crowd of cheering men were round the four travellers. "Up with them! up with them!" cried a hundred voices. In a moment four figures shot up above the crowd. In vain they strove to break loose. They were held in their lofty places of honour. It would have been hard to let them down if it had been wished, so dense was the crowd around them. "Regent Street! Regent Street!" sounded the voices. There was a swirl in the packed multitude, and a slow current, bearing the four upon their shoulders, made for the door. Out in the street the scene was extraordinary. An assemblage of not less than a hundred thousand people was waiting. The close-packed throng extended from the other side of the Langham Hotel to Oxford Circus. A roar of acclamation greeted the four adventurers as they appeared, high above the heads of the people, under the vivid electric lamps outside the hall. "A procession! A procession!" was the cry. In a dense phalanx, blocking the streets from side to side, the crowd set forth, taking the route of Regent Street, Pall Mall, St. James's Street, and Piccadilly. The whole central traffic of London was held up, and many collisions were reported between the demonstrators upon the one side and the police and taxi-cabmen upon the other. Finally, it was not until after midnight that the four travellers were released at the entrance to Lord John Roxton's chambers in the Albany, and that the exuberant crowd, having sung "They are Jolly Good Fellows" in chorus, concluded their programme with "God Save the King." So ended one of the most remarkable evenings that London has seen for a considerable time.'

So far my friend Macdona; and it may be taken as a fairly accurate, if florid, account of the proceedings. As to the main incident, it was a bewildering surprise to the audience, but not, I need hardly say, to us. The reader will remember how I met Lord John Roxton upon the very occasion when, in his protective crinoline, he had gone to bring the 'Devil's chick' as he called it, for Professor Challenger. I have hinted also at the trouble which the Professor's baggage gave us when we left the plateau, and had I described our voyage I might have said a good deal of the worry we had to coax with putrid fish the appetite of our filthy companion. If I have not said much about it before, it was, of course, that the Professor's earnest desire was that no possible rumour of the unanswerable argument which we carried should be allowed to leak out until the moment came when his enemies were to be confuted.

One word as to the fate of the London pterodactyl. Nothing can be said to be certain upon this point. There is the evidence of two frightened women that it perched upon the roof of the Queen's Hall and remained there like a diabolical statue for some hours. The next day it came out in the evening papers that Private Miles, of the Coldstream Guards, on duty outside Marlborough House, had deserted his post without leave, and was therefore court-martialled. Private Miles' account, that he dropped his rifle and took to his heels down the Mall because on looking up he had suddenly seen the devil between him and the moon, was not accepted by the Court, and yet it may have a direct bearing upon the point at issue. The only other evidence which I can adduce is from the log of the S.S. *Friesland*, a Dutch-American liner, which asserts that at nine next morning, Start Point being at the time ten miles upon their starboard quarter, they were passed by something between a flying goat and a monstrous bat, which was heading at a prodigious pace south and west. If its homing instinct led it upon the right line, there can be no doubt that somewhere out in the wastes of the Atlantic the last European pterodactyl found its end.

And Gladys – oh, my Gladys! – Gladys of the mystic lake, now to be re-named the Central, for never shall she have immortality through me. Did I not always see some hard fibre in her nature? Did I not, even at the time when I was proud to obey her behest, feel that it was surely a poor love which could drive a lover to his death or the danger of it? Did I not, in my truest thoughts, always recurring and always dismissed, see past the beauty of the face, and, peering into the soul, discern the twin shadows of selfishness and of fickleness glooming at the back of it? Did she love the heroic and the spectacular for its own noble sake, or was it for the glory which might, without effort of sacrifice, be reflected upon herself? Or are these thoughts the vain wisdom which comes after the event? It was the shock of my life. For a moment it had turned me to a cynic. But already, as I write, a week has passed, and we have had our momentous interview with Lord John Roxton and – well, perhaps things might be worse.

Let me tell it in a few words. No letter or telegram had come to me at Southampton, and I reached the little villa at Streatham about ten o'clock that night in a fever of alarm. Was she dead or alive? Where were all my nightly dreams of the open arms, the smiling face, the words of praise for her man who had risked his life to humour her whim? Already I was down from the high peaks and standing flat-footed upon earth. Yet some good reasons given might still lift me to the clouds once more. I rushed down the garden path, hammered at the door, heard the voice of Gladys within, pushed past the staring maid, and strode into the sitting-room. She was seated in a low settee under the shaded standard lamp by the piano. In three steps I was across the room and had both her hands in mine.

'Gladys!' I cried, 'Gladys!'

She looked up with amazement in her face. She was altered in some subtle way. The expression of her eyes, the hard upward stare, the set of the lips, was new to me. She drew back her hands.

'What do you mean?' she said.

'Gladys!' I cried. 'What is the matter? You are my Gladys, are you not – little Gladys Hungerton?'

'No,' said she, 'I am Gladys Potts. Let me introduce you to my husband.'

How absurd life is! I found myself mechanically bowing and shaking hands with a little ginger-haired man who was coiled up in the deep arm-chair which had once been sacred to my own use. We bobbed and grinned in front of each other.

'Father lets us stay here. We are getting our house ready,' said Gladys.

'Oh, yes,' said I.

'You didn't get my letter at Para, then?'

'No, I got no letter.'

'Oh, what a pity! It would have made all clear.'

'It is quite clear,' said I.

'I've told William all about you,' said she. 'We have no secrets. I am so sorry about it. But it couldn't have been so very deep, could it, if you could go off to the other end of the world and leave me here alone. You're not crabby, are you?'

'No, no, not at all. I think I'll go.'

'Have some refreshment,' said the little man, and he added, in a confidential way, 'It's always like this, ain't it? And must be unless you had polygamy, only the other way round; you understand.' He laughed like an idiot, while I made for the door.

I was through it, when a sudden fantastic impulse came upon me, and I went back to my successful rival, who looked nervously at the electric push.

'Will you answer a question?' I asked.

'Well, within reason,' said he.

'How did you do it? Have you searched for hidden treasure, or discovered a pole, or done time on a pirate, or flown the channel, or what? Where is the glamour of romance? How did you get it?'

He stared at me with a hopeless expression upon his vacuous, good-natured, scrubby little face.

'Don't you think all this is a little too personal?' he said.

'Well, just one question,' I cried. 'What are you? What is your profession?'

'I am a solicitor's clerk,' said he. 'Second man at Johnson and Merivale's, 41, Chancery Lane.'

'Good-night!' said I, and vanished, like all disconsolate and broken-hearted heroes, into the darkness, with grief and rage and laughter all simmering within me like a boiling pot.

One more little scene, and I have done. Last night we all supped at Lord John Roxton's rooms, and sitting together afterwards we smoked in good comradeship and talked our adventures over. It was strange under these altered surroundings to see the old, well-known faces and figures. There was Challenger, with his smile of conde-scension, his drooping eyelids, his intolerant eyes, his aggressive beard, his huge chest, swelling and puffing as he laid down the law to Summerlee. And Summerlee, too, there he was with his short briar between his thin moustache and his grey goat's-beard, his worn face protruded in eager debate as he queried all Challenger's propositions. Finally, there was our host, with his rugged, eagle face, and his cold, blue, glacier eyes with always a shimmer of devil-ment and of humour down in the depths of them. Such is the last picture of them that I have carried away. It was after supper, in his own sanctum – the room of the pink radiance and the innumerable trophies – that Lord John Roxton had something to say to us. From a cupboard he had brought an old cigar box, and this he laid before him on the table.

'There's one thing,' said he, 'that maybe I should have spoken about before this, but I wanted to know a little more clearly where I was. No use to raise hopes and let them down again. But it's facts, not hopes, with us now. You may remember that day we found the pterodactyl rookery in the swamp – what? Well, somethin' in the lie of the land took my notice. Perhaps it has escaped you, so I will tell you. It was a volcanic vent full of blue clay.'

The Professors nodded.

'Well, now, in the whole world I've only had to do with one place that was a volcanic vent of blue clay. That was the great De Beers Diamond Mine of Kimberley – what? So you see I got diamonds into my head. I rigged up a contraption to hold off those stinking beasts, and I spent a happy day there with a spud. This is what I got.'

He opened his cigar-box, and tilting it over he poured about twenty or thirty rough stones, varying from the size of beans to that of chestnuts, on the table.

'Perhaps you think I should have told you then. Well, so I should, only I know there are a lot of traps for the unwary, and that stones may be of any size and yet of little value where colour and consistency are clean off. Therefore, I brought them back, and on the first day at home I took one round to Spink's and asked him to have it roughly cut and valued.'

He took a pill-box from his pocket, and spilled out of it a beautiful glittering diamond, one of the finest stones that I have ever seen.

'There's the result,' said he. 'He prices the lot at a minimum of two hundred thousand pounds. Of course it is fair shares between us. I won't hear of anythin' else. Well, Challenger, what will you do with your fifty thousand?'

'If you really persist in your generous view,' said the Professor, 'I should found a private museum, which has long been one of my dreams.'

'And you, Summerlee?'

'I would retire from teaching, and so find time for my final classification of the chalk fossils.'

'I'll use my own,' said Lord John Roxton, 'in fitting a well-formed expedition and having another look at the dear old plateau. As to you, young fellah, you, of course, will spend yours in gettin' married.'

'Not just yet,' said I, with a rueful smile. 'I think, if you will have me, that I would rather go with you.'

Lord Roxton said nothing, but a brown hand was stretched out to me across the table.

THE END

THE POISON BELT

CHAPTER I

The Blurring of the Lines

IT IS IMPERATIVE THAT NOW AT ONCE, while these stupendous events are still clear in my mind, I should set them down with that exactness of detail which time may blur. But even as I do so, I am overwhelmed by the wonder of the fact that it should be our little group of the 'Lost World' – Professor Challenger, Professor Summerlee, Lord John Roxton, and myself – who have passed through this amazing experience.

When, some years ago, I chronicled in the *Daily Gazette* our epoch-making journey in South America, I little thought that it should ever fall to my lot to tell an even stranger personal experience, one which is unique in all human annals, and must stand out in the records of history as a great peak among the humble foothills which surround it. The event itself will always be marvellous, but the circumstances that we four were together at the time of this extraordinary episode came about in a most natural and, indeed, inevitable fashion. I will explain the events which led up to it as shortly and as clearly as I can, though I am well aware that the fuller the detail upon such a subject the more welcome it will be to the reader, for the public curiosity has been and still is insatiable.

It was upon Friday, the twenty-seventh of August – a date for ever memorable in the history of the world – that I went down to the office of my paper and asked for three days' leave of absence from Mr. McArdle, who still presided over our news department. The good old Scotchman shook his head, scratched his dwindling fringe of ruddy fluff, and finally put his reluctance into words.

'I was thinking, Mr. Malone, that we could employ you to advantage these days. I was thinking there was a story that you are the only man that could handle as it should be handled.'

'I am sorry for that,' said I, trying to hide my disappointment. 'Of course if I am needed, there is an end of the matter. But the engagement was important and intimate. If I could be spared –'

'Well, I don't see that you can.'

It was bitter, but I had to put the best face I could upon it. After all, it was my own fault, for I should have known by this time that a journalist has no right to make plans of his own.

'Then I'll think no more of it,' said I, with as much cheerfulness as I could assume at so short a notice. 'What was it that you wanted me to do?'

'Well, it was just to interview that deevil of a man down at Rotherfield.'

'You don't mean Professor Challenger?' I cried.

'Aye, it's just him that I do mean. He ran young Alec Simpson, of the *Courier*, a mile down the high road last week by the collar of his coat and the slack of his breeches. You'll have read of it, likely, in the police report. Our boys would as soon interview a loose alligator in the Zoo. But you could do it, I'm thinking – an old friend like you.'

'Why,' said I, greatly relieved, 'this makes it all easy. It so happens that it was to visit Professor Challenger at Rotherfield that I was asking for leave of absence. The fact is, that it is the anniversary of our main adventure on the plateau three years ago, and he has asked our whole party down to his house to see him and celebrate the occasion.'

'Capital!' cried McArdle, rubbing his hands and beaming through his glasses. 'Then you will be able to get his opeenions out of him. In any other man I would say it was all moonshine, but the fellow has made good once, and who knows but he may again!'

'Get what out of him?' I asked. 'What has he been doing?'

'Haven't you seen his letter on "Scientific Possibeelities" in to-day's *Times*?'

'No.'

McArdle dived down and picked a copy from the floor.

'Read it aloud,' said he, indicating a column with his finger. 'I'd be glad to hear it again, for I am not sure now that I have the man's meaning clear in my head.'

This was the letter which I read to the news editor of the *Gazette*:

'SCIENTIFIC POSSIBILITIES'

'SIR, – I have read with amusement, not wholly unmixed with some less complimentary emotion, the complacent and wholly fatuous letter of James Wilson MacPhail, which has lately appeared in your columns upon the subject of the blurring of Frauenhofer's lines in the spectra both of the planets and of the fixed stars. He dismisses the matter as of no significance. To a wider intelligence it may well seem of very great possible importance – so great as to involve the ultimate welfare of every man, woman, and child upon this planet. I can hardly hope, by the use of scientific language, to convey any sense of my meaning to those ineffectual people who gather their ideas from the columns of a daily newspaper. I will endeavour, therefore, to condescend to their limitation, and to indicate the situation by the use of a homely analogy which will be within the limits of the intelligence of your readers.'

'Man, he's a wonder – a living wonder!' said McArdle, shaking his head reflectively. 'He'd put up the feathers of a sucking-dove and set up a riot in a Quaker's meeting. No wonder he has made London too hot for him. It's a peety, Mr. Malone, for it's a grand brain! Well, let's have the analogy.'

'We will suppose,' I read, 'that a small bundle of connected corks was launched in a sluggish current upon a voyage across the Atlantic. The corks drift slowly on from day to day with the same conditions all round them. If the corks were sentient we could imagine that they would consider these conditions to be permanent and assured. But we, with our superior knowledge, know that many things might happen to surprise the corks. They might possibly float up against a ship, or a sleeping whale, or become entangled in seaweed. In any case, their voyage would probably end by their being thrown up on the rocky coast of Labrador. But what could they know of all this while they drifted so gently day by day in what they thought was a limitless and homogeneous ocean?

'Your readers will possibly comprehend that the Atlantic, in this parable, stands for the mighty ocean of ether through which we drift, and that the bunch of corks represents the little and obscure planetary system to which we belong. A third-rate sun, with its rag-tag and bobtail of insignificant satellites, we float under the same daily conditions towards some unknown end, some squalid catastrophe which will overwhelm us at the ultimate confines of space, where we are swept over an etheric Niagara, or dashed upon some unthinkable Labrador. I see no room here for the shallow and ignorant optimism of your correspondent, Mr. James Wilson MacPhail, but many reasons why we should watch with a very close and interested attention every indication of change in those cosmic surroundings upon which our own ultimate fate may depend.'

'Man, he'd have made a grand meenister,' said McArdle. 'It just booms like an organ. Let's get doun to what it is that's troubling him.'

'The general blurring and shifting of Frauenhofer's lines of the spectrum point, in my opinion, to a widespread cosmic change of a subtle and singular character. Light from a planet is the reflected light of the sun. Light from a star is a self-produced light. But the spectra both from planets and stars have, in this instance, all undergone the same change. Is it, then, a change in those planets and stars? To me such an idea is inconceivable. What common change could simultaneously come upon them all? Is it a change in our own atmosphere? It is possible, but in the highest degree improbable, since we see no signs of it around us, and chemical analysis has failed to reveal it. What, then, is the third possibility? That it may be a change in the conducting medium, in that infinitely fine ether which extends from star to star and pervades the whole universe. Deep in that ocean we are floating upon a slow current. Might that current not drift us into belts of ether which are novel and have properties of which we have never conceived? There is a change somewhere. This cosmic disturbance of the spectrum proves it. It may be a good change. It may be an evil one. It may be a neutral one. We do not know. Shallow observers may treat the matter as one which can be disregarded, but one who like myself is possessed of the deeper intelligence of the true philosopher will understand that the possibilities of the universe are incalculable and that the wisest man is he who holds himself ready for the unexpected. To take an obvious example, who would undertake to say that the mysterious and universal outbreak of illness, recorded in your columns this very morning as having broken out among the indigenous races of Sumatra, has no connection with some cosmic change to which they may respond more quickly than the more complex peoples of Europe? I throw out the idea for what it is worth. To assert it is, in the present stage, as unprofitable as to deny it, but it is an unimaginative numskull who is too dense to perceive that it is well within the bounds of scientific possibility.

                                        'Yours faithfully,
                               'GEORGE EDWARD CHALLENGER.
'THE BRIARS, ROTHERFIELD.'

'It's a fine, steemulating letter,' said McArdle, thoughtfully, fitting a cigarette into the long glass tube which he used as a holder. 'What's your opeenion of it, Mr. Malone?'

I had to confess my total and humiliating ignorance of the subject at issue. What, for example, were Frauenhofer's lines? McArdle had just been studying the matter with the aid of our tame scientist at the office, and he picked from his desk two of those many-coloured spectral bands which bear a general resemblance to the hat-ribbons of some young and ambitious cricket club. He pointed out to me that there were certain black lines which formed cross-bars upon the series of brilliant colours extending from the red at one end, through gradations of orange, yellow, green, blue, and indigo, to the violet at the other.

'Those dark bands are Frauenhofer's lines,' said he. 'The colours are just light itself. Every light, if you can split it up with a prism, gives the same colours. They tell us nothing. It is the lines that count, because they vary according to what it may be that produces the light. It is these lines that have been blurred instead of clear this last week, and all the astronomers have been quarrelling over the reason. Here's a photograph of the blurred lines for our issue tomorrow. The public have taken no interest in the matter up to now, but this letter of Challenger's in *The Times* will make them wake up, I'm thinking.'

'And this about Sumatra?'

'Well, it's a long cry from a blurred line in a spectrum to a sick nigger in Sumatra. And yet the chiel has shown us once before that he knows what he's talking about. There is some queer illness down yonder, that's beyond all doubt, and to-day there's a cable just come in from Singapore that the lighthouses are out of action in the Straits of Sunda, and two ships on the beach in consequence. Anyhow, it's good enough for you to interview Challenger upon. If you get anything definite, let us have a column by Monday.'

I was coming out from the news editor's room, turning over my new mission in my mind, when I heard my name called from the waiting-room below. It was a telegraph-boy with a wire which had been forwarded from my lodgings at Streatham. The message was from the very man we had been discussing, and ran thus:

'Malone, 17, Hill Street, Streatham. – Bring oxygen. – CHALLENGER.'

'Bring oxygen!' The Professor, as I remembered him, had an ele- phantine sense of humour capable of the most clumsy and unwieldy gambollings. Was this one of those jokes which used to reduce him to uproarious laughter, when his eyes would disappear, and he was all gaping mouth and wagging beard, supremely indif- ferent to the gravity of all around him? I turned the words over, but could make nothing even remotely jocose out of them. Then surely it was a concise order – though a very strange one. He was the last man in the world whose deliberate command I should care to disobey. Possibly some chemical experiment was afoot; possibly – Well, it was no business of mine to speculate upon why he wanted it. I must get it. There was nearly an hour before I should catch the train at Victoria. I took a taxi, and having ascertained the address from the telephone book, I made for the Oxygen Tube Supply Company in Oxford Street.

As I alighted on the pavement at my destination, two youths emerged from the door of the establishment carrying an iron cylinder, which, with some trouble, they hoisted into a waiting motor-car. An elderly man was at their heels scolding and direct-ing in a creaky, sardonic voice. He turned towards me. There was no mistaking those austere features and that goatee beard. It was my old cross-grained companion, Professor Summerlee.

'What!' he cried. 'Don't tell me that you have had one of these preposterous telegrams for oxygen?'

I exhibited it.

'Well, well! I have had one, too, and, as you see, very much against the grain, I have acted upon it. Our good friend is as impos-sible as ever. The need for oxygen could not have been so urgent that he must desert the usual means of supply and encroach upon the time of those who are really busier than himself. Why could he not order it direct?'

I could only suggest that he probably wanted it at once.

'Or thought he did, which is quite another matter. But it is super-fluous now for you to purchase any, since I have this considerable supply.'

'Still, for some reason he seems to wish that I should bring oxygen too. It will be safer to do exactly what he tells me.'

Accordingly, in spite of many grumbles and remonstrances from Summerlee, I ordered an additional tube, which was placed with the other in his motor-car, for he had offered me a lift to Victoria.

I turned away to pay off my taxi, the driver of which was very cantankerous and abusive over his fare. As I came back to Professor Summerlee, he was having a furious altercation with the men who had carried down the oxygen, his little white goat's beard jerking with indignation. One of the fellows called him, I remember, 'a silly old bleached cockatoo,' which so enraged his chauffeur that he bounded out of his seat to take the part of his insulted master, and it was all we could do to prevent a riot in the street.

These little things may seem trivial to relate, and passed as mere incidents at the time. It is only now, as I look back, that I see their relation to the whole story which I have to unfold.

The chauffeur must, as it seemed to me, have been a novice or else have lost his nerve in this disturbance, for he drove vilely on the way to the station. Twice we nearly had collisions with other equally erratic vehicles, and I remember remarking to Summerlee that the standard of driving in London had very much declined. Once we brushed the very edge of a great crowd which was watching a fight at the corner of the Mall. The people, who were much excited, raised cries of anger at the clumsy driving, and one fellow sprang upon the step and waved a stick above our heads. I pushed him off, but we were glad when we had got clear of them and safe out of the park. These little events, coming one after the other, left me very jangled in my nerves, and I could see from my companion's petulant manner that his own patience had got to a low ebb.

But our good humour was restored when we saw Lord John Roxton waiting for us upon the platform, his tall, thin figure clad in a yellow tweed shooting-suit. His keen face, with those unforgettable eyes, so fierce and yet so humorous, flushed with pleasure at the sight of us. His ruddy hair was shot with grey, and the furrows upon his brow had been cut a little deeper by Time's chisel, but in all else he was the Lord John who had been our good comrade in the past.

'Hullo, Herr Professor! Hullo, young fellah!' he shouted as he came towards us.

He roared with amusement when he saw the oxygen cylinders upon the porter's trolly behind us.

'So you've got them, too!' he cried. 'Mine is in the van. Whatever can the old dear be after?'

'Have you seen his letter in *The Times*?' I asked.

'What was it?'

'Stuff and nonsense!' said Summerlee, harshly.

'Well, it's at the bottom of this oxygen business, or I am mistaken,' said I.

'Stuff and nonsense!' cried Summerlee again, with quite unnecessary violence.

We had all got into a first-class smoker, and he had already lit the short and charred old briar pipe which seemed to singe the end of his long, aggressive nose.

'Friend Challenger is a clever man,' said he, with great vehemence. 'No one can deny it. It's a fool that denies it. Look at his hat. There's a sixty-ounce brain inside it – a big engine, running smooth, and turning out clean work. Show me the engine-house and I'll tell you the size of the engine. But he is a born charlatan – you've heard me tell him so to his face – a born charlatan, with a kind of dramatic trick of jumping into the limelight. Things are quiet, so friend Challenger sees a chance to set the public talking about him. You don't imagine that he seriously believes all this non-sense about a change in the ether and a danger to the human race? Was ever such a cock-and-bull story in this life?'

He sat like an old white raven, croaking and shaking with sar-donic laughter.

A wave of anger passed through me as I listened to Summerlee. It was disgraceful that he should speak thus of the leader who had been the source of all our fame and given us such an experience as no men have ever enjoyed. I had opened my mouth to utter some hot retort, when Lord John got before me.

'You had a scrap once before with old man Challenger,' said he, sternly, 'and you were down and out inside ten seconds. It seems to me, Professor Summerlee, he's beyond your class, and the best you can do with him is to walk wide and leave him alone.'

'Besides,' said I, 'he has been a good friend to every one of us. Whatever his faults may be, he is as straight as a line, and I don't believe he ever speaks evil of his comrades behind their backs.'

'Well said, young fellah-my-lad,' said Lord John Roxton. Then, with a kindly smile, he slapped Professor Summerlee upon his shoulder. 'Come, Herr Professor, we're not going to quarrel at this time of day. We've seen too much together. But keep off the grass when you get near Challenger, for this young fellah and I have a bit of a weakness for the old dear.'

But Summerlee was in no humour for compromise. His face was screwed up in rigid disapproval, and thick curls of angry smoke rolled up from his pipe.

'As to you, Lord John Roxton,' he creaked, 'your opinion upon a matter of science is of as much value in my eyes as my views upon a new type of shot-gun would be in yours. I have my own judgment, sir, and I use it in my own way. Because it has misled me once, is that any reason why I should accept without criticism anything, however far-fetched, which this man may care to put forward? Are we to have a Pope of science, with infallible decrees laid down *ex cathedra*, and accepted without question by the poor humble public? I tell you, sir, that I have a brain of my own, and that I should feel myself to be a snob and a slave if I did not use it. If it pleases you to believe this rigmarole about ether and Frauenhofer's lines upon the spectrum, do so by all means, but do not ask one who is older and wiser than yourself to share in your folly. Is it not evident that if the ether were affected to the degree which he maintains, and if it were obnoxious to human health, the result of it would already be apparent upon ourselves?' Here he laughed with uproarious triumph over his own argument. 'Yes, sir, we should already be very far from our normal selves, and instead of sitting quietly discussing scientific problems in a railway train we should be showing actual symptoms of the poison which was working within us. Where do we see any signs of this poisonous cosmic disturbance? Answer me that, sir! Answer me that! Come, come, no evasion! I pin you to an answer!'

I felt more and more angry. There was something very irritating and aggressive in Summerlee's demeanour.

'I think that if you knew more about the facts you might be less positive in your opinion,' said I.

Summerlee took his pipe from his mouth and fixed me with a stony stare.

'Pray what do you mean, sir, by that somewhat impertinent observation?'

'I mean that when I was leaving the office the news editor told me that a telegram had come in confirming the general illness of the Sumatra natives, and adding that the lights had not been lit in the Strait of Sunda.'

'Really, there should be some limits to human folly!' cried Summerlee, in a positive fury. 'Is it possible that you do not realize that ether, if for a moment we adopt Challenger's preposterous supposition, is a universal substance which is the same here as at the other side of the world? Do you for an instant suppose that there is an English ether and a Sumatran ether? Perhaps you imagine that the ether of Kent is in some way superior to the ether of Surrey, through which this train is now bearing us. There really are no bounds to the credulity and ignorance of the average layman. Is it conceivable that the ether in Sumatra should be so deadly as to cause total insensibility at the very time when the ether here has had no appreciable effect upon us whatever? Personally, I can truly say that I never felt stronger in body or better balanced in mind in my life.'

'That may be. I don't profess to be a scientific man,' said I, 'though I have heard somewhere that the science of one generation is usually the fallacy of the next. But it does not take much common sense to see that as we seem to know so little about ether it might be affected by some local conditions in various parts of the world, and might show an effect over there which would only develop later with us.'

'With "might" and "may" you can prove anything,' cried Summerlee furiously. 'Pigs may fly. Yes, sir, pigs *may* fly – but they don't. It is not worth arguing with you. Challenger has filled you with his nonsense and you are both incapable of reason. I had as soon lay arguments before those railway cushions.'

'I must say, Professor Summerlee, that your manners do not seem to have improved since I last had the pleasure of meeting you,' said Lord John, severely.

'You lordlings are not accustomed to hear the truth,' Summerlee answered, with a bitter smile. 'It comes as a bit of a shock, does it not, when someone makes you realize that your title leaves you none the less a very ignorant man?'

'Upon my word, sir,' said Lord John, very stern and rigid, 'if you were a younger man you would not dare to speak to me in so offensive a fashion.'

Summerlee thrust out his chin, with its little wagging tuft of goatee beard.

'I would have you know, sir, that, young or old, there has never been a time in my life when I was afraid to speak my mind to an ignorant coxcomb – yes, sir, an ignorant coxcomb, if you had as many titles as slaves could invent and fools could adopt.'

For a moment Lord John's eyes blazed, and then, with a tremendous effort, he mastered his anger and leaned back in his seat with arms folded and a bitter smile upon his face. To me all this was dreadful and deplorable. Like a wave, the memory of the past swept over me, the good comradeship, the happy, adventurous days – all that we had suffered and worked for and won. That it should have come to this – to insults and abuse! Suddenly I was sobbing – sobbing in loud, gulping, uncontrollable sobs which refused to be concealed. My companions looked at me in surprise. I covered my face with my hands.

'It's all right,' said I. 'Only – only it *is* such a pity!'

'You're ill, young fellah, that's what's amiss with you,' said Lord John. 'I thought you were queer from the first.'

'Your habits, sir, have not mended in these three years,' said Summerlee, shaking his head. 'I also did not fail to observe your strange manner the moment we met. You need not waste your sympathy, Lord John. These tears are, purely alcoholic. The man has been drinking. By the way, Lord John, I called you a coxcomb just now, which was perhaps, unduly severe. But the word reminds me of a small accomplishment, trivial but amusing, which I used to possess. You know me as the austere man of science. Can you believe that I once had a well-deserved reputation in several nurseries as a farmyard imitator? Perhaps I can help you to pass the time in a pleasant way. Would it amuse you to hear me crow like a cock?'

'No, sir,' said Lord John, who was still greatly offended; 'it would not amuse me.'

'My imitation of the clucking hen who had just laid an egg was also considered rather above the average. Might I venture?'

'No, sir, no – certainly not.'

But in spite of this earnest prohibition, Professor Summerlee laid down his pipe and for the rest of our journey he entertained – or failed to entertain – us by a succession of bird and animal cries which seemed so absurd that my tears were suddenly changed into boisterous laughter, which must have become quite hysterical as I sat opposite this grave Professor and saw him – or rather heard him – in the character of the uproarious rooster or the puppy whose tail had been trodden upon. Once Lord John passed across his newspaper, upon the margin of which he had written in pencil, 'Poor devil! Mad as a hatter.' No doubt it was very eccentric, and yet the performance struck me as extraordinarily clever and amusing.

While this was going on Lord John leaned forward and told me some interminable story about a buffalo and an Indian rajah, which seemed to me to have neither beginning nor end. Professor Summerlee had just begun to chirrup like a canary, and Lord John to get to the climax of his story, when the train drew up at Jarvis Brook, which had been given us as the station for Rotherfield.

And there was Challenger to meet us. His appearance was glorious. Not all the turkey-cocks in creation could match the slow, high-stepping dignity with which he paraded his own railway station, and the benignant smile of condescending encouragement with which he regarded everybody around him. If he had changed in anything since the days of old, it was that his points had become accentuated. The huge head and broad sweep of forehead, with its plastered lock of black hair, seemed even greater than before. His black beard poured forward in a more impressive cascade, and his clear grey eyes, with their insolent and sardonic eyelids, were even more masterful than of yore.

He gave me the amused handshake and encouraging smile which the headmaster bestows upon the small boy, and, having greeted the others and helped to collect their bags and their cylinders of oxygen, he stowed us and them away in a large motor-car which was driven by the same impassive Austin, the man of few words, whom I had seen in the character of butler upon the occasion of my first eventful visit to the Professor. Our journey led us up a winding hill through beautiful country. I sat in front with the chauffeur, but behind me my three comrades seemed to me to be all talking together. Lord John was still struggling with his buffalo story, so far as I could make out, while once again I heard, as of old, the deep rumble of Challenger and the insistent accents of Summerlee, as their brains locked in high and fierce scientific debate. Suddenly Austin slanted his mahogany face towards me without taking his eyes from his steering-wheel.

'I'm under notice,' said he.

'Dear me!' said I.

Everything seemed strange to-day. Everyone said queer, unexpected things. It was like a dream.

'It's forty-seven times,' said Austin, reflectively.

'When do you go?' I asked, for want of some better observation.

'I don't go,' said Austin.

The conversation seemed to have ended there, but presently he came back to it.

'If I was to go, who would look after 'im?' He jerked his head towards his master. 'Who would 'e get to serve 'im?'

'Someone else,' I suggested lamely.

'Not 'e. No one would stay a week. If I was to go, that 'ouse would run down like a watch with the mainspring out. I'm telling you because you're 'is friend, and you ought to know. If I was to take 'im at 'is word – but there, I wouldn't have the 'eart. 'E and the missus would be like two babes left out in a bundle. I'm just everything. And then 'e goes and gives me notice.'

'Why would no one stay?' I asked.

'Well, they wouldn't make allowances, same as I do. 'E's a very clever man, the master – so clever that 'e's clean balmy sometimes. I've seen 'im right off 'is onion, and no error. Well, look what 'e did this morning.'

'What did he do?'

Austin bent over to me.

' 'E bit the 'ousekeeper,' said he, in a hoarse whisper.

'Bit her?'

'Yes, sir. Bit 'er on the leg. I saw 'er with my own eyes startin' a Marathon from the 'all-door.'

'Good gracious!'

'So you'd say, sir, if you could see some of the goings-on. 'E don't make friends with the neighbours. There's some of them thinks that when 'e was up among those monsters you wrote about, it was just " 'Ome, Sweet 'Ome," for the master, and 'e was never in fitter company. That's what they say. But I've served 'im ten years, and I'm fond of 'im, and, mind you, 'e's a great man, when all's said an' done, and it's an honour to serve 'im. But 'e does try one cruel at times. Now look at that, sir. That ain't what you might call old-fashioned 'ospitality, is it now? Just you read it for yourself.'

The car on its lowest speed had ground its way up a steep, curving ascent. At the corner a notice-board peered over a well-clipped hedge. As Austin said, it was not difficult to read, for the words were few and arresting: –

> ### WARNING.
> ———
> Visitors, Pressmen, and Mendicants
> are not encouraged.
> G. E. CHALLENGER.

'No, it's not what you might call 'earty,' said Austin, shaking his head and glancing up at the deplorable placard. 'It wouldn't look well in a Christmas-card. I beg your pardon, sir, for I haven't spoke as much as this for many a long year, but to-day my feelings seem to 'ave got the better of me. 'E can sack me till 'e's blue in the face, but I ain't going, and that's flat. I'm 'is man and 'e's my master, and so it will be, I expect, to the end of the chapter.'

We had passed between the white posts of a gate and up a curving drive, lined with rhododendron bushes. Beyond stood a low brick house, picked out with white woodwork, very comfortable and pretty. Mrs. Challenger, a small, dainty, smiling figure, stood in the open doorway to welcome us.

'Well, my dear,' said Challenger, bustling out of the car, 'here are our visitors. It is something new for us to have visitors, is it not? No love lost between us and our neighbours, is there? If they could get rat poison into our baker's cart, I expect it would be there.'

'It's dreadful – dreadful!' cried the lady, between laughter and tears. 'George is always quarrelling with everyone. We haven't a friend on the countryside.'

'It enables me to concentrate my attention upon my incomparable wife,' said Challenger, passing his short, thick arm round her waist. Picture a gorilla and a gazelle, and you have the pair of them. 'Come, come, these gentlemen are tired from the journey, and luncheon should be ready. Has Sarah returned?'

The lady shook her head ruefully, and the Professor laughed loudly and stroked his beard in his masterful fashion.

'Austin,' he cried, 'when you have put up the car you will kindly help your mistress to lay the lunch. Now, gentlemen, will you please step into my study, for there are one or two very urgent things which I am anxious to say to you.'

CHAPTER II

The Tide of Death

As WE CROSSED THE HALL the telephone-bell rang, and we were the involuntary auditors of Professor Challenger's end of the ensuing dialogue. I say 'we,' but no one within a hundred yards could have failed to hear the booming of that monstrous voice, which reverberated through the house. His answers lingered in my mind.

'Yes, yes, of course, it is I. . . . Yes, certainly, the Professor Challenger, the famous Professor, who else? . . . Of course, every word of it, otherwise I should not have written it. . . . I shouldn't be surprised. . . . There is every indication of it. . . . Within a day or so at the furthest. . . . Well, I can't help that, can I? . . . Very unpleasant, no doubt, but I rather fancy it will affect more important people than you. There is no use whining about it. . . . No, I couldn't possibly. You must take your chance. . . . That's enough, sir. Nonsense! I have something more important to do than to listen to such twaddle.'

He shut off with a crash and led us upstairs into a large, airy apartment which formed his study. On the great mahogany desk seven or eight unopened telegrams were lying.

'Really,' he said, as he gathered them up, 'I begin to think that it would save my correspondents' money if I were to adopt a telegraphic address. Possibly "Noah, Rotherfield," would be the most appropriate.'

As usual when he made an obscure joke, he leaned against the desk and bellowed in a paroxysm of laughter, his hands shaking so that he could hardly open the envelopes.

'Noah! Noah!' he gasped, with a face of beetroot, while Lord John and I smiled in sympathy, and Summerlee, like a dyspeptic goat, wagged his head in sardonic disagreement. Finally Challenger, still rumbling and exploding, began to open his telegrams. The three of us stood in the bow window and occupied ourselves in admiring the magnificent view.

It was certainly worth looking at. The road in its gentle curves had really brought us to a considerable elevation – seven hundred feet, as we afterwards discovered. Challenger's house was on the very edge of the hill, and from its southern face, in which was the study window, one looked across the vast stretch of the Weald to where the gentle curves of the South Downs formed an undulating horizon. In a cleft of the hills a haze of smoke marked the position of Lewes. Immediately at our feet there lay a rolling plain of heather, with the long, vivid green stretches of the Crowborough golf course, all dotted with the players. A little to the south, through an opening in the woods, we could see a section of the main line from London to Brighton. In the immediate foreground, under our very noses, was a small enclosed yard, in which stood the car which had brought us from the station.

An ejaculation from Challenger caused us to turn. He had read his telegrams and had arranged them in a little methodical pile upon his desk. His broad, rugged face, or as much of it as was visible over the matted beard, was still deeply flushed, and he seemed to be under the influence of some strong excitement.

'Well, gentlemen,' he said, in a voice as if he was addressing a public meeting, 'this is indeed an interesting reunion, and it takes place under extraordinary – I may say unprecedented – circumstances. May I ask if you have observed anything upon your journey from town?'

'The only thing which I observed,' said Summerlee, with a sour smile, 'was that our young friend here has not improved in his manners during the years that have passed. I am sorry to state that I have had to seriously complain of his conduct in the train, and I should be wanting in frankness if I did not say that it has left a most unpleasant impression in my mind.'

'Well, well, we all get a bit prosy sometimes,' said Lord John. 'The young fellah meant no real harm. After all, he's an International, so if he takes half an hour to describe a game of football he has more right to do it than most folk.'

'Half an hour to describe a game!' I cried, indignantly. 'Why, it was you that took half an hour with some long-winded story about a buffalo. Professor Summerlee will be my witness.'

'I can hardly judge which of you was the most utterly wearisome,' said Summerlee. 'I declare to you, Challenger, that I never wish to hear of football or of buffaloes so long as I live.'

'I have never said one word to-day about football,' I protested.

Lord John gave a shrill whistle, and Summerlee shook his head sadly.

'So early in the day, too,' said he. 'It is indeed deplorable. As I sat there in sad but thoughtful silence –'

'In silence!' cried Lord John. 'Why, you were doin' a music-hall turn of imitations all the way – more like a runaway gramophone than a man.'

Summerlee drew himself up in bitter protest.

'You are pleased to be facetious, Lord John,' said he, with a face of vinegar.

'Why, dash it all, this is clear madness,' cried Lord John. 'Each of us seems to know what the others did and none of us knows what he did himself. Let's put it all together from the first. We got into a first-class smoker, that's clear, ain't it? Then we began to quarrel over friend Challenger's letter in *The Times*.'

'Oh, you did, did you?' rumbled our host, his eyelids beginning to droop.

'You said, Summerlee, that there was no possible truth in his contention.'

'Dear me!' said Challenger, puffing out his chest and stroking his beard. 'No possible truth! I seem to have heard the words before. And may I ask with what arguments the great and famous Professor Summerlee proceeded to demolish the humble individual who had ventured to express an opinion upon a matter of scientific possibility? Perhaps before he exterminates that unfortunate nonentity he will condescend to give some reasons for the adverse views which he has formed.'

He bowed and shrugged and spread open his hands as he spoke with his elaborate and elephantine sarcasm.

'The reason was simple enough,' said the dogged Summerlee. 'I contended that, if the ether surrounding the earth was so toxic in one quarter that it produced dangerous symptoms, it was hardly likely that we three in the railway carriage should be entirely unaffected.'

The explanation only brought uproarious merriment from Challenger. He laughed until everything in the room seemed to rattle and quiver.

'Our worthy Summerlee is, not for the first time, somewhat out of touch with the facts of the situation,' said he at last, mopping his heated brow. 'Now, gentlemen, I cannot make my point better than by detailing to you what I have myself done this morning. You will the more easily condone any mental aberration upon your own part when you realize that even I have had moments when my balance has been disturbed. We have had for some years in this household a housekeeper – one Sarah, with whose second name I have never attempted to burden my memory. She is a woman of a severe and forbidding aspect, prim and demure in her bearing, very impassive in her nature, and never known within our experience to show signs of any emotion. As I sat alone at my breakfast – Mrs. Challenger is in the habit of keeping her room of a morning – it suddenly entered my head that it would be entertaining and instructive to see whether I could find any limits to this woman's imperturbability. I devised a simple but effective experiment. Having upset a small vase of flowers which stood in the centre of the cloth, I rang the bell and slipped under the table. She entered, and, seeing the room empty, imagined that I had withdrawn to the study. As I had expected, she approached and leaned over the table to replace the vase. I had a vision of a cotton stocking and an elastic-sided boot. Protruding my head, I sank my teeth into the calf of her leg. The experiment was successful beyond belief. For some moments she stood paralysed, staring down at my head. Then with a shriek she tore herself free and rushed from the room. I pursued her with some thoughts of an explanation, but she flew down the drive, and some minutes after-wards I was able to pick her out with my field-glasses travelling very rapidly in a south-westerly direction. I tell you the anecdote for what it is worth. I drop it into your brains and await its germination. Is it illuminative? Has it conveyed anything to your minds? What do you think of it, Lord John?'

Lord John shook his head gravely.

'You'll be gettin' into serious trouble some of these days if you don't put a brake on,' said he.

'Perhaps you have some observation to make, Summerlee?'

'You should drop all work instantly, Challenger, and take three months in a German watering-place,' said he.

'Profound! profound!' cried Challenger. 'Now, my young friend, is it possible that wisdom may come from you where your seniors have so signally failed?'

And it did. I say it with all modesty, but it did. Of course, it all seems obvious enough to you who know what occurred, but it was not so very clear when everything was new. But it came on me sud-denly with the full force of absolute conviction.

'Poison!' I cried.

Then, even as I said the word, my mind flashed back over the whole morning's experiences, past Lord John with his buffalo, past my own hysterical tears, past the outrageous conduct of Professor Summerlee, to the queer happenings in London, the row in the park, the driving of the chauffeur, the quarrel at the oxygen ware-house. Everything fitted suddenly into its place.

'Of course,' I cried again. 'It is poison. We are all poisoned.'

'Exactly,' said Challenger, rubbing his hands; 'we are all poi-soned. Our planet has swum into the poison belt of ether, and is now flying deeper into it at the rate of some millions of miles a minute. Our young friend has expressed the cause of all our trou-bles and perplexities in a single word, "Poison." '

We looked at each other in amazed silence. No comment seemed to meet the situation.

'There is a mental inhibition by which such symptoms can be checked and controlled,' said Challenger. 'I cannot expect to find it developed in all of you to the same point which it has reached in me, for I suppose that the strength of our different mental processes bears some proportion to each other. But no doubt it is appreciable even in our young friend here. After the little outburst of high spirits which so alarmed my domestic I sat down and rea-soned with myself. I put it to myself that I had never before felt impelled to bite any of my household. The impulse had then been an abnormal one. In an instant I perceived the truth. My pulse upon examination was ten beats above the usual, and my reflexes were increased. I called upon my higher and saner self, the real G. E. C., seated serene and impregnable behind all mere molecular disturbance. I summoned him, I say, to watch the foolish and mental tricks which the poison would play. I found that I was indeed the master. I could recognize and control a disordered mind. It was a remarkable exhibition of the victory of mind over matter, for it was a victory over that particular form of matter which is most intimately connected with mind. I might almost say that mind was at fault, and that personality controlled it. Thus, when my wife came downstairs and I was impelled to slip behind the door and alarm her by some wild cry as she entered, I was able to stifle the impulse and to greet her with dignity and restraint. An overpowering desire to quack like a duck was met and mastered in the same fashion. Later, when I descended to order the car and found Austin bending over it absorbed in repairs, I controlled my open hand even after I had lifted it, and refrained from giving him an experience which would possibly have caused him to follow in the steps of the housekeeper. On the contrary, I touched him on the shoulder and ordered the car to be at the door in time to meet your train. At the present instant I am most forcibly tempted to take Professor Summerlee by that silly old beard of his, and to shake his head violently backwards and forwards. And yet, as you see, I am perfectly restrained. Let me commend my example to you.'

'I'll look out for that buffalo,' said Lord John.

'And I for the football match.'

'It may be that you are right, Challenger,' said Summerlee, in a chastened voice. 'I am willing to admit that my turn of mind is critical rather than constructive, and that I am not a ready convert to any new theory, especially when it happens to be so unusual and fantastic as this one. However, as I cast my mind back over the events of the morning, and as I reconsider the fatuous conduct of my companions, I find it easy to believe that some poison of an exciting kind was responsible for their symptoms.'

Challenger slapped his colleague good-humouredly upon the shoulder. 'We progress,' said he. 'Decidedly we progress.'

'And pray, sir,' asked Summerlee, humbly, 'what is your opinion as to the present outlook?'

'With your permission I will say a few words upon that subject.' He seated himself upon his desk, his short, stumpy legs swinging in front of him. 'We are assisting at a tremendous and awful function. It is, in my opinion, the end of the world.'

The end of the world! Our eyes turned to the great bow-window and we looked out at the summer beauty of the countryside, the long slopes of heather, the great country houses, the cosy farms, the pleasure-seekers upon the links. The end of the world! One had often heard the words, but the idea that they could ever have an immediate practical significance, that it should not be at some vague date, but now, to-day, that was a tremendous, a staggering thought. We were all struck solemn and waited in silence for Challenger to continue. His overpowering presence and appearance lent such force to the solemnity of his words that for a moment all the crudities and absurdities of the man vanished, and he loomed before us as something majestic and beyond the range of ordinary humanity. Then to me, at least, there came back the cheering recollection of how twice since we had entered the room he had roared with laughter. Surely, I thought, there are limits to mental detachment. The crisis cannot be so great or so pressing, after all.

'You will conceive a bunch of grapes,' said he, 'which are covered by some infinitesimal but noxious bacillus. The gardener passes it through a disinfecting medium. It may be that he desires his grapes to be cleaner. It may be that he needs space to breed some fresh bacillus less noxious than the last. He dips it into the poison and they are gone. Our Gardener is, in my opinion, about to dip the solar system, and the human bacillus, the little mortal vibrio which twisted and wriggled upon the outer rind of the earth, will in an instant be sterilized out of existence.'

Again there was silence. It was broken by the high trill of the telephone-bell.

'There is one of our bacilli squeaking for help,' said he, with a grim smile. 'They are beginning to realize that their continued existence is not really one of the necessities of the Universe.'

He was gone from the room for a minute or two. I remember that none of us spoke in his absence. The situation seemed beyond all words or comments.

'The medical officer of health for Brighton,' said he, when he returned. 'The symptoms are for some reason developing more rapidly upon the sea-level. Our seven hundred feet of elevation give us an advantage. Folk seem to have learned that I am the first authority upon the question. No doubt it comes from my letter in *The Times*. That was the mayor of a provincial town with whom I talked when we first arrived. You may have heard me upon the telephone. He seemed to put an entirely inflated value upon his own life. I helped him to re-adjust his ideas.'

Summerlee had risen and was standing by the window. His thin, bony hands were trembling with his emotion.

'Challenger,' said he, earnestly, 'this thing is too serious for mere futile argument. Do not suppose that I desire to irritate you by any question I may ask. But I put it to you whether there may not be some fallacy in your information or in your reasoning. There is the sun shining as brightly as ever in the blue sky. There are the heather and the flowers and the birds. There are the folk enjoying themselves upon the golf-links, and the labourers yonder cutting the corn. You tell us that they and we may be upon the very brink of destruction – that this sunlit day may be that day of doom which the human race has so long awaited. So far as we know, you found this tremendous judgment upon what? Upon some abnormal lines in a spectrum – upon rumours from Sumatra – upon some curious personal excitement which we have discerned in each other. This latter symptom is not so marked but that you and we could, by a deliberate effort, control it. You need not stand on ceremony with us, Challenger. We have all faced death together before now. Speak out, and let us know exactly where we stand, and what, in your opinion, are our prospects for our future.'

It was a brave, good speech, a speech from that staunch and strong spirit which lay behind all the acidities and angularities of the old zoologist. Lord John rose and shook him by the hand.

'My sentiment to a tick,' said he. 'Now, Challenger, it's up to you to tell us where we are. We ain't nervous folk, as you know well; but when it comes to makin' a week-end visit and finding you've run full butt into the Day of Judgment, it wants a bit of explainin'. What's the danger, and how much of it is there, and what are we goin' to do to meet it?'

He stood, tall and strong, in the sunshine at the window, with his brown hand upon the shoulder of Summerlee. I was lying back in an arm-chair, an extinguished cigarette between my lips, in that sort of half-dazed state in which impressions become exceedingly distinct. It may have been a new phase of the poisoning, but the delirious promptings had all passed away, and were succeeded by an exceedingly languid and, at the same time, perceptive state of mind. I was a spectator. It did not seem to be any personal concern of mine. But here were three strong men at a great crisis, and it was fascinating to observe them. Challenger bent his heavy brows and stroked his beard before he answered. One could see that he was very carefully weighing his words.

'What was the last news when you left London?' he asked.

'I was at the *Gazette* office about ten,' said I. 'There was a Reuter just come in from Singapore to the effect that the sickness seemed to be universal in Sumatra, and that the lighthouses had not been lit in consequence.'

'Events have been moving somewhat rapidly since then,' said Challenger, picking up his pile of telegrams. 'I am in close touch both with the authorities and with the Press, so that news is converging upon me from all parts. There is, in fact, a general and very insistent demand that I should come to London; but I see no good end to be served. From the accounts the poisonous effect begins with mental excitement; the rioting in Paris this morning is said to have been very violent, and the Welsh colliers are in a state of uproar. So far as the evidence to hand can be trusted, this stimulative stage, which varies much in races and in individuals, is succeeded by a certain exaltation and mental lucidity – I seem to discern some signs of it in our young friend here – which, after an appreciable interval, turns to coma, deepening rapidly into death. I fancy, so far as my toxicology carries me, that there are some vegetable nerve poisons –'

'Datura,' suggested Summerlee.

'Excellent!' cried Challenger. 'It would make for scientific precision if we named our toxic agent. Let it be daturon. To you, my dear Summerlee, belongs the honour – posthumous, alas! but none the less unique – of having given a name to the universal destroyer, the great Gardener's disinfectant. The symptoms of daturon, then, may be taken to be such as I indicate. That it will involve the whole world and that no life can possibly remain behind seems to me to be certain, since ether is a universal medium. Up to now it has been capricious in the places which it has attacked, but the difference is only a matter of a few hours, and it is like an advancing tide which covers one strip of sand and then another, running hither and thither in irregular streams, until at last it has submerged it all. There are laws at work in connection with the action and distribution of daturon which would have been of deep interest had the time at our disposal permitted us to study them. So far as I can trace them' – here he glanced over his telegrams – 'the less developed races have been the first to respond to its influence. There are deplorable accounts from Africa, and the Australian aborigines appear to have been already exterminated. The Northern races have as yet shown greater resisting power than the Southern. This, you see, is dated from Marseilles at nine-forty-five this morning. I give it to you verbatim: –

' "All night delirious excitement throughout Provence. Tumult of vine growers at Nîmes. Socialistic upheaval at Toulon. Sudden illness attended by coma attacked population this morning. *Peste foudroyant*. Great numbers of dead in the streets. Paralysis of business and universal chaos."

'An hour later came the following, from the same source: –

' "We are threatened with utter extermination. Cathedrals and churches full to overflowing. The dead outnumber the living. It is inconceivable and horrible. Decease seems to be painless, but swift and inevitable."

'There is a similar telegram from Paris, where the development is not yet as acute. India and Persia appear to be utterly wiped out. The Slavonic population of Austria is down, while the Teutonic has hardly been affected. Speaking generally, the dwellers upon the plains and upon the seashore seem, so far as my limited information goes, to have felt the effects more rapidly than those inland or on the heights. Even a little elevation makes a considerable difference, and perhaps if there be a survivor of the human race, he will again be found upon the summit of some Ararat. Even our own little hill may presently prove to be a temporary island amid a sea of disaster. But at the present rate of advance a few short hours will submerge us all.'

Lord John Roxton wiped his brow.

'What beats me,' said he, 'is how you could sit there laughin' with that stack of telegrams under your hand. I've seen death as often as most folk; but universal death – it's awful!'

'As to the laughter,' said Challenger, 'you will bear in mind that, like yourselves, I have not been exempt from the stimulating cerebral effects of the etheric poison. But as to the horror with which universal death appears to inspire you, I would put it to you that it is somewhat exaggerated. If you were sent to sea alone in an open boat to some unknown destination, your heart might well sink within you. The isolation, the uncertainty, would oppress you. But if your voyage were made in a goodly ship, which bore within it all your relations and your friends, you would feel that, however uncertain your destination might still remain, you would at least have one common and simultaneous experience which would hold you to the end in the same close communion. A lonely death may be terrible, but a universal one, as painless as this would appear to be, is not, in my judgment, a matter for apprehension. Indeed, I could sympathize with the person who took the view that the horror lay in the idea of surviving when all that is learned, famous, and exalted had passed away.'

'What, then, do you propose to do?' asked Summerlee, who had for once nodded his assent to the reasoning of his brother scientist.

'To take our lunch,' said Challenger, as the boom of a gong sounded through the house. 'We have a cook whose omelettes are only excelled by her cutlets. We can but trust that no cosmic disturbance has dulled her excellent abilities. My Scharzberger of '96 must also be rescued, so far as our earnest and united efforts can do it, from what would be a deplorable waste of a great vintage.' He levered his great bulk off the desk, upon which he had sat while he announced the doom of the planet. 'Come,' said he. 'If there is little time left, there is the more need that we should spend it in sober and reasonable enjoyment.'

And, indeed, it proved to be a very merry meal. It is true that we could not forget our awful situation. The full solemnity of the event loomed ever at the back of our minds and tempered our thoughts. But surely it is the soul which has never faced Death which shies strongly from it at the end. To each of us men it had, for one great epoch in our lives, been a familiar presence. As to the lady, she leaned upon the strong guidance of her mighty husband and was well content to go whither his path might lead. The future was our Fate. The present was our own. We passed it in goodly comradeship and gentle merriment. Our minds were, as I have said, singularly lucid. Even I struck sparks at times. As to Challenger, he was wonderful! Never have I so realized the elemental greatness of the man, the sweep and power of his understanding. Summerlee drew him on with his chorus of subacid criticism, while Lord John and I laughed at the contest; and the lady, her hand upon his sleeve, controlled the bellowings of the philosopher. Life, death, fate, the destiny of man – these were the stupendous subjects of that memorable hour, made vital by the fact that as the meal progressed strange, sudden exaltations in my mind and tinglings in my limbs proclaimed that the invisible tide of Death was slowly and gently rising around us. Once I saw Lord John put his hand suddenly to his eyes, and once Summerlee dropped back for an instant in his chair. Each breath we breathed was charged with strange forces. And yet our minds were happy and at ease. Presently Austin laid the cigarettes upon the table and was about to withdraw.

'Austin!' said his master.

'Yes, sir?'

'I thank you for your faithful service.'

A smile stole over the servant's gnarled face.

'I've done my duty, sir.'

'I'm expecting the end of the world to-day, Austin.'

'Yes, sir. What time, sir?'

'I can't say, Austin. Before evening.'

'Very good, sir.'

The taciturn Austin saluted and withdrew. Challenger lit a cigarette, and, drawing his chair to his wife's, he took her hand in his.

'You know how matters stand, dear,' said he. 'I have explained it also to our friends here. You're not afraid, are you?'

'It won't be painful, George?'

'No more than laughing-gas at the dentist's. Every time you have had it you have practically died.'

'But that is a pleasant sensation.'

'So may death be. The worn-out bodily machine can't record its impression, but we know the mental pleasure which lies in a dream or a trance. Nature may build a beautiful door and hang it with many a gauzy and shimmering curtain to make an entrance to the new life for our wondering souls. In all my probings of the actual, I have always found wisdom and kindness at the core; and if ever the frightened mortal needs tenderness, it is surely as he makes the passage perilous from life to life. No, Summerlee, I will have none of your materialism, for I, at least, am too great a thing to end in mere physical constituents, a packet of salts and three bucketfuls of water. Here – here' – and he beat his great head with his huge, hairy fist – 'there is something which uses matter, but is not of it – something which might destroy death, but which Death can never destroy.'

'Talkin' of death,' said Lord John. 'I'm a Christian of sorts, but it seems to me there was somethin' mighty natural in those ancestors of ours who were buried with their axes and bows and arrows and the like, same as if they were livin' on just the same as they used to. I don't know,' he added, looking round the table in a shamefaced way, 'that I wouldn't feel more homely myself if I was put away with my old .450 Express and the fowlin'-piece, the shorter one with the rubbered stock, and a clip or two of cartridges – just a fool's fancy, of course, but there it is. How does it strike you, Herr Professor?'

'Well,' said Summerlee, 'since you ask my opinion, it strikes me as an indefensible throwback to the Stone Age or before it. I'm of the twentieth century myself, and would wish to die like a reasonable civilized man. I don't know that I am more afraid of death than the rest of you, for I am an oldish man, and, come what may, I can't have very much longer to live; but it is all against my nature to sit waiting without a struggle like a sheep for the butcher. Is it quite certain, Challenger, that there is nothing we can do?'

'To save us – nothing,' said Challenger. 'To prolong our lives a few hours, and thus to see the evolution of this mighty tragedy before we are actually involved in it – that may prove to be within my powers. I have taken certain steps –'

'The oxygen?'

'Exactly. The oxygen.'

'But what can oxygen effect in the face of a poisoning of the ether? There is not a greater difference in quality between a brick-bat and a gas than there is between oxygen and ether. They are different planes of matter. They cannot impinge upon one another. Come, Challenger, you could not defend such a proposition.'

'My good Summerlee, this etheric poison is most certainly influenced by material agents. We see it in the methods and distribution of the outbreak. We should not *a priori* have expected it, but it is undoubtedly a fact. Hence I am strongly of opinion that a gas like oxygen, which increases the vitality and the resisting power of the body, would be extremely likely to delay the action of what you have so happily named the daturon. It may be that I am mistaken, but I have every confidence in the correctness of my reasoning.'

'Well,' said Lord John, 'if we've got to sit suckin' at those tubes like so many babies with their bottles, I'm not takin' any.'

'There will be no need for that,' Challenger answered. 'We have made arrangements – it is to my wife that you chiefly owe it – that her boudoir shall be made as airtight as is practicable. With matting and varnished paper.'

'Good heavens, Challenger, you don't suppose you can keep out ether with varnished paper?'

'Really, my friend, you are a trifle perverse in missing the point. It is not to keep out the ether that we have gone to such trouble. It is to keep in the oxygen. I trust that if we can ensure an atmosphere hyper-oxygenated to a certain point, we may be able to retain our senses. I had two tubes of the gas and you have brought me three more. It is not much, but it is something.'

'How long will they last?'

'I have not an idea. We will not turn them on until our symptoms become unbearable. Then we shall dole the gas out as it is urgently needed. It may give us some hours, possibly even some days, on which we may look out upon a blasted world. Our own fate is delayed to that extent, and we will have the very singular experience, we five, of being, in all probability, the absolute rearguard of the human race upon its march into the unknown. Perhaps you will be kind enough now to give me a hand with the cylinders. It seems to me that the atmosphere already grows somewhat more oppressive.'

CHAPTER III

Submerged

THE CHAMBER WHICH WAS DESTINED to be the scene of our unforgettable experience was a charmingly feminine sitting-room, some fourteen or sixteen feet square. At the end of it, divided by a curtain of red velvet, was a small apartment which formed the Professor's dressing-room. This in turn opened into a large bedroom. The curtain was still hanging, but the boudoir and dressing-room could be taken as one chamber for the purposes of our experiment. One door and the window-frame had been plastered round with varnished paper, so as to be practically sealed. Above the other door, which opened on to the landing, there hung a fanlight which could be drawn by a cord when some ventilation became absolutely necessary. A large shrub in a tub stood in each corner.

'How to get rid of our excessive carbon dioxide without unduly wasting our oxygen is a delicate and vital question,' said Challenger, looking round him after the five iron tubes had been laid side by side against the wall. 'With longer time for preparation I could have brought the whole concentrated force of my intelligence to bear more fully upon the problem, but as it is we must do what we can. The shrubs will be of some small service. Two of the oxygen tubes are ready to be turned on at an instant's notice, so that we cannot be taken unawares. At the same time, it would be well not to go far from the room, as the crisis may be a sudden and urgent one.'

There was a broad, low window opening out upon a balcony. The view beyond was the same as that which we had already admired from the study. Looking out, I could see no sign of disorder anywhere. There was a road curving down the side of the hill, under my very eyes. A cab from the station, one of those prehistoric survivals which are only to be found in our country villages, was toiling slowly up the hill. Lower down was a nurse-girl wheeling a perambulator and leading a second child by the hand. The blue reeks of smoke from the cottages gave the whole widespread landscape an air of settled order and homely comfort. Nowhere in the blue heaven or on the sunlit earth was there any foreshadowing of a catastrophe. The harvesters were back in the fields once more and the golfers, in pairs and fours, were still streaming round the links. There was so strange a turmoil within my own head, and such a jangling of my overstrung nerves, that the indifference of these people was amazing.

'Those fellows don't seem to feel any ill effects,' said I, pointing down at the links.

'Have you played golf?' asked Lord John.

'No, I have not.'

'Well, young fellah, when you do you'll learn that once fairly out on a round, it would take the crack of doom to stop a true golfer. Halloa! There's that telephone-bell again.'

From time to time during and after lunch the high, insistent ring had summoned the Professor. He gave us the news as it came through to him in a few curt sentences. Such terrific items had never been registered in the world's history before. The great shadow was creeping up from the South like a rising tide of death. Egypt had gone through its delirium and was now comatose. Spain and Portugal, after a wild frenzy in which the Clericals and the Anarchists had fought most desperately, were now fallen silent. No cable messages were received any longer from South America. In North America the Southern States, after some terrible racial rioting, had succumbed to the poison. North of Maryland the effect was not yet marked, and in Canada it was hardly perceptible. Belgium, Holland, and Denmark had each in turn been affected. Despairing messages were flashing from every quarter to the great centres of learning, to the chemists and the doctors of world-wide repute, imploring their advice. The astronomers, too, were deluged with inquiries. Nothing could be done. The thing was universal and beyond our human knowledge or control. It was death – painless but inevitable – death for young and old, for weak and strong, for rich and poor, without hope or possibility of escape. Such was the news which, in scattered distracted messages, the telephone had brought us. The great cities already knew their fate, and so far as we could gather were preparing to meet it with dignity and resignation. Yet here were our golfers and labourers like the lambs who gambol under the shadow of the knife. It seemed amazing. And yet how could they know? It had all come upon us in one giant stride. What was there in the morning paper to alarm them? And now it was but three in the afternoon. Even as we looked some rumour seemed to have spread, for we saw the reapers hurrying from the fields. Some of the golfers were returning to the club-house. They were running as if taking refuge from a shower. Their little caddies trailed behind them. Others were continuing their game. The nurse had turned and was pushing her perambulator hurriedly up the hill again. I noticed that she had her hand to her brow. The cab had stopped and the tired horse, with his head sunk to his knees, was resting. Above there was a perfect summer sky – one huge vault of unbroken blue, save for a few fleecy white clouds over the distant downs. If the human race must die to-day, it was at least upon a glorious deathbed. And yet all that gentle loveliness of Nature made this terrific and wholesale destruction the more pitiable and awful. Surely it was too goodly a residence that we should be so swiftly, so ruthlessly, evicted from it!

But I have said that the telephone-bell had rung once more. Suddenly I heard Challenger's tremendous voice from the hall.

'Malone!' he cried. 'You are wanted.'

I rushed down to the instrument. It was McArdle speaking from London.

'That you, Mr. Malone?' cried his familiar voice. 'Mr. Malone, there are terrible goings-on in London. For God's sake, see if Professor Challenger can suggest anything that can be done.'

'He can suggest nothing, sir,' I answered. 'He regards the crisis as universal and inevitable. We have some oxygen here, but it can only defer our fate for a few hours.'

'Oxygen!' cried the agonized voice. 'There is no time to get any. The office has been a perfect pandemonium ever since you left in the morning. Now half of the staff are insensible. I am weighed down with heaviness myself. From my window I can see the people lying thick in Fleet Street. The traffic is all held up. Judging by the last telegrams, the whole world –'

His voice had been sinking, and suddenly stopped. An instant later I heard through the telephone a muffled thud, as if his head had fallen forward on the desk.

'Mr. McArdle!' I cried. 'Mr. McArdle!'

There was no answer. I knew as I replaced the receiver that I should never hear his voice again.

At that instant, just as I took a step backwards from the telephone, the thing was on us. It was as if we were bathers, up to our shoulders in water, who suddenly are submerged by a rolling wave. An invisible hand seemed to have quietly closed round my throat and to be gently pressing the life from me. I was conscious of immense oppression upon my chest, great tightness within my head, a loud singing in my ears, and bright flashes before my eyes. I staggered to the balustrades of the stair. At the same moment, rushing and snorting like a wounded buffalo, Challenger dashed past me, a terrible vision, with red-purple face, engorged eyes, and bristling hair. His little wife, insensible to all appearance, was slung over his great shoulder, and he blundered and thundered up the stair, scrambling and tripping, but carrying himself and her through sheer will-force through that mephitic atmosphere to the haven of temporary safety. At the sight of his effort I too rushed up the steps, clambering, falling, clutching at the rail, until I tumbled half senseless upon my face on the upper landing. Lord John's fingers of steel were in the collar of my coat, and a moment later I was stretched upon my back, unable to speak or move, on the boudoir carpet. The woman lay beside me and Summerlee was bunched in a chair by the window, his head nearly touching his knees. As in a dream I saw Challenger, like a monstrous beetle, crawling slowly across the floor, and a moment later I heard the gentle hissing of the escaping oxygen. Challenger breathed two or three times with enormous gulps, his lungs roaring as he drew in the vital gas.

'It works!' he cried exultantly. 'My reasoning has been justified!' He was up on his feet again, alert and strong. With a tube in his hand he rushed over to his wife and held it to her face. In a few seconds she moaned, stirred, and sat up. He turned to me, and I felt the tide of life stealing warmly through my arteries. My reason told me that it was but a little respite, and yet, carelessly as we talk of its value, every hour of existence now seemed an inestimable thing. Never have I known such a thrill of sensuous joy as came with that freshet of life. The weight fell away from my lungs, the band loosened from my brow, a sweet feeling of peace and gentle, languid comfort stole over me. I lay watching Summerlee revive under the same remedy, and finally Lord John took his turn. He sprang to his feet and gave me a hand to rise, while Challenger picked up his wife and laid her on the settee.

'Oh, George, I am so sorry you brought me back,' she said, holding him by the hand. 'The door of death is indeed, as you said, hung with beautiful, shimmering curtains; for, once the choking feeling had passed, it was all unspeakably soothing and beautiful. Why have you dragged me back?'

'Because I wish that we make the passage together. We have been together so many years. It would be sad to fall apart at the supreme moment.'

For a moment in his tender voice I caught a glimpse of a new Challenger, something very far from the bullying, ranting, arrogant man who had alternately amazed and offended his generation. Here in the shadow of death was the innermost Challenger, the man who had won and held a woman's love. Suddenly his mood changed and he was our strong captain once again.

'Alone of all mankind I saw and foretold this catastrophe,' said he, with a ring of exultation and scientific triumph in his voice. 'As to you, my good Summerlee, I trust your last doubts have been resolved as to the meaning of the blurring of the lines in the spectrum, and that you will no longer contend that my letter in *The Times* was based upon a delusion.'

For once our pugnacious colleague was deaf to a challenge. He could but sit gasping and stretching his long, thin limbs, as if to assure himself that he was still really upon this planet. Challenger walked across to the oxygen tube, and the sound of the loud hissing fell away till it was the most gentle sibilation.

'We must husband our supply of the gas,' said he. 'The atmosphere of the room is now strongly hyper-oxygenated, and I take it that none of us feel any distressing symptoms. We can only determine by actual experiments what amount added to the air will serve to neutralize the poison. Let us see how that will do.'

We sat in silent nervous tension for five minutes or more, observing our own sensations. I had just begun to fancy that I felt the constriction round my temples again when Mrs. Challenger called out from the sofa that she was fainting. Her husband turned on more gas.

'In pre-scientific days,' said he, 'they used to keep a white mouse in every submarine, as its more delicate organization gave signs of a vicious atmosphere before it was perceived by the sailors. You, my dear, will be our white mouse. I have now increased the supply and you are better.'

'Yes, I am better.'

'Possibly we have hit upon the correct mixture. When we have ascertained exactly how little will serve we shall be able to compute how long we shall be able to exist. Unfortunately, in resuscitating ourselves we have already consumed a considerable proportion of this first tube.'

'Does it matter?' asked Lord John, who was standing with his hands in his pockets close to the window. 'If we have to go, what is the use of holdin' on? You don't suppose there's any chance for us?'

Challenger smiled and shook his head.

'Well, then, don't you think there is more dignity in takin' the jump and not waitin' to be pushed in? If it must be so I'm for sayin' our prayers, turnin' off the gas, and openin' the window.'

'Why not?' said the lady, bravely. 'Surely, George, Lord John is right and it is better so.'

'I most strongly object,' cried Summerlee, in a querulous voice. 'When we must die let us by all means die; but to deliberately anticipate death seems to me to be a foolish and unjustifiable action.'

'What does our young friend say to it?' asked Challenger.

'I think we should see it to the end.'

'And I am strongly of the same opinion,' said he.

'Then, George, if you say so, I think so too,' cried the lady.

'Well, well, I'm only puttin' it as an argument,' said Lord John. 'If you all want to see it through I am with you. It's dooced interestin', and no mistake about that. I've had my share of adventures in my life, and as many thrills as most folk, but I'm endin' on my top note.'

'Granting the continuity of life,' said Challenger.

'A large assumption!' cried Summerlee.

Challenger stared at him in silent reproof.

'Granting the continuity of life,' said he, in his most didactic manner, 'none of us can predicate what opportunities of observation one may have from what we may call the spirit plane to the plane of matter. It surely must be evident to the most obtuse person' (here he glared at Summerlee) 'that it is while we are ourselves material that we are most fitted to watch and form a judgment upon material phenomena. Therefore it is only by keeping alive for these few extra hours that we can hope to carry on with us to some future existence a clear conception of the most stupendous event that the world, or the universe so far as we know it, has ever encountered. To me it would seem a deplorable thing that we should in any way curtail by so much as a minute so wonderful an experience.'

'I am strongly of the same opinion,' cried Summerlee.

'Carried without a division,' said Lord John. 'By George, that poor devil of a chauffeur of yours down in the yard has made his last journey. No use makin' a sally and bringin' him in?'

'It would be absolute madness,' cried Summerlee.

'Well, I suppose it would,' said Lord John. 'It couldn't help him and would scatter our gas all over the house, even if we ever got back alive. My word, look at the little birds under the trees!'

We drew four chairs up to the long, low window, the lady still resting with closed eyes upon the settee. I remember that the monstrous and grotesque idea crossed my mind – the illusion may have been heightened by the heavy stuffiness of the air which we were breathing – that we were in four front seats of the stalls at the last act of the drama of the world.

In the immediate foreground, beneath our very eyes, was the small yard with the half-cleaned motor-car standing in it. Austin, the chauffeur, had received his final notice at last, for he was sprawling beside the wheel, with a great black bruise upon his forehead where it had struck the step or mud-guard in falling. He still held in his hand the nozzle of the hose with which he had been washing down his machine. A couple of small plane trees stood in the corner of the yard, and underneath them lay several pathetic little balls of fluffy feathers, with tiny feet uplifted. The sweep of Death's scythe had included everything great and small within its swathe.

Over the wall of the yard we looked down upon the winding road, which led to the station. A group of the reapers whom we had seen running from the fields were lying all pellmell, their bodies crossing each other, at the bottom of it. Farther up the nurse-girl lay with her head and shoulders propped against the slope of the grassy bank. She had taken the baby from the perambulator, and it was a motionless bundle of wraps in her arms. Close behind her a tiny patch upon the roadside showed where the little boy was stretched. Still nearer to us was the dead cab-horse kneeling between the shafts. The old driver was hanging over the splash-board like some grotesque scarecrow, his arms dangling absurdly in front of him. Through the window we could dimly discern that a young man was seated. The door was swinging open, and his hand was grasping the handle, as if he had attempted to leap forth at the last instant. In the middle distance lay the golf links, dotted as they had been in the morning with the dark figures of the golfers, lying motionless upon the grass of the course, or among the heather which skirted it. On one particular green there were eight bodies stretched where a foursome with its caddies had held to their game to the last. No bird flew in the blue vault of heaven, no man or beast moved upon the vast countryside which lay before us. The evening sun shone its peaceful radiance across it, but there brooded over it all the stillness and the silence of universal death – a death in which we were so soon to join. At the present instant that one frail sheet of glass, by holding in the extra oxygen, which counteracted the poisoned ether, shut us off from the fate of all our kind. For a few short hours the knowledge and foresight of one man could preserve our little oasis of life in the vast desert of death, and save us from participation in the common catastrophe. Then the gas would run low, we too should lie gasping upon that cherry-coloured boudoir carpet, and the fate of the human race and of all earthly life would be complete. For a long time, in a mood which was too solemn for speech, we looked out at the tragic world.

'There is a house on fire,' said Challenger, at last, pointing to a column of smoke which rose above the trees. 'There will, I expect, be many such – possibly whole cities in flames – when we consider how many folk may have dropped with lights in their hands. The fact of combustion is in itself enough to show that the proportion of oxygen in the atmosphere is normal, and that it is the ether which is at fault. Ah, there you see another blaze on the top of Crowborough Hill. It is the golf clubhouse, or I am mistaken. There is the church clock chiming the hour. It would interest our philosophers to know that man-made mechanism has survived the race who made it.'

'By George!' cried Lord John, rising excitedly from his chair. 'What's that puff of smoke? It's a train.'

We heard the roar of it, and presently it came flying into sight, going at what seemed to me to be a prodigious speed. Whence it had come, or how far, we had no means of knowing. Only by some miracle of luck could it have gone any distance. But now we were to see the terrific end of its career. A train of coal-trucks stood motionless upon the line. We held our breath as the express roared along the same track. The crash was horrible. Engine and carriages piled themselves into a hill of splintered wood and twisted iron. Red spurts of flame flickered up from the wreckage until it was all ablaze. For half an hour we sat with hardly a word, stunned by the stupendous sight.

'Poor, poor people!' cried Mrs. Challenger, at last, clinging with a whimper to her husband's arm.

'My dear, the passengers on that train were no more animate than the coals into which they crashed, or the carbon which they have now become,' said Challenger, stroking her hand soothingly. 'It was a train of the living when it left Victoria, but it was driven and freighted by the dead long before it reached its fate.'

'All over the world the same thing must be going on,' said I, as a vision of strange happenings rose before me. 'Think of the ships at sea – how they will steam on and on, until the furnaces die down, or until they run full tilt upon some beach. The sailing ships, too – how they will back and fill with their cargoes of dead sailors, while their timbers rot and their joints leak, till one by one they sink below the surface. Perhaps a century hence the Atlantic may still be dotted with the old drifting derelicts.'

'And the folk in the coal-mines,' said Summerlee, with a dismal chuckle. 'If ever geologists should by any chance live upon earth again they will have some strange theories of the existence of man in carboniferous strata.'

'I don't profess to know about such things,' remarked Lord John, 'but it seems to me the earth will be "To let, empty," after this. When once our human crowd is wiped off it, how will it ever get on again?'

'The world was empty before,' Challenger answered, gravely. 'Under laws which in their inception are beyond and above us, it became peopled. Why may the same process not happen again?'

'My dear Challenger, you can't mean that?'

'I am not in the habit, Professor Summerlee, of saying things which I do not mean. The observation is trivial.' Out went the beard and down came the eyelids.

'Well, you lived an obstinate dogmatist, and you mean to die one,' said Summerlee, sourly.

'And you, sir, have lived an unimaginative obstructionist, and never can hope now to emerge from it.'

'Your worst critics will never accuse you of lacking imagination,' Summerlee retorted.

'Upon my word!' said Lord John, 'It would be like you if you used up our last gasp of oxygen in abusing each other. What can it matter whether folk come back or not? It surely won't be in our time.'

'In that remark, sir, you betray your own very pronounced limitations,' said Challenger severely. 'The true scientific mind is not to be tied down by its own conditions of time and space. It builds itself an observatory erected upon the border line of present, which separates the infinite past from the infinite future. From this sure post it makes its sallies even to the beginning and to the end of all things. As to death, the scientific mind dies at its post working in normal and methodic fashion to the end. It disregards so petty a thing as its own physical dissolution as completely as it does all other limitations upon the plane of matter. Am I right, Professor Summerlee?'

Summerlee grumbled an ungracious assent.

'With certain reservations, I agree,' said he.

'The ideal scientific mind,' continued Challenger – 'I put it in the third person rather than appear to be too self-complacent – the ideal scientific mind should be capable of thinking out a point of abstract knowledge in the interval between its owner falling from a balloon and reaching the earth. Men of this strong fibre are needed to form the conquerors of Nature and the bodyguard of truth.'

'It strikes me Nature's on top this time,' said Lord John, looking out of the window. 'I've read some leadin' articles about you gentlemen controllin' her, but she's gettin' a bit of her own back.'

'It is but a temporary set-back,' said Challenger, with conviction. 'A few million years, what are they in the great cycle of time? The vegetable world has, as you can see, survived. Look at the leaves of that plane tree. The birds are dead, but the plant flourishes. From this vegetable life in pond and in marsh will come, in time, the tiny crawling microscopic slugs which are the pioneers of that great army of life in which for the instant we five have the extraordinary duty of serving as rearguard. Once the lowest form of life has established itself, the final advent of Man is as certain as the growth of the oak from the acorn. The old circle will swing round once more.'

'But the poison?' I asked. 'Will that not nip life in the bud?'

'The poison may be a mere stratum or layer in the ether – a mephitic Gulf Stream across that mighty ocean in which we float. Or tolerance may be established, and life accommodate itself to a new condition. The mere fact that with a comparatively small hyper-oxygenation of our blood we can hold out against it is surely a proof in itself that no very great change would be needed to enable animal life to endure it.'

The smoking house beyond the trees had burst into flames. We could see the high tongues of fire shooting up into the air.

'It's pretty awful,' muttered Lord John, more impressed than I had ever seen him.

'Well, after all, what does it matter?' I remarked. 'The world is dead. Cremation is surely the best burial.'

'It would shorten us up if this house went ablaze.'

'I foresaw the danger,' said Challenger, 'and asked my wife to guard against it.'

'Everything is quite safe, dear. But my head begins to throb again. What a dreadful atmosphere!'

'We must change it,' said Challenger. He bent over his cylinder of oxygen.

'It's nearly empty,' said he. 'It has lasted us some three hours. It is now close on eight o'clock. We shall get through the night comfortably. I should expect the end about nine o'clock to-morrow morning. We shall see one sunrise, which shall be our own.'

He turned on his second tube and opened for half a minute the fanlight over the door. Then as the air became perceptibly better, but our own symptoms more acute, he closed it once again.

'By the way,' said he, 'man does not live upon oxygen alone. It's dinner time and over. I assure you, gentlemen, that when I invited you to my home and to what I had hoped would be an interesting reunion, I had intended that my kitchen should justify itself. However, we must do what we can. I am sure that you will agree with me that it would be folly to consume our air too rapidly by lighting an oil-stove. I have some small provision of cold meats, bread, and pickles, which, with a couple of bottles of claret, may serve our turn. Thank you, my dear – now as ever you are the queen of managers.'

It was indeed wonderful how, with the self-respect and sense of propriety of the British housekeeper, the lady had within a few minutes adorned the central table with a snow-white cloth, laid the napkins upon it, and set forth the simple meal with all the elegance of civilization, including an electric torch lamp in the centre. Wonderful, also, was it to find that our appetites were ravenous.

'It is the measure of our emotion,' said Challenger, with that air of condescension with which he brought his scientific mind to the explanation of humble facts. 'We have gone through a great crisis. That means molecular disturbance. That in turn means the need for repair. Great sorrow or great joy should bring intense hunger – not abstinence from food, as our novelists will have it.'

'That's why the country folk have great feasts at funerals,' I hazarded.

'Exactly. Our young friend has hit upon an excellent illustration. Let me give you another slice of tongue.'

'The same with savages,' said Lord John, cutting away at the beef. 'I've seen them buryin' a chief up the Aruwimi River, and they ate a hippo that must have weighed as much as a tribe. There are some of them down New Guinea way that eat the late-lamented himself, just by way of a last tidy up. Well, of all the funeral feasts on this earth, I suppose the one we are takin' is the queerest.'

'The strange thing is,' said Mrs. Challenger, 'that I find it impossible to feel grief for those who are gone. There are my father and mother at Bedford. I know that they are dead, and yet in this tremendous universal tragedy I can feel no sharp sorrow for any individuals, even for them.'

'And my old mother in her cottage in Ireland,' said I. 'I can see her in my mind's eye, with her shawl and her lace cap, lying back with closed eyes in the old high-backed chair near the window, her glasses and her book beside her. Why should I mourn her? She has passed and I am passing, and I may be nearer her in some other life than England is to Ireland. Yet I grieve to think that that dear body is no more.'

'As to the body,' remarked Challenger, 'we do not mourn over the parings of our nails nor the cut locks of our hair, though they were once part of ourselves. Neither does a one-legged man yearn sentimentally over his missing member. The physical body has rather been a source of pain and fatigue to us. It is the constant index of our limitations. Why then should we worry about its detachment from our psychical selves?'

'If they can indeed be detached,' Summerlee grumbled. 'But, anyhow, universal death is dreadful.'

'As I have already explained,' said Challenger, 'a universal death must in its nature be far less terrible than an isolated one.'

'Same in a battle,' remarked Lord John. 'If you saw a single man lying on that floor with his chest knocked in and a hole in his face it would turn you sick. But I've seen ten thousand on their backs in the Soudan, and it gave me no such feelin', for when you are makin' history the life of any man is too small a thing to worry over. When a thousand million pass over together, same as happened to-day, you can't pick your own partic'lar out of the crowd.'

'I wish it were well over with us,' said the lady, wistfully. 'Oh, George, I am so frightened.'

'You'll be the bravest of us all, little lady, when the time comes. I've been a blusterous old husband to you, dear, but you'll just bear in mind that G. E. C. is as he was made and couldn't help himself. After all, you wouldn't have had anyone else?'

'No one in the whole wide world, dear,' said she, and put her arms round his bull neck. We three walked to the window, and stood amazed at the sight which met our eyes.

Darkness had fallen and the dead world was shrouded in gloom. But right across the southern horizon was one long vivid scarlet streak, waxing and waning in vivid pulses of life, leaping suddenly to a crimson zenith and then dying down to a glowing line of fire.

'Lewes is ablaze!' I cried.

'No, it is Brighton which is burning,' said Challenger, stepping across to join us. 'You can see the curved back of the downs against the glow. That fire is miles on the farther side of it. The whole town must be alight.'

There were several red glares at different points, and the pile of *débris* upon the railway line was still smouldering darkly, but they all seemed mere pin-points of light compared to that monstrous conflagration throbbing beyond the hills. What copy it would have made for the *Gazette*! Had ever a journalist such an opening and so little chance of using it – the scoop of scoops, and no one to appreciate it? And then, suddenly, the old instinct of recording came over me. If these men of science could be so true to their life's work to the very end, why should not I, in my humble way, be as constant? No human eye might ever rest upon what I had done. But the long night had to be passed somehow, and for me, at least, sleep seemed to be out of the question. My notes would help to pass the weary hours and to occupy my thoughts. Thus it is that now I have before me the notebook with its scribbled pages, written confusedly upon my knee in the dim, waning light of our one electric torch. Had I the literary touch, they might have been worthy of the occasion. As it is, they may still serve to bring to other minds the long-drawn emotions and tremors of that awful night.

CHAPTER IV

A Diary of the Dying

HOW STRANGE THE WORDS LOOK scribbled at the top of the empty page of my book! How stranger still that it is I, Edward Malone, who have written them – I who started only some twelve hours ago from my rooms in Streatham without one thought of the marvels which the day was to bring forth! I look back at the chain of incidents, my interview with McArdle, Challenger's first note of alarm in *The Times*, the absurd journey in the train, the pleasant luncheon, the catastrophe, and now it has come to this – that we linger alone upon an empty planet, and so sure is our fate that I can regard these lines, written from mechanical professional habit and never to be seen by human eyes, as the words of one who is already dead, so closely does he stand to the shadowed borderland over which all outside this one little circle of friends have already gone. I feel how wise and true were the words of Challenger when he said that the real tragedy would be if we were left behind when all that is noble and good and beautiful had passed. But of that there can surely be no danger. Already our second tube of oxygen is drawing to an end. We can count the poor dregs of our lives almost to a minute.

We have just been treated to a lecture, a good quarter of an hour long, from Challenger, who was so excited that he roared and bellowed as if he were addressing his old rows of scientific sceptics in the Queen's Hall. He had certainly a strange audience to harangue: his wife perfectly acquiescent and absolutely ignorant of his meaning, Summerlee seated in the shadow, querulous and critical, but interested, Lord John lounging in a corner somewhat bored by the whole proceeding, and myself beside the window watching the scene with a kind of detached attention as if it were all a dream or something in which I had no personal interest whatever. Challenger sat at the centre table with the electric light illuminating the slide under the microscope which he had brought from his dressing-room. The small vivid circle of white light from the mirror left half of his rugged, bearded face in brilliant radiance, and half in deepest shadow. He had, it seems, been working of late upon the lowest forms of life, and what excited him at the present moment was that in the microscopic slide made up the day before he found the amœba to be still alive.

'You can see it for yourselves,' he kept repeating, in great excitement. 'Summerlee, will you step across and satisfy yourself upon the point? Malone, will you kindly verify what I say? The little spindle-shaped things in the centre are diatoms, and may be disregarded since they are probably vegetable rather than animal. But at the right-hand side you will see an undoubted amœba, moving sluggishly across the field. The upper screw is the fine adjustment. Look at it for yourselves.'

Summerlee did so, and acquiesced. So did I, and perceived a little creature which looked as if it were made of ground glass flowing in a sticky way across the lighted circle. Lord John was prepared to take him on trust.

'I'm not troublin' my head whether he's alive or dead,' said he. 'We don't so much as know each other by sight, so why should I take it to heart? I don't suppose he's worryin' himself over the state of *our* health.'

I laughed at this, and Challenger looked in my direction with his coldest and most supercilious stare. It was a most petrifying experience.

'The flippancy of the half-educated is more obstructive to science than the obtuseness of the ignorant,' said he. 'If Lord John Roxton would condescend –'

'My dear George, don't be so peppery,' said his wife, with her hand on the black mane that drooped over the microscope. 'What can it matter whether the amœba is alive or not?'

'It matters a great deal,' said Challenger, gruffly.

'Well, let's hear about it,' said Lord John, with a good-humoured smile. 'We may as well talk about that as anything else. If you think I've been too offhand with the thing, or hurt its feelin's in any way, I'll apologize.'

'For my part,' remarked Summerlee, in his creaky, argumentative voice, 'I can't see why you should attach such importance to the creature being alive. It is in the same atmosphere as ourselves, so naturally the poison does not act upon it. If it were outside of this room it would be dead, like all other animal life.'

'Your remarks, my good Summerlee,' said Challenger, with enormous condescension (oh, if I could paint that over-bearing, arrogant face in the vivid circle of reflection from the microscope mirror!) – 'your remarks show that you imperfectly appreciate the situation. This specimen was mounted yesterday and was hermetically sealed. None of our oxygen can reach it. But the ether, of course, has penetrated to it, as to every other point upon the universe. Therefore, it has survived the poison. Hence, we may argue that every amœba outside this room, instead of being dead, as you have erroneously stated, has really survived the catastrophe.'

'Well, even now I don't feel inclined to hip-hurrah about it,' said Lord John. 'What does it matter?'

'It just matters this, that the world is a living instead of a dead one. If you had the scientific imagination, you would cast your mind forward from this one fact, and you would see some few millions of years hence – a mere passing moment in the enormous flux of the ages – the whole world teeming once more with the animal and human life which will spring from this tiny root. You have seen a prairie fire, where the flames have swept every trace of grass or plant from the surface of the earth and left only a blackened waste. You would think that it must be for ever desert. Yet the roots of growth have been left behind, and when you pass the place a few years hence you can no longer tell where the black scars used to be. Here in this tiny creature are the roots of growth of the animal world, and by its inherent development, and evolution, it will surely in time remove every trace of this incomparable crisis in which we are now involved.'

'Dooced interestin'!' said Lord John, lounging across and looking through the microscope. 'Funny little chap to hang number one among the family portraits. Got a fine big shirt-stud on him!'

'The dark object is his nucleus,' said Challenger, with the air of a nurse teaching letters to a baby.

'Well, we needn't feel lonely,' said Lord John, laughing. 'There's somebody livin' besides us on the earth.'

'You seem to take it for granted, Challenger,' said Summerlee, 'that the object for which this world was created was that it should produce and sustain human life.'

'Well, sir, and what object do you suggest?' asked Challenger, bristling at the least hint of contradiction.

'Sometimes I think that it is only the monstrous conceit of mankind which makes him think that all this stage was erected for him to strut upon.'

'We cannot be dogmatic about it, but at least without what you have ventured to call monstrous conceit we can surely say that we are the highest thing in Nature.'

'The highest of which we have cognizance.'

'That, sir, goes without saying.'

'Think of all the millions and possibly billions of years that the earth swung empty through space – or, if not empty, at least without a sign or thought of the human race. Think of it, washed by the rain and scorched by the sun, and swept by the wind for those unnumbered ages. Man only came into being yesterday so far as geological time goes. Why, then, should it be taken for granted that all this stupendous preparation was for his benefit?'

'For whose then – or for what?'

Summerlee shrugged his shoulders.

'How can we tell? For some reason altogether beyond our conception – and man may have been a mere accident, a by-product evolved in the process. It is as if the scum upon the surface of the ocean imagined that the ocean was created in order to produce and sustain it, or a mouse in a cathedral thought that the building was its own proper ordained residence.'

I have jotted down the very words of their argument; but now it degenerates into a mere noisy wrangle with much polysyllabic scientific jargon upon each side. It is no doubt a privilege to hear two such brains discuss the highest questions; but as they are in perpetual disagreement plain folk like Lord John and I get little that is positive from the exhibition. They neutralize each other and we are left as they found us. Now the hubbub has ceased, and Summerlee is coiled up in his chair, while Challenger, still fingering the screws of his microscope, is keeping up a continual low, deep, inarticulate growl like the sea after a storm. Lord John comes over to me, and we look out together into the night.

There is a pale new moon – the last moon that human eyes will ever rest upon – and the stars are most brilliant. Even in the clear plateau air of South America I have never seen them brighter. Possibly this etheric change has some effect upon light. The funeral pyre of Brighton is still blazing, and there is a very distant patch of scarlet in the western sky, which may mean trouble at Arundel or Chichester, possibly even at Portsmouth. I sit and muse and make an occasional note. There is a sweet melancholy in the air. Youth and beauty and chivalry and love – is this to be the end of it all? The starlit earth looks a dreamland of gentle peace. Who would imagine it as the terrible Golgotha strewn with the bodies of the human race? Suddenly, I find myself laughing.

'Halloa, young fellah!' says Lord John, staring at me in surprise. 'We could do with a joke in these hard times. What was it, then?'

'I was thinking of all the great unsolved questions,' I answer; 'the questions that we spent so much labour and thought over. Think of Anglo-German competition, for example – or the Persian Gulf that my old chief was so keen about. Whoever would have guessed, when we fumed and fretted so, how they were to be eventually solved?'

We fall into silence again. I fancy that each of us is thinking of friends that have gone before. Mrs. Challenger is sobbing quietly, and her husband is whispering to her. My mind turns to all the most unlikely people, and I see each of them lying white and rigid as poor Austin does in the yard. There is McArdle, for example, I know exactly where he is, with his face upon his writing-desk and his hand on his own telephone, just as I heard him fall. Beaumont, the editor, too – I suppose he is lying upon the blue-and-red Turkey carpet which adorned his sanctum. And the fellows in the reporters' room – Macdona and Murray and Bond. They had certainly died hard at work on their job, with note-books full of vivid impressions and strange happenings in their hands. I could just imagine how this one would have been packed off to the doctors, and that other to Westminster, and yet a third to St. Paul's. What glorious rows of headlines they must have seen as a last vision beautiful, never destined to materialize in printer's ink! I could see Macdona among the doctors – 'Hope in Harley Street' – Mac had always a weakness for alliteration. 'Interview with Mr. Soley Wilson.' 'Famous Specialist says "Never despair!" ' 'Our Special Correspondent found the eminent scientist seated upon the roof, whither he had retreated to avoid the crowd of terrified patients who had stormed his dwelling. With a manner which plainly showed his appreciation of the immense gravity of the occasion, the celebrated physician refused to admit that every avenue of hope had been closed.' That's how Mac would start. Then there was Bond; he would probably do St. Paul's. He fancied his own literary touch. My word, what a theme for him! 'Standing in the little gallery under the dome, and looking down upon that packed mass of despairing humanity, grovelling at this last instant before a Power which they had so persistently ignored, there rose to my ears from the swaying crowd such a low moan of entreaty and terror, such a shuddering cry for help to the Unknown, that –' and so forth.

Yes, it would be a great end for a reporter, though, like myself, he would die with the treasures still unused. What would Bond not give, poor chap, to see 'J. H. B.' at the foot of a column like that?

But what drivel I am writing! It is just an attempt to pass the weary time. Mrs. Challenger has gone to the inner dressing-room, and the Professor says that she is asleep. He is making notes and consulting books at the central table, as calmly as if years of placid work lay before him. He writes with a very noisy quill pen which seems to be screeching scorn at all who disagree with him.

Summerlee has dropped off in his chair, and gives from time to time a peculiarly exasperating snore. Lord John lies back with his hands in his pockets, and his eyes closed. How people can sleep under such conditions is more than I can imagine.

Three-thirty a.m. I have just awakened with a start. It was five minutes past eleven when I made my last entry. I remember winding up my watch and noting the time. So I have wasted some five hours of the little span still left to us. Who would have believed it possible? But I feel very much fresher, and ready for my fate – or try to persuade myself that I am. And yet, the fitter a man is, and the higher his tide of life, the more must he shrink from death. How wise and how merciful is that provision of Nature by which his earthly anchor is usually loosened by many little imperceptible tugs, until his consciousness has drifted out of its untenable earthly harbour into the great sea beyond!

Mrs. Challenger is still in the dressing-room. Challenger has fallen asleep in his chair. What a picture! His enormous frame leans back, his huge, hairy hands are clasped across his waistcoat, and his head is so tilted that I can see nothing above his collar save a tangled bristle of luxuriant beard. He shakes with the vibration of his own snoring. Summerlee adds his occasional high tenor to Challenger's sonorous bass. Lord John is sleeping also, his long body doubled up sideways in a basket-chair. The first cold light of dawn is just stealing into the room, and everything is grey and mournful.

I look out at the sunrise – that fateful sunrise which will shine upon an unpeopled world. The human race is gone, extinguished in a day, but the planets swing round and the tides rise or fall, and the wind whispers, and all Nature goes her way, down, as it would seem, to the very amœba, with never a sign that he who styled himself the lord of creation had ever blessed or cursed the universe with his presence. Down in the yard lies Austin with sprawling limbs, his face glimmering white in the dawn, and the hose-nozzle still projecting from his dead hand. The whole of human kind is typified in that one half-ludicrous and half-pathetic figure, lying so helpless beside the machine which it used to control.

Here end the notes which I made at the time. Henceforward events were too swift and too poignant to allow me to write, but they are too clearly outlined in my memory that any detail could escape me.

Some chokiness in my throat made me look at the oxygen cylinders, and I was startled at what I saw. The sands of our lives were running very low. At some period in the night Challenger had switched the tube from the third to the fourth cylinder. Now it was clear that this also was nearly exhausted. That horrible feeling of constriction was closing in upon me. I ran across and, unscrewing the nozzle, I changed it to our last supply. Even as I did so my conscience pricked me, for I felt that perhaps if I had held my hand all of them might have passed in their sleep. The thought was banished, however, by the voice of the lady from the inner room, crying:

'George, George, I am stifling!'

'It is all right, Mrs. Challenger,' I answered, as the others started to their feet. 'I have just turned on a fresh supply.'

Even at such a moment I could not help smiling at Challenger, who with a great hairy fist in each eye was like a huge, bearded baby, new wakened out of sleep. Summerlee was shivering like a man with the ague, human fears, as he realized his position, rising for an instant above the stoicism of the man of science. Lord John, however, was as cool and alert as if he had just been roused on a hunting morning.

'Fifthly and lastly,' said he, glancing at the tube. 'Say, young fellah, don't tell me you've been writin' up your impressions in that paper on your knee.'

'Just a few notes to pass the time.'

'Well, I don't believe anyone but an Irishman would have done that. I expect you'll have to wait till little brother amœba gets grown up before you'll find a reader. He don't seem to take much stock of things just at present. Well, Herr Professor, what are the prospects?'

Challenger was looking out at the great drifts of morning mist which lay over the landscape. Here and there the wooded hills rose like conical islands out of this woolly sea.

'It might be a winding-sheet,' said Mrs. Challenger, who had entered in her dressing-gown. 'There's that song of yours, George, "Ring out the old, ring in the new." It was prophetic. But you are shivering, my poor dear friends. I have been warm under a coverlet all night, and you cold in your chairs. But I'll soon set you right.'

The brave little creature hurried away, and presently we heard the sizzling of a kettle. She was back soon with five steaming cups of cocoa upon a tray.

'Drink these,' said she. 'You will feel so much better.'

And we did. Summerlee asked if he might light his pipe, and we all had cigarettes. It steadied our nerves, I think, but it was a mistake, for it made a dreadful atmosphere in that stuffy room. Challenger had to open the ventilator.

'How long, Challenger?' asked Lord John.

'Possibly three hours,' he answered, with a shrug.

'I used to be frightened,' said his wife. 'But the nearer I get to it, the easier it seems. Don't you think we ought to pray, George?'

'You will pray, dear, if you wish,' the big man answered, very gently. 'We all have our own ways of praying. Mine is a complete acquiescence in whatever Fate may send me – a cheerful acquiescence. The highest religion and the highest science seem to unite on that.'

'I cannot truthfully describe my mental attitude as acquiescence and far less cheerful acquiescence,' grumbled Summerlee, over his pipe. 'I submit because I have to. I confess that I should have liked another year of life to finish my classification of the chalk fossils.'

'Your unfinished work is a small thing,' said Challenger, pompously, 'when weighed against the fact that my own *magnum opus*, "The Ladder of Life," is still in the first stages. My brain, my reading, my experience – in fact, my whole unique equipment – were to be condensed into that epoch-making volume. And yet, as I say, I acquiesce.'

'I expect we've all left some loose ends stickin' out,' said Lord John. 'What are yours, young fellah?'

'I was working at a book of verses,' I answered.

'Well, the world has escaped that, anyhow,' said Lord John. 'There's always compensation somewhere if you grope around.'

'What about you?' I asked.

'Well, it just so happens, that I was tidied up and ready. I'd promised Merivale to go to Tibet for a snow-leopard in the spring. But it's hard on you, Mrs. Challenger, when you have just built up this pretty home.'

'Where George is, there is my home. But, oh, what would I not give for one last walk together in the fresh morning air upon those beautiful downs!'

Our hearts re-echoed her words. The sun had burst through the gauzy mists which veiled it, and the whole broad Weald was washed in golden light. Sitting in our dark and poisonous atmosphere that glorious, clean, windswept country-side seemed a very dream of beauty. Mrs. Challenger held her hand stretched out to it in her longing. We drew up chairs and sat in a semicircle in the window. The atmosphere was already very close. It seemed to me that the shadows of death were drawing in upon us – the last of our race. It was like an invisible curtain closing down upon every side.

'That cylinder is not lastin' too well,' said Lord John, with a long gasp for breath.

'The amount contained is variable,' said Challenger, 'depending upon the pressure and care with which it has been bottled. I am inclined to agree with you, Roxton, that this one is defective.'

'So we are to be cheated out of the last hour of our lives,' Summerlee remarked, bitterly. 'An excellent final illustration of the sordid age in which we have lived. Well, Challenger, now is your time if you wish to study the subjective phenomena of physical dissolution.'

'Sit on the stool at my knee and give me your hand,' said Challenger to his wife. 'I think, my friends, that a further delay in this insufferable atmosphere is hardly advisable. You would not desire it, dear, would you?'

His wife gave a little groan and sank her face against his leg.

'I've seen the folk bathin' in the Serpentine in winter,' said Lord John. 'When the rest are in, you see one or two shiverin' on the bank, envyin' the others that have taken the plunge. It's the last that have the worst of it. I'm all for a header and have done with it.'

'You would open the window and face the ether?'

'Better be poisoned than stifled.'

Summerlee nodded his reluctant acquiescence, and held out his thin hand to Challenger.

'We've had our quarrels in our time, but that's all over,' said he. 'We were good friends and had a respect for each other under the surface. Good-bye!'

'Good-bye, young fellah!' said Lord John. 'The window's plastered up. You can't open it.'

Challenger stooped and raised his wife, pressing her to his breast, while she threw her arms round his neck.

'Give me that field glass, Malone,' said he, gravely.

I handed it to him.

'Into the hands of the Power that made us we render ourselves again!' he shouted in his voice of thunder, and at the words he hurled the field-glass through the window.

Full in our flushed faces, before the last tinkle of falling fragments had died away, there came the wholesome breath of the wind, blowing strong and sweet.

I don't know how long we sat in amazed silence. Then, as in a dream, I heard Challenger's voice once more.

'We are back in normal conditions,' he cried. 'The world has cleared the poison belt, but we alone of all mankind are saved.'

CHAPTER V

The Dead World

I REMEMBER THAT WE ALL SAT GASPING in our chairs, with that sweet, wet south-western breeze, fresh from the sea, flapping the muslin curtains and cooling our flushed faces. I wonder how long we sat! None of us afterwards could agree at all on that point. We were bewildered, stunned, semi-conscious. We had all braced our courage for death, but this fearful and sudden new fact – that we must continue to live after we had survived the race to which we belonged – struck us with the shock of a physical blow, and left us prostrate. Then gradually the suspended mechanism began to move once more; the shuttles of memory worked; ideas weaved themselves together in our minds. We saw, with vivid, merciless clearness, the relations between the past, the present, and the future – the lives that we had led and the lives which we would have to live. Our eyes turned in silent horror upon those of our companions and found the same answering look in theirs. Instead of the joy which men might have been expected to feel who had so narrowly escaped an imminent death, a terrible wave of darkest depression submerged us. Everything on earth that we loved had been washed away into the great, infinite, unknown ocean, and here were we marooned upon this desert island of a world, without companions, hopes, or aspirations. A few years' skulking like jackals among the graves of the human race and then our belated and lonely end would come.

'It's dreadful, George, dreadful!' the lady cried, in an agony of sobs. 'If we had only passed with the others! Oh, why did you save us? I feel as if it is we that are dead and everyone else alive.'

Challenger's great eyebrows were drawn down in concentrated thought, while his huge, hairy paw closed upon the outstretched hand of his wife. I had observed that she always held out her arms to him in trouble as a child would to its mother.

'Without being a fatalist to the point of non-resistance,' said he, 'I have always found that the highest wisdom lies in an acquiescence with the actual.' He spoke slowly, and there was a vibration of feeling in his sonorous voice.

'I do *not* acquiesce,' said Summerlee, firmly.

'I don't see that it matters a row of pins whether you acquiesce or whether you don't,' remarked Lord John. 'You've got to take it, whether you take it fightin' or take it lyin' down, so what's the odds whether you acquiesce or not? I can't remember that anyone asked our permission before the thing began, and nobody's likely to ask it now. So what difference can it make what we may think of it?'

'It is just all the difference between happiness and misery,' said Challenger, with an abstracted face, still patting his wife's hand. 'You can swim with the tide and have peace in mind and soul, or you can thrust against it and be bruised and weary. This business is beyond us, so let us accept it as it stands and say no more.'

'But what in the world are we to do with our lives?' I asked, appealing in desperation to the blue, empty heaven. 'What am I to do, for example? There are no newspapers, so there's an end of my vocation.'

'And there's nothin' left to shoot, and no more soldierin', so there's an end of mine,' said Lord John.

'And there are no students, so there's an end of mine,' cried Summerlee.

'But I have my husband and my house, so I can thank Heaven that there is no end of mine,' said the lady.

'Nor is there an end of mine,' remarked Challenger, 'for science is not dead, and this catastrophe in itself will offer us many more absorbing problems for investigation.'

He had now flung open the windows and we were gazing out upon the silent and motionless landscape.

'Let me consider,' he continued. 'It was about three, or a little after, yesterday afternoon that the world finally entered the poison belt to the extent of being completely submerged. It is now nine o'clock. The question is, at what hour did we pass out from it?'

'The air was very bad at daybreak,' said I.

'Later than that,' said Mrs Challenger. 'As late as eight o'clock I distinctly felt the same choking at my throat which came at the outset.'

'Then we shall say that it passed just after eight o'clock. For seventeen hours the world has been soaked in the poisonous ether. For that length of time the Great Gardener has sterilized the human mould which had grown over the surface of His fruit. Is it possible that the work is incompletely done – that others may have survived besides ourselves?'

'That's what I was wonderin',' said Lord John. 'Why should we be the only pebbles on the beach?'

'It is absurd to suppose that anyone besides ourselves can possibly have survived,' said Summerlee, with conviction. 'Consider that the poison was so virulent that even a man who is as strong as an ox, and has not a nerve in his body, like Malone here, could hardly get up the stairs before he fell unconscious. Is it likely that anyone could stand seventeen minutes of it, far less hours?'

'Unless someone saw it coming and made preparation, same as old friend Challenger did.'

'That, I think, is hardly probable,' said Challenger, projecting his beard and sinking his eyelids. 'The combination of observation, inference, and anticipatory imagination which enabled me to foresee the danger is what one can hardly expect twice in the same generation.'

'Then your conclusion is that everyone is certainly dead?'

'There can be little doubt of that. We have to remember, however, that the poison worked from below upwards, and would possibly be less virulent in the higher strata of the atmosphere. It is strange, indeed, that it should be so; but it presents one of those features which will afford us in the future a fascinating field for study. One could imagine, therefore, that if one had to search for survivors one would turn one's eyes with best hopes of success to some Tibetan village or some Alpine farm, many thousands of feet above the sea-level.'

'Well, considerin' that there are no railroads and no steamers you might as well talk about survivors in the moon,' said Lord John. 'But what I'm askin' myself is whether it's really over or whether it's only half-time.'

Summerlee craned his neck to look round the horizon.

'It seems clear and fine,' said he, in a dubious voice; 'but so it did yesterday. I am by no means assured that it is all over.'

Challenger shrugged his shoulders.

'We must come back once more to our fatalism,' said he. 'If the world has undergone this experience before, which is not outside the range of possibility, it was certainly a very long time ago. Therefore, we may reasonably hope that it will be very long before it occurs again.'

'That's all very well,' said Lord John; 'but if you get an earthquake shock you are mighty likely to have a second one right on the top of it. I think we'd be wise to stretch our legs and have a breath of air while we have the chance. Since our oxygen is exhausted we may just as well be caught outside as in.'

It was strange the absolute lethargy which had come upon us as a reaction after our tremendous emotions of the last twenty-four hours. It was both mental and physical, a deep-lying feeling that nothing mattered and that everything was a weariness and a profit-less exertion. Even Challenger had succumbed to it, and sat in his chair, with his great head leaning upon his hands, and his thoughts far away, until Lord John and I, catching him by each arm, fairly lifted him on to his feet, receiving only the glare and growl of an angry mastiff for our trouble. However, once we had got out of our narrow haven of refuge into the wider atmosphere of everyday life, our normal energy came gradually back to us once more.

But what were we to begin to do in that graveyard of a world? Could ever men have been faced with such a question since the dawn of time? It is true that our own physical needs, and even our luxuries, were assured for the future. All the stores of food, all the vintages of wine, all the treasures of art were ours for the taking. But what were we to *do*? Some few tasks appealed to us at once, since they lay ready to our hands. We descended into the kitchen, and laid the two domestics upon their respective beds. They seemed to have died without suffering, one in the chair by the fire, the other upon the scullery floor. Then we carried in poor Austin from the yard. His muscles were set as hard as a board in the most exag-gerated rigor mortis, while the contraction of the fibres had drawn his mouth into a hard sardonic grin. This symptom was prevalent among all who had died from the poison. Wherever we went we were confronted by those grinning faces, which seemed to mock at our dreadful position, smiling silently and grimly at the ill-fated survivors of their race.

'Look here,' said Lord John, who had paced restlessly about the dining-room whilst we partook of some food, 'I don't know how you fellows feel about it, but for my part, I simply *can't* sit here and do nothin'.'

'Perhaps,' Challenger answered, 'you would have the kindness to suggest what you think we ought to do.'

'Get a move on us and see all that has happened.'

'That is what I should myself propose.'

'But not in this little country village. We can see from the window all that this place can teach us.'

'Where should we go, then?'

'To London!'

'That's all very well,' grumbled Summerlee. 'You may be equal to a forty-mile walk, but I'm not so sure about Challenger, with his stumpy legs, and I am perfectly sure about myself.'

Challenger was very much annoyed.

'If you could see your way, sir, to confining your remarks to your own physical peculiarities, you would find that you had an ample field for comment,' he cried.

'I had no intention to offend you, my dear Challenger,' cried our tactless friend. 'You can't be held responsible for your own physique. If Nature has given you a short, heavy body you cannot possibly help having stumpy legs.'

Challenger was too furious to answer. He could only growl and blink and bristle. Lord John hastened to intervene before the dispute became more violent.

'You talk of walking. Why should we walk?' said he.

'Do you suggest taking a train?' asked Challenger, still simmering.

'What's the matter with the motor-car? Why should we not go in that?'

'I am not an expert,' said Challenger, pulling at his beard, reflectively. 'At the same time, you are right in supposing that the human intellect in its higher manifestations should be sufficiently flexible to turn itself to anything. Your idea is an excellent one, Lord John. I myself will drive you all to London.'

'You will do nothing of the kind,' said Summerlee, with decision.

'No, indeed, George!' cried his wife. 'You only tried once, and you remember how you crashed through the gate of the garage.'

'It was a momentary want of concentration,' said Challenger, complacently. 'You can consider the matter settled. I will certainly drive you all to London.'

The situation was relieved by Lord John.

'What's the car?' he asked.

'A twenty-horse Humber.'

'Why, I've driven one for years,' said he. 'By George!' he added. 'I never thought I'd live to take the whole human race in one load. There's just room for five, as I remember it. Get your things on, and I'll be ready at the door by ten o'clock.'

Sure enough, at the hour named, the car came purring and crackling from the yard with Lord John at the wheel. I took my seat beside him, while the lady, a useful buffer state, was squeezed in between the two men of wrath at the back. Then Lord John released his brakes, slid his lever rapidly from first to third, and we sped off upon the strangest drive that ever human beings have taken since man first came upon the earth.

You are to picture the loveliness of Nature upon that August day, the freshness of the morning air, the golden glare of the summer sunshine, the cloudless sky, the luxuriant green of the Sussex woods, and the deep purple of heather-clad downs. As you looked round upon the many-coloured beauty of the scene all thought of a vast catastrophe would have passed from your mind had it not been for one sinister sign – the solemn, all-embracing silence. There is a gentle hum of life which pervades a closely-settled country, so deep and constant that one ceases to observe it as the dweller by the sea loses all sense of the constant murmur of the waves. The twitter of birds, the buzz of insects, the far-off echo of voices, the lowing of cattle, the distant barking of dogs, roar of trains, and rattle of carts – all these form one low, unremitting note, striking unheeded upon the ear. We missed it now. This deadly silence was appalling. So solemn was it, so impressive, that the buzz and rattle of our motor-car seemed an unwarrantable intrusion, an indecent disregard of this reverent stillness which lay like a pall over and round the ruins of humanity. It was this grim hush, and the tall clouds of smoke which rose here and there over the countryside from smouldering buildings, which cast a chill into our hearts as we gazed round at the glorious panorama of the Weald.

And then there were the dead! At first those endless groups of drawn and grinning faces filled us with a shuddering horror. So vivid and mordant was the impression that I can live over again that slow descent of the Station Hill, the passing by the nurse-girl with the two babes, the sight of the old horse on his knees between the shafts, the cabman twisted across his seat, and the young man inside with his hand upon the open door in the very act of springing out. Lower down were six reapers all in a litter, their limbs crossing, their dead, unwinking eyes gazing upwards at the glare of heaven. These things I see as in a photograph. But soon, by the merciful provision of Nature, the over-excited nerve ceased to respond. The very vastness of the horror took away from its personal appeal. Individuals merged into groups, groups into crowds, crowds into a universal phenomenon which one soon accepted as the inevitable detail of every scene. Only here and there, where some particularly brutal or grotesque incident caught the attention, did the mind come back with a sudden shock to the personal and human meaning of it all.

Above all there was the fate of the children. That, I remember, filled us with the strongest sense of intolerable injustice. We could have wept – Mrs. Challenger did weep – when we passed a great Council school and saw the long trail of tiny figures scattered down the road which led from it. They had been dismissed by their terrified teachers, and were speeding for their homes when the poison caught them in its net. Great numbers of people were at the open windows of the houses. In Tunbridge Wells there was hardly one which had not its staring, smiling face. At the last instant the need of air, that very craving for oxygen which we alone had been able to satisfy, had sent them flying to the window. The side walks, too, were littered with men and women, hatless and bonnet-less, who had rushed out of the houses. Many of them had fallen in the road-way. It was a lucky thing that in Lord John we had found an expert driver, for it was no easy matter to pick one's way. Passing through the villages or towns we could only go at a walking pace, and once, I remember, opposite the school at Tonbridge, we had to halt some time while we carried aside the bodies which blocked our path.

A few small, definite pictures stand out in my memory from amid that long panorama of death upon the Sussex and Kentish high roads. One was that of a great, glittering motor-car standing outside the inn at the village of Southborough. It bore, as I should guess, some pleasure party upon their return from Brighton or from East-bourne. There were three gaily dressed women, all young and beau-tiful, one of them with a Peking spaniel upon her lap. With them were a rakish-looking elderly man and a young aristocrat, his eye-glass still in his eye, his cigarette burned down to the stub between the fingers of his begloved hand. Death must have come on them in an instant and fixed them as they sat. Save that the elderly man had at the last moment torn out his collar in an effort to breathe, they might all have been asleep. On one side of the car a waiter with some broken glasses beside a tray was huddled near the step. On the other two very ragged tramps, a man and a woman, lay where they had fallen, the man with his long, thin arm still outstretched, even as he had asked for alms in his lifetime. One instant of time had put aristocrat, waiter, tramp, and dog upon one common footing of inert and dissolving protoplasm.

I remember another singular picture, some miles on the London side of Sevenoaks. There is a large convent upon the left, with a long, green slope in front of it. Upon this slope were assembled a great number of school children, all kneeling at prayer. In front of them was a fringe of nuns, and higher up the slope, facing towards them, a single figure whom we took to be the Mother Superior. Unlike the pleasure-seekers in the motor-car, these people seemed to have had warning of their danger, and to have died beautifully together, the teachers and the taught, assembled for their last common lesson.

My mind is still stunned by that terrific experience, and I grope vainly for means of expression by which I can reproduce the emo-tions which we felt. Perhaps it is best and wisest not to try, but merely to indicate the facts. Even Summerlee and Challenger were crushed, and we heard nothing of our companions behind us save an occasional whimper from the lady. As to Lord John, he was too intent upon his wheel and the difficult task of threading his way along such roads to have time or inclination for conversation. One phrase he used with such wearisome iteration that it stuck in my memory, and at last almost made me laugh as a comment upon the day of doom.

'Pretty doin's! What!'

That was his ejaculation as each fresh tremendous combination of death and disaster displayed itself before us. 'Pretty doin's! What!' he cried, as we descended the Station Hill at Rotherfield, and it was still 'Pretty doin's! What!' as we picked our way through a wilderness of death in the High Street of Lewisham and the Old Kent Road.

It was here that we received a sudden and amazing shock. Out of the window of a humble corner house there appeared a fluttering handkerchief waving at the end of a long, thin human arm. Never had the sight of unexpected death caused our hearts to stop and then throb so wildly as did this amazing indication of life. Lord John ran the motor to the kerb, and in an instant we had rushed through the open door of the house and up the staircase to the second-floor front room from which the signal proceeded.

A very old lady sat in a chair by the open window, and close to her, laid across a second chair, was a cylinder of oxygen, smaller but of the same shape as those which had saved our own lives. She turned her thin, drawn, bespectacled face towards us as we crowded in at the doorway.

'I feared that I was abandoned here for ever,' said she, 'for I am an invalid and cannot stir.'

'Well, madam,' Challenger answered, 'it is a lucky chance that we happened to pass.'

'I have one all-important question to ask you,' said she. 'Gentlemen, I beg that you will be frank with me. What effect will these events have upon London and North-Western Railway shares?'

We should have laughed had it not been for the tragic eagerness with which she listened for our answer. Mrs. Burston, for that was her name, was an aged widow, whose whole income depended upon a small holding of this stock. Her life had been regulated by the rise or fall of the dividend, and she could form no conception of existence save as it was effected by the quotation of her shares. In vain we pointed out to her that all the money in the world was hers for the taking, and was useless when taken. Her old mind would not adapt itself to the new idea, and she wept loudly over her vanished stock. 'It was all I had,' she wailed. 'If that is gone I may as well go too.'

Amid her lamentations we found out how this frail old plant had lived where the whole great forest had fallen. She was a confirmed invalid and an asthmatic. Oxygen had been prescribed for her malady, and a tube was in her room at the moment of the crisis. She had naturally inhaled some as had been her habit when there was a difficulty with her breathing. It had given her relief, and by doling out her supply she had managed to survive the night. Finally she had fallen asleep and been awakened by the buzz of our motor-car. As it was impossible to take her on with us, we saw that she had all necessaries of life and promised to communicate with her in a couple of days at the latest. So we left her, still weeping bitterly over her vanished stock.

As we approached the Thames the block in the streets became thicker and the obstacles more bewildering. It was with difficulty that we made our way across London Bridge. The approaches to it upon the Middlesex side were choked from end to end with frozen traffic which made all further advance in that direction impossible. A ship was blazing brightly alongside one of the wharves near the bridge, and the air was full of drifting smuts and of a heavy acrid smell of burning. There was a cloud of dense smoke somewhere near the Houses of Parliament, but it was impossible from where we were to see what was on fire.

'I don't know how it strikes you,' Lord John remarked, as he brought his engine to a standstill, 'but it seems to me the country is more cheerful than the town. Dead London is gettin' on my nerves. I'm for a cast round and then gettin' back to Rotherfield.'

'I confess that I do not see what we can hope for here,' said Professor Summerlee.

'At the same time,' said Challenger, his great voice booming strangely amid the silence, 'it is difficult for us to conceive that out of seven millions of people there is only this one old woman who by some peculiarity of constitution or some accident of occupation has managed to survive this catastrophe.'

'If there should be others, how can we hope to find them, George?' asked the lady. 'And yet I agree with you that we cannot go back until we have tried.'

Getting out of the car, and leaving it by the kerb, we walked with some difficulty along the crowded pavement of King William

Street, and entered the open door of a large insurance office. It was a corner house, and we chose it as commanding a view in every direction. Ascending the stair, we passed through what I suppose to have been the board-room, for eight elderly men were seated round a long table in the centre of it. The high window was open and we all stepped out upon the balcony. From it we could see the crowded City streets radiating in every direction, while below us the road was black from side to side with the tops of the motionless taxis. All, or nearly all, had their heads pointed outwards, showing how the terrified men of the City had at the last moment made a vain endeavour to rejoin their families in the suburbs or the country. Here and there amid the humbler cabs towered the great brass-spangled motor-car of some wealthy magnate, wedged hopelessly among the dammed stream of arrested traffic. Just beneath us there was such a one of great size and luxurious appearance, with its owner, a fat old man, leaning out, half his gross body through the window, and his podgy hand, gleaming with diamonds, outstretched as he urged his chauffeur to make a last effort to break through the press.

A dozen motor-buses towered up like islands in this flood, the passengers who crowded the roofs lying all huddled together and across each others' laps like a child's toys in a nursery. On a broad lamp pedestal, in the centre of the roadway, a burly policeman was standing, leaning his back against the post in so natural an attitude that it was hard to realize that he was not alive, while at his feet there lay a ragged newsboy with his bundle of papers on the ground beside him. A paper-cart had got blocked in the crowd, and we could read in large letters, black upon yellow, 'Scene at Lord's. County match interrupted.' This must have been the earliest edition, for there were other placards bearing the legend, 'Is it the End? Great Scientist's Warning.' And another, 'Is Challenger Justified? Ominous Rumours.'

Challenger pointed the latter placard out to his wife, as it thrust itself like a banner above the throng. I could see him throw out his chest and stroke his beard as he looked at it. It pleased and flattered that complex mind to think that London had died with his name and his words still present in their thoughts. His feelings were so evident that they aroused the sardonic comment of his colleague.

'In the limelight to the last, Challenger,' he remarked.

'So it would appear,' he answered, complacently. 'Well,' he added, as he looked down the long vista of the radiating streets, all silent and all choked up with death, 'I really see no purpose to be served by our staying any longer in London. I suggest that we return at once to Rotherfield, and then take counsel as to how we shall most profitably employ the years which lie before us.'

Only one other picture shall I give of the scenes which we carried back in our memories from the dead City. It is a glimpse which we had of the interior of the old church of St. Mary's, which is at the very point where our car was awaiting us. Picking our way among the prostrate figures upon the steps, we pushed open the swing door and entered. It was a wonderful sight. The church was crammed from end to end with kneeling figures in every posture of supplication and abasement. At the last dreadful moment, brought suddenly face to face with the realities of life, those terrific realities which hand over us even while we follow the shadows, the terrified people had rushed into those old City churches which for generations had hardly ever held a congregation. There they huddled as close as they could kneel, many of them in their agitation still wearing their hats, while above them in the pulpit a young man in lay dress had apparently been addressing them when he and they had been over-whelmed by the same fate. He lay now, like Punch in his booth, with his head and two limp arms hanging over the ledge of the pulpit. It was a nightmare, the grey, dusty church, the rows of ago-nized figures, the dimness and silence of it all. We moved about with hushed whispers, walking upon our tiptoes.

And then suddenly I had an idea. At one corner of the church, near the door, stood the ancient font, and behind it a deep recess in which there hung the ropes for the bell-ringers. Why should we not send a message out over London which would attract to us anyone who might still be alive? I ran across, and pulling at the list-covered rope I was surprised to find how difficult it was to swing the bell. Lord John had followed me.

'By George, young fellah!' said he, pulling off his coat. 'You've hit on a dooced good notion. Give me a grip and we'll soon have a move on it.'

But, even then, so heavy was the bell that it was not until Chal-lenger and Summerlee had added their weight to ours that we heard the roaring and clanging above our heads which told us that the great clapper was ringing out its music. Far over dead London resounded our message of comradeship, and hope to any fellow-man surviving. It cheered our own hearts, that strong, metallic call, and we turned the more earnestly to our work, dragged two feet off the earth with each upward jerk of the rope, but all straining together on the downward heave, Challenger the lowest of all, bending all his great strength to the task, and flopping up and down like a monstrous bull-frog, croaking with every pull. It was at that moment that an artist might have taken a picture of the four adventurers, the comrades of many strange perils in the past, whom fate had now chosen for so supreme an experience. For half an hour we worked, the sweat dropping from our faces, our arms and backs aching with the exertion. Then we went out into the portico of the church, and looked eagerly up and down the silent, crowded streets. Not a sound, not a motion, in answer to our summons.

'It's no use. No one is left,' I cried.

'We can do nothing more,' said Mrs. Challenger. 'For God's sake, George, let us get back to Rotherfield. Another hour of this dreadful, silent City would drive me mad.'

We got into the car without another word. Lord John backed her round and turned her to the South. To us the chapter seemed closed. Little did we foresee the strange new chapter which was to open.

CHAPTER VI

The Great Awakening

AND NOW I COME TO THE END of this extraordinary incident so overshadowing in its importance, not only in our own small, individual lives, but in the general history of the human race. As I said when I began my narrative, when that history comes to be written this occurrence will surely stand out among all other events like a mountain towering among its foothills. Our generation has been reserved for a very special fate since it has been chosen to experience so wonderful a thing. How long its effect may last – how long mankind may preserve the humility and reverence which this great shock has taught it, can only be shown by the future. I think it is safe to say that things can never be quite the same again. Never can one realize how powerless and ignorant one is, and how one is upheld by an unseen hand, until for an instant that hand has seemed to close and to crush. Death has been imminent upon us. We know that at any moment it may be again. That grim presence shadows our lives, but who can deny that in that shadow the sense of duty, the feeling of sobriety and responsibility, the appreciation of the gravity and of the objects of life, the earnest desire to develop and improve, have grown and become real with us to a degree that has leavened our whole society from end to end? It is something beyond sects and beyond dogmas. It is rather an alteration of perspective, a shifting of our sense of proportion, a vivid realization that we are insignificant and evanescent creatures, existing on sufferance and at the mercy of the first chill wind from the unknown. But if the world has grown graver with this knowledge it is not, I think, a sadder place in consequence. Surely we are agreed that the more sober and restrained pleasures of the present are deeper as well as wiser than the noisy, foolish hustle which passed so often for enjoyment in the days of old – days so recent and yet already so inconceivable. Those empty lives which were wasted in aimless visiting and being visited, in the worry of great and unnecessary households, in the arranging and eating of elaborate and tedious meals, have now found rest and health in the reading, the music, the gentle family communion which comes from a simpler and saner division of their time. With greater health and greater pleasure they are richer than before, even after they have paid those increased contributions to the common fund which have so raised the standard of life in these islands.

There is some clash of opinion as to the exact hour of the great awakening. It is generally agreed that, apart from the difference of clocks, there may have been local causes which influenced the action of the poison. Certainly, in each separate district the resurrection was practically simultaneous. There are numerous witnesses that Big Ben pointed to ten minutes past six at the moment. The Astronomer Royal has fixed the Greenwich time at twelve past six. On the other hand, Laird Johnson, a very capable East Anglia observer, has recorded six-twenty as the hour. In the Hebrides it was as late as seven. In our own case there can be no doubt whatever, for I was seated in Challenger's study with his carefully-tested chronometer in front of me at the moment. The hour was a quarter-past six.

An enormous depression was weighing upon my spirits. The cumulative effect of all the dreadful sights which we had seen upon our journey was heavy upon my soul. With my abounding animal health and great physical energy any kind of mental clouding was a rare event. I had the Irish faculty of seeing some gleam of humour in every darkness. But now the obscurity was appalling and unrelieved. The others were downstairs making their plans for the future. I sat by the open window, my chin resting upon my hand, and my mind absorbed in the misery of our situation. Could we continue to live? That was the question which I had begun to ask myself. Was it possible to exist upon a dead world? Just as in physics the greater body draws to itself the lesser, would we not feel an overpowering attraction from that vast body of humanity which had passed into the unknown? How would the end come? Would it be from a return of the poison? Or would the earth be uninhabitable from the mephitic products of universal decay? Or, finally, might our awful situation prey upon and unbalance our minds? A group of insane folk upon a dead world! My mind was brooding upon this last dreadful idea when some slight noise caused me to look down upon the road beneath me. The old cab-horse was coming up the hill!

I was conscious at the same instant of the twittering of birds, of someone coughing in the yard below, and of a background of movement in the landscape. And yet I remember that it was that absurd, emaciated, superannuated cab-horse which held my gaze. Slowly and wheezily it was climbing the slope. Then my eye travelled to the driver sitting hunched up upon the box, and finally to the young man who was leaning out of the window in some excitement and shouting a direction. They were all indubitably, aggressively alive!

Everybody was alive once more! Had it all been a delusion? Was it conceivable that this whole poison belt incident had been an elaborate dream? For an instant my startled brain was really ready to believe it. Then I looked down, and there was the rising blister on my hand where it was frayed by the rope of the City bell. It had really been so, then. And yet here was the world resuscitated – here was life come back in an instant full tide to the planet. Now, as my eyes wandered all over the great landscape, I saw it in every direction – and moving, to my amazement, in the very same groove in which it had halted. There were the golfers. Was it possible that they were going on with their game? Yes, there was a fellow driving off from a tee, and that other group upon the green were surely putting for the hole. The reapers were slowly trooping back to their work. The nurse-girl slapped one of her charges and then began to push the perambulator up the hill. Everyone had unconcernedly taken up the thread at the very point where they had dropped it.

I rushed downstairs, but the hall door was open, and I heard the voices of my companions, loud in astonishment and congratulation, in the yard. How we all shook hands and laughed as we came together, and how Mrs. Challenger kissed us all in her emotion, before she finally threw herself into the bear-hug of her husband!

'But they could not have been asleep!' cried Lord John. 'Dash it all Challenger, you don't mean to believe that those folk were asleep with their staring eyes and stiff limbs, and that awful death-grin on their faces!'

'It can only have been the condition that is called catalepsy,' said Challenger. 'It has been a rare phenomenon in the past and has constantly been mistaken for death. While it endures the temperature falls, the respiration disappears, the heart-beat is indistinguishable – in fact, it *is* death, save that it is evanescent. Even the most comprehensive mind' – here he closed his eyes and simpered – 'could hardly conceive a universal outbreak of it in this fashion.'

'You may label it catalepsy,' remarked Summerlee, 'but, after all, that is only a name, and we know as little of the result as we do of the poison which has caused it. The most we can say is that the vitiated ether has produced a temporary death.'

Austin was seated all in a heap on the step of the car. It was his coughing which I had heard from above. He had been holding his head in silence, but now he was muttering to himself and running his eyes over the car.

'Young fat-head!' he grumbled. 'Can't leave things alone!'

'What's the matter, Austin?'

'Lubricators left running, sir. Someone has been fooling with the car. I expect it's that young garden boy, sir.'

Lord John looked guilty.

'I don't know what's amiss with me,' continued Austin, staggering to his feet. 'I expect I came over queer when I was hosing her down. I seem to remember flopping over by the step. But I'll swear I never left those lubricator taps on.'

In a condensed narrative the astonished Austin was told what had happened to himself and the world. The mystery of the dripping lubricators was also explained to him. He listened with an air of deep distrust when told how an amateur had driven his car, and with absorbed interest to the few sentences in which our experiences of the sleeping City were recorded. I can remember his comment when the story was concluded.

'Was you outside the Bank of England, sir?'

'Yes, Austin –'

'With all them millions inside and everybody asleep?'

'That was so.'

'And I not there!' he groaned, and turned dismally once more to the hosing of his car.

There was a sudden grinding of wheels upon gravel. The old cab had actually pulled up at Challenger's door. I saw the young occupant step out from it. An instant later the maid, who looked as tousled and bewildered as if she had that instant been roused from the deepest sleep, appeared with a card upon a tray. Challenger snorted ferociously as he looked at it, and his thick black hair seemed to bristle up in his wrath.

'A Pressman!' he growled. Then with a deprecating smile: 'After all, it is natural that the whole world should hasten to know what I think of such an episode.'

'That can hardly be his errand,' said Summerlee, 'for he was on the road in his cab before ever the crisis came.'

I looked at the card: 'James Baxter, London Correspondent, *New York Monitor.*'

'You'll see him?' said I.

'Not I.'

'Oh, George! You should be kinder and more considerate to others. Surely you have learned something from what we have undergone.'

He tut-tutted and shook his big, obstinate head.

'A poisonous breed! Eh, Malone? The worst breed in modern civilization, the ready tool of the quack and the hindrance of the self-respecting man! When did they ever say a good word for me?'

'When did you ever say a good word to them?' I answered. 'Come, sir, this is a stranger who has made a journey to see you. I am sure that you won't be rude to him.'

'Well, well,' he grumbled, 'you come with me and do the talking. I protest in advance against any such outrageous invasion of my private life.' Muttering and mumbling, he came rolling after me like an angry and rather ill-conditioned mastiff.

The dapper young American pulled out his notebook and plunged instantly into his subject.

'I came down, sir,' said he, 'because our people in America would very much like to hear more about this danger which is, in your opinion, pressing upon the world.'

'I know of no danger which is now pressing upon the world,' Challenger answered, gruffly.

The Pressman looked at him in mild surprise.

'I meant, sir, the chances that the world might run into a belt of poisonous ether.'

'I do not now apprehend any such danger,' said Challenger.

The Pressman looked even more perplexed.

'You are Professor Challenger, are you not?' he asked.

'Yes, sir; that is my name.'

'I cannot understand, then, how you can say that there is no such danger. I am alluding to your own letter, published above your name in the London *Times* of this morning.'

It was Challenger's turn to look surprised.

'This morning?' said he. 'No London *Times* was published this morning.'

'Surely, sir,' said the American, in mild remonstrance, 'you must admit that the London *Times* is a daily paper.' He drew out a copy from his inside pocket. 'Here is the letter to which I refer.'

Challenger chuckled and rubbed his hands.

'I begin to understand,' said he. 'So you read this letter this morning?'

'Yes, sir.'

'And came at once to interview me?'

'Yes, sir.'

'Did you observe anything unusual upon the journey down?'

'Well, to tell the truth, your people seemed more lively and generally human than I have ever seen them. The baggage man set out to tell me a funny story, and that's a new experience for me in this country.'

'Nothing else?'

'Why, no, sir, not that I can recall.'

'Well, now, what hour did you leave Victoria?'

The American smiled.

'I came here to interview you, Professor, but it seems to be a case of "Is this nigger fishing, or is this fish niggering?" You're doing most of the work.'

'It happens to interest me. Do you recall the hour?'

'Sure. It was half-past twelve.'

'And you arrived?'

'At a quarter-past two.'

'And you hired a cab?'

'That was so.'

'How far do you suppose it is to the station?'

'Well, I should reckon the best part of two miles.'

'So how long do you think it took you?'

'Well, half an hour, maybe, with that asthmatic in front.'

'So it should be three o'clock?'

'Yes, or a trifle after it.'

'Look at your watch.'

The American did so, and then stared at us in astonishment.

'Say!' he cried. 'It's run down. That horse has broken every record, sure. The sun is pretty low, now that I come to look at it. Well, there's something here I don't understand.'

'Have you no remembrance of anything remarkable as you came up the hill?'

'Well, I seem to recollect that I was mighty sleepy once. It comes back to me that I wanted to say something to the driver, and that I couldn't make him heed me. I guess it was the heat, but I felt swimmy for a moment. That's all.'

'So it is with the whole human race,' said Challenger to me. 'They have all felt swimmy for a moment. None of them have as yet any comprehension of what has occurred. Each will go on with his interrupted job as Austin has snatched up his hose-pipe or the golfer continued his game. Your editor, Malone, will continue the issue of his papers, and very much amazed he will be at finding that an issue is missing. Yes, my young friend,' he added, to the American reporter, with a sudden mood of amused geniality, 'it may interest you to know that the world has swum through the poisonous current which swirls like the Gulf Stream through the ocean of ether. You will also kindly note for your own future convenience that to-day is not Friday, August the twenty-seventh, but Saturday, August the twenty-eighth, and that you sat senseless in your cab for twenty-eight hours upon the Rotherfield Hill.'

And 'right here,' as my American colleague would say, I may bring this narrative to an end. It is, as you are probably aware, only a fuller and more detailed version of the account which appeared in the Monday edition of the *Daily Gazette* – an account which has been universally admitted to be the greatest journalistic scoop of all time, which sold no fewer than three-and-a-half million copies of the paper. Framed upon the wall of my sanctum I retain those magnificent headlines:

TWENTY-EIGHT HOURS' WORLD COMA
UNPRECEDENTED EXPERIENCE
CHALLENGER JUSTIFIED
OUR CORRESPONDENT ESCAPES
ENTHRALLING NARRATIVE
THE OXYGEN ROOM
WEIRD MOTOR DRIVE
DEAD LONDON
REPLACING THE MISSING PAGE
GREAT FIRES AND LOSS OF LIFE
WILL IT RECUR?

Underneath this glorious scroll came nine-and-a-half columns of narrative, in which appeared the first, last, and only account of the history of the planet, so far as one observer could draw it, during one long day of its existence. Challenger and Summerlee have treated the matter in a joint scientific paper, but to me alone was left the popular account. Surely I can sing 'Nunc Dimittis.' What is left but anti-climax in the life of a journalist after that!

But let me not end on sensational headlines and a merely personal triumph. Rather let me quote the sonorous passages in which the greatest of daily papers ended its admirable leader upon the subject – a leader which might well be filed for reference by every thoughtful man.

'It has been a well-worn truism,' said *The Times*, 'that our human race are a feeble folk before the infinite latent forces which surround us. From the prophets of old and from the philosophers of our own time the same message and warning have reached us. But, like all oft-repeated truths, it has in time lost something of its actuality and cogency. A lesson, an actual experience, was needed to bring it home. It is from that salutory but terrible ordeal that we have just emerged, with minds which are still stunned by the suddenness of the blow, and with spirits which are chastened by the realization of our own limitations and impotence. The world has paid a fearful price for its schooling. Hardly yet have we learned the full tale of disaster, but the destruction by fire of New York, of Orleans, and of Brighton constitutes in itself one of the greatest tragedies in the history of our race. When the account of the railway and shipping accidents has been completed, it will furnish grim reading, although there is evidence to show that in the vast majority of cases the drivers of trains and engineers of steamers succeeded in shutting off their motive power before succumbing to the poison. But the material damage, enormous as it is both in life and in property, is not the consideration which will be uppermost in our minds to-day. All this may in time be forgotten. But what will not be forgotten, and what will and should continue to obsess our imaginations, is this revelation of the possibilities of the universe, this destruction of our ignorant self-complacency, and this demonstration of how narrow is the path of our material existence, and what abysses may lie upon either side of it. Solemnity and humility are at the base of our emotions to-day. May they be the foundations upon which a more earnest and reverent race may build a more worthy temple.'

THE END

THE LAND OF MIST

CHAPTER I

In Which Our Special Commissioners Make a Start

THE GREAT PROFESSOR CHALLENGER has been – very improperly and imperfectly – used in fiction. A daring author placed him in impossible and romantic situations in order to see how he would react to them. He reacted to the extent of a libel action, an abortive appeal for suppression, a riot in Sloane Street, two personal assaults, and the loss of his position as lecturer upon Physiology at the London School of Sub-Tropical Hygiene. Otherwise, the matter passed more peaceably than might have been expected.

But he was losing something of his fire. Those huge shoulders were a little bowed. The spade-shaped Assyrian beard showed tangles of grey amid the black, his eyes were a trifle less aggressive, his smile less self-complacent, his voice as monstrous as ever but less ready to roar down all opposition. Yet he was dangerous, as all around him were painfully aware. The volcano was not extinct, and constant rumblings threatened some new explosion. Life had much yet to teach him, but he was a little less intolerant in learning.

There was a definite date for the change which had been wrought in him. It was the death of his wife. That little bird of a woman had made her nest in the big man's heart. He had all the tenderness and chivalry which the strong can have for the weak. By yielding everything she had won everything, as a sweet-natured, tactful woman can. And when she died suddenly from virulent pneumonia following influenza, the man staggered and went down. He came up again, smiling ruefully like the stricken boxer, and ready to carry on for many a round with Fate. But he was not the same man, and if it had not been for the help and comradeship of his daughter Enid, he might have never rallied from the blow. She it was who, with clever craft, lured him into every subject which would excite his combative nature and infuriate his mind, until he lived once more in the present and not the past. It was only when she saw him turbulent in controversy, violent to pressmen, and generally offensive to those around him, that she felt he was really in a fair way to recovery.

Enid Challenger was a remarkable girl and should have a paragraph to herself. With the raven-black hair of her father, and the blue eyes and fresh colour of her mother, she was striking, if not beautiful, in appearance. She was quiet, but she was very strong. From her infancy she had either to take her own part against her father, or else to consent to be crushed and to become a mere automaton worked by his strong fingers. She was strong enough to hold her own in a gentle, elastic fashion, which bent to his moods and reasserted itself when they were past. Lately she had felt the constant pressure too oppressive and she had relieved it by feeling out for a career of her own. She did occasional odd jobs for the London press, and did them in such fashion that her name was beginning to be known in Fleet Street. In finding this opening she had been greatly helped by an old friend of her father – and possibly of the reader – Mr. Edward Malone of the *Daily Gazette*.

Malone was still the same athletic Irishman who had once won his international cap at Rugby, but life had toned him down also, and made him a more subdued and thoughtful man. He had put away a good deal when last his football-boots had been packed away for good. His muscles may have wilted and his joints stiffened, but his mind was deeper and more active. The boy was dead and the man was born. In person he had altered little, but his moustache was heavier, his back a little rounded, and some lines of thought were tracing themselves upon his brow. Post-war conditions and new world problems had left their mark. For the rest he had made his name in journalism and even to a small degree in literature. He was still a bachelor, though there were some who thought that his hold on that condition was precarious, and that Miss Enid Challenger's little white fingers could disengage it. Certainly they were very good chums.

It was a Sunday evening in October, and the lights were just beginning to twinkle out through the fog which had shrouded London from early morning. Professor Challenger's flat at Victoria West Gardens was upon the third floor, and the mist lay thick upon the windows, while the low hum of the attenuated Sunday traffic rose up from an invisible highway beneath, which was outlined only by scattered patches of dull radiance. Professor Challenger sat with his thick, bandy legs outstretched to the fire, and his hands thrust deeply into his trouser pockets. His dress had a little of the eccentricity of genius, for he wore a loose-collared shirt, a large knotted maroon-coloured silk tie, and a black velvet smoking-jacket, which, with his flowing beard, gave him the appearance of an elderly and Bohemian artist. On one side of him ready for an excursion, with bowl hat, short-skirted dress of black, and all the other fashionable devices with which women contrive to deform the beauties of nature, there sat his daughter, while Malone, hat in hand, waited by the window.

'I think we should get off, Enid. It is nearly seven,' said he.

They were writing joint articles upon the religious denominations of London, and on each Sunday evening they sallied out together to sample some new one and get copy for the next week's issue of the *Gazette*.

'It's not till eight, Ted. We have lots of time.'

'Sit down, sir! Sit down!' boomed Challenger, tugging at his beard as was his habit if his temper was rising. 'There is nothing annoys me more than having anyone standing behind me. A relic of atavism and the fear of a dagger, but still persistent. That's right. For heaven's sake put your hat down! You have a perpetual air of catching a train.'

'That's the journalistic life,' said Malone. 'If we don't catch the perpetual train we get left. Even Enid is beginning to understand that. But still, as you say, there is time enough.'

'How far have you got?' asked Challenger.

Enid consulted a business-like little reporter's notebook. 'We have done seven. There was Westminster Abbey for the Church in its most picturesque form, and Saint Agatha for the High Church, and Tudor Place for the Low. Then there was the Westminster Cathedral for Catholics, Endell Street for Presbyterians, and Gloucester Square for Unitarians. But to-night we are trying to introduce some variety. We are doing the Spiritualists.'

Challenger snorted like an angry buffalo.

'Next week the lunatic asylums, I presume,' said he. 'You don't mean to tell me, Malone, that these ghost people have got churches of their own.'

'I've been looking into that,' said Malone. 'I always look up cold facts and figures before I tackle a job. They have over four hundred registered churches in Great Britain.'

Challenger's snorts now sounded like a whole herd of buffaloes.

'There seems to me to be absolutely no limit to the inanity and credulity of the human race. *Homo Sapiens! Homo idioticus!* Who do they pray to – the ghosts?'

'Well, that's what we want to find out. We should get some copy out of them. I need not say that I share your view entirely, but I've seen something of Atkinson of St. Mary's Hospital lately. He is a rising surgeon, you know.'

'I've heard of him – cerebro-spinal.'

'That's the man. He is level-headed and is looked on as an authority on psychic research, as they call the new science which deals with these matters.'

'Science, indeed!'

'Well, that is what they call it. He seems to take these people seriously. I consult him when I want a reference, for he has the literature at his fingers' end. "Pioneers of the Human Race" – that was his description.'

'Pioneering them to Bedlam,' growled Challenger. 'And literature! What literature have they?'

'Well, that was another surprise. Atkinson has five hundred volumes, but complains that his psychic library is very imperfect. You see, there is French, German, Italian, as well as our own.'

'Well, thank God all the folly is not confined to poor old England. Pestilential nonsense!'

'Have you read it up at all, Father?' asked Enid.

'Read it up! I, with all my interests and no time for one-half of them! Enid, you are too absurd.'

'Sorry, Father. You spoke with such assurance, I thought you knew something about it.'

Challenger's huge head swung round and his lion's glare rested upon his daughter.

'Do you conceive that a logical brain, a brain of the first order, needs to read and to study before it can detect a manifest absurdity? Am I to study mathematics in order to confute the man who tells me that two and two are five? Must I study physics once more and take down my *Principia* because some rogue or fool insists that a table can rise in the air against the law of gravity? Does it take five hundred volumes to inform us of a thing which is proved in every police-court when an impostor is exposed? Enid, I am ashamed of you!'

His daughter laughed merrily.

'Well, Dad, you need not roar at me any more. I give in. In fact, I have the same feeling that you have.'

'None the less,' said Malone, 'some good men support them. I don't see that you can laugh at Lodge and Crookes and the others.'

'Don't be absurd, Malone. Every great mind has its weaker side. It is a sort of reaction against all the good sense. You come suddenly upon a vein of positive nonsense. That is what is the matter with these fellows. No, Enid, I haven't read their reasons, and I don't mean to, either; some things are beyond the pale. If we re-open all the old questions, how can we ever get ahead with the new ones? This matter is settled by common sense, the law of England, and by the universal assent of every sane European.'

'So that's that!' said Enid.

'However,' he continued, 'I can admit that there are occasional excuses for misunderstandings upon the point.' He sank his voice, and his great grey eyes looked sadly up into vacancy. 'I have known cases where the coldest intellect – even my own intellect – might, for a moment have been shaken.'

Malone scented copy.

'Yes, sir?'

Challenger hesitated. He seemed to be struggling with himself. He wished to speak, and yet speech was painful. Then, with an abrupt, impatient gesture, he plunged into his story:

'I never told you, Enid. It was too . . . too intimate. Perhaps too absurd. I was ashamed to have been so shaken. But it shows how even the best balanced may be caught unawares.'

'Yes, sir?'

'It was after my wife's death. You knew her, Malone. You can guess what it meant to me. It was the night after the cremation . . . horrible, Malone, horrible! I saw the dear little body slide down, down . . . and then the glare of flame and the door clanged to.' His great body shook and he passed his big, hairy hand over his eyes.

'I don't know why I tell you this; the talk seemed to lead up to it. It may be a warning to you. That night – the night after the cremation – I sat up in the hall. She was there,' he nodded at Enid. 'She had fallen asleep in a chair, poor girl. You know the house at Rotherfield, Malone. It was in the big hall. I sat by the fireplace, the room all draped in shadow, and my mind draped in shadow also. I should have sent her to bed, but she was lying back in her chair and I did not wish to wake her. It may have been one in the morning – I remember the moon shining through the stained-glass window. I sat and I brooded. Then suddenly there came a noise.'

'Yes, sir?'

'It was low at first – just a ticking. Then it grew louder and more distinct – it was a clear rat-tat-tat. Now comes the queer coincidence, the sort of thing out of which legends grow when credulous folk have the shaping of them. You must know that my wife had a peculiar way of knocking at a door. It was really a little tune which she played with her fingers. I got into the same way so that we could each know when the other knocked. Well, it seemed to me – of course my mind was strained and abnormal – that the taps shaped themselves into the well-known rhythm of her knock. I couldn't localize it. You can think how eagerly I tried. It was above me, somewhere on the woodwork. I lost sense of time. I daresay it was repeated a dozen times at least.'

'Oh, Dad, you never told me!'

'No, but I woke you up. I asked you to sit quiet with me for a little.'

'Yes, I remember that.'

'Well, we sat, but nothing happened. Not a sound more. Of course it was a delusion. Some insect in the wood; the ivy on the outer wall. My own brain furnished the rhythm. Thus do we make fools and children of ourselves. But it gave me an insight. I saw how even a clever man could be deceived by his own emotions.'

'But how do you know, sir, that it was *not* your wife?'

'Absurd, Malone! Absurd, I say! I tell you I saw her in the flames. What was there left?'

'Her soul, her spirit.'

Challenger shook his head sadly.

'When that dear body dissolved into its elements – when its gases went into the air and its residue of solids sank into a grey dust – it was the end. There was no more. She had played her part, played it beautifully, nobly. It was done. Death ends all, Malone. This soul talk is the Animism of savages. It is a superstition, a myth. As a physiologist I will undertake to produce crime or virtue by vascular control or cerebral stimulation. I will turn a Jekyll into a Hyde by a surgical operation. Another can do it by a psychological suggestion. Alcohol will do it. Drugs will do it. Absurd, Malone, absurd! As the tree falls, so does it lie. There is no next morning . . . night – eternal night . . . and long rest for the weary worker.'

'Well, it's a sad philosophy.'

'Better a sad than a false one.'

'Perhaps so. There is something virile and manly in facing the worst. I would not contradict. My reason is with you.'

'But my instincts are against!' cried Enid. 'No, no, never can I believe it.' She threw her arms round the great bull neck. 'Don't tell me, Daddy, that you with all your complex brain and wonderful self are a thing with no more life hereafter than a broken clock!'

'Four buckets of water and a bagful of salts,' said Challenger as he smilingly detached his daughter's grip. 'That's your daddy, my lass, and you may as well reconcile your mind to it. Well, it's twenty to eight. Come back, if you can, Malone, and let me hear your adventures among the insane.'

CHAPTER II

Which Describes an Evening in Strange Company

THE LOVE-AFFAIR OF ENID CHALLENGER and Edward Malone is not of the slightest interest to the reader, for the simple reason that it is not of the slightest interest to the writer. The unseen, unnoticed lure of the unborn babe is common to all youthful humanity. We deal in this chronicle with matters which are less common and of higher interest. It is only mentioned in order to explain those terms of frank and intimate comradeship which the narrative discloses. If the human race has obviously improved in anything – in Anglo-Celtic countries, at least – it is that the prim affectations and sly deceits of the past are lessened, and that young men and women can meet in an equality of clean and honest comradeship.

A taxi took the adventurers down Edgware Road and into the side-street called 'Helbeck Terrace.' Halfway down, the dull line of brick houses was broken by one glowing gap, where an open arch threw a flood of light into the street. The cab pulled up and the man opened the door.

'This is the Spiritualist Church, sir,' said he. Then, as he saluted to acknowledge his tip, he added in the wheezy voice of the man of all weathers: 'Tommy-rot, I call it, sir.' Having eased his conscience thus, he climbed into his seat and a moment later his red rear-lamp was a waning circle in the gloom. Malone laughed.

'*Vox populi*, Enid. That is as far as the public has got at present.'

'Well, it is as far as we have got, for that matter.'

'Yes, but we are prepared to give them a show. I don't suppose Cabby is. By Jove, it will be hard luck if we can't get in!'

There was a crowd at the door and a man was facing them from the top of the step, waving his arms to keep them back.

'It's no good, friends. I am very sorry, but we can't help it. We've been threatened twice with prosecution for over-crowding.' He turned facetious. 'Never heard of an Orthodox Church getting into trouble for that. No, sir, no.'

'I've come all the way from 'Ammersmith,' wailed a voice. The light beat upon the eager, anxious face of the speaker, a little woman in black with a baby in her arms.

'You've come for clairvoyance, Mam,' said the usher, with intelligence. 'See here, give me the name and address and I will write you, and Mrs. Debbs will give you a sitting gratis. That's better than taking your chance in the crowd when, with all the will in the world, you can't all get a turn. You'll have her to yourself. No, sir, there's no use shovin' . . . What's that? . . . Press?'

He had caught Malone by the elbow.

'Did you say Press? The Press boycott us, sir. Look at the weekly list of services in a Saturday's *Times* if you doubt it. You wouldn't know there was such a thing as Spiritualism. . . . What paper, sir? . . . "The *Daily Gazette.*" Well, well, we are getting on. And the lady, too? . . . Special article – my word! Stick to me, sir, and I'll see what I can do. Shut the doors, Joe. No use, friends. When the building fund gets on a bit we'll have more room for you. Now, Miss, this way, if you please.'

This way proved to be down the street and round a side-alley which brought them to a small door with a red lamp shining above it.

'I'll have to put you on the platform – there's no standing room in the body of the hall.'

'Good gracious!' cried Enid.

'You'll have a fine view, Miss, and maybe get a readin' for your-self if your lucky. It often happens that those nearest the medium get the best chance. Now, sir, in here!'

Here was a frowsy little room with some hats and topcoats drap-ing the dirty, white-washed walls. A thin, austere woman, with eyes which gleamed from behind her glasses, was warming her gaunt hands over a small fire. With his back to the fire in the traditional British attitude was a large, fat man with a bloodless face, a ginger moustache and curious, light-blue eyes – the eyes of a deep-sea mariner. A little bald-headed man with huge horn-rimmed specta-cles, and a very handsome and athletic youth in a blue lounge-suit completed the group.

'The others have gone on the platform, Mr. Peeble. There's only five seats left for ourselves.' It was the fat man talking.

'I know, I know,' said the man who had been addressed as Peeble, a nervous, stringy, dried-up person as he now appeared in the light. 'But this is the Press, Mr. Bolsover. *Daily Gazette* – special article. . . . Malone, the name and Challenger. This is Mr. Bolsover, our Presi-dent. This is Mrs. Debbs of Liverpool, the famous clairvoyante. Here is Mr. James, and this tall young gentleman is Mr. Hardy Williams, our energetic secretary. Mr. Williams is a nailer for the buildin' fund. Keep your eye on your pockets if Mr. Williams is around.'

They all laughed.

'Collection comes later,' said Mr. Williams, smiling.

'A good, rousing article is our best collection,' said the stout president. 'Ever been to a meeting before, sir?'

'No,' said Malone.

'Don't know much about it, I expect.'

'No, I don't.'

'Well, well, we must expect a slating. They get it from the humorous angle at first. We'll have you writing a very comic account. I never could see anything very funny in the spirit of one's dead wife, but it's a matter of taste and of knowledge also. If they don't know, how can they take it seriously? I don't blame them. We were mostly like that ourselves once. I was one of Bradlaugh's men, and sat under Joseph MacCabe until my old Dad came and pulled me out.'

'Good for him!' said the Liverpool medium.

'It was the first time I found I had powers of my own. I saw him like I see you now.'

'Was he one of us in the body?'

'Knew no more than I did. But they come on amazin' at the other side if the right folk get hold of them.'

'Time's up!' said Mr. Peeble, snapping his watch. 'You are on the right of the chair, Mrs. Debbs. Will you go first? Then you, Mr. Chairman. Then you two and myself. Get on the left, Mr. Hardy Williams, and lead the singin'. They want warmin' up and you can do it. Now then, if *you* please!'

The platform was already crowded, but the newcomers threaded their way to the front amid a decorous murmur of welcome. Mr. Peeble shoved and exhorted and two end seats emerged upon which Enid and Malone perched themselves. The arrangement suited them well, for they could use their notebooks freely behind the shelter of the folk in front.

'What is your reaction?' whispered Enid.

'Not impressed as yet.'

'No, nor I,' said Enid, 'but it's very interesting all the same.'

People who are in earnest are always interesting, whether you agree with them or not, and it was impossible to doubt that these people were extremely earnest. The hall was crammed, and as one looked down one saw line after line of upturned faces, curiously alike in type, women predominating, but men running them close. That type was not distinguished nor intellectual, but it was undeniably healthy, honest and sane. Small trades-folk, male and female shopwalkers, better class artisans, lower middle-class women worn with household cares, occasional young folk in search of a sensation – these were the impressions which the audience conveyed to the trained observation of Malone.

The fat president rose and raised his hand.

'My friends,' said he, 'we have had once more to exclude a great number of people who desired to be with us to-night. It's all a question of the building fund, and Mr. Williams on my left will be glad to hear from any of you. I was in a hotel last week and they had a notice hung up in the reception bureau: "No cheques accepted". That's not the way Brother Williams talks. You just try him.'

The audience laughed. The atmosphere was clearly that of the lecture-hall rather than of the Church.

'There's just one more thing I want to say before I sit down. I'm not here to talk. I'm here to hold this chair down and I mean to do it. It's a hard thing I ask. I want Spiritualists to keep away on Sunday nights. They take up the room that inquirers should have. You can have the morning service. But it's better for the cause that there should be room for the stranger. You've had it. Thank God for it. Give the other man a chance.' The president plumped back into his chair.

Mr. Peeble sprang to his feet. He was clearly the general utility man who emerges in every society and probably becomes its autocrat. With his thin, eager face and darting hands he was more than a live wire – he was a whole bundle of live wires. Electricity seemed to crackle from his fingertips.

'Hymn One!' he shrieked.

A harmonium droned and the audience rose. It was a fine hymn and lustily sung:

> 'The world hath felt a quickening breath
>   From Heaven's eternal shore,
> And souls triumphant over death
>   Return to earth once more.'

There was a ring of exultation in the voices as the refrain rolled out:

> 'For this we hold our Jubilee
>   For this with joy we sing,
> Oh Grave, where is thy victory,
>   Oh Death, where is thy sting?'

Yes, they were in earnest, these people. And they did not appear to be mentally weaker than their fellows. And yet both Enid and Malone felt a sensation of great pity as they looked at them. How sad to be deceived upon so intimate a matter as this, to be duped by impostors who used their most sacred feelings and their beloved dead as counters with which to cheat them. What did they know of the laws of evidence, of the cold, immutable decrees of scientific law? Poor earnest, honest, deluded people!

'Now!' screamed Mr. Peeble. 'We shall ask Mr. Munro from Australia to give us the invocation.'

A wild-looking old man with a shaggy beard and slumbering fire in his eyes rose up and stood for a few seconds with his gaze cast down. Then he began a prayer, very simple, very unpremeditated. Malone jotted down the first sentence: 'Oh, Father, we are very ignorant folk and do not well know how to approach you, but we will pray to you the best we know how.' It was all cast in that humble key. Enid and Malone exchanged a swift glance of appreciation.

There was another hymn, less successful than the first, and the chairman then announced that Mr. James Jones of North Wales would now deliver a trance address which would embody the views of his well-known control, Alasha the Atlantean.

Mr. James Jones, a brisk and decided little man in a faded check suit, came to the front and, after standing a minute or so as if in deep thought, gave a violent shudder and began to talk. It must be admitted that save for a certain fixed stare and vacuous glazing of the eye there was nothing to show that anything save Mr. James Jones of North Wales was the orator. It has also to be stated that if Mr. Jones shuddered at the beginning it was the turn of his audience to shudder afterwards. Granting his own claim, he had proved clearly that an Atlantean spirit might be a portentous bore. He droned on with platitudes and ineptitudes while Malone whispered to Enid that if Alasha was a fair specimen of the population it was just as well that his native land was safely engulfed in the Atlantic Ocean. When, with another rather melodramatic shudder, he emerged from his trance, the chairman sprang to his feet with an alacrity which showed that he was taking no risks lest the Atlantean should return.

'We have present with us to-night,' he cried, 'Mrs. Debbs, the well-known clairvoyante of Liverpool. Mrs. Debbs is, as many of you know, richly endowed with several of those gifts of the spirit of which Saint Paul speaks, and the discerning of spirits is among them. These things depend upon laws which are beyond our control, but a sympathetic atmosphere is essential, and Mrs. Debbs will ask for your good wishes and your prayers while she endeavours to get into touch with some of those shining ones on the other side who may honour us with their presence to-night.'

The president sat down and Mrs. Debbs rose amid discreet applause. Very tall, very pale, very thin, with an aquiline face and eyes shining brightly from behind her gold-rimmed glasses, she stood facing her expectant audience. Her head was bent. She seemed to be listening.

'Vibrations!' she cried at last. 'I want helpful vibrations. Give me a verse on the harmonium, please.'

The instrument droned out 'Jesu, Lover of my soul.' The audience sat in silence, expectant and a little awed. The hall was not too well lit and dark shadows lurked in the corners. The medium still bent her head as if her ears were straining. Then she raised her hand and the music stopped.

'Presently! Presently! All in good time,' said the woman, addressing some invisible companion. Then to the audience, 'I don't feel that the conditions are very good to-night. I will do my best and so will they. But I must talk to you first.'

And she talked. What she said seemed to the two strangers to be absolute gabble. There was no consecutive sense in it, though now and again a phrase or sentence caught the attention. Malone put his stylo in his pocket. There was no use reporting a lunatic. A Spiritualist next him saw his bewildered disgust and leaned towards him.

'She's tuning in. She's getting her wave length,' he whispered. 'It's all a matter of vibration. Ah, there you are!'

She had stopped in the very middle of a sentence. Her long arm and quivering forefinger shot out. She was pointing at an elderly woman in the second row.

'You! Yes, you, with the red feather. No, not you. The stout lady in front. Yes, you! There is a spirit building up behind you. It is a man. He is a tall man – six foot maybe. High forehead, eyes grey or blue, a long chin, brown moustache, lines on his face. Do you recognize him, friend?'

The stout woman looked alarmed, but shook her head.

'Well, see if I can help you. He is holding up a book – brown book with a clasp. It's a ledger same as they have in offices. I get the words "Caledonian Insurance". Is that any help?'

The stout woman pursed her lips and shook her head.

'Well, I can give you a little more. He died after a long illness. I get chest trouble – asthma.'

The stout woman was still obdurate, but a small, angry, red-faced person, two places away from her, sprang to her feet.

'It's my 'usband, ma'm. Tell 'im I don't want to 'ave any more dealin's with him.' She sat down with decision.

'Yes, that's right. He moves to you now. He was nearer the other. He wants to say he's sorry. It doesn't do, you know, to have hard feelings to the dead. Forgive and forget. It's all over. I get a message for you. It is: "Do it and my blessing go with you"! Does that mean anything to you?'

The angry woman looked pleased and nodded.

'Very good.' The clairvoyante suddenly darted out her finger towards the crowd at the door. 'It's for the soldier.'

A soldier in khaki, looking very much amazed, was in the front of the knot of people.

'Wot's for me?' he asked.

'It's a soldier. He has a corporal's stripes. He is a big man with grizzled hair. He has a yellow tab on his shoulders. I get the initials J. H. Do you know him?'

'Yes – but he's dead,' said the soldier.

He had not understood that it was a Spiritualistic Church, and the whole proceedings had been a mystery to him. They were rapidly explained by his neighbours. 'My Gawd!' cried the soldier, and vanished amid a general titter. In the pause Malone could hear the constant mutter of the medium as she spoke to someone unseen.

'Yes, yes, wait your turn! Speak up, woman! Well, take your place near him. How should I know? Well, I will if I can.' She was like a janitor at the theatre marshalling a queue.

Her next attempt was a total failure. A solid man with bushy side-whiskers absolutely refused to have anything to do with an elderly gentleman who claimed kinship. The medium worked with admirable patience, coming back again and again with some fresh detail, but no progress could be made.

'Are you a Spiritualist, friend?'

'Yes, for ten years.'

'Well, you know there are difficulties.'

'Yes, I know that.'

'Think it over. It may come to you later. We must just leave it at that. I am only sorry for your friend.'

There was a pause during which Enid and Malone exchanged whispered confidences.

'What do you make of it, Enid?'

'I don't know. It confuses me.'

'I believe it is half guess-work and the other half a case of confederates. These people are all of the same church, and naturally they know each other's affairs. If they don't know they can inquire.'

'Someone said it was Mrs. Debbs' first visit.'

'Yes but they could easily coach her up. It is all clever quackery and bluff. It *must* be, for just think what is implied if it is not.'

'Telepathy, perhaps.'

'Yes, some element of that also. Listen! She is off again.'

Her next attempt was more fortunate. A lugubrious man at the back of the hall readily recognized the description and claims of his deceased wife.

'I get the name Walter.'

'Yes, that's me.'

'She called you Wat?'

'No.'

'Well, she calls you Wat now. "Tell Wat to give my love to the children". That's how I get it. She is worrying about the children.'

'She always did.'

'Well, they don't change. Furniture. Something about furniture. She says you gave it away. Is that right?'

'Well, I might as well.'

The audience tittered. It was strange how the most solemn and comic were eternally blended – strange and yet very natural and human.

'She has a message: "The man will pay up and all will be well. Be a good man, Wat, and we will be happier here when ever we were on earth".'

The man put his hand over his eyes. As the seeress stood irresolute the tall young secretary half rose and whispered something in her ear. The woman shot a swift glance over her left shoulder in the direction of the visitors.

'I'll come back to it,' said she.

She gave two more descriptions to the audience, both of them rather vague, and both recognized with some reservations. It was a curious fact that her details were such as she could not possibly see at the distance. Thus, dealing with a form which she claimed had built up at the far end of the hall, she could none the less give the colour of the eyes and small points of the face. Malone noted the point as one which he could use for destructive criticism. He was just jotting it down when the woman's voice sounded louder and, looking up, he found that she had turned her head and her spectacles were flashing in his direction.

'It is not often I give a reading from the platform,' said she, her
face rotating between him and the audience, 'but we have friends
here to-night, and it may interest them to come in contact with the
spirit people. There is a presence building up behind the gentleman
with a moustache – the gentleman who sits next to the young lady.
Yes, sir, behind you. He is a man of middle size, rather inclined to
shortness. He is old, over sixty, with white hair, curved nose and a
white, small beard of the variety that is called goatee. He is no relation, I gather, but a friend. Does that suggest anyone to you, sir?'

Malone shook his head with some contempt. 'It would nearly fit
any old man,' he whispered to Enid.

'We will try to get a little closer. He has deep lines on his face. I
should say he was an irritable man in his lifetime. He was quick and
nervous in his ways. Does that help you?'

Again Malone shook his head.

'Rot! Perfect rot,' he muttered.

'Well, he seems very anxious, so we must do what we can for him.
He holds up a book. It is a learned book. He opens it and I see diagrams in it. Perhaps he wrote it – or perhaps he taught from it. Yes,
he nods. He taught from it. He was a teacher.'

Malone remained unresponsive.

'I don't know that I can help him any more. Ah! there is one
thing. He has a mole over his right eyebrow.'

Malone started as if he had been stung.

'One mole?' he cried.

The spectacles flashed round again.

'Two moles – one large, one small.'

'My God!' gasped Malone. 'It's Professor Summerlee!'

'Ah, you've got it. There's a message: "Greetings to old –" It's a
long name and begins with a C. I can't get it. Does it mean
anything?'

'Yes.'

In an instant she had turned and was describing something or
someone else. But she had left a badly-shaken man upon the platform behind her.

It was at this point that the orderly service had a remarkable
interruption which surprised the audience as much as it did the two
visitors. This was the sudden appearance beside the chairman of a
tall, pale-faced bearded man dressed like a superior artisan, who
held up his hand with a quietly impressive gesture as one who was
accustomed to exert authority. He then half-turned and said a word
to Mr. Bolsover.

'This is Mr. Miromar of Dalston,' said the chairman. 'Mr. Miromar has a message to deliver. We are always glad to hear from Mr. Miromar.'

The reporters could only get a half-view of the newcomer's face, but both of them were struck by his noble bearing and by the massive outline of his head which promised very unusual intellectual power. His voice when he spoke rang clearly and pleasantly through the hall.

'I have been ordered to give the message wherever I think that there are ears to hear it. There are some here who are ready for it, and that is why I have come. They wish that the human race should gradually understand the situation so that there shall be the less shock or panic. I am one of several who are chosen to carry the news.'

'A lunatic, I'm afraid!' whispered Malone, scribbling hard upon his knee. There was a general inclination to smile among the audience. And yet there was something in the man's manner and voice which made them hang on every word.

'Things have now reached a climax. The very idea of progress has been made material. It is progress to go swiftly, to send swift messages, to build new machinery. All this is a diversion of real ambition. There is only one real progress – spiritual progress. Mankind gives it a lip tribute but presses on upon its false road of material science.

'The Central Intelligence recognized that amid all the apathy there was also much honest doubt which had outgrown old creeds and had a right to fresh evidence. Therefore fresh evidence was sent – evidence which made the life after death as clear as the sun in the heavens. It was laughed at by scientists, condemned by the churches, became the butt of the newspapers, and was discarded with contempt. That was the last and greatest blunder of humanity.'

The audience had their chins up now. General speculations were beyond their mental horizon. But this was very clear to their comprehension. There was a murmur of sympathy and applause.

'The thing was now hopeless. It had got beyond all control. Therefore something sterner was needed since Heaven's gift had been disregarded. The blow fell. Ten million young men were laid dead upon the ground. Twice as many were mutilated. That was God's first warning to mankind. But it was vain. The same dull materialism prevailed as before. Years of grace were given, and save the stirrings of the spirit seen in such churches as these, no change was anywhere to be seen. The nations heaped up fresh loads of sin, and sin must ever be atoned for. Russia became a cesspool. Germany was unrepentant of her terrible materialism which had been the prime cause of the war. Spain and Italy were sunk in alternate atheism and superstition. France had no religious ideal. Britain was confused and distracted, full of wooden sects which had nothing of life in them. America had abused her glorious opportunities and, instead of being the loving younger brother to a stricken Europe, she held up all economic reconstruction by her money claims; she dishonoured the signature of her own president, and she refused to join that League of Peace which was the one hope of the future. All have sinned, but some more than others, and their punishment will be in exact proportion.

'And that punishment soon comes. These are the exact words I have been asked to give you. I read them lest I should in any way garble them.'

He took a slip of paper from his pocket and read:

' "What we want is, not that folk should be frightened, but that they should begin to change themselves – to develop themselves on more spiritual lines. We are not trying to make people nervous, but to prepare while there is yet time. The world cannot go on as it has done. It would destroy itself if it did. Above all we must sweep away the dark cloud of theology which has come between mankind and God".'

He folded up the paper and replaced it in his pocket.

'That is what I have been asked to tell you. Spread the news where there seems to be a window in the soul. Say to them, "Repent! Reform! the Time is at hand".'

He had paused and seemed about to turn. The spell was broken. The audience rustled and leaned back in its seats. Then a voice from the back:

'Is this the end of the world, mister?'

'No,' said the stranger, curtly.

'Is it the Second Coming?' asked another voice.

'Yes.'

With quick light steps he threaded his way among the chairs on the platform and stood near the door. When Malone next looked round he was gone.

'He is one of these Second-Coming fanatics,' he whispered to Enid. 'There are a lot of them – Christadelphians, Russellites, Bible Students and what-not. But he was impressive.'

'Very,' said Enid.

'We have, I am sure, been very interested in what our friend has told us,' said the chairman. 'Mr. Miromar is in hearty sympathy with our movement even though he cannot be said actually to belong to it. I am sure he is always welcome upon our platforms. As to his prophecy, it seems to me the world has had enough trouble without our anticipating any more. If it is as our friend says, we can't do much to mend the matter. We can only go about our daily jobs, do them as well as we can, and await the event in full confidence of help from above. If it's the Day of Judgment to-morrow,' he added, smiling, 'I mean to look after my provision store at Hammersmith to-day. We shall now continue with the service.'

There was a vigorous appeal for money and a great deal about the building-fund from the young secretary. 'It's a shame to think that there are more left in the street than in the building on a Sunday night. We all give our services. No one takes a penny. Mrs. Debbs is here for her bare expenses. But we want another thousand pounds before we can start. There is one brother here who mortgaged his house to help us. That's the spirit that wins. Now let us see what you can do for us to-night.'

A dozen soup-plates circulated, and a hymn was sung to the accompaniment of much chinking of coin. Enid and Malone conversed in undertones.

'Professor Summerlee died, you know, at Naples last year.'

'Yes, I remember him well.'

'And "old C" was, of course, your father.'

'It was really remarkable.'

'Poor old Summerlee. He thought survival was an absurdity. And here he is – or here he seems to be.'

The soup-plates returned – it was mostly brown soup, unhappily, and they were deposited on the table where the eager eye of the secretary appraised their value. Then the little shaggy man from Australia gave a benediction in the same simple fashion as the opening prayer. It needed no Apostolic succession or laying-on of hands to make one feel that his words were from a human heart and might well go straight to a Divine one. Then the audience rose and sang their final farewell hymn – a hymn with a haunting tune and a sad, sweet refrain of 'God keep you safely till we meet once more.' Enid was surprised to feel the tears running down her cheeks. These earnest, simple folks with their direct methods had wrought upon her more than all the gorgeous service and rolling music of the cathedral.

Mr. Bolsover, the stout president, was in the waiting-room and so was Mrs. Debbs.

'Well, I expect you are going to let us have it,' he laughed. 'We are used to it Mr. Malone. We don't mind. But you will see the turn some day. These articles may rise up in judgment.'

'I will treat it fairly, I assure you.'

'Well, we ask no more.'

The medium was leaning with her elbow on the mantel-piece, austere and aloof.

'I am afraid you are tired,' said Enid.

'No, young lady, I am never tired in doing the work of the spirit people. They see to that.'

'May I ask,' Malone ventured, 'whether you ever knew Professor Summerlee?'

The medium shook her head.

'No, sir, no. They always think I know them. I know none of them. They come and I describe them.'

'How do you get the message?'

'Clairaudient. I hear it. I hear them all the time. The poor things all want to come through and they pluck at me and pull me and pester me on the platform. "Me next – me – me"! That's what I hear. I do my best, but I can't handle them all.'

'Can you tell me anything of that prophetic person?' asked Malone of the chairman. Mr. Bolsover shrugged his shoulders with a deprecating smile.

'He is an Independent. We see him now and again as a sort of comet passing across us. By the way, it comes back to me that he prophesied the war. I'm a practical man myself. Sufficient for the day is the evil thereof. We get plenty in ready cash without any bills for the future. Well, good night! Treat us as well as you can.'

'Good night,' said Enid.

'Good night,' said Mrs. Debbs. 'By the way, young lady, you are a medium yourself. Good night!'

And so they found themselves in the street once more inhaling long draughts of the night air. It was sweet after that crowded hall. A minute later they were in the rush of the Edgware Road and Malone had hailed a cab to carry them back to Victoria Gardens.

CHAPTER III

In Which Professor Challenger Gives His Opinion

ENID HAD STEPPED INTO THE CAB and Malone was following when his name was called and a man came running down the street. He was tall, middle-aged, handsome and well-dressed, with the clean-shaven, self-confident face of the successful surgeon.

'Hullo, Malone! Stop!'

'Why, it's Atkinson! Enid, let me introduce you. This is Mr. Atkinson of St. Mary's about whom I spoke to your father. Can we give you a lift? We are going towards Victoria.'

'Capital!' The surgeon followed them into the cab. 'I was amazed to see you at a Spiritualist meeting.'

'We were only there professionally. Miss Challenger and I are both on the Press.'

'Oh, really! The *Daily Gazette*, I suppose, as before. Well, you will have one more subscriber, for I shall want to see what you made of to-night's show.'

'You'll have to wait till next Sunday. It is one of a series.'

'Oh, I say, I can't wait as long as that. What *did* you make of it?'

'I really don't know. I shall have to read my notes carefully to-morrow and think it over, and compare impressions with my colleague here. She has the intuition, you see, which goes for so much in religious matters.'

'And what is your intuition, Miss Challenger?'

'Good – oh yes, good! But, dear me, what an extraordinary mixture!'

'Yes, indeed. I have been several times and it always leaves the same mixed impression upon my own mind. Some of it is ludicrous, and some of it might be dishonest, and yet again some of it is clearly wonderful.'

'But you are not on the Press. Why were *you* there?'

'Because I am deeply interested. You see, I am a student of psychic matters and have been for some years. I am not a convinced one but I am sympathetic, and I have sufficient sense of proportion to realize that while I seem to be sitting in judgment upon the subject it may in truth be the subject which is sitting in judgment upon me.'

Malone nodded appreciation.

'It is enormous. You will realize that as you get to close grips with it. It is half a dozen great subjects in one. And it is all in the hands of these good humble folk who, in the face of every discouragement and personal loss, have carried it on for more than seventy years. It is really very like the rise of Christianity. It was run by slaves and underlings until it gradually extended upwards. There were three hundred years between Cæsar's slave and Cæsar getting the light.'

'But the preacher!' cried Enid in protest.

Mr. Atkinson laughed.

'You mean our friend from Atlantis. What a terrible bore the fellow was! I confess I don't know what to make of performances like that. Self-deception, I think, and the temporary emergence of some fresh strand of personality which dramatizes itself in this way. The only thing I am quite sure of is that it is not really an inhabitant of Atlantis who arrives from his long voyage with this awful cargo of platitudes. Well, here we are!'

'I have to deliver this young lady safe and sound to her father,' said Malone. 'Look here, Atkinson, don't leave us. The Professor would really like to see you.'

'What at this hour! Why, he would throw me down the stairs.'

'You've been hearing stories,' said Enid. 'Really it is not so bad as that. Some people annoy him, but I am sure you are not one of them. Won't you chance it?'

'With that encouragement, certainly.' And the three walked down the bright outer corridor to the lift.

Challenger, clad now in a brilliant blue dressing-gown, was eagerly awaiting them. He eyed Atkinson as a fighting bulldog eyes some canine stranger. The inspection seemed to satisfy him, however, for he growled that he was glad to meet him.

'I've heard of your name, sir, and of your rising reputation. Your resection of the cord last year made some stir, I understand. But have you been down among the lunatics also?'

'Well, if you call them so,' said Atkinson with a laugh.

'Good Heavens, what else could I call them? I remember now that my young friend here' (Challenger had a way of alluding to Malone as if he were a promising boy of ten) 'told me you were studying the subject.' He roared with offensive laughter. ' "The proper study of mankind is spooks", eh, Mr. Atkinson?'

'Dad really knows nothing about it, so don't be offended with him,' said Enid. 'But I assure you, Dad, you would have been interested.' She proceeded to give a sketch of their adventures, though interrupted by a running commentary of groans, grunts and derisive jeers. It was only when the Summerlee episode was reached that Challenger's indignation and contempt could no longer be restrained. The old volcano blew his head off and a torrent of red-hot invective descended upon his listeners.

'The blasphemous rascals!' he shouted. 'To think that they can't let poor old Summerlee rest in his grave. We had our differences in his time and I will admit that I was compelled to take a moderate view of his intelligence, but if he came back from the grave he would certainly have something worth hearing to say to us. It is an absurdity – a wicked, indecent absurdity upon the face of it. I object to any friend of mine being made a puppet for the laughter of an audience of fools. They didn't laugh! They must have laughed when they heard an educated man, a man whom I have met upon equal terms, talking such nonsense. I say it *was* nonsense. Don't contradict me, Malone. I won't have it! His message might have been the postscript of a schoolgirl's letter. Isn't that nonsense, coming from such a source? Are you not in agreement, Mr. Atkinson? No! I had hoped better things from you.'

'But the description?'

'Good Heavens, where are your brains? Have not the names of Summerlee and Malone been associated with my own in some peculiarly feeble fiction which attained some notoriety? Is it not also known that you two innocents were doing the Churches week by week? Was it not patent that sooner or later you would come to a Spiritualist gathering? Here was a chance for a convert! They set a bait and poor old gudgeon Malone came along and swallowed it. Here he is with the hook still stuck in his silly mouth. Oh, yes, Malone, plain speaking is needed and you shall have it.' The Professor's black mane was bristling and his eyes glaring from one member of the company to another.

'Well, we want every view expressed,' said Atkinson. 'You seem very qualified, sir, to express the negative one. At the same time I would repeat in my own person the words of Thackeray. He said to some objector: "What you say is natural, but if you had seen what I have seen you might alter your opinion". Perhaps sometime you will be able to look into the matter, for your high position in the scientific world would give your opinion great weight.'

'If I have a high place in the scientific world as you say, it is because I have concentrated upon what is useful and discarded what is nebulous or absurd. My brain, sir, does not pare the edges. It cuts right through. It has cut right through this and has found fraud and folly.'

'Both are there at times,' said Atkinson, 'and yet . . . and yet! Ah, well, Malone, I'm some way from home and it is late. You will excuse me, Professor. I am honoured to have met you.'

Malone was leaving also and the two friends had a few minutes' chat before they went their separate ways, Atkinson to Wimpole Street and Malone to South Norwood, where he was now living.

'Grand old fellow!' said Malone, chuckling. 'You must never get offended with him. He means no harm. He is splendid.'

'Of course he is. But if anything could make me a real out-and-out Spiritualist it is that sort of intolerance. It is very common, though it is generally cast rather in the tone of the quiet sneer than of the noisy roar. I like the latter best. By the way, Malone, if you care to go deeper into this subject I may be able to help you. You've heard of Linden?'

'Linden, the professional medium. Yes, I've been told he is the greatest blackguard unhung.'

'Ah, well, they usually talk of them like that. You must judge for yourself. He put his knee-cap out last winter and I put it in again, and that has made a friendly bond between us. It's not always easy to get him, and of course a small fee, a guinea I think, is usual, but if you wanted a sitting I could work it.'

'You think him genuine?'

Atkinson shrugged his shoulders.

'I daresay they all take the line of least resistance. I can only say that I have never detected him in fraud. You must judge for yourself.'

'I will,' said Malone. 'I am getting hot on this trail. And there is copy in it, too. When things are more easy I'll write to you, Atkinson, and we can go more deeply into the matter.'

CHAPTER IV

Which Describes Some Strange Doings in Hammersmith

THE ARTICLE BY THE JOINT COMMISSIONERS (such was their glorious title) aroused interest and contention. It had been accompanied by a deprecating leaderette from the sub-editor which was meant to calm the susceptibilities of his orthodox readers, as who should say: 'These things have to be noticed and seem to be true, but of course you and I recognize how pestilential it all is.' Malone found himself at once plunged into a huge correspondence, for and against, which in itself was enough to show how vitally the question was in the minds of men. All the previous articles had only elicited a growl here or there from a hide-bound Catholic or from an iron-clad Evangelical, but now his post-bag was full. Most of them were ridiculing the idea that psychic forces existed and many were from writers who, whatever they might know of psychic forces, had obviously not yet learned to spell. The Spiritualists were in many cases not more pleased than the others, for Malone had – even while his account was true – exercised a journalist's privilege of laying an accent on the more humorous sides of it.

One morning in the succeeding week Mr. Malone was aware of a large presence in the small room wherein he did his work at the office. A page-boy, who preceded the stout visitor, had laid a card on the corner of the table which bore the legend "James Bolsover, Provision Merchant, High Street, Hammersmith." It was none other than the genial president of last Sunday's congregation. He wagged a paper accusingly at Malone, but his good-humoured face was wreathed in smiles.

'Well, well,' said he. 'I told you that the funny side would get you.'

'Don't you think it a fair account?'

'Well, yes, Mr. Malone, I think you and the young woman have done your best for us. But, of course, you know nothing and it all seems queer to you. Come to think of it, it would be a deal queerer if all the clever men who leave this earth could not among them find some way of getting a word back to us.'

'But it's such a stupid word sometimes.'

'Well, there are a lot of stupid people leave the world. They don't change. And then, you know, one never knows what sort of message is needed. We had a clergyman in to see Mrs. Debbs yesterday. He was broken-hearted because he had lost his daughter. Mrs. Debbs got several messages through that she was happy and that only his grief hurt her. "That's no use", said he. "Anyone could say that. That's not my girl". And then suddenly she said: "But I wish to goodness you would not wear a Roman collar with a coloured shirt". That sounded a trivial message, but the man began to cry. "That's her", he sobbed. "She was always chipping me about my collars". It's the little things that count in this life – just the homely, intimate things, Mr. Malone.'

Malone shook his head.

'Anyone would remark on a coloured shirt and a clerical collar.'

Mr. Bolsover laughed. 'You're a hard proposition. So was I once, so I can't blame you. But I called here with a purpose. I expect you are a busy man and I know that I am, so I'll get down to the brass tacks. First, I wanted to say that all our people that have any sense are pleased with the article. Mr. Algernon Mailey wrote me that it would do good, and if he is pleased we are all pleased.'

'Mailey the barrister?'

'Mailey, the religious reformer. That's how he will be known.'

'Well, what else?'

'Only that we would help you if you and the young lady wanted to go further in the matter. Not for publicity, mind you, but just for your own good – though we don't shrink from publicity, either. I have psychical phenomena seances at my own home without a professional medium, and if you would like . . .'

'There's nothing I would like so much.'

'Then you shall come – both of you. I don't have many outsiders. I wouldn't have one of those psychic research people inside my doors. Why should I go out of my way to be insulted by all their suspicions and their traps? They seem to think that folk have no feelings. But you have some ordinary common sense. That's all we ask.'

'But I don't believe. Would that not stand in the way?'

'Not in the least. So long as you are fair-minded and don't disturb the conditions, all is well. Spirits out of the body don't like disagreeable people any more than spirits in the body do. Be gentle and civil, same as you would to any other company.'

'Well, I can promise that.'

'They are funny sometimes,' said Mr. Bolsover, in reminiscent vein. 'It is as well to keep on the right side of them. They are not allowed to hurt humans, but we all do things we're not allowed to do, and they are very human themselves. You remember how *The Times* correspondent got his head cut open with the tambourine in one of the Davenport Brothers' seances. Very wrong, of course, but it happened. No friend ever got his head cut open. There was another case down Stepney way. A moneylender went to a seance. Some victim that he had driven to suicide got into the medium. He got the moneylender by the throat and it was a close thing for his life. But I'm off, Mr. Malone. We sit once a week and have done for four years without a break. Eight o'clock Thursdays. Give us a day's notice and I'll get Mr. Mailey to meet you. He can answer questions better than I. Next Thursday! Very good.' And Mr. Bolsover lurched out of the room.

Both Malone and Enid Challenger had, perhaps, been more shaken by their short experience than they had admitted, but both were sensible people who agreed that every possible natural cause should be exhausted – and very thoroughly exhausted – before the bounds of what is possible should be enlarged. Both of them had the utmost respect for the ponderous intellect of Challenger and were affected by his strong views, though Malone was compelled to admit in the frequent arguments in which he was plunged that the opinion of a clever man who has had no experience is really of less value than that of the man in the street who has actually been there.

These arguments, as often as not, were with Mervin, editor of the psychic paper *Dawn*, which dealt with every phase of the occult, from the lore of the Rosicrucians to the strange regions of the students of the Great Pyramid, or of those who uphold the Jewish origin of our blonde Anglo-Saxons. Mervin was a small, eager man with a brain of a high order, which might have carried him to the most lucrative heights of his profession had he not determined to sacrifice worldly prospects in order to help what seemed to him to be a great truth. As Malone was eager for knowledge and Mervin was equally keen to impart it, the waiters at the Literary Club found it no easy matter to get them away from the corner-table in the window at which they were wont to lunch. Looking down at the long, grey curve of the Embankment and the noble river with its vista of bridges, the pair would linger over their coffee, smoking cigarettes and discussing various sides of this most gigantic and absorbing subject, which seemed already to have disclosed new horizons to the mind of Malone.

There was one warning given by Mervin which aroused impatience amounting almost to anger in Malone's mind. He had the hereditary Irish objection to coercion and it seemed to him to be appearing once more in an insidious and particularly objectionable form.

'You are going to one of Bolsover's family seances,' said Mervin. 'They are, of course, well known among our people, though few have been actually admitted, so you may consider yourself privileged. He has clearly taken a fancy to you.'

'He thought I wrote fairly about them.'

'Well, it wasn't much of an article, but still among the dreary, purblind nonsense that assails us it did show some traces of dignity and balance and sense of proportion.'

Malone waved a deprecating cigarette.

'Bolsover's seances and others like them are, of course, things of no moment to the real psychic. They are like the rude foundations of a building which certainly help to sustain the edifice, but are forgotten when once you come to inhabit it. It is the higher superstructure with which we have to do. You would think that the physical phenomena were the whole subject – those and a fringe of ghosts and haunted houses – if you were to believe the cheap papers who cater for the sensationalist. Of course, these physical phenomena have a use of their own. They rivet the attention of the inquirer and encourage him to go further. Personally, having seen them all, I would not go across the road to see them again. But I would go across many roads to get high messages from the beyond.'

'Yes, I quite appreciate the distinction, looking at it from your point of view. Personally, of course, I am equally agnostic as to the messages and the phenomena.'

'Quite so. St. Paul was a good psychic. He makes the point so neatly that even his ignorant translators were unable to disguise the real occult meanings as they have succeeded in doing in so many cases.'

'Can you quote it?'

'I know my New Testament pretty well, but I am not letter-perfect. It is the passage where he says that the gift of tongues, which was an obvious sensational thing, was for the uninstructed, but that prophecies, that is real spiritual messages, were for the elect. In other words that an experienced Spiritualist has no need of phenomena.'

'I'll look that passage up.'

'You will find it in Corinthians, I think. By the way, there must have been a pretty high average of intelligence among those old congregations if Paul's letters could have been read aloud to them and thoroughly comprehended.'

'That is generally admitted, is it not?'

'Well, it is a concrete example of it. However, I am down a side-track. What I wanted to say to you is that you must not take Bolsover's little spirit circus too seriously. It is honest as far as it goes, but it goes a mighty short way. It's a disease, this phenomena hunting. I know some of our people, women mostly, who buzz around seance rooms continually, seeing the same thing over and over, sometimes real, sometimes, I fear, imitation. What better are they for that as souls or as citizens or in any other way? No, when your foot is firm on the bottom rung don't mark time on it, but step up to the next rung and get firm upon that.'

'I quite get your point. But I'm still on the solid ground.'

'Solid!' cried Mervin. 'Good Lord! But the paper goes to press to-day and I must get down to the printer. With a circulation of ten thousand or so we do things modestly, you know – not like you plu-tocrats of the daily press. I am practically the staff.'

'You said you had a warning.'

'Yes, yes, I wanted to give you a warning.' Mervin's thin, eager face became intensely serious. 'If you have any ingrained religious or other prejudices which may cause you to turn down this subject after you have investigated it, then don't investigate at all – for it is dangerous.'

'What do you mean – dangerous?'

'They don't mind honest doubt, or honest criticism, but if they are badly treated they are dangerous.'

'Who are "they"?'

'Ah, who are they? I wonder. Guides, controls, psychic entities of some kind. Who the agents of vengeance – or I should say justice – are, is really not essential. The point is that they exist.'

'Oh, rot, Mervin!'

'Don't be too sure of that.'

'Pernicious rot! These are the old theological bogies of the Middle Ages coming up again. I am surprised at a sensible man like you!'

Mervin smiled – he had a whimsical smile, but his eyes, looking out from under bushy yellow brows, were as serious as ever.

'You may come to change your opinion. There are some queer sides to this question. As a friend I put you wise to this one.'

'Well, put me wise, then.'

Thus encouraged, Mervin went into the matter. He rapidly sketched the career and fate of a number of men who had, in his opinion, played an unfair game with these forces, become an obstruction, and suffered for it. He spoke of judges who had given prejudiced decisions against the cause, of journalists who had worked up stunt cases for sensational purposes and to throw discredit on the movement; of others who had interviewed mediums to make game of them, or who, having started to investigate, had drawn back alarmed, and given a negative decision when their inner soul knew that the facts were true. It was a formidable list, for it was long and precise; but Malone was not to be driven.

'If you pick your cases I have no doubt one could make such a list about any subject. Mr. Jones said that Raphael was a bungler, and Mr. Jones died of angina pectoris. Therefore it is dangerous to criticize Raphael. That seems to be the argument.'

'Well, if you like to think so.'

'Take the other side. Look at Morgate. He has always been an enemy, for he is a convinced materialist. But he prospers – look at his professorship.'

'Ah, an honest doubter. Certainly. Why not?'

'And Morgan who at one time exposed mediums.'

'If they were really false he did good service.'

'And Falconer who has written so bitterly about you?'

'Ah, Falconer! Do you know anything of Falconer's private life? No. Well, take it from me he has got his dues. He doesn't know why. Some day these gentlemen will begin to compare notes and then it may dawn on them. But they get it.'

He went on to tell a horrible story of one who had devoted his considerable talents to picking Spiritualism to pieces, though really convinced of its truth, because his worldly ends were served thereby. The end was ghastly – too ghastly for Malone.

'Oh, cut it out, Mervin!' he cried impatiently. 'I'll say what I think, no more and no less, and I won't be scared by you or your spooks into altering my opinions.'

'I never asked you to.'

'You got a bit near it. What you have said strikes me as pure superstition. If what you say is true you should have the police after you.'

'Yes, if we did it. But it is out of our hands. However, Malone, for what it's worth I have given you the warning and you can now go your way. Bye-bye! You can always ring me up at the office of *Dawn*.'

If you want to know if a man is of the true Irish blood there is one infallible test. Put him in front of a swing-door with 'Push' or 'Pull' printed upon it. The Englishman will obey like a sensible man. The Irishman, with less sense but more individuality, will at once and with vehemence do the opposite. So it was with Malone. Mervin's well meant warning simply raised a rebellious spirit within him, and when he called for Enid to take her to the Bolsover seance he had gone back several degrees in his dawning sympathy for the subject. Challenger bade them farewell with many gibes, his beard projecting forward and his eyes closed with upraised eyebrows, as was his wont when inclined to be facetious.

'You have your powder-bag, my dear Enid. If you see a particularly good specimen of ectoplasm in the course of the evening don't forget your father. I have a microscope, chemical reagents and everything ready. Perhaps even a small *poltergeist* might come your way. Any trifle would be welcome.'

His bull's bellow of laughter followed them into the lift.

The provision merchant's establishment of Mr. Bolsover proved to be a euphemism for an old-fashioned grocer's shop in the most crowded part of Hammersmith. The neighbouring church was chiming out the three-quarters as the taxi drove up, and the shop was full of people. So Enid and Malone walked up and down outside. As they were so engaged another taxi drove up and a large, untidy looking, ungainly bearded man in a suit of Harris tweed stepped out of it. He glanced at his watch and then began to pace the pavement. Presently he noted the others and came up to them.

'May I ask if you are the journalists who are going to attend the seance? . . . I thought so. Old Bolsover is terribly busy so you were wise to wait. Bless him, he is one of God's saints in his way.'

'You are Mr. Algernon Mailey, I presume?'

'Yes. I am the gentleman whose credulity is giving rise to considerable anxiety upon the part of my friends, as one of the rags remarked the other day.' His laugh was so infectious that the others were bound to laugh also. Certainly, with his athletic proportions, which had run a little to seed but were still notable, and with his virile voice and strong if homely face, he gave no impression of instability.

'We are all labelled with some stigma by our opponents,' said he. 'I wonder what yours will be.'

'We must not sail under false colours, Mr. Mailey,' said Enid. 'We are not yet among the believers.'

'Quite right. You should take your time over it. It is infinitely the most important thing in the world, so it is worth taking time over. I took many years myself. Folk can be blamed for neglecting it, but no one can be blamed for being cautious in examination. Now I am all out for it, as you are aware, because I *know* it is true. There is such a difference between believing and knowing. I lecture a good deal. But I never want to convert my audience. I don't believe in sudden conversions. They are shallow, superficial things. All I want is to put the thing before the people as clearly as I can. I just tell them the truth and why we know it is the truth. Then my job is done. They can take it or leave it. If they are wise they will explore along the paths that I indicate. If they are unwise they miss their chance. I don't want to press them or to proselytize. It's their affair, not mine.'

'Well, that seems a reasonable view,' said Enid, who was attracted by the frank manner of their new acquaintance. They were standing now in the full flood of light cast by Bolsover's big plate-glass window. She had a good look at him, his broad forehead, his curious grey eyes, thoughtful and yet eager, his straw-coloured beard which indicated the outline of an aggressive chin. He was solidity personified – the very opposite of the fanatic whom she had imagined. His name had been a good deal in the papers lately as a protagonist in the long battle, and she remembered that it had never been mentioned without an answering snort from her father.

'I wonder,' she said to Malone, 'what would happen if Mr. Mailey were locked up in a room with Dad!'

Malone laughed. 'There used to be a schoolboy question as to what would occur if an irresistible force were to strike an invincible obstacle.'

'Oh, you are the daughter of Professor Challenger,' said Mailey with interest. 'He is a big figure in the scientific world. What a grand world it would be if it would only realize its own limitations.'

'I don't quite follow you.'

'It is this scientific world which is at the bottom of much of our materialism. It has helped us in comfort – if comfort is any use to us. Otherwise it has usually been a curse to us, for it has called itself progress and given us a false impression that we are making progress, whereas we are really drifting very steadily backwards.'

'Really, I can't quite agree with you there, Mr. Mailey,' said Malone, who was getting restive under what seemed to him dogmatic assertion. 'Look at wireless. Look at the S.O.S. call at sea. Is that not a benefit to mankind!'

'Oh, it works out all right sometimes. I value my electric reading-lamp, and that is a product of science. It gives us, as I said before, comfort and occasionally safety.'

'Why, then, do you depreciate it?'

'Because it obscures the vital thing – the object of life. We were not put into this planet in order that we should go fifty miles an hour in a motor-car, or cross the Atlantic in an airship, or send messages either with or without wires. These are the mere trimmings and fringes of life. But these men of science have so riveted our attention on these fringes that we forget the central object.'

'I don't follow you.'

'It is not how fast you go that matters, it is the object of your journey. It is not how you send a message, it is what the value of the message may be. At every stage this so-called progress may be a curse, and yet as long as we use the word we confuse it with real progress and imagine that we are doing that for which God sent us into the world.'

'Which is?'

'To prepare ourselves for the next phase of life. There is mental preparation and spiritual preparation, and we are neglecting both. To be in an old age better men and women, more unselfish, more broadminded, more genial and tolerant, that is what we are for. It is a soul factory, and it is turning out a bad article. But – Hullo!' he burst into his infectious laugh. 'Here I am delivering my lecture in the street. Force of habit, you see. My son says that if you press the third button of my waistcoat I automatically deliver a lecture. But here is the good Bolsover to your rescue.'

The worthy grocer had caught sight of them through the window and came bustling out, untying his white apron.

'Good evening, all! I won't have you waiting in the cold. Besides, there's the clock, and time's up. It does not do to keep them waiting. Punctuality for all – that's my motto and theirs. My lads will shut up the shop. This way, and mind the sugar-barrel.'

They threaded their way amid boxes of dried fruits and piles of cheese, finally passing between two great casks which hardly left room for the grocer's portly form. A narrow door beyond opened into the residential part of the establishment. Ascending the narrow stair, Bolsover threw open a door and the visitors found themselves in a considerable room in which a number of people were seated round a large table. There was Mrs. Bolsover herself, large, cheerful and buxom like her husband. Three daughters were all of the same pleasing type. There was an elderly woman who seemed to be some relation, and two other colourless females who were described as neighbours and Spiritualists. The only other man was a little grey-headed fellow with a pleasant face and quick, twinkling eyes, who sat at a harmonium in the corner.

'Mr. Smiley, our musician,' said Bolsover. 'I don't know what we could do without Mr. Smiley. It's vibrations, you know. Mr. Mailey could tell you about that. Ladies, you know Mr. Mailey, our very good friend. And these are the two inquirers – Miss Challenger and Mr. Malone.'

The Bolsover family all smiled genially, but the nondescript elderly person rose to her feet and surveyed them with an austere face.

'You're very welcome here, you two strangers,' she said. 'But we would say to you that we want outward reverence. We respect the shining ones and we will not have them insulted.'

'I assure you we are very earnest and fairminded,' said Malone.

'We've had our lesson. We haven't forgotten the Meadows' affair, Mr. Bolsover.'

'No, no, Mrs. Seldon. That won't happen again. We were rather upset over that,' Bolsover added, turning to the visitors. 'That man came here as our guest, and when the lights were out he poked the other sitters with his finger so as to make them think it was a spirit hand. Then he wrote the whole thing up as an exposure in the public Press, when the only fraudulent thing present had been himself.'

Malone was honestly shocked. 'I can assure you we are incapable of such conduct.'

The old lady sat down, but still regarded them with a suspicious eye. Bolsover bustled about and got things ready.

'You sit here, Mr. Mailey. Mr. Malone, will you sit between my wife and my daughter? Where would the young lady like to sit?'

Enid was feeling rather nervous. 'I think,' said she, 'that I would like to sit next to Mr. Malone.'

Bolsover chuckled and winked at his wife.

'Quite so. Most natural, I am sure.' They all settled into their places. Mr. Bolsover had switched off the electric light, but a candle burned in the middle of the table. Malone thought what a picture it would have made for a Rembrandt. Deep shadows draped it in, but the yellow light flickered upon the circle of faces – the strong, homely, heavy features of Bolsover, the solid line of his family circle, the sharp, austere countenance of Mrs. Seldon, the earnest eyes and yellow beard of Mailey, the worn, tired faces of the two Spiritualist women, and finally the firm, noble profile of the girl who sat beside him. The whole world had suddenly narrowed down to that one little group, so intensely concentrated upon its own purpose.

On the table there was scattered a curious collection of objects, which had all the same appearance of tools which had long been used. There was a battered brass speaking-trumpet, very discoloured, a tambourine, a musical-box, and a number of smaller objects. 'We never know what they may want,' said Bolsover, waving his hand over them. 'If Wee One calls for a thing and it isn't there she lets us know all about it – oh, yes, something shocking!'

'She has a temper of her own has Wee One,' remarked Mrs. Bolsover.

'Why not, the pretty dear?' said the austere lady. 'I expect she has enough to try it with researchers and whatnot. I often wonder she troubles to come at all.'

'Wee One is our little girl guide,' said Bolsover. 'You'll hear her presently.'

'I do hope she will come,' said Enid.

'Well, she never failed us yet, except when that man Meadows clawed hold of the trumpet and put it outside the circle.'

'Who is the medium?' asked Malone.

'Well, we don't know ourselves. We all help, I think. Maybe, I give as much as anyone. And mother, she is a help.'

'Our family is a co-operative store,' said his wife, and everyone laughed.

'I thought one medium was necessary.'

'It is usual but not necessary,' said Mailey in his deep, authoritative voice. 'Crawford showed that pretty clearly in the Gallagher seances when he proved, by weighing chairs, that everyone in the circle lost from half to two pounds at a sitting, though the medium, Miss Kathleen, lost as many as ten or twelve. Here the long series of sittings – How long, Mr. Bolsover?'

'Four years unbroken.'

'The long series has developed everyone to some extent, so that there is a high average output from each, instead of an extraordinary amount from one.'

'Output of what?'

'Animal magnetism, ectoplasm – in fact, power. That is the most comprehensive word. The Christ used that word. "Much power has gone out of me". It is "dunamis" in the Greek, but the translators missed the point and translated it "virtue". If a good Greek scholar who was also a profound occult student was to re-translate the New Testament we should get some eye-openers. Dear old Ellis Powell did a little in that direction. His death was a loss to the world.'

'Aye, indeed,' said Bolsover in a reverent voice. 'But now, before we get to work, Mr. Malone, I want you just to note one or two things. You see the white spots on the trumpet and the tambourine? Those are luminous points so that we can see where they are. The table is just our dining-table, good British oak. You can examine it if you like. But you'll see things that won't depend upon the table. Now, Mr. Smiley, out goes the light and we'll ask you for "The Rock of Ages".'

The harmonium droned in the darkness and the circle sang. They sang very tunefully, too, for the girls had fresh voices and true ears. Low and vibrant, the solemn rhythm became most impressive when no sense but that of hearing was free to act. Their hands, according to instructions, were laid lightly upon the table, and they were warned not to cross their legs. Malone, with his hand touching Enid's, could feel the little quiverings which showed that her nerves were highly strung. The homely, jovial voice of Bolsover relieved the tension.

'That should do it,' he said. 'I feel as if the conditions were good to-night. Just a touch of frost in the air, too. I'll ask you now to join with me in prayer.'

It was effective, that simple, earnest prayer in the darkness – an inky darkness which was only broken by the last red glow of a dying fire.

'Oh, great Father of us all,' said the voice. 'You who are beyond our thoughts and who yet pervade our lives, grant that all evil may be kept from us this night and that we may be privileged to get in touch, if only for an hour, with those who dwell upon a higher plane than ours. You are our Father as well as theirs. Permit us, for a short space, to meet in brotherhood, that we may have an added knowledge of that eternal life which awaits us, and so be helped during our years of waiting in this lower world.' He ended with the 'Our Father', in which we all joined. Then they all sat in expectant silence. Outside was the dull roar of traffic and the occasional ill-tempered squawk of a passing car. Inside there was absolute still-ness. Enid and Malone felt every sense upon the alert and every nerve on edge as they gazed out into the gloom.

'Nothing doing, mother,' said Bolsover at last. 'It's the strange company. New vibrations. They have to tune them in to get har-mony. Give us another tune, Mr. Smiley.'

Again the harmonium droned. It was still playing when a woman's voice cried: 'Stop! Stop! They are here!'

Again they waited without result.

'Yes! Yes! I heard Wee One. She is here, right enough. I'm sure of it.'

Silence again, and then it came – such a marvel to the visitors, such a matter of course to the circle.

'Gooda evenin'!' cried a voice.

There was a burst of greeting and of welcoming laughter from the circle. They were all speaking at once. 'Good evening, Wee One!' 'There you are, dear!' 'I knew you would come!' 'Well done, little girl guide!'

'Gooda evenin', all!' replied the voice. 'Wee One so glad see Daddy and Mummy and the rest. Oh, what big man with beard! Mailey, Mister Mailey, I meet him before. He big Mailey, I little femaley. Glad to see you, Mr. Big Man.'

Enid and Malone listened with amazement, but it was impossible to be nervous in face of the perfectly natural way in which the com-pany accepted it. The voice was very thin and high – more so than any artificial falsetto could produce. It was the voice of a female child. That was certain. Also that there was no female child in the room unless one had been smuggled in after the light went out. That was possible. But the voice seemed to be in the middle of the table. How could a child get there?

'Easy get there, Mr. Gentleman,' said the voice, answering his unspoken thought. 'Daddy strong man. Daddy lift Wee One on to table. Now I show what Daddy not able to do.'

'The trumpet's up!' cried Bolsover.

The little circle of luminous paint rose noiselessly into the air. Now it was swaying above their heads.

'Go up and hit the ceiling!' cried Bolsover.

Up it went and they heard the metallic tapping above them. Then the high voice came from above:

'Clever Daddy! Daddy got fishing-rod and put trumpet up to ceiling. But how Daddy make the voice, eh? What you say, pretty English Missy? Here is a present from Wee One.'

Something soft dropped on Enid's lap. She put her hand down and felt it.

'It's a flower – a chrysanthemum. Thank you, Wee One!'

'An apport?' asked Mailey.

'No, no, Mr. Mailey,' said Bolsover. 'They were in the vase on the harmonium. Speak to her, Miss Challenger. Keep the vibrations going.'

'Who are you, Wee One?' asked Enid, looking up at the moving spot above her.

'I am little black girl. Eight-year-old little black girl.'

'Oh, come, dear,' said mother in her rich, coaxing voice. 'You were eight when you came to us first, and that was years ago.'

'Years ago to you. All one time to me. I to do my job as eight-year child. When job done then Wee One become Big One all in one day. No time here, same as you have. I always eight-year-old.'

'In the ordinary way they grow up exactly as we do here,' said Mailey. 'But if they have a special bit of work for which a child is needed, then as a child they remain. It's a sort of arrested development.'

'That's me. "Rested envelopment",' said the voice proudly. 'I learn good England when big man here.'

They all laughed. It was the most genial, free-and-easy association possible. Malone heard Enid's voice whispering in his ear.

'Pinch me from time to time, Edward – just to make me sure that I am not in a dream.'

'I have to pinch myself, too.'

'What about your song, Wee One?' asked Bolsover.

'Oh, yes, indeeda! Wee One sing to you.' She began some simple song, but faded away in a squeak, while the trumpet clattered on to the table.

'Ah, power run down!' said Mailey. 'I think a little more music will set us right. "Lead, Kindly Light", Smiley.'

They sang the beautiful hymn together. As the verse closed an amazing thing happened – amazing, at least, to the novices, though it called for no remark from the circle.

The trumpet still shone upon the table, but two voices, those apparently of a man and a woman, broke out in the air above them and joined very tunefully in the singing. The hymn died away and all was silence and tense expectancy once more.

It was broken by a deep male voice from the darkness. It was an educated English voice, well modulated, a voice which spoke in a fashion to which the good Bolsover could never attain.

'Good evening, friends. The power seems good to-night.'

'Good evening, Luke. Good evening!' cried everyone. 'It is our teaching guide,' Bolsover explained. 'He is a high spirit from the sixth sphere who gives us instruction.'

'I may seem high to you,' said the voice. 'But what am I to those in turn who instruct me! It is not *my* wisdom. Give me no credit. I do but pass it on.'

'Always like that,' said Bolsover. 'No swank. It's a sign of his height.'

'I see you have two inquirers present. Good evening, young lady! You know nothing of your own powers or destiny. You will find them out. Good evening, sir, you are on the threshold of great knowledge. Is there any subject upon which you would wish me to say a few words? I see that you are making notes.'

Malone had, as a fact, disengaged his hand in the darkness and was jotting down in shorthand the sequence of events.

'What shall I speak of?'

'Of love and marriage,' suggested Mrs. Bolsover, nudging her husband.

'Well, I will say a few words on that. I will not take long, for others are waiting. The room is crowded with spirit people. I wish you to understand that there is one man, and only one, for each woman, and one woman only for each man. When those two meet they fly together and are one through all the endless chain of existence. Until they meet all unions are mere accidents which have no meaning. Sooner or later each couple becomes complete. It may not be here. It may be in the next sphere where the sexes meet as they do on earth. Or it may be further delayed. But every man and every woman has his or her affinity, and will find it. Of earthly marriages perhaps one in five is permanent. The others are accidental. Real marriage is of the soul and spirit. Sex actions are a mere external symbol which mean nothing and are foolish, or even pernicious, when the thing which they should symbolize is wanting. Am I clear?'

'Very clear,' said Mailey.

'Some have the wrong mate here. Some have no mate, which is more fortunate. But all will sooner or later get the right mate. That is certain. Do not think that you will not necessarily have your present husband when you pass over.'

'Gawd be praised! Gawd be thanked!' cried a voice.

'No. Mrs. Melder, it is love – real love – which unites us here. He goes his way. You go yours. You are on separate planes, perhaps. Some day you will each find your own, when your youth has come back as it will over here.'

'You speak of love. Do you mean sexual love?' asked Mailey.

'Where are we gettin' to?' murmured Mrs. Bolsover.

'Children are not born here. That is only on the earth plane. It was this aspect of marriage to which the great Teacher referred when he said: "There will be neither marriage nor giving in marriage". No! It is purer, deeper, more wonderful, a unity of souls, a complete merging of interests and knowledge without a loss of individuality. The nearest you ever get to it is the first high passion, too beautiful for physical expression when two high-souled lovers meet upon your plane. They find lower expression afterwards, but they will always in their hearts know that the first delicate, exquisite soul-union was the more lovely. So it is with us. Any question?'

'If a woman loves two men equally, what then?' asked Malone.

'It seldom happens. She nearly always knows which is really nearest to her. If she really did so, then it would be a proof that neither was the real affinity, for he is bound to stand high above all. Of course, if she . . .'

The voice trailed off and the trumpet fell.

'Sing "Angels are hoverin' around"!' cried Bolsover. 'Smiley, hit that old harmonium. The vibrations are at zero.'

Another bout of music, another silence, and then a most dismal voice. Never had Enid heard so sad a voice. It was like clods on a coffin. At first it was a deep mutter. Then it was a prayer – a Latin prayer apparently – for twice the word *Domine* sounded and once the word *peccavimus*. There was an indescribable air of depression and desolation in the room. 'For God's sake what is it?' cried Malone.

The circle was equally puzzled.

'Some poor chap out of the lower spheres, I think,' said Bolsover. 'Orthodox folk say we should avoid them. I say we should hurry up and help them.'

'Right, Bolsover!' said Mailey, with hearty approval. 'Get on with it, quick!'

'Can we do anything for you, friend?'

There was silence.

'He doesn't know. He doesn't understand the conditions. Where is Luke? He'll know what to do.'

'What is it, friend?' asked the pleasant voice of the guide.

'There is some poor fellow here. We want to help him.'

'Ah! yes, yes, he has come from the outer darkness,' said Luke in a sympathetic voice. 'He doesn't know. He doesn't understand. They come over here with a fixed idea, and when they find the real thing is quite different from anything they have been taught by the Churches, they are helpless. Some adapt themselves and they go on. Others don't, and they just wander on unchanging, like this man. He was a cleric, and a very narrow, bigoted one. This is the growth of his own mental seed sown upon earth – sown in ignorance and reaped in misery.'

'What is amiss with him?'

'He does not know he is dead. He walks in the mist. It is all an evil dream to him. He has been years so. To him it seems an eternity.'

'Why do you not tell him – instruct him?'

'We cannot. We –'

The trumpet crashed.

'Music, Smiley, music! Now the vibrations should be better.'

'The higher spirits cannot reach earth-bound folk,' said Mailey. 'They are in very different zones of vibration. It is we who are near them and can help them.'

'Yes, you! you!' cried the voice of Luke.

'Mr. Mailey, speak to him. You know him!' The low mutter had broken out again in the same weary monotone.

'Friend, I would have a word with you,' said Mailey in a firm, loud voice. The mutter ceased and one felt that the invisible presence was straining its attention. "Friend, we are sorry at your condition. You have passed on. You see us and you wonder why we do not see you. You are in the other world. But you do not know it, because it is not as you expected. You have not been received as you imagined. It is because you imagined wrong. Understand that all is well, and that God is good, and that all happiness is awaiting you if you will but raise your mind and pray for help, and above all think less of your own condition and more of those other poor souls who are round you.'

There was a silence and Luke spoke again.

'He has heard you. He wants to thank you. He has some glimmer now of his condition. It will grow within him. He wants to know if he may come again.'

'Yes! yes!' cried Bolsover. 'We have quite a number who report progress from time to time. God bless you, friend. Come as often as you can.' The mutter had ceased and there seemed to be a new feeling of peace in the air. The high voice of Wee One was heard.

'Plenty power still left. Red Cloud here. Show what he can do, if Daddy likes.'

'Red Cloud is our Indian control. He is usually busy when any purely physical phenomena have to be done. You there, Red Cloud?'

Three loud thuds, like a hammer on wood, sounded from the darkness.

'Good evening, Red Cloud!'

A new voice, slow, staccato, laboured, sounded above them.

'Good day, Chief! How the squaw? How the papooses? Strange faces in wigwam to-night.'

'Seeking knowledge, Red Cloud. Can you show what you can do?'

'I try. Wait a little. Do all I can.'

Again there was a long hush of expectancy. Then the novices were faced once more with the miraculous.

There came a dull glow in the darkness. It was apparently a wisp of luminous vapour. It whisked across from one side to the other and then circled in the air. By degrees it condensed into a circular disc of radiance about the size of a bull's-eye lantern. It cast no reflection round it and was simply a clean-cut circle in the gloom. Once it approached Enid's face and Malone saw it clearly from the side.

'Why, there is a hand holding it!' he cried, with sudden suspicion.

'Yes, there is a materialized hand,' said Mailey. 'I can see it clearly.'

'Would you like it to touch you, Mr. Malone?'

'Yes, if it will.'

The light vanished and an instant afterwards Malone felt pressure upon his own hand. He turned it palm upwards and clearly felt three fingers laid across it, smooth, warm fingers of adult size. He closed his own fingers and the hand seemed to melt away in his grasp.

'It has gone!' he gasped.

'Yes! Red Cloud is not very good at materializations. Perhaps we don't give him the proper sort of power. But his lights are excellent.'

Several more had broken out. They were of different types, slow-moving clouds and little dancing sparks like glow-worms. At the same time both visitors were conscious of a cold wind which blew upon their faces. It was no delusion, for Enid felt her hair stream across her forehead.

'You feel the rushing wind,' said Mailey. 'Some of these lights would pass for tongues of fire, would they not? Pentecost does not seem such a very remote or impossible thing, does it?'

The tambourine had risen in the air, and the dot of luminous paint showed that it was circling round. Presently it descended and touched their heads each in turn. Then with a jingle it quivered down upon the table.

'Why a tambourine? It seems always to be a tambourine,' remarked Malone.

'It is a convenient little instrument,' Mailey explained. 'The only one which shows automatically by its noise where it is flying. I don't know what other I could suggest except a musical-box.'

'Our box here flies round somethin' amazin',' said Mrs. Bolsover. 'It thinks nothing of winding itself up in the air as it flies. It's a heavy box too.'

'Nine pounds,' said Bolsover. 'Well, we seem to have got to the end of things. I don't think we shall get much more to-night. It has not been a bad sitting – what I should call a fair average sitting. We must wait a little before we turn on the light. Well, Mr. Malone, what do you think of it? Let's have any objections now before we part. That's the worst of you inquirers, you know. You often bottle things up in your own minds and let them loose afterwards, when it would have been easy to settle it at the time. Very nice and polite to our faces, and then we are a gang of swindlers in the report.'

Malone's head was throbbing and he passed his hand over his heated brow.

'I am confused,' he said, 'but impressed. Oh, yes, certainly impressed. I've read of these things, but it is very different when you see them. What weighs most with me is the obvious sincerity and sanity of all you people. No one could doubt that.'

'Come. We're gettin' on,' said Bolsover.

'I try to think of the objections which would be raised by others who were not present. I'll have to answer them. First, there is the oddity of it all. It is so different to our preconceptions of spirit people.'

'We must fit our theories to the facts,' said Mailey. 'Up to now we have fitted the facts to our theories. You must remember that we have been dealing to-night – with all respect to our dear good hosts – with a simple, primitive, earthly type of spirit, who has his very definite uses, but is not to be taken as an average type. You might as well take the stevedore whom you see on the quay as being a representative Englishman.'

'There's Luke,' said Bolsover.

'Ah, yes, he is, of course, very much higher. You heard him and could judge. What else, Mr. Malone?'

'Well, the darkness! Everything done in darkness. Why should all mediumship be associated with gloom?'

'You mean all physical mediumship. That is the only branch of the subject which needs darkness. It is purely chemical, like the darkness of the photographic room. It preserves the delicate physical substance which, drawn from the human body, is the basis of these phenomena. A cabinet is used for the purpose of condensing this same vaporous substance and helping it to solidify. Am I clear?'

'Yes, but it is a pity all the same. It gives a horrible air of deceit to the whole business.'

'We get it now and again in the light, Mr. Malone,' said Bolsover. 'I don't know if Wee One is gone yet. Wait a bit! Where are the matches?' He lit the candle, which set them all blinking after their long darkness, 'Now let us see what we can do.'

There was a round wood platter or circle of wood lying among the miscellaneous objects littered over the table to serve as playthings for the strange forces. Bolsover stared at it. They all stared at it. They had risen but no one was within three feet of it.

'Please, Wee One, please!' cried Mrs. Bolsover.

Malone could hardly believe his eyes. The disc began to move. It quivered and then rattled upon the table, exactly as the lid of a boiling pot might do.

'Up with it, Wee One!' They were all clapping their hands.

The circle of wood, in the full light of the candle, rose upon edge and stood there shaking, as if trying to keep its balance.

'Give three tilts, Wee One.'

The disc inclined forward three times. Then it fell flat and remained so.

'I am so glad you have seen that,' said Mailey. 'There is Telekinesis in its simplest and most decisive form.'

'I could not have believed it!' cried Enid.

'Nor I,' said Malone. 'I have extended my knowledge of what is possible. Mr. Bolsover, you have enlarged my views.'

'Good, Mr. Malone!'

'As to the power at the back of these things I am still ignorant. As to the thing themselves I have now and henceforward not the slightest doubt in the world. I *know* that they are true. I wish you all good night. It is not likely that Miss Challenger or I will ever forget the evening that we have spent under your roof.'

It was like another world when they came out into the frosty air, and saw the taxis bearing back the pleasure-seekers from the theatre or cinema palace. Mailey stood beside them while they waited for a cab.

'I know exactly how you feel,' he said, smiling. 'You look at all these bustling, complacent people, and you marvel to think how little they know of the possibilities of life. Don't you want to stop them? Don't you want to tell them? And yet they would only think you a liar or a lunatic. Funny situation, is it not?'

'I've lost all my bearings for the moment.'

'They will come back to-morrow morning. It is curious how fleeting these impressions are. You will persuade yourselves that you have been dreaming. Well, good-bye – and let me know if I can help your studies in the future.'

The friends – one could hardly yet call them lovers – were absorbed in thought during their drive home. When he reached Victoria Gardens Malone escorted Enid to the door of the flat, but he did not go in with her. Somehow the jeers of Challenger which usually rather woke sympathy within him would now get upon his nerves. As it was he heard his greeting in the hall.

'Well, Enid. Where's your spook? Spill him out of the bag on the floor and let us have a look at him.'

His evening's adventure ended as it had begun, with a bellow of laughter which pursued him down the lift.

CHAPTER V

Where Our Commissioners Have a Remarkable Experience

MALONE SAT AT THE SIDE TABLE of the smoking-room of the Literary Club. He had Enid's impressions of the seance before him – very subtle and observant they were – and he was endeavouring to merge them in his own experience. A group of men were smoking and chatting round the fire. This did not disturb the journalist, who found, as many do, that his brain and his pen worked best sometimes when they were stimulated by the knowledge that he was part of a busy world. Presently, however, somebody who observed his presence brought the talk round to psychic subjects, and then it was more difficult for him to remain aloof. He leaned back in his chair and listened.

Polter, the famous novelist, was there, a brilliant man with a subtle mind, which he used too often to avoid obvious truth and to defend some impossible position for the sake of the empty dialectic exercise. He was holding forth now to an admiring, but not entirely a subservient audience.

'Science,' said he, 'is gradually sweeping the world clear of all these old cobwebs of superstition. The world was like some old, dusty attic, and the sun of science is bursting in, flooding it with light, while the dust settles gradually to the floor.'

'By science,' said someone maliciously, 'you mean, of course, men like Sir William Crookes, Sir Oliver Lodge, Sir William Barrett, Lombroso, Richet, and so forth.'

Polter was not accustomed to be countered, and usually became rude.

'No, sir, I mean nothing so preposterous,' he answered, with a glare. 'No name, however eminent, can claim to stand for science so long as he is a member of an insignificant minority of scientific men.'

'He is, then, a crank,' said Pollifex, the artist, who usually played jackal to Polter.

The objector, one Millworthy, a free-lance of journalism, was not to be so easily silenced.

'Then Galileo was a crank in his day,' said he. 'And Harvey was a crank when he was laughed at over the circulation of the blood.'

'It's the circulation of the *Daily Gazette* which is at stake,' said Marrible, the humorist of the club. 'If they get off their stunt I don't suppose they care a tinker's curse what is truth or what is not.'

'Why such things should be examined at all, except in a police court, I can't imagine,' said Polter. 'It is a dispersal of energy, a misdirection of human thought into channels which lead nowhere. We have plenty of obvious, material things to examine. Let us get on with our job.'

Atkinson, the surgeon, was one of the circle, and had sat silently listening. Now he spoke.

'I think the learned bodies should find more time for the consideration of psychic matters.'

'Less,' said Polter.

'You can't have less than nothing. They ignore them altogether. Some time ago I had a series of cases of telepathic *rapport* which I wished to lay before the Royal Society. My colleague Wilson, the zoologist, also had a paper which he proposed to read. They went in together. His was accepted and mine rejected. The title of his paper was "The Reproductive System of the Dung-Beetle".'

There was a general laugh.

'Quite right, too,' said Polter. 'The humble dung-beetle was at least a fact. All this psychic stuff is not.'

'No doubt you have good grounds for your views,' chirped the mischievous Millworthy, a mild youth with a velvety manner. 'I have little time for solid reading, so I should like to ask you which of Dr. Crawford's three books you consider the best?'

'I never heard of the fellow.'

Millworthy simulated intense surprise.

'Good Heavens, man! Why, he is *the* authority. If you want pure laboratory experiments those are the books. You might as well lay down the law about zoology and confess that you had never heard of Darwin.'

'This is not science,' said Polter, emphatically.

'What is really not science,' said Atkinson, with some heat, 'is the laying down of the law on matters which you have not studied. It is talk of that sort which has brought me to the edge of Spiritualism, when I compare this dogmatic ignorance with the earnest search for truth conducted by the great Spiritualists. Many of them took twenty years of work before they formed their conclusions.'

'But their conclusions are worthless because they are upholding a formed opinion.'

'But each of them fought a long fight before he formed that opinion. I know a few of them, and there is not one who did not take a lot of convincing.'

Polter shrugged his shoulders.

'Well, they can have their spooks if it makes them happier so long as they let me keep my feet firm on the ground.'

'Or stuck in the mud,' said Atkinson.

'I would rather be in the mud with sane people than in the air with lunatics,' said Polter. 'I know some of these Spiritualists people and I believe that you can divide them equally into fools and rogues.'

Malone had listened with interest and then with a growing indignation. Now he suddenly took fire.

'Look here, Polter,' he said, turning his chair towards the company, 'it is fools and dolts like you which are holding back the world's progress. You admit that you have read nothing of this, and I'll swear you have seen nothing. Yet you use the position and the name which you have won in other matters in order to discredit a number of people who, whatever they may be, are certainly very earnest and very thoughtful.'

'Oh,' said Polter, 'I had no idea you had got so far. You don't dare to say so in your articles. You *are* a Spiritualist then. That rather discounts your views, does it not?'

'I am not a Spiritualist, but I am an honest inquirer, and that is more than you have ever been. You call them rogues and fools, but, little as I know, I am sure that some of them are men and women whose boots you are not worthy to clean.'

'Oh, come, Malone!' cried one or two voices, but the insulted Polter was on his feet. 'It's men like you who empty this club,' he cried, as he swept out. 'I shall certainly never come here again to be insulted.'

'I say, you've done it, Malone!'

'I felt inclined to help him out with a kick. Why should he ride roughshod over other people's feelings and beliefs? He has got on and most of us haven't, so he thinks it's a condescension to come among us.'

'Dear old Irishman!' said Atkinson, patting his shoulder. 'Rest, perturbed spirit, rest! But I wanted to have a word with you. Indeed, I was waiting here because I did not want to interrupt you.'

'I've had interruptions enough!' cried Malone. 'How could I work with that damned donkey braying in my ear?'

'Well, I've only a word to say. I've got a sitting with Linden, the famous medium of whom I spoke to you, at the Psychic College to-night. I have an extra ticket. Would you care to come?'

'Come? I should think so!'

'I have another ticket. I should have asked Polter if he had not been so offensive. Linden does not mind sceptics, but objects to scoffers. Who should I ask?'

'Let Miss Enid Challenger come. We work together, you know.'

'Why, of course I will. Will you let her know?'

'Certainly.'

'It's at seven o'clock to-night. The Psychic College. You know the place down at Holland Park.'

'Yes, I have the address. Very well, Miss Challenger and I will certainly be there.'

Behold the pair, then, upon a fresh psychic adventure. They picked Atkinson up at Wimpole Street, and then traversed that long, roaring rushing, driving belt of the great city which extends through Oxford Street and Bayswater to Notting Hill and the stately Victorian houses of Holland Park. It was at one of these that the taxi drew up, a large, imposing building, standing back a little from the road. A smart maid admitted them, and the subdued light of the tinted hall-lamp fell upon shining linoleum and polished woodwork with the gleam of white marble statuary in the corner. Enid's female perceptions told her of a well-run, well-appointed establishment, with a capable direction at the head. This direction took the shape of a kindly Scottish lady who met them in the hall and greeted Mr. Atkinson as an old friend. She was, in turn, introduced to the journalists as Mrs. Ogilvy. Malone had already heard how her husband and she had founded and run this remarkable institute, which is the centre of psychic experiment in London, at a very great cost, both in labour and in money, to themselves.

'Linden and his wife have gone up,' said Mrs. Ogilvy. 'He seems to think that the conditions are favourable. The rest are in the drawing-room. Won't you join them for a few minutes?'

Quite a number of people had gathered for the seance, some of them old psychic students who were mildly interested; others, beginners who looked about them with rather startled eyes, wondering what was going to happen next. A tall man was standing near the door who turned and disclosed the tawny beard and open face of Algernon Mailey. He shook hands with the newcomers.

'Another experience, Mr. Malone? Well, I thought you gave a very fair account of the last. You are still a neophyte, but you are well within the gates of the temple. Are you alarmed, Miss Challenger?'

'I don't think I could be while you were around,' she answered.

He laughed.

'Of course, a materialization seance is a little different to any other – more impressive, in a way. You'll find it very instructive, Malone, as bearing upon psychic photography and other matters. By the way, you should try for a psychic picture. The famous Hope works upstairs.'

'I always thought that that at least was fraud.'

'On the contrary, I should say it was the best established of all phenomena, the one which leaves the most permanent proof. I've been a dozen times under every possible test conditions. The real trouble is, not that it lends itself to fraud, but that it lends itself to exploitation by that villainous journalism which cares only for a sensation. Do you know anyone here?'

'No, we don't.'

'The tall, handsome lady is the Duchess of Rossland. Then, there are Lord and Lady Montnoir, the middle-aged couple near the fire. Real, good folk and among the very few of the aristocracy who have shown earnestness and moral courage in this matter. The talkative lady is Miss Badley, who lives for seances, a jaded Society woman in search of new sensations – always visible, always audible, and always empty. I don't know the two men. I heard someone say they were researchers from the university. The stout man with the lady in black is Sir James Smith – they lost two boys in the war. The tall, dark person, is a weird man named Barclay, who lives, I understand, in one room and seldom comes out save for a seance.'

'And the man with the horn glasses?'

'That is a pompous ass named Weatherby. He is one of those who wander about on the obscure edges of Masonry, talking with whispers and reverence of mysteries where no mystery is. Spiritual-ism, with its very real and awful mysteries, is, to him, a vulgar thing because it brought consolation to common folk, but he loves to read papers on the Palladian Cultus, ancient and accepted Scottish rites, and Baphometic figures. Eliphas Levi is his prophet.'

'It sounds very learned,' said Enid.

'Or very absurd. But, hullo! Here are mutual friends.'

The two Bolsovers had arrived, very hot and frowsy and genial. There is no such leveller of classes as Spiritualism, and the char-woman with psychic force is the superior of the millionaire who lacks it. The Bolsovers and the aristocrats fraternized instantly. The Duchess was just asking for admission to the grocer's circle, when Mrs. Ogilvy bustled in.

'I think everyone is here now,' she said. 'It is time to go upstairs.'

The seance room was a large, comfortable chamber on the first floor, with a circle of easy chairs, and a curtain-hung divan which served as a cabinet. The medium and his wife were waiting there. Mr. Linden was a gentle, large-featured man, stoutish in build, deep-chested, clean-shaven, with dreamy, blue eyes and flaxen, curly hair which rose in a pyramid at the apex of his head. He was of middle age. His wife was rather younger, with the sharp, querulous expression of the tired housekeeper, and quick, critical eyes, which softened into something like adoration when she looked at her hus-band. Her role was to explain matters, and to guard his interests while he was unconscious.

'The sitters had better just take their own places,' said the medium. 'If you can alternate the sexes it is as well. Don't cross your knees, it breaks the current. If we have a materialization, don't grab at it. If you do, you are liable to injure me.'

The two sleuths of the Research Society looked at each other knowingly. Mailey observed it.

'Quite right,' he said. 'I have seen two cases of dangerous hæmorrhage in the medium brought on by that very cause.'

'Why?' asked Malone.

'Because the ectoplasm used is drawn from the medium. It recoils upon him like a snapped elastic band. Where it comes through the skin you get a bruise. Where it comes from mucous membrane you get bleeding.'

'And when it comes from nothing, you get nothing,' said the researcher with a grin.

'I will explain the procedure in a few words,' said Mrs. Ogilvy, when everyone was seated. 'Mr. Linden does not enter the cabinet at all. He sits outside it, and as he tolerates red light you will be able to satisfy yourselves that he does not leave his seat. Mrs. Linden sits on the other side. She is there to regulate and explain. In the first place we would wish you to examine the cabinet. One of you will also please lock the door on the inside and be responsible for the key.'

The cabinet proved to be a mere tent of hangings, detached from the wall and standing on a solid platform. The researchers ferreted about inside it and stamped on the boards. All seemed solid.

'What is the use of it?' Malone whispered to Mailey.

'It serves as a reservoir and condensing place for the ectoplasmic vapour from the medium, which would otherwise diffuse over the room.'

'It has been known to serve other purposes also,' remarked one of the researchers, who overheard the conversation.

'That's true enough,' said Mailey philosophically. 'I am all in favour of caution and supervision.'

'Well, it seems fraud-proof on this occasion, if the medium sits outside.' The two researchers were agreed on this.

The medium was seated on one side of the little tent, his wife on the other. The light was out, and a small red lamp near the ceiling was just sufficient to enable outlines to be clearly seen. As the eyes became accustomed to it some detail could also be observed.

'Mr. Linden will begin by some clairvoyant readings,' said Mrs. Linden. Her whole attitude, seated beside the cabinet with her hands on her lap and the air of a proprietor, made Enid smile, for she thought of Mrs. Jarley and her waxworks.

Linden, who was not in a trance, began to give clairvoyance. It was not very good. Possibly the mixed influence of so many sitters of various types at close quarters was too disturbing. That was the excuse which he gave himself when several of his descriptions were unrecognized. But Malone was more shocked by those which were recognized, since it was so clear that the word was put into the medium's mouth. It was the folly of the sitter rather than the fault of the medium, but it was disconcerting all the same.

'I see a young man with brown eyes and a rather drooping moustache.'

'Oh, darling, darling, have you then come back!' cried Miss Badley. 'Oh, has he a message?'

'He sends his love and does not forget.'

'Oh, how evidential! It is so exactly what the dear boy would have said! My first lover, you know,' she added, in a simpering voice to the company. 'He never fails to come. Mr. Linden has brought him again and again.'

'There is a young fellow in khaki building up on the left. I see a symbol over his head. It might be a Greek cross.'

'Jim – it is surely Jim!' cried Lady Smith.

'Yes. He nods his head.'

'And the Greek cross is probably a propeller,' said Sir James. 'He was in the Air Service, you know.'

Malone and Enid were both rather shocked. Mailey was also uneasy.

'This is not good,' he whispered to Enid. 'Wait a bit! You will get something better.'

There were several good recognitions, and then someone resembling Summerlee was described for Malone. This was wisely discounted by him, since Linden might have been in the audience on the former occasion. Mrs. Debbs' exhibition seemed to him far more convincing than that of Linden.

'Wait a bit!' Mailey repeated.

'The medium will now try for materializations,' said Mrs. Linden. 'If the figures appear I would ask you not to touch them, save by request. Victor will tell you if you may do so. Victor is the medium's control.'

The medium had settled down in his chair and he now began to draw long, whistling breaths with deep intakes, puffing the air out between his lips. Finally he steadied down and seemed to sink into a deep coma, his chin upon his breast. Suddenly he spoke, but it seemed that his voice was better modulated and more cultivated than before.

'Good evening, all!' said the voice.

There was a general murmur of 'Good evening, Victor.'

'I am afraid that the vibrations are not very harmonious. The sceptical element is present, but not, I think, predominant, so that we may hope for results. Martin Lightfoot is doing what he can.'

'That is the Indian control,' Mailey whispered.

'I think that if you would start the gramophone it would be helpful. A hymn is always best, though there is no real objection to secular music. Give us what you think best, Mrs. Ogilvy.'

There was the rasping of a needle which had not yet found its grooves. Then 'Lead, Kindly Light' was churned out. The audience joined in in a subdued fashion. Mrs. Ogilvy then changed it to 'O, God, our help in ages past'.

'They often change the records themselves,' said Mrs. Ogilvy, 'but to-night there is not enough power.'

'Oh, yes,' said the voice. 'There *is* enough power, Mrs. Ogilvy, but we are anxious to conserve it all for the materializations. Martin says they are building up very well.'

At this moment the curtain in front of the cabinet began to sway. It bellied out as if a strong wind were behind it. At the same time a breeze was felt by all who were in the circle, together with a sensation of cold.

'It is quite chilly,' whispered Enid, with a shiver.

'It is not a subjective feeling,' Mailey answered. 'Mr. Harry Price has tested it with thermometric readings. So did Professor Crawford.'

'My God!' cried a startled voice. It belonged to the pompous dabbler in mysteries, who was suddenly faced with a real mystery. The curtains of the cabinet had parted and a human figure had stolen noiselessly out. There was the medium clearly outlined on one side. There was Mrs. Linden, who had sprung to her feet, on the other. And, between them, the little black, hesitating figure, which seemed to be terrified at its own position. Mrs. Linden soothed and encouraged it.

'Don't be alarmed, dear. It is all quite right. No one will hurt you.'

'It is someone who has never been through before,' she explained to the company. 'Naturally it seems very strange to her. Just as strange as if we broke into their world. That's right, dear. You are gaining strength, I can see. Well done!'

The figure was moving forward. Everyone sat spellbound, with staring eyes. Miss Badley began to giggle hysterically. Weatherby lay back in his chair, gasping with horror. Neither Malone nor Enid felt any fear, but were consumed with curiosity. How marvellous to hear the humdrum flow of life in the street outside and to be face to face with such a sight as that.

Slowly the figure moved round. Now it was close to Enid and between her and the red light. Stooping, she could get the silhouette sharply outlined. It was that of a little, elderly woman, with sharp, clear-cut features.

'It's Susan!' cried Mrs. Bolsover. 'Oh, Susan, don't you know me?'

The figure turned and nodded her head.

'Yes, yes, dear, it is your sister Susie,' cried her husband. 'I never saw her in anything but black. Susan, speak to us!'

The head was shaken.

'They seldom speak the first time they come,' said Mrs. Linden, whose rather blasé, business-like air was in contrast to the intense emotion of the company. 'I'm afraid she can't hold together long. Ah, there! She has gone!'

The figure had disappeared. There had been some backward movement towards the cabinet, but it seemed to the observers that she sank into the ground before she reached it. At any rate, she was gone.

'Gramophone, please!' said Mrs. Linden. Everyone relaxed and sat back with a sigh. The gramophone struck up a lively air. Suddenly the curtains parted, and a second figure appeared.

It was a young girl, with flowing hair down her back. She came forward swiftly and with perfect assurance to the centre of the circle.

Mrs. Linden laughed in a satisfied way.

'Now you will get something good,' she said. 'Here is Lucille.'

'Good evening, Lucille!' cried the Duchess. 'I met you last month, you will remember, when your medium came to Maltraver Towers.'

'Yes, yes, lady, I remember you. You have a little boy, Tommy, on our side of life. No, no, not dead, lady! We are far more alive than you are. All the fun and frolic are with us!' She spoke in a high clear voice and perfect English.

'Shall I show you what we do over here?' She began a graceful, gliding dance, while she whistled as melodiously as a bird. 'Poor Susan could not do that. Susan has had no practice. Lucille knows how to use a built-up body.'

'Do you remember me, Lucille?' asked Mailey.

'I remember you, Mr. Mailey. Big man with yellow beard.'

For the second time in her life Enid had to pinch herself hard to satisfy herself that she was not dreaming. Was this graceful creature, who had now sat down in the centre of the circle, a real materialization of ectoplasm, used for the moment as a machine for expression by a soul that had passed, or was it an illusion of the senses, or was it a fraud? There were the three possibilities. An illusion was absurd when all had the same impression. Was it a fraud? But this was certainly not the little old woman. She was inches taller and fair, not dark. And the cabinet was fraud-proof. It had been meticulously examined. Then it was true. But if it were true, what a vista of possibilities opened out. Was it not far the greatest matter which could claim the attention of the world!

Meanwhile, Lucille had been so natural and the situation was so normal that even the most nervous had relaxed. The girl answered most cheerfully to every question, and they rained upon her from every side.

'Where did you live, Lucille?'

'Perhaps I had better answer that,' interposed Mrs. Linden. 'It will save the power. Lucille was bred in South Dakota in the United States, and passed over at the age of fourteen. We have verified some of her statements.'

'Are you glad you died, Lucille?'

'Glad for my own sake. Sorry for mother.'

'Has your mother seen you since?'

'Poor mother is a shut box. Lucille cannot open the lid.'

'Are you happy?'

'Oh, yes, so gloriously happy.'

'Is it right that you can come back?'

'Would God allow it if it were not right? What a wicked man you must be to ask!'

'What religion were you?'

'We were Roman Catholics.'

'Is that the right religion?'

'All religions are right if they make you better.'

'Then it does not matter.'

'It is what people do in daily life, not what they believe.'

'Tell us more, Lucille.'

'Lucille has little time. There are others who wish to come. If Lucille uses too much power, the others have less. Oh, God is very good and kind! You poor people on earth do not know how good and kind He is because it is grey down there. But it is grey for your own good. It is to give you your chance to earn all the lovely things which wait for you. But you can only tell how wonderful He is when you get over here.'

'Have you seen him?'

'Seen Him! How could you see God? No, no, He is all round us and in us and in everything, but we do not see Him. But I have seen the Christ. Oh, He was glorious, glorious! Now, good-bye – good-bye!' She backed towards the cabinet and sank into the shadows.

Now came a tremendous experience for Malone. A small, dark, rather broad figure of a woman appeared slowly from the cabinet. Mrs. Linden encouraged her, and then came across to the journalist.

'It is for you. You can break the circle. Come up to her.'

Malone advanced and peered, awestruck, into the face of the apparition. There was not a foot between them. Surely that large head, that solid, square outline was familiar! He put his face still nearer – it was almost touching. He strained his eyes. It seemed to him that the features were semi-fluid, moulding themselves into a shape, as if some unseen hand was modelling them in putty.

'Mother!' he cried. 'Mother!'

Instantly the figure threw up both her hands in a wild gesture of joy. The motion seemed to destroy her equilibrium and she vanished.

'She had not been through before. She could not speak,' said Mrs. Linden, in her business-like way. 'It was your mother.'

Malone went back half-stunned to his seat. It is only when these things come to one's own address that one understands their full force. His mother! Ten years in her grave and yet standing before him. Could he *swear* it was his mother? No, he could not. Was he morally certain that it was his mother? Yes, he was morally certain. He was shaken to the core.

But other wonders diverted his thoughts. A young man had emerged briskly from the cabinet and had advanced to the front of Mailey, where he had halted.

'Hullo, Jock! Dear old Jock!' said Mailey. 'My nephew,' he explained to the company. 'He always comes when I am with Linden.'

'The power is sinking,' said the lad, in a clear voice. 'I can't stay very long. I am so glad to see you, Uncle. You know, we can see quite clearly in this light, even if you can't.'

'Yes, I know you can. I say, Jock. I wanted to tell you that I told your mother I had seen you. She said her Church taught her it was wrong.'

'I know. And that I was a demon. Oh, it is rotten, rotten, rotten, and rotten things will fall!' His voice broke in a sob.

'Don't blame her Jock, she believes this.'

'No, no, I don't blame her! She will know better some day. The day is coming soon when all truth will be manifest and all these corrupt Churches will be swept off the earth with their cruel doctrines and their caricatures of God.'

'Why, Jock, you are becoming quite a heretic!'

'Love, Uncle! Love! That is all that counts. What matter what you believe if you are sweet and kind and unselfish as the Christ was of old?'

'Have you seen Christ?' asked someone.

'Not yet. Perhaps the time may come.'

'Is he not in Heaven, then?'

'There are many heavens. I am in a very humble one. But it is glorious all the same.'

Enid had thrust her head forward during this dialogue. Her eyes had got used to the light and she could see more clearly than before. The man who stood within a few feet of her was not human. Of that she had no doubt whatever, and yet the points were very subtle. Something in his strange, yellow-white colouring as contrasted with the faces of her neighbours. Something, also, in the curious stiffness of his carriage, as of a man in very rigid stays.

'Now, Jock,' said Mailey, 'give an address to the company. Tell them a few words about your life.'

The figure hung his head, exactly as a shy youth would do in life.

'Oh, Uncle, I can't.'

'Come, Jock, we love to listen to you.'

'Teach the folk what death is,' the figure began. 'God wants them to know. That is why He lets us come back. It is nothing. You are no more changed than if you went into the next room. You can't believe you are dead. I didn't. It was only when I saw old Sam that I knew, for I was certain that he was dead, anyhow. Then I came back to mother. And' – his voice broke – 'she would not receive me.'

'Never mind, dear old Jock,' said Mailey. 'She will learn wisdom.'

'Teach them the truth! Teach it to them! Oh, it is so much more important than all the things men talk about. If papers for one week gave as much attention to psychic things as they do to football, it would be known to all. It is ignorance which stands –'

The observers were conscious of a sort of flash towards the cabinet, but the youth had disappeared.

'Power run down,' said Mailey. 'Poor lad, he held on to the last. He always did. That was how he died.'

There was a long pause. The gramophone started again. Then

there was a movement of the curtains. Something was emerging. Mrs. Linden sprang up and waved the figure back. The medium for the first time stirred in his chair and groaned.

'What is the matter, Mrs. Linden?'

'Only half-formed,' she answered. 'The lower face had not materialized. Some of you would have been alarmed. I think that we shall have no more to-night. The power has sunk very low.'

So it proved. The lights were gradually turned on. The medium lay with a white face and a clammy brow in his chair, while his wife sedulously watched over him, unbuttoning his collar and bathing his face from a water-glass. The company broke into little groups, discussing what they had seen.

'Oh, wasn't it thrilling?' cried Miss Badley. 'It really was most exciting. But what a pity we could not see the one with the semi-materialized face.'

'Thanks, I have seen quite enough,' said the pompous mystic, all the pomposity shaken out of him. 'I confess that it has been rather too much for my nerves.'

Mr. Atkinson found himself near the psychic researchers. 'Well, what do you make of it?' he asked.

'I have seen it better done at Maskelyne's Hall,' said one.

'Oh, come, Scott!' said the other. 'You've no right to say that. You admitted that the cabinet was fraud-proof.'

'Well, so do the committees who go on the stage at Maskelyne's.'

'Yes, but it is Maskelyne's own stage. This is not Linden's own stage. He has no machinery.'

'*Populus vult decipi*,' the other answered, shrugging his shoulders. 'I should certainly reserve judgment.' He moved away with the dignity of one who cannot be deceived, while his more rational companion still argued with him as they went.

'Did you hear that?' said Atkinson. 'There is a certain class of psychic researcher who is absolutely incapable of receiving evidence. They misuse their brains by straining them to find a way round when the road is quite clear before them. When the human race advances into its new kingdom, these intellectual men will form the absolute rear.'

'No, no,' said Mailey, laughing. 'The bishops are predestined to be the rearguard. I see them all marching in step, a solid body, with their gaiters and cassocks – the last in the whole world to reach spiritual truth.'

'Oh, come,' said Enid, 'that is too severe. They are all good men.'

'Of course they are. It's quite physiological. They are a body of elderly men, and the elderly brain is sclerosed and cannot record new impressions. It's not their fault, but the fact remains. You are very silent, Malone.'

But Malone was thinking of a little, squat, dark figure which waved its hands in joy when he spoke to it. It was with that image in his mind that he turned from this room of wonders and passed down into the street.

CHAPTER VI

In Which the Reader is Shown the Habits of a Notorious Criminal

WE WILL NOW LEAVE THAT LITTLE GROUP with whom we have made our first exploration of these grey and ill-defined, but immensely important, regions of human thought and experiences. From the researchers we will turn to the researched. Come with me and we will visit Mr. Linden at home, and will examine the lights and shades which make up the life of a professional medium

To reach him we will pass down the crowded thoroughfare of Tottenham Court Road, where the huge furniture emporia flank the way, and we will turn into a small street of drab houses which leads eastwards towards the British Museum. Tullis Street is the name and 40 the number. Here it is, one of a row, flat-faced, dull-coloured and commonplace, with railed steps leading up to a dis-coloured door, and one front-room window, in which a huge gilt-edged Bible upon a small round table reassures the timid visi-tor. With the universal pass-key of imagination we open the dingy door, pass down a dark passage and up a narrow stair. It is nearly ten o'clock in the morning and yet it is in his bedroom that we must seek the famous worker of miracles. The fact is that he has had, as we have seen, an exhausting sitting the night before, and that he has to conserve his strength in the mornings.

At the moment of our inopportune, but invisible, visit he was sit-ting up, propped by the pillows, with a breakfast-tray upon his knees. The vision he presented would have amused those who have prayed with him in the humble Spiritualist temples, or had sat with awe at the seances where he had exhibited the modern equivalents of the gifts of the Spirit. He looked unhealthily pallid in the dim morning light, and his curly hair rose up in a tangled pyramid above his broad, intellectual brow. The open collar of his nightshirt dis-played a broad, bull's neck, and the depth of his chest and spread of his shoulders showed that he was a man of considerable personal strength. He was eating his breakfast with avidity while he conversed with the little, eager, dark-eyed wife who was seated on the side of the bed.

'And you reckon it a good meeting, Mary?'

'Fair to middling, Tom. There was two of them researchers raking round with their feet and upsetting everybody. D'ye think those folk in the Bible would have got their phenomena if they had chaps of that sort on the premises? "Of one accord", that's what they say in the Book.'

'Of course!' cried Linden heartily. 'Was the Duchess pleased?'

'Yes, I think she was very pleased. So was Mr. Atkinson, the surgeon. There was a new man there called Malone of the Press. Then Lord and Lady Montnoir got evidence, and so did Sir James Smith and Mr. Mailey.'

'I wasn't satisfied with the clairvoyance,' said the medium. 'The silly idiots kept on putting things into my mind. "That's surely my Uncle Sam", and so forth. It blurs me so that I can see nothing clear.'

'Yes, and they think they are helping! Helping to muddle you and deceive themselves. I know the kind.'

'But I went under nicely and I am glad there were some fine materializations. It took it out of me, though. I'm a rag this morning.'

'They work you too hard, dear. I'll take you to Margate and build you up.'

'Well, maybe at Easter we could do a week. It would be fine. I don't mind readings and clairvoyance, but the physicals do try you. I'm not as bad as Hallows. They say he just lies white and gasping on the floor after them.'

'Yes,' cried the woman bitterly. 'And then they run to him with whisky, and so they teach him to rely on the bottle and you get another case of a drunken medium. I know them. You keep off it, Tom!'

'Yes, one of our trade should stick to soft drinks. If he can stick to vegetables, too, he's all the better, but I can't preach that while I am wolfin' up ham and eggs. By Gosh, Mary! it's past ten and I have a string of them comin' this morning. I'm going to make a bit to-day.'

'You give it away as quick as you make it, Tom.'

'Well, some hard cases come my way. So long as we can make both ends meet what more do we want? I expect *they* will look after us all right.'

'They have let down a lot of other poor mediums who did good work in their day.'

'It's the rich folk that are to blame not the Spirit-people,' said Tom Linden hotly. 'It makes me see red when I remember these folk, Lady This and Countess That, declaring all the comfort they have had, and then leaving those who gave it to die in the gutter or rot in the workhouse. Poor old Tweedy and Soames and the rest all living on old-age pensions and the papers talking of the money that mediums make, while some damned conjuror makes more than all of us put together by a rotten imitation with two tons of machinery to help him.'

'Don't worry, dear,' cried the medium's wife, putting her thin hand caressingly upon the tangled mane of her man. 'It all comes level in time and everybody pays the price for what they have done.'

Linden laughed loudly. 'It's my Welsh half that comes out when I flare up. Let the conjurors take their dirty money and let the rich folk keep their purses shut. I wonder what they think money is for. Paying death duties is about the only fun some of them seem to get out of it. If I had their money . . .'

There was a knock at the door.

'Please, sir, your brother Silas is below.'

The two looked at each other with some dismay.

'More trouble,' said Mrs. Linden sadly.

Linden shrugged his shoulders. 'All right, Susan!' he cried. 'Tell him I'll be down. Now, dear, you keep him going and I'll be with you in a quarter of an hour.'

In less time than he named he was down in the front-room – his consulting room – where his wife was evidently having some difficulty in making agreeable conversation with their visitor. He was a big, heavy man, not unlike his elder brother, but with all the genial chubbiness of the medium coarsened into pure brutality. He had the same pile of curly hair, but he was clean-shaven with a heavy, obstinate jowl. He sat by the window with his huge freckled hands upon his knees. A very important part of Mr. Silas Linden lay in those hands, for he had been a formidable professional boxer, and at one time was fancied for the welter-weight honours of England. Now, as his stained tweed suit and frayed boots made clear, he had fallen on evil days, which he endeavoured to mitigate by cadging on his brother.

'Mornin', Tom,' he said in a husky voice. Then as the wife left the room: 'Got a drop of Scotch about? I've a head on me this morning. I met some of the old set last night down at "The Admiral

Vernon". Quite a reunion it was – chaps I hadn't seen since my best ring days.'

'Sorry, Silas,' said the medium, seating himself behind his desk. 'I keep nothing in the house.'

'Spirits enough, but not the right sort,' said Silas. 'Well, the price of a drink will do as well. If you've got a Bradbury about you I could do with it, for there's nothing coming my way.'

Tom Linden took a pound note from his desk.

'Here you are, Silas. So long as I have any you have your share. But you had two pounds last week. Is it gone?'

'Gone! I should say so!' He put the note in his pocket. 'Now, look here, Tom, I want to speak to you very serious as between man and man.'

'Yes, Silas, what is it?'

'You see that!' He pointed to a lump on the back of his hand. 'That's a bone! See? It will never be right. It was when I hit Curly Jenkins third round and outed him at the N.S.C. I outed myself for life that night. I can put up a show fight and exhibition bout, but I'm done for the real thing. My right has gone west.'

'It's a hard case, Silas.'

'Damned hard! But that's neither here nor there. What matters is that I've got to pick up a living and I want to know how to do it. An old scrapper don't find many openings. Chucker-out at a pub with free drinks. Nothing doing there. What I want to know, Tom, is what's the matter with my becoming a medium?'

'A medium?'

'Why the devil should you stare at me! If it's good enough for you it's good enough for me.'

'But you are *not* a medium.'

'Oh, come! Keep that for the newspapers. It's all in the family, and between you an' me, how d'ye do it?'

'I don't do it. I do nothing.'

'And get four or five quid a week for it. That's a good yarn. Now you can't fool me. Tom, I'm not one o' those duds that pay you a thick 'un for an hour in the dark. We're on the square, you an' me. How d'ye do it?'

'Do what?'

'Well, them raps, for example. I've seen you sit there at your desk, as it might be, and raps come answerin' questions over yonder on the bookshelf. It's damned clever – fair puzzles 'em every time. How d'ye get them?'

'I tell you I don't. It's outside myself.'

'Rats! You can tell me, Tom. I'm Griffiths, the safe man. It would set me up for life if I could do it.'

For the second time in one morning the medium's Welsh strain took control.

'You're an impudent, blasphemous rascal, Silas Linden. It's men like you who come into our movement and give it a bad name. You should know me better than to think that I am a cheat. Get out of my house, you ungrateful rascal!'

'Not too much of your lip,' growled the ruffian.

'Out you go, or I'll put you out, brother or no brother.'

Silas doubled his great fists and looked ugly for a moment. Then the anticipation of favours to come softened his mood.

'Well, well, no harm meant,' he growled, as he made for the door. 'I expect I can make a shot at it without your help.' His grievance suddenly overcame his prudence as he stood in the doorway. 'You damned, canting, hypocritical box-of-tricks. I'll be even with you yet.'

The heavy door slammed behind him.

Mrs. Linden had rushed in to her husband.

'The hulking blackguard!' she cried. 'I 'eard 'im. What did 'e want?'

'Wanted me to put him wise to mediumship. Thinks it's a trick of some sort that I could teach him.'

'The foolish lump! Well, it's a good thing, for he won't dare show his face here again.'

'Oh, won't he?'

'If he does I'll slap it for him. To think of his upsettin' you like this. Why, you're shakin' all over!'

'I suppose I wouldn't be a medium if I wasn't high strung. Someone said we were poets, only more so. But it's bad just when work is beginning.'

'I'll give you healing.'

She put her little work-worn hands over his high forehead and held them there in silence.

'That's better!' said he. 'Well done, Mary. I'll have a cigarette in the kitchen. That will finish it.'

'No, there's someone here.' She had looked out of the window. 'Are you fit to see her? It's a woman.'

'Yes, yes. I am all right now. Show her in.'

An instant later a woman entered, a pale, tragic figure in black, whose appearance told its own tale. Linden motioned her to a chair away from the light. Then he looked through his papers.

'You are Mrs. Blount, are you not? You had an appointment?'

'Yes – I wanted to ask –'

'Please ask me nothing. It confuses me.'

He was looking at her with the medium's gaze in his light grey eyes – that gaze which looks round and through a thing rather than at it.

'You have been wise to come, very wise. There is someone beside you who has an urgent message which could not be delayed. I get a name . . . Francis . . . yes, Francis.'

The woman clasped her hands.

'Yes, yes, it is the name.'

'A dark man, very sad, very earnest – oh, so earnest. He will speak. He must speak! It is urgent. He says, "Tink-a-bell". Who is Tink-a-bell?'

'Yes, yes, he called me so. Oh, Frank, Frank, speak to me! Speak!'

'He is speaking. His hand is on your head. "Tink-a-bell", he says, "If you do what you purpose doing it will make a gap that it will take many years to cross". Does that mean anything?'

She sprang from her chair. 'It means everything. Oh, Mr. Linden, this was my last chance. If this had failed – if I found that I had really lost him I meant to go and seek him. I would have taken poison this night.'

'Thank God that I have saved you. It is a terrible thing, madame, to take one's life. It breaks the law of Nature, and Nature's laws cannot be broken without punishment. I rejoice that he has been able to save you. He has more to say to you. His message is, "If you will live and do your duty I will for ever be by your side, far closer to you than ever I was in life. My presence will surround you and guard both you and our three babes." '

It was marvellous the change! The pale, worn woman who had entered the room was now standing with flushed cheeks and smiling lips. It is true that tears were pouring down her face, but they were tears of joy. She clapped her hands. She made little convulsive movements as if she would dance.

'He's not dead! He's not dead! How can he be dead if he can speak to me and be closer to me than ever? Oh, it's glorious! Oh, Mr. Linden, what can I do for you? You have saved me from shameful death! You have restored my husband to me! Oh, what a God-like power you have!'

The medium was an emotional man and his own tears were moist upon his cheeks.

'My dear lady, say no more. It is not I. I do nothing. You can thank God Who in His mercy permits some of His mortals to discern a spirit or to carry a message. Well, well, a guinea is my fee, if you can afford it. Come back to me if ever you are in trouble.'

'I am content now,' she cried, drying her eyes, 'to await God's will and to do my duty in the world until such time as it shall be ordained that we unite once more.'

The widow left the house walking on air. Tom Linden also felt that the clouds left by his brother's visit had been blown away by this joyful incident, for there is no happiness like giving happiness and seeing the beneficent workings of one's own power. He had hardly settled down in his chair, however, before another client was ushered in. This time it was a smartly-dressed, white-spatted, frock-coated man of the world, with a bustling air as of one to whom minutes are precious.

'Mr. Linden, I believe? I have heard, sir, of your powers. I am told that by handling an object you can often get some clue as to the person who owned it?'

'It happens sometimes. I cannot command it.'

'I should like to test you. I have a letter here which I received this morning. Would you try your powers upon that?'

The medium took the folded letter, and, leaning back in his chair, he pressed it upon his forehead. He sat with his eyes closed for a minute or more. Then he returned the paper.

'I don't like it,' he said. 'I get a feeling of evil. I see a man dressed all in white. He has a dark face. He writes at a bamboo table. I get a sensation of heat. The letter is from the tropics.'

'Yes, from Central America.'

'I can tell you no more.'

'Are the spirits so limited? I thought they knew everything.'

'They do not know everything. Their power and knowledge are as closely limited as ours. But this is not a matter for the spirit people. What I did then was psychometry, which, so far as we know, is a power of the human soul.'

'Well, you are right as far as you have gone. This man, my correspondent, wants me to put up the money for the half-share in an oil boring. Shall I do it?'

Tom Linden shook his head.

'These powers are given to some of us, sir, for the consolation of humanity and for a proof of immortality. They were never meant for worldly use. Trouble always comes of such use, trouble to the medium and trouble to the client. I will not go into the matter.'

'Money's no object,' said the man, drawing a wallet from his inner pocket.

'No, sir, nor to me. I am poor, but I have never ill-used my gift.'

'A fat lot of use the gift is, then!' said the visitor, rising from his chair. 'I can get all the rest from the parsons who are licensed, and you are not. There is your guinea, but I have not had the worth of it.'

'I am sorry, sir, but I cannot break a rule. There is a lady beside you – near your left shoulder – an elderly lady . . .'

'Tut! tut!' said the financier, turning towards the door.

'She wears a large gold locket with an emerald cross upon her breast.'

The man stopped, turned and stared.

'Where did you pick that up?'

'I see it before me, now.'

'Why, dash it, man, that is what my mother always wore! D'you tell me you can see her?'

'No, she is gone.'

'What was she like? What was she doing?'

'She *was* your mother. She said so. She was weeping.'

'Weeping! My mother! Why, she is in heaven if ever a woman was. They don't weep in heaven!'

'Not in the imaginary heaven. They do in the real heaven. It is only we who ever make them weep. She left a message.'

'Give it to me!'

'The message was: "Oh, Jack! Jack! you are drifting ever further from my reach".'

The man made a contemptuous gesture.

'I was a damned fool to let you have my name when I made the appointment. You have been making inquiries. You don't take me in with your tricks. I've had enough of it – more than enough!'

For the second time that morning the door was slammed by an angry visitor.

'He didn't like his message.' Linden explained to his wife. 'It was his poor mother. She is fretting over him. Lord! If folk only knew these things it would do them more good than all the forms and ceremonies.'

'Well, Tom, it's not your fault if they don't,' his wife answered. 'There are two women waiting to see you. They have not an introduction but they seem in great trouble.'

'I've a bit of a headache. I haven't got over last night. Silas and I are the same in that. Our night's work finds us out next morning. I'll just take these and no more, for it is bad to send anyone sorrowin' away if one can help it.'

The two women were shown in, both of them austere figures dressed in black, one a stern-looking person of fifty, the other about half that age.

'I believe your fee is a guinea,' said the elder, putting that sum upon the table.

'To those who can afford it,' Linden answered. As a matter of fact, the guinea often went the other way.

'Oh yes, I can afford it,' said the woman. 'I am in sad trouble and they told me maybe you could help me.'

'Well, I will if I can. That's what I am for.'

'I lost my poor husband in the war – killed at Ypres he was. Could I get in touch with him?'

'You don't seem to bring any influence with you. I get no impression. I am sorry but we can't command these things. I get the name Edmund. Was that his name?'

'No.'

'Or Albert?'

'No.'

'I am sorry, but it seems confused – cross vibrations, perhaps, and a mix-up of messages like crossed telegraph wires.'

'Does the name Pedro help you?'

'Pedro! Pedro! No, I get nothing. Was Pedro an elderly man?'

'No, not elderly.'

'I can get no impression.'

'It was about this girl of mine that I really wanted advice. My husband would have told me what to do. She has got engaged to a young man, a fitter by trade, but there are one or two things against it and I want to know what to do.'

'Do give us some advice,' said the young woman, looking at the medium with a hard eye.

'I would if I could, my dear. Do you love this man?'

'Oh yes, he's all right.'

'Well, if you don't feel more than that about him, I should leave him alone. Nothing but unhappiness comes of such a marriage.'

'Then you see unhappiness waiting for her?'

'I see a good chance of it. I think she should be careful.'

'Do you see anyone else coming along?'

'Everyone, man or woman, meets their mate sometime somewhere.'

'Then she will get a mate?'

'Most certainly she will.'

'I wonder if I should have any family?' asked the girl.

'Nay, that's more than I can say.'

'And money – will she have money? We are down-hearted, Mr. Linden, and we want a little –'

At this moment there came a most surprising interruption. The door flew open and little Mrs. Linden rushed into the room with pale face and blazing eyes.

'They are policewomen, Tom. I've had a warning about them. It's only just come. Get out of this house, you pair of snivelling hypocrites. Oh, what a fool! What a fool I was not to recognize what you were.'

The two women had risen.

'Yes, you are rather late, Mrs. Linden,' said the senior. 'The money has passed.'

'Take it back! Take it back! It's on the table.'

'No, no, the money has passed. We have had our fortune told. You will hear more of this, Mr. Linden.'

'You brace of frauds! You talk of frauds when it is you who are the frauds all the time! He would not have seen you if it had not been for compassion.'

'It is no use scolding us,' the woman answered. 'We do our duty and we did not make the law. So long as it is on the Statute Book we have to enforce it. We must report the case at headquarters.'

Tom Linden seemed stunned by the blow, but, when the policewomen had disappeared, he put his arm round his weeping wife and consoled her as best he might.

'The typist at the police office sent down the warning,' she said. 'Oh, Tom, it is the second time!' she cried. 'It means gaol and hard labour for you.'

'Well, dear, so long as we are conscious of having done no wrong and of having done God's work to the best of our power, we must take what comes with a good heart.'

'But where were they? How could they let you down so? Where was your guide?'

'Yes, Victor,' said Tom Linden, shaking his head at the air above him, 'where were you? I've got a crow to pick with you. You know, dear,' he added, 'just as a doctor can never treat his own case, a medium is very helpless when things come to his own address. That's the law. And yet I should have known. I was feeling in the dark. I had no inspiration of any sort. It was just a foolish pity and sympathy that led me on when I had no sort of a real message. Well, dear Mary, we will take what's coming to us with a brave heart. Maybe they have not enough to make a case, and maybe the beak is not as ignorant as most of them. We'll hope for the best.'

In spite of his brave words the medium was shaking and quivering at the shock. His wife had put her hands upon him and was endeavouring to steady him, when Susan, the maid, who knew nothing of the trouble, admitted a fresh visitor into the room. It was none other than Edward Malone.

'He can't see you,' said Mrs. Linden, 'the medium is ill. He will see no one this morning.'

But Linden had recognized his visitor.

'This is Mr. Malone, my dear, of the *Daily Gazette*. He was with us last night. We had a good sitting, had we not, sir?'

'Marvellous!' said Malone. 'But what is amiss?'

Both husband and wife poured out their sorrows.

'What a dirty business!' cried Malone, with disgust. 'I am sure the public does not realize how this law is enforced, or there would be a row. This agent-provocateur business is quite foreign to British justice. But in any case, Linden, you are a *real* medium. The law was made to suppress false ones.'

'There are no real mediums in British law,' said Linden, ruefully. 'I expect the more real you are the greater the offence. If you are a medium at all and take money you are liable. But how can a medium live if he does not take money? It's a man's whole work and needs all his strength. You can't be a carpenter all day and a first-class medium in the evening.'

'What a wicked law! It seems to be deliberately stifling all physical proofs of spiritual power.'

'Yes, that is just what it is. If the Devil passed a law it would be just that. It is supposed to be for the protection of the public and yet no member of the public has ever been known to complain. Every case is a police trap. And yet the police know as well as you or I that every Church charity garden-party has got its clairvoyante or its fortune-teller.'

'It does seem monstrous. What will happen now?'

'Well, I expect a summons will come along. Then a police court case. Then fine or imprisonment. It's the second time, you see.'

'Well, your friends will give evidence for you and we will have a good man to defend you.'

Linden shrugged his shoulders.

'You never know who are your friends. They slip away like water when it comes to the pinch.'

'Well, I won't, for one,' said Malone, heartily. 'Keep me in touch with what is going on. But I called because I had something to ask you.'

'I am sorry, but I am really not fit.' Linden held out a quivering hand.

'No, no, nothing psychic. I simply wanted to ask you whether the presence of a strong sceptic would stop all your phenomena?'

'Not necessarily. But, of course, it makes everything more difficult. If they will be quiet and reasonable we can get results. But they know nothing, break every law, and ruin their own sittings. There was old Sherbank, the doctor, the other day. When the raps came on the table he jumped up, put his hand on the wall, and cried, "Now then, put a rap on the palm of my hand within five seconds". Because he did not get it he declared it was all humbug and stamped out of the room. They will not admit that there are fixed laws in this as in everything else.'

'Well, I must confess that the man I am thinking of might be quite as unreasonable. It is the great Professor Challenger.'

'Oh, yes, I've heard he is a hard case.'

'Would you give him a sitting?'

'Yes, if you desired it.'

'He won't come to you or to any place you name. He imagines all sorts of wires and contrivances. You might have to come down to his country house.'

'I would not refuse if it might convert him.'

'And when?'

'I can do nothing until this horrible affair is over. It will take a month or two.'

'Well, I will keep in touch with you till then. When all is well again we shall make our plans and see if we can bring these facts before him, as they have been brought before me. Meanwhile, let me say how much I sympathize. We will form a committee of your friends and all that can will surely be done.'

CHAPTER VII

In Which the Notorious Criminal Gets What the British Law Considers to be His Deserts

BEFORE WE PURSUE FURTHER the psychic adventures of our hero and heroine, it would be well to see how the British law dealt with that wicked man, Mr. Tom Linden.

The two policewomen returned in triumph to Bardley Square Station where Inspector Murphy, who had sent them, was waiting for their report. Murphy was a jolly-looking, red-faced, black-moustached man who had a cheerful, fatherly way with women which was by no means justified by his age or virility. He sat behind his official table, his papers strewn in front of him.

'Well, girls,' he said as the two women entered, 'what luck?'

'I think it's a go, Mr. Murphy,' said the elder policewoman. 'We have the evidence you want.'

The Inspector took up a written list of questions from his desk.

'You ran it on the general lines that I suggested?' he asked.

'Yes. I said my husband was killed at Ypres.'

'What did he do?'

'Well, he seemed sorry for me.'

'That, of course, is part of the game. He'll be sorry for himself before he is through with it. He didn't say, "You are a single woman and never had a husband?" '

'No.'

'Well, that's one up against his spirits, is it not? That should impress the Court. What more?'

'He felt round for names. They were all wrong.'

'Good!'

'He believed me when I said that Miss Bellinger here was my daughter.'

'Good again! Did you try the Pedro stunt?'

'Yes, he considered the name, but I got nothing.'

'Ah, that's a pity. But, anyhow, he did not know that Pedro was your Alsatian dog. He considered the name. That's good enough. Make the jury laugh and you have your verdict. Now about fortune-telling? Did you do what I suggested?'

'Yes, I asked about Amy's young man. He did not give much that was definite.'

'Cunning devil! He knows his business.'

'But he did say that she would be unhappy if she married him.'

'Oh, he did, did he? Well, if we spread that a little we have got all we want. Now sit down and dictate your report while you have it fresh. Then we can go over it together and see how we can put it best. Amy must write one, also.'

'Very good, Mr. Murphy.'

'Then we shall apply for the warrant. You see, it all depends upon which magistrate it comes before. There was Mr. Dalleret who let a medium off last month. He is no use to us. And Mr. Lancing has been mixed up with these people. Mr. Melrose is a stiff materialist. We could depend on him, and have timed the arrest accordingly. It would never do to fail to get our conviction.'

'Couldn't you get some of the public to corroborate?'

The inspector laughed.

'We are supposed to be protecting the public, but between you and me none of the public have ever yet asked to be protected. There are no complaints. Therefore it is left to us to uphold the law as best we can. As long as it is there we have got to enforce it. Well, good-bye, girls! Let me have the report by four o'clock.'

'Nothing for it, I suppose?' said the elder woman, with a smile.

'You wait, my dear. If we get twenty-five pounds fine it has got to go somewhere – Police Fund, of course, but there may be something over. Anyhow, you go and cough it up and then we shall see.'

Next morning a scared maid broke into Linden's modest study. 'Please sir, it's an officer.'

The man in blue followed hard at her heels.

'Name of Linden?' said he, and handing a folded sheet of foolscap he departed.

The stricken couple who spent their lives in bringing comfort to others were sadly in need of comfort themselves. She put her arm round his neck while they read the cheerless document:

To THOMAS LINDEN of 40, Tullis Street, N.W.
Information has been laid this day by Patrick Murphy, Inspector of Police, that you the said Thomas Linden on the 10th day of November at the above dwelling did profess to Henrietta Dresser and to Amy Bellinger to tell fortunes to deceive and impose on certain of His Majesty's subjects to wit those above mentioned. You are therefore summoned to appear before the Magistrate of the Police Court in Bardsley Square on Wednesday next, the 17th, at the hour of 11 in the forenoon to answer to the said information.
Dated the 10th day of November.
(Signed) B. J. WITHERS.

On the same afternoon Mailey called upon Malone and they sat in consultation over this document. Then they went together to see Summerway Jones, an acute solicitor and an earnest student of psychic affairs. Incidentally, he was a hard rider to hounds, a good boxer, and a man who carried a fresh-air flavour into the mustiest law chambers. He arched his eyebrows over the summons.

'The poor devil has not an earthly!' said he. 'He's lucky to have a summons. Usually they act on a warrant. Then the man is carted right off, kept in the cells all night, and tried next morning with no one to defend him. The police are cute enough, of course, to choose either a Roman Catholic or a materialist as the magistrate. Then, by the beautiful judgment of Chief Justice Lawrence – the first judgment, I believe, that he delivered in that high capacity – the profession of mediumship or wonder-working is in itself a legal crime, whether it be genuine or no, so that no defence founded upon good results has a look in. It's a mixture of religious persecution and police blackmail. As to the public, they don't care a damn! Why should they? If they don't want their fortune told, they don't go. The whole thing is the most absolute bilge and a disgrace to our legislature.'

'I'll write it up,' said Malone, glowing with Celtic fire. 'What do you call the Act?'

'Well, there are two Acts, each more putrid than the other, and both passed long before Spiritualism was ever heard of. There is the Witchcraft Act dating from George the Second. That has become too absurd, so they only use it as a second string. Then there is the Vagrancy Act of 1824. It was passed to control the wandering gipsy folk on the roadside, and was never intended, of course, to be used like this.' He hunted among his papers. 'Here is the beastly thing. "Every person professing to tell fortunes or using any subtle craft, means or device to deceive and impose on any of His Majesty's subjects shall be deemed a rogue and a vagabond", and so on and so forth. The two Acts together would have roped in the whole Early Christian movement just as surely as the Roman persecution did.'

'Lucky there are no lions now,' said Malone.

'Jackasses!' said Mailey. 'That's the modern substitute. But what are we to do?'

'I'm damned if I know!' said the solicitor, scratching his head. 'It's perfectly hopeless!'

'Oh, dash it all!' cried Malone, 'we can't give it up so easily. We know the man is an honest man.'

Mailey turned and grasped Malone's hand.

'I don't know if you call yourself a Spiritualist yet,' he said, 'but you are the kind of chap we want. There are too many white-livered folk in our movement who fawn on a medium when all is well, and desert him at the first breath of an accusation. But, thank God! there are a few stalwarts. There is Brookes and Rodwin and Sir James Smith. We can put up a hundred or two among us.'

'Right-o!' said the solicitor, cheerily. 'If you feel like that we will give you a run for your money.'

'How about a K.C.?'

'Well, they don't plead in police courts. If you'll leave it in my hands I fancy I can do as well as anyone, for I've had a lot of these cases. It will keep the costs down, too.'

'Well, we are with you. And we will have a few good men at our back.'

'If we do nothing else we shall ventilate it,' said Malone. 'I believe in the good old British public. Slow and stupid, but sound at the core. They will not stand for injustice if you can get the truth into their heads.'

'They damned well need trepanning before you can get it there,' said the solicitor. 'Well, you do your bit and I'll do mine and we will see what comes of it.'

The fateful morning arrived and Linden found himself in the dock facing a spruce, middle-aged man with rat-trap jaws, Mr. Melrose, the redoubtable police magistrate. Mr. Melrose had a reputation for severity with fortune-tellers and all who foretold the future, though he spent the intervals in his court by reading up the sporting prophets, for he was an ardent follower of the Turf, and his trim, fawn-coloured coat and rakish hat were familiar objects at every race meeting which was within his reach. He was in no particularly good humour this morning as he glanced at the charge-sheet and then surveyed the prisoner. Mrs. Linden had secured a position below the dock, and occasionally extended her hand to pat that of the prisoner which rested on the edge. The court was crowded and many of the prisoner's clients had attended to show their sympathy.

'Is this case defended?' asked Mr. Melrose.

'Yes, your worship,' said Summerway Jones. 'May I, before it opens, make an objection?'

'If you think it worth while, Mr. Jones.'

'I beg to respectfully request your ruling before the case is proceeded with. My client is not a vagrant, but a respectable member of the community, living in his own house, paying rates and taxes, and on the same footing as every other citizen. He is now prosecuted under the fourth section of the Vagrancy Act of 1824, which is styled, "An Act for punishing idle and disorderly persons, and rogues and vagabonds". The Act was intended, as the words imply, to restrain lawless gipsies and others, who at that time infested the country. I ask your worship to rule that my client is clearly not a person within the purview of this Act or liable to its penalties.'

The magistrate shook his head.

'I fear, Mr. Jones, that there have been too many precedents for the Act to be now interpreted in this limited fashion. I will ask the solicitor prosecuting on behalf of the Commissioner of Police to put forward his evidence.'

A little bull of a man with side-whiskers and a raucous voice sprang to his feet.

'I call Henrietta Dresser.'

The elder policewoman popped up in the box with the alacrity of one who is used to it. She held an open notebook in her hand.

'You are a policewoman, are you not?'

'Yes, sir.'

'I understand that you watched the prisoner's home the day before you called on him?'

'Yes, sir.'

'How many people went in?'

'Fourteen, sir.'

'Fourteen people. And I believe the prisoner's average fee is ten and sixpence.'

'Yes.'

'Seven pounds in one day! Pretty good wages when many an honest man is content with five shillings.'

'These were the tradespeople!' cried Linden.

'I must ask you not to interrupt. You are already very efficiently represented,' said the magistrate severely.

'Now, Henrietta Dresser,' continued the prosecutor, wagging his pince-nez. 'Let's hear what occurred when you and Amy Bellinger visited the prisoner.'

The policewoman gave an account which was in the main true, reading it from her book. She was not a married woman, but the medium had accepted her statement that she was. He had fumbled with several names and had seemed greatly confused. The name of a dog – Pedro – had been submitted to him, but he had not recognized it as such. Finally, he had answered questions as to the future of her alleged daughter, who was, in fact, no relation to her, and had foretold that she would be unhappy in her marriage.

'Any questions, Mr. Jones?' asked the magistrate.

'Did you come to this man as one who needed consolation? And did he attempt to give it?'

'I suppose you might put it so.'

'You professed deep grief, I understand.'

'I tried to give that impression.'

'You do not consider that to be hypocrisy?'

'I did what was my duty.'

'You saw no signs of psychic power, or anything abnormal?' asked the prosecutor.

'No, he seemed a very nice, ordinary sort of man.'

Amy Bellinger was the next witness. She appeared with her note-book in her hand.

'May I ask, your worship, whether it is in order that these wit-nesses should read their evidence?' asked Mr. Jones.

'Why not?' queried the magistrate. 'We desire the exact facts, do we not?'

'*We* do. Possibly Mr. Jones does not,' said the prosecuting solicitor.

'It is clearly a method of securing that the evidence of these two witnesses shall be in accord,' said Jones. 'I submit that these accounts are carefully prepared and collated.'

'Naturally, the police prepare their case,' said the magistrate. 'I do not see that you have any grievance, Mr. Jones. Now, witness, let us hear your evidence.'

It followed on the exact lines of the other.

'You asked questions about your fiancé? You had no fiancé,' said Mr. Jones.

'That is so.'

'In fact, you both told a long sequence of lies?'

'With a good object in view.'

'You thought the end justified the means?'

'I carried out my instructions.'

'Which were given you beforehand?'

'Yes, we were told what to ask.'

'I think,' said the magistrate, 'that the policewomen have given their evidence very fairly and well. Have you any witnesses for the defence, Mr. Jones?'

'There are a number of people in court, your worship, who have received great benefit from the mediumship of the prisoner. I have subpœnaed one woman who was, by her own account, saved from suicide that very morning by what he told her. I have another man who was an atheist, and had lost all belief in future life. He was completely converted by his experience of psychic phenomena. I can produce men of the highest eminence in sci-ence and literature who will testify to the real nature of Mr. Linden's powers.'

The magistrate shook his head.

'You must know, Mr. Jones, that such evidence would be quite beside the question. It has been clearly laid down by the ruling of the Lord Chief Justice and others that the law of this country does not recognize supernatural powers of any sort whatever, and that a pretence of such powers where payment is involved constitutes a crime in itself. Therefore your suggestion that you should call witnesses could not possibly lead to anything save a wasting of the time of the court. At the same time, I am, of course, ready to listen to any observations which you may care to make after the solicitor for the prosecution has spoken.'

'Might I venture to point out, your worship,' said Jones, 'that such a ruling would mean the condemnation of any sacred or holy person of whom we have any record, since even holy persons have to live, and have therefore to receive money.'

'If you refer to Apostolic times, Mr. Jones,' said the magistrate sharply, 'I can only remind you that the Apostolic age is past and also that Queen Anne is dead. Such an argument is hardly worthy of your intelligence. Now, sir, if you have anything to add . . .'

Thus encouraged the prosecutor made a short address, stabbing the air at intervals with his pince-nez as if every stab punctured afresh all claims of the spirit. He pictured the destitution among the working-classes, and yet charlatans, by advancing wicked and blasphemous claims, were able to earn a rich living. That they had real powers was, as had been observed, beside the question, but even that excuse was shattered by the fact that these policewomen, who had discharged an unpleasant duty in a most exemplary way, had received nothing but nonsense in return for their money. Was it likely that other clients fared any better? These parasites were increasing in number, trading upon the finer feelings of bereaved parents, and it was high time that some exemplary punishment should warn them that they would be wise to turn their hands to some more honest trade.

Mr. Summerway Jones replied as best he might. He began by pointing out that the Acts were being used for a purpose for which they were never intended. ('That point has already been considered!' snapped the magistrate.) The whole position was open to criticism. The convictions were secured by evidence from agents-provocateurs, who, if any crime had been committed, were obviously inciters to it and also participants. The fines obtained were often deflected for purposes in which the police had a direct interest.

'Surely, Mr. Jones, you do not mean to cast a reflection upon the honesty of the police!'

The police were human, and were naturally inclined to stretch a point where there own interests were affected. All these cases were artificial. There was no record at any time of any real complaint from the public or any demand for protection. There were frauds in every profession, and if a man deliberately invested and lost a guinea in a false medium he had no more right to protection than the man who invested his money in a bad company on the stock market. Whilst the police were wasting time upon such cases, and their agents were weeping crocodile tears in the character of forlorn mourners, many of her branches of real crime received far less attention than they deserved. The law was quite arbitrary in its action. Every big garden-party, even, as he had been informed, every police fête was incomplete without its fortune-teller or palmist.

Some years ago the *Daily Mail* had raised an outcry against fortune-tellers. That great man, the late Lord Northcliffe, had been put in the box by the defence, and it had been shown that one of his other papers was running a palmistry column, and that the fees received were divided equally between the palmist and the proprietors. He mentioned this in no spirit which was derogatory to the memory of this great man, but merely as an example of the absurdity of the law as it was now administered. Whatever might be the individual opinion of members of that court, it was incontrovertible that a large number of intelligent and useful citizens regarded this power of mediumship as a remarkable manifestation of the power of spirit, making for the great improvement of the race. Was it not a most fatal policy in these days of materialism to crush down by law that which in its higher manifestation might work for the regeneration of mankind? As to the undoubted fact that information received by the policewomen was incorrect and that their lying statements were not detected by the medium, it was a psychic law that harmonious conditions were essential for true results, and that deceit on one side produced confusion on the other. If the court would for a moment adopt the Spiritualistic hypothesis, they would realize how absurd it would be to expect that angelic hosts would descend in order to answer the questions of two mercenary and hypocritical inquirers.

Such, in a short synopsis, was the general line of Mr. Summerway Jones's defence which reduced Mrs. Linden to tears and threw the magistrate's clerk into a deep slumber. The magistrate himself rapidly brought the matter to a conclusion.

'Your quarrel, Mr. Jones, seems to be with the law, and that is outside my competence. I administer it as I find it, though I may remark that I am entirely in agreement with it. Such men as the defendant are the noxious fungi which collect on a corrupt society, and the attempt to compare their vulgarities with the holy men of old, or to claim similar gifts, must be reprobated by all right-thinking men.

'As to you, Linden,' he added, fixing his stern eyes upon the prisoner, 'I fear that you are a hardened offender since a previous conviction has not altered your ways. I sentence you, therefore, to two months' hard labour without the option of a fine.'

There was a scream from Mrs. Linden.

'Good-bye, dear, don't fret,' said the medium, glancing over the side of the dock. An instant later he had been hurried down to the cell.

Summerway Jones, Mailey and Malone met in the hall, and Mailey volunteered to escort the poor stricken woman home.

'What had he ever done but bring comfort to all?' she moaned. 'Is there a better man living in the whole great City of London?'

'I don't think there is a more useful one,' said Mailey. 'I'll venture to say that the whole of Crockford's Directory with the Archbishops at their head could not prove the things of religion as I have seen Tom Linden prove them, or convert an atheist as I have seen Linden convert him.'

'It's a shame! A damned shame!' said Malone, hotly.

'The touch about vulgarity was funny,' said Jones. 'I wonder if he thinks the Apostles were very cultivated people. Well, I did my best. I had no hopes, and it has worked out as I thought. It is a pure waste of time.'

'Not at all,' Malone answered. 'It has ventilated an evil. There were reporters in court. Surely some of them have some sense. They will note the injustice.'

'Not they,' said Mailey. 'The Press is hopeless. My God, what a responsibility these people take on themselves, and how little they guess the price that each will pay! I know. I have spoken with them while they were paying it.'

'Well, I for one will speak out,' said Malone, 'and I believe others will also. The Press is more independent and intelligent than you seem to think.'

But Mailey was right, after all. When he had left Mrs. Linden in her lonely home and had reached Fleet Street once more, Malone bought a *Planet*. As he opened it a scare head-line met his eye:

IMPOSTOR IN THE POLICE COURT.

Dog Mistaken for Man.
Who Was Pedro?
Exemplary Sentence.

He crumpled the paper up in his hand.

'No wonder these Spiritualists feel bitterly,' he thought. 'They have good cause.'

Yes, poor Tom Linden had a bad Press. He went down into his miserable cell amid universal objurgation. The *Planet*, an evening paper which depended for its circulation upon the sporting forecasts of Captain Touch-and-go, remarked upon the absurdity of forecasting the future. *Honest John*, a weekly journal which had been mixed up with some of the greatest frauds of the century, was of opinion that the dishonesty of Linden was a public scandal. A rich country rector wrote to *The Times* to express his indignation that anyone should profess to sell the gifts of the spirit. The *Churchman* remarked that such incidents arose from the growing infidelity, while the *Freethinker* saw in them a reversion to superstition. Finally Mr. Maskelyne showed the public, to the great advantage of his box office, exactly how the swindle was perpetrated. So for a few days Tom Linden was what the French call a 'succés d'execration.' Then the world moved on and he was left to his fate.

CHAPTER VIII

In Which Three Investigators Come Upon a Dark Soul

LORD ROXTON HAD RETURNED from a Central African heavy game shooting, and had at once carried out a series of Alpine ascents which had satisfied and surprised everyone except himself.

'Top of the Alps is becomin' a perfect bear-garden,' said he. 'Short of Everest there don't seem to be any decent privacy left.'

His advent into London was acclaimed by a dinner given in his honour at the "Travellers" by the Heavy Game Society. The occasion was private and there were no reporters, but Lord Roxton's speech was fixed *verbatim* in the minds of all his audience and has been imperishably preserved. He writhed for twenty minutes under the flowery and eulogistic periods of the president, and rose himself in the state of confused indignation which the Briton feels when he is publicly approved. 'Oh, I say! By Jove! What!' was his oration, after which he resumed his seat and perspired profusely.

Malone was first aware of Lord Roxton's return through McArdle, the crabbed old red-headed news editor, whose bald dome projected further and further from its ruddy fringe as the years still found him slaving at the most grinding of tasks. He retained his keen scent of what was good copy, and it was this sense of his which caused him one winter morning to summon Malone to his presence. He removed the long glass tube which he used as a cigarette-holder from his lips, and he blinked through his big round glasses at his subordinate.

'You know that Lord Roxton is back in London?'

'I had not heard.'

'Aye, he's back. Dootless you've heard that he was wounded in the war. He led a small column in East Africa and made a wee war of his own till he got an elephant bullet through his chest. Oh, he's done fine since then, or he couldn't be climbin' these mountains. He's a deevil of a man and aye stirring up something new.'

'What is the latest?' asked Malone, eyeing a slip of paper which McArdle was waving between his finger and thumb.

'Well, that's where he impinges on you. I was thinking maybe you could hunt in couples and, there would be copy in it. There's a leaderette in the *Evening Standard.*' He handed it over. It ran thus:

'A quaint advertisement in the columns of a contemporary shows that the famous Lord John Roxton, third son of the Duke of Pomfret, is seeking fresh worlds to conquer. Having exhausted the sporting adventures of this terrestrial globe, he is now turning to those of the dim, dark and dubious regions of psychic research. He is in the market apparently for any genuine specimen of a haunted house, and is open to receive information as to any violent or dangerous manifestation which called for investigation. As Lord John Roxton is a man of resolute character and one of the best revolver shots in England, we would warn any practical joker that he would be well-advised to stand aside and leave this matter to those who are said to be as impervious to bullets as their supporters are to common sense.'

McArdle gave his dry chuckle at the concluding words. 'I'm thinking they are getting pairsonal there, friend Malone, for if you are no a supporter, you're well on the way. But are you no of the opeenion that this chiel and you between you might put up a spook and get two racy columns off him?'

'Well, I can see Lord Roxton,' said Malone. 'He's still, I suppose, in his old rooms in the Albany. I would wish to call in any case, so I can open this up as well.'

Thus it was that in the late afternoon just as the murk of London broke into dim circles of silver, the pressman found himself once more walking down Vigo Street and accosting the porter at the dark entrance of the old-fashioned chambers. Yes, Lord John Roxton was in, but a gentleman was with him. He would take a card. Presently he returned with word that in spite of the previous visitor, Lord Roxton would see Malone at once. An instant later, he had been ushered into the old luxurious rooms with their trophies of war and of the chase. The owner of them with outstretched hand was standing at the door, long, thin, austere, with the same gaunt, whimsical, Don Quixote face as of old. There was no change save that he was more aquiline, and his eyebrows jutted more thickly over his reckless, restless eyes.

'Hullo, young fellah!' he cried. 'I was hopin' you'd draw this old covert once more. I was comin' down to the office to look you up. Come in! Come in! Let me introduce you to the Reverend Charles Mason.'

A very tall, thin clergyman, who was coiled up in a large basket chair, gradually unwound himself and held out a bony hand to the newcomer. Malone was aware of two very earnest and human grey eyes looking searchingly into his, and of a broad, welcoming smile which disclosed a double row of excellent teeth. It was a worn and weary face, the tired face of the spiritual fighter, but it was very kindly and companionable, none the less. Malone had heard of the man, a Church of England vicar, who had left his model parish and the church which he had built himself in order to preach freely the doctrines of Christianity, with the new psychic knowledge super-added.

'Why, I never seem to get away from the Spiritualists!' he exclaimed.

'You never will, Mr. Malone,' said the lean clergyman, chuckling. 'The world never will until it has absorbed this new knowledge which God has sent. You can't get away from it. It is too big. At the present moment, in this great city there is not a place where men or women meet that it does not come up. And yet you would not know it from the Press.'

'Well, you can't level that reproach at the *Daily Gazette*,' said Malone. 'Possibly you may have read my own descriptive articles.'

'Yes, I read them. They are at least better than the awful sensational nonsense which the London Press usually serves up, save when they ignore it altogether. To read a paper like *The Times* you would never know that this vital movement existed at all. The only editorial allusion to it that I can ever remember was in a leading article when the great paper announced that it would believe in it when it found it could, by means of it, pick out more winners on a race-card than by other means.'

'Doosed useful, too,' said Lord Roxton. 'It's just what I should have said myself. What!'

The clergyman's face was grave and he shook his head. 'That brings me back to the object of my visit,' he said. He turned to Malone. 'I took the liberty of calling upon Lord Roxton in connection with his advertisement to say that if he went on such a quest with a good intention, no better work could be found in the world, but if he did it out of a love of sport, following some poor earth-bound soul in the same spirit as he followed the white rhinoceros of the Lido, he might be playing with fire.'

'Well, padre, I've been playin' with fire all my life and that's nothin' new. What I mean – if you want me to look at this ghost business from the religious angle, there's nothin' doin', for the Church of England that I was brought up in fills my very modest need. But if it's got a spice of danger, as you say, then it's worth while. What!'

The Rev. Charles Mason smiled his kindly, toothsome grin.

'Incorrigible, is he not?' he said to Malone. 'Well, I can only wish you a fuller comprehension of the subject.' He rose as if to depart.

'Wait a bit, padre!' cried Lord Roxton, hurriedly. 'When I'm explorin', I begin by ropin' in a friendly native. I expect you're just the man. Won't you come with me?'

'Where to?'

'Well, sit down and I'll tell you.' He rummaged among a pile of letters on his desk. 'Fine selection of spooks!' he said. 'I got on the track of over twenty by the first post. This is an easy winner, though. Read it for yourself. Lonely house, man driven mad, tenants boltin' in the night, horrible spectre. Sounds all right – what!'

The clergyman read the letter with puckered brows. 'It seems a bad case,' said he.

'Well, suppose you come along. What! Maybe you can help clear it up.'

The Rev. Mason pulled out a pocket-almanac. 'I have a service for ex-Service men on Wednesday, and a lecture the same evening.'

'But we could start to-day.'

'It's a long way.'

'Only Dorsetshire. Three hours.'

'What is your plan?'

'Well, I suppose a night in the house should do it.'

'If there is any poor soul in trouble it becomes a duty. Very well, I will come.'

'And surely there is room for me,' pleaded Malone.

'Of course there is, young fellah! What I mean – I expect that old, red-headed bird at the office sent you round with no other purpose. Ah, I thought so. Well, you can write an adventure that is not perfect bilge for a change – what! There's a train from Victoria at eight o'clock. We can meet there, and I'll have a look in at old man Challenger as I pass.'

They dined together in the train and after dinner reassembled in their first-class carriage, which is the snuggest mode of travel which the world can show. Roxton, behind a big black cigar, was full of his visit to Challenger.

'The old dear is the same as ever. Bit my head off once or twice in his own familiar way. Talked unadulterated tripe. Says I've got brain-softenin', if I could think there was such a thing as a real spook. "When you're dead you're dead". That's the old man's cheery slogan. Surveyin' his contemporaries, he said, extinction was a doosed good thing! "It's the only hope of the world", said he. "Fancy the awful prospect if they survived". Wanted to give me a bottle of chlorine to chuck at the ghost. I told him that if my automatic was not a spook-stopper, nothin' else would serve. Tell me, padre, is this the first time you've been on safari after this kind of game?'

'You treat the matter too lightly, Lord John,' said the clergyman gravely. 'You have clearly had no experience of it. In answer to your question I may say that I have several times tried to help in similar cases.'

'And you take it seriously?' asked Malone, making notes for his article.

'Very, very seriously.'

'What do you think these influences are?'

'I am no authority upon the general question. You know Algernon Mailey, the barrister, do you not? He could give you facts and figures. I approach the subject rather perhaps from the point of view of instinct and emotion. I remember Mailey lecturing on Professor Bozzano's book on ghosts where over five hundred well-authenticated instances were given, every one of them sufficient to establish an *a priori* case. There is Flammarion, too. You can't laugh away evidence of that kind.'

'I've read Bozzano and Flammarion, too,' said Malone, 'but it is your own experience and conclusions that I want.'

'Well, if you quote me, remember that I do not look on myself as a great authority on psychic research. Wiser brains than mine may come along and give some other explanation. Still, what I have seen has led me to certain conclusions. One of them is to think that there is some truth in the theosophical idea of shells.'

'What is that?'

'They imagined that all spirit bodies near the earth were empty shells or husks from which the real entity had departed. Now, of course, we know that a general statement of that sort is nonsense, for we could not get the glorious communications which we do get from anything but high intelligences. But we also must beware of generalizations. They are not *all* high intelligences. Some are so low that I think the creature is purely external and is an appearance rather than a reality.'

'But why should it be there?'

'Yes, that is the question. It is usually allowed that there is the natural body, as St. Paul called it, which is dissolved at death, and the etheric or spiritual body which survives and functions upon an etheric plane. Those are the essential things. But we may really have as many coats as an onion and there may be a mental body which may shed itself at any spot where great mental or emotional strain has been experienced. It may be a dull automatic simulacrum and yet carry something of our appearance and thoughts.'

'Well,' said Malone, 'that would to some extent get over the difficulty, for I could never imagine that a murderer or his victim could spend whole centuries re-acting the old crime. What would be the sense of it?'

'Quite right, young fellah,' said Lord Roxton. 'There was a pal of mine, Archie Soames, the gentleman Jock, who had an old place in Berkshire. Well, Nell Gwynne had lived there once, and he was ready to swear he met her a dozen times in the passage. Archie never flinched at the big jump at the Grand National, but, by Jove! he flinched at those passages after dark. Doosed fine woman she was and all that, but dash it all! What I mean – one has to draw the line – what!'

'Quite so!' the clergyman answered. 'You can't imagine that the real soul of a vivid personality like Nell could spend centuries walking those passages. But if by chance she had ate her heart out in that house, brooding and fretting, one could think that she might have cast a shell and left some thought-image of herself behind her.'

'You said you had experiences of your own.'

'I had one before ever I knew anything of Spiritualism. I hardly expect that you will believe me, but I assure you it is true. I was a very young curate up in the north. There was a house in the village which had a poltergeist, one of those very mischievous influences which cause so much trouble. I volunteered to exorcize it. We have an official form of exorcism in the Church, you know, so I thought that I was well-armed. I stood in the drawing-room which was the centre of the disturbances, with all the family on their knees beside me, and I read the service. What do you think happened?'

Mason's gaunt face broke into a sweetly humorous laugh. 'Just as I reached Amen, when the creature should have been slinking away abashed, the big bearskin hearthrug stood up on end and simply enveloped me. I am ashamed to say that I was out of that house in two jumps. It was then that I learned that no formal religious proceeding has any effect at all.'

'Then what has?'

'Well, kindness and reason may do something. You see, they vary greatly. Some of these earthbound or earth-interested creatures are neutral, like these simulacra or shells that I speak of. Others are essentially good like these monks of Glastonbury, who have manifested so wonderfully of late years and are recorded by Bligh Bond. They are held to earth by a pious memory. Some are mischievous children like the poltergeists. And some – only a few, I hope – are deadly beyond words, strong, malevolent creatures too heavy with matter to rise above our earth plane – so heavy with matter that their vibrations may be low enough to affect the human retina and to become visible. If they have been cruel, cunning brutes in life, they are cruel and cunning still with more power to hurt. It is evil monsters of this kind who are let loose by our system of capital punishment, for they die with unused vitality which may be expended upon revenge.'

'This Dryfont spook has a doosed bad record,' said Lord Roxton.

'Exactly. That is why I disapprove of levity. He seems to me to be the very type of the creature I speak of. Just as an octopus may have his den in some ocean cave, and come floating out a silent image of horror to attack a swimmer, so I picture such a spirit lurking in the dark of the house which he curses by his presence, and ready to float out upon all whom he can injure.'

Malone's jaw began to drop.

'I say!' he exclaimed, 'have we no protection?'

'Yes, I think we have. If we had not, such a creature could devastate the earth. Our protection is that there are white forces as well as dark ones. We may call them "guardian angels" as the

Catholics do, or "guides" or "controls", but whatever you call them, they really do exist and they guard us from evil on the spiritual plane.'

'What about the chap who was driven mad, padre? Where was your guide when the spook put the rug round you? What!'

'The power of our guides may depend upon our own worthiness. Evil may always win for a time. Good wins in the end. That's my experience in life.'

Lord Roxton shook his head.

'If good wins, then it runs a doosed long waitin' race, and most of us never live to see the finish. Look at those rubber devils that I had a scrap with up the Putomayo River. Where are they? What! Mostly in Paris havin' a good time. And the poor niggers they murdered. What about them?'

'Yes, we need faith sometimes. We have to remember that we don't see the end. "To be continued in our next" is the conclusion of every life-story. That's where the enormous value of the other world accounts come in. They give us at least one chapter more.'

'Where can I get that chapter?' asked Malone.

'There are many wonderful books, though the world has not yet learned to appreciate them – records of the life beyond. I remember one incident – you may take it as a parable, if you like – but it is really more than that. The dead rich man pauses before the lovely dwelling. His sad guide draws him away. "It is not for you. It is for your gardener". He shows him a wretched shack. "You gave us nothing to build with. It was the best that we could do". That may be the next chapter in the story of our rubber millionaires.'

Roxton laughed grimly.

'I gave some of them a shack that was six foot long and two foot deep,' said he. 'No good shakin' your head, padre. What I mean – I don't love my neighbour as myself, and never shall. I hate some of 'em like poison.'

'Well, we should hate sin, and, for my own part, I have never been strong enough to separate sin from the sinner. How can I preach when I am as human and weak as anyone?'

'Why, that's the only preachin' I could listen to,' said Lord Roxton. 'The chap in the pulpit is over my head. If he comes down to my level I have some use for him. Well, it strikes me we won't get much sleep to-night. We've just an hour before we reach Dryfont. Maybe we had better use it.'

It was past eleven o'clock of a cold, frosty night when the party reached their destination. The station of the little watering-place was almost deserted, but a small, fat man in a fur overcoat ran forward to meet them, and greeted them warmly.

'I am Mr. Belchamber, owner of the house. How do you do, gentlemen? I got your wire, Lord Roxton, and everything is in order. It is indeed kind of you to come down. If you can do anything to ease my burden I shall indeed be grateful.'

Mr. Belchamber led them across to the little Station Hotel where they partook of sandwiches and coffee, which he had thoughtfully ordered. As they ate he told them something of his troubles.

'It isn't as if I was a rich man, gentlemen. I am a retired grazier and all my savings are in three houses. That is one of them, the Villa Maggiore. Yes, I got it cheap, that's true. But how could I think there was anything in this story of the mad doctor?'

'Let's have the yarn,' said Lord Roxton, munching at a sandwich.

'He was there away back in Queen Victoria's time. I've seen him myself. A long, stringy, dark-faced kind of man, with a round back and a queer, shuffling way of walking. They say he had been in India all his life, and some thought he was hiding from some crime, for he would never show his face in the village and seldom came out till after dark. He broke a dog's leg with a stone, and there was some talk of having him up for it, but the people were afraid of him, and no one would prosecute. The little boys would run past, for he would sit glowering and glooming in the front window. Then one day he didn't take the milk in, and the same next day, and so they broke the door open, and he was dead in his bath – but it was a bath of blood, for he opened the veins of his arm. Tremayne was his name. No one here forgets it.'

'And you bought the house?'

'Well, it was re-papered and painted and fumigated, and done up outside. You'd have said it was a new house. Then, I let it to Mr. Jenkins of the Brewery. Three days he was in it. I lowered the rent, and Mr. Beale, the retired grocer, took it. It was he who went mad – clean mad – after a week of it. And I've had it on my hands ever since – sixty pounds out of my income, and taxes to pay on it, into the bargain. If you gentlemen can do anything, for God's sake do it! If not, it would pay me to burn it down.'

The Villa Maggiore stood about half a mile from the town on the slope of a low hill. Mr. Belchamber conducted them so far, and even up to the hall door. It was certainly a depressing place, with a huge, gambrel roof which came down over the upper windows and nearly obscured them. There was a half-moon, and by its light they could see that the garden was a tangle of scraggy, winter vegetation, which had, in some places, almost overgrown the path. It was all very still, very gloomy and very ominous.

'The door is not locked,' said the owner. 'You will find some chairs and a table in the sitting-room on the left of the hall. I had a fire lit there, and there is a bucketful of coals. You will be pretty comfortable, I hope. You won't blame me for not coming in, but my nerves are not so good as they were.' With a few apologetic words, the owner slipped away, and they were alone with their task.

Lord Roxton had brought a strong electric torch. On opening the mildewed door, he flashed a tunnel of light down the passage, uncarpeted and dreary, which ended in a broad, straight, wooden staircase leading to the upper floor. There were doors on either side of the passage. That on the right led into a large, cheerless, empty room, with a derelict lawn-mower in one corner and a pile of old books and journals. There was a corresponding room upon the left which was a much more cheery apartment. A brisk fire burned in the grate, there were three comfortable chairs, and a deal table with a water carafe, a bucket of coals, and a few other amenities. It was lit by a large oil-lamp. The clergyman and Malone drew up to the fire, for it was very cold, but Lord Roxton completed his preparations. From a little hand-bag he extracted his automatic pistol, which he put upon the mantelpiece. Then he produced a packet of candles, placing two of them in the hall. Finally he took a ball of worsted and tied strings of it across the back passage and across the opposite door.

'We will have one look round,' said he, when his preparations were complete. 'Then we can wait down here and take what comes.'

The upper passage led at right angles to left and right from the top of the straight staircase. On the right were two large, bare, dusty rooms, with the wallpaper hanging in strips and the floor littered with scattered plaster. On the left was a single large room in the same derelict condition. Out of it was the bathroom of tragic memory, with the high, zinc bath still in position. Great blotches of red lay within it, and though they were only rust stains, they seemed to be terrible reminders from the past. Malone was surprised to see the clergyman stagger and support himself against the door. His face was ghastly white and there was moisture on his brow. His two comrades supported him down the stairs, and he sat for a little, as one exhausted, before he spoke.

'Did you two really feel nothing?' he asked. 'The fact is that I am mediumistic myself and very open to psychic impressions. This particular one was horrible beyond description.'

'What did you get, padre?'

'It is difficult to describe these things. It was a sinking of my heart, a feeling of utter desolation. All my senses were affected. My eyes went dim. I smelt a terrible odour of putrescence. The strength seemed to be sapped out of me. Believe me, Lord Roxton, it is no light thing which we are facing to-night.'

The sportsman was unusually grave. 'So I begin to think,' said he. 'Do you think you are fit for the job?'

'I am sorry to have been so weak,' Mr. Mason answered. 'I shall certainly see the thing through. The worse the case, the more need for my help. I am all right now,' he added, with his cheery laugh, drawing an old charred briar from his pocket. 'This is the best doctor for shaken nerves. I'll sit here and smoke till I'm wanted.'

'What shape do you expect it to take?' asked Malone of Lord Roxton.

'Well, it is something you can see. That's certain.'

'That's what I cannot understand, in spite of all my reading,' said Malone. 'These authorities are all agreed that there is a material basis, and that this material basis is drawn from the human body. Call it ectoplasm, or what you like, it is human in origin, is it not?'

'Certainly,' Mason answered.

'Well, then, are we to suppose that this Dr. Tremayne builds up his own appearance by drawing stuff from me and you?'

'I think, so far as I understand it, that in most cases a spirit does so. I believe that when the spectator feels that he goes cold, that his hair rises and the rest of it, he is really conscious of this draft upon his own vitality which may be enough to make him faint or even to kill him. Perhaps he was drawing on me then.'

'Suppose we are not mediumistic? Suppose we give out nothing?'

'There is a very full case that I read lately,' Mr. Mason answered. 'It was closely observed – reported by Professor Neillson of Iceland. In that case the evil spirit used to go down to an unfortunate photographer in the town, draw his supplies from him, and then come back and use them. He would openly say, "Give me time to get down to So-and-so. Then I will show you what I can do". He was a most formidable creature and they had great difficulty in mastering him.'

'Strikes me, young fellah, we have taken on a larger contract than we knew,' said Lord Roxton. 'Well, we've done what we could. The passage is well lit. No one can come at us except down the stair without breaking the worsted. There is nothing more we can do except just to wait.'

So they waited. It was a weary time. A carriage clock had been placed on the discoloured wooden mantelpiece, and slowly its hands crept on from one to two and from two to three. Outside an owl was hooting most dismally in the darkness. The villa was on a by-road, and there was no human sound to link them up with life. The padre lay dozing in his chair. Malone smoked incessantly. Lord Roxton turned over the pages of a magazine. There were the occasional strange tappings and creakings which come in the silence of the night. Nothing else until . . .

Someone came down the stair.

There could not be a doubt of it. It was a furtive, and yet a clear footstep. Creak! Creak! Creak! Then it had reached the level. Then it had reached their door. They were all sitting erect in their chairs, Roxton grasping his automatic. Had it come in? The door was ajar, but had not further opened. Yet all were aware of a sense that they were not alone, that they were being observed. It seemed suddenly colder, and Malone was shivering. An instant later the steps were retreating. They were low and swift – much swifter than before. One could imagine that a messenger was speeding back with intelligence to some great master who lurked in the shadows above.

The three sat in silence, looking at each other.

'By Jove!' said Lord Roxton at last. His face was pale but firm. Malone scribbled some notes and the hour. The clergyman was praying.

'Well, we are up against it,' said Roxton after a pause. 'We can't leave it at that. We have to go through with it. I don't mind tellin' you, padre, that I've followed a wounded tiger in thick jungle and never had quite the feelin' I've got now. If I'm out for sensations, I've got them. But I'm going upstairs.'

'We will go, too,' cried his comrades, rising from their chairs.

'Stay here, young fellah! And you, too, padre. Three of us make too much noise. I'll call you if I want you. My idea is just to steal out and wait quiet on the stair. If that thing, whatever it was, comes again, it will have to pass me.'

All three went into the passage. The two candles were throwing out little circles of light, and the stair was deeply illuminated, with heavy shadows at the top. Roxton sat down half-way up the stair, pistol in hand. He put his finger to his lips and impatiently waved his companions back to the room. Then they sat by the fire, waiting, waiting.

Half an hour, three-quarters – and then, suddenly it came. There was a sound as of rushing feet, the reverberation of a shot, a scuffle and a heavy fall, with a loud cry for help. Shaking with horror, they rushed into the hall. Lord Roxton was lying on his face amid a litter of plaster and rubbish. He seemed half dazed as they raised him, and was bleeding where the skin had been grazed from his cheek and hands. Looking up the stair, it seemed that the shadows were blacker and thicker at the top.

'I'm all right,' said Roxton, as they led him to his chair. 'Just give me a minute to get my wind and I'll have another round with the devil – for if this is not the devil, then none ever walked the earth.'

'You shan't go alone this time,' said Malone.

'You never should,' added the clergyman. 'But tell us what happened.'

'I hardly know myself. I sat, as you saw, with my back to the top landing. Suddenly I heard a rush. I was aware of something dark right on the top of me. I half-turned and fired. The next instant I was chucked down as if I had been a baby. All that plaster came showering down after me. That's as much as I can tell you.'

'Why should we go further in the matter?' said Malone. 'You are convinced that this is more than human, are you not?'

'There is no doubt of that.'

'Well, then, you have had your experience. What more can you want?'

'Well, I, at least, want something more,' said Mr. Mason. 'I think our help is needed.'

'Strikes me that *we* shall need the help,' said Lord Roxton, rubbing his knee. 'We shall want a doctor before we get through. But I'm with you, padre. I feel that we must see it through. If you don't like it, young fellah –'

The mere suggestion was too much for Malone's Irish blood.

'I am going up alone!' he cried, making for the door.

'No, indeed. I am with you.' The clergyman hurried after him.

'And you don't go without me!' cried Lord Roxton, limping in the rear.

They stood together in the candle-lit, shadow-draped passage. Malone had his hand on the balustrade and his foot on the lower step, when it happened.

What was it? They could not tell themselves. They only knew that the black shadows at the top of the staircase had thickened, had coalesced, had taken a definite, batlike shape. Great God! They were moving! They were rushing swiftly and noiselessly downwards! Black, black as night, huge, ill-defined, semi-human and altogether evil and damnable. All three men screamed and blundered for the door. Lord Roxton caught the handle and threw it open. It was too late; the thing was upon them. They were conscious of a warm, glutinous contact, of a purulent smell, of a half-formed, dreadful face and of entwining limbs. An instant later all three were lying half-dazed and horrified, hurled outwards on to the gravel of the drive. The door had shut with a crash.

Malone whimpered and Roxton swore, but the clergyman was silent as they gathered themselves together, each of them badly shaken and bruised, but with an inward horror which made all bodily ill seem insignificant. There they stood in a little group in the light of the sinking moon, their eyes turned upon the black square of the door.

'That's enough,' said Roxton, at last.

'More than enough,' said Malone. 'I wouldn't enter that house again for anything Fleet Street could offer.'

'Are you hurt?'

'Defiled, degraded – oh, it was loathsome!'

'Foul!' said Roxton. 'Did you get the reek of it? And the purulent warmth?'

Malone gave a cry of disgust. 'Featureless – save for the dreadful eyes! Semi-materialized! Horrible!'

'What about the lights?'

'Oh, damn the lights! Let them burn. I am not going in again!'

'Well, Belchamber can come in the morning. Maybe he is waiting for us now at the inn.'

'Yes, let us go to the inn. Let us get back to humanity.'

Malone and Roxton turned away, but the clergyman stood fast. He had drawn a crucifix from his pocket.

'You can go,' said he. 'I am going back.'

'What! Into the house?'

'Yes, into the house.'

'Padre, this is madness! It will break your neck. We were all like stuffed dolls in its clutch.'

'Well, let it break my neck. I am going.'

'You are not! Here, Malone, catch hold of him!'

But it was too late. With a few quick steps, Mr. Mason had reached the door, flung it open, passed in and closed it behind him. As his comrades tried to follow, they heard a creaking clang upon the further side. The padre had bolted them out. There was a great slit where the letter-box had been. Through it Lord Roxton entreated him to return.

'Stay there!' said the quick, stern voice of the clergyman. 'I have my work to do. I will come when it is done.'

A moment later he began to speak. His sweet, homely, affectionate accents rang through the hall. They could only hear snatches outside, bits of prayer, bits of exhortation, bits of kindly greeting. Looking through the narrow opening, Malone could see the straight, dark figure in the candlelight, its back to the door, its face to the shadows of the stair, the crucifix held aloft in its right hand.

His voice sank into silence and then there came one more of the miracles of this eventful night. A voice answered him. It was such a sound as neither of the auditors had heard before – a guttural, rasping, croaking utterance, indescribably menacing. What it said was short, but it was instantly answered by the clergyman, his tone sharpened to a fine edge by emotion. His utterance seemed to be exhortation and was at once answered by the ominous voice from beyond. Again and again, and yet again came the speech and the answer, sometimes shorter, sometimes longer, varying in every key of pleading, arguing, praying, soothing, and everything save upbraiding. Chilled to the marrow, Roxton and Malone crouched by the door, catching snatches of that inconceivable dialogue. Then, after what seemed a weary time, though it was less than an hour, Mr. Mason, in a loud, full, exultant tone, repeated the 'Our Father.' Was it fancy, or echo, or was there really some accompanying voice in the darkness beyond him? A moment later the light went out in the left-hand window, the bolt was drawn, and the clergyman emerged carrying Lord Roxton's bag. His face looked ghastly in the moonlight, but his manner was brisk and happy.

'I think you will find everything here,' he said, handing over the bag.

Roxton and Malone took him by either arm and hurried him down to the road.

'By Jove! You don't give us the slip again!' cried the nobleman. 'Padre, you should have a row of Victoria Crosses.'

'No, no, it was my duty. Poor fellow, he needed help so badly. I am but a fellow-sinner and yet I was able to give it.'

'You did him good?'

'I humbly hope so. I was but the instrument of the higher forces. The house is haunted no longer. He promised. But I will not speak of it now. It may be easier in days to come.'

The landlord and the maids stared at the three adventurers in amazement when, in the chill light of the winter dawn, they presented themselves at the inn once more. Each of them seemed to have aged five years in the night. Mr. Mason, with the re-action upon him, threw himself down upon the horsehair sofa in the humble coffee-room and was instantly asleep.

'Poor chap! He looks pretty bad!' said Malone. Indeed, his white, haggard face and long, limp limbs might have been those of a corpse.

'We will get a cup of hot tea into him,' Lord Roxton answered, warming his hands at the fire, which the maid had just lit. 'By Jove! We shall be none the worse for some ourselves. Well, young fellah, we've got what we came for. I've had my sensation, and you've had your copy.'

'And he has had the saving of a soul. Well, we must admit that our objects seem very humble compared to his.'

They caught the early train to London, and had a carriage to themselves. Mason had said little and seemed to be lost in thought. Suddenly he turned to his companions.

'I say, you two, would you mind joining me in prayer?'

Lord Roxton made a grimace. 'I warn you, padre, I am rather out of practice.'

'Please kneel down with me. I want your aid.'

They knelt down, side by side, the padre in the middle. Malone made a mental note of the prayer.

'Father, we are all Your children, poor, weak, helpless creatures, swayed by Fate and circumstance. I implore You that You will turn eyes of compassion upon the man, Rupert Tremayne, who wandered far from You, and is now in the dark. He has sunk deep, very deep, for he had a proud heart which would not soften, and a cruel mind, which was filled with hate. But now he would turn to the light, and so I beg help for him and for the woman, Emma, who, for the love of him, has gone down into the darkness. May she raise him, as she had tried to do. May they both break the bonds of evil memory which tie them to earth. May they, from to-night, move up towards that glorious light which sooner or later shines upon even the lowest.'

They rose from their knees.

'That's better!' cried the padre, thumping his chest with his bony hand, and breaking out into his expansive, toothsome grin. 'What a night! Good Lord, what a night!'[1]

---

[1]*Vide* Appendix.

CHAPTER IX

Which Introduces Some Very Physical Phenomena

MALONE SEEMED DESTINED to be entangled in the affairs of the Linden family, for he had hardly seen the last of the unfortunate Tom before he became involved in a very much more unpleasant fashion with his unsavoury brother.

The episode began by a telephone ring in the morning and the voice of Algernon Mailey at the far end of the wire.

'Are you clear for this afternoon?'

'At your service.'

'I say, Malone, you are a hefty man. You played Rugger for Ireland, did you not? You don't mind a possible rough-and-tumble, do you?'

Malone grinned over the receiver.

'You can count me in.'

'It may be really rather formidable. We shall have possibly to tackle a prize-fighter.'

'Right-o!' said Malone, cheerfully.

'And we want another man for the job. Do you know any fellow who would come along just for the sake of the adventure. If he knows anything about psychic matters, all the better.'

Malone puzzled for a moment. Then he had an inspiration.

'There is Roxton,' said he. 'He's not a chicken, but he is a useful man in a row. I think I could get him. He has been keen on your subject since his Dorsetshire experience.'

'Right! Bring him along! If he can't come, we shall have to tackle the job ourselves. Forty-one, Belshaw Gardens, S.W. Near Earl's Court Station. Three p.m. Right!'

Malone at once rang up Lord Roxton, and soon heard the familiar voice.

'What's that, young fellah? . . . A scrap? Why, certainly. What . . . I mean I had a golf match at Richmond Deer Park, but this sounds more attractive. . . . What? Very good. I'll meet you there.'

And so it came about that at the hour of three, Mailey, Lord Roxton and Malone found themselves seated round the fire in the comfortable drawing-room of the barrister. His wife, a sweet and beautiful woman, who was his helpmate in his spiritual as well as in his material life, was there to welcome them.

'Now, dear, you are not on in this act,' said Mailey. 'You will retire discreetly into the wings. Don't worry if you hear a row.'

'But I do worry, dear. You'll get hurt.'

Mailey laughed.

'I think your furniture may possibly get hurt. You have nothing else to fear, dear. And it's all for the good of the Cause. That always settles it,' he explained, as his wife reluctantly left the room. 'I really think she would go to the stake for the Cause. Her great, loving, womanly heart knows what it would mean for this grey earth if people could get away from the shadow of death, and realize the great happiness that is to come. By Jove! she is an inspiration to me . . . . Well,' he went on with a laugh, 'I must not get on to that subject. We have something very different to think of – something as hideous and vile as she is beautiful and good. It concerns Tom Linden's brother.'

'I've heard of the fellow,' said Malone. 'I used to box a bit and I am still a member of the N.S.C. Silas Linden was very nearly champion in the Welters.'

'That's the man. He is out of a job and thought he would take up mediumship. Naturally I and other Spiritualists took him seriously, for we all love his brother, and these powers often run in families, so that his claim seemed reasonable. So we gave him a trial last night.'

'Well, what happened?'

'I suspected the fellow from the first. You understand that it is hardly possible for a medium to deceive an experienced Spiritualist. When there is deception it is at the expense of outsiders. I watched him carefully from the first, and I seated myself near the cabinet. Presently he emerged clad in white. I broke the contact by prearrangement with my wife who sat next me, and I felt him as he passed me. He was, of course, in white. I had a pair of scissors in my pocket and snipped off a bit from the edge.'

Mailey drew a triangular piece of linen from his pocket.

'There it is, you see. Very ordinary linen. I have no doubt the fellow was wearing his night-gown.'

'Why did you not have a show-up at once?' asked Lord Roxton.

'There were several ladies there, and I was the only really able-bodied man in the room.'

'Well, what do you propose?'

'I have appointed that he come here at three-thirty. He is due now. Unless he has noticed the small cut in his linen, I don't think he has any suspicion why I want him.'

'What will you do?'

'Well, that depends on him. We have to stop him at any cost. That is the way our Cause gets bemired. Some villain who knows nothing about it comes into it for money and so the labours of the honest mediums get discounted. The public very naturally brackets them all together. With your help I can talk to this fellow on equal terms which I certainly could not do if I were alone. By Jove, here he is!'

There was a heavy step outside. The door was opened and Silas Linden, fake medium and ex-prize-fighter, walked in. His small, piggy grey eyes under their shaggy brows looked round with suspicion at the three men. Then he forced a smile and nodded to Mailey.

'Good day, Mr. Mailey. We had a good evening last night, had we not?'

'Sit down, Linden,' said Mailey, indicating a chair. 'It's about last night that I want to talk to you. You cheated us.'

Silas Linden's heavy face flushed red with anger.

'What's that?' he cried, sharply.

'You cheated us. You dressed up and pretended to be a spirit.'

'You are a damned liar!' cried Linden. 'I did nothing of the sort.'

Mailey took the rag of linen from his pocket and spread it on his knee.

'What about that?' he asked.

'Well, what about it?'

'It was cut out of the white gown you wore. I cut it out myself as you stood in front of me. If you examine the gown you will find the place. It's no use, Linden. The game is up. You can't deny it.'

For a moment the man was completely taken aback. Then he burst into a stream of horrible profanity.

'What's the game?' he cried, glaring round him. 'Do you think I am easy and that you can play me for a sucker? Is it a frame-up, or what? You've chose the wrong man for a try-on of that sort.'

'There is no use being noisy or violent, Linden,' said Mailey quietly, 'I could bring you up in the police court to-morrow. I don't want any public scandal, for your brother's sake. But you don't leave this room until you have signed a paper that I have here on my desk.'

'Oh, I don't, don't I? Who will stop me?'

'We will.'

The three men were between him and the door.

'You will! Well, try that!' He stood before them with rage in his eyes and his great hands knotted. 'Will you get out of the way?'

They did not answer, but they all three gave the fighting snarl which is perhaps the oldest of all human expressions. The next instant Linden was upon them, his fists flashing out with terrific force. Mailey, who had boxed in his youth, stopped one blow, but the next beat in his guard and he fell with a crash against the door. Lord Roxton was hurled to one side, but Malone, with a footballer's instinct, ducked his head and caught the prize-fighter round the knees. If a man is too good for you on his feet, then put him on his back, for he cannot be scientific there. Over went Linden, crashing through an armchair before he reached the ground. He staggered to one knee and got in a short jolt to the chin, but Malone had him down again and Roxton's bony hand had closed upon his throat. Silas Linden had a yellow streak in him and he was cowed.

'Let up!' he cried. 'That's enough!'

He lay now spread-eagled upon his back. Malone and Roxton were bending over him. Mailey had gathered himself together, pale and shaken after his fall.

'I'm all right!' he cried, in answer to a feminine voice at the other side of the door. 'No, not yet, dear, but we shall soon be ready for you. Now, Linden, there's no need for you to get up, for you can talk very nicely where you are. You've got to sign this paper before you leave the room.'

'What is the paper?' croaked Linden, as Roxton's grip upon his throat relaxed.

'I'll read it to you.'

Mailey took it from the desk and read aloud.

' "I, Silas Linden, hereby admit that I have acted as a rogue and a scoundrel by simulating to be a spirit, and I swear that I will never again in my life pretend to be a medium. Should I break this oath, then this signed confession may be used for my conviction in the police court."

'Will you sign that?'

'No, I am damned if I will!'

'Shall I give him another squeeze?' asked Lord Roxton. 'Perhaps I could choke some sense into him – what!'

'Not at all,' said Mailey. 'I think that his case now would do good in the police court, for it would show the public that we are determined to keep our house clean. I'll give you one minute for consideration, Linden, and then I ring up the police.'

But it did not take a minute for the impostor to make up his mind.

'All right,' said he in a sulky voice, 'I'll sign.'

He was allowed to rise with a warning that if he played any tricks he would not get off so lightly the second time. But there was no kick left in him and he scrawled a big, coarse 'Silas Linden' at the bottom of the paper without a word. The three men signed as witnesses.

'Now, get out!' said Mailey, sharply. 'Find some honest trade in future and leave sacred things alone!'

'Keep your damned cant to yourself!' Linden answered, and so departed, grumbling and swearing, into the outer darkness from which he had come. He had hardly passed before Mrs. Mailey had rushed into the room to reassure herself as to her husband. Once satisfied as to this she mourned over her broken chair, for like all good women she took a personal pride and joy in every detail of her little *ménage*.

'Never mind, dear. It's a cheap price to pay in order to get that blackguard out of the movement. Don't go away, you fellows. I want to talk to you.'

'And tea is just coming in.'

'Perhaps something stronger would be better,' said Mailey, and indeed, all three were rather exhausted, for it was sharp while it lasted. Roxton, who had enjoyed the whole thing immensely, was full of vitality, but Malone was shaken and Mailey had narrowly escaped serious injury from that ponderous blow.

'I have heard,' said Mailey, as they all settled down round the fire, 'that this blackguard has sweated money out of poor Tom Linden for years. It was a form of blackmail, for he was quite capable of denouncing him. By Jove!' he cried, with sudden inspiration, 'that would account for the police raid. Why should they pick Linden out of all the mediums in London? I remember now that Tom told me the fellow had asked to be taught to be a medium, and that he had refused to teach him.'

'Could he teach him?' asked Malone.

Mailey was thoughtful over this question. 'Well, perhaps he could,' he said at last. 'But Silas Linden as a false medium would be very much less dangerous than Silas Linden as a true medium.'

'I don't follow you.'

'Mediumship can be developed,' said Mrs. Mailey. 'One might almost say it was catching.'

'That was what the laying-on of hands meant in the early Church,' Mailey explained. 'It was the conferring of thaumaturgic powers. We can't do it now as rapidly as that. But if a man or woman sits with the desire of development, and especially if that sitting is in the presence of a real medium, the chance is that powers will come.'

'But why do you say that would be worse than false mediumship?'

'Because it could be used for evil. I assure you, Malone, that the talk of black magic and of evil entities is not an invention of the enemy. Such things do happen and centre round the wicked medium. You can get down into a region which is akin to the popular idea of witchcraft. It is dishonest to deny it.'

'Like attracts like,' explained Mrs. Mailey, who was quite as capable an exponent as her husband. 'You get what you deserve. If you sit with wicked people you get wicked visitors.'

'Then there *is* a dangerous side to it?'

'Do you know anything on earth which has not a dangerous side if it is mishandled and exaggerated? This dangerous side exists quite apart from orthodox Spiritualism, and our knowledge is the surest way to counteract it. I believe that the witchcraft of the Middle Ages was a very real thing, and that the best way to meet such practices is to cultivate the higher powers of the spirit. To leave the thing entirely alone is to abandon the field to the forces of evil.'

Lord Roxton interposed in an unexpected way.

'When I was in Paris last year,' said he, 'there was a fellah called La Paix who dabbled in the black magic business. He held circles and the like. What I mean, there was no great harm in the thing, but it wasn't what you would call very spiritual, either.'

'It's a side that I as a journalist would like to see something of, if I am to report impartially upon the subject,' said Malone.

'Quite right!' Mailey agreed. 'We want all the cards on the table.'

'Well, young fellah, if you would give me a week of your time and come to Paris, I'll introduce you to La Paix,' said Roxton.

'It is a curious thing, but I also had a Paris visit in my mind for our friend here,' said Mailey. 'I have been asked over by Dr. Maupuis of the Institut Métapsychique to see some of the experiments which he is conducting upon a Galician medium. It is really the religious side of this matter which interests me, and that is conspicuously wanting in the minds of these scientific men of the Continent; but for accurate, careful examination of the psychic facts they are ahead of anyone except poor Crawford of Belfast, who stood in a class by himself. I promised Maupuis to run across and he has certainly been having some wonderful – in some respects, some rather alarming results.'

'Why alarming?'

'Well, his materializations lately have not been human at all.

That is confirmed by photographs. I won't say more, for it is best that, if you go, you should approach it with an open mind.'

'I shall certainly go,' said Malone. 'I am sure my chief would wish it.'

Tea had arrived to interrupt the conversation in the irritating way that our bodily needs intrude upon our higher pursuits. But Malone was too keen to be thrown off his scent.

'You speak of these evil forces. Have you ever come in contact with them?'

Mailey looked at his wife and smiled.

'Continually,' he said. 'It is part of our job. We specialize on it.'

'I understood that when there was an intrusion of that kind you drove it away.'

'Not necessarily. If we can help any lower spirit we do so, and we can only do it by encouraging it to tell us its troubles. Most of them are not wicked. They are poor, ignorant, stunted creatures who are suffering the effects of the narrow and false views which they have learned in this world. We try to help them – and we do.'

'How do you know that you do?'

'Because they report to us afterwards and register their progress. Such methods are often used by our people. They are called "rescue circles".'

'I have heard of rescue circles. Where could I attend one? This thing attracts me more and more. Fresh gulfs seem always opening. I would take it as a great favour if you would help me to see this fresh side of it.'

Mailey became thoughtful.

'We don't want to make a spectacle of these poor creatures. On the other hand, though we can hardly claim you yet as a Spiritualist, you have treated the subject with some understanding and sympathy.' He looked enquiringly at his wife, who smiled and nodded.

'Ah, you have permission. Well then, you must know that we run our own little rescue circle, and that at five o'clock to-day we have our weekly sitting. Mr. Terbane is our medium. We don't usually have anyone else except Mr. Charles Mason, the clergyman. But if you both care to have the experience, we shall be very happy if you will stay. Terbane should be here immediately after tea. He is a railway-porter, you know, so his time is not his own. Yes, psychic power in its varied manifestations is found in humble quarters, but surely that has been its main characteristic from the beginning – fishermen, carpenters, tentmakers, camel drivers, these were the prophets of old. At this moment some of the highest psychic gifts in

England lie in a miner, a cotton operative, a railway-porter, a barge-man and a charwoman. Thus does history repeat itself, and that foolish beak, with Tom Linden before him, was but Felix judging Paul. The old wheel goes round.'

CHAPTER X

De Profundis

THEY WERE STILL HAVING TEA when Mr. Charles Mason was ushered in. Nothing draws people together into such intimate soul-to-soul relationship as psychic quest, and thus it was that Roxton and Malone, who had only known him in the one episode, felt more near to this man than to others with whom they had associated for years. This close vital comradeship is one of the outstanding features of such communion. When his loosely-built, straggling, lean clerical figure appeared, with that gaunt, worn face illuminated by its human grin and dignified by its earnest eyes, through the doorway, they both felt as if an old friend had entered. His own greeting was equally cordial.

'Still exploring!' he cried, as he shook them by the hand. 'We will hope your new experiences will not be so nerve-racking as our last.'

'By Jove, padre!' said Roxton. 'I've worn out the brim of my hat taking it off to you since then.'

'Why, what did he do?' asked Mrs. Mailey.

'No, no!' cried Mason. 'I tried in my poor way to guide a dark-ened soul. Let us leave it at that. But that is exactly what we are here for now, and what these dear people do every week of their lives. It was from Mr. Mailey here that I learned how to attempt it.'

'Well, certainly we have plenty of practice,' said Mailey. 'You have seen enough of it, Mason, to know that.'

'But I can't get the focus of this at all!' cried Malone. 'Could you clear my mind a little on the point? I accept, for the moment, your hypothesis that we are surrounded by material earth-bound spirits who find themselves under strange conditions which they don't understand, and who want counsel and guidance. That more or less expresses it, does it not?'

The Maileys both nodded their agreement.

'Well, their dead friends and relatives are presumably on the other side and cognizant of their benighted condition. They know the truth. Could they not minister to the wants of these afflicted ones far better than we can?'

'It is a most natural question,' Mailey answered. 'Of course we put that objection to them and we can only accept their answer. They appear to be actually anchored to the surface of this earth, too heavy and gross to rise. The others are, presumably, on a spiritual level and far separated from them. They explain that they are much nearer to us and that they are cognizant of us, but not of anything higher. Therefore it is we who can reach them best.'

'There was one poor dear dark soul –'

'My wife loves everybody and everything,' Mailey explained. 'She is capable of talking of the poor dear devil.'

'Well, surely they are to be pitied and loved!' cried the lady. 'This poor fellow was nursed along by us, week by week. He had really come from the depths. Then one day he cried in rapture, "My mother has come! My mother is here!" We naturally said, "But why did she not come before?" "How could she", said he, "when I was in so dark a place that she could not see me?" '

'That's very well,' said Malone, 'but so far as I can follow your methods it is some guide or control or higher spirit who regulates the whole matter and brings the sufferer to you. If he can be cognizant, one would think other higher spirits could also be.'

'No, for it is his particular mission,' said Mailey. 'To show how marked the divisions are I can remember one occasion when we had a dark soul here. Our own people came through and did not know he was there until we called their attention to it. When we said to the dark soul, "Don't you see our friends beside you?" he answered, "I can see a light but nothing else".'

At this point the conversation was interrupted by the arrival of Mr. John Terbane from Victoria Station, where his mundane duties lay. He was dressed now in civil garb and appeared as a pale, sad-faced, clean-shaven, plump-featured man with dreamy, thoughtful eyes, but no other indication of the remarkable uses to which he was put.

'Have you my record?' was his first question.

Mrs. Mailey, smiling, handed him an envelope. 'We kept it all ready for you but you can read it at home. You see,' she explained, 'poor Mr. Terbane is in trance and knows nothing of the wonderful work of which he is the instrument, so after each sitting my husband and I draw up an account for him.'

'Very much astonished I am when I read it,' said Terbane.

'And very proud, I should think,' added Mason.

'Well, I don't know about that,' Terbane answered humbly. 'I don't see that the tool need to be proud because the worker happens to use it. Yet it is a privilege, of course.'

'Good old Terbane!' said Mailey, laying his hand affectionately on the railwayman's shoulder. 'The better the medium the more unselfish. That is my experience. The whole conception of a medium is one who gives himself up for the use of others, and that is incompatible with selfishness. Well, I suppose we had better get to work or Mr. Chang will scold us.'

'Who is he?' asked Malone.

'Oh, you will soon make the acquaintance of Mr. Chang! We need not sit round the table. A semi-circle round the fire does very well. Lights half-down. That is all right. You'll make yourself comfortable, Terbane. Snuggle among the cushions.'

The medium was in the corner of a comfortable sofa, and had fallen at once into a doze. Both Mailey and Malone sat with notebooks upon their knees awaiting developments.

They were not long in coming. Terbane suddenly sat up, his dreamy self transformed into a very alert and masterful individuality. A subtle change had passed over his face. An ambiguous smile fluttered upon his lips, his eyes seemed more oblique and less open, his face projected. The two hands were thrust into the sleeves of his blue lounge jacket.

'Good evening,' said he, speaking crisply and in short staccato sentences. 'New faces! Who these?'

'Good evening, Chang,' said the master of the house. 'You know Mr. Mason. This is Mr. Malone who studies our subject. This is Lord Roxton who has helped me to-day.'

As each name was mentioned, Terbane made a sweeping Oriental gesture of greeting, bringing his hand down from his forehead. His whole bearing was superbly dignified and very different from the humble little man who had sat down a few minutes before.

'Lord Roxton!' he repeated. 'An English milord! I knew Lord – Lord Macart – No – I – I cannot say it. Alas! I called him "foreign devil" then. Chang, too, had much to learn.'

'He is speaking of Lord Macartney. That would be over a hundred years ago. Chang was a great living philosopher then,' Mailey explained.

'Not lose time!' cried the control. 'Much to do to-day. Crowd waiting. Some new, some old. I gather strange folk in my net. Now I go.' He sank back among the cushions.

A minute elapsed, then he suddenly sat up.

'I want to thank you,' he said, speaking perfect English. 'I came two weeks ago. I have thought over all you said. The path is lighter.'

'Were you the spirit who did not believe in God?'

'Yes, yes! I said so in my anger. I was so weary – so weary. Oh, the time, the endless time, the grey mist, the heavy weight of remorse! Hopeless! Hopeless! And you brought me comfort, you and this great Chinese spirit. You gave me the first kind words I have had since I died.'

'When was it that you died?'

'Oh! It seems an eternity. We do not measure as you do. It is a long, horrible dream without change or break.'

'Who was king in England?'

'Victoria was queen. I had attuned my mind to matter and so it clung to matter. I did not believe in a future life. Now I know that I was all wrong, but I could not adapt my mind to new conditions.'

'Is it bad where you are?'

'It is all – all grey. That is the awful part of it. One's surroundings are so horrible.'

'But there are many more. You are not alone.'

'No, but they know no more than I. They, too, scoff and doubt and are miserable.'

'You will soon get out.'

'For God's sake, help me to do so!'

'Poor soul!' said Mrs. Mailey in her sweet, caressing voice, a voice which could bring every animal to her side. 'You have suffered much. But do not think of yourself. Think of these others. Try to bring one of them up and so you will best help yourself.'

'Thank you, lady, I will. There is one here whom I brought. He has heard you. We will go on together. Perhaps some day we may find the light.'

'Do you like to be prayed for?'

'Yes, yes, indeed I do!'

'I will pray for you,' said Mason. 'Could you say the "Our Father" now?' He uttered the old universal prayer, but before he had finished Terbane had collapsed again among the cushions. He sat up again as Chang.

'He come on well,' said the control. 'He give up time for others who wait. That is good. Now I have hard case. Ow!'

He gave a comical cry of disapprobation and sank back.

Next moment he was up, his face long and solemn, his hands palm to palm.

'What is this?' he asked in a precise and affected voice. 'I am at a loss to know what right this Chinese person has to summon me here. Perhaps you can enlighten me.'

'It is that we may perhaps help you.'

'When I desire help, sir, I ask for it. At present I do not desire it. The whole proceeding seems to me to be a very great liberty. So far as this Chinaman can explain it, I gather that I am the involuntary spectator of some sort of religious service.'

'We are a spiritualistic circle.'

'A most pernicious sect. A most blasphemous proceeding. As a humble parish priest I protest against such desecrations.'

'You are held back, friend, by those narrow views. It is you who suffer. We want to relieve you.'

'Suffer? What do you mean, sir?'

'You realize that you have passed over?'

'You are talking nonsense!'

'Do you realize that you are dead?'

'How can I be dead when I am talking to you?'

'Because you are using this man's body.'

'I have certainly wandered into an asylum.'

'Yes, an asylum for bad cases. I fear you are one of them. Are you happy where you are?'

'Happy? No, sir. My present surroundings are perfectly inexplicable to me.'

'Have you any recollection of being ill?'

'I was very ill indeed.'

'So ill that you died.'

'You are certainly out of your senses.'

'How do you know you are not dead?'

'Sir, I must give you some religious instruction. When one dies and has led an honourable life, one assumes a glorified body and one associates with the angels. I am now in exactly the same body as in life, and I am in a very dull, drab place. Such companions as I have are not such as I have been accustomed to associate with in life, and certainly no one could describe them as angels. Therefore your absurd conjecture may be dismissed.'

'Do not continue to deceive yourself. We wish to help you. You can never progress until you realize your position.'

'Really, you try my patience too far. Have I not said – ?'

The medium fell back among the cushions. An instant later the Chinese control, with his whimsical smile and his hands tucked away in his sleeves, was talking to the circle.

'He good man – fool man – learn sense soon. Bring him again. Not waste more time. Oh, my God! My God! Help! Mercy! Help!'

He had fallen full length upon the sofa, face upwards, and his cries were so terrible that the little audience all sprang to their feet. 'A saw! A saw! Fetch a saw!' yelled the medium. His voice sank into a moan.

Even Mailey was agitated. The rest were horrified.

'Someone has obsessed him. I can't understand it. It may be some strong evil entity.'

'Shall I speak to him?' asked Mason.

'Wait a moment! Let it develop. We shall soon see.'

The medium writhed in agony. 'Oh, my God! Why don't you fetch a saw!' he cried. 'It's here across my breast-bone. It is cracking! I feel it! Hawkin! Hawkin! Pull me from under! Hawkin! Push up the beam! No, no, that's worse! And it's on fire! Oh, horrible! Horrible!'

His cries were blood-curdling. They were all chilled with horror. Then in an instant the Chinaman was blinking at them with his slanting eyes.

'What you think of that, Mister Mailey?'

'It was terrible, Chang. What was it?'

'It was for him,' nodding towards Malone. 'He want newspaper story, I give him newspaper story. He will understand. No time 'splain now. Too many waiting. Sailor man come next. Here he come!'

The Chinaman was gone, and a jovial, puzzled grin passed over the face of the medium. He scratched his head.

'Well, damn me,' said he. 'I never thought I would take orders from a Chink, but he says "hist!" and by crums you've got to hist and no back talk either. Well, here I am. What did you want?'

'We wanted nothing.'

'Well, the Chink seemed to think you did, for he slung me in here.'

'It was you that wanted something. You wanted knowledge.'

'Well, I've lost my bearings, that's true. I know I am dead 'cause I've seen the gunnery lootenant, and he was blown to bits before my eyes. If he's dead I'm dead and all the rest of us, for we are over to the last man. But we've got the laugh on our sky-pilot, for he's as puzzled as the rest of us. Damned poor pilot, I call him. We're all taking our own soundings now.'

'What was your ship?'

'The *Monmouth*.'

'She that went down in battle with the German?'

'That's right. South American waters. It was clean hell. Yes, it was hell.' There was a world of emotion in his voice. 'Well,' he added more cheerfully, 'I've heard our mates got level with them later. That is so, sir, is it not?'

'Yes, they all went to the bottom.'

'We've seen nothing of them this side. Just as well, maybe. We don't forget nothing.'

'But you must,' said Mailey. 'That's what is the matter with you. That is why the Chinese control brought you through. We are here to teach you. Carry our message to your mates.'

'Bless your heart, sir, they are all here behind me.'

'Well, then, I tell you and them that the time for hard thoughts and worldly strife is over. Your faces are to be turned forward, not back. Leave this earth which still holds you by the ties of thought and let all your desire be to make yourself unselfish and worthy of a higher, more peaceful, more beautiful life. Can you understand?'

'I hear you, sir. So do they. We want steering, sir, for, indeed, we've had wrong instructions, and we never expected to find ourselves cast away like this. We had heard of heaven and we had heard of hell, but this don't seem to fit in with either. But this Chinese gent. says time is up, and we can report again next week. I thank you, sir, for self and company. I'll come again.'

There was silence.

'What an incredible conversation!' gasped Malone. 'If I were to put down that man's sailor talk and slang as emanating from a world of spirits, what would the public say?'

Mailey shrugged his shoulders.

'Does it matter what the public says? I started as a fairly sensitive person, and now a tank takes as much notice of small shot as I do of newspaper attacks. They honestly don't even interest me. Let us just stick fast to truth as near as we can get it, and leave all else to find its own level.'

'I don't pretend to know much of these things,' said Roxton, 'but what strikes me most is that these folk are very decent ordinary people. What? Why should they be wanderin' about in the dark, and hauled up here by this Chinaman when they've done no partic'lar harm in life?'

'It is the strong earth tie and the absence of any spiritual nexus in each case,' Mailey explained. 'Here is a clergyman with his mind entangled with formulas and ritual. Here is a materialist who has deliberately attuned himself to matter. Here is a seaman brooding over revengeful thoughts. They are there by the million million.'

'Where?' asked Malone.

'Here,' Mailey answered. 'Actually on the surface of the earth.

Well, you saw it for yourself, I understand, when you went down to Dorsetshire. That was on the surface, was it not? That was a very gross case, and that made it more visible and obvious, but it did not change the general law. I believe that the whole globe is infested with the earth-bound, and that when a great cleansing comes, as is prophesied, it will be for their benefit as much as for that of the living.'

Malone thought of the strange visionary Miromar and his speech at the Spiritualistic Church on the first night of his quest.

'Do you, then, believe in some impending event?' he asked.

Mailey smiled. 'That is rather a large subject to open up,' he said. 'I believe – But here is Mr. Chang again!'

The control joined in the conversation.

'I heard you. I sit and listen,' said he. 'You speak now of what is to come. Let it be! Let it be! The Time is not yet. You will be told when it is good that you know. Remember this. All is best. Whatever come all is best. God makes no mistakes. Now others here who wish your help, I leave you.'

Several spirits came through in quick succession. One was an architect who said that he had lived at Bristol. He had not been an evil man, but had simply banished all thoughts of the future. Now he was in the dark and needed guidance. Another had lived in Birmingham. He was an educated man but a materialist. He refused to accept the assurances of Mailey, and was by no means convinced that he was really dead. Then came a very noisy and violent man of a crudely-religious and narrow, intolerant type, who spoke repeatedly of 'the blood'.

'What is this ribald nonsense?' he asked several times.

'It is not nonsense. We are here to help,' said Mailey.

'Who wants to be helped by the devil?'

'Is it likely that the devil would wish to help souls in trouble?'

'It is part of his deceit. I tell you it is of the devil! Be warned! I will take no further part in it.'

The placid, whimsical Chinaman was back like a flash. 'Good man. Foolish man,' he repeated once more. 'Plenty time. He learn better some day. Now I bring bad case – very bad case. Ow!'

He reclined his head in the cushion and did not raise it as the voice, a feminine voice, broke out:

'Janet! Janet!'

There was a pause.

'Janet, I say! Where is the morning tea? Janet! This is intolerable! I have called you again and again! Janet!' The figure sat up, blinking and rubbing his eyes.

'What is this?' cried the voice. 'Who are you? What right have you here? Are you aware that this is my house?'

'No, friend, this is my house.'

'Your house! How can it be your house when this is my bed-room? Go away this moment!'

'No, friend. You do not understand your position.'

'I will have you put out. What insolence! Janet! Janet! Will no one look after me this morning?'

'Look round you, lady. Is this your bedroom?'

Terbane looked round with a wild stare.

'It is a room I never saw in my life. Where am I? What is the meaning of it? You look like a kind lady. Tell me, for God's sake, what is the meaning of it? Oh, I am so terrified, so terrified! Where are John and Janet?'

'What do you last remember?'

'I remember speaking severely to Janet. She is my maid, you know. She has become so very careless. Yes, I was very angry with her. I was so angry that I was ill. I went to bed feeling very ill. They told me that I should not get excited. How can one help getting excited? Yes, I remember being breathless. That was after the light was out. I tried to call Janet. But why should I be in another room?'

'You passed over in the night.'

'Passed over? Do you mean I died?'

'Yes, lady, you died.'

There was a long silence. Then there came a shrill scream. 'No, no, no! It is a dream! A nightmare! Wake me! Wake me! How can I be dead? I was not ready to die! I never thought of such a thing. If I am dead, why am I not in heaven or hell? What is this room? This room is a real room.'

'Yes, lady, you have been brought here and allowed to use this man's body –'

'A man?' She convulsively felt the coat and passed her hand over the face. 'Yes, it is a man. Oh, I am dead! I am dead! What shall I do?'

'You are here that we may explain to you. You have been, I judge, a worldly woman – a society woman. You have lived always for material things.'

'I went to church. I was at St. Saviour's every Sunday.'

'That is nothing. It is the inner daily life that counts. You were material. Now you are held down to the world. When you leave this man's body you will be in your own body once more and in your old surroundings. But no one will see you. You will remain there unable to show yourself. Your body of flesh will be buried. You will still persist, the same as ever.'

'What am I to do? Oh, what can I do?'

'You will take what comes in a good spirit and understand that it is for your cleansing. We only clear ourselves of matter by suffering. All will be well. We will pray for you.'

'Oh, do! I need it so! Oh my God! . . .' The voice trailed away.

'Bad case,' said the Chinaman, sitting up. 'Selfish woman! Bad woman! Live for pleasure. Hard on those around her. She have much to suffer. But you put her feet on the path. Now my medium tired. Plenty waiting, but no more to-day.'

'Have we done good, Chang?'

'Plenty good. Plenty good.'

'Where are all these people, Chang?'

'I tell you before.'

'Yes, but I want these gentlemen to hear.'

'Seven spheres round the world, heaviest below, lightest above. First sphere is on the earth. These people belong to that sphere. Each sphere is separate from the other. Therefore it is easier for you to speak with these people than for those in any other sphere.'

'And easier for them to speak to us?'

'Yes. That why you should be plenty careful when you do not know to whom you talk. Try the spirits.'

'What sphere do you belong to, Chang?'

'I come from Number Four sphere.'

'Which is the first really happy sphere?'

'Number Three. Summerland. Bible book called it the third heaven. Plenty sense in Bible book, but people do not understand.'

'And the seventh heaven?'

'Ah! That is where the Christs are. All come there at last – you, me, everybody.'

'And after that?'

'Too much question, Mr. Mailey. Poor old Chang not know so much as that. Now good-bye! God bless you! I go.'

It was the end of the sitting of the rescue circle. A few minutes later Terbane was sitting up smiling and alert, but with no apparent recollection of anything which had occurred. He was pressed for time and lived afar, so that he had to make his departure, unpaid save by the blessing of those who he had helped. Modest little unvenal man, where will he stand when we all find our real places in the order of creation upon the further side?

The circle did not break up at once. The visitors wanted to talk, and the Maileys to listen.

'What I mean,' said Roxton, 'it's doosed interestin' and all that, but there is a sort of variety-show element in it. What! Difficult to be sure it's really real, if you take what I mean.'

'That is what I feel also,' said Malone. 'Of course on its face value it is simply unspeakable. It is a thing so great that all ordinary happenings become commonplace. That I grant. But the human mind is very strange. I've read that case Moreton Prince examined, and Miss Beauchamp and the rest; also the results of Charcot, the great Nancy hypnotic school. They could turn a man into anything. The mind seems to be like a rope which can be unravelled into its various threads. Then each thread is a different personality which may take dramatic form, and act and speak as such. That man is honest, and he could not normally produce these effects. But how do we know that he is not self-hypnotized, and that under those conditions one strand of him becomes Mr. Chang and another becomes a sailor and another a society lady, and so forth?'

Mailey laughed. 'Every man his own Cinquevalli,' said he, 'but it is a rational objection and has to be met.'

'We have traced some of the cases,' said Mrs. Mailey. 'There is not a doubt of it – names, addresses, everything.'

'Well, then, we have to consider the question of Terbane's normal knowledge. How can you possibly know what he has learned? I should think a railway-porter is particularly able to pick up such information.'

'You have seen one sitting,' Mailey answered. 'If you had been present at as many as we and noted the cumulative effect of the evidence you would not be sceptical.'

'That is very possible,' Malone answered. 'And I daresay my doubts are very annoying to you. And yet one is bound to be brutally honest in a case like this. Anyhow, whatever the ultimate cause, I have seldom spent so thrilling an hour. Heavens! If it only *is* true, and if you had a thousand circles instead of one, what regeneration would result?'

'That will come,' said Mailey in his patient, determined fashion. 'We shall live to see it. I am sorry the thing has not forced conviction upon you. However, you must come again.'

But it so chanced that a further experience became unnecessary. Conviction came in a full flood and in a strange fashion that very evening. Malone had hardly got back to the office, and was seated at his desk drawing up some sort of account from his notes of all that had happened in the afternoon, when Mailey burst into the room, his yellow beard bristling with excitement. He was waving an *Evening News* in his hand. Without a word he seated himself beside Malone and turned the paper over. Then he began to read:

ACCIDENT IN THE CITY.

This afternoon shortly after five o'clock, an old house, said to date from the fifteenth century, suddenly collapsed. It was situated between Lesser Colman Street and Elliot Square, and next door to the Veterinary Society's Headquarters. Some preliminary crackings warned the occupants and most of them had time to escape. Three of them, however, James Beale, William Moorson, and a woman whose name has not been ascertained, were caught by the falling rubbish. Two of these seem to have perished at once, but the third, James Beale, was pinned down by a large beam and loudly demanded help. A saw was brought, and one of the occupants of the house, Samuel Hawkin, showed great gallantry in an attempt to free the unfortunate man. Whilst he was sawing the beam, however, a fire broke out among the debris around him, and though he persevered most manfully, and continued until he was himself badly scorched, it was impossible for him to save Beale, who probably died from suffocation. Hawkin was removed to the London Hospital, and it is reported to-night that he is in no immediate danger.

'That's that!' said Mailey, folding up the paper. 'Now Mr. Thomas Didymus, I leave you to your conclusions,' and the enthusiast vanished out of the office as precipitately as he had entered.

For the incidents recorded in this chapter *vide* Appendix

CHAPTER XI

Where Silas Linden Comes Into His Own

SILAS LINDEN, prize-fighter and fake-medium, had had some good days in his life – days crowded with incidents for good or evil. There was the time when he had backed Rosalind at 100 to 1 in the Oaks and had spent twenty-four hours of brutal debauchery on the strength of it. There was the day also when his favourite right uppercut had connected in most accurate and rhythmical fashion with the protruded chin of Bull Wardell of Whitechapel, whereby Silas put himself in the way of a Lonsdale Belt and a try for the championship. But never in all his varied career had he such a day as this supreme one, so it is worth our while to follow him to the end of it. Fanatical believers have urged that it is dangerous to cross the path of spiritual things when the heart is not clean. Silas Linden's name might be added to their list of examples, but his cup of sin was full and overflowing before the judgment fell.

He emerged from the room of Algernon Mailey with every reason to know that Lord Roxton's grip was as muscular as ever. In the excitement of the struggle he had hardly realized his injuries, but now he stood outside the door with his hand to his bruised throat and a hoarse stream of oaths pouring through it. His breast was aching also where Malone had planted his knee, and even the successful blow which had struck Mailey down had brought retribution, for it had jarred that injured hand of which he had complained to his brother. Altogether, if Silas Linden was in a most cursed temper, there was a very good reason for his mood.

'I'll get you one at a time,' he growled, looking back with his angry pigs' eyes at the outer door of the flats. 'You wait my lads, and see!' Then with sudden purpose he swung off down the street.

It was to the Bardsley Square Police Station that he made his way, and he found the jovial, rubicund, black-moustached Inspector Murphy seated at his desk.

'Well, what do *you* want?' asked the inspector in no very friendly voice.

'I hear you got that medium right and proper.'

'Yes, we did. I learn he was your brother.'

'That's neither here nor there. I don't hold with such things in any man. But you got your conviction. What is there for me in it?'

'Not a shilling!'

'What? Wasn't it I that gave the information? Where would you have been if I had not given you the office?'

'If there had been a fine we might have allowed you something. We would have got something, too. Mr. Melrose sent him to gaol. There is nothing for anybody.'

'So say you. I'm damned sure you and those two women got something out of it. Why the hell should I give away my own brother for the sake of the likes of you? You'll find your own bird next time.'

Murphy was a choleric man with a sense of his own importance. He was not to be bearded thus in his own seat of office. He rose with a very red face.

'I'll tell you what, Silas Linden, I could find my own bird and never move out of this room. You had best get out of this quick, or you may chance to stay here longer than you like. We've had complaints of your treatment of those two children of yours, and the children's protection folk are taking an interest. Look out that we don't take an interest, too.'

Silas Linden flung out of the room with his temper hotter than ever, and a couple of rum-and-waters on his way home did not help to appease him. On the contrary, he had always been a man who grew more dangerous in his cups. There were many of his trade who refused to drink with him.

Silas lived in one of a row of small brick houses named Bolton's Court, lying at the back of Tottenham Court Road. His was the end house of a cul-de-sac, with the side wall of a huge brewery beyond. These dwellings were very small, which was probably the reason why the inhabitants, both adults and children, spent most of their time in the street. Several of the elders were out now, and as Silas passed under the solitary lamp-post, they scowled at his thick-set figure, for though the morality of Bolton's Court was of no high order, it was none the less graduated and Silas was at zero. A tall Jewish woman, Rebecca Levi, thin, aquiline and fierce-eyed, lived next to the prize-fighter. She was standing at her door now, with a child holding her apron.

'Mr. Linden,' she said as he passed, 'them children of yours want more care than they get. Little Margery was in here to-day. That child don't get enough to eat.'

'You mind your own business, curse you!' growled Silas. 'I've told you before now not to push that long, sheeny beak of yours into my affairs. If you was a man I'd know better how to speak to you.'

'If I was a man maybe you wouldn't dare to speak to me so. I say it's a shame, Silas Linden, the way them children is treated. If it's a police-court case, I'll know what to say.'

'Oh, go to hell!' said Silas, and kicked open his own unlatched door. A big, frowsy woman with a shock of dyed hair and some remains of a florid beauty, now long over-ripe, looked out from the sitting-room door.

'Oh, it's you, is it?' said she.

'Who did you think it was? The Dook of Wellington?'

'I thought it was a mad bullock maybe got strayin' down the lane, and buttin' down our door.'

'Funny, ain't you?'

'Maybe I am, but I hain't got much to be funny about. Not a shilling in the 'ouse, nor so much as a pint o' beer, and these damned children of yours for ever upsettin' me.'

'What have they been a-doin' of?' asked Silas with a scowl. When this worthy pair could get no change out of each other, they usually united their forces against the children. He had entered the sitting-room and flung himself down in the wooden armchair.

'They've been seein' Number One again.'

'How d'ye know that?'

'I 'eard 'im say somethin' to 'er about it. "Mother was there", 'e says. Then afterwards 'e 'ad one 'o them sleepy fits.'

'It's in the family.'

'Yes, it is,' retorted the woman. 'If you 'adn't sleepy fits you'd get some work to do, like other men.'

'Oh, shut it, woman! What I mean is, that my brother Tom gets them fits, and this lad o' mine is said to be the livin' image of his uncle. So he had a trance, had he? What did you do?'

The woman gave an evil grin.

'I did what you did.'

'What, the sealin'-wax again?'

'Not much of it. Just enough to wake 'im. It's the only way to break 'im of it.'

Silas shrugged his shoulders.

' 'Ave a care, my lass! There is talk of the p'lice, and if they see those burns, you and I may be in the dock together.'

'Silas Linden, you are a fool! Can't a parent c'rect 'is own child?'

'Yes, but it ain't *your* own child, and stepmothers has a bad name, see? There's that Jew woman next door. She saw you when you took the clothes' rope to little Margery last washin'-day. She spoke to me about it and again to-day about the food.'

'What's the matter with the food? The greedy little bastards! They had a 'unch of bread each when I 'ad my dinner. A bit of real starvin' would do them no 'arm, and I would 'ave less sauce.'

'What, has Willie sauced you?'

'Yes, when 'e woke up.'

'After you'd dropped the hot sealin'-wax on him?'

'Well, I did it for 'is good, didn't I? It was to cure 'im of a bad 'abit.'

'Wot did he say?'

'Cursed me good and proper, 'e did. All about his mother – wot 'is mother would do to me. I'm dam' well sick of 'is mother!'

'Don't say too much about Amy. She was a good woman.'

'So you say now, Silas Linden, but by all accounts you 'ad a queer way of showin' it when she was alive.'

'Hold your jaw, woman! I've had enough to vex me to-day with-out you startin' your tantrums. You're jealous of the grave. That's wot's the matter with you.'

'And her brats can insult me as they like – me that 'as cared for you these five years.'

'No, I didn't say that. If he insulted you, it's up to me to deal with him. Where's that strap? Go, fetch him in!'

The woman came across and kissed him.

'I've only you, Silas.'

'Oh hell! don't muck me about. I'm not in the mood. Go and fetch Willie in. You can bring Margery also. It takes the sauce out of her also, for I think she feels it more than he does.'

The woman left the room but was back, in a moment. ' 'E's off again!' said she. 'It fair gets on my nerves to see him. Come 'ere, Silas! 'Ave a look!'

They went together into the back kitchen. A small fire was smouldering in the grate. Beside it, huddled up in a chair, sat a fair-haired boy of ten. His delicate face was upturned to the ceiling. His eyes were half-closed, and only the whites visible. There was a look of great peace upon his thin, spiritual features. In the corner a poor little cowed mite of a girl, a year or two younger, was gazing with sad, frightened eyes at her brother.

'Looks awful, don't 'e?' said the woman. 'Don't seem to belong to this world. I wish to God 'e'd make a move for the other. 'E don't do much good 'ere.'

'Here, wake up!' cried Silas. 'None of your foxin'! Wake up! D'ye hear?' He shook him roughly by the shoulder, but the boy still slumbered on. The backs of his hands, which lay upon his lap, were covered with bright scarlet blotches.

'My word, you've dropped enough hot wax on him. D'you mean to tell me, Sarah, it took all that to wake him?'

'Maybe I dropped one or two extra for luck. 'E does aggravate me so that I can 'ardly 'old myself. But you wouldn't believe 'ow little 'e can feel when 'e's like that. You can 'owl in 'is ear. It's all lost on 'im. See 'ere!'

She caught the lad by the hair and shook him violently. He groaned and shivered. Then he sank back into his serene trance.

'Say!' cried Silas, stroking his stubbled chin as he looked thought-fully at his son, 'I think there is money in this if it is handled to rights. Wot about a turn on the halls, eh? "The Boy Wonder or How is it Done?" There's a name for the bills. Then folk know his uncle's name, so they will be able to take him on trust.'

'I thought you was going into the business yourself.'

'That's a wash-out,' snarled Silas. 'Don't you talk of it. It's finished.'

'Been caught out already?'

'I tell you not to talk about it, woman!' the man shouted. 'I'm just in the mood to give you the hidin' of your life, so don't you get my goat, or you'll be sorry.' He stepped across and pinched the boy's arm with all his force. 'By Cripes, he's a wonder! Let us see how far it will go.'

He turned to the sinking fire and with the tongs he picked out a half-red ember. This he placed on the boy's head. There was a smell of burning hair, then of roasting flesh, and suddenly, with a scream of pain, the boy came back to his senses.

'Mother! Mother!' he cried. The girl in the corner took up the cry. They were like two lambs bleating together.

'Damn your mother!' cried the woman, shaking Margery by the collar of her frail black dress. 'Stop squallin', you little stinker!' She struck the child with her open hand across the face. Little Willie ran at her and kicked her shins until a blow from Silas knocked him into the corner. The brute picked up a stick and lashed the two cowering children, while they screamed for mercy, and tried to cover their little bodies from the cruel blows.

'You stop that!' cried a voice in the passage.

'It's that blasted Jewess!' said the woman. She went to the kitchen door. 'What the 'ell are you doing in our 'ouse? 'Op it, quick, or it will be the worse for you!'

'If I hear them children cry out once more, I'm off for the police.'

'Get out of it! 'Op it, I tell you!' The frowsy stepmother bore down in full sail, but the lean, lank Jewess stood her ground. Next instant they met. Mrs. Silas Linden screamed, and staggered back with blood running down her face where four nails had left as many red furrows. Silas, with an oath, pushed his wife out of the way, seized the intruder round the waist, and slung her bodily through the door. She lay in the roadway with her long gaunt limbs sprawling about like some half-slain fowl. Without rising, she shook her clenched hands in the air and screamed curses at Silas, who slammed the door and left her, while neighbours ran from all sides to hear particulars of the fray. Mrs. Linden, staring through the front blind, saw with some relief that her enemy was able to rise and to limp back to her own door, whence she could be heard delivering a long shrill harangue as to her wrongs. The wrongs of a Jew are not lightly forgotten, for the race can both love and hate.

'She's all right, Silas. I thought maybe you 'ad killed 'er.'

'It's what she wants, the damned canting sheeny. It's bad enough to have her in the street without her daring to set foot inside my door. I'll cut the hide off that young Willie. He's the cause of it all. Where is he?'

'They ran up to their room. I heard them lock the door.'

'A lot of good that will do them.'

'I wouldn't touch 'em now, Silas. The neighbours is all up and about and we needn't ask for trouble.'

'You're right!' he grumbled. 'It will keep till I come back.'

'Where are you goin'?'

'Down to the "Admiral Vernon". There's a chance of a job as sparrin' partner to Long Davis. He goes into training on Monday and needs a man of my weight.'

'Well, I'll expect you when I see you. I get too much of that pub of yours. I know what the "Admiral Vernon" means.'

'It means the only place in God's earth where I get any peace or rest,' said Silas.

'A fat lot I get – or ever 'ave 'ad since I married you.'

'That's right. Grouse away!' he growled. 'If grousin' made a man happy, you'd be the champion.'

He picked up his hat and slouched off down the street, his heavy tread resounding upon the great wooden flap which covered the cellars of the brewery.

Up in a dingy attic two little figures were seated on the side of a wretched straw-stuffed bed, their arms enlacing each other, their cheeks touching, their tears mingling. They had to cry in silence, for any sound might remind the ogre downstairs of their existence. Now and again one would break into an uncontrollable sob, and the other would whisper, 'Hush! Hush! Oh hush!' Then suddenly they heard the slam of the outer door and that heavy tread booming over the wooden flap. They squeezed each other in their joy. Perhaps when he came back he might kill them, but for a few short hours at least they were safe from him. As to the woman, she was spiteful and vicious, but she did not seem so deadly as the man. In a dim way they felt that he had hunted their mother into her grave and might do as much for them.

The room was dark save for the light which came through the single dirty window. It cast a bar across the floor, but all round was black shadow. Suddenly the little boy stiffened, clasped his sister with a tighter grip, and stared rigidly into the darkness.

'She's coming!' he muttered. 'She's coming!'

Little Margery clung to him.

'Oh, Willie, is it mother?'

'It is a light – a beautiful yellow light. Can you not see it, Margery?'

But the little girl, like all the world, was without vision. To her all was darkness.

'Tell me, Willie,' she whispered, in a solemn voice. She was not really frightened, for many times before had the dead mother returned in the watches of the night to comfort her stricken children.

'Yes. Yes, she is coming now. Oh, mother! Mother!'

'What does she say, Willie?'

'Oh, she is beautiful. She is not crying. She is smiling. It is like the picture we saw of the angel. She looks so happy. Dear, dear mother! Now she is speaking. "It is over", she says. "It is all over". She says it again. Now she beckons with her hand. We are to follow. She has moved to the door.'

'Oh, Willie, I dare not.'

'Yes, yes, she nods her head. She bids us fear nothing. Now she has passed through the door. Come, Margery, come, or we shall lose her.'

The two little mites crept across the room and Willie unlocked the door. The mother stood at the head of the stair beckoning them onwards. Step by step they followed her down into an empty kitchen. The woman seemed to have gone out. All was still in the house. The phantom still beckoned them on.

'We are to go out.'

'Oh, Willie, we have no hats.'

'We must follow, Madge. She is smiling and waving.'

'Father will kill us for this.'

'She shakes her head. She says we are to fear nothing. Come!'

They threw open the door and were in the street. Down the deserted court they followed the gleaming gracious presence, and through a tangle of low streets, and so out into the crowded rush of Tottenham Court Road. Once or twice amid all that blind torrent of humanity, some man or woman, blessed with the precious gift of discernment, would start and stare as if they were aware of an angel presence and of two little white-faced children who followed behind, the boy with fixed, absorbed gaze, the girl glancing ever in terror over her shoulder. Down the long street they passed, then again amid humbler dwellings, and so at last to a quiet drab line of brick houses. On the step of one the spirit had halted.

'We are to knock,' said Willie.

'Oh, Willie, what shall we say? We don't know them.'

'We are to knock,' he repeated, stoutly. Rat-tat! 'It's all right, Madge. She is clapping her hands and laughing.'

So it was that Mrs. Tom Linden, sitting lonely in her misery and brooding over her martyr in gaol, was summoned suddenly to the door, and found two little apologetic figures outside it. A few words, a rush of woman's instinct, and her arms were round the children. These battered little skiffs, who had started their life's voyage so sadly, had found a harbour of peace where no storm should vex them more.

There were some strange happenings in Bolton's Court that night. Some folk thought they had no relation to each other. One or two thought they had. The British Law saw nothing and had nothing to say.

In the second last house, a keen, hawklike face peered from behind a window-blind into the darkened street. A shaded candle was behind that fearful face, dark as death, remorseless as the tomb. Behind Rebecca Levi stood a young man whose features showed that he sprang from the same Oriental race. For an hour – for a second hour – the woman had sat without a word, watching, watching . . . At the entrance to the court there was a hanging lamp which cast a circle of yellow light. It was on this pool of radiance that her brooding eyes were fixed.

Then suddenly she saw what she had waited for. She started and hissed out a word. The young man rushed from the room and into the street. He vanished through a side door into the brewery.

Drunken Silas Linden was coming home. He was in a gloomy, sulken state of befuddlement. A sense of injury filled his mind. He had not gained the billet he sought. His injured hand had been against him. He had hung about the bar waiting for drinks and had got some, but not enough. Now he was in a dangerous mood. Woe to the man, woman or child, who crossed his path! He thought savagely of the Jewess who lived in that darkened house. He thought savagely of all his neighbours. They would stand between him and his children, would they? He would show them. The very next morning he would take them both out into the street and strap them within an inch of their lives. That would show them all what Silas Linden thought of their opinions. Why should he not do it now? If he were to waken the neighbours up with the shrieks of his children, it would show them once for all that they could not defy him with impunity. The idea pleased him. He stepped more briskly out. He was almost at his door when . . .

It was never quite clear how it was that the cellar-flap was not securely fastened that night. The jury were inclined to blame the brewery, but the coroner pointed out that Linden was a heavy man, that he might have fallen on it if he were drunk, and that all reasonable care had been taken. It was an eighteen-foot fall upon jagged stones, and his back was broken. They did not find him till next morning, for, curiously enough, his neighbour, the Jewess, never heard the sound of the accident. The doctor seemed to think that death had not come quickly. There were horrible signs that he had lingered. Down in the darkness, vomiting blood and beer, the man ended his filthy life with a filthy death.

One need not waste words or pity over the woman whom he had left. Relieved from her terrible mate, she returned to that music-hall stage from which he, by force of his virility and bull-like strength, had lured her. She tried to regain her place with:

> 'Hi! Hi! Hi! I'm the *dernier cri*,
> The girl with the cart-wheel hat.'

which was the ditty which had won her her name. But it became too painfully evident that she was anything but the *dernier cri*, and that she could never get back. Slowly she sank from big halls to small halls, from small halls to pubs, and so ever deeper and deeper, sucked into the awful silent quicksands of life which drew her down and down until that vacuous painted face and frowsy head were seen no more.

CHAPTER XII

There are Heights and there are Depths

THE INSTITUT MÉTAPSYCHIQUE was an imposing stone building in the Avenue Wagram with a door like a baronial castle. Here it was that the three friends presented themselves late in the evening. A footman showed them into a reception-room where they were presently welcomed by Dr. Maupuis in person. The famous authority on psychic science was a short, broad man with a large head, a clean-shaven face, and an expression in which worldly wisdom and kindly altruism were blended. His conversation was in French with Mailey and Roxton, who both spoke the language well, but he had to fall back upon broken English with Malone, who could only utter still more broken French in reply. He expressed his pleasure at their visit, as only a graceful Frenchman can, said a few words as to the wonderful qualities of Panbek, the Galician medium, and finally led the way downstairs to the room in which the experiments were to be conducted. His air of vivid intelligence and penetrating sagacity had already shown the strangers how preposterous were those theories which tried to explain away his wonderful results by the supposition that he was a man who was the easy victim of impostors.

Descending a winding stair they found themselves in a large chamber which looked at first glance like a chemical laboratory, for shelves full of bottles, retorts, test-tubes, scales and other apparatus lined the walls. It was more elegantly furnished, however, than a mere workshop, and a large massive oak table occupied the centre of the room with a fringe of comfortable chairs. At one end of the room was a large portrait of Professor Crookes, which was flanked by a second of Lombroso, while between them was a remarkable picture of one of Eusapia Palladino's seances. Round the table there was gathered a group of men who were talking in low tones, too much absorbed in their own conversation to take much notice of the newcomers.

'Three of these are distinguished visitors like yourselves,' said Dr. Maupuis. 'Two others are my laboratory assistants, Dr. Sauvage and Dr. Buisson. The others are Parisians of note. The Press is represented to-day by Mr. Forte, sub-editor of the *Matin*. The tall, dark man who looks like a retired general you probably know. . . . Not? That is Professor Charles Richet, our honoured doyen, who has shown great courage in this matter, though he has not quite reached the same conclusions as you, Monsieur Mailey. But that also may come. You must remember that we have to show policy, and that the less we mix this with religion, the less trouble we shall have with the Church, which is still very powerful in this country. The distinguished looking man with the high forehead is the Count de Grammont. The gentleman with the head of a Jupiter and the white beard is Flammarion, the astronomer. Now, gentlemen,' he added, in a louder voice, 'if you will take your places we shall get to work.'

They sat at random round the long table, the three Britons keeping together. At one end a large photographic camera was reared aloft. Two zinc buckets also occupied a prominent position upon a side table. The door was locked and the key given to Professor Richet. Dr. Maupuis sat at one end of the table with a small middle-aged man, moustached, bald-headed and intelligent, upon his right.

'Some of you have not met Monsieur Panbek,' said the doctor. 'Permit me to present him to you. Monsieur Panbek, gentlemen, has placed his remarkable powers at our disposal for scientific investigation, and we all owe him a debt of gratitude. He is now in his forty-seventh year, a man of normal health, of a neuro-arthritic disposition. Some hyper-excitability of his nervous system is indicated, and his reflexes are exaggerated, but his blood-pressure is normal. The pulse is now at seventy-two, but rises to one hundred under trance conditions. There are zones of marked hyper-æsthesia on his limbs. His visual field and pupillary reaction is normal. I do not know that there is anything to add.'

'I might say,' remarked Professor Richet, 'that the hyper-sensibility is moral as well as physical. Panbek is impressionable and full of emotion, with the temperament of the poet and all those little weaknesses, if we may call them so, which the poet pays as a ransom for his gifts. A great medium is a great artist and is to be judged by the same standards.'

'He seems to me, gentlemen, to be preparing you for the worst,' said the medium with a charming smile, while the company laughed in sympathy.

'We are sitting in the hopes that some remarkable materializations which we have recently had may be renewed in such a form that we may get a permanent record of them.' Dr. Maupuis was talking in his dry, unemotional voice. 'These materializations have taken very unexpected forms of late, and I would beg the company to repress any feelings of fear, however strange these forms may be, as a calm and judicial atmosphere is most necessary. We shall now turn out the white light and begin with the lowest degree of red light until the conditions will admit of further illumination.'

The lamps were controlled from Dr. Maupuis' seat at the table. For a moment they were plunged in utter darkness. Then a dull red glow came in the corner, enough to show the dim outlines of the men round the table. There was no music and no religious atmosphere of any sort. The company conversed in whispers.

'This is different to your English procedure,' said Malone.

'Very,' Mailey answered. 'It seems to me that we are wide open to anything which may come. It's all wrong. They don't realize the danger.'

'What danger can there be?'

'Well, from my point of view, it is like sitting at the edge of a pond which may have harmless frogs in it, or may have man-eating crocodiles. You can't tell what may come.'

Professor Richet, who spoke excellent English, overheard the words.

'I know your views, Mr. Mailey,' said he. 'Don't think that I treat them lightly. Some things which I have seen make me appreciate your comparison of the frog and the crocodile. In this very room I have been conscious of the presence of creatures which could, if moved to anger, make our experiments seem rather hazardous. I believe with you that evil people here might bring an evil reflection into our circle.'

'I am glad, sir, that you are moving in our direction,' said Mailey, for like everyone else he regarded Richet as one of the world's great men.

'Moving, perhaps, and yet I cannot claim to be altogether with you yet. The latent powers of the human incarnate spirit may be so wonderful that they may extend to regions which seem at present to be quite beyond their scope. As an old materialist, I fight every inch of the ground, though I admit that I have lost several lines of trenches. My illustrious friend Challenger still holds his front intact, as I understand.'

'Yes, sir,' said Malone, 'and yet I have some hopes –'

'Hush!' cried Maupuis in an eager voice.

There was dead silence. Then there came a sound of uneasy movement with a strange flapping vibration.

'The bird!' said an awestruck whisper.

There was silence and then once again came the sound of movement and an impatient flap.

'Have you all ready, René?' asked the doctor.

'All is ready.'

'Then shoot!'

The flash of the luminant mixture filled the room, while the shutter of the camera fell. In that sudden glare of light the visitors had a momentary glimpse of a marvellous sight. The medium lay with his head upon his hands in apparent insensibility. Upon his rounded shoulders there was perched a huge bird of prey – a large falcon or an eagle. For one instant the strange picture was stamped upon their retinas even as it was upon the photographic plate. Then the darkness closed down again, save for the two red lamps, like the eyes of some baleful demon lurking in the corner.

'My word!' gasped Malone. 'Did you see it?'

'A crocodile out of the pond,' said Mailey.

'But harmless,' added Professor Richet. 'The bird has been with us several times. He moves his wings, as you have heard, but otherwise is inert. We may have another and a more dangerous visitor.'

The flash of the light had, of course, dispelled all ectoplasm. It was necessary to begin again. The company may have sat for a quarter of an hour when Richet touched Mailey's arm.

'Do you smell anything, Monsieur Mailey?'

Mailey sniffed the air.

'Yes, surely, it reminds me of our London Zoo.'

'There is another more ordinary analogy. Have you been in a warm room with a wet dog?'

'Exactly,' said Mailey. 'That is a perfect description. But where is the dog?'

'It is not a dog. Wait a little! Wait!'

The animal smell became more pronounced. It was overpowering. Then suddenly Malone became conscious of something moving round the table. In the dim red light he was aware of a mis-shapen figure, crouching, ill-formed, with some resemblance to man. He silhouetted it against the dull radiance. It was bulky, broad, with a bullet-head, a short neck, heavy, clumsy shoulders. It slouched slowly round the circle. Then it stopped, and a cry of surprise, not unmixed with fear, came from one of the sitters.

'Do not be alarmed,' said Dr. Maupuis' quiet voice. 'It is the Pithecanthropus. He is harmless.' Had it been a cat which had strayed into the room the scientist could not have discussed it more calmly.

'It has long claws. It laid them on my neck,' cried a voice.

'Yes, yes. He means it as a caress.'

'You may have my share of his caresses!' cried the sitter in a quavering voice.

'Do not repulse him. It might be serious. He is well disposed. But he has his feelings, no doubt, like the rest of us.'

The creature had resumed its stealthy progress. Now it turned the end of the table and stood behind the three friends. Its breath came in quick puffs at the back of their necks. Suddenly Lord Roxton gave a loud exclamation of disgust.

'Quiet! Quiet!' said Maupuis.

'It's licking my hand!' cried Roxton.

An instant later Malone was aware of a shaggy head extended between Lord Roxton and himself. With his left hand he could feel long, coarse hair. It turned towards him, and it needed all his self-control to hold his hand still when a long soft tongue caressed it. Then it was gone.

'In heaven's name, what is it?' he asked.

'We have been asked not to photograph it. Possibly the light would infuriate it. The command through the medium was definite.

We can only say that it is either an ape-like man or a man-like ape. We have seen it more clearly than to-night. The face is Simian, but the brow is straight; the arms long, the hands huge, the body covered with hair.'

'Tom Linden gave us something better than that,' whispered Mailey. He spoke low but Richet caught the words.

'All Nature is the field of our study, Mr. Mailey. It is not for us to choose. Shall we classify the flowers but neglect the fungi?'

'But you admit it is dangerous.'

'The X-rays were dangerous. How many martyrs lost their arms, joint by joint, before those dangers were realized? And yet it was necessary. So it is with us. We do not know yet what it is that we are doing. But if we can indeed show the world that this Pithecanthropus can come to us from the Invisible, and depart again as it came, then the knowledge is so tremendous that even if he tore us to pieces with those formidable claws it would none the less be our duty to go forward with our experiments.'

'Science can be heroic,' said Mailey. 'Who can deny it? And yet I have heard these very scientific men tell us that we imperil our reason when we try to get in touch with spiritual forces. Gladly would we sacrifice our reason, or our lives, if we could help mankind. Should we not do as much for spiritual advance as they for material?'

The lights had been turned up and there was a pause for relaxation before the great experiment of the evening was attempted. The men broke into little groups, chatting in hushed tones over their recent experience. Looking round at the comfortable room with its up-to-date appliances, the strange bird and the stealthy monster seemed like dreams. And yet they had been very real, as was shown presently by the photographer, who had been allowed to leave and now rushed excitedly from the adjacent dark room waving the plate which he had just developed and fixed. He held it up against the light, and there, sure enough, was the bald head of the medium sunk between his hands, and crouching closely over his shoulders the outline of that ominous figure. Dr. Maupuis rubbed his little fat hands with glee. Like all pioneers he had endured much persecution from the Parisian Press, and every fresh phenomenon was another weapon for his own defence.

'*Nous marchons! Hein! Nous marchons!*' he kept on repeating, while Richet, lost in thought, answered mechanically:

'*Oui, mon ami, vous marchez!*'

The little Galician was sitting nibbling a biscuit with a glass of red wine before him. Malone went round to him and found that he had been in America and could talk a little English.

'Are you tired? Does it exhaust you?'

'In moderation, no. Two sittings a week. Behold my allowance. The doctor will allow no more.'

'Do you remember anything?'

'It comes to me like dreams. A little here – a little there.'

'Has the power always been with you?'

'Yes, yes, ever since a child. And my father, and my uncle. Their talk was of visions. For me, I would go and sit in the woods and strange animals would come round me. It did me such a surprise when I found that the other children could not see them.'

'*Est ce que vous êtes prêtes?*' asked Dr. Maupuis.

'*Parfaitement,*' answered the medium, brushing away the crumbs. The doctor lit a spirit-lamp under one of the zinc buckets.

'We are about to co-operate in an experiment, gentlemen, which should, once and for all, convince the world as to the existence of these ectoplasmic forms. Their nature may be disputed, but their objectivity will be beyond doubt from now onwards unless my plans miscarry. I would first explain these two buckets to you. This one, which I am warming, contains paraffin, which is now in process of liquefaction. This other contains water. Those who have not been present before must understand that Panbek's phenomena occur usually in the same order, and that at this stage of the evening we may expect the apparition of the old man. To-night we lie in wait for the old man, and we shall, I hope, immortalize him in the history of psychic research. I resume my seat, and I switch on the red light, Number Three, which allows of greater visibility.'

The circle was now quite visible. The medium's head had fallen forward and his deep snoring showed that he was already in trance. Every face was turned towards him, for the wonderful process of materialization was going on before their very eyes. At first it was a swirl of light, steam-like vapour which circled round his head. Then there was a waving, as of white diaphanous drapery, behind him. It thickened. It coalesced. It hardened in outline and took definite shape. There was a head. There were shoulders. Arms grew out from them. Yes, there could not be a doubt of it – there was a man, an old man, standing behind the chair. He moved his head slowly from side to side. He seemed to be peering in indecision towards the company. One could imagine that he was asking himself, 'Where am I, and what am I here for?'

'He does not speak, but he hears and has intelligence,' said Dr.

Maupuis, glancing over his shoulder at the apparition. 'We are here, sir, in the hope that you will aid us in a very important experiment. May we count upon your co-operation?'

The figure bowed his head in assent.

'We thank you. When you have attained your full power you will, no doubt, move away from the medium.'

The figure again bowed, but remained motionless. It seemed to Malone that it was growing denser every moment. He caught glimpses of the face. It was certainly an old man, heavy-faced, long-nosed, with a curiously projecting lower lip. Suddenly with a brusque movement it stood clear from Panbek and stepped out into the room.

'Now, sir,' said Maupuis in his precise fashion. 'You will perceive the zinc bucket upon the left. I would beg you to have the kindness to approach it and to plunge your right hand into it.'

The figure moved across. He seemed interested in the buckets, for he examined them with some attention. Then he dipped one of his hands into that which the doctor had indicated.

'Excellent!' cried Maupuis, his voice shrill with excitement. 'Now, sir, might I ask you to have the kindness to dip the same hand into the cold water of the other bucket.'

The form did so.

'Now, sir, you would bring our experiment to complete success if you would lay your hand upon the table, and while it is resting there you would yourself dematerialize and return into the medium.'

The figure bowed its comprehension and assent. Then it slowly advanced towards the table, stooped over it, extended its hand – and vanished. The heavy breathing of the medium ceased and he moved uneasily as if about to wake. Maupuis turned on the white light, and threw up his hands with a loud cry of wonder and joy which was echoed by the company.

On the shining wooden surface of the table there lay a delicate yellow-pink glove of paraffin, broad at the knuckles, thin at the wrist, two of the fingers bent down to the palm. Maupuis was beside himself with delight. He broke off a small bit of the wax from the wrist and handed it to an assistant, who hurried from the room.

'It is final!' he cried. 'What can they say now? Gentlemen, I appeal to you. You have seen what occurred. Can any of you give any rational explanation of that paraffin mould, save that it was the result of dematerialization of the hand within it?'

'I can see no other solution,' Richet answered. 'But you have to do with very obstinate and very prejudiced people. If they cannot deny it, they will probably ignore it.'

'The Press is here and the Press represents the public,' said Maupuis. 'For the Press Engleesh, Monsieur Malone,' he went on in his broken way. 'Is it that you can see any answer?'

'I can see none,' Malone answered.

'And you, monsieur?' addressing the representative of the *Matin*. The Frenchman shrugged his shoulders.

'For us who had the privilege of being present it was indeed convincing,' said he, 'and yet you will certainly be met with objections. They will not realize how fragile this thing is. They will say that the medium brought it on his person and laid it upon the table.'

Maupuis clapped his hands triumphantly. His assistant had just brought him a slip of paper from the next room.

'Your objection is already answered,' he cried, waving the paper in the air. 'I had foreseen it and I had put some cholesterine among the paraffin in the zinc pail. You may have observed that I broke off a corner of the mould. It was for purpose of chemical analysis. This has now been done. It is here and cholesterine has been detected.'

'Excellent!' said the French journalist. 'You have closed the last hole. But what next?'

'What we have done once we can do again,' Maupuis answered. 'I will prepare a number of these moulds. In some cases I will have fists and hands. Then I will have plaster casts made from them. I will run the plaster inside the mould. It is delicate, but it can be done. I will have dozens of them so treated, and I will send them broadcast to every capital in the world that people may see with their own eyes. Will that not at last convince them of the reality of our conclusions?'

'Do not hope for too much, my poor friend,' said Richet, with his hand upon the shoulder of the enthusiast. 'You have not yet realized the enormous *vis inertia* of the world. But as you have said, "*Vous marchez – vous marchez toujours*".'

'And our march is regulated,' said Mailey. 'There is a gradual release to accommodate it to the receptivity of mankind.'

Richet smiled and shook his head.

'Always transcendental, Monsieur Mailey! Always seeing more than meets the eye and changing science into philosophy! I fear you are incorrigible. Is your position reasonable?'

'Professor Richet,' said Mailey, very earnestly, 'I would beg you to answer the same question. I have a deep respect for your talents and complete sympathy with your caution, but have you not come to the dividing of the ways? You are now in the position that you admit – you must admit – that an intelligent apparition in human

370 THE LOST WORLD & OTHER STORIES

form, built up from the substance which you have yourself named ectoplasm, can walk the room and carry out instructions while the medium lay senseless under our eyes, and yet you hesitate to assert that spirit has an independent existence. Is *that* reasonable?'

Richet smiled and shook his head. Without answering he turned and bid farewell to Dr. Maupuis, and to offer him his congratulations. A few minutes later the company had broken up and our friends were in a taxi speeding towards their hotel.

Malone was deeply impressed with what he had seen, and he sat up half the night drawing up a full account of it for the Central News, with the names of those who had endorsed the result – honourable names which no one in the world could associate with folly or deception.

'Surely, surely, this will be a turning point and an epoch.' So ran his dream. Two days later he opened the great London dailies one after the other. Columns about football. Columns about golf. A full page as to the value of shares. A long and earnest correspondence in *The Times* about the habits of the lapwing. Not one word in any of them as to the wonders which he had seen and reported. Mailey laughed at his dejected face.

'A mad world, my masters,' said he. 'A crazy world! But the end is not yet!'

CHAPTER XIII

In Which Professor Challenger Goes Forth to Battle

PROFESSOR CHALLENGER WAS IN A BAD HUMOUR, and when that was so his household were made aware of it. Neither were the effects of his wrath confined to those around him, for most of those terrible letters which appeared from time to time in the Press, flaying and scarifying some unhappy opponent, were thunderbolt flashes from an offended Jove who sat in sombre majesty in his study-throne on the heights of a Victoria flat. Servants would hardly dare to enter the room where, glooming and glowering, the maned and bearded head looked up from his papers as a lion from a bone. Only Enid could dare him at such a time, and even she felt occasionally that sinking of the heart which the bravest of tamers may experience as he unbars the gate of the cage. She was not safe from the acridity of his tongue but at least she need not fear physical violence, which was well within the possibilities for others.

Sometimes these berserk fits of the famous Professor arose from material causes. 'Hepatic, sir, hepatic!' he would explain in extenuation after some aggravated assault. But on this particular occasion he had a very definite cause for discontent. It was Spiritualism!

He never seemed to get away from the accursed superstition – a thing which ran counter to the whole work and philosophy of his lifetime. He attempted to pooh-pooh it, to laugh at it, to ignore it with contempt, but the confounded thing would insist upon obtruding itself once more. On Monday he would write it finally off his books, and before Saturday he would be up to his neck in it again. And the thing was so absurd! It seemed to him that his mind was being drawn from the great pressing material problems of the Universe in order to waste itself upon Grimm's fairy tales or the ghosts of a sensational novelist.

Then things grew worse. First Malone, who had in his simple fashion been an index figure representing the normal clear-headed human being, had in some way been bedevilled by these people and had committed himself to their pernicious views. Then Enid, his wee-lamb, his one real link with humanity, had also been corrupted. She had agreed with Malone's conclusions. She had even hunted up a good deal of evidence of her own. In vain he had himself investigated a case and proved beyond a shadow of a doubt that the medium was a designing villain who brought messages from a widow's dead husband in order to get the woman into his power. It was a clear case and Enid admitted it. But neither she nor Malone would allow any general application. 'There are rogues in every line of life,' they would say. 'We must judge every movement by the best and not by the worst.'

All this was bad enough, but worse still was in store. He had been publicly humiliated by the Spiritualists – and that by a man who admitted that he had had no education and would in any other subject in the world have been seated like a child at the Professor's feet. And yet in public debate . . . but the story must be told.

Be it known, then, that Challenger, greatly despising all opposition and with no knowledge of the real strength of the case to be answered, had, in a fatal moment, actually asserted that he would descend from Olympus and would meet in debate any representative whom the other party should select. 'I am well aware,' he wrote, 'that by such condescension I, like any other man of science of equal standing, run the risk of giving a dignity to these absurd and grotesque aberrations of the human brain which they could otherwise not pretend to claim, but we must do our duty to the public, and we must occasionally turn from our serious work and spare a moment in order to sweep away those ephemeral cobwebs which might collect and become offensive if they were not dispersed by the broom of Science.' Thus, in a most self-confident fashion, did Goliath go forth to meet his tiny antagonist, an ex-printer's assistant and now the editor of what Challenger would describe as an obscure print devoted to matters of the spirit.

The particulars of the debate are public property, and it is not necessary to tell in any great detail that painful event. It will be remembered that the great man of Science went down to the Queen's Hall accompanied by many rationalist sympathizers who desired to see the final destruction of the visionaries. A large number of these poor deluded creatures also attended, hoping against hope that their champion might not be entirely immolated upon the altar of outraged Science. Between them the two factions filled the hall, and glared at each other with as much enmity as did the Blues and the Greens a thousand years before in the Hippodrome of Constantinople. There on the left of the platform were the solid ranks of those hard and unbending rationalists who look upon the Victorian agnostics as credulous, and refresh their faith by the periodical perusal of the *Literary Gazette* and the *Freethinker*.

There, too, was Dr. Joseph Baumer, the famous lecturer upon the absurdities of religion, together with Mr. Edward Mould, who has insisted so eloquently upon man's claim to ultimate putridity of the body and extinction of the soul. On the other side Mailey's yellow beard flamed like an oriflamme. His wife sat on one side of him and Mervin, the journalist, on the other, while dense ranks of earnest men and women from the Queen Square Spiritual Alliance, from the Psychic College, from the Stead Bureau, and from the outlying churches, assembled in order to encourage their champion in his hopeless task. The genial faces of Bolsover, the grocer, with his Hammersmith friends, Terbane, the railway medium, the Reverend Charles Mason, with his ascetic features, Tom Linden, now happily released from bondage, Mrs. Linden, the Crewe circle, Dr. Atkinson, Lord Roxton, Malone, and many other familiar faces were to be picked out amid that dense wall of humanity. Between the two parties, solemn and stolid and fat, sat Judge Gaverson of the King's Bench, who had consented to preside. It was an interesting and suggestive fact that in this critical debate at which the very core or vital centre of real religion was the issue, the organized churches were entirely aloof and neutral. Drowsy and semi-conscious, they could not discern that the live intellect of the nation was really holding an inquisition upon their bodies to determine whether they were doomed to the extinction towards which they were rapidly drifting, or whether a resuscitation in other forms was among the possibilities of the future.

In front, on one side, with his broad-browed disciples behind him, sat Professor Challenger, portentous and threatening, his Assyrian beard projected in his most aggressive fashion, a half-smile upon his lips, and his eyelids drooping insolently over his intolerant grey eyes. On the corresponding position on the other side was perched a drab and unpretentious person over whose humble head Challenger's hat would have descended to the shoulders. He was pale and apprehensive, glancing across occasionally in apologetic and deprecating fashion at his leonine opponent. Yet those who knew James Smith best were the least alarmed, for they were aware that behind his commonplace and democratic appearance there lay a knowledge of his subject, practical and theoretical, such as few living men possessed. The wise men of the Psychical Research Society are but children in psychic knowledge when compared with such practising Spiritualists as James Smith – men whose whole lives are spent in various forms of communion with the unseen. Such men often lose touch with the world in which they dwell and are useless for its everyday purposes, but the editorship of a live paper and the administration of a widespread, scattered community had kept Smith's feet solid upon earth, while his excellent natural faculties, uncorrupted by useless education, had enabled him to concentrate upon the one field of knowledge which offers in itself a sufficient scope for the greatest human intellect. Little as Challenger could appreciate it, the contest was really one between a brilliant discursive amateur and a concentrated highly-specialized professional.

It was admitted on all sides that Challenger's opening half-hour was a magnificent display of oratory and argument. His deep organ voice – such a voice as only a man with a fifty-inch chest can produce – rose and fell in a perfect cadence which enchanted his audience. He was born to sway an assembly – an obvious leader of mankind. In turn he was descriptive, humorous and convincing. He pictured the natural growth of animism among savages cowering under the naked sky, unable to account for the beat of the rain or the roar of the thunder, and seeing a benevolent or malicious intelligence behind those operations of Nature which Science had now classified and explained.

Hence on false premises was built up that belief in spirits or invisible beings outside ourselves, which by some curious atavism was

re-emerging in modern days among the less educated strata of
mankind. It was the duty of Science to resist retrogressive tendencies
of the sort, and it was a sense of that duty which had reluctantly
drawn him from the privacy of his study to the publicity of this platform. He rapidly sketched the movement as depicted by its malign-
ers. It was a most unsavoury story as he told it, a story of cracking
toe joints, of phosphorescent paint, of muslin ghosts, of a nauseous
sordid commission trade betwixt dead men's bones on one side, and
widow's tears upon the other. These people were the hyenas of the
human race who battened upon the graves. (Cheers from the Rationalists and ironical laughter from the Spiritualists.) They were not
all rogues. ('Thank you, Professor!' from a stentorian opponent). But
the others were fools (laughter). Was it exaggeration to call man a
fool who believed that his grandmother could rap out absurd messages with the leg of a dining-room table? Had any savages
descended to so grotesque a superstition? These people had taken
dignity from death and had brought their own vulgarity into the
serene oblivion of the tomb. It was a hateful business. He was sorry
to have to speak so strongly, but only the knife or the cautery could
deal with so cancerous a growth. Surely man need not trouble himself with grotesque speculations as to the nature of life beyond the
grave. We had enough to do in this world. Life was a beautiful thing.
The man who appreciated its real duties and beauties would have
sufficient to employ him without dabbling in pseudo sciences which
had their roots in frauds, exposed already a hundred times and yet
finding fresh crowds of foolish devotees whose insane credulity and
irrational prejudice made them impervious to all argument.

Such is a most bald and crude summary of this powerful opening
argument. The materialists roared their applause; the Spiritualists
looked angry and uneasy, while their spokesman rose, pale but resolute, to answer the ponderous onslaught.

His voice and appearance had none of those qualities which made
Challenger magnetic, but he was clearly audible and made his
points in a precise fashion like a workman who is familiar with his
tools. He was so polite and so apologetic at first that he gave the
impression of having been cowed. He felt that it was almost pre-
sumptuous upon one who had so little advantage of education to
measure mental swords for an instant with so renowned an antagonist, one whom he had long revered. It seemed to him, however,
that in the long list of the Professor's accomplishments – accomplishments which had made him a household word throughout the
world – there was one missing, and unhappily it was just this one

upon which he had been tempted to speak. He had listened to that speech with admiration so far as its eloquence was concerned, but with surprise, and he might almost say with contempt, when he analysed the assertions which were contained in it. It was clear that the Professor had prepared his case by reading all the anti-Spiritualist literature which he could lay his hands upon – a most tainted source of information – while neglecting the works of those who spoke from experience and conviction.

All this talk of cracking joints and other fraudulent tricks was mid-Victorian in its ignorance, and as to the grandmother talking through the leg of a table he, the speaker, could not recognize it as a fair description of Spiritualistic phenomena. Such comparisons reminded one of the jokes about the dancing frogs which impeded the recognition of Volta's early electrical experiments. They were unworthy of Professor Challenger. He must surely be aware that the fraudulent medium was the worst enemy of Spiritualism, that he was denounced by name in the psychic journals whenever he was discovered, and that such exposures were usually made by the Spiritualists themselves who had spoken of 'human hyenas' as indignantly as his opponent had done. One did not condemn banks because forgers occasionally used them for nefarious purposes. It was wasting the time of so chosen an audience to descend to such a level of argument. Had Professor Challenger denied the religious implications of Spiritualism while admitting the phenomena, it might have been harder to answer him, but in denying everything he had placed himself in an absolutely impossible position. No doubt Professor Challenger had read the recent work of Professor Richet, the famous physiologist. That work had extended over thirty years. Richet had verified all the phenomena.

Perhaps Professor Challenger would inform the audience what personal experience he had himself had which gave him the right to talk of Richet, or Lombroso, or Crookes, as if they were superstitious savages. Possibly his opponent had conducted experiments in private of which the world knew nothing. In that case he should give them to the world. Until he did so it was unscientific and really indecent to deride men, hardly inferior in scientific reputation to himself, who actually had done such experiments and laid them before the public.

As to the self-sufficiency of this world, a successful Professor with a eupeptic body might take such a view, but if one found oneself with cancer of the stomach in a London garret, one might question the doctrine that there was no need to yearn for any state of being save that in which we found ourselves.

It was a workmanlike effort illustrated with facts, dates and figures. Though it rose to no height of eloquence it contained much which needed an answer. And the sad fact emerged that Challenger was not in a position to answer. He had read up his own case but had neglected that of his adversary, accepting too easily the facile and specious presumptions of incompetent writers who handled a matter which they had not themselves investigated. Instead of answering, Challenger lost his temper. The lion began to roar. He tossed his dark mane and his eyes glowed, while his deep voice reverberated through the hall. Who were these people who took refuge behind a few honoured but misguided names? What right had they to expect serious men of science to suspend their labours in order to waste time in examining their wild surmises? Some things were self-evident and did not require proof. The onus of proof lay with those who made the assertions. If this gentleman, whose name is unfamiliar, claims that he can raise spirits, let him call one up now before a sane and unprejudiced audience. If he says that he receives messages, let him give us the news in advance of the general agencies. ('It has often been done!' from the Spiritualists.) So you say, but I deny it. I am too accustomed to your wild assertions to take them seriously. (Uproar, and Judge Gaverson upon his feet.) If he claims that he has higher inspiration, let him solve the Peckham Rye murder. If he is in touch with angelic beings, let him give us a philosophy which is higher than mortal mind can evolve. This false show of science, this camouflage of ignorance, this babble about ectoplasm and other mythical products of the psychic imagination was mere obscurantism, the bastard offspring of superstition and darkness. Wherever the matter was probed one came upon corruption and mental putrescence. Every medium was a deliberate impostor. ('You are a liar!' in a woman's voice from the neighbourhood of the Lindens.) The voices of the dead had uttered nothing but childish twaddle. The asylums were full of the supporters of the cult and would be fuller still if everyone had his due.

It was a violent but not an effective speech. Evidently the great man was rattled. He realized that there was a case to be met and that he had not provided himself with the material wherewith to meet it. Therefore he had taken refuge in angry words and sweeping assertions which can only be safely made when there is no antagonist present to take advantage of them. The Spiritualists seemed more amused than angry. The materialists fidgeted uneasily in their seats. Then James Smith rose for his last innings. He wore a mischievous smile. There was quiet menace in his whole bearing.

He must ask, he said, for a more scientific attitude from his illustrious opponent. It was an extraordinary fact that many scientific men, when their passions and prejudices were excited, showed a ludicrous disregard for all their own tenets. Of these tenets there was none more rigid than that a subject should be examined before it was condemned. We have seen of late years, in such matters as wireless or heavier-than-air machines, that the most unlikely things may come to pass. It is most dangerous to say *a priori* that a thing is impossible. Yet this was the error into which Professor Challenger had fallen. He had used the fame which he had rightly won in subjects which he had mastered in order to cast discredit upon a subject which he had not mastered. The fact that a man was a great physiologist and physicist did not in itself make him an authority upon psychic science.

It was perfectly clear that Professor Challenger had not read the standard works upon the subject on which he posed as an authority. Could he tell the audience what the name of Schrenck Notzing's medium was? He paused for a reply. Could he then tell the name of Dr. Crawford's medium? Not? Could he tell them who had been the subject of Professor Zollner's experiments at Leipzig? What, still silent? But these were the essential points of the discussion. He had hesitated to be personal, but the Professor's robust language called for corresponding frankness upon his part. Was the Professor aware that this ectoplasm which he derided had been examined lately by twenty German professors – the names were here for reference – and that all had testified to its existence? How could Professor Challenger deny that which these gentlemen asserted? Would he contend that they also were criminals or fools? The fact was that the Professor had come to this hall entirely ignorant of the facts and was now learning them for the first time. He clearly had no perception that Psychic Science had any laws whatever, or he would not have formulated such childish requests as that an ectoplasmic figure should manifest in full light upon this platform when every student was aware that ectoplasm was soluble in light. As to the Peckham Rye murder it had never been claimed that the angel world was an annexe to Scotland Yard. It was mere throwing of dust in the eyes of the public for a man like Professor Challenger –

It was at this moment that the explosion occurred. Challenger had wriggled in his chair. Challenger had tugged at his beard. Challenger had glared at the speaker. Now he suddenly sprang to the side of the chairman's table with the bound of a wounded lion. That gentleman had been lying back half asleep with his fat hands clutched across his ample paunch, but at this sudden apparition he gave a convulsive start which nearly carried him into the orchestra.

'Sit down, sir! Sit down!' he cried.

'I refuse to sit down,' roared Challenger. 'Sir, I appeal to you as chairman! Am I here to be insulted? These proceedings are intolerable. I will stand it no longer. If my private honour is touched I am justified in taking the matter into my own hands.'

Like many men who override the opinions of others, Challenger was exceedingly sensitive when anyone took a liberty with his own. Each successive incisive sentence of his opponent had been like a barbed bandarillo in the flanks of a foaming bull. Now, in speechless fury, he was shaking his huge hairy fist over the chairman's head in the direction of his adversary, whose derisive smile stimulated him to more furious plunges with which he butted the fat president along the platform. The assembly had in an instant become a pandemonium. Half the rationalists were scandalized, while the other half shouted 'Shame! Shame!' as a sign of sympathy with their champion. The Spiritualists had broken into derisive shouts, while some rushed forward to protect their champion from physical assault.

'We must get the old dear out,' said Lord Roxton to Malone. 'He'll be had for manslaughter if we don't. What I mean, he's not responsible – he'll sock someone and be lagged for it.'

The platform had become a seething mob, while the auditorium was little better. Through the crush Malone and Roxton elbowed their way until they reached Challenger's side, and partly by judicious propulsion, partly by artful persuasion, they got him, still bellowing his grievances, out of the building. There was a perfunctory vote to the chairman, and the meeting broke up in riot and confusion. 'The whole episode,' remarked *The Times* next morning, 'was a deplorable one, and forcibly illustrates the danger of public debates where the subjects are such as to inflame the prejudices of either speakers or audience. Such terms as "Microcephalous idiot!" or "Simian survival!" when applied by a world-renowned Professor to an opponent, illustrate the lengths to which such disputants may permit themselves to go.'

Thus by a long interpolation we have got back to the fact that Professor Challenger was in the worst of humours as he sat with the above-mentioned copy of *The Times* in his hand and a heavy scowl upon his brow. And yet it was that very moment that the injudicious Malone had chosen in order to ask him the most intimate question which one man can address to another.

Yet perhaps it is hardly fair to our friend's diplomacy to say that he had 'chosen' the moment. He had really called in order to see for himself that the man for whom, in spite of his eccentricities, he had a deep reverence and affection, had not suffered from the events of the night before. On that point he was speedily reassured.

'Intolerable!' roared the Professor, in a tone so unchanged that he might have been at it all night. 'You were there yourself, Malone. In spite of your inexplicable and misguided sympathy for the fatuous views of these people, you must admit that the whole conduct of the proceedings was intolerable, and that my righteous protest was more than justified. It is possible that when I threw the chairman's table at the President of the Psychic College I passed the bounds of decorum, but the provocation had been excessive. You will remember that this Smith or Brown person – his name is most immaterial – dared to accuse me of ignorance and of throwing dust in the eyes of the audience.'

'Quite so,' said Malone, soothingly. 'Never mind, Professor. You got in one or two pretty hard knocks yourself.'

Challenger's grim features unbent and he rubbed his hands with glee.

'Yes, yes, I fancy that some of my thrusts went home. I imagine that they will not be forgotten. When I said that the asylums would be full if every man of them had his due I could see them wince. They all yelped, I remember, like a kennelful of puppies. It was their preposterous claim that I should read their hare-brained literature which caused me to display some little heat. But I hope, my boy, that you have called round this morning in order to tell me that what I said last night has had some effect upon your own mind, and that you have reconsidered these views which are, I confess, a considerable tax upon our friendship.'

Malone took his plunge like a man.

'I had something else in my mind when I came here,' said he. 'You must be aware that your daughter Enid and I have been thrown together a good deal of late. To me, sir, she has become the one woman in the world, and I shall never be happy until she is my wife. I am not rich, but a good sub-editorship has been offered to me and I could well afford to marry. You have known me for some time and I hope you have nothing against me. I trust, therefore, that I may count upon your approval in what I am about to do.'

Challenger stroked his beard and his eyelids drooped dangerously over his eyes.

'My perceptions,' said he, 'are not so dull that I should have failed to observe the relations which have been established between my daughter and yourself. This question however, has become entangled with the other which we were discussing. You have both, I fear, imbibed this poisonous fallacy which I am more and more inclined to devote my life to extirpating. If only on the ground of eugenics, I could not give my sanction to a union which was built up on such a foundation, I must ask you, therefore, for a definite assurance that your views have become more sane. I shall ask the same from her.'

And so Malone suddenly found himself also enrolled among the noble army of martyrs. It was a hard dilemma, but he faced it like the man that he was.

'I am sure, sir, that you would not think the better of me if I allowed my views as to truth, whether they be right or wrong, to be swayed by material considerations. I cannot change my opinions even to win Enid. I am sure that she would take the same view.'

'Did you not think I had the better last night?'

'I thought your address was very eloquent.'

'Did I not convince you?'

'Not in the face of the evidence of my own senses.'

'Any conjuror could deceive your senses.'

'I fear, sir, that my mind is made up on this point.'

'Then my mind is made up also,' roared Challenger, with a sudden glare. 'You will leave this house, sir, and you will return when you have regained your sanity.'

'One moment!' said Malone. 'I beg, sir, that you will not be precipitate. I value your friendship too much to risk the loss of it if it can, in any way, be avoided. Possibly if I had your guidance I would better understand these things that puzzle me. If I should be able to arrange it would you mind being present personally at one of these demonstrations so that your own trained powers of observation may throw a light upon the things that have puzzled me.'

Challenger was enormously open to flattery. He plumed and preened himself now like some great bird.

'If, my dear Malone, I can help you to get this taint – what shall we call it? – *microbus spiritualensis* – out of your system, I am at your service. I shall be happy to devote a little of my spare time to exposing those specious fallacies to which you have fallen so easy a victim. I would not say that you are entirely devoid of brains, but that your good nature is liable to be imposed upon. I warn you that I shall be an exacting inquirer and bring to the investigation those laboratory methods of which it is generally admitted that I am a master.'

'That is what I desire.'

'Then you will prepare the occasion and I shall be there. But meanwhile you will clearly understand that I insist upon a promise that this connection with my daughter shall go no further.'

Malone hesitated.

'I give my promise for six months,' he said at last.

'And what will you do at the end of that time?'

'I will decide when the time comes,' Malone answered diplomatically, and so escaped from a dangerous situation with more credit than at one time seemed probable.

It chanced that, as he emerged upon the landing, Enid who had been engaged in her morning's shopping, appeared in the lift. Malone's easy Irish conscience allowed him to think that the six months need not start on the instant, so he persuaded Enid to descend in the lift with him. It was one of those lifts which are handled by whoever uses them, and on this occasion it so happened that, in some way best known to Malone, it stuck between the landing stages, and in spite of several impatient rings it remained stuck for a good quarter of an hour. When the machinery resumed its functions, and when Enid was able at last to reach her home and Malone the street, the lovers had prepared themselves to wait for six months with every hope of a successful end to their experiment.

CHAPTER XIV

In Which Challenger Meets a Strange Colleague

PROFESSOR CHALLENGER WAS NOT A MAN who made friends easily. In order to be his friend you had also to be his dependant. He did not admit of equals. But as a patron he was superb. With his Jovian air, his colossal condescension, his amused smile, his general suggestion of the god descending to the mortal, he could be quite overpowering in his amiability. But he needed certain qualities in return. Stupidity disgusted him. Physical ugliness alienated him. Independence repulsed him. He coveted the man whom all the world would admire, but who in turn would admire the superman above him. Such a man was Dr. Ross Scotton, and for this reason he had been Challenger's favourite pupil.

And now he was sick unto death. Dr. Atkinson of St. Mary's who had already played some minor part in this record, was attending him, and his reports were increasingly depressing. The illness was that dread disease disseminated sclerosis, and Challenger was aware that Atkinson was no alarmist when he said that a cure was a most remote and unlikely possibility. It seemed a terrible instance of the unreasonable nature of things that a young man of science, capable before he reached his prime of two such works as *The Embryology of the Sympathetic Nervous System* or *The Fallacy of the Obsonic Index*, should be dissolved into his chemical elements with no personal or spiritual residue whatever. And yet the Professor shrugged his huge shoulders, shook his massive head, and accepted the inevitable. Every fresh message was worse than the last, and, finally, there was an ominous silence. Challenger went down once to his young friend's lodging in Gower Street. It was a racking experience, and he did not repeat it. The muscular cramps which are characteristic of the complaint were tying the sufferer into knots, and he was biting his lips to shut down the screams which might have relieved his agony at the expense of his manhood. He seized his mentor by the hand as a drowning man seizes a plank.

'Is it really as you have said? Is there no hope beyond the six months of torture which I see lying before me? Can you with all your wisdom and knowledge see no spark of light or life in the dark shadow of eternal dissolution?'

'Face it, my boy, face it!' said Challenger. 'Better to look fact in the face than to console oneself with fancies.'

Then the lips parted and the long-pent scream burst forth. Challenger rose and rushed from the room.

But now an amazing development occurred. It began by the appearance of Miss Delicia Freeman.

One morning there came a knock at the door of the Victoria flat. The austere and taciturn Austin looking out at the level of his eyes perceived nothing at all. On glancing downwards, however, he was aware of a small lady, whose delicate face and bright bird-like eyes were turned upwards to his own.

'I want to see the Professor,' said she, diving into her handbag for a card.

'Can't see you,' said Austin.

'Oh, yes, he can,' the small lady answered serenely. There was not a newspaper office, a statesman's sanctum, or a political chancellory which had ever presented a barrier strong enough to hold her back where she believed that there was good work to be done.

'Can't see you,' repeated Austin.

'Oh, but really I must, you know,' said Miss Freeman, and made a sudden dive past the butler. With unerring instinct she made for the door of the sacred study, knocked, and forthwith entered.

The lion head looked up from behind a desk littered with papers. The lion eyes glared.

'What is the meaning of this intrusion?' the lion roared. The small lady was, however, entirely unabashed. She smiled sweetly at the glowering face.

'I am so glad to make your acquaintance,' she said. 'My name is Delicia Freeman.'

'Austin!' shouted the Professor. The butler's impassive face appeared round the angle of the door. 'What is this, Austin. How did this person get here?'

'I couldn't keep her out,' wailed Austin. 'Come, miss, we've had enough of it.'

'No, no! You must not be angry – you really must not,' said the lady sweetly. 'I was told that you were a perfectly terrible person, but really you are rather a dear.'

'Who are you? What do you want? Are you aware that I am one of the most busy men in London?'

Miss Freeman fished about in her bag once more. She was always fishing in that bag, extracting sometimes a leaflet on Armenia, sometimes a pamphlet on Greece, sometimes a note on Zenana Missions, and sometimes a psychic manifesto. On this occasion it was a folded bit of writing-paper which emerged.

'From Dr. Ross Scotton,' she said.

It was hastily folded and roughly scribbled – so roughly as to be hardly legible. Challenger bent his heavy brows over it.

Please, dear friend and guide, listen to what this lady says. I know it is against all your views. And yet I had to do it. You said yourself that I had no hope. I have tested it and it works. I know it seems wild and crazy. But any hope is better than no hope. If you were in my place you would have done the same. Will you not cast out prejudice and see for yourself? Dr. Felkin comes at three.

J. Ross Scotton.

Challenger read it twice over and sighed. The brain was clearly involved in the lesion: 'He says I am to listen to you. What is it? Cut it as short as you can.'

'It's a spirit doctor,' said the lady.

Challenger bounded in his chair.

'Good God, am I never to get away from this nonsense!' he cried. 'Can they not let this poor devil lie quiet on his deathbed but they must play their tricks upon him?'

Miss Delicia clapped her hands and her quick little eyes twinkled with joy.

'It's *not* his deathbed. He is going to get well.'

'Who said so?'

'Dr. Felkin. He never is wrong.'

Challenger snorted.

'Have you seen him lately?' she asked.

'Not for some weeks.'

'But you wouldn't recognise him. He is nearly cured.'

'Cured! Cured of diffused sclerosis in a few weeks!'

'Come and see.'

'You want me to aid and abet in some infernal quackery. The next thing, I should see my name on this rascal's testimonials. I know the breed. If I did come I should probably take him by the collar and throw him down the stair.'

The lady laughed heartily.

'He would say with Aristides: "Strike, but hear me". You will hear him first, however, I am sure. Your pupil is a real chip of yourself. He seems quite ashamed of getting well in such an unorthodox way. It was I who called Dr. Felkin in against his wish.'

'Oh, you did, did you? You took a great deal upon yourself.'

'I am prepared to take any responsibility, so long as I *know* I am right. I spoke to Dr. Atkinson. He knows a little of psychic matters. He is far less prejudiced than most of you scientific gentlemen. He took the view that when a man was dying, in any case it could matter little what you did. So Dr. Felkin came.'

'And pray how did this quack doctor proceed to treat the case?'

'That is what Dr. Ross Scotton wants you to see.' She looked at a watch which she dragged from the depths of the bag. 'In an hour he will be there. I'll tell your friend you are coming. I am sure you would not disappoint him. Oh!' She dived into the bag again. 'Here is a recent note upon the Bessarabian question. It is much more serious than people think. You will just have time to read it before you come. So good-bye, dear Professor, and *au revoir!*'

She beamed at the scowling lion and departed.

But she had succeeded in her mission, which was a way she had. There was something compelling in the absolutely unselfish enthusiasm of this small person who would, at a moment's notice, take on anyone from a Mormon Elder to an Albanian brigand, loving the culprit and mourning the sin. Challenger came under the spell, and shortly after three he stumped his way up the narrow stair and blocked the door of the humble bedroom where his favourite pupil lay stricken. Ross Scotton lay stretched upon the bed in a red dressing-gown, and his teacher saw, with a start of surprised joy, that his face had filled out and that the light of life and hope had come back into his eyes.

'Yes, I'm beating it!' he cried. 'Ever since Felkin held his first consultation with Atkinson I have felt the life-force stealing back into me. Oh, chief, it is a fearful thing to lie awake at night and feel these cursed microbes nibbling away at the very roots of your life! I could almost hear them at it. And the cramps when my body – like a badly articulated skeleton – would all get twisted into one rigid tangle! But now, except some dyspepsia and urticaria of the palms, I am free from pain. And all on account of this dear fellow here who has helped me.'

He motioned with his hand as if alluding to someone present. Challenger looked round with a glare, expecting to find some smug charlatan behind him. But no doctor was there. A frail young woman, who seemed to be a nurse, quiet, unobtrusive, and with a wealth of brown hair, was dozing in a corner. Miss Delicia, smiling demurely, stood in the window.

'I am glad you are better, my dear boy,' said Challenger. 'But do not tamper with your reason. Such a complaint has its natural systole and diastole.'

'Talk to him, Dr. Felkin. Clear his mind for him,' said the invalid.

Challenger looked up at the cornice and round at the skirting. His pupil was clearly addressing some doctor in the room and yet none was visible. Surely his aberration had not reached the point when he thought that actual floating apparitions were directing his cure.

'Indeed, it needs some clearing,' said a deep and virile voice at his elbow. He bounded round. It was the frail young woman who was talking.

'Let me introduce you to Dr. Felkin,' said Miss Delicia, with a mischievous laugh.

'What tomfoolery is this?' cried Challenger.

The young woman rose and fumbled at the side of her dress. Then she made an impatient gesture with her hand.

'Time was, my dear colleague, when a snuff-box was as much part of my equipment as my phlebotomy case. I lived before the days of Laennec, and we carried no stethoscope, but we had our little chirurgical battery, none the less. But the snuff-box was a peace-offering, and I was about to offer it to you, but, alas! it has had its day.'

Challenger stood with staring eyes and dilated nostrils while this speech was delivered. Then he turned to the bed.

'Do you mean to say that this is your doctor – that you take the advice of this person?'

The young girl drew herself up very stiffly.

'Sir, I will not bandy words with you. I perceive very clearly that you are one of those who have been so immersed in material knowledge that you have had no time to devote to the possibilities of the spirit.'

'I certainly have no time for nonsense,' said Challenger.

'My dear chief!' cried a voice from the bed. 'I beg you to bear in mind how much Dr. Felkin has already done for me. You saw how I was a month ago, and you see how I am now. You would not offend my best friend.'

'I certainly think, Professor, that you owe dear Dr. Felkin an apology,' said Miss Delicia.

'A private lunatic asylum!' snorted Challenger. Then, playing up to his part, he assumed the ponderous elephantine irony which was one of his most effective weapons in dealing with recalcitrant students.

'Perhaps, young lady – or shall I say elderly and most venerable Professor? – you will permit a mere raw earthly student, who has no more knowledge than this world can give, to sit humbly in a corner and possibly to learn a little from your methods and your teaching.' This speech was delivered with his shoulders up to his ears, his eyelids over his eyes, and his palms extended in front – an alarming statue of sarcasm. Dr. Felkin, however, was striding with heavy and impatient steps about the room, and took little notice.

'Quite so! Quite so!' she said carelessly. 'Get into the corner and stay there. Above all, stop talking, as this case calls for all my faculties.' He turned with a masterful air towards the patient. 'Well, well, you are coming along. In two months you will be in the class-room.'

'Oh, it is impossible!' cried Ross Scotton, with a half sob.

'Not so. I guarantee it. I do not make false promises.'

'I'll answer for that,' said Miss Delicia. 'I say, dear Doctor, do tell us who you were when you were alive.'

'Tut! tut! The unchanging woman. They gossiped in my time and they gossip still. No! no! We will have a look at our young friend here. Pulse! The intermittent beat has gone. That is something gained. Temperature – obviously normal. Blood pressure – still higher than I like. Digestion – much to be desired. What you moderns call a hunger-strike would not be amiss. Well, the general conditions are tolerable. Let us see the local centre of the mischief. Pull your shirt down, sir! Lie on your face. Excellent!' She passed her fingers with great force and precision down the upper part of the spine, and then dug in her knuckles with a sudden force which made the sufferer yelp. 'That is better! There is – as I have explained – a slight want of alignment in the cervical vertebræ which has, as I perceive it, the effect of lessening the foramina through which the nerve roots emerge. This has caused compression, and as these nerves are really the conductors of vital force, it has upset the whole equilibrium of the parts supplied. My eyes are the same as your clumsy X-rays, and I clearly perceive that the position is almost restored, and the fatal constriction removed. I hope, sir,' to Challenger, 'that I make the pathology of this interesting case intelligible to you.'

Challenger grunted his general hostility and disagreement.

'I will clear up any little difficulties which may linger in your mind. But, meantime, my dear lad, you are a credit to me, and I rejoice in your progress. You will present my compliments to my colleague of earth, Dr. Atkinson, and tell him that I can suggest nothing more. The medium is a little weary, poor girl, so I will not remain longer to-day.'

'But you said you would tell us who you were.'

'Indeed, there is little to say. I was a very undistinguished practitioner. I sat under the great Abernethy in my youth, and perhaps imbibed something of his methods. When I passed over in early middle age I continued my studies, and was permitted, if I could find some suitable means of expression, to do something to help humanity. You understand, of course, that it is only by serving and self-abnegation that we advance in the higher world. This is my service, and I can only thank kind Fate that I was able to find in this girl a being whose vibrations so correspond with my own that I can easily assume control of her body.'

'And where is she?' asked the patient.

'She is waiting beside me and will presently re-enter her own frame. As to you, sir,' turning to Challenger, 'you are a man of character and learning, but you are clearly embedded in that materialism which is the special curse of your age. Let me assure you that the medical profession, which is supreme upon earth for the disinterested work of its members, has yielded too much to the dogmatism of such men as you, and has unduly neglected that spiritual element in man which is far more important than your herbs and your minerals. There is a life-force, sir, and it is in the control of this life force that the medicine of the future lies. If you shut your mind to it, it can only mean that the confidence of the public will turn to those who are ready to adopt every means of cure, whether they have the approval of your authorities or not.'

Never could young Ross Scotton forget that scene. The Professor, the master, the supreme chief, he who had to be addressed with bated breath sat with half-opened mouth and staring eyes, leaning forward in his chair, while in front of him the slight young woman shaking her mop of brown hair and wagging an admonitory forefinger, spoke to him as a father speaks to a refractory child. So intense was her power that Challenger, for the instant, was constrained to accept the situation. He gasped and grunted, but no retort came to his lips. The girl turned away and sat down on a chair.

'He is going,' said Miss Delicia.

'But not yet gone,' replied the girl with a smile. 'Yes, I must go, for I have much to do. This is not my only medium of expression, and I am due in Edinburgh in a few minutes. But be of good heart, young man. I will set my assistant with two extra batteries to increase your vitality so far as your system will permit. As to you, sir,' to Challenger, 'I would implore you to beware of the egotism of brain and the self-concentration of intellect. Store what is old, but be ever receptive to what is new; and judge it not as you may wish it, but as God has designed it.'

She gave a deep sigh and sank back in her chair. There was a minute of dead silence while she lay with her head upon her breast. Then, with another sigh and a shiver, she opened a pair of very bewildered blue eyes.

'Well, has he been?' she asked in a gentle feminine voice.

'Indeed, yes!' cried the patient. 'He was great. He says I shall be in the class-room in two months.'

'Splendid! Any directions for me?'

'Just the special massage as before. But he is going to put on two new spirit batteries if I can stand it.'

'My word, he won't be long now!' Suddenly the girl's eyes lit on Challenger and she stopped in confusion

'This is Nurse Ursula,' said Miss Delicia. 'Nurse, let me present you to the famous Professor Challenger.'

Challenger was great in his manner towards women, especially if the particular woman happened to be a young and pretty girl. He advanced now as Solomon may have advanced to the Queen of Sheba, took her hand, and patted her hair with patriarchal assurance.

'My dear, you are far too young and charming for such deceit. Have done with it for ever. Be content to be a bewitching nurse and resign all claim to the higher functions of doctor. Where, may I ask, did you pick up all this jargon about cervical vertebræ and posterior foramina?'

Nurse Ursula looked helplessly round as one who finds herself suddenly in the clutches of a gorilla.

'She does not understand a word you say!' cried the man on the bed. 'Oh, chief, you must make an effort to face the real situation! I know what a readjustment it means. In my small way I have had to undergo it myself. But, believe me, you see everything through a prism instead of through plate-glass until you understand the spiritual factor.'

Challenger continued his paternal attentions, though the frightened lady had begun to shrink from him.

'Come now,' said he, 'who was the clever doctor with whom you acted as nurse – the man who taught you all these fine words? You must feel that it is hopeless to deceive me. You will be much happier, dear child, when you have made a clean breast of it all, and when we can laugh together over the lecture which you inflicted upon me.'

An unexpected interruption came to check Challenger's exploration of the young woman's conscience or motives. The invalid was sitting up, a vivid red patch against his white pillows, and he was speaking with an energy which was in itself an indication of his coming cure.

'Professor Challenger!' he cried, 'you are insulting my best friend. Under this roof at least she shall be safe from the sneers of scientific prejudice. I beg you to leave the room if you cannot address Nurse Ursula in a more respectful manner.'

Challenger glared, but the peacemaking Delicia was at work in a moment.

'You are far too hasty, dear Dr. Ross Scotton!' she cried. 'Professor Challenger has had no time to understand this. You were just as sceptical yourself at first. How can you blame him?'

'Yes, yes, that is true,' said the young doctor. 'It seemed to me to open the door to all the quackery in the Universe – indeed it does, but the fact remains.'

' "One thing I know that whereas I was blind now I see",' quoted Miss Delicia. 'Ah, Professor, you may raise your eyebrows and shrug your shoulders, but we've dropped something into your big mind this afternoon which will grow and grow until no man can see the end of it.' She dived into the bag. 'There is a little slip here "Brain *versus* Soul". I do hope, dear Professor, that you will read it and then pass it on.'

CHAPTER XV

In Which Traps are Laid for a Great Quarry

MALONE WAS BOUND IN HONOUR not to speak of love to Enid Challenger, but looks can speak, and so their communications had not broken down completely. In all other ways he adhered closely to the agreement, though the situation was a difficult one. It was the more difficult since he was a constant visitor to the Professor, and now that the irritation of the debate was over, a very welcome one. The one object of Malone's life was to get the great man's sympathetic consideration of those psychic subjects which had gained such a hold upon himself. This he pursued with assiduity, but also with great caution, for he knew that the lava was thin, and that a fiery explosion was always possible. Once or twice it came and caused Malone to drop the subject for a week or two, until the ground seemed a little more firm.

Malone developed a remarkable cunning in his approaches. One favourite device was to consult Challenger upon some scientific point – on the zoological importance of the Straits of Banda, for example, or the Insects of the Malay Archipelago, and lead him on until Challenger in due course would explain that our knowledge on the point was due to Alfred Russel Wallace. 'Oh, really! To Wallace the Spiritualist!' Malone would say in an innocent voice, on which Challenger would glare and change the topic.

Sometimes it was Lodge that Malone would use as a trap. 'I suppose you think highly of him.'

'The first brain in Europe,' said Challenger.

'He is the greatest authority on ether, is he not?'

'Undoubtedly.'

'Of course, I only know him by his psychic works.'

Challenger would shut up like a clam. Then Malone would wait a few days and remark casually: 'Have you ever met Lombroso?'

'Yes, at the Congress at Milan.'

'I have been reading a book of his.'

'Criminology, I presume?'

'No, it was called *After Death – What?*'

'I have not heard of it.'

'It discusses the psychic question.'

'Ah, a man of Lombroso's penetrating brain would make short work of the fallacies of these charlatans.'

'No, it is written to support them.'

'Well, even the greatest mind has its inexplicable weakness.' Thus, with infinite patience and cunning did Malone drop his little drops of reason in the hope of slowly wearing away the casing of prejudice, but no very visible effects could be seen. Some stronger measure must be adopted, and Malone determined upon direct demonstration. But how, when, and where? Those were the all-important points upon which he determined to consult Algernon Mailey. One spring afternoon found him back in that drawing-room where he had once rolled upon the carpet in the embrace of Silas Linden. He found the Reverend Charles Mason, and Smith, the hero of the Queen's Hall debate, in deep consultation with Mailey upon a subject which may seem much more important to our descendants than those topics which now bulk large in the eyes of the public. It was no less than whether the psychic movement in Britain was destined to take a Unitarian or a Trinitarian course. Smith had always been in favour of the former, as had the old leaders of the movement and the present organized Spiritualist Churches. On the other hand, Charles Mason was a loyal son of the Anglican Church, and was the spokesman of a host of others, including such weighty names as Lodge and Barrett among the laymen, or Wilberforce, Haweis and Chambers among the clergy, who clung fast to the old teachings while admitting the fact of spirit communication. Mailey stood between the two parties, and, like the zealous referee in a boxing-match who separated the two combatants, he always took a chance of getting a knock from each. Malone was only too glad to listen, for now that he realized that the future of the world might be bound up in this movement, every phase of it was of intense interest to him. Mason was holding forth in his earnest but good-humoured way as he entered.

'The people are not ready for a great change. It is not necessary. We have only to add our living knowledge and direct communion of the saints to the splendid liturgy and traditions of the Church, and you will have a driving force which will revitalize all religion. You can't pull a thing up from the roots like that. Even the early

Christians found that they could not, and so they made all sorts of concessions to the religions around them.'

'Which was exactly what ruined them,' said Smith 'That was the real end of the Church in its original strength and purity.'

'It lasted, anyhow.'

'But it was never the same from the time that villain Constantine laid his hands on it.'

'Oh, come!' said Mailey. 'You must not write down the first Christian emperor as a villain.'

But Smith was a forthright, uncompromising, bull-doggy antagonist. 'What other name will you give to a man who murdered half his own family?'

'Well, his personal character is not the question. We were talking of the organization of the Christian Church.'

'You don't mind my frankness, Mr. Mason?'

Mason smiled his jolly smile. 'So long as you grant me the existence of the New Testament I don't care what you do. If you were to prove that our Lord was a myth, as that German Drews tried to do, it would not in the least affect me so long as I could point to that body of sublime teaching. It must have come from somewhere, and I adopt it and say, "That is my creed".'

'Oh, well, there is not so much between us on that point,' said Smith. 'If there is any better teaching I have not seen it. It is good enough to go on with, anyhow. But we want to cut out the frills and superfluities. Where did they all come from? They were compromises with many religions, so that our friend C. could get uniformity in his world-wide Empire. He made a patchwork quilt of it. He took an Egyptian ritual – vestments, mitre, crozier, tonsure, marriage ring – all Egyptian. The Easter ceremonies are pagan and refer to the vernal equinox. Confirmation is mithraism. So is baptism, only it was blood instead of water. As to the sacrificial meal . . .'

Mason put his fingers in his ears. 'This is some old lecture of yours,' he laughed. 'Hire a hall, but don't obtrude it in a private house. But, seriously, Smith, all this is beside the question. If it is true it will not affect my position at all, which is that we have a great body of doctrine which is working well, and which is regarded with veneration by many people, your humble servant included, and that it would be wrong and foolish to scrap it. Surely you must agree.'

'No, I don't,' Smith answered, setting his obstinate jaw. 'You are thinking too much of the feelings of your blessed church-goers. But you have also to think of the nine people out of ten who never enter into a church. They have been choked off by what they, including your humble servant, consider to be unreasonable and fantastic. How will you gain them while you continue to offer them the same things, even though you mix spirit-teaching with it? If, however, you approach these agnostic or atheistic ones, and say to them: "I quite agree that all this is unreal and is tainted by a long history of violence and reaction. But here we have something pure and new. Come and examine it!" In that way I could coax them back into a belief in God and in all the fundamentals of religion without their having to do violence to their reason by accepting your theology.'

Mailey had been tugging at his tawny beard while he listened to these conflicting counsels. Knowing the two men he was aware that there was not really much between them, when one got past mere words, for Smith revered the Christ as a God-like man, and Mason as a man-like God, and the upshot was much the same. At the same time he knew that their more extreme followers on either side were in very truth widely separated, so that compromise became impossible.

'What I can't understand,' said Malone, 'is why you don't ask your spirit friends these questions and abide by their decisions.'

'It is not so simple as you think,' Mailey answered. 'We all carry on our earthly prejudices after death, and we all find ourselves in an atmosphere which more or less represents them. Thus each would echo his old views at first. Then in time the spirit broadens out and it ends in a universal creed which includes only the brotherhood of man and the fatherhood of God. But that takes time. I have heard most furious bigots talking through the veil.'

'So have I, for that matter,' said Malone, 'and in this very room. But what about the materialists? They at least cannot remain unchanged.'

'I believe their mind influences their state and that they lie inert for ages sometimes, under their own obsession that nothing can occur. Then at last they wake, realize their own loss of time, and finally, in many cases, get to the head of the procession, since they are often men of fine character and influenced by lofty motives however mistaken in their views.'

'Yes, they are often among the salt of the earth,' said the clergyman heartily.

'And they offer the very best recruits for our movement,' said Smith. 'There comes such a reaction when they find by the evidence of their own senses that there really is intelligent force outside themselves, that it gives them an enthusiasm that makes them ideal missionaries. You fellows who have a religion and then add to it cannot even imagine what it means to the man who has a complete vacuum and suddenly finds something to fill it. When I meet some poor earnest chap feeling out into the darkness I just yearn to put it into his hand.'

At this stage, tea and Mrs. Mailey appeared together. But the conversation did not flag. It is one of the characteristics of those who explore psychic possibilities that the subject is so many-sided and the interest so intense that when they meet together they plunge into the most fascinating exchange of views and experiences. It was with some difficulty that Malone got the conversation round to that which had been the particular object of his visit. He could have found no group of men more fit to advise him, and all were equally keen that so great a man as Challenger should have the best available.

Where should it be? On that they were unanimous. The large seance room of the Psychic College was the most select, the most comfortable, in every way the best appointed in London. When should it be? The sooner the better. Every spiritualist and every medium would surely put any engagement aside in order to help on such an occasion.

Who should the medium be? Ah! There was the rub. Of course, the Bolsover circle would be ideal. It was private and unpaid, but Bolsover was a man of quick temper and Challenger was sure to be very insulting and annoying. The meeting might end in riot and fiasco. Such a chance should not be taken. Was it worth while to take him over to Paris? But who would take the responsibility of letting loose such a bull in Dr. Maupuis' china-shop?

'He would probably seize pithecanthropus by the throat and risk every life in the room,' said Mailey. 'No, no, it would never do.'

'There is no doubt that Banderby is the strongest physical medium in England,' said Smith. 'But we all know what his personal character is. You could not rely upon him.'

'Why not?' asked Malone. 'What's the matter with him?'

Smith raised his hand to his lips.

'He has gone the way that many a medium has gone before him.'

'But surely,' said Malone, 'that is a strong argument against our cause. How can a thing be good if it leads to such a result?'

'Do you consider poetry to be good?'

'Why, of course I do!'

'Yet Poe was a drunkard, and Coleridge an addict, and Byron a rake, and Verlaine a degenerate. You have to separate the man from the thing. The genius has to pay a ransom for his genius in the instability of his temperament. A great medium is even more sensitive than a genius. Many are beautiful in their lives. Some are not. The excuse for them is great. They practise a most exhausting profession and stimulants are needed. Then they lose control. But their physical mediumship carries on all the same.'

'Which reminds me of a story about Banderby,' said Mailey. 'Perhaps you have not seen him, Malone. He is a funny figure at any time – a little, round, bouncing man who has not seen his own toes for years. When drunk he is funnier still. A few weeks ago I got an urgent message that he was in the bar of a certain hotel, and too far gone to get home unassisted. A friend and I set forth to rescue him. We got him home after some unsavoury adventures, and what would the man do but insist upon holding a seance. We tried to restrain him, but the trumpet was on a side-table, and he suddenly switched off the light. In an instant the phenomena began. Never were they more powerful. But they were interrupted by Princeps, his control, who seized the trumpet and began belabouring him with it. "You rascal! You drunken rascal! How dare you!" The trumpet was all dinted with the blows. Banderby ran bellowing out of the room, and we took our departure.'

'Well, it wasn't the medium that time, at any rate,' said Mason. 'But about Professor Challenger – it would never do to risk the chance.'

'What about Tom Linden?' asked Mrs. Mailey.

Mailey shook his head.

'Tom has never been quite the same since his imprisonment. These fools not only persecute our precious mediums, but they ruin their powers. It is like putting a razor into a damp place and then expecting it to have a fine edge.'

'What! Has he lost his powers?'

'Well, I would not go so far as that. But they are not so good as they were. He sees a disguised policeman in every sitter and it distracts him. Still, he is dependable so far as he goes. Yes, on the whole we had better have Tom.'

'And the sitters?'

'I expect Professor Challenger may wish to bring a friend or two of his own.'

'They will form a horrible block of vibrations. We must have some of our own sympathetic people to counteract it. There is Delicia Freeman. She would come. I would come myself. You would come, Mason?'

'Of course I would.'

'And you, Smith?'

'No, no! I have my paper to look after, three services, two burials, one marriage, and five meetings all next week.'

'Well, we can easily get one or two more. Eight is Linden's favourite number. So now, Malone, you have only to get the great man's consent and the date.'

'And the spirit of confirmation,' said Mason, seriously. 'We must take our partners into consultation.'

'Of course we must, padre. That is the right note to strike. Well, that's settled, Malone, and we can only await the event.'

As it chanced, a very different event was awaiting Malone that evening, and he came upon one of those chasms which unexpectedly open across the path of life. When, in his ordinary routine, he reached the office of the *Gazette*, he was informed by the commissionaire that Mr. Beaumont desired to see him. Malone's immediate superior was the old Scotch sub-editor, Mr. McArdle, and it was rare indeed for the supreme editor to cast a glimpse down from that peak whence he surveyed the kingdoms of the world, or to show any cognizance of his humble fellow-workers upon the slopes beneath him. The great man, clean-shaven, prosperous and capable, sat in his palatial sanctum amid a rich assortment of old oak furniture and sealing-wax-red leather. He continued his letter when Malone entered, and only raised his shrewd, grey eyes after some minutes' interval.

'Ah, Mr. Malone, good evening! I have wanted to see you for some little time. Won't you sit down? It is in reference to these articles on psychic matters which you have been writing. You opened them in a tone of healthy scepticism, tempered by humour, which was very acceptable both to me and to our public. I regret, however, to observe that your view changed as you proceeded, and that you have now assumed a position in which you really seem to condone some of these practices. That, I need not say, is not the policy of the *Gazette*, and we should have discontinued the articles had it not been that we had announced a series by an impartial investigator. We have to continue but the tone must change.'

'What do you wish me to do, sir?'

'You must get the funny side of it again. That is what our public loves. Poke fun at it all. Call up the maiden aunt and make her talk in an amusing fashion. You grasp my meaning?'

'I am afraid, sir, it has ceased to seem funny in my eyes. On the contrary, I take it more and more seriously.'

Beaumont shook his solemn head.

'So, unfortunately, do our subscribers.' He had a small pile of letters upon the desk beside him and he took one up.

'Look at this: "I had always regarded your paper as a God-fearing publication, and I would remind you that such practices as your correspondent seems to condone are expressly forbidden both in Leviticus and Deuteronomy. I should share your sin if I continued to be a subscriber".'

'Bigoted ass!' muttered Malone.

'So he may be, but the penny of a bigoted ass is as good as any other penny. Here is another letter: "Surely in this age of freethought and enlightenment you are not helping a movement which tries to lead us back to the exploded idea of angelic and diabolic intelligences outside ourselves. If so, I must ask you to cancel my subscription".'

'It would be amusing, sir, to shut these various objectors up in a room and let them settle it among themselves.'

'That may be, Mr. Malone, but what I have to consider is the circulation of the *Gazette*.'

'Don't you think, sir, that possibly you underrate the intelligence of the public, and that behind these extremists of various sorts there is a vast body of people who have been impressed by the utterances of so many great and honourable witnesses? Is it not our duty to keep these people abreast of the real facts without making fun of them?'

Mr. Beaumont shrugged his shoulders.

'The Spiritualists must fight their own battle. This is not a propaganda newspaper, and we make no pretence to lead the public on religious beliefs.'

'No, no, I only meant as to the actual facts. Look how systematically they are kept in the dark. When, for example, did one ever read an intelligent article upon ectoplasm in any London paper? Who would imagine that this all-important substance has been examined and described and endorsed by men of science with innumerable photographs to prove their words?'

'Well, well,' said Beaumont, impatiently. 'I am afraid I am too busy to argue the question. The point of this interview is that I have had a letter from Mr. Cornelius to say that we must at once take another line.'

Mr. Cornelius was the owner of the *Gazette*, having become so, not from any personal merit, but because his father left him some millions, part of which he expended upon this purchase. He seldom was seen in the office himself, but occasionally a paragraph in the paper recorded that his yacht had touched at Mentone and that he had been seen at the Monte Carlo tables, or that he was expected in Leicestershire for the season. He was a man of no force of brain or character, though occasionally he swayed public affairs by a manifesto printed in larger type upon his own front page. Without being dissolute, he was a free liver, living in a constant luxury which placed him always on the edge of vice and occasionally over the border. Malone's hot blood flushed to his head as he thought of this trifler, this insect, coming between mankind and a message of instruction and consolation descending from above. And yet those clumsy, childish fingers could actually turn the tap and cut off the divine stream, however much it might break through in other quarters.

'So that is final, Mr. Malone,' said Beaumont, with the manner of one who ends an argument.

'Quite final!' said Malone. 'So final that it marks the end of my connection with your paper. I have a six months' contract. When it ends, I go!'

'Please yourself, Mr. Malone.' Mr. Beaumont went on with his writing.

Malone, with the flush of battle still upon him, went into McArdle's room and told him what had happened. The old Scotch sub-editor was very perturbed.

'Eh, man, it's that Irish blood of yours. A drop o' Scotch is a good thing, either in your veins or at the bottom o' a glass. Go back, man, and say you have reconseedered!'

'Not I! The idea of this man Cornelius, with his pot-belly and red face, and – well, you know all about his private life – the idea of such a man dictating what folk are to believe, and asking me to make fun of the holiest thing on this earth!'

'Man, you'll be ruined!'

'Well, better men than I have been ruined over this cause. But I'll get another job.'

'Not if Cornelius can stop you. If you get the name of an insubordinate dog there is no place for you in Fleet Street.'

'It's a damned shame!' cried Malone. 'The way this thing has been treated is a disgrace to journalism. It's not Britain alone. America is worse. We seem to have the lowest, most soulless folk that ever lived on the Press – good-hearted fellows too, but material to a man. And these are the leaders of the people! It's awful!'

McArdle put a fatherly hand upon the young man's shoulder.

'Weel, weel, lad, we take the world as we find it. We didn't make it and we're no reesponsible. Give it time! Give it time! We're a' in such a hurry. Gang hame, now, think it over, remember your career, that young leddy of yours, and then come back and eat the old pie that all of us have to eat if we are to keep our places in the world.'

CHAPTER XVI

In Which Challenger Has the Experience of His Lifetime

SO NOW THE NETS WERE SET and the pit was dug and the hunters were all ready for the great quarry, but the question was whether the creature would allow himself to be driven in the right direction. Had Challenger been told that the meeting was really held in the hope of putting convincing evidence before him as to the truth of spirit inter-course with the aim of his eventual conversion, it would have roused mingled anger and derision in his breast. But the clever Malone, aided and abetted by Enid, still put forward the idea that his presence would be a protection against fraud, and that he would be able to point out to them how and why they had been deceived. With this thought in his mind, Challenger gave a contemptuous and conde-scending consent to the proposal that he should grace with his pres-ence a proceeding which was, in his opinion, more fitted to the stone cabin of a neolithic savage than to the serious attention of one who represented the accumulated culture and wisdom of the human race.

Enid accompanied her father, and he also brought with him a curious companion who was strange both to Malone and to the rest of the company. This was a large, raw-boned Scottish youth, with a freckled face, a huge figure, and a taciturnity which nothing could penetrate. No question could discover where his interests in psychic research might lie, and the only positive thing obtained from him was that his name was Nicholl. Malone and Mailey went together to the rendezvous at Holland Park, where they found awaiting them Delicia Freeman, the Rev. Charles Mason, Mr. and Mrs. Ogilvy of the College, Mr. Bolsover of Hammersmith, and Lord Roxton, who had become assiduous in his psychic studies, and was rapidly pro-gressing in knowledge. There were nine in all, a mixed, inharmo-nious assembly, from which no experienced investigator could expect great results. On entering the seance room Linden was found seated in the armchair, his wife beside him, and was intro-duced collectively to the company, most of whom were already his friends. Challenger took up the matter at once with the air of a man who will stand no nonsense.

'Is this the medium?' he asked, eyeing Linden with much disfavour.

'Yes.'

'Has he been searched?'

'Not yet.'

'Who will search him?'

'Two men of the company have been selected.'

Challenger sniffed his suspicions.

'Which men?' he asked.

'It is suggested that you and your friend, Mr. Nicholl, shall do so. There is a bedroom next door.'

Poor Linden was marched off between them in a manner which reminded him unpleasantly of his prison experiences. He had been nervous before, but this ordeal and the overpowering presence of Challenger made him still more. He shook his head mournfully at Mailey when he reappeared.

'I doubt we will get nothing to-day. Maybe it would be wise to postpone the sitting,' said he.

Mailey came round and patted him on the shoulder, while Mrs. Linden took his hand.

'It's all right, Tom,' said Mailey. 'Remember that you have a bodyguard of friends round you who won't see you ill-used.' Then Mailey spoke to Challenger in a sterner way than was his wont. 'I beg you to remember, sir, that a medium is as delicate an instrument as any to be found in your laboratories. Do not abuse it. I presume that you found nothing compromising upon his person?'

'No, sir, I did not. And as a result he assures us that we will get nothing to-day.'

'He says so because your manner has disturbed him. You must treat him more gently.'

Challenger's expression did not promise any amendment. His eyes fell upon Mrs. Linden.

'I understand that this person is the medium's wife. She should also be searched.'

'That is a matter of course,' said the Scotsman Ogilvy. 'My wife and your daughter will take her out. But I beg you, Professor Challenger, to be as harmonious as you can, and to remember that we are all as interested in the results as you are, so that the whole company will suffer if you should disturb the conditions.'

Mr. Bolsover, the grocer, rose with as much dignity as if he were presiding at his favourite temple.

'I move,' said he, 'that Professor Challenger be searched.'

Challenger's beard bristled with anger.

'Search me! What do you mean, sir?'

Bolsover was not to be intimidated.

'You are here not as our friend but as our enemy. If you was to prove fraud it would be a personal triumph for you – see? Therefore I, for one, says as you should be searched.'

'Do you mean to insinuate, sir, that I am capable of cheating?' trumpeted Challenger.

'Well, Professor, we are all accused of it in turn,' said Mailey smiling. 'We all feel as indignant as you are at first, but after a time you get used to it. I've been called a liar, a lunatic – goodness knows what. What does it matter?'

'It is a monstrous proposition,' said Challenger, glaring all round him.

'Well, sir,' said Ogilvy, who was a particularly pertinacious Scot. 'Of course, it is open to you to walk out of the room and leave us. But if you sit, you must sit under what we consider to be scientific conditions. It is not scientific that a man who is known to be bitterly hostile to the movement should sit with us in the dark with no check as to what he may have in his pockets.'

'Come, come!' cried Malone. 'Surely we can trust to the honour of Professor Challenger.'

'That's all very well,' said Bolsover. 'I did not observe that Professor Challenger trusted so very much to the honour of Mr. and Mrs. Linden.'

'We have cause to be careful,' said Ogilvy. 'I can assure you that there are frauds practised on mediums just as there are frauds practised by mediums. I could give you plenty of examples. No, sir, you will have to be searched.'

'It won't take a minute,' said Lord Roxton. 'What I mean, young Malone here and I could give you a once over in no time.'

'Quite so, come on!' said Malone.

And so Challenger, like a red-eyed bull with dilating nostrils, was led from the room. A few minutes later, all preliminaries being completed, they were seated in the circle and the seance had begun.

But already the conditions had been destroyed. Those meticulous researchers who insist upon tying up a medium until the poor creature resembles a fowl trussed for roasting, or who glare their suspicions at him before the lights are lowered, do not realize that they are like people who add moisture to gunpowder and then expect to explode it. They ruin their own results, and then when those results do not occur imagine that their own astuteness, rather than their own lack of understanding, has been the cause.

Hence it is that at humble gatherings all over the land, in an atmosphere of sympathy and of reverence, there are such happenings as the cold man of 'Science' is never privileged to see.

All the sitters felt churned up by the preliminary altercation, but how much more did it mean to the sensitive centre of it all! To him the room was filled with conflicting rushes and eddies of psychic power, whirling this way or that, and as difficult for him to navigate as the rapids below Niagara. He groaned in his despair. Everything was mixed and confused. He was beginning as usual with his clairvoyance, but names buzzed in his etheric ears without sequence or order. The word 'John' seemed to predominate, so he said. Did 'John' mean anything to anyone? A cavernous laugh from Challenger was the only reply. Then he had the surname of Chapman. Yes, Mailey had lost a friend named Chapman. But, it was years ago and there seemed no reason for his presence, nor could he furnish his Christian name. 'Budworth' – no; no one would own to a friend named Budworth. Definite messages came across, but they seemed to have no reference to the present company. Everything was going amiss, and Malone's spirits sank to zero. Challenger sniffed so loudly that Ogilvy remonstrated.

'You make matters worse, sir, when you show your feelings,' said he. 'I can assure you that in ten years of constant experience I have never known the medium so far out, and I attribute it entirely to your own conduct.'

'Quite so,' said Challenger with satisfaction.

'I am afraid it is no use, Tom,' said Mrs. Linden. 'How are you feeling now, dear? Would you wish to stop?'

But Linden under all his gentle exterior, was a fighter. He had in another form those same qualities which had brought his brother within an ace of the Lonsdale Belt.

'No, I think, maybe, it is only the mental part that is confused. If I am in trance I'll get past that. The physicals may be better. Anyhow I'll try.'

The lights were turned lower until they were a mere crimson glimmer. The curtain of the cabinet was drawn. Outside it on the one side, dimly outlined to his audience, Tom Linden, breathing stertorously in his trance, lay back in a wooden armchair. His wife kept watch and ward at the other side of the cabinet.

But nothing happened.

Quarter of an hour passed. Then another quarter of an hour. The company was patient, but Challenger had begun to fidget in his seat. Everything seemed to have gone cold and dead. Not only was nothing happening, but somehow all expectation of anything happening seemed to have passed away.

'It's no use!' cried Mailey at last.

'I fear not,' said Malone.

The medium stirred and groaned; he was waking up. Challenger gave an ostentatious yawn.

'Is not this a waste of time?' he asked.

Mrs. Linden was passing her hand over the medium's head and brow. His eyes had opened.

'Any results?' he asked.

'It's no use, Tom. We shall have to postpone.'

'I think so, too,' said Mailey.

'It is a great strain upon him under these adverse conditions,' remarked Ogilvy, looking angrily at Challenger.

'I should think so,' said the latter with a complacent smile.

But Linden was not to be beaten.

'The conditions are bad,' said he. 'The vibrations are all wrong. But I'll try inside the cabinet. It concentrates the force.'

'Well, it's the last chance,' said Mailey. 'We may as well try it.'

The armchair was lifted inside the cloth tent and the medium followed, drawing the curtain behind him

'It condenses the ectoplasmic emanations,' Ogilvy explained.

'No doubt,' said Challenger. 'At the same time in the interests of truth, I must point out that the disappearance of the medium is most regrettable.'

'For goodness sake, don't start wrangling again,' cried Mailey with impatience. 'Let us get some results, and then it will be time enough to discuss their value.'

Again there was a weary wait. Then came some hollow groanings from inside the cabinet. The Spiritualists sat up expectantly.

'That's ectoplasm,' said Ogilvy. 'It always causes pain on emission.'

The words were hardly out of his mouth when the curtains were torn open with sudden violence and a rattling of all the rings. In the dark aperture there was outlined a vague white figure. It advanced slowly and with hesitation into the centre of the room. In the red-tinted gloom all definite outline was lost, and it appeared simply as a moving white patch in the darkness. With the deliberation which suggested fear it came, step by step, until it was opposite the professor.

'Now!' he bellowed in his stentorian voice.

There was a shout, a scream, a crash. 'I've got him!' roared some-one. 'Turn up the lights!' yelled another. 'Be careful! You may kill the medium!' cried a third. The circle was broken. Challenger rushed to the switch and put on all the lights. The place was so flooded with radiance that it was some seconds before the bewildered and half-blinded spectators could see the details.

When they had recovered their sight and their balance, the spectacle was a deplorable one for the majority of the company. Tom Linden, looking white, dazed, and ill, was seated upon the ground. Over him stood the huge young Scotsman who had borne him to earth; while Mrs. Linden, kneeling beside her husband, was glaring up at his assailant. There was a silence as the company surveyed the scene. It was broken by Professor Challenger.

'Well, gentlemen, I presume that there is no more to be said. Your medium has been exposed as he deserved to be. You can see now the nature of your ghosts. I must thank Mr. Nicholl, who, I may remark, is the famous football player of that name, for the prompt way in which he has carried out his instructions.'

'I collared him low,' said the tall youth. 'He was easy.'

'You did it very effectively. You have done public service by helping to expose a heartless cheat. I need not say that a prosecution will follow.'

But Mailey now intervened and with such authority that Challenger was forced to listen.

'Your mistake is not unnatural, sir, though the course which you adopted in your ignorance is one which might well have been fatal to the medium.'

'My ignorance indeed! If you speak like that I warn you that I will look upon you not as dupes, but as accomplices.'

'One moment, Professor Challenger. I would ask you one direct question, and I ask for an equally direct reply. Was not the figure which we all saw before this painful episode a white figure?'

'Yes, it was.'

'You see now that the medium is entirely dressed in black. Where is the white garment?'

'It is immaterial to me where it is. No doubt his wife and himself are prepared for all eventualities. They have their own means of secreting the sheet, or whatever it may have been. These details can be explained in the police court.'

'Examine now. Search the room for anything white.'

'I know nothing of the room. I can only use my common sense.

The man is exposed masquerading as a spirit. Into what corner or crevice he has thrust his disguise is a matter of small importance.'

'On the contrary, it is a vital matter. What you have seen has not been an imposture, but has been a very real phenomenon.'

Challenger laughed.

'Yes, sir, a very real phenomenon. You have seen a transfiguration which is the half-way state of materialization. You will kindly realize that spirit guides, who conduct such affairs, care nothing for your doubts and suspicions. They set themselves to get certain results, and if they are prevented by the infirmities of the circle from getting them one way they get them in another, without consulting your prejudice or convenience. In this case being unable, owing to the evil conditions which you have yourself created, to build up an ectoplasmic form they wrapped the unconscious medium in an ectoplasmic covering, and sent him forth from the cabinet. He is as innocent of imposture as you are.'

'I swear to God,' said Linden, 'that from the time I entered the cabinet until I found myself upon the floor I knew nothing.' He had staggered to his feet and was shaking all over in his agitation, so that he could not hold the glass of water which his wife had brought him.

Challenger shrugged his shoulders.

'Your excuses,' he said, 'only open up fresh abysses of credulity. My own duty is obvious, and it will be done to the uttermost. Whatever you have to say will, no doubt, receive such consideration as it deserves from the magistrate.' Then Professor Challenger turned to go as one who has triumphantly accomplished that for which he came. 'Come, Enid!' said he.

And now occurred a development so sudden, so unexpected, so dramatic, that no one present will ever cease to have it in vivid memory.

No answer was returned to Challenger's call.

Everyone else had risen to their feet. Only Enid remained in her chair. She sat with her head on one shoulder, her eyes closed, her hair partly loosened – a model for a sculptor.

'She is asleep,' said Challenger. 'Wake up, Enid. I am going.'

There was no response from the girl. Mailey was bending over her.

'Hush! Don't disturb her! She is in trance.'

Challenger rushed forward. 'What have you done? Your infernal hankey-pankey has frightened her. She has fainted.'

Mailey had raised her eyelid.

'No, no, her eyes are turned up. She is in trance. Your daughter, sir, is a powerful medium.'

'A medium! You are raving. Wake up girl! Wake up!'

'For God's sake leave her! You may regret it all your life if you don't. It is not safe to break abruptly into the mediumistic trance.'

Challenger stood in bewilderment. For once his presence of mind had deserted him. Was it possible that his child stood on the edge of some mysterious precipice and that he might push her over?

'What shall I do?' he asked helplessly.

'Have no fear. All will be well. Sit down! Sit down, all of you. Ah! she is about to speak.'

The girl had stirred. She had sat straight in her chair. Her lips trembled. One hand was outstretched:

'For him!' she cried, pointing to Challenger. 'He must not hurt my Medi. It is a message. For him.'

There was breathless silence among the persons who had gathered round the girl.

'Who speaks?' asked Mailey.

'Victor speaks. Victor. He shall not hurt my Medi. I have a message. For him!'

'Yes, yes. What is the message?'

'His wife is here.'

'Yes!'

'She says that she has been once before. That she came through this girl. It was after she was cremated. She knock and he hear her knocking, but not understand.'

'Does this mean anything to you, Professor Challenger?'

His great eyebrows were bunched over his suspicious, questioning eyes, and he glared like a beast at bay from one to the other of the faces round him. There was a trick – a vile trick. They had suborned his own daughter. It was damnable. He would expose them, every one. No, he had no questions to ask. He could see through it all. She had been won over. He could not have believed it of her, and yet it must be so. She was doing it for Malone's sake. A woman would do anything for a man she loved. Yes, it was damnable. Far from being softened he was more vindictive than ever. His furious face, his broken words, expressed his convictions.

Again the girl's arm shot out, pointing in front of her.

'Another message!'

'To whom?'

'To him. The man who wanted to hurt my Medi. He must not hurt my Medi. A man here – two men – wish to give him a message.'

'Yes, Victor, let us have it.'

'First man's name is . . .' The girl's head slanted and her ear was upturned, as if listening. 'Yes, yes, I have it! It is Al-Al-Aldridge.'

'Does that mean anything to you?'

Challenger staggered. A look of absolute wonder had come upon his face.

'What is the second man?' he asked.

'Ware. Yes that is it. Ware.'

Challenger sat down suddenly. He passed his hand over his brow. He was deadly pale. His face was clammy with sweat.

'Do you know them?'

'I knew two men of those names.'

'They have message for you,' said the girl.

Challenger seemed to brace himself for a blow.

'Well, what is it?'

'Too private. Not speak, all these people here.'

'We shall wait outside,' said Mailey. 'Come, friends, let the Professor have his message.'

They moved towards the door leaving the man seated in front of his daughter. An unwonted nervousness seemed suddenly to seize him. 'Malone, stay with me!'

The door closed and the three were left together.

'What is the message?'

'It is about a powder.'

'Yes, yes.'

'A grey powder?'

'Yes.'

'The message that men want me to say is: "You did not kill us".'

'Ask them then – ask them – how did they die?' His voice was broken and his great frame was quivering with his emotion.

'They die disease.'

'What disease?'

'New – new . . . What that? . . . Pneumonia.'

Challenger sank back in his chair with an immense sigh of relief. 'My God!' he cried, wiping his brow. Then:

'Call in the others, Malone.'

They had waited on the landing and now streamed into the room. Challenger had risen to meet them. His first words were to Tom Linden. He spoke like a shaken man whose pride for the instant was broken.

'As to you, sir, I do not presume to judge you. A thing has occurred to me which is so strange, and also so certain, since my own trained senses have attested it, that I am not prepared to deny any explanation which has been offered of your previous conduct. I beg to withdraw any injurious expressions I may have used.'

Tom Linden was a true Christian in his character. His forgiveness was instant and sincere.

'I cannot doubt that my daughter has some strange power which bears out much which you, Mr. Mailey, have told me. I was justified in my scientific scepticism, but you have to-day offered me some incontrovertible evidence.'

'We all go through the same experience, Professor. We doubt, and then in turn we are doubted.'

'I can hardly conceive that my word will be doubted upon such a point,' said Challenger, with dignity. 'I can truly say that I have had information to-night which no living person upon this earth was in a position to give. So much is beyond all question.'

'The young lady is better,' said Mrs. Linden.

Enid was sitting up and staring round her with bewildered eyes.

'What has happened, Father? I seem to have been asleep.'

'All right, dear. We will talk of that later. Come home with me now. I have much to think over. Perhaps you will come back with us, Malone. I feel that I owe you some explanation.'

When Professor Challenger reached his flat, he gave Austin orders that he was on no account to be disturbed, and he led the way into his library, where he sat in his big armchair with Malone upon his left and his daughter upon his right. He had stretched out his great paw and enclosed Enid's small hand.

'My dear,' he said, after a long silence, 'I cannot doubt that you are possessed of a strange power, for it has been shown to me to-night with a fullness and a clearness which is final. Since you have it I cannot deny that others may have it also, and the general idea of mediumship has entered within my conceptions of what is possible. I will not discuss the question, for my thoughts are still confused upon the subject, and I will need to thrash the thing out with you, young Malone, and with your friends, before I can get a more definite idea. I will only say that my mind has received a shock, and that a new avenue of knowledge seems to have opened up before me.'

'We shall be proud indeed,' said Malone, 'if we can help you.'

Challenger gave a wry smile.

'Yes, I have no doubt that a headline in your paper, "Conversion of Professor Challenger" would be a triumph. I warn you that I have not got so far.'

'We certainly would do nothing premature and your opinions may remain entirely private.'

'I have never lacked the moral courage to proclaim my opinions when they are formed, but the time has not yet come. However, I have received two messages to-night, and I can only ascribe to them an extra-corporeal origin. I take it for granted, Enid, that you were indeed insensible.'

'I assure you, Father, that I knew nothing.'

'Quite so. You have always been incapable of deceit. First there came a message from your mother. She assured me that she had indeed produced those sounds which I heard and of which I have told you. It is clear now that you were the medium and that you were not in sleep but in trance. It is incredible, inconceivable, grotesquely wonderful – but it would seem to be true.'

'Crookes used almost those very words,' said Malone. He wrote that it was all "perfectly impossible and absolutely true".'

'I owe him an apology. Perhaps I owe a good many people an apology.'

'None will ever be asked for,' said Malone. 'These people are not made that way.'

'It is the second case which I would explain.' The Professor fidgeted uneasily in his chair. 'It is a matter of great privacy – one to which I have never alluded, and which no one on earth could have known. Since you heard so much you may as well hear all.

'It happened when I was a young physician, and it is not too much to say that it cast a cloud over my life – a cloud which has only been raised to-night. Others may try to explain what has occurred by telepathy, by subconscious mind action, by what they will, but I cannot doubt – it is impossible to doubt – that a message has come to me from the dead.

'There was a new drug under discussion at that time. It is useless to enter into details which you would be incapable of appreciating. Suffice it that it was of the datura family which supplies deadly poisons as well as powerful medicines. I had received one of the earliest specimens, and I desired my name to be associated with the first exploration of its properties. I gave it to two men, Ware and Aldridge. I gave it in what I thought was a safe dose. They were patients, you understand, in my ward in a public hospital. Both were found dead in the morning.

'I had given it secretly. None knew of it. There was no scandal for they were both very ill, and their death seemed natural. But in my own heart I had fears. I believed that I had killed them. It has always been a dark background to my life. You heard yourselves to-night that it was from the disease, and not from the drug that they died.'

'Poor Dad!' whispered Enid patting the great hirsute hand. 'Poor Dad! What you must have suffered!'

Challenger was too proud a man to stand pity, even from his own daughter. He pulled away his hand.

'I worked for science,' he said. 'Science must take risks. I do not know that I am to blame. And yet – and yet – my heart is very light to-night.'

CHAPTER XVII

Where the Mists Clear Away

MALONE HAD LOST HIS BILLET and had found his way in Fleet Street blocked by the rumour of his independence. His place upon the staff had been taken by a young and drunken Jew, who had at once won his spurs by a series of highly humorous articles upon psychic matters, peppered with assurances that he approached the subject with a perfectly open and impartial mind. His final device of offering five thousand pounds if the spirits of the dead would place the three first horses in the coming Derby, and his demonstration that ectoplasm was in truth the froth of bottle porter artfully concealed by the medium, are newspaper stunts, which are within the recollection of the reader.

But the path which closed on one side had opened on the other. Challenger, lost in his daring dreams and ingenious experiments, had long needed an active, clear-headed man to manage his business interests, and to control his world-wide patents. There were many devices, the fruits of his life's work, which brought in income, but had to be carefully watched and guarded. His automatic alarm for ships in shallow waters, his device for deflecting a torpedo, his new and economical method of separating nitrogen from the air, his radical improvements in wireless transmission and his novel treatment of pitch blend, were all money-makers. Enraged by the attitude of Cornelius, the Professor placed the management of all these in the hands of his prospective son-in-law, who diligently guarded his interests.

Challenger had himself altered. His colleagues, and those about him, observed the change without clearly perceiving the cause. He was a gentler, humbler, and more spiritual man. Deep in his soul was the conviction that he, the champion of scientific method and of truth, had, in fact, for many years been unscientific in his methods, and a formidable obstruction to the advance of the human soul through the jungle of the unknown. It was this self-condemnation which had wrought the change in his character. Also, with characteristic energy, he had plunged into the wonderful literature of the subject, and as, without the prejudice which had formerly darkened his brain, he read the illuminating testimony of Hare, de Morgan, Crookes, Lombroso, Barrett, Lodge, and so many other great men, he marvelled that he could ever for one instant have imagined that such a consensus of opinion could be founded upon error. His violent and whole-hearted nature made him take up the psychic cause with the same vehemence, and even occasionally the same intolerance with which he had once denounced it, and the old lion bared his teeth and roared back at those who had once been his associates.

His remarkable article in the *Spectator* began, 'The obtuse incredulity and stubborn unreason of the prelates who refused to look through the telescope of Galileo and to observe the moons of Jupiter, has been far transcended in our own days by those noisy controversialists, who rashly express extreme opinions upon those psychic matters which they have never had either the time, or the inclination to examine'; while in a final sentence he expressed his conviction that his opponents 'did not in truth represent the thought of the twentieth century, but might rather be regarded as mental fossils dug from some early Pliocene horizon'. Critics raised their hands in horror, as is their wont, against the robust language of the article, though violence of attack has for so many years been condoned in the case of those who are in opposition. So we may leave Challenger, his black mane slowly turning to grey, but his great brain growing ever stronger and more virile as it faces such problems as the future had in store – a future which had ceased to be bounded by the narrow horizon of death, and which now stretches away into the infinite possibilities and developments of continued survival of personality, character and work.

The marriage had taken place. It was a quiet function, but no prophet could ever have foretold the guests whom Enid's father had assembled in the Whitehall Rooms. They were a happy crowd, all welded together by the opposition of the world, and united in one common knowledge. There was the Rev. Charles Mason, who had officiated at the ceremony, and if ever a saint's blessing consecrated a union, so it had been that morning. Now in his black garb with his cheery toothsome smile, he was moving about among the crowd carrying peace and kindliness with him. The yellow-bearded Mailey, the old warrior, scarred with many combats and eager for more, stood beside his wife, the gentle squire who bore his weapons and nerved his arm. There was Dr. Maupuis from Paris, trying to make the waiter understand that he wanted coffee, and being presented with tooth-picks, while the gaunt Lord Roxton viewed his efforts with cynical amusement. There, too, was the good Bolsover with several of the Hammersmith circle, and Tom Linden with his wife, and Smith, the fighting bulldog from the north, and Dr. Atkinson, and Mervin the psychic editor with his kind wife, and the two Ogilvies, and little Miss Delicia with her bag and her tracts, and Dr. Ross Scotton, now successfully cured, and Dr. Felkin who had cured him so far as his earthly representative, Nurse Ursula, could fill his place. All these and many more were visible to our two-inch spectrum of colour, and audible to our four octaves of sound. How many others, outside those narrow limitations, may have added their presence and their blessing – who shall say?

One last scene before we close the record. It was in a sitting-room of the Imperial Hotel at Folkestone. At the window sat Mr. and Mrs. Edward Malone gazing westwards down Channel at an angry evening sky. Great purple tentacles, threatening forerunners from what lay unseen and unknown beyond the horizon, were writhing up towards the zenith. Below, the little Dieppe boat was panting eagerly homewards. Far out the great ships were keeping mid-channel as scenting danger to come. The vague threat of that menacing sky acted subconsciously upon the minds of both of them.

'Tell me, Enid,' said Malone, 'of all our wonderful psychic experiences, which is now most vivid in your mind?'

'It is curious that you should ask, Ned, for I was thinking of it at that moment. I suppose it was the association of ideas with that terrible sky. It was of Miromar I was thinking, the strange mystery man with his words of doom.'

'And so was I.'

'Have you heard of him since?'

'Once and once only. It was on a Sunday morning in Hyde Park. He was speaking to a little group of men. I mixed with the crowd and listened. It was the same warning.'

'How did they take it? Did they laugh?'

'Well, you have seen and heard him. You could not laugh, could you?'

'No, indeed. But you don't take it seriously, Ned, do you? Look at the solid old earth of England. Look at our great hotel and the people on the Lees, and the stodgy morning papers and all the settled order of a civilized land. Do you really think that anything could come to destroy it all?'

'Who knows? Miromar is not the only one who says so.'

'Does he call it the end of the world?'

'No, no, it is the rebirth of the world – of the true world, the world as God meant it to be.'

'It is a tremendous message. But what is amiss? Why should so dreadful a Judgment fall?'

'It is the materialism, the wooden formalities of the churches, the alienation of all spiritual impulses, the denial of the Unseen, the ridicule of this new revelation – these are the causes according to him.'

'Surely the world has been worse before now?'

'But never with the same advantages – never with the education and knowledge and so-called civilization, which should have led it to higher things. Look how everything has been turned to evil. We got the knowledge of airships. We bomb cities with them. We learn how to steam under the sea. We murder seamen with our new knowledge. We gain command over chemicals. We turn them into explosives or poison gases. It goes from worse to worse. At the present moment every nation upon earth is plotting secretly how it can best poison the others. Did God create the planet for this end, and is it likely that He will allow it to go on from bad to worse?'

'Is it you or Miromar who is talking now?'

'Well, I have myself been brooding over the matter, and all my thoughts seem to justify his conclusions. I read a spirit message which Charles Mason wrote. It was: "The most dangerous condition for a man or a nation is when his intellectual side is more developed than his spiritual". Is that not exactly the condition of the world to-day?'

'And how will it come?'

'Ah, there I can only take Miromar's word for it. He speaks of a breaking of all the phials. There is war, famine, pestilence, earthquake, flood, tidal waves – all ending in peace and glory unutterable.'

The great purple streamers were right across the sky. A dull crimson glare, a lurid angry glow, was spreading in the west. Enid shuddered as she watched it.

'One thing we have learned,' said he. 'It is that two souls, where real love exists, go on and on without a break through all the spheres. Why, then, should you and I fear death, or anything which life or death can bring?'

She smiled and put her hand in his.

'Why indeed?' said she.

THE END

APPENDICES

NOTE ON CHAPTER II

CLAIRVOYANCE IN SPIRITUALISTIC CHURCHES

THIS PHENOMENON, as exhibited in Spiritualistic churches or temples, as the Spiritualists usually call them, varies very much in quality. So uncertain is it that many congregations have given it up entirely, as it has become rather a source of scandal than of edification. On the other hand there are occasions, the conditions being good, the audience sympathetic and the medium in good form, when the results are nothing short of amazing. I was present on one occasion when Mr. Tom Tyrell, of Blackburn, speaking in a sudden call at Doncaster – a town with which he was unfamiliar – got not only the descriptions but even the names of a number of people which were recognized by the different individuals to whom he pointed. I have known Mr. Vout Peters also to give forty descriptions in a foreign city (Liège) where he had never been before, with only one failure, which was afterwards explained. Such results are far above coincidence. What their true *raison d'être* may be has yet to be determined. It has seemed to me sometimes that the vapour which becomes visible as a solid in ectoplasm, may in its more volatile condition fill the hall, and that a spirit coming within it may show up as an invisible shooting star comes into view when it crosses the atmosphere of the earth. No doubt the illustration is only an analogy but it may suggest a line of thought.

I remember being present on two occasions in Boston, Massachusetts, when clergymen gave clairvoyance from the steps of the altar, and with complete success. It struck me as an admirable reproduction of those apostolic conditions when they taught 'not only by words but also by power'. All this has to come back into the Christian religion before it will be revitalized and restored to its pristine power. It cannot, however, be done in a day. We want less faith and more knowledge.

NOTE ON CHAPTER IX

EARTHBOUND SPIRITS

THIS CHAPTER MAY BE REGARDED AS SENSATIONAL, but as a fact there is no incident in it for which chapter and verse may not be given. The incident of Nell Gwynne, mentioned by Lord Roxton, was told me by Colonel Cornwallis West as having occurred in a country house of his own. Visitors had met the wraith in the passages and had afterwards, when they saw the portrait of Nell Gwynne which hung in a sitting-room, exclaimed, 'Why, there is the woman I met'.

The adventure of the terrible occupant of the deserted house is taken with very little change from the experience of Lord St. Audries in a haunted house near Torquay. This gallant soldier told the story himself in *The Weekly Dispatch* (Dec., 1921), and it is admirably retold in Mrs. Violet Tweedale's *Phantoms of the Dawn*. As to the conversation carried on between the clergyman and the earthbound spirit, the same authoress has described a similar one when recording the adventures of Lord and Lady Wynford in Glamis Castle (*Ghosts I Have Seen*, p. 175).

Whence such a spirit draws its stock of material energy is an unsolved problem. It is probably from some mediumistic individual in the neighbourhood. In the extremely interesting case quoted by the Rev. Chas. Mason in the narrative and very carefully observed by the Psychic Research Society of Reykjavik in Iceland, the formidable earthbound creature proclaimed how it got its vitality. The man was in life a fisherman of rough and violent character who had committed suicide. He attached himself to the medium, followed him to the seances of the Society, and caused indescribable confusion and alarm, until he was exorcised by some such means as described in the story. A long account appeared in the *Proceedings of the American Society of Psychic Research* and also in the organ of the Psychic College, *Psychic Research* for January, 1925. Iceland, it may be remarked, is very advanced in psychic science, and in proportion to its population or opportunities is probably ahead of any other country. The Bishop of Reykjavik is President of the Psychic Society, which is surely a lesson to our own prelates whose disassociation from the study of such matters is little less than a scandal. The matter relates to the nature of the soul and to its fate in the Beyond, yet there are, I believe, fewer students of the matter among our spiritual guides than among any other profession.

NOTE ON CHAPTER X

RESCUE CIRCLES

THE SCENES IN THIS CHAPTER are drawn very closely either from personal experience or from the reports of careful and trustworthy experimenters. Among the latter are Mr. Tozer of Melbourne, and Mr. McFarlane of Southsea, both of whom have run methodical circles for the purpose of giving help to earthbound spirits. Detailed accounts of experiences which I have personally had in the former circles are to be found in Chapters IV and VI of my *Wanderings of a Spiritualist*. I may add that in my own domestic circle, under my wife's mediumship, we have been privileged to bring hope and knowledge to some of these unhappy beings.

Full reports of a number of these dramatic conversations are to be found in the last hundred pages of the late Admiral Usborne Moore's *Glimpses of the Next State*. It should be said that the Admiral was not personally present at these sittings, but that they were carried out by people in whom he had every confidence, and that they were confirmed by sworn affidavits of the sitters. 'The high character of Mr. Leander Fisher', says the Admiral, 'is sufficient voucher for their authenticity'. The same may be said of Mr. E. G. Randall, who has published many such cases. He is one of the leading lawyers of Buffalo, while Mr. Fisher is a Professor of Music in that city.

The natural objection is that, granting the honesty of the investigators, the whole experience may be in some way subjective and have no relation to real facts. Dealing with this the Admiral says: 'I made inquiries as to whether any of the spirits, thus brought to understand that they had entered a new state of consciousness, had been satisfactorily identified. The reply was that many had been discovered, but after several had been verified it was considered useless to go on searching for the relatives and places of abode in earth life of the remainder. Such inquiries involved much time and labour, and always ended with the same result'. In one of the cases cited (*op. cit.*, p. 524) there is the prototype of the fashionable woman who died in her sleep, as depicted in the text. In all these instances the returning spirit did not realize that its earth life was over.

The case of the clergyman and of the sailor from the *Monmouth* both occurred in my presence at the circle of Mr. Tozer.

The dramatic case where the spirit of a man (it was the case of several men in the original) manifested at the very time of the accident which caused their death, and where the names were afterwards verified in the newspaper report, is given by Mr. E. G. Randall. Another example given by that gentleman may be added for the consideration of those who have not realized how cogent is the evidence, and how necessary for us to reconsider our views of death. It is in *The Dead Have Never Died* (p. 104).

'I recall an incident that will appeal to the purely materialistic. I was one of my father's executors, and after his dissolution and the settlement of his estate, speaking to me from the next plane, he told me one night that I had overlooked an item that he wanted to mention to me.

'I replied: "Your mind was ever centred on the accumulation of money. Why take up the time that is so limited with the discussion of your estate? It has already been divided".

' "Yes", he answered, "I know that, but I worked too hard for my money to have it lost, and there is an asset remaining that you have not discovered".

' "Well", I said "if that be true, tell me about it".

'He answered: "Some years before I left I loaned a small sum of money to Susan Stone, who resided in Pennsylvania, and I took from her a promissory note upon which, under the laws of that State, I was entitled to enter a judgment at once without suit. I was somewhat anxious about the loan, so, before its maturity, I took the note and filed it with the prothonotary at Erie, Pennsylvania, and he entered judgment, which became a lien on her property. In my books of account there was no reference to that note or judgement. If you will go to the prothonotary's office in Erie, you will find the judgment on record, and I want you to collect it. There are many things that you don't know about and this is one of them".

'I was much surprised at the information thus received, and naturally sent for a transcript of that judgment. I found it entered Oct. 21, 1896, and with that evidence of the indebtedness I collected from the judgment debtor 70 dollars with interest. I question if anyone knew of that transaction besides the makers of the note and the prothonotary at Erie. Certainly I did not know about it. I had no reason to suspect it. The psychic present at that interview could not have known about the matter, and I certainly collected the money. My father's voice was clearly recognizable on that occasion, as it has been on hundreds of others, and I cite this instance for the benefit of those who measure everything from a monetary standpoint.'

The most striking, however, of all these posthumous communications are to be found in *Thirty Years Among the Dead*, by Dr. Wickland of Los Angeles. This, like many other valuable books of the sort, can only be obtained in Great Britain at the Psychic Bookshop in Victoria Street, S.W.

Dr. Wickland and his heroic wife have done work which deserves the very closest attention from the alienists of the world. If he makes his point, and the case is a strong one, he not only revolutionizes all our ideas about insanity, but he cuts deep also into our views of criminology, and may well show that we have been punishing as criminals people who were more deserving of commiseration than of censure.

Having framed the view that many cases of mania were due to obsession from undeveloped entities, and having found out by some line of inquiry, which is not clear to me, that such entities are exceedingly sensitive to static electricity when it is passed through the body which they have invaded, he founded his treatment with remarkable results upon this hypothesis. The third factor in his system was the discovery that such entities were more easily dislodged if a vacant body was provided for their temporary reception. Therein lies the heroism of Mrs. Wickland, a very charming and cultivated lady, who sits in hypnotic trance beside the subject ready to receive the invader when he is driven forth. It is through the lips of this lady that the identity and character of the undeveloped spirit are determined.

The subject having been strapped to the electric chair – the strapping is very necessary as many are violent maniacs – the power is turned on. It does not affect the patient, since it is static in its nature, but it causes acute discomfort to the parasitical spirit, who rapidly takes refuge in the unconscious form of Mrs. Wickland. Then follow the amazing conversations which are chronicled in this volume. The spirit is cross-questioned by the doctor, is admonished, instructed, and finally dismissed either in the care of some ministering spirit who superintends the proceedings, or relegated to the charge of some sterner attendant who will hold him in check should he be unrepentant.

To the scientist who is unfamiliar with psychic work such a bald statement sounds wild, and I do not myself claim that Dr. Wickland has finally made out his case, but I do say that our experiences at rescue circles bear out the general idea, and that he has admittedly cured many cases which others have found intractable. Occasionally there is very cogent confirmation. Thus in the case of one female spirit who bitterly bewailed that she had not taken enough carbolic acid the week before, the name and address being correctly given (*op. cit.*, p. 39).

It is not apparently everyone who is open to this invasion, but only those who are in some peculiar way psychic sensitives. The discovery, when fully made out, will be one of the root facts of the psychology and jurisprudence of the future.

NOTE ON CHAPTER XII

DR. MAUPUIS'S EXPERIMENTS

THE DR. MAUPUIS OF THE NARRATIVE IS, as every student of psychic research will realize, the late Dr. Geley, whose splendid work on this subject will ensure his permanent fame. His was a brain of the first order, coupled with a moral courage which enabled him to face with equanimity the cynicism and levity of his critics. With rare judgment he never went further than the facts carried him, and yet never flinched from the furthest point which his reason and the evidence would justify. By the munificence of Mr. Jean Meyer he had been placed at the head of the Institut Métapsychique, admirably equipped for scientific work, and he got the full value out of that equipment. When a British Jean Meyer makes his appearance he will get no return for his money if he does not choose a progressive brain to drive his machine. The great endowment left to the Stanford University of California has been practically wasted, because those in charge of it were not Geleys or Richets.

The account of Pithecanthropus is taken from the *Bulletin de l'Institut Métapsychique.* A well-known lady has described to me how the creature pressed between her and her neighbour, and how she placed her hand upon his shaggy skin. An account of this seance is to be found in Geley's *L'Ectoplasmie et la Clairvoyance* (Felix Alcau), p. 345. On page 296 is a photograph of the strange bird of prey upon the medium's head. It would take the credulity of a MacCabe to imagine that all this is imposture.

These various animal types may assume very bizarre forms. In an unpublished manuscript by Colonel Ochorowitz, which I have been privileged to see, some new developments are described which are not only formidable but also unlike any creature with which we are acquainted.

Since animal forms of this nature have materialized under the mediumship both of Kluski and of Guzik, their formation would seem to depend rather upon one of the sitters than upon either of the mediums unless we can disconnect them entirely from the circle. It is usually an axiom among Spiritualists that the spirit visitors to a circle represent in some way the mental and spiritual tendency of the circle. Thus, in nearly forty years of experience, I have never heard an obscene or blasphemous word at a seance because such seances have been run in a reverent and religious fashion. The question therefore may arise whether sittings which are held for purely scientific and experimental purposes, without the least recognition of their extreme religious significance, may not evoke less desirable manifestations of psychic force. The high character, however, of men like Richet and Geley ensure that the general tendency shall be good.

It might be argued that a subject with such possibilities had better be left alone. The answer seems to be that these manifestations are, fortunately, very rare, whereas the daily comfort of spirit intercourse illumines thousands of lives. We do not abandon exploration because the land explored contains some noxious creatures. To abandon the subject would be to hand it over to such forces of evil as chose to explore it while depriving ourselves of that knowledge which would aid us in understanding and counteracting their results.

THE DISINTEGRATION MACHINE

The Disintegration Machine

PROFESSOR CHALLENGER was in the worst possible humour. As I stood at the door of his study, my hand upon the handle and my foot upon the mat, I heard a monologue which ran like this, the words booming and reverberating through the house:

'Yes, I say it is the second wrong call. The *second* in one morning. Do you imagine that a man of science is to be distracted from essential work by the constant interference of some idiot at the end of a wire? I will not have it. Send this instant for the manager. Oh! you *are* the manager. Well, why don't you manage? Yes, you certainly manage to distract me from work the importance of which your mind is incapable of understanding. I want the superintendent. He is away? So I should imagine. I will carry you to the law courts if this occurs again. Crowing cocks have been adjudicated upon. I myself have obtained a judgment. If crowing cocks, why not jangling bells? The case is clear. A written apology. Very good. I will consider it. *Good* morning.'

It was at this point that I ventured to make my entrance. It was certainly an unfortunate moment. I confronted him as he turned from the telephone – a lion in its wrath. His huge black beard was bristling, his great chest was heaving with indignation, and his arrogant grey eyes swept me up and down as the backwash of his anger fell upon me.

'Infernal, idle, overpaid rascals!' he boomed. 'I could hear them laughing while I was making my just complaint. There is a conspiracy to annoy me. And now, young Malone, you arrive to complete a disastrous morning. Are you here, may I ask, on your own account, or has your rag commissioned you to obtain an interview? As a friend you are privileged – as a journalist you are outside the pale.'

I was hunting in my pocket for McArdle's letter when suddenly some new grievance came to his memory. His great hairy hands fumbled about among the papers upon his desk and finally extracted a press cutting.

'You have been good enough to allude to me in one of your

recent lucubrations,' he said, shaking the paper at me. 'It was in the course of your somewhat fatuous remarks concerning the recent Saurian remains discovered in the Solenhofen Slates. You began a paragraph with the words: "Professor G. E. Challenger, who is among our greatest living scientists –" '

'Well, sir?' I asked.

'Why these invidious qualifications and limitations? Perhaps you can mention who these other predominant scientific men may be to whom you impute equality, or possibly superiority to myself?'

'It was badly worded. I should certainly have said: "Our greatest living scientist," ' I admitted. It was after all my own honest belief. My words turned winter into summer.

'My dear young friend, do not imagine that I am exacting, but surrounded as I am by pugnacious and unreasonable colleagues, one is forced to take one's own part. Self-assertion is foreign to my nature, but I have to hold my ground against opposition. Come now! Sit here! What is the reason of your visit?'

I had to tread warily, for I knew how easy it was to set the lion roaring once again. I opened McArdle's letter.

'May I read you this, sir? It is from McArdle, my editor.'

'I remember the man – not an unfavourable specimen of his class.'

'He has, at least, a very high admiration for you. He has turned to you again and again when he needed the highest qualities in some investigation. That is the case now.'

'What does he desire?' Challenger plumed himself like some unwieldy bird under the influence of flattery. He sat down with his elbows upon the desk, his gorilla hands clasped together, his beard bristling forward, and his big grey eyes, half covered by his drooping lids, fixed benignly upon me. He was huge in all that he did, and his benevolence was even more overpowering than his truculence.

'I'll read you his note to me. He says:

"Please call upon our esteemed friend, Professor Challenger, and ask for his co-operation in the following circumstances. There is a Latvian gentleman named Theodore Nemor living at White Friars Mansions, Hampstead, who claims to have invented a machine of a most extraordinary character which is capable of disintegrating any object placed within its sphere of influence. Matter dissolves and returns to its molecular or atomic condition. By reversing the process it can be reassembled. The claim seems to be an extravagant one, and yet there is solid evidence that there is some basis for it and that the man has stumbled upon some remarkable discovery.

"I need not enlarge upon the revolutionary character of such an invention, nor of its extreme importance as a potential weapon of war. A force which could disintegrate a battleship, or turn a battalion, if it were only for a time, into a collection of atoms, would dominate the world. For social and for political reasons not an instant is to be lost in getting to the bottom of the affair. The man courts publicity as he is anxious to sell his invention, so that there is no difficulty in approaching him. The enclosed card will open his doors. What I desire is that you and Professor Challenger shall call upon him, inspect his invention, and write for the *Gazette* a considered report upon the value of the discovery. I expect to hear from you to-night. – R. McARDLE."

'There are my instructions, Professor,' I added, as I refolded the letter. 'I sincerely hope that you will come with me, for how can I, with my limited capacities, act alone in such a matter?'

'True, Malone! True!' purred the great man. 'Though you are by no means destitute of natural intelligence, I agree with you that you would be somewhat over-weighted in such a matter as you lay before me. These unutterable people upon the telephone have already ruined my morning's work, so that a little more can hardly matter. I am engaged in answering that Italian buffoon, Mazotti, whose views upon the larval development of the tropical termites have excited my derision and contempt, but I can leave the complete exposure of the impostor until evening. Meanwhile, I am at your service.'

And thus it came about that on that October morning I found myself in the deep level tube with the Professor speeding to the North of London in what proved to be one of the most singular experiences of my remarkable life.

I had, before leaving Enmore Gardens, ascertained by the much-abused telephone that our man was at home, and had warned him of our coming. He lived in a comfortable flat in Hampstead, and he kept us waiting for quite half an hour in his ante-room whilst he carried on an animated conversation with a group of visitors, whose voices, as they finally bade farewell in the hall, showed that they were Russians. I caught a glimpse of them through the half-opened door, and had a passing impression of prosperous and intelligent men, with astrakhan collars to their coats, glistening top-hats, and every appearance of that bourgeois well-being which the successful Communist so readily assumes. The hall door closed behind them, and the next instant Theodore Nemor entered our apartment. I can see him now as he stood with the sunlight full upon him, rubbing his long, thin hands together and surveying us with his broad smile and his cunning yellow eyes.

He was a short, thick man, with some suggestion of deformity in his body, though it was difficult to say where that suggestion lay.

One might say that he was a hunchback without the hump. His large, soft face was like an underdone dumpling, of the same colour and moist consistency, while the pimples and blotches which adorned it stood out the more aggressively against the pallid background. His eyes were those of a cat, and catlike was the thin, long, bristling moustache above his loose, wet, slobbering mouth. It was all low and repulsive until one came to the sandy eyebrows. From these upwards there was a splendid cranial arch such as I have seldom seen. Even Challenger's hat might have fitted that magnificent head. One might read Theodore Nemor as a vile, crawling conspirator below, but above he might take rank with the great thinkers and philosophers of the world.

'Well, gentlemen,' said he, in a velvety voice with only the least trace of a foreign accent, 'you have come, as I understand from our short chat over the wires, in order to learn more of the Nemor Disintegrator. Is it so?'

'Exactly.'

'May I ask whether you represent the British Government?'

'Not at all. I am a correspondent of the *Gazette*, and this is Professor Challenger.'

'An honoured name – a European name.' His yellow fangs gleamed in obsequious amiability. 'I was about to say that the British Government has lost its chance. What else it has lost it may find out later. Possibly its Empire as well. I was prepared to sell to the first Government which gave me its price, and if it has now fallen into hands of which you may disapprove, you have only yourselves to blame.'

'Then you have sold your secret?'

'At my own price.'

'You think the purchaser will have a monopoly?'

'Undoubtedly he will.'

'But others know the secret as well as you.'

'No, sir.' He touched his great forehead. 'This is the safe in which the secret is securely locked – a better safe than any of steel, and secured by something better than a Yale key. Some may know one side of the matter: others may know another. No one in the world knows the whole matter save only I.'

'And these gentlemen to whom you have sold it.'

'No, sir; I am not so foolish as to hand over the knowledge until the price is paid. After that it is I whom they buy, and they move this safe' – he again tapped his brow – 'with all its contents to whatever point they desire. My part of the bargain will then be done –

faithfully, ruthlessly done. After that, history will be made.' He rubbed his hands together and the fixed smile upon his face twisted itself into something like a snarl.

'You will excuse me, sir,' boomed Challenger, who had sat in silence up to now, but whose expressive face registered most complete disapproval of Theodore Nemor, 'we should wish before we discuss the matter to convince ourselves that there is something to discuss. We have not forgotten a recent case where an Italian, who proposed to explode mines from a distance, proved upon investigation to be an arrant impostor. History may well repeat itself. You will understand, sir, that I have a reputation to sustain as a man of science – a reputation which you have been good enough to describe as European, though I have every reason to believe that it is not less conspicuous in America. Caution is a scientific attribute, and you must show us your proofs before we can seriously consider your claims.'

Nemor cast a particularly malignant glance from the yellow eyes at my companion, but the smile of affected geniality broadened upon his face.

'You live up to your reputation, Professor. I had always heard that you were the last man in the world who could be deceived. I am prepared to give you an actual demonstration which cannot fail to convince you, but before we proceed to that I must say a few words upon the general principle.

'You will realize that the experimental plant which I have erected here in my laboratory is a mere model, though within its limits it acts most admirably. There would be no possible difficulty, for example, in disintegrating you and reassembling you, but it is not for such a purpose as that that a great Government is prepared to pay a price which runs into millions. My model is a mere scientific toy. It is only when the same force is invoked upon a large scale that enormous practical effects could be achieved.'

'May we see this model?'

'You will not only see it, Professor Challenger, but you will have the most conclusive demonstration possible upon your own person, if you have the courage to submit to it.'

'If!' the lion began to roar. 'Your "if," sir, is in the highest degree offensive.'

'Well, well. I had no intention to dispute your courage. I will only say that I will give you an opportunity to demonstrate it. But I would first say a few words upon the underlying laws which govern the matter.

'When certain crystals, salt, for example, or sugar, are placed in water they dissolve and disappear. You would not know that they have ever been there. Then by evaporation or otherwise you lessen the amount of water, and lo! there are your crystals again, visible once more and the same as before. Can you conceive a process by which you, an organic being, are in the same way dissolved into the cosmos, and then by a subtle reversal of the conditions reassembled once more?'

'The analogy is a false one,' cried Challenger. 'Even if I make so monstrous an admission as that our molecules could be dispersed by some disrupting power, why should they reassemble in exactly the same order as before?'

'The objection is an obvious one, and I can only answer that they do so reassemble down to the last atom of the structure. There is an invisible framework and every brick flies into its true place. You may smile, Professor, but your incredulity and your smile may soon be replaced by quite another emotion.'

Challenger shrugged his shoulders. 'I am quite ready to submit it to the test.'

'There is another case which I would impress upon you, gentlemen, and which may help you to grasp the idea. You have heard both in Oriental magic and in Western occultism of the phenomenon of the *apport* when some object is suddenly brought from a distance and appears in a new place. How can such a thing be done save by the loosening of the molecules, their conveyance upon an etheric wave, and their reassembling, each exactly in its own place, drawn together by some irresistible law? That seems a fair analogy to that which is done by my machine.'

'You cannot explain one incredible thing by quoting another incredible thing,' said Challenger. 'I do not believe in your *apports*, Mr. Nemor, and I do not believe in your machine. My time is valuable, and if we are to have any sort of a demonstration I would beg you to proceed with it without further ceremony.'

'Then you will be pleased to follow me,' said the inventor. He led us down the stair of the flat and across a small garden which lay behind. There was a considerable outhouse, which he unlocked and we entered.

Inside was a large whitewashed room with innumerable copper wires hanging in festoons from the ceiling, and a huge magnet balanced upon a pedestal. In front of this was what looked like a prism of glass, three feet in length and about a foot in diameter. To the right of it was a chair which rested upon a platform of zinc, and which had a burnished copper cap suspended above it. Both the cap and the chair had heavy wires attached to them, and at the side was a sort of ratchet with numbered slots and a handle covered with indiarubber which lay at present in the slot marked zero.

'Nemor's Disintegrator,' said this strange man, waving his hand towards the machine.

'This is the model which is destined to be famous, as altering the balance of power among the nations. Who holds this rules the world. Now, Professor Challenger, you have, if I may say so, treated me with some lack of courtesy and consideration in this matter. Will you dare to sit upon that chair and to allow me to demonstrate upon your own body the capabilities of the new force?'

Challenger had the courage of a lion, and anything in the nature of a defiance roused him in an instant to a frenzy. He rushed at the machine, but I seized his arm and held him back.

'You shall not go,' I said. 'Your life is too valuable. It is monstrous. What possible guarantee of safety have you? The nearest approach to that apparatus which I have ever seen was the electrocution chair at Sing Sing.'

'My guarantee of safety,' said Challenger, 'is that you are a witness and that this person would certainly be held for manslaughter at the least should anything befall me.'

'That would be a poor consolation to the world of science, when you would leave work unfinished which none but you can do. Let me, at least, go first, and then, when the experience proves to be harmless, you can follow.'

Personal danger would never have moved Challenger, but the idea that his scientific work might remain unfinished hit him hard. He hesitated, and before he could make up his mind I had dashed forward and jumped into the chair. I saw the inventor put his hand to the handle. I was aware of a click. Then for a moment there was a sensation of confusion and a mist before my eyes. When they cleared, the inventor with his odious smile was standing before me, and Challenger, with his apple-red cheeks drained of blood and colour, was staring over his shoulder.

'Well, get on with it!' said I.

'It is all over. You responded admirably,' Nemor replied. 'Step out, and Professor Challenger will now, no doubt, be ready to take his turn.'

I have never seen my old friend so utterly upset. His iron nerve had for a moment completely failed him. He grasped my arm with a shaking hand.

'My God, Malone, it is true,' said he. 'You vanished. There is not a doubt of it. There was a mist for an instant and then vacancy.'

'How long was I away?'

'Two or three minutes. I was, I confess, horrified. I could not imagine that you would return. Then he clicked this lever, if it is a lever, into a new slot and there you were upon the chair, looking a little bewildered but otherwise the same as ever. I thanked God at the sight of you!' He mopped his moist brow with his big red handkerchief.

'Now, sir,' said the inventor. 'Or perhaps your nerve has failed you?'

Challenger visibly braced himself. Then, pushing my protesting hand to one side, he seated himself upon the chair. The handle clicked into number three. He was gone.

I should have been horrified but for the perfect coolness of the operator. 'It is an interesting process, is it not?' he remarked. 'When one considers the tremendous individuality of the Professor it is strange to think that he is at present a molecular cloud suspended in some portion of this building. He is now, of course, entirely at my mercy. If I choose to leave him in suspension there is nothing on earth to prevent me.'

'I would very soon find means to prevent you.'

The smile once again became a snarl. 'You cannot imagine that such a thought ever entered my mind. Good heavens! Think of the permanent dissolution of the great Professor Challenger – vanished into cosmic space and left no trace! Terrible! Terrible! At the same time he has not been as courteous as he might. Don't you think some small lesson – ?'

'No, I do not.'

'Well, we will call it a curious demonstration. Something that would make an interesting paragraph in your paper. For example, I have discovered that the hair of the body being on an entirely different vibration to the living organic tissues can be included or excluded at will. It would interest me to see the bear without his bristles. Behold him!'

There was the click of the lever. An instant later Challenger was seated upon the chair once more. But what a Challenger! What a shorn lion! Furious as I was at the trick that had been played upon him I could hardly keep from roaring with laughter.

His huge head was as bald as a baby's and his chin was as smooth as a girl's. Bereft of his glorious mane the lower part of his face was heavily jowled and ham-shaped, while his whole appearance was that of an old fighting gladiator, battered and bulging, with the jaws of a bulldog over a massive chin.

It may have been some look upon our faces – I have no doubt that the evil grin of my companion had widened at the sight – but, however that may be, Challenger's hand flew up to his head and he became conscious of his condition. The next instant he had sprung out of his chair, seized the inventor by the throat, and had hurled him to the ground. Knowing Challenger's immense strength I was convinced that the man would be killed.

'For God's sake be careful. If you kill him we can never get matters right again!' I cried.

That argument prevailed. Even in his maddest moments Challenger was always open to reason. He sprang up from the floor, dragging the trembling inventor with him. 'I give you five minutes,' he panted in his fury. 'If in five minutes I am not as I was, I will choke the life out of your wretched little body.'

Challenger in a fury was not a safe person to argue with. The bravest man might shrink from him, and there were no signs that Mr. Nemor was a particularly brave man. On the contrary, those blotches and warts upon his face had suddenly become much more conspicuous as the face behind them changed from the colour of putty, which was normal, to that of a fish's belly. His limbs were shaking and he could hardly articulate.

'Really, Professor!' he babbled, with his hand to his throat, 'this violence is quite unnecessary. Surely a harmless joke may pass among friends. It was my wish to demonstrate the powers of the machine. I had imagined that you wanted a full demonstration. No offence, I assure you, Professor, none in the world!'

For answer Challenger climbed back into the chair.

'You will keep your eye upon him, Malone. Do not permit any liberties.'

'I'll see to it, sir.'

'Now then, set that matter right or take the consequences.'

The terrified inventor approached his machine. The reuniting power was turned on to the full, and in an instant, there was the old lion with his tangled mane once more. He stroked his beard affectionately with his hands and passed them over his cranium to be sure that the restoration was complete. Then he descended solemnly from his perch.

'You have taken a liberty, sir, which might have had very serious consequences to yourself. However, I am content to accept your explanation that you only did it for purposes of demonstration.

Now, may I ask you a few direct questions upon this remarkable power which you claim to have discovered?'

'I am ready to answer anything save what the source of the power is. That is my secret.'

'And do you seriously inform us that no one in the world knows this except yourself?'

'No one has the least inkling.'

'No assistants?'

'No, sir. I work alone.'

'Dear me! That is most interesting. You have satisfied me as to the reality of the power, but I do not yet perceive its practical bearings.'

'I have explained, sir, that this is a model. But it would be quite easy to erect a plant upon a large scale. You understand that this acts vertically. Certain currents above you, and certain others below you, set up vibrations which either disintegrate or reunite. But the process could be lateral. If it were so conducted it would have the same effect, and cover a space in proportion to the strength of the current.'

'Give an example.'

'We will suppose that one pole was in one small vessel and one in another; a battleship between them would simply vanish into molecules. So also with a column of troops.'

'And you have sold this secret as a monopoly to a single European Power?'

'Yes, sir, I have. When the money is paid over they shall have such power as no nation ever had yet. You don't even now see the full possibilities if placed in capable hands – hands which did not fear to wield the weapon which they held. They are immeasurable.' A gloating smile passed over the man's evil face. 'Conceive a quarter of London in which such machines have been erected. Imagine the effect of such a current upon the scale which could easily be adopted. Why,' he burst into laughter, 'I could imagine the whole Thames valley being swept clean, and not one man, woman, or child left of all these teeming millions!'

The words filled me with horror – and even more the air of exultation with which they were pronounced. They seemed, however, to produce quite a different effect upon my companion. To my surprise he broke into a genial smile and held out his hand to the inventor.

'Well, Mr. Nemor, we have to congratulate you,' said he. 'There is no doubt that you have come upon a remarkable property of nature which you have succeeded in harnessing for the use of man. That this use should be destructive is no doubt very deplorable, but Science knows no distinctions of the sort, but follows knowledge wherever it may lead. Apart from the principle involved you have, I suppose, no objection to my examining the construction of the machine?'

'None in the least. The machine is merely the body. It is the soul of it, the animating principle, which you can never hope to capture.'

'Exactly. But the mere mechanism seems to be a model of ingenuity.' For some time he walked round it and fingered its several parts. Then he hoisted his unwieldy bulk into the insulated chair.

'Would you like another excursion into the cosmos?' asked the inventor.

'Later, perhaps – later! But meanwhile there is, as no doubt you know, some leakage of electricity. I can distinctly feel a weak current passing through me.'

'Impossible. It is quite insulated.'

'But I assure you that I feel it.' He levered himself down from his perch.

The inventor hastened to take his place.

'I can feel nothing.'

'Is there not a tingling down your spine?'

'No, sir, I do not observe it.'

There was a sharp click and the man had disappeared. I looked with amazement at Challenger. 'Good heavens! did you touch the machine, Professor?'

He smiled at me benignly with an air of mild surprise.

'Dear me! I may have inadvertently touched the handle,' said he. 'One is very liable to have awkward incidents with a rough model of this kind. This lever should certainly be guarded.'

'It is in number three. That is the slot which causes disintegration.'

'So I observed when you were operated upon.'

'But I was so excited when he brought you back that I did not see which was the proper slot for the return. Did you notice it?'

'I may have noticed it, young Malone, but I do not burden my mind with small details. There are many slots and we do not know their purpose. We may make the matter worse if we experiment with the unknown. Perhaps it is better to leave matters as they are.'

'And you would –'

'Exactly. It is better so. The interesting personality of Mr. Theodore Nemor has distributed itself throughout the cosmos, his machine is worthless, and a certain foreign Government has been deprived of knowledge by which much harm might have been wrought. Not a bad morning's work, young Malone. Your rag will no doubt have an interesting column upon the inexplicable disappearance of a Latvian inventor shortly after the visit of its own special correspondent. I have enjoyed the experience. These are the lighter moments which come to brighten the dull routine of study. But life has its duties as well as its pleasures, and I now return to the Italian Mazotti and his preposterous views upon the larval development of the tropical termites.'

Looking back, it seemed to me that a slight oleaginous mist was still hovering round the chair. 'But surely –' I urged.

'The first duty of the law-abiding citizen is to prevent murder,' said Professor Challenger. 'I have done so. Enough, Malone, enough! The theme will not bear discussion. It has already disengaged my thoughts too long from matters of more importance.'

WHEN THE WORLD SCREAMED

When the World Screamed

I HAD A VAGUE RECOLLECTION of having heard my friend Edward Malone, of the *Gazette*, speak of Professor Challenger, with whom he had been associated in some remarkable adventures. I am so busy, however, with my own profession, and my firm has been so overtaxed with orders, that I know little of what is going on in the world outside my own special interests. My general recollection was that Challenger had been depicted as a wild genius of a violent and intolerant disposition. I was greatly surprised to receive a business communication from him which was in the following terms:

'14 (Bis), Enmore Gardens,
Kensington.

'Sir, –
'I have occasion to engage the services of an expert in Artesian borings. I will not conceal from you that my opinion of experts is not a high one, and that I have usually found that a man who, like myself, has a well-equipped brain can take a sounder and broader view than the man who professes a special knowledge (which, alas, is so often a mere profession), and is therefore limited in his outlook. None the less, I am disposed to give you a trial. Looking down the list of Artesian authorities, a certain oddity – I had almost written absurdity – in your name attracted my attention, and I found upon inquiry that my young friend, Mr. Edward Malone, was actually acquainted with you. I am therefore writing to say that I should be glad to have an interview with you, and that if you satisfy my requirements, and my standard is no mean one, I may be inclined to put a most important matter into your hands. I can say no more at present as the matter is one of extreme secrecy, which can only be discussed by word of mouth. I beg, therefore, that you will at once cancel any engagement which you may happen to have, and that you will call upon me at the above address at 10.30 in the morning of next Friday. There is a scraper as well as a mat, and Mrs. Challenger is most particular.
'I remain, Sir, as I began,
'George Edward Challenger.'

I handed this letter to my chief clerk to answer, and he informed the Professor that Mr. Peerless Jones would be glad to keep the appointment as arranged. It was a perfectly civil business note, but it began with the phrase: 'Your letter (undated) has been received.' This drew a second epistle from the Professor:

> 'Sir,' he said – and his writing looked like a barbed wire fence – 'I observe that you animadvert upon the trifle that my letter was undated. Might I draw your attention to the fact that, as some return for a monstrous taxation, our Government is in the habit of affixing a small circular sign or stamp upon the outside of the envelope which notifies the date of posting? Should this sign be missing or illegible your remedy lies with the proper postal authorities. Meanwhile, I would ask you to confine your observations to matters which concern the business over which I consult you, and to cease to comment upon the form which my own letters may assume.'

It was clear to me that I was dealing with a lunatic, so I thought it well before I went any further in the matter to call upon my friend Malone, whom I had known since the old days when we both played Rugger for Richmond. I found him the same jolly Irishman as ever, and much amused at my first brush with Challenger.

'That's nothing, my boy,' said he. 'You'll feel as if you had been skinned alive when you have been with him five minutes. He beats the world for offensiveness.'

'But why should the world put up with it?'

'They don't. If you collected all the libel actions and all the rows and all the police-court assaults –'

'Assaults!'

'Bless you, he would think nothing of throwing you downstairs if you have a disagreement. He is a primitive cave-man in a lounge suit. I can see him with a club in one hand and a jagged bit of flint in the other. Some people are born out of their proper century, but he is born out of his millennium. He belongs to the early neolithic or thereabouts.'

'And he a professor!'

'There is the wonder of it! It's the greatest brain in Europe, with a driving force behind it that can turn all his dreams into facts. They do all they can to hold him back for his colleagues hate him like poison, but a lot of trawlers might as well try to hold back the *Berengaria*. He simply ignores them and steams on his way.'

'Well,' said I, 'one thing is clear. I don't want to have anything to do with him. I'll cancel that appointment.'

'Not a bit of it. You will keep it to the minute – and mind that it *is* to the minute or you will hear of it.'

'Why should I?'

'Well, I'll tell you. First of all, don't take too seriously what I have said about old Challenger. Everyone who gets close to him learns to love him. There is no real harm in the old bear. Why, I remember how he carried an Indian baby with the smallpox on his back for a hundred miles from the back country down to the Madeira river. He is big every way. He won't hurt you if you get right with him.'

'I won't give him the chance.'

'You will be a fool if you don't. Have you ever heard of the Hengist Down Mystery – the shaft-sinking on the South Coast?'

'Some secret coal-mining exploration, I understand.'

Malone winked.

'Well, you can put it down as that if you like. You see, I am in the old man's confidence, and I can't say anything until he gives the word. But I may tell you this, for it has been in the Press. A man, Betterton, who made his money in rubber, left his whole estate to Challenger some years ago, with the provision that it should be used in the interests of science. It proved to be an enormous sum – several millions. Challenger then bought a property at Hengist Down, in Sussex. It was worthless land on the north edge of the chalk country, and he got a large tract of it, which he wired off. There was a deep gully in the middle of it. Here he began to make an excavation. He announced' – here Malone winked again – 'that there was petroleum in England and that he meant to prove it. He built a little model village with a colony of well-paid workers who are all sworn to keep their mouths shut. The gully is wired off as well as the estate, and the place is guarded by bloodhounds. Several pressmen have nearly lost their lives, to say nothing of the seats of their trousers, from these creatures. It's a big operation, and Sir Thomas Morden's firm has it in hand, but they also are sworn to secrecy. Clearly the time has come when Artesian help is needed. Now, would you not be foolish to refuse such a job as that, with all the interest and experience and a big fat cheque at the end of it – to say nothing of rubbing shoulders with the most wonderful man you have ever met or are ever likely to meet?'

Malone's arguments prevailed, and Friday morning found me on my way to Enmore Gardens. I took such particular care to be in time that I found myself at the door twenty minutes too soon. I was waiting in the street when it struck me that I recognized the Rolls-Royce with the silver arrow mascot at the door. It was certainly that of Jack Devonshire, the junior partner of the great Morden firm. I had always known him as the most urbane of men, so that it was rather a shock to me when he suddenly appeared, and standing outside the door he raised both his hands to heaven and said with great fervour: 'Damn him! Oh, damn him!'

'What is up, Jack? You seem peeved this morning.'

'Hullo, Peerless! Are you in on this job, too?'

'There seems a chance of it.'

'Well, you will find it chastening to the temper.'

'Rather more so than yours can stand, apparently.'

'Well, I should say so. The butler's message to me was: "The Professor desired me to say, sir, that he was rather busy at present eating an egg, and that if you would call at some more convenient time he would very likely see you." That was the message delivered by a servant. I may add that I had called to collect forty-two thousand pounds that he owes us.'

I whistled.

'You can't get your money?'

'Oh, yes, he is all right about money. I'll do the old gorilla the justice to say that he is open-handed with money. But he pays when he likes and how he likes, and he cares for nobody. However, you go and try your luck and see how you like it.' With that he flung himself into his motor and was off.

I waited with occasional glances at my watch until the zero hour should arrive. I am, if I may say so, a fairly hefty individual, and a runner-up for the Belsize Boxing Club middle-weights, but I have never faced an interview with such trepidation as this. It was not physical, for I was confident I could hold my own if this inspired lunatic should attack me, but it was a mixture of feelings in which fear of some public scandal and dread of losing a lucrative contract were mingled. However, things are always easier when imagination ceases and action begins. I snapped up my watch and made for the door.

It was opened by an old wooden-faced butler, a man who bore an expression, or an absence of expression, which gave the impression that he was so inured to shocks that nothing on earth would surprise him.

'By appointment, sir?' he asked.

'Certainly.'

He glanced at a list in his hand.

'Your name, sir? . . . Quite so, Mr. Peerless Jones. . . . Ten-thirty. Everything is in order. We have to be careful, Mr. Jones, for we are much annoyed by journalists. The Professor, as you may be aware, does not approve of the Press. This way, sir. Professor Challenger is now receiving.'

The next instant I found myself in the presence. I believe that my friend, Ted Malone, has described the man in his 'Lost World' yarn better than I can hope to do, so I'll leave it at that. All I was aware of was a huge trunk of a man behind a mahogany desk, with a great spade-shaped black beard and two large grey eyes half covered with insolent drooping eyelids. His big head sloped back, his beard bristled forward, and his whole appearance conveyed one single impression of arrogant intolerance. 'Well, what the devil do *you* want?' was written all over him. I laid my card on the table.

'Ah yes,' he said, picking it up and handling it as if he disliked the smell of it. 'Of course. You are the expert – so-called. Mr. Jones – Mr. Peerless Jones. You may thank your godfather, Mr. Jones, for it was this ludicrous prefix which first drew my attention to you.'

'I am here, Professor Challenger, for a business interview and not to discuss my own name,' said I, with all the dignity I could master.

'Dear me, you seem to be a very touchy person, Mr. Jones. Your nerves are in a highly irritable condition. We must walk warily in dealing with you, Mr. Jones. Pray sit down and compose yourself. I have been reading your little brochure upon the reclaiming of the Sinai Peninsula. Did you write it yourself?'

'Naturally, sir. My name is on it.'

'Quite so! Quite so! But it does not always follow, does it? However, I am prepared to accept your assertion. The book is not without merit of a sort. Beneath the dullness of the diction one gets glimpses of an occasional idea. There are germs of thought here and there. Are you a married man?'

'No, sir. I am not.'

'Then there is some chance of your keeping a secret.'

'If I promised to do so, I would certainly keep my promise.'

'So you say. My young friend, Malone' – he spoke as if Ted were ten years of age – 'has a good opinion of you. He says that I may trust you. This trust is a very great one, for I am engaged just now in one of the greatest experiments – I may even say *the* greatest experiment – in the history of the world. I ask for your participation.'

'I shall be honoured.'

'It is indeed an honour. I will admit that I should have shared my labours with no one were it not that the gigantic nature of the undertaking calls for the highest technical skill. Now, Mr. Jones, having obtained your promise of inviolable secrecy, I come down to the essential point. It is this – that the world upon which we live is itself a living organism, endowed, as I believe, with a circulation, a respiration, and a nervous system of its own.'

Clearly the man was a lunatic.

'Your brain, I observe,' he continued, 'fails to register. But it will gradually absorb the idea. You will recall how a moor or heath resembles the hairy side of a giant animal. A certain analogy runs through all nature. You will then consider the secular rise and fall of land, which indicates the slow respiration of the creature. Finally, you will note the fidgetings and scratchings which appear to our Lilliputian perceptions as earthquakes and convulsions.'

'What about volcanoes?' I asked.

'Tut, tut! They correspond to the heat spots upon our own bodies.'

My brain whirled as I tried to find some answer to these monstrous contentions.

'The temperature!' I cried. 'Is it not a fact that it rises rapidly as one descends, and that the centre of the earth is liquid heat?'

He waved my assertion aside.

'You are probably aware, sir, since Council schools are now compulsory, that the earth is flattened at the poles. This means that the pole is nearer to the centre than any other point and would therefore be most affected by this heat of which you spoke. It is notorious, of course, that the conditions of the poles are tropical, is it not?'

'The whole idea is utterly new to me.'

'Of course it is. It is the privilege of the original thinker to put forward ideas which are new and usually unwelcome to the common clay. Now, sir, what is this?' He held up a small object which he had picked from the table.

'I should say it is a sea-urchin.'

'Exactly!' he cried, with an air of exaggerated surprise, as when an infant has done something clever. 'It is a sea-urchin – a common echinus. Nature repeats itself in many forms regardless of the size. This echinus is a model, a prototype, of the world. You perceive that it is roughly circular, but flattened at the poles. Let us then regard the world as a huge echinus. What are your objections?'

My chief objection was that the thing was too absurd for argument, but I did not dare to say so. I fished around for some less sweeping assertion.

'A living creature needs food,' I said. 'Where could the world sustain its huge bulk?'

'An excellent point – excellent!' said the Professor, with a huge air of patronage. 'You have a quick eye for the obvious, though you are slow in realizing the more subtle implications. How does the world get nourishment? Again we turn to our little friends the echinus. The water which surrounds it flows through the tubes of this small creature and provides its nutrition.'

'Then you think that the water –'

'No, sir. The ether. The earth browses upon a circular path in the fields of space, and as it moves the ether is continually pouring through it and providing its vitality. Quite a flock of other little world-echini are doing the same thing, Venus, Mars, and the rest, each with its own field for grazing.'

The man was clearly mad, but there was no arguing with him. He accepted my silence as agreement and smiled at me in most benefi-cent fashion.

'We are coming on, I perceive,' said he. 'Light is beginning to break in. A little dazzling at first, no doubt, but we will soon get used to it. Pray give me your attention while I found one or two more observations upon this little creature in my hand.

'We will suppose that on this outer hard rind there were certain infinitely small insects which crawled upon the surface. Would the echinus ever be aware of their existence?'

'I should say not.'

'You can well imagine then, that the earth has not the least idea of the way in which it is utilized by the human race. It is quite unaware of this fungus growth of vegetation and evolution of tiny animalcules which has collected upon it during its travels round the sun as barnacles gather upon the ancient vessel. That is the present state of affairs, and that is what I propose to alter.'

I stared in amazement. 'You propose to alter it?'

'I propose to let the earth know that there is at least one person, George Edward Challenger, who calls for attention – who, indeed, insists upon attention. It is certainly the first intimation it has ever had of the sort.'

'And how, sir, will you do this?'

'Ah, there we get down to business. You have touched the spot. I will again call your attention to this interesting little creature which I hold in my hand. It is all nerves and sensibility beneath that pro-tective crust. Is it not evident that if a parasitic animalcule desired to call its attention it would sink a hole in its shell and so stimulate its sensory apparatus?'

'Certainly.'

'Or, again, we will take the case of the homely flea or a mosquito which explores the surface of the human body. We may be unaware of its presence. But presently, when it sinks its proboscis through the skin, which is our crust, we are disagreeably reminded that we are not altogether alone. My plans now will no doubt begin to dawn upon you. Light breaks in the darkness.'

'Good heavens! You propose to sink a shaft through the earth's crust?'

He closed his eyes with ineffable complacency.

'You see before you,' he said, 'the first who will ever pierce that horny hide. I may even put it in the present tense and say who *has* pierced it.'

'You have done it!'

'With the very efficient aid of Morden and Co., I think I may say that I have done it. Several years of constant work which has been carried on night and day, and conducted by every known species of drill, borer, crusher, and explosive, has at last brought us to our goal.'

'You don't mean to say you are through the crust!'

'If your expressions denote bewilderment they may pass. If they denote incredulity –'

'No, sir, nothing of the kind.'

'You will accept my statement without question. We are through the crust. It was exactly fourteen thousand four hundred and forty-two yards thick, or roughly eight miles. In the course of our sinking it may interest you to know that we have exposed a fortune in the matter of coal-beds which would probably in the long run defray the cost of the enterprise. Our chief difficulty has been the springs of water in the lower chalk and Hastings sands, but these we have overcome. The last stage has now been reached – and the last stage is none other than Mr. Peerless Jones. You, sir, represent the mosquito. Your Artesian borer takes the place of the stinging proboscis. The brain has done its work. Exit the thinker. Enter the mechanical one, the peerless one, with his rod of metal. Do I make myself clear?'

'You talk of eight miles!' I cried. 'Are you aware, sir, that five thousand feet is considered nearly the limit for Artesian borings? I am acquainted with one in upper Silesia which is six thousand two hundred feet deep, but it is looked upon as a wonder.'

'You misunderstand me, Mr. Peerless. Either my explanation or your brain is at fault, and I will not insist upon which. I am well aware of the limits of Artesian borings, and it is not likely that I would have spent millions of pounds upon my colossal tunnel if a six-inch boring would have met my needs. All that I ask you is to have a drill ready which shall be as sharp as possible, not more than a hundred feet in length, and operated by an electric motor. An ordinary percussion drill driven home by a weight will meet every requirement.'

'Why by an electric motor?'

'I am here, Mr. Jones, to give orders, not reasons. Before we finish it may happen – it *may*, I say, happen – that your very life may depend upon this drill being started from a distance by electricity. It can, I presume, be done?'

'Certainly it can be done.'

'Then prepare to do it. The matter is not yet ready for your actual presence, but your preparations may now be made. I have nothing more to say.'

'But it is essential,' I expostulated, 'that you should let me know what soil the drill is to penetrate. Sand, or clay, or chalk would each need different treatment.'

'Let us say jelly,' said Challenger. 'Yes, we will for the present suppose that you have to sink your drill into jelly. And now, Mr. Jones, I have matters of some importance to engage my mind, so I will wish you good morning. You can draw up a formal contract with mention of your charges for my Head of Works.'

I bowed and turned, but before I reached the door my curiosity overcame me. He was already writing furiously with a quill pen screeching over the paper, and he looked up angrily at my interruption.

'Well, sir, what now? I had hoped you were gone.'

'I only wished to ask you, sir, what the object of so extraordinary an experiment can be?'

'Away, sir, away!' he cried, angrily. 'Raise your mind above the base mercantile and utilitarian needs of commerce. Shake off your paltry standards of business. Science seeks knowledge. Let the knowledge lead us where it will, we still must seek it. To know once for all what we are, why we are, where we are, is that not in itself the greatest of all human aspirations? Away, sir, away!'

His great black head was bowed over his papers once more and blended with his beard. The quill pen screeched more shrilly than ever. So I left him, this extraordinary man, with my head in a whirl at the thought of the strange business in which I now found myself to be his partner.

When I got back to my office I found Ted Malone waiting with a broad grin upon his face to know the result of my interview.

'Well!' he cried. 'None the worse? No case of assault and battery? You must have handled him very tactfully. What do you think of the old boy?'

'The most aggravating, insolent, intolerant, self-opinionated man I have ever met, but –'

'Exactly!' cried Malone. 'We all come to that "but." Of course, he is all you say and a lot more, but one feels that so big a man is not to be measured in our scale, and that we can endure from him what we would not stand from any other living mortal. Is that not so?'

'Well, I don't know him well enough yet to say, but I will admit that if he is not a mere bullying megalomaniac, and if what he says is true, then he certainly is in a class by himself. But *is* it true?'

'Of course it is true. Challenger always delivers the goods. Now, where are you exactly in the matter? Has he told you about Hengist Down?'

'Yes, in a sketchy sort of way.'

'Well, you may take it from me that the whole thing is colossal – colossal in conception and colossal in execution. He hates press-men, but I am in his confidence, for he knows that I will publish no more than he authorizes. Therefore I have his plans, or some of his plans. He is such a deep old bird that one never is sure if one has really touched bottom. Anyhow, I know enough to assure you that Hengist Down is a practical proposition and nearly completed. My advice to you now is simply to await events, and meanwhile to get your gear all ready. You'll hear soon enough either from him or from me.'

As it happened, it was from Malone himself that I heard. He came round quite early to my office some weeks later, as the bearer of a message.

'I've come from Challenger,' said he.

'You are like the pilot fish to the shark.'

'I'm proud to be anything to him. He really is a wonder. He has done it all right. It's your turn now, and then he is ready to ring up the curtain.'

'Well, I can't believe it till I see it, but I have everything ready and loaded on a lorry. I could start it off at any moment.'

'Then do so at once. I've given you a tremendous character for energy and punctuality, so mind you don't let me down. In the meantime, come down with me by rail and I will give you an idea of what has to be done.'

It was a lovely spring morning – May 22nd, to be exact – when we made that fateful journey which brought me on to a stage which is destined to be historical. On the way Malone handed me a note from Challenger which I was to accept as my instructions.

'Sir,' (it ran) –

'Upon arriving at Hengist Down you will put yourself at the disposal of Mr. Barforth, the Chief Engineer, who is in possession of my plans. My young friend, Malone, the bearer of this, is also in touch with me and may protect me from any personal contact. We have now experienced certain phenomena in the shaft at and below the fourteen thousand-foot level which fully bear out my views as to the nature of a planetary body, but some more sensational proof is needed before I can hope to make an impression upon the torpid intelligence of the modern scientific world. That proof you are destined to afford, and they to witness. As you descend in the lifts you will observe, presuming that you have the rare quality of observation, that you pass in succession the secondary chalk beds, the coal measures, some Devonian and Cambrian indications, and finally the granite, through which the greater part of our tunnel is conducted. The bottom is now covered with tarpaulin, which I order you not to tamper with, as any clumsy handling of the sensitive inner cuticle of the earth might bring about premature results. At my instruction, two strong beams have been laid across the shaft twenty feet above the bottom, with a space between them. This space will act as a clip to hold up your Artesian tube. Fifty feet of drill will suffice, twenty of which will project below the beams. so that the point of the drill comes nearly down to the tarpaulin. As you value your life do not let it go further. Thirty feet will then project upwards in the shaft, and when you have released it we may assume that not less than forty feet of drill will bury itself in the earth's substance. As this substance is very soft I find that you will probably need no driving power, and that simply a release of the tube will suffice by its own weight to drive it into the layer which we have uncovered. These instructions would seem to be sufficient for any ordinary intelligence, but I have little doubt that you will need more, which can be referred to me through our young friend, Malone.

'GEORGE EDWARD CHALLENGER.'

It can be imagined that when we arrived at the station of Storrington, near the northern foot of the South Downs I was in a state of considerable nervous tension. A weather-worn Vauxhall thirty landaulette was awaiting us, and bumped us for six or seven miles over by-paths and lanes which, in spite of their natural seclusion, were deeply rutted and showed every sign of heavy traffic. A broken lorry lying in the grass at one point showed that others had found it rough going as well as we. Once a huge piece of machinery which seemed to be the valves and piston of a hydraulic pump projected itself, all rusted, from a clump of furze.

'That's Challenger's doing,' said Malone, grinning. 'Said it was one-tenth of an inch out of estimate, so he simply chucked it by the wayside.'

'With a lawsuit to follow, no doubt.'

'A lawsuit! My dear chap, we should have a court of our own. We have enough to keep a judge busy for a year. Government, too. The old devil cares for no one. Rex *v.* George Challenger and George Challenger *v.* Rex. A nice devil's dance the two will have from one court to another. Well, here we are. All right, Jenkins, you can let us in!'

A huge man with a notable cauliflower ear was peering into the car, a scowl of suspicion upon his face. He relaxed and saluted as he recognized my companion.

'All right, Mr. Malone. I thought it was the American Associated Press.'

'Oh, they are on the track, are they?'

'They to-day, and *The Times* yesterday. Oh, they are buzzing round proper. Look at that!' He indicated a distant dot upon the sky-line. 'See that glint! That's the telescope of the Chicago *Daily News*. Yes, they are fair after us now. I've seen 'em in rows, same as the crows, along the Beacon yonder.'

'Poor old Press gang!' said Malone, as we entered a gate in a formidable barbed wire fence. 'I am one of them myself, and I know how it feels.'

At this moment we heard a plaintive bleat behind us of 'Malone! Ted Malone!' It came from a fat little man who had just arrived upon a motor-bike and was at present struggling in the Herculean grasp of the gatekeeper.

'Here, let me go!' he sputtered. 'Keep your hands off! Malone, call off this gorilla of yours.'

'Let him go, Jenkins! He's a friend of mine!' cried Malone. 'Well, old bean, what is it? What are you after in these parts? Fleet Street is your stamping ground – not the wilds of Sussex.'

'You know what I am after perfectly well,' said our visitor. 'I've got the assignment to write a story about Hengist Down and I can't go home without the copy.'

'Sorry, Roy, but you can't get anything here. You'll have to stay on that side of the wire. If you want more you must go and see Professor Challenger and get his leave.'

'I've been,' said the journalist, ruefully. 'I went this morning.'

'Well, what did he say?'

'He said he would put me through the window.'

Malone laughed.

'And what did you say?'

'I said, "What's wrong with the door?" and I skipped through it just to show there was nothing wrong with it. It was no time for argument. I just went. What with that bearded Assyrian bull in London, and this Thug down here, who has ruined my clean celluloid, you seem to be keeping queer company, Ted Malone.'

'I can't help you, Roy; I would if I could. They say in Fleet Street that you have never been beaten, but you are up against it this time. Get back to the office, and if you just wait a few days I'll give you the news as soon as the old man allows.'

'No chance of getting in?'

'Not an earthly.'

'Money no object?'

'You should know better than to say that.'

'They tell me it's a short cut to New Zealand.'

'It will be a short cut to the hospital if you butt in here, Roy. Good-bye, now. We have some work to do of our own.

'That's Roy Perkins, the war correspondent,' said Malone as we walked across the compound. 'We've broken his record, for he is supposed to be undefeatable. It's his fat little innocent face that carries him through everything. We were on the same staff once. Now there' – he pointed to a cluster of pleasant red-roofed bungalows – 'are the quarters of the men. They are a splendid lot of picked workers who are paid far above ordinary rates. They have to be bachelors and teetotallers, and under oath of secrecy. I don't think there has been any leakage up to now. That field is their football ground and the detached house is their library and recreation room. The old man is some organizer, I can assure you. This is Mr. Barforth, the head engineer-in-charge.'

A long, thin, melancholy man with deep lines of anxiety upon his face had appeared before us.

'I expect you are the Artesian engineer,' said he, in a gloomy voice. 'I was told to expect you. I am glad you've come, for I don't mind telling you that the responsibility of this thing is getting on my nerves. We work away, and I never know if it's a gush of chalk water, or a seam of coal, or a squirt of petroleum, or maybe a touch of hell fire that is coming next. We've been spared the last up to now, but you may make the connection for all I know.'

'Is it so hot down there?'

'Well, it's hot. There's no denying it. And yet maybe it is not hotter than the barometric pressure and the confined space might account for. Of course, the ventilation is awful. We pump the air down, but two-hour shifts are the most the men can do – and they are willing lads too. The Professor was down yesterday, and he was very pleased with it all. You had best join us at lunch, and then you will see it for yourself.'

After a hurried and frugal meal we were introduced with loving assiduity upon the part of the manager to the contents of his engine-house, and to the miscellaneous scrapheap of disused implements with which the grass was littered. On one side was a huge dismantled Arrol hydraulic shovel, with which the first excavations had been rapidly made. Beside it was a great engine which worked a continuous steel rope on which the skips were fastened which drew up the *débris* by successive stages from the bottom of the shaft. In the power-house were several Escher Wyss turbines of great horse-power running at one hundred and forty revolutions a minute and governing hydraulic accumulators which evolved a pressure of fourteen hundred pounds per square inch, passing in three-inch pipes down the shaft and operating four rock drills with hollow cutters of the Brandt type. Abutting upon the engine-house was the electric house supplying power for a very large lighting instalment, and next to that again was an extra turbine of two hundred horse-power, which drove a ten-foot fan forcing air down a twelve-inch pipe to the bottom of the workings. All these wonders were shown with many technical explanations by their proud operator, who was well on his way to boring me stiff, as I may in turn have done my reader. There came a welcome interruption, however, when I heard the roar of wheels and rejoiced to see my Leyland three-tonner come rolling and heaving over the grass, heaped up with my tools and sections of tubing, and bearing my foreman, Peters, and a very grimy assistant in front. The two of them set to work at once to unload my stuff and to carry it in. Leaving them at their work, the manager, with Malone and myself, approached the shaft.

It was a wondrous place, on a very much larger scale than I had imagined. The spoil banks, which represented the thousands of tons removed, had been built up into a great horseshoe around it, which now made a considerable hill. In the concavity of this horseshoe, composed of chalk, clay, coal, and granite, there rose up a bristle of iron pillars and wheels from which the pumps and the lifts were operated. They connected with the brick power building which filled up the gap in the horseshoe. Beyond it lay the open mouth of the shaft, a huge yawning pit, some thirty or forty feet in diameter, lined and topped with brick and cement. As I craned my neck over the side and gazed down into the dreadful abyss, which I had been assured was eight miles deep, my brain reeled at the thought of what it represented. The sunlight struck the mouth of it diagonally, and I could only see some hundreds of yards of dirty white chalk, bricked here and there where the surface had seemed unstable. Even as I looked, however, I saw, far, far down in the darkness, a tiny speck of light, the smallest possible dot, but clear and steady against the inky background.

'What is that light?' I asked.

Malone bent over the parapet beside me.

'That's one of the cages coming up,' said he. 'Rather wonderful, is it not? That is a mile or more from us, and that little gleam is a powerful arc lamp. It travels quickly, and will be here in a few minutes.'

Sure enough the pin-point of light came larger and larger, until it flooded the tube with its silvery radiance, and I had to turn away my eyes from its blinding glare. A moment later the iron cage clashed up to the landing stage, and four men crawled out of it and passed on to the entrance.

'Nearly all in,' said Malone. 'It is no joke to do a two-hour shift at that depth. Well, some of your stuff is ready to hand here. I suppose the best thing we can do is to go down. Then you will be able to judge the situation for yourself.'

There was an annexe to the engine-house into which he led me. A number of baggy suits of the lightest tussore material were hanging from the wall. Following Malone's example I took off every stitch of my clothes, and put on one of these suits, together with a pair of rubber-soled slippers. Malone finished before I did and left the dressing-room. A moment later I heard a noise like ten dog-fights rolled into one, and rushing out I found my friend rolling on the ground with his arms round the workman who was helping to stack my artesian tubing. He was endeavouring to tear something from him to which the other was most desperately clinging. But Malone was too strong for him, tore the object out of his grasp, and danced upon it until it was shattered to pieces. Only then did I recognize that it was a photographic camera. My grimy-faced artisan rose ruefully from the floor.

'Confound you, Ted Malone!' said he. 'That was a new ten-guinea machine.'

'Can't help it, Roy. I saw you take the snap, and there was only one thing to do.'

'How the devil did you get mixed up with my outfit?' I asked, with righteous indignation.

The rascal winked and grinned. 'There are always ways and means,' said he. 'But don't blame your foreman. He thought it was just a rag. I swapped clothes with his assistant, and in I came.'

'And out you go,' said Malone. 'No use arguing, Roy. If Challenger were here he would set the dogs on you. I've been in a hole myself, so I won't be hard, but I am watchdog here, and I can bite as well as bark. Come on! Out you march!'

So our enterprising visitor was marched by two grinning workmen out of the compound. So now the public will at last understand the genesis of that wonderful four-column article headed 'Mad Dream of a Scientist,' with the subtitle 'A Bee-line to Australia,' which appeared in *The Adviser* some days later and brought Challenger to the verge of apoplexy, and the editor of *The Adviser* to the most disagreeable and dangerous interview of his lifetime. The article was a highly coloured and exaggerated account of the adventure of Roy Perkins, 'our experienced war correspondent,' and it contained such purple passages as 'this hirsute bully of Enmore Gardens,' 'a compound guarded by barbed wire, plug-uglies, and bloodhounds,' and finally, 'I was dragged from the edge of the Anglo-Australian tunnel by two ruffians, the more savage being a jack-of-all-trades whom I had previously known by sight as a hanger-on of the journalistic profession, while the other, a sinister figure in a strange tropical garb, was posing as an Artesian engineer, though his appearance was more reminiscent of Whitechapel.' Having ticked us off in this way, the rascal had an elaborate description of rails at the pit mouth, and of a zigzag excavation by which funicular trains were to burrow into the earth. The only practical inconvenience arising from the article was that it notably increased that line of loafers who sat upon the South Downs waiting for something to happen. The day came when it did happen and when they wished themselves elsewhere.

My foreman with his faked assistant had littered the place with all my apparatus, my bellbox, my crowsfoot, the V-drills, the rods, and the weight, but Malone insisted that we disregard all that and descend ourselves to the lowest level. To this end we entered the cage, which was of latticed steel, and in the company of the chief engineer we shot down into the bowels of the earth. There were a series of automatic lifts, each with its own operating station hollowed out in the side of the excavation. They operated with great speed, and the experience was more like a vertical railway journey than the deliberate fall which we associate with the British lift.

Since the cage was latticed and brightly illuminated, we had a clear view of the strata through which we passed. I was conscious of each of them as we flashed past. There were the sallow lower chalk, the coffee-coloured Hastings beds, the lighter Ashburnham beds, the dark carboniferous clays, and then, gleaming in the electric light, band after band of jet-black, sparkling coal alternating with the rings of clay. Here and there brickwork had been inserted, but as a rule the shaft was self-supported, and one could but marvel at the immense labour and mechanical skill which it represented. Beneath the coal-beds I was conscious of jumbled strata of a concrete-like appearance, and then we shot down into the primitive granite, where the quartz crystals gleamed and twinkled as if the dark walls were sown with the dust of diamonds. Down we went and ever down – lower now than ever mortals had before penetrated. The archaic rocks varied wonderfully in colour, and I can never forget one broad belt of rose-coloured felspar, which shone with an unearthly beauty before our powerful lamps. Stage after stage, and lift after lift, the air getting ever closer and hotter until even the light tussore garments were intolerable and the sweat was pouring down into those rubber-soled slippers. At last, just as I was thinking that I could stand it no more, the last lift came to a stand and we stepped out upon a circular platform which had been cut in the rock. I noticed that Malone gave a curiously suspicious glance round at the walls as he did so. If I did not know him to be among the bravest of men, I should say that he was exceedingly nervous.

'Funny-looking stuff,' said the chief engineer, passing his hand over the nearest section of rock. He held it to the light and showed that it was glistening with a curious slimy scum. 'There have been shiverings and tremblings down here. I don't know what we are dealing with. The Professor seems pleased with it, but it's all new to me.'

'I am bound to say I've seen that wall fairly shake itself,' said Malone. 'Last time I was down here we fixed those two cross-beams for your drill, and when we cut into it for the supports it winced at every stroke. The old man's theory seemed absurd in solid old London town, but down here, eight miles under the surface, I am not so sure about it.'

'If you saw what was under that tarpaulin you would be even less sure,' said the engineer. 'All this lower rock cut like cheese, and when we were through it we came on a new formation like nothing on earth. "Cover it up! Don't touch it!" said the Professor. So we tarpaulined it according to his instructions and there it lies.'

'Could we not have a look?'

A frightened expression came over the engineer's lugubrious countenance.

'It's no joke disobeying the Professor,' said he. 'He is so damn cunning, too, that you never know what check he has set on you. However, we'll have a peep and chance it.' He turned down our reflector lamp so that the light gleamed upon the black tarpaulin. Then he stooped and, seizing a rope which connected up with the corner of the covering, he disclosed half-a-dozen square yards of the surface beneath it.

It was a most extraordinary and terrifying sight. The floor consisted of some greyish material, glazed and shiny, which rose and fell in slow palpitation. The throbs were not direct, but gave the impression of a gentle ripple or rhythm, which ran across the surface. This surface itself was not entirely homogeneous, but beneath it, seen as through ground glass, there were dim whitish patches or vacuoles, which varied constantly in shape and size. We stood all three gazing spell-bound at this extraordinary sight.

'Does look rather like a skinned animal,' said Malone in an awed whisper. 'The old man may not be so far out with his blessed echinus.'

'Good Lord!' I cried. 'And am I to plunge a harpoon into that beast!'

'That's your privilege, my son,' said Malone, 'and, sad to relate, unless I give it a miss in baulk, I shall have to be at your side when you do it.'

'Well, I won't,' said the head engineer, with decision. 'I was never clearer on anything than I am on that. If the old man insists, then I resign my portfolio. Good Lord, look at that!'

The grey surface gave a sudden heave upwards, welling towards us as a wave does when you look down from the bulwarks. Then it subsided and the dim beatings and throbbings continued as before. Barforth lowered the rope and replaced the tarpaulin.

'Seemed almost as if it knew we were here,' said he. 'Why should it swell up towards us like that? I expect the light had some sort of effect upon it.'

'What am I expected to do now?' I asked.

Mr. Barforth pointed to two beams which lay across the pit just under the stopping place of the lift. There was a interval of about nine inches between them.

'That was the old man's idea,' said he. 'I think I could have fixed it better, but you might as well try to argue with a mad buffalo. It is easier and safer just to do whatever he says. His idea is that you should use your six-inch bore and fasten it in some way between these supports.'

'Well, I don't think there would be much difficulty about that,' I answered. 'I'll take the job over as from to-day.'

It was, as one might imagine, the strangest experience of my very varied life which has included well-sinking in every continent upon earth. As Professor Challenger was so insistent that the operation should be started from a distance, and as I began to see a good deal of sense in his contention, I had to plan some method of electric control, which was easy enough as the pit was wired from top to bottom. With infinite care my foreman, Peters, and I brought down our lengths of tubing and stacked them on the rocky ledge. Then we raised the stage of the lowest lift so as to give ourselves room. As we proposed to use the percussion system, for it would not do to trust entirely to gravity, we hung our hundred-pound weight over a pulley beneath the lift, and ran our tubes down beneath it with a V-shaped terminal. Finally, the rope which held the weight was secured to the side of the shaft in such a way that an electrical discharge would release it. It was delicate and difficult work done in a more than tropical heat, and with the ever-present feeling that a slip of a foot or the dropping of a tool upon the tarpaulin beneath us might bring about some inconceivable catastrophe. We were awed, too, by our surroundings. Again and again I have seen a strange quiver and shiver pass down the walls, and have even felt a dull throb against my hands as I touched them. Neither Peters nor I were very sorry when we signalled for the last time that we were ready for the surface, and were able to report to Mr. Barforth that Professor Challenger could make his experiment as soon as he chose.

And it was not long that we had to wait. Only three days after my date of completion my notice arrived.

It was an ordinary invitation card such as one uses for 'at homes,' and it ran thus:

PROFESSOR G. E. CHALLENGER,

F.R.S., M. D., D. Sc., etc.

(late President Zoological Institute and holder of so many honorary degrees and appointments that they overtax the capacity of this card)

requests the attendance of

MR. JONES (no lady)

at 11.30 a.m. of Tuesday, June 21st, to witness a remarkable triumph of mind over matter

at

HENGIST DOWN, SUSSEX

Special train Victoria 10.5. Passengers pay their own fares. Lunch after the experiment or not – according to circumstances. Station, Storrington.

R.S.V.P. (and at once with name in block letters), 14 Bis, Enmore Gardens, S.W.

I found that Malone had just received a similar missive over which he was chuckling.

'It is mere swank sending it to us,' said he. 'We have to be there whatever happens, as the hangman said to the murderer. But I tell you this has set all London buzzing. The old man is where he likes to be, with a pin-point limelight right on his hairy old head.'

And so at last the great day came. Personally I thought it well to go down the night before so as to be sure that everything was in order. Our borer was fixed in position, the weight was adjusted, the electric contacts could be easily switched on, and I was satisfied that my own part in this strange experiment would be carried out without a hitch. The electric controls were operated at a point some five hundred yards from the mouth of the shaft, to minimize any personal danger. When on the fateful morning, an ideal English summer day, I came to the surface with my mind assured, I climbed half-way up the slope of the Down in order to have a general view of the proceedings.

All the world seemed to be coming to Hengist Down. As far as we could see the roads were dotted with people. Motor-cars came bumping and swaying down the lanes, and discharged their passengers at the gate of the compound. This was in most cases the end of their progress. A powerful band of janitors waited at the entrance, and no promises or bribes, but only the production of the coveted buff tickets, could get them any farther. They dispersed therefore and joined the vast crowd which was already assembling on the side of the hill and covering the ridge with a dense mass of spectators. The place was like Epsom Downs on the Derby Day. Inside the compound certain areas had been wired off, and the various privileged people were conducted to the particular pen to which they had been allotted. There was one for peers, one for members of the House of Commons, and one for the heads of learned societies and the men of fame in the scientific world, including Le Pellier of the Sorbonne and Dr. Driesinger of the Berlin Academy. A special reserved enclosure with sandbags and a corrugated iron roof was set aside for three members of the Royal Family.

At a quarter past eleven a succession of chars-à-bancs brought up the specially-invited guests from the station and I went down into the compound to assist at the reception. Professor Challenger stood by the select enclosure, resplendent in frock-coat, white waistcoat, and burnished top-hat, his expression a blend of over-powering and almost offensive benevolence, mixed with most por-tentous self-importance. 'Clearly a typical victim of the Jehovah complex,' as one of his critics described him. He assisted in con-ducting and occasionally in propelling his guests into their proper places, and then, having gathered the *élite* of the company around him, he took his station upon the top of a convenient hillock and looked around him with the air of the chairman who expects some welcoming applause. As none was forthcoming, he plunged at once into his subject, his voice booming to the farthest extremities of the enclosure.

'Gentlemen,' he roared, 'upon this occasion I have no need to include the ladies. If I have not invited them to be present with us this morning it is not, I can assure you, for want of appreciation, for I may say' – with elephantine humour and mock modesty – 'that the relations between us upon both sides have always been excellent, and indeed intimate. The real reason is that some small element of danger is involved in our experiment, though it is not sufficient to justify the discomposure which I see upon many of your faces. It will interest the members of the Press to know that I have reserved very special seats for them upon the spoil banks which immediately overlook the scene of the operation. They have shown an interest which is sometimes indistinguishable from impertinence in my affairs, so that on this occasion at least they cannot complain that I have been remiss in studying their convenience. If nothing happens, which is always possible, I have at least done my best for them. If, on the other hand, something does happen, they will be in an excel-lent position to experience and record it, should they ultimately feel equal to the task.

'It is, as you will readily understand, impossible for a man of sci-ence to explain to what I may describe, without undue disrespect, as the common herd, the various reasons for his conclusions or his actions. I hear some unmannerly interruptions, and I will ask the gentleman with the horn spectacles to cease waving his umbrella. (A voice: "Your description of your guests, sir, is most offensive.") Pos-sibly it is my phrase, "the common herd," which has ruffled the gen-tleman. Let us say, then, that my listeners are a most uncommon herd. We will not quibble over phrases. I was about to say, before I was interrupted by this unseemly remark, that the whole matter is very fully and lucidly discussed in my forthcoming volume upon the earth, which I may describe with all due modesty as one of the epoch-making books of the world's history. (General interruption and cries of "Get down to the facts!" "What are we here for?" "Is this a practical joke?") I was about to make the matter clear, and if I have any further interruption I shall be compelled to take means to preserve decency and order, the lack of which is so painfully obvious. The position is, then, that I have sunk a shaft through the crust of the earth and that I am about to try the effect of a vigorous stimulation of its sensory cortex, a delicate operation which will be carried out by my subordinates, Mr. Peerless Jones, a self-styled expert in Artesian borings, and Mr. Edward Malone, who represents myself upon this occasion. The exposed and sensitive substance will be pricked, and how it will react is a matter for conjecture. If you will now kindly take your seats these two gentlemen will descend into the pit and make the final adjustments. I will then press the electric button upon this table and the experiment will be complete.'

An audience after one of Challenger's harangues usually felt as if, like the earth, its protective epidermis had been pierced and its nerves laid bare. This assembly was no exception, and there was a dull murmur of criticism and resentment as they returned to their places. Challenger sat alone on the top of the mound, a small table beside him, his black mane and beard vibrating with excitement, a most portentous figure. Neither Malone nor I could admire the scene, however, for we hurried off upon our extraordinary errand. Twenty minutes later we were at the bottom of the shaft, and had pulled the tarpaulin from the exposed surface.

It was an amazing sight which lay before us. By some strange cosmic telepathy the old planet seemed to know that an unheard-of liberty was about to be attempted. The exposed surface was like a boiling pot. Great grey bubbles rose and burst with a crackling report. The air-spaces and vacuoles below the skin separated and coalesced in an agitated activity. The transverse ripples were stronger and faster in their rhythm than before. A dark purple fluid appeared to pulse in the tortuous anastomoses of channels which lay under the surface. The throb of life was in it all. A heavy smell made the air hardly fit for human lungs.

My gaze was fixed upon this strange spectacle when Malone at my elbow gave a sudden gasp of alarm. 'My God, Jones!' he cried. 'Look there!'

I gave one glance, and the next instant I released the electric connection and I sprang into the lift. 'Come on!' I cried. 'It may be a race for life!'

What we had seen was indeed alarming. The whole lower shaft, it would seem, had shared in the increased activity which we had observed below, and the walls were throbbing and pulsing in sympathy. This movement had reacted upon the holes in which the beams rested, and it was clear that with a very little further retraction – a matter of inches – the beams would fall. If they did so then the sharp end of my rod would, of course, penetrate the earth quite independently of the electric release. Before that happened it was vital that Malone and I should be out of the shaft. To be eight miles down in the earth with the chance any instant of some extraordinary convulsion taking place was a terrible prospect. We fled wildly for the surface.

Shall either of us ever forget that nightmare journey? The lifts whizzed and buzzed and yet the minutes seemed to be hours. As we reached each stage we sprang out, jumped into the next lift, touched the release and flew onwards. Through the steel latticed roof we could see far away the little circle of light which marked the mouth of the shaft. Now it grew wider and wider, until it came full circle and our glad eyes rested upon the brickwork of the opening. Up we shot, and up – and then at last in a glad mad moment of joy and thankfulness we sprang out of our prison and had our feet upon the green sward once more. But it was touch and go. We had not gone thirty paces from the shaft when far down in the depths my iron dart shot into the nerve ganglion of old Mother Earth and the great moment had arrived.

What was it happened? Neither Malone nor I was in a position to say, for both of us were swept off our feet as by a cyclone and swirled along the grass, revolving round and round like two curling stones upon an ice rink. At the same time our ears were assailed by the most horrible yell that ever yet was heard. Who is there of all the hundreds who have attempted it who has ever yet described adequately that terrible cry? It was a howl in which pain, anger, menace, and the outraged majesty of Nature all blended into one hideous shriek. For a full minute it lasted, a thousand sirens in one, paralysing all the great multitude with its fierce insistence, and floating away through the still summer air until it went echoing along the whole South Coast and even reached our French neighbours across the Channel. No sound in history has ever equalled the cry of the injured Earth.

Dazed and deafened, Malone and I were aware of the shock and of the sound, but it is from the narrative of others that we learned the other details of that extraordinary scene.

The first emergence from the bowels of the earth consisted of the lift cages. The other machinery being against the walls escaped the blast, but the solid floors of the cages took the full force of the upward current. When several separate pellets are placed in a blow-pipe they still shoot forth in their order and separately from each other. So the fourteen lift cages appeared one after the other in the air, each soaring after the other, and describing a glorious parabola which landed one of them in the sea near Worthing pier, and a second one in a field not far from Chichester. Spectators have averred that of all the strange sights that they had ever seen nothing could exceed that of the fourteen lift cages sailing serenely through the blue heavens.

Then came the geyser. It was an enormous spout of vile treacly substance of the consistence of tar, which shot up into the air to a height which has been computed at two thousand feet. An inquisitive aeroplane, which had been hovering over the scene, was picked off as by an Archie and made a forced landing, man and machine buried in filth. This horrible stuff, which had a most penetrating and nauseous odour, may have represented the life blood of the planet, or it may be, as Professor Driesinger and the Berlin School maintain, that it is a protective secretion, analogous to that of the skunk, which Nature has provided in order to defend Mother Earth from intrusive Challengers. If that were so the prime offender, seated on his throne upon the hillock, escaped untarnished, while the unfortunate Press were so soaked and saturated, being in the direct line of fire, that none of them was capable of entering decent society for many weeks. This gush of putridity was blown south-wards by the breeze, and descended upon the unhappy crowd who had waited so long and so patiently upon the crest of the Downs to see what would happen. There were no casualties. No home was left desolate, but many were made odoriferous, and still carry within their walls some souvenir of that great occasion.

And then came the closing of the pit. As Nature slowly closes a wound from below upwards, so does the Earth with extreme rapid-ity mend any rent which is made in its vital substance. There was a prolonged high-pitched crash as the sides of the shaft came together, the sound, reverberating from the depths and then rising higher and higher until with a deafening bang the brick circle at the orifice flattened out and clashed together, while a tremor like a small earthquake shook down the spoil banks and piled a pyramid fifty feet high of *débris* and broken iron over the spot where the hole had been. Professor Challenger's experiment was not only finished, it was buried from human sight for ever. If it were not for the obelisk which has now been erected by the Royal Society it is doubtful if our descendants would ever know the exact site of that remarkable occurrence.

And then came the grand finale. For a long period after these successive phenomena there was a hush and a tense stillness as folk reassembled their wits and tried to realize exactly what had occurred and how it had come about. And then suddenly the mighty achievement, the huge sweep of the conception, the genius and wonder of the execution, broke upon their minds. With one impulse they turned upon Challenger. From every part of the field there came the cries of admiration, and from his hillock he could look down upon the lake of upturned faces broken only by the rise and fall of the waving handkerchiefs. As I look back I see him best as I saw him then. He rose from his chair, his eyes half closed, a smile of conscious merit upon his face, his left hand upon his hip, his right buried in the breast of his frock-coat. Surely that picture will be fixed for ever, for I heard the cameras clicking round me like crickets in a field. The June sun shone golden upon him as he turned gravely bowing to each quarter of the compass. Challenger the super scientist, Challenger the arch pioneer, Challenger the first man of all men whom Mother Earth had been compelled to recognize.

Only a word by way of epilogue. It is of course well known that the effect of the experiment was a world-wide one. It is true that nowhere did the injured planet emit such a howl as at the actual point of penetration, but she showed that she was indeed one entity by her conduct elsewhere. Through every vent and every volcano she voiced her indignation. Hecla bellowed until the Icelanders feared a cataclysm. Vesuvius blew its head off. Etna spewed up a quantity of lava, and a suit of half-a-million lira damages has been decided against Challenger in the Italian Courts for the destruction of vineyards. Even in Mexico and in the belt of Central America there were signs of intense Plutonic indignation, and the howls of Stromboli filled the whole Eastern Mediterranean. It has been the common ambition of mankind to set the whole world talking. To set the whole world screaming was the privilege of Challenger alone.

WORDSWORTH CLASSICS

General Editors: Marcus Clapham & Clive Reynard

JANE AUSTEN
Emma
Mansfield Park
Northanger Abbey
Persuasion
Pride and Prejudice
Sense and Sensibility

ARNOLD BENNETT
Anna of the Five Towns

R. D. BLACKMORE
Lorna Doone

ANNE BRONTË
Agnes Grey
The Tenant of
Wildfell Hall

CHARLOTTE BRONTË
Jane Eyre
The Professor
Shirley
Villette

EMILY BRONTË
Wuthering Heights

JOHN BUCHAN
Greenmantle
Mr Standfast
The Thirty-Nine Steps

SAMUEL BUTLER
The Way of All Flesh

LEWIS CARROLL
Alice in Wonderland

CERVANTES
Don Quixote

G. K. CHESTERTON
Father Brown:
Selected Stories
The Man who was
Thursday

ERSKINE CHILDERS
The Riddle of the Sands

JOHN CLELAND
Memoirs of a Woman of
Pleasure: Fanny Hill

WILKIE COLLINS
The Moonstone
The Woman in White

JOSEPH CONRAD
Heart of Darkness
Lord Jim
The Secret Agent

J. FENIMORE COOPER
The Last of the
Mohicans

STEPHEN CRANE
The Red Badge of
Courage

THOMAS DE QUINCEY
Confessions of an English
Opium Eater

DANIEL DEFOE
Moll Flanders
Robinson Crusoe

CHARLES DICKENS
Bleak House
David Copperfield
Great Expectations
Hard Times
Little Dorrit
Martin Chuzzlewit
Oliver Twist
Pickwick Papers
A Tale of Two Cities

BENJAMIN DISRAELI
Sybil

THEODOR DOSTOEVSKY
Crime and Punishment

SIR ARTHUR CONAN
DOYLE
The Adventures of
Sherlock Holmes
The Case-Book of
Sherlock Holmes
The Lost World &
Other Stories
The Return of
Sherlock Holmes
Sir Nigel

GEORGE DU MAURIER
Trilby

ALEXANDRE DUMAS
The Three Musketeers

MARIA EDGEWORTH
Castle Rackrent

GEORGE ELIOT
The Mill on the Floss
Middlemarch
Silas Marner

HENRY FIELDING
Tom Jones

F. SCOTT FITZGERALD
A Diamond as Big as the
Ritz & Other Stories
The Great Gatsby
Tender is the Night

GUSTAVE FLAUBERT
Madame Bovary

JOHN GALSWORTHY
In Chancery
The Man of Property
To Let

ELIZABETH GASKELL
Cranford
North and South

KENNETH GRAHAME
The Wind in the
Willows

GEORGE & WEEDON
GROSSMITH
Diary of a Nobody

RIDER HAGGARD
She

THOMAS HARDY
Far from the
Madding Crowd
The Mayor of Casterbridge
The Return of the
Native
Tess of the d'Urbervilles
The Trumpet Major
Under the Greenwood
Tree

NATHANIEL HAWTHORNE
The Scarlet Letter

O. HENRY
Selected Stories

HOMER
The Iliad
The Odyssey

E. W. HORNUNG
Raffles: The Amateur Cracksman

VICTOR HUGO
The Hunchback of Notre Dame
Les Misérables: volume 1
Les Misérables: volume 2

HENRY JAMES
The Ambassadors
Daisy Miller & Other Stories
The Golden Bowl
The Turn of the Screw & The Aspern Papers

M. R. JAMES
Ghost Stories

JEROME K. JEROME
Three Men in a Boat

JAMES JOYCE
Dubliners
A Portrait of the Artist as a Young Man

RUDYARD KIPLING
Captains Courageous
Kim
The Man who would be King & Other Stories
Plain Tales from the Hills

D. H. LAWRENCE
The Rainbow
Sons and Lovers
Women in Love

SHERIDAN LE FANU
(edited by M. R. James)
Madam Crowl's Ghost & Other Stories

JACK LONDON
Call of the Wild & White Fang

HERMAN MELVILLE
Moby Dick
Typee

H. H. MUNRO
The Complete Stories of Saki

EDGAR ALLAN POE
Tales of Mystery and Imagination

FREDERICK ROLFE
Hadrian the Seventh

SIR WALTER SCOTT
Ivanhoe

WILLIAM SHAKESPEARE
All's Well that Ends Well
Antony and Cleopatra
As You Like It
A Comedy of Errors
Hamlet
Henry IV Part 1
Henry IV part 2
Henry V
Julius Caesar
King Lear
Macbeth
Measure for Measure
The Merchant of Venice
A Midsummer Night's Dream
Othello
Richard II
Richard III
Romeo and Juliet
The Taming of the Shrew
The Tempest
Troilus and Cressida
Twelfth Night
A Winter's Tale

MARY SHELLEY
Frankenstein

ROBERT LOUIS STEVENSON
Dr Jekyll and Mr Hyde

BRAM STOKER
Dracula

JONATHAN SWIFT
Gulliver's Travels

W. M. THACKERAY
Vanity Fair

TOLSTOY
War and Peace

ANTHONY TROLLOPE
Barchester Towers
Dr Thorne
Framley Parsonage
The Last Chronicle of Barset
The Small House at Allington
The Warden

MARK TWAIN
Tom Sawyer & Huckleberry Finn

JULES VERNE
Around the World in 80 Days &
Five Weeks in a Balloon
20,000 Leagues Under the Sea

VOLTAIRE
Candide

EDITH WHARTON
The Age of Innocence

OSCAR WILDE
Lord Arthur Savile's Crime & Other Stories
The Picture of Dorian Gray

VIRGINIA WOOLF
Orlando
To the Lighthouse

P. C. WREN
Beau Geste

DISTRIBUTION

AUSTRALIA & PAPUA NEW GUINEA
Peribo Pty Ltd
58 Beaumont Road, Mount Kuring-Gai
NSW 2080, Australia
Tel: (02) 457 0011 Fax: (02) 457 0022

CYPRUS
Huckleberry Trading
Othos Appis 3, Tala, Paphos
Tel: 06 653585

CZECH REPUBLIC
Bohemian Ventures s r o.,
Delnicka 13, 170 00 Prague 7
Tel: 042 2 877837 Fax: 042 2 801498

FRANCE
Copernicus Diffusion
23 Rue Saint Dominique, Paris 75007
Tel: 1 44 11 33 20 Fax: 1 44 11 33 21

GERMANY & AUSTRIA
**GLBmbH (Bargain, Promotional
& Remainder Shops)**
Postfach 51 06 04, 50942 Köln
Tel: (0)221 936438-0 Fax: (0)221 936438-3

Tradis Verlag und Vertrieb GmbH (Bookshops)
Postfach 90 03 69, D-51113 Köln
Tel: 022 03 31059 Fax: 022 03 39340

GREAT BRITAIN & IRELAND
Wordsworth Editions Ltd
Cumberland House, Crib Street
Ware, Hertfordshire SG12 9ET
Tel: 01920 465167 Fax: 01920 462267

INDIA
Rupa & Co
Post Box No 7071,
7/16 Makhanlal Street, Ansari Road,
Daryaganj, New Delhi – 110 002
Tel: 3278586 Fax: (011) 3277294

ISRAEL
Sole Agent – **Timmy Marketing Limited**
Israel Ben Zeev 12, Ramont Gimmel, Jerusalem
Tel: 972-2-5865266 Fax: 972-2-5860035
Sole Distributor – Sefer ve Sefel Ltd
Tel & Fax: 972-2-6248237

ITALY
Magis Books s.p.a.
Via Raffaello 31/C, Zona Ind Mancasale
42100 Reggio Emilia
Tel: 0522 920999 Fax: 0522 920666

NEW ZEALAND & FIJI
Allphy Book Distributors Ltd
4-6 Charles Street, Eden Terrace, Auckland,
Tel: (09) 3773096 Fax: (09) 3022770

MALAYSIA & BRUNEI
Vintrade SDN BHD
5 & 7 Lorong Datuk Sulaiman 7
Taman Tun Dr Ismail
60000 Kuala Lumpur, Malaysia
Tel: (603) 717 3333 Fax: (603) 719 2942

MALTA & GOZO
Agius & Agius Ltd
42A South Street, Valletta VLT 11
Tel: 234038 - 220347 Fax: 241175

PHILIPPINES
I J Sagun Enterprises
P O Box 4322 CPO Manila
2 Topaz Road, Greenheights Village,
Taytay, Rizal
Tel: 631 80 61 TO 66

PORTUGAL
International Publishing Services Ltd
Rua da Cruz da Carreira, 4B, 1100 Lisbon
Tel: 01 570051 Fax: 01 3522066

SOUTHERN & CENTRAL AFRICA
Southern Book Publishers (Pty) Ltd
P.O.Box 3103
Halfway House 1685, South Africa
Tel: (011) 315-3633/4/5/6
Fax: (011) 315-3810

EAST AFRICA & KENYA
P.M.C. International Importers & Exporters CC
Unit 6, Ben-Sarah Place, 52-56 Columbine Place, Glen
Anil, Kwa-Zulu Natal 4051,
P.O.Box 201520,
Durban North, Kwa-Zulu Natal 4016
Tel: (031) 844441 Fax: (031) 844466

SINGAPORE
Paul & Elizabeth Book Services Pte Ltd
163 Tanglin Road No 03-15/16
Tanglin Mall, Singapore 1024
Tel: (65) 735 7308 Fax: (65) 735 9747

SLOVAK REPUBLIC
Slovak Ventures s r o.,
Stefanikova 128, 949 01 Nitra
Tel/Fax: 042 87 525105/6/7

SPAIN
Ribera Libros, S.L.
Poligono Martiartu, Calle 1 - no 6
48480 Arrigorriaga, Vizcaya
Tel: 34 4 6713607 (Almacen)
     34 4 4418787 (Libreria)
Fax: 34 4 6713608 (Almacen)
     34 4 4418029 (Libreria)

UNITED ARAB EMIRATES
Nadoo Trading LLC
P.O.Box 3186
Dubai,
United Arab Emirates
Tel: 04-359793 Fax: 04-487157

UNITED STATES OF AMERICA
NTC/Contemporary Publishing Company
4225 West Touhy Avenue
Lincolnwood (Chicago)
Illinois 60646-4622
USA
Tel: (847) 679 5500 Fax: (847) 679 2494

DIRECT MAIL
Bibliophile Books 5 Thomas Road, London E14 7BN,
Tel: 0171-515 9222 Fax: 0171-538 4115
Order hotline 24 hours Tel: 0171-515 9555 **Cash with order + £2.00 p&p (UK)**